D0181799

DAW titles by Jennifer Roberson

THE SWORD-DANCER SAGA
SWORD-DANCER
SWORD-SINGER
SWORD-MAKER
SWORD-BREAKER
SWORD-BORN
SWORD-SWORN*

CHRONICLES OF THE CHEYSULI
SHAPECHANGER'S SONG
(Omnibus One)
LEGACY OF THE WOLF
(Omnibus Two)
CHILDREN OF THE LION
(Omnibus Three)
THE LION THRONE
(Omnibus Four)

THE GOLDEN KEY
(with Melanie Rawn and Kate Elliott)

ANTHOLOGIES
(as editor)
RETURN TO AVALON
HIGHWAYMEN: ROBBERS AND ROGUES

*forthcoming from DAW Books

Jennifer Roberson

THE LION THRONE

THE CHRONICLES OF THE CHEYSULI

OMNIBUS FOUR

Book Seven
FLIGHT OF THE RAVEN

Book Eight
A TAPESTRY OF LIONS

DAW BOOKS, INC.

DONALD A. WOLLHEIM, FOUNDER

375 Hudson Street, New York, NY 10014

ELIZABETH R. WOLLHEIM
SHEILA E. GILBERT
PUBLISHERS

First Paperback Printing, October 2001
1 2 3 4 5 6 7 8 9

DAW TRADEMARK REGISTERED
U.S. PAT OFF AND FOREIGN COUNTRIES
—MARCA REGISTRADA.
HECHO EN USA

PRINTED IN THE U.S.A.

THE
LION THRONE

FLIGHT
OF THE RAVEN

Prologue

He was small, so very small, but desperation lent him strength. The *need* lent him strength, even though fright and tension threatened to undermine it. He placed small hands on the hammered silver door and *pushed* as hard as he could, grunting with the effort; pushing with all his might.

The door opened slightly. Then fell back again, scraping, as his meager strength failed.

"*No,*" he muttered aloud between clenched teeth. "No, I will not *let* you."

He shoved very hard again. This time he squeezed into the opening before the door could shut. When it shut, it shut on *him;* gasping shock and fright, Aidan thrust himself through. His sleeping robe tore, but he did not care. It did not matter. He was in at last.

Once in, he froze. The Great Hall was cavernous. Darker than night—a thick, heavy blackness trying to squash him flat. Darkness and *something* calling to him.

He would not be squashed. He would *not*—and yet his belly knotted. Who was he to do this? Who was he to come to his grandsire's Great Hall, to confront the Lion Throne?

Small hands tugged at hair, twisting a lock through fingers. Black hair by night; by day a dark russet, red in the light of the sun. He peered the length of the hall, feeling cold stone beneath his feet. His mother would have told him to put on his slippers. But the *need* had been so great that nothing else mattered but that he confront the Lion, and the thing in the Lion's lap.

He shivered. Not from cold: from *fear.*

Compulsion drove him. Aidan moaned a little. He wanted to leave the hall. He wanted to turn his back on the Lion, the big black beast who waited to devour him. But the need, so overwhelming, would not let him.

No candles had been left lighted. The firepit coals glowed only vaguely. What little moon there was shone fitfully through the casements, its latticed light distorted by stained glass panes.

If only he could *see.*

No. He knew better. If he could see the Lion, he would fear it more.

Or would he? The light of day was no better. The Lion still glared, still bared wooden teeth. Now he could barely see it, acrouch on the marble dais. Could it see him?

Aidan bit a finger. Bowels turned to water; he wanted the chamber pot. But he was prince and also Cheysuli. If he retreated now, he would dishonor the blood in his veins.

But, oh, how he wanted to leave!

Aidan rocked a little. "*Jehana . . .*" he whispered, not knowing that he spoke.

In the darkness, the Lion waited.

So did something else.

Aidan drew in a strangled breath in three gulping inhalations very noisy in the silence. Pressure in his bladder increased. He bit into his finger, then slowly took a step.

One. Then two. Then three. He lost count of them all. But eventually all the steps merged and took him the length of the hall, where he stood before the Lion. He looked at eyes, teeth, nostrils. All of it wood, all of it. *He* was made of flesh. *He* would rule the Lion.

With effort, Aidan looked into the lap. In dim light, something glowed.

It was a chain, made of gold. Heavy, hammered gold, alive with promises. More than wealth, or power: the chain was heritage. His past, and his future: legacy of the gods. He reached for it, transfixed, wanting it, *needing* it, knowing it was for him; but when his trembling hand closed over a link the size of a large man's wrist, the chain shapechanged to dust.

He cried out. Urine stained his nightrobe. Shame flooded him, but so did desperation. It had been right *there;* now there was nothing. Nothing at all remained. The dust—and the chain—was gone.

He did not want to cry. He did not *intend* to cry, but the tears came anyway. Which made him cry all the harder, ashamed of his emotion. Ashamed of his loss of control. Of his too-Homanan reaction; Cheysuli warriors did not cry. Grief was not expressed.

But he was more than merely Cheysuli. And no one let him forget.

Only one more bloodline needed. One more outcross required, and the prophecy was complete. But even he, at six, knew how impossible it was. He had heard it often enough in the halls of Homana-Mujhar.

No Cheysuli warrior will ever lie down with an Ihlini and sire a child upon her.

But even he, a boy, knew better. A Cheysuli warrior *had;* in fact, *two* had: his grandsire's brother, Ian, and his own father, the Prince of Homana, who one day would be Mujhar.

Even at six, he knew. And knew what he was meant for; what blood ran in his veins. But it was all very confusing, and he chose to leave it so.

Grief renewed itself. *I want my chain.*

But the chain—*his* chain—had vanished.

A small ferocity was born: *I want my CHAIN—*

One of the doors scraped open. Aidan twitched and swung around unsteadily, clutching the sodden nightrobe in both hands. It was his mother, he knew. Who else would come looking for a boy not in his bed? And she would see, she would *know*—

"Aidan? Aidan—what are ye doing here? 'Tis far past your bedtime!"

Shame made him hot. He fought tears and trembling.

She was white-faced, distraught, though trying to hide it. He knew what she felt; could *feel* it, as if her skin was his. But she tried so hard to hide it.

The familiar lilt of Erinn echoed in the Great Hall. "What are ye doing, my lad? Paying homage to the Lion?" Aileen's laugh was forced. "'Twill be *your* beastie, one day—there's no need for you to come in the night to see it!"

She meant well, he knew. She always meant well. But he sensed her fear, her anguish, beneath forced cheerfulness.

She hurried the length of the hall, gathering folds of a heavy robe. By the doors stood a servant holding a lamp. Light glowed in the hall. The Lion leaped out of the shadows.

Aidan fell back, thrusting up a warding arm, then realized it was no more than it ever was: a piece of wood shaped by man. And then his mother was beside him, asking him things fear distorted, until she gathered the reins of her worry and knotted them away.

She saw his hands doubled up in a soaked nightrobe. She saw

the urine stain. Anguish flared anew—he felt it most distinctly, like a burning band thrust into his spirit—but she said nothing of it. She merely knelt down at his side, putting a hand on his shoulder. "Aidan—why are you here? Your nurse came, speaking of a nightmare . . . but when I, came, you were gone. What are you doing here?"

He looked up into her face as she knelt down next to him. Into eyes green as glass; green as Erinnish turf. " 'Tis gone," he told her plainly, unconsciously adopting her accent.

She wore blue velvet chamber robe over white linen nightshift. Her hair was braided for sleeping: a single thick red plait, hanging down her back. "*What's* gone, my lad?"

"The chain," he explained, though he knew she would not understand. No one understood; no one *could* understand.

Sudden anguish was overwhelming. He craved reassurance as much as understanding. The former he could get. As the hated tears renewed themselves, he went willingly into her arms.

She pressed her cheek against his head, twining arms around small shoulders to still the wracking sobs. "Oh, Aidan, Aidan . . . 'twas only a dream, my lad . . . a wee bit of a dream come to trouble your sleep. There's no harm in it, I promise, but you mustn't be thinking 'tis real."

" *'Twas* real," he insisted, crying hard into her shoulder. " 'Twas real—I *swear* . . . and the Lion—the Lion meant to *eat* me—"

"Aidan, no. Oh, my sweet bairn, no. There's naught to the Lion's teeth but bits of rotting wood."

" 'Twas real—'twas *there*—"

"Aidan, hush—"

"It woke me up, calling . . ." He drew his head away so he could see her face, to judge what she thought. "It wanted me to come—"

"The Lion?"

Fiercely, he shook his head. "Not the Lion—the *chain*—"

"Oh, Aidan—"

She did not believe him. He hurled himself against her, trembling from a complex welter of fear, anguish, insistence: he needed her to believe him. She was his rock, his anchor—if *she* did not believe him—

In Erinnish, she tried to soothe him. He needed her warmth, her compassion, her love, but he was aware, if distantly, he also required something more. Something very real, no matter what she said: the solidity of the chain in his small-fingered child's hands, because it was his *tahlmorra*. Because he knew, without knowing why, the golden links in his dreams bound him as fully as his blood.

A sound: the whisper of leather on stone, announcing someone's presence. Pressed against his mother, Aidan peered one-eyed over a velveted shoulder and saw his father in the hall. His tall, black-haired father with eyes undeniably yellow, feral as Aidan's own; a creature of the shadows as much as flesh and bone. Brennan's dress was haphazard and the black hair mussed. Alarm and concern stiffened the flesh of his face.

"The nursemaid came—what is wrong?"

Aidan felt his mother turn on her knees even as her arms tightened slightly. "Oh, naught but a bad dream. Something to do with the Lion." Forced lightness. Forced calm. But Aidan read the nuances. For him, a simple task.

The alarm faded as Brennan walked to the dais. The tension in his features relaxed. "Ah, well, there was a time it frightened *me*."

Aidan did not wait. "I wanted the chain, *jehan*. It called me. It *wanted* me . . . and I needed *it*."

Brennan frowned. "The chain?"

"In the Lion. The chain." Aidan twisted in Aileen's arms and pointed. " 'Twas *there*," he insisted. "I came to fetch it because it wanted me to. But the Lion swallowed it."

Brennan's smile was tired. Aidan knew his father sat up late often to discuss politics with the Mujhar. "No one ever said the Lion does not hunger. But it does not eat little boys. Not even little princes."

Vision blurred oddly. "It will eat *me* . . ."

"Aidan, hush. 'Tis fanciful foolishness," Aileen admonished, rising to stand. "We'll be having no more of it."

A dark-skinned, callused hand was extended for Aidan to grasp. Brennan smiled kindly. "Come, little prince. Time you were safe in bed."

It was shock, complete and absolute. *They do not believe me,* either *of them*—

His mother and his father, so wise and trustworthy, did not *believe* him. Did not believe their *son*.

He gazed blindly at the hand still extended from above. Then he looked into the face. A strong, angular face, full of planes and hollows; of heritage and power.

His father knew everything. But if his father did not *believe* him.

Aidan felt cold. And hollow. And old. Something inside flared painfully, then crumbled into ash.

They will think I am LYING.

It hurt very badly.

"Aidan." Brennan wiggled fingers. "Are you coming with me?"

A new resolve was born. *If I tell them nothing, they cannot think I am lying.*

"Aidan," Aileen said, "go with your father. 'Tis time you were back in bed."

Where I might dream again.

He shivered. He gazed up at the hand.

"Aidan," Aileen murmured. Then, in a flare of stifled impatience, "Take him to bed, Brennan. If he cannot be taking himself."

That hurt, too,

Neither of them believe me.

The emptiness increased.

Will anyone *believe me?*

"Aidan," Brennan said. "Would you have me carry you?"

For a moment, he wanted it. But the new knowledge was too painful. Betrayal was not a word he knew, but was beginning to comprehend.

Slowly he reached out and took the hand. It was callused, large, warm. For a moment he forgot about the betrayal: the hand of his father was a talisman of power; it would chase away the dreams.

Aidan went with his father, followed by his mother. Behind them, in the darkness, crouched the Lion Throne of Homana, showing impotent teeth.

He clutched his father's hand. Inside his head, rebelling, he said it silently: *I want my chain.*

Gentle fingers touched his hair, feathering it from his brow. " 'Twas only a dream," she promised.

Foreboding knotted his belly. But he did not tell her she lied. He wanted his mother to sleep, even if he could not.

PART I

Chapter One

Deirdre's solar had become a place of comfort to all of them. Of renewal. A place where rank did not matter, nor titles, nor the accent with which one spoke: Erinnish, Cheysuli, Homanan. It was, Aileen felt, a place where *all* of them could gather, regardless of differing bloodlines, to share the heavy, unspoken bonds of heritage. It had nothing to do with magic, breeding, or homeland. Only with the overriding knowledge of what it was to rule.

She knew what Keely would say; *had* said, often enough, phrased in many different—and explicit—ways. That women had no place in the male-dominated succession lining up for the Lion Throne. But Aileen knew better. Keely would not agree—she seldom agreed with anything concerning the disposition of women—but it was true. Women *did* have a place in the line of succession. As long as kings needed queens to bear sons for the Lion, women would have a place.

Not the place Keely—or others—might want, but it was something nonetheless. It made women important, if for womb instead of brain.

Aileen's womb had given Homana one son. Twin boys, enough to shore up Aidan's tenuous place in the succession, were miscarried; the ordeal had left her barren. She was, therefore, a princess of precarious reknown, and potentially threatened future. Brennan would not, she knew, set her aside willingly—he had made that clear—but there were others to be reckoned with besides the Prince of Homana. He *was* only a prince; kings bore precedence. And while the Mujhar showed no signs of concern regarding her son's odd habits, she knew very well even Niall was not the sole arbiter. There was also the Homanan Council. She was the daughter of a king, albeit the island was small; nonetheless, she understood the demands of a kingship. The demands of a council.

Only one son for Homana. One son who was—different.

She shivered. The solar was comfortable, but her peace of mind nonexistent. It was why she had gone to Deirdre.

Aileen stood rigidly before the casement in the solar with sunlight in her hair, setting it ablaze. A wisp drifted near her eyes; distracted, she stripped it back. The gesture was abrupt, impatient, lacking the grace she had mastered after twenty-four years as Princess of Homana; twenty-four years as her aunt's protégée, in blood as well as deportment.

She folded arms beneath her breasts and hugged herself, hard. "I've *tried,*" she said in despair. "I've tried to understand, to believe 'twould all pass . . . but there's no hiding from it now. It started in childhood . . . he thinks we're not knowing . . . he believes he's fooled us all, but servants know the truth. They *always* know the truth—d'ye think they'd keep it secret?" Her tone now echoed the rumors. "The heir to Homana rarely spends a whole night in sleep—and he goes to talk to the Lion, to rail against a *chair* . . ." She let it trail off, then hugged herself harder. "What are we to do? I think he'll *never* be—right." Her voice broke on the last word. With it her hardwon composure; tears welled into green eyes. "What are we to do? How can he hold the throne if everyone thinks him mad?"

Deirdre of Erinn, seated near the window with lap full of yarn and linen, regarded Aileen with compassion and sympathy. At more than sixty years of age she was no longer young—brass-blonde hair was silver, green eyes couched in creases, the flesh less taut on her bones—but her empathy was undiminished even if beauty was. She knew what it was like to fear for a child; she had borne the Mujhar a daughter. But Maeve, for all her troubles, had never been like Aidan. Her niece's fears were legitimate. They all realized Aidan was—different.

Deirdre knew better than to attempt to placate Aileen with useless platitudes, no matter how well-meant. So she gave her niece the truth: " 'Twill be years before Aidan comes close to inheriting. There is Brennan to get through first, and Niall is nowhere near dying. Don't be borrowing trouble, or wishing it on others."

Aileen made a jerky gesture meant to dispel the bad wishing, a thing Erinnish abhorred. "No, no . . . gods willing—" she grimaced "—*or* their eternal *tahlmorras*—Aidan *will* be old . . . but am I wrong to worry? 'Twas one thing to dream as a child—he's a grown man now, and the dreams are worse than ever!"

Deirdre's mouth tightened. "Has he said nothing of it? You used to be close, you and Aidan—and he as close to Brennan. What has he said to you?"

Aileen's expulsion of breath was underscored with bitterness. "Aidan? Aidan says nothing. Aye, once we were close—when he was so little . . . but now he says nothing. Not to either of us. 'Tis as if he cannot *trust* us—" She pressed the palms of her hands against temples, trying to massage away the ache. "If I say aught to him—if I ask him what troubles him, he tells me nothing. He *lies* to me, Deirdre! And he knows I know it. But does it change his answer? No, not his . . . he is, if nothing else, stubborn as a blind mule."

"Aye, well, he's getting that from both sides of his heritage." Deirdre's smile was kind. "He is but twenty-three. Young men are often secretive."

"No—not like Aidan." Aileen, pacing before the window, lifted a hand, then let it drop to slap against her skirts. "The whole palace knows it . . . the whole *city* knows it—likely all of Homana." She stopped, swung to face Deirdre, half-sitting against the casement sill. "Some of them go so far as to say he's mad, mad as Gisella."

"Enough!" Deirdre said sharply. "Do you want to give fuel to such talk? You're knowing as well as I there's nothing in that rumor. He could no more inherit insanity than *I* did, or you." She sat straighter in her chair, unconscious of creased linen. "He's Erinnish, too, as well as Cheysuli . . . how d'ye know he's not showing a bit of *our* magic? There's more than a little in the House of Eagles—"

Aileen cut her off. "Oh, aye, I know . . . but the Cheysuli is so dominant I doubt our magic can show itself."

Deirdre lifted an eyebrow. "That's not so certain, I'm thinking, with your hair on his head."

Aileen grimaced, one hand drifting to brilliant locks. Aidan's was darker, but still red; only the eyes were Cheysuli. "There's nothing about my son that bespeaks Erinnish roots—he's as bad as any of *them.*"

Deirdre's smile was faint. "By 'them,' you're meaning Cheysuli?"

"Cheysuli," Aileen echoed, forehead creased in absent concern. "One moment they're all so human . . . the next, they're *alien.*"

"Aye, well, they could say the same of us." Deirdre took up the forgotten embroidery in her lap, examining it critically. Her skills faded year by year, but not her desire. The worst thing about aging, she thought, was the inability physically to do what her mind wanted. "I think women have made that complaint many times before, whether the man in their bed is a shapechanger, or nothing more than a *man*."

For the first time Aileen smiled. She had never been beautiful, but beauty was not what made her Aileen. The beauty of Erinn's eagles lay in vividness of spirit, and a crude physical splendor. "You wouldn't be saying that of the Mujhar."

"I would," Deirdre retorted. "No doubt he's said it of me; no man understands a woman."

Aileen's brief smile faded, "Does a mother understand her son?"

Deirdre's hands slowed. "I'll not say you've naught to think about, with Aidan, but there's no madness in him. And there are worse things to a man than dreams; worse things to a throne than a dreamer."

"I wonder," Aileen murmured.

Deirdre schooled her tone into idle inquiry. "What does Brennan say?"

"Nothing." Aileen shifted on the sill, cocking one knee against the glazing so that her weight was on the stone. "He feels it as much as I, but d'ye think he'll admit it? Admit he doubts his son?" The line of her mouth flattened. "When Aidan was little, and so sick, Brennan and I shared everything. But Aidan withdrew, and then so did Brennan. There was nothing left between us. Now, when he speaks of it at all, he says merely 'tis Aidan's *tahlmorra* to hold the Lion Throne."

Deirdre sighed. "So says his birthright. But there are times, to my way of thinking, they put too much weight on what they believe instead of on what they feel."

"They believe in the prophecy, each and every one of them." Then Aileen laughed. Bitterness was manifest. "Except, of course, for Teirnan and his *a'saii*, lost in the woods of Homana."

Deirdre's mouth tightened. "Teirnan was a fool."

"You only say that because he seduced your daughter . . . you're not caring a whit what Teirnan thinks about anything else, after what he did to Maeve." Aileen shifted restlessly, adjusting heavy skirts. "Maeve is happy now, in Erinn, and perfectly safe—my son is neither, I'm thinking."

"Your son will do well enough." Deirdre bit through a thread. "As you said, Maeve is happy—and who would have thought *that* possible after what Teirnan did to her?" Deirdre sighed, untangling colors. "I thank the oldfolk of Erinn for hearing a mother's pleas . . . Rory Redbeard's a good man, and has made her a good husband."

"Since he couldn't be having Keely. " Aileen smiled briefly. "He wanted her, you know. For all she was meant for Sean, and the Redbeard came here knowing . . ." She let it trail off. "Maeve is nothing like Keely. If that was what Rory wanted, he got something other than expected."

Deirdre raised a brow. "By the time Keely and Sean sailed for Erinn, only a fool would have thought he yet had a chance. After Teirnan's bastard was born, Rory took Maeve for Maeve's *own* sake, not as a replacement for Keely. "

Aileen laughed aloud. "There is no replacement for Keely."

"And no replacement for Aidan . . . the boy will be whatever it is he's meant to be."

Brief amusement fled. Aileen stared at her aunt. Deirdre's composure occasionally irked, because she claimed so little herself. Just now, it made her want to shatter it, even as she longed for Deirdre's serenity. It was a thing unknown to her, with a son such as Aidan.

"There is something wrong with him. There is something not *right*." Aileen stared at her aunt, daring her to disagree. "Next time you see him," she said intensely, "look into his eyes. Then ask yourself these questions: "Is my grandson happy? Is my grandson *sane?*"

Deirdre stared, aghast. "I'd *never* do such a thing!"

"Ask," Aileen suggested. "Better yet, ask *him*. But don't listen to what he says—look in his eyes, instead. 'Tis where you'll find the truth. Cheysuli eyes or no, 'tis where you'll find the truth."

Chapter Two

He was up and out of his bed before he knew who or where he was; before he knew what he wanted. The need drove him to it. The compulsion preempted everything: thought, logic, comprehension, much as *lir*-sickness had. It overtook his body and carried him to the door, where he pressed himself against it in mute appeal for passage.

Inside his head tolled a certainty tainted with a plea: *This time I can touch it . . . this time it will be real—THIS time, I know—*

But the declaration faded, along with certainty, as he came sluggishly to himself from the depths of unsettling dreams. He realized, in despair, it had happened yet again.

Sweat filmed him. He slept nude, as always, disliking the bindings of sleepclothes, the excess warmth of covers. So now, damp with dreams and fear, he shivered in the chill of a cool summer night, and cursed himself for a fool.

With great effort he stilled his breathing, pressing his brow against the heavy door as if the pressure of flesh on wood might drive out the dream he dreamed. But it never did, never, no matter how hard he tried, and at last he turned, giving up, scraping shoulder blades against wood, and stared blindly into darkness.

"Why?" he whispered raggedly, through the headache only beginning. "Why does this happen to *me?*"

In the darkness, something stirred. But no answer was offered him; after too many years of the asking, he no longer expected one.

The pounding of his heart slowed. He swallowed heavily twice, disliking the bitter aftertaste of the dream, and scratched irritably at a scalp itchy from dream-fear and reaction. He shivered once, controlled it, then stood up at last from the door.

He lingered only a moment, considering what might happen if he simply went back to bed; he knew better. He knew very well, having tasted futility more often than dreamless slumber. So he gave up the sweet contemplation of what it might be like if he could simply *sleep*, as other people slept, and stumbled to the nearest clothing chest to pull out age-softened leather leggings.

No more: only leggings, enough for now, he thought; more would be too much. More would be too *hot;* the summer night was cool, but dreams banished comfort and basted him with warmth.

It would not be so bad, he thought wryly, *if at least I dreamed of women. They are worth the discomfort of a night become too hot.*

He had been a man, as manhood is reckoned, for nearly eight years. He had dreamed, and spilled his seed, into women and into his bed. But it was not of women he dreamed when the dreams were sent by gods.

A servant always left him a lighted candle; he always blew it out. Warrior training—and common sense—taught him safety lay in eyes well-accustomed to heavy darkness instead of blinded by too much light. But his room was an outer one, narrow casements slit the walls, and torchlight from the baileys crept through to bathe his chamber. Pale light burnished his arms: faceted *lir*-bands gleamed.

Bare of chest and feet, he swung back toward the door. He paused there, eyes shut, cursing himself for a fool.

"Leave it alone—*ignore* it—" Aidan bit into his lip. "Who is in control: a piece of wood, or you?"

Inside his head, the Lion roared. Aidan's belly knotted.

"Leave it alone," he repeated. "Gods—leave *me* alone—"

Time to go, someone said. *How can you turn back now? It has become ritual . . . and you are not the kind who changes anything regardless of the need.*

Stung, Aidan turned to glare through darkness at the rustling in the corner. "What am I to change? Would you have it be my *tahlmorra?*"

Now the tone was scornful. *You do not even have an inkling what your* tahlmorra *IS.*

Through the link, he lashed out. *I know very well what it is— Do you?*

I have known all along. What do you think I am? Are YOU not proof that my tahlmorra *is undertaken?*

Because I exist? No. The tone, now, was cool. *I exist because I am. Because the gods created me.*

To be my lir.

The tone spilled into smugness. *Or you to be mine.*

Aidan swore beneath his breath. Mockingly, he asked, "Has any warrior ever revoked the *lir*-link?"

No living *warrior.*

It reminded Aidan of something, as it was meant to do: the precariousness of his race. "Has any warrior petitioned the gods for a new *lir?*"

Undoubtedly others have asked. But it is not my duty to tell you how the gods deal with ungrateful children.

"Ungrateful," Aidan muttered. "How could any man be so foolish as to consider how peaceful life might be if his *lir* was other than you?"

How can any warrior contemplate peace when he stands ready to fight a chair made of wood?

"Agh, gods . . ." Aidan put his hand on the latch. "You do not need to come, Teel. Stay in the corner and sulk; I can find my own way."

He jerked open the heavy door and stepped through, leaving it ajar. He thought for the merest moment he *would* be unaccompanied, but the rustling grew louder. And then the raven left the darkness and flew to perch on his shoulder.

Aidan extended an arm. "Try my hand," he suggested. "Like this, you scratch my shoulder."

Too soft, his *lir* chided, but exchanged shoulder for hand.

Aidan briefly considered taking a lamp with him, but decided against it. No corridor in the massive palace was left completely without light so guards or servants, if needed, could see to serve or protect, but unnecessary torches and lamps were extinguished. And he was, after all, Cheysuli, with yellow Cheysuli eyes; he saw what there was to see whether light existed or not.

"A fool," Aidan muttered, but set off anyway. Ignoring the stubborn compulsion gained him nothing but sleepless nights.

He had known, for as long as he could remember, he was *different*. The dreams of childhood had faded during adolescence, dissipated by the intense need for and the bonding with his *lir*, but once adulthood was reached the dreams returned in force. Now, at twenty-three, he was accounted a warrior in the clans and a full-grown man by the Homanans who called him a prince, but he was still plagued by dreams. By the vision of the chain. By the *substance* of the chain—until he put out a hand to touch it, and the links dispersed into dust.

As a child, it had frightened him. Growing older, he believed it merely a manifestation of a want and desire he could not fully understand. But of late the dreams had worsened. The desire had become a *demand*. And Aidan fully believed, with a dreadful certainty, he was somehow, someway, tainted.

"Tainted," he murmured aloud, aware of familiar tension.

Perhaps, the raven agreed. *But why would gods choose a tool that is tainted?* Teel paused significantly. *Unless they merely forgot—*

It was not precisely the sort of reassurance he craved. It was true the *lir* were a gift of the gods, but he preferred to think of himself as a man, not a tool. Not even a divine one; he asked no favors of the gods, for fear they might give him one.

Enough, he said dismissively, sending it through the link.

Well? Well? Why would *they?*

Firmly, Aidan said: *We are not discussing gods.*

Perhaps we should *discuss them. You discuss everything else, yet very little of substance.*

He gritted teeth, but did not answer. He merely walked, saying nothing, passing out of shadows into torchlight, into darkness again. Through countless corridors and passageways, knowing them all by heart, until he reached the Great Hall.

There are times, the raven commented, *even Cheysuli are fools.*

Aidan, searching for release from the tension, settled on irony. *It is because of the other blood.*

Teel considered it. *I think not,* he replied. *I think it is merely you.*

Muttering under his breath, Aidan shoved open the doors.

Go back to bed, Teel suggested. *You know how you feel in the morning when you spend the night chasing dreams. You know how you* look.

Irritated, Aidan shifted back into human speech as he shouldered into the hall. Against his flesh he felt the texture of the silver, the whorls and angles and patterns set by craftsmen into the metal. "You know very well when I try to ignore the dream, it only gets worse."

Because you allow it to.

He let the door fall closed behind him, hearing its distant grate. Irritation spilled away. Fear trickled back. He recalled all the nights very clearly. Especially the first, when he had come at the age of six to find the chain of gold in the lap of the Lion Throne.

And how he had shamed himself, frightened by something of wood; and by things he could not fathom.

All came rushing back. Humiliation caused him to squirm; why could he not forget?

Tension made him curt. "Is it there?"

Probably, Teel observed dryly. *Is it not always there?*

Aidan sighed and moved away from the heavy silver doors. The flames of the firepit had died to coals, lending dim illumination to the cavernous hall. Shadows cloaked the walls: tapestries and banners; history set in cloth. Wheels of swords and daggers painstakingly bracketed in a perfect and deadly symmetry. Spears and pikes sprouted from display blocks set in corners; flagsticks dangled silk. In the folds crouched Homana. Beyond the pit, on the dais, crouched the Lion Throne.

Teel rode Aidan's hand easily, considerably lighter than the hawks, falcons, and eagles other warriors claimed. It was, Aidan felt, a facet of his very *differentness* that his *lir* was a raven. The bird was hardly unknown in the history of the clans, but neither was it common. Aidan considered it a jest played on him by capricious gods. In addition to sending him dreams, they gave him an irascible *lir.*

Teel pecked his thumb. *I have ridden faster rocks.*

"Then get off my hand and go sit on one."

Obligingly, the raven lifted and flew the length of the hall. But he did not sit on a rock. He sat on the head of the Lion.

Aidan, ruddy brows lifted, stopped at the foot of the dais. "Surely sacrilegious—you profane the Mujhar's throne."

Teel fluffed a wing. *Considering the Mujhar is only the Mujhar because of* lir *like myself, I think it is allowed.*

Steadfastly, Aidan stared at the raven. Then, drawing a breath, he made himself look down at the cushion on which his grandsire sat when he inhabited the throne.

So, Teel observed, *the dream remains constant.*

Aidan shut his eyes. The painfully familiar sense of loss and oppression rushed in from out of the shadows.

Stiffly, he knelt. He waited. Felt the coldness of glossy marble through the leather of his leggings. Smelled ash, old wood, oil; the scent of ancient history, intangible yet oddly vivid.

Let me touch it, he begged. *Let me know the chain is real.*

But when he put out a hesitant hand, the links dissolved to dust. Breath spilled raggedly. "Oh, gods . . . oh, *gods*—why do this to me? What have I done to deserve it? What do you want from me?"

But even as he asked, futility overwhelmed him, much as it had the very first time. And, like that time, what he wanted was to cry. But he was twenty-three: a man fully grown. An acknowledged Cheysuli warrior with a *lir* to call his own . . . if Teel condescended to let him.

Aidan did not cry. He was no longer six years old.

Though there are times I wish I were, so I could begin again.

Teel's tone was cool. *What use in that?* he asked. *The gods made the child. Now the rest is up to the* man.

"Stop," Aidan declared.

When you *do.*

"I swear, you will drive me mad, hag-riding me to death."

Teel's irony slipped, replaced with an odd kindness. *I will keep you sane when you hag-ride* yourself *to death.*

Aidan let it go. He was too weary, too worn. There was something he had come for. The ritual to perform.

He sighed, cursing himself out of habit. He knew what he would find, but Aidan put hand to cushion. Touched the worn nap of the velvet. Felt nothing but the fabric. Not even the grit of dust.

Futility was overpowering. *"Why?"* The shout filled the hall. "Why do I always come back when I know what will happen?"

"Because the gods, when they are playful, are sometimes cruel instead of kind."

Aidan lurched to his feet and spun around, catching himself against the Lion. He had heard nothing, nothing at all; no scrape of silver on marble, no steps the length of the hall. He stared hard like a wolf at bay, thinking of how he looked; of what appearance he presented—hair in disarray, half dressed, haranguing a wooden beast. Heat flooded him. Humiliation stung his armpits. He wanted to shout aloud, to send the man from the hall, away from his royal—but embarrassed—presence; he did not. Because he looked at the man who faced him and recognition shamed him.

His grandfather smiled. "I know what you are thinking; it is written on your face. But it is unworthy of you, Aidan . . . you have as much right to be here, no matter what the hour, as I do myself."

On the headpiece of the Lion, the bright-eyed raven preened. *I have told you that, myself.*

Aidan ignored his *lir*. Embarrassment had not receded; if anything, he felt worse. What he wanted most was to apologize and flee—*this man is the Mujhar!*—but he managed to stand his ground.

After a moment's hesitation, he wet his lips and spoke quietly. "I may have the right to be here, but not to disturb your rest."

"The rest of an old man?" Niall's tone was amused, "Ah, well . . . when you are as old as I you will understand that sleep does not always come when you want it to."

He began to feel a little better; the Mujhar was now his grandsire. Wryly, Ajdan smiled. "I know that already."

"So." Niall advanced, holding a fat candle in its cup of gleaming gold. "Why have you said nothing to me of these dreams? Do you think I have no time for my grandson?"

Aidan stared at the man who, by right of gods and men, held the Lion Throne of Homana. He, like Deirdre, was past sixty, yet as undiminished by age. Still tall, still fit, still unmistakably regal, though no longer youthful. Tawny hair had silvered, fading like tarnished gilt; Homanan-fair skin had creased, displaying a delicately drawn fretwork born of years of responsibility; of the eyes, one was blue and bright as ever, the other, an empty socket couched in talon scars, was hidden behind a patch.

Aidan drew in a breath, answering his grandfather's question with one of his own. "How can you have the time? You are the Mujhar."

"I am also a man who sired five children, and who now reaps the benefits of my children's fertility." Briefly, Niall eyed the raven perched upon his throne. "You I know better than the others, since you live here in Homana, but there are times I fully believe I *know* you least of all."

Aidan smiled. "It is nothing, grandsire."

Niall arched a brow.

"Nothing," Aidan repeated.

"Ah." Niall smiled faintly. "Then it pains me to know my grandson feels he cannot confide in me."

Guilt flickered deep inside. "No grandsire—'tisn't that. 'Tis only . . ." Aidan shrugged. "There is nothing to speak about."

Niall's gaze was steady. "I am neither a fool, nor blind—though I have but one eye I still see."

Heat coursed through Aidan's flesh. The sweat of shame dotted a thin line above his lips. He made a futile gesture. "They are just—dreams. Nothing more."

"Then I must assume the servants are embroidering the truth."

The tone was very quiet, but compelling nonetheless. "I think it is time you spoke. If not to Aileen or to Brennan, then to me. I have some stake in this."

Aidan clenched his teeth briefly. "*Dreams*, nothing more—as anyone dreams. Fragments of sleep. Thoughts all twisted up, born of many things."

The Mujhar of Homana forbore to sit in his throne, usurped by a black-eyed raven who, as a *lir*, had more claim than any human, Cheysuli-bred or not. Or so Teel told them. Instead, Niall sat down upon the dais, setting down the candle cup with its wax and smoking flame. "Tell me about them,"

Aidan rubbed damp fingertips against soft leather. *Tell him. Tell him? Just like that?*

Niall's tone was kind. "Locking things away only adds to the problem. Believe me, I know; I spent far too many years denying myself peace because I believed myself unworthy of this creature looming behind me."

Aidan glanced only briefly at the Lion. Then sat down on the dais next to Niall, putting his back to the beast. He felt a vast impatience—how could he share what no one would believe?—but attempted to honor his grandsire by fulfilling part of the request. "This has nothing at all to do with unworthiness. I promise, grandsire, I know who I am and the task I am meant for: to rule as Mujhar of Homana." Easily, he made the palm-up Cheysuli gesture denoting *tahlmorra,* and his acceptance of it. "I think I will do as well as the next man when my time comes—you and my *jehan* have taught me very well; how could I *not* be worthy?" He flicked fingers dismissively, thinking it enough.

Niall waited in silence.

Discomfited, Aidan stirred. "No one can understand. Why *should* I speak of it? When I was a child, I tried to tell them about it. But neither of them believed me."

"Who did not?"

"*Jehan* and *jehana*. They both said I was a child, and that what I dreamed was not real. That I would *outgrow* it . . ." Bitterness underscored the tone; Aidan pushed it away with effort. "Would you speak of a thing people would ridicule you for?"

"Aileen and Brennan would never ridicule you."

Aidan grimaced. "Not *them,* perhaps . . . not so obviously. But what is a child to feel when his parents call him a liar?"

Niall's brows knit. "I have never known you to be that. I doubt they have, either; nor would ever say such a thing."

"There is such a thing as *implying*—"

"They would not even do that."

It was definitive. Aidan shifted his buttocks and stared gloomily into the hall. "I wish there were a way I *could* explain what I feel. What I *fear*."

"Try," Niall suggested. "Tell me the truth, as you know it. Tell me what disturbs your sleep."

Aidan rubbed gritty eyes. What he needed most *was* sleep.

No. What he needed most was *the chain*.

He sighed and let it go. "What I fear is the meaning behind my dream. The same one over and over." Now it was begun. Tension began to ease. With it went strength. Slumping, he braced elbows on his knees and leaned his chin into cupped hands. "For as long as I can recall, the *same* dream over and over. I think it will drive me mad."

Niall said nothing. His patience was manifest.

Aidan sighed heavily and sat upright, scraping hair back from his face. In the poor light his thick auburn hair was an odd reddish-black, falling across bare shoulders too fair for a Cheysuli. A man, looking at him, would name him all Homanan, or call him Erinnish-born. Until he saw the eyes.

"There is a chain," Aidan began. "A chain made of gold. It is in the lap of the Lion."

The Mujhar did not give in to the urge to turn and look. Mutely, Niall waited.

Aidan, abruptly restless, thrust himself upright and paced away from dais, Lion, Mujhar. Away from his *lir*, uncharacteristically silent. He stared in disgust at the firepit, letting the coals dazzle his eyes, then swung back to face his grandsire.

"I know—I *know* how it sounds . . . but it is what I feel, what I *dream*—"

"Aidan," Niall said quietly, "stop trying to look through my eyes."

Brought up short, Aidan shut his mouth and waited. He had been carefully tutored.

Niall's gaze was kind. "You are wasting too much time trying to imagine what I will think. Simply say it. *Tell* it; you may find me less ignorant than you believe."

Aidan clenched his teeth; how could anyone, kin or not, fully understand?

But in the end, it was very easy. "I have to have it," he said plainly. "If I do not, the world ends."

Niall's expression was startled. "The world—*ends?*"

Aidan gestured acknowledgment; it sounded as odd to him. "The entire world," he agreed dryly. "At least—for me." And then he gestured again. "I know, I *know*—now I am being selfish, to think of the entire world, and its fate, being determined by what I do . . . but that is what I dream. Over and over again."

He waited. Before him the old man sat hunched on the dais, silvered brows knit with thought. Niall frowned pensively, but his expression gave nothing away.

The thought was fleeting and, unwelcome. *There is madness in my kinfolk—*

But Aidan knew better than to say it. Niall would only deny it; or, rather, deny its cause as anything other than accident. He had said, time and time again, the madness of Aidan's Atvian granddame, Gisella, was induced by an early, traumatic birth—but Aidan sometimes wondered. He was capable of intense thoughts and impulses, sometimes as disturbing as his dreams, though he always suppressed them. He had heard the same said of Gisella. And he knew from repeated stories his *su'fala*, Keely, had never been fully convinced the madness was not hereditary.

"Well," Niall said finally, "everyone dreams. *My* dreams are odd enough—"

For the first time in his life, Aidan cut him off. "I *have to have it,* grandsire. Do you understand? It is a need as strong as the need of a man for a woman . . . as the need of warrior for *lir.* There is no difference, grandsire . . . it *makes* me come here. Every time I dream it."

Niall stared at him, clearly startled by the passion. "If it disturbs you this much—"

Aidan laughed aloud. "Disturbs me? Aye, that is one way of saying it . . ." He banished the desperation with effort, striving for equanamity. "Grandsire, perhaps it is better put like so: what if, as you reached to take her into your arms, Deirdre was turned to dust? To *nothingness* in your hands, even as you touched her, wanting her so badly you think you might burst with it."

Niall's expression was arrested. Aidan knew, as he always knew, the emotions his grandsire felt. Shock. Disbelief. The merest trace of anger, that Aidan could compare a chain to the Mujhar's beloved *meijha* . . . and then the comprehension of what the failure meant.

After a moment, Niall got up with a muffled grunt of effort and mounted the dais steps. He paused before the Lion, placed a hand upon it, then turned awkwardly and sat down. It was not, Aidan knew, an attempt to use his rank, but the desire of an old man wishing for softness under his buttocks while be contemplated his grandson.

The Mujhar rubbed at deep scar-creases mostly hidden beneath the patch, as if the empty socket ached. "What happens, then, when you come looking for this chain?"

Aidan shrugged, trying to diminish the desperation he always felt. "I put out my hand to take it, and the chain is changed to dust."

"Dust," Niall echoed thoughtfully.

Aidan extended his right hand. It shook; he tried to suppress it. "I have to have it, grandsire . . . I *have to have the chain*—and yet when I touch it, only dust is left." He shut his hand tightly. "But even the dust goes before I can really touch it."

Niall's single eye was steady. "Have you seen the priests?"

Aidan grinned derisively, slapping his hand down. "They are Homanans."

A silver brow arched. Mildly, the Mujhar said, "They are also men of the gods."

Aidan made an impatient gesture. "They would laugh."

Niall rubbed meditatively at his bottom lip. "No priest of Homana-Mujhar would ever deign to laugh at the man who will one day rule."

Aidan sighed. "No, perhaps not . . . but they would tell those stories. *Already* people tell stories." He tapped his bare chest. "The servants are full of gossip about the Prince of Homana's fey son—the man who walks by night because he requires no sleep."

Niall's smile was faint. "Oh, you require it. And they should know it, too—they have only to look at your face."

"So it shows . . ." He had known it did, to him; he had hoped others were blind to it. "I have done so many things, trying to banish the dreams. Petitions to the gods. Even turning to women," His mouth twisted in self-contempt. "I have lost count of how many women . . . each one I hoped could do it, could banish all the feelings by substituting others. It is a sweet release, grandsire, but it gave me no freedom." He sighed heavily. "None of them was un-grateful—it was the heir to the Prince of Homana, grandson to the Mujhar!—and I like women too much to cast them off indis-creetly . . . but after a while, it palled. Physical satisfaction was no longer enough . . . all the dreams came back."

Niall said nothing.

"Gods—now I am started . . ." Aidan laughed a little. "*And* liquor! I have drunk myself into a stupor more times than I can count, hoping to banish the dream. And for a night, it may work—but in the morning, when all a man in his cups desires is for the sun to set again so it does not blind his eyes, the dream slips through the cracks." Aidan smiled wryly. "I'll be telling you plain, grand-sire, the dream is bad enough when I've been having no liquor—'tis *worse* when I'm in my cups."

Niall's smile widened. "Did you know that when you are upset, you sound very like your *jehana?*"

Aidan's mouth twitched. "Or is it I sound like Deirdre?"

"No, no—Dierdre has been in Homana too long . . . most of Erinn is banished, in her . . ." Niall flicked dismissive fingers and straightened in the throne. "But we are not here to speak of ac-cents. Aidan, if you will not go to Homanan priests, what of the *shar tahls?*"

Aidan stilled. "Clankeep?"

"There may be an answer for you."

"Or no answer at all."

"Aidan—"

"I thought of it," he admitted. "Many, many times, and each time I did I convinced myself not to go."

Niall frowned. "Why? Clankeep is your home as much as Homana-Mujhar."

"Is it?" Aidan shook his head. "Homana-Mujhar is my home—Clankeep is merely a *place.*"

For a moment his grandsire's expression was frozen. And then the fretwork of Niall's face seemed to collapse inwardly. His eye, oddly, was empty of all expression, until realization crept into it. Followed by blatant grief and regret.

His tone was ragged. "So, it comes to pass . . . Teirnan was right after all." He slumped back in the throne, digging at the leather strap bisecting his brow. "All those times he said we would be swallowed up by Homanans; are you the first, I wonder? Is this the Homanan revenge; if Cheysuli must hold the Lion, we make the Cheysuli Homanan?"

Aidan stared in startled dismay. "Grandsire—"

Niall waved a hand. "No, no, I am not mad . . . nor am I grown suddenly too old for sense." He pulled himself upright in the massive throne. Now the tone was bitter. "I am speaking of Tiernan, your kinsman—cousin to your *jehan*, son to my dead *rujholla*. The one who renounced the prophecy and founded his own clan."

Aidan frowned faintly. "I know who he is. We all know who Teirnan is—or *was*." He shrugged. "How many years has it been since anyone has seen him? Fifteen? Twenty? He may well be dead."

Niall's expression was pensive. "He took his clan into the deepwood somewhere in Homana . . . he is still out there, Aidan—he still plots to take the Lion."

Aidan did not really believe his grandsire was too old to rule, or growing feeble in his wits, but he did think perhaps too much weight was given to a man no one had seen for too many years. The Ihlini were past masters at waiting year after year to strike at their enemies, but from what he knew of his kinsman, Teirnan was not that kind.

"Grandsire—"

Niall did not listen. He heaved himself out of the Lion and bent to retrieve the candle in its cup. He straightened and looked his grandson dead in the eyes. "Go to Clankeep, Aidan. Discover your true heritage before it is too late."

Dumbfounded, Aidan automatically gave way to his grandfather's passage and watched him go, saying nothing. Then turned to look at his *lir* once the silver doors had closed. "What does that mean?"

Teel observed him thoughtfully. *I did not know you were deaf.*

Aidan scowled. "No, I am not deaf . . . but what good will Clankeep do?"

Give you ears to hear with. Give you eyes with which to see. Teel rustled feathers. *Go back to bed, deaf* lir. *No more dreams tonight.*

Aidan thought about retorting. Then thought instead about his bed and the sweetness of dreamless sleep. "Coming?" he asked acerbically, turning away from the dais.

Teel flew ahead. *I could ask the same of you.*

Chapter Three

The stallion was old, growing older, but retained enough of his spirit to make handling him occasionally difficult. The horseboys and grooms of Homana-Mujhar had long ago learned the tending of the black—appropriately named Bane—was best left to his owner, who had a true gift. They dealt with him as they could, then gave him gladly into Brennan's keeping whenever the prince came down to the stableyard.

He came now, dismissing the horseboys flocking to offer attendance, and went into the wood-and-brick stable to see the stallion. But a true horseman never merely *looks;* he can but tie his hands to keep from touching the flesh, from the strong-lipped, velveted muzzle, blowing warmly against his palms.

Bane, by right of rank, had the largest stall in the stable block; a second block housed the Mujhar's favorite mounts. Brennan slipped the latch and entered the straw-bedded stall. The stallion laid back ears, cocked a hoof, then shifted stance to adjust his weight. One black hip briefly pressed Brennan into the stall; automatically slapped, the hip duly shifted itself, ritual completed. Raven ears came up. One dark eye slewed around to look as Brennan moved in close. Bane blew noisily, then bestowed his chin upon Brennan's shoulder, waiting for the fingers that knew *just* where to scratch.

The murmured words were familiar. Bane spoke neither Homanan nor the Old Tongue of the Cheysuli; Bane spoke motion and voice and touch and smell, the language of horse and rider. He listened but vaguely to the words Brennan crooned, hearing instead the tones and nuances, knowing nothing of meaning. Only the promise of affection. The attendance upon a king by a royal-born man himself.

Bane did not mark the underlying anguish in Brennan's tone, the soft subtleties of despair. He was horse, not human; he did not answer to anything unless it concerned his few wants and needs. But even if he *were* human, even a Homanan, the emotions would escape him. Cheysuli-born were different. The unblessed, regardless of bloodlines, of humanness, were deaf to things unsaid. Blind to things suppressed.

But Ian was not unblessed. Ian was Cheysuli. His own share of anguish and despair, though mostly vanquished by time, made him party to them in his nephew.

He moved close to the stall, pausing at the door. Briefly he watched Brennan with his stallion, noting tension in the movements, marking worry in the expression. Seeing such indications was what he had learned to do as liege man to the Mujhar, and as kin to volatile fledglings not always cognizant of caution.

"I have," Ian began quietly, "spent much of my life offering succor—or merely an attentive ear—to those of my kin in need. You have always held yourself apart, depending in great measure on a natural reserve and full understanding of your place, But I have never known a Lion's cub to be beyond the need of comfort."

Brennan, startled, stiffened into unaccustomed awkwardness, then turned. One arm rested on Bane's spine, as if maintaining contact might lend him strength. The other fell to his side. The gold on his arms gleamed in a latticework of sunlight, vented through laddered slats in the outside stable walls. "Did *jehan* send you?"

Ian, hooking elbows on the top of the stall door, smiled with serene good humor. His arms, like Brennan's, were bare of sleeves, displaying Cheysuli gold. "I am not always in his keeping, any more than you. Give me credit for seeing your pain independent of the Mujhar."

Brennan grimaced, looking away from his uncle's discerning eyes to the black silk of Bane's heavy rump. Idly he smoothed it, slicking fingers against the thin cloak of summer coat. Thinking private things. "It was always *jehan* you went to, or Hart—then Keely, when Hart was gone. There were times I wanted to come, but with so many others to tend, I thought your compassion might be all used up."

Ian's eyes were on Bane. He was, like the stallion, past his prime, with hair more gray than black, and white creeping in. By casual reckoning, he was perhaps fifty; in truth, nearly seventy. It was the good fortune of the Cheysuli that age came on them slowly, except for prematurely graying hair. The bones and muscles stiffened, the skin loosened, the hair bleached to white. But nothing about Ian's manner divulged a weakening of spirit any more than in the stallion.

He shifted slightly, rustling boots in straw and hay and bits of grain dropped by Bane over the door. "Niall's children cannot escape the often too-heavy weight of *tahlmorra*, except perhaps for Maeve." Still-black brows rose in brief consideration. "But even then, I wonder—who are we to say there is no magic in her? Niall's blood runs true . . . even in Aidan."

Brennan winced. And Ian, who had baited the hook with quiet deliberation, saw it swallowed whole.

"Oh, aye," Brennan sighed wearily. "The blood runs true in Aidan . . . including Gisella's, I wonder? It is what every one *else* wonders, regardless of the truth." Brennan turned again to the stallion. A lock of raven hair, showing the first threading of early silver, fell across a dark brow deeply furrowed with concern. "You know and I know my *jehana*'s madness is not hereditary, but the Homanans overlook it. All they see is his *difference*, then they mutter about Gisella."

"You cannot ask a man to hide his true self," Ian said gently, "and yet Aidan does so."

Brennan's mouth tightened. "You refer to what *jehan* told me. About Aidan's dreams."

"There was a time he would have told you himself."

Brennan's expression was bleak. "Not for many years. He changed, *su'fali* . . . somehow, some*when*, he changed."

"Perhaps he believed he had to."

The tone now was anguished. "I did not *want* him to! Why would I? After so many years of sickness . . . after so much worry and fear . . ." Brennan sighed, shutting his eyes. "We thought he would die, *su'fali*. In fever, he often babbled. We learned not to - listen."

"Because what you heard made no sense."

Mutely, Brennan nodded.

"And so now he does not speak." Ian shook his head. "Aidan is perhaps not what you expected . . . but trying to reforge a sword will only make the steel brittle."

Brennan swung abruptly from the horse. "Have I tried?" he cried. "He is as much a man and warrior as you or I. There is nothing in him I would curse, wishing for alteration . . . he came through a sickly childhood in better fashion than we hoped for, and now there are no doubts he will live to inherit the Lion. But I cannot say what he *thinks*—" Brennan broke it off. The stallion shifted restlessly, disturbed by the raw tone. "*Su'fali*, have you never seen him look through you? Not *at* you, but through. As if you were not present. As if *he* were not, but in another place."

Ian felt serenity slipping. He was one of those men others spoke to freely, finding him easy to confide in. It was a trait not well known among the Cheysuli, who had, in the old days, forbidden the showing of private emotions before others for fear of divulging a weakness to enemies. But those days were past. Things changed within the clans—some said too many things—and he saw no oddity in listening to the sometimes illogical initial commentary of a man—or a woman—trying to find the proper way. It had been so with Niall, and with Hart, and Keely. Brennan had needed no one; Corin had *wanted* no one, unless she be twin-born Keely. But even that had changed.

As everything changed. Now Brennan needed someone to explain a son to his father. And Ian could not do it.

"So you have," Brennan said dully. "You have seen it as well."

Ian sighed. "How can I give you an answer? How can anyone? Aidan is like none of us in many ways, while very like us in others. I see Aileen in him. I see you in him. But perhaps all of us look too hard for unimportant things, such as who he resembles or sounds like. Perhaps Aidan is merely *Aidan*—"

"That bird." Brennan's tone was intent. "That raven—"

Ian smiled. "Teel is a *lir*."

Brennan shook his head. "More. I swear, he is more. Have you seen the look in Aidan's eyes when he goes into the link?"

Ian's smile broadened. "If Keely were here, no doubt she could tell us what it is they converse about, but I would imagine what they say to one another—or what Teel says to him—is little different from what we say to our own *lir*. You should see *your* expression when Sleeta links with you."

"Aye, well, she is sometimes difficult to deal with." Brennan's brow smoothed as a faint smile pulled his mouth crooked. "Aidan himself has said Teel hag-rides him unmercifully."

Ian stepped aside as Brennan left Bane and unlatched the door to exit the stall. "For too many years he was sick, too many times close to death. It marks a man, Brennan. It marked your *jehan*. It marked you. It marked Hart and Corin and Keely. Did you think your son would escape it?"

Brennan swung shut the door and slammed the latch into place. "The Lion requires a man who can rule with intellect, not with dreams and fancies."

"Ah," Ian murmured. "Is that why you allowed yourself none?"

Brennan's face hardened, "You understand what responsibility is, *su'fali*. Do you blame me? When it comes to levying war, dare a king think of dreams?"

"There is no war in Homana. Nor in Solinde. Nor in Erinn or Atvia. What war are you fighting, *harani?*"

Brennan shook his head. "No one understands what it is to look at Aidan and wonder what he will be. To wonder what he *is*."

Ian refrained from answering at once. There was wildness in the Cheysuli, for all they practiced control; he knew from personal experience how difficult it was to maintain balance under trying circumstances. Some said it was the beast in the blood. Ian knew better. There was a price to pay for control: the occasional loss of it.

His royal nephew, for all Brennan's reknowned maturity, was as capable of anger as his volatile brother, Corin, or Keely, his prickly sister. He simply did not show it as much, yet Ian thought it best now to avoid provocation. It was next to impossible to make a man see reason if his mouth was busy shouting.

He watched Brennan a moment, marking redoubled tension. "Do you wonder, then, why he says nothing to you? Why he goes so often to the Lion? If you have, in any fashion, caused him to wonder if he is—*askew*—in any way, should he trust himself with a throne shaped like a mythical beast? Or believe it an enemy?"

"By the gods, Ian, he is a grown man, a *warrior*."

"This began when he was a child. Children view things differently."

"Children are often too fanciful. They frighten themselves." Brennan's eyes, oddly, were black. "Do you think I know nothing of that? Even within Bane's stall, knowing the door is *there,* I still feel the fear of being closed in."

"Do you blame yourself for that?"

Brennan's expression was ravaged. "I was locked in the Womb for a very short time . . . and yet I believed it days." He raked a hand through his hair. "Gods—how I frightened myself. I made all those *lir* into beasts . . . *carved marble shapes,* I remade into living beasts. And now I reap the reward . . . shut me up in darkness, and I lose myself utterly."

Ian nodded slightly. "And so the *jehan,* seeing a child's fear fed by fancies, told him it was not real. Over and over again, until the child thought it best to keep everything to himself."

Desperation threaded Brennan's tone. "They are *dreams,* Ian. What else was I to do? Allow him to frighten himself?"

Ian shrugged a single shoulder. "I have no answer for you. But Aidan still dreams . . . fear or no fear, *something* is real to him."

"And I gave it no credence, ever." Brennan collapsed against the wall, mouth pulled awry. "I am not and have never been the most discerning of men."

Ian watched him closely. Quietly, he suggested, "I think Aileen might understand what you feel. She has as much stake in Aidan's future as you."

Brennan's expression was bleak. "She says nothing of it to me."

Ian did not smile. "Have you ever thought to ask her?"

Brennan shrugged. "She is too quick to defend him. She hears nothing of my concern, gives no weight to what I say." He grimaced. "He is her only child; she will hear no wrong of him."

Ian shook his head. "Aileen is neither blind nor deaf. She defends him to *others;* is there need to do that with you?"

The stallion, now turned, thrust his head over the door, blocking their view of one another. Brennan cupped a hand over the bone of the nose and pulled the black head down so he could see his uncle. "I have the right to worry."

Ian stroked the silken neck. "No one will take that from you. But Aileen might help you bear it."

Brennan's expression was odd. "He needs to sire a son."

Ian's motion was arrested. "Why? Do you think it might be best if you replaced your son with a grandson? Just *in case*—"

"No!" The response came too quickly. "But he is twenty-three, *su'fali* . . . I had a son by then. My *jehan* had three of his own, as well as two daughters."

Ian said nothing a moment. Then, in precise, staccato, tones, "Have you never thought that, given more time, you and Aileen might have made a true match? One much like Niall's and Deirdre's?"

"There was Corin—"

"That was very nearly twenty-five years ago!"

Muscles clenched in Brennan's jaw. "You are saying I should give Aidan time."

"There is enough of it yet; aye. You know the price you and Aileen have paid . . . why ask *him* to pay it?"

Brennan's tone was as clipped. "Kings must beget sons."

Ian lost his patience. "The present king is living. His own heir is perfectly healthy, and *he* has an heir. I think the Lion, just this moment, requires no more than that."

Brennan shut his eyes. When he opened them, Ian saw bleak despair. "And if my son is mad? How do I get another? Aileen can give me no more . . . and I will not set her aside. I *need* a son from Aidan."

Ian shook his head. "Aidan is not mad. Aidan is only— different."

Brennan cupped Bane's black muzzle. "Kings cannot be different. It makes the Homanans afraid."

His uncle's expression was compassionate. "No more afraid than you."

The day was gray, growing grayer. Aidan, who had ridden out of Mujhara not long after a mid-morning meal, scowled irritably at the pewter-hued sky. Teel was in it somewhere, riding out the wind; Aidan looked, found him, sent his feelings through the link.

As if to spite the wind, Teel's tone was undiminished. *Some things are worth discomfort.*

"But it is *summer*," Aiden protested. "Summer rain I understand—*this* feels more like winter!"

Only yesterday you complained of the heat . . . I think you are merely perverse.

He could be, Aidan admitted. But now was not one of those times. Yesterday, it *had* been hot; now it was much too cold. Not so cold as to make him shiver, but enough to make him wish he had brought at least a fall cloak. Arms left bare by Cheysuli jerkin protested the chill. *Lir*-bands felt icy.

Wind changed direction and blew ruddy hair into pale eyes. Aidan stripped it back, peeling strands free of lashes, then forgot about hair altogether as his horse shied violently sideways to make his own discomfort known. The dun gelding did not bolt, but only because Aidan was ready for him.

"No," he said calmly, speaking also through the reins. "I think it would be best for both of us if you let me do the choosing of whether we walk or run."

Lir. Teel's voice. *The storm is growing worse.*

Aidan, who could feel the blast of the wind as well as the raven, offered no comment. He was too busy with the horse, who threatened to run again. Aidan did not really blame him. If he himself were a horse, he might run as well. The wind was full of urging, wailing down hilly croftlands. Its song was one of winter; of hearthfires and steaming wine. Or, if he were a horse, of windtight stable and warm bedding straw, with grain for the asking.

"Summer," Aidan muttered. "What will winter be like, I wonder?"

There was nothing for it but to ride on, to reach the fringes of the wood that would provide some protection. The track, warded by trees and foliage, would be free of much of the wind, and he could go on to Clankeep screened from the worst of the weather.

Debris littered the air: leaves, dirt, torn petals of wind-tattered flowers. Aidan ducked his head, squinted, spat, urged the gelding a little faster. And then faster still.

"Go ahead," he agreed, giving the dun his head. "A bit of a run will do no harm, and will get us there the faster."

The gelding required no urging. By the time they reached the trees, Aidan was almost sorry. A gallop through the wind blew away the dull dregs of a troubled night's sleep, leaving him refreshed and in good spirits. He gloried in the sensation of horse against the storm, himself bent over the neck so as to give the wind no purchase. But he did not give into the impulse that told him to run again; the gelding deserved a rest, and the track was littered with stormwrack, providing treacherous footing for a horse already spooked.

"*Shansu,*" he said, patting the gelding's neck. "Another time, I promise—for now we will walk."

The dun was ordinarily a well-mannered, settled horse, neither young nor old, and not given to coltish antics. But clearly the storm had set him on edge; now, as Aidan attempted to calm him, he pawed and swished his tail, indicating displeasure.

Aidan lifted an arm and pointed. "That way," he suggested.

The dun backed in a circle, eyeing the way they had come.

"No, I said *that* way—" Aidan turned him forcibly. "We have been to Clankeep uncountable times before . . . there is no reason for this. If there were danger, Teel would say so; I trust him more than you."

The gelding protested, snorting nosily. Dark eyes rolled.

Frowning, Aidan went into the link. Lir—is *there danger?*

So much for trust, Teel answered. *No, there is no danger . . . nothing but the storm.*

Relieved, Aidan aimed the dun yet again toward the east. "If this is a show of will, I could choose a better time . . . shall we discuss this a bit later?"

The gelding stood still and quivered.

Aidan stroked the ocher-brown neck again. "*Shansu,* my lad, my boy—'tis naught but a bit of a blow . . . d'ye think I'd be wanting you harmed?"

Erinnish, many held, was a tongue made for horses, but the gelding was Homanan. He chose to misunderstand.

Wind roared through the trees. The dun bolted and ran.

It was, Aidan thought grimly, an entirely horselike flight. After refusing to go east, fright had forced the gelding. If the storm had not worsened matters, Aidan might have let him run on since he was heading toward their destination. But he dared not in the wind. The track was fouled with debris. If the gelding tripped and went down—

"Never *mind,*" Aidan muttered, cursing imagination.

He drew the reins in tautly and attempted to apply force of will to the restraint. He had gentled many a colt and won many a horse's trust, sharing much of his father's skill. But the gelding was having none of it.

Concern instantly deepened. Aidan knew the feel of it: the bit had been rolled forward, free of tender bars, and now was lodged in teeth. The horse was in control. The man on his back was nothing more than a minor inconvenience not worth the trouble of throwing off.

Aidan, amused by the all-too-accurate vision, grinned, then wished he had not as dirt fouled his teeth. He spat. *I could simply take* lir-*shape and let this fool of a boy run on* without *me*—

But the thought of risking the gelding made him reconsider. His father had trained him too well; when it came to welfare, he thought of the horse's in place of his own.

Or, I could—

But what else he could—or could not—do, went unthought. Without altering his pace, the gelding dodged off the track and crashed into deadfall and foliage, neatly avoiding a tree trunk. Aidan also avoided the trunk, but did not miss the limb sweeping down from the rack of low boughs.

In reflex, he thrust out a warding forearm, knowing it much too late. *Lir*—

It was all Aidan managed as the tree limb embraced his ribs and swept him out of the saddle.

Chapter Four

He dreamed. He dreamed he was made of smoke and fire in place of flesh and blood. His heart was a white flame and his soul whiter still, so brilliant it was blinding. Out of the white flame of his heart and the whiter brilliance of his soul came the music that poured through his veins like quicksilver, burning what it touched with a pain exquisitely sweet. He wanted to cry with its beauty, but knew he dared not.

Water extinguishes flame. Extinguished, I will die.

He saw himself, but it was not himself. The Aidan he saw was another man, insubstantial, incorporeal, substantive as smoke. He drifted this way, that way, shredding himself as he moved, then forming himself again. And then the man of smoke congealed into anther shape, taking the form of a raven, also made of smoke, and the raven flew swiftly skyward in a bid for needed freedom.

South, to an island: away from Homana-Mujhar and all the Cheysuli Keeps; away from the world everyone else called home, until the raven found a new home among the standing stones now fallen, cold and green and gray, where he perched upon a shattered, rune-scribed altar as if he wished to speak of gods.

The altar was overturned. From beneath it, something glinted with the dull brilliance of muddied gold. The raven, knowing need, left his perch and descended.

A chain. Coiled beneath the altar, perfect and unblemished. Its beauty was so compelling that even the raven was moved to desire it. But a raven has no hands; he shapechanged himself to a man and knelt down to pick up the chain.

He touched it. It was whole. He lifted it. It was whole. He took it from the shadows, unable to breathe, and held it in the light.

The links were the size of a man's forearm. Seamless, flawless gold, filled with twisted runes too intertwined to decipher.

He dared to breathe on it. One of the links broke.

Grief swallowed him. *Why do I destroy when all I want is to make things whole?*

He still held half of the chain. The other half had fallen, spilled on leaf-molded floor.

A sound. He turned, still kneeling, still grasping his half of the chain, and saw the shadowed figure in the tumbled doorway of lichen-clad stones.

The voice was firm and commanding. "You hold me in your hand. What do you want from me?"

Aidan tried not to gape. Where had the stranger come from? For that matter, where was *he?*

"Who are you?" he blurted.

Disbelief was manifest: black brows arched up, then snapped together over a blade-straight nose. "The Mujhar," he said. Clearly the stranger believed Aidan could surely name him; only a fool could not, or a man with no eyes to see.

Aidan heard the undertone of expectation couched in blatant arrogance. But he *heard* it, he did not *feel* it; something was not right. Something was not *real.*

The Mujhar—? he echoed blankly.

Certainly the man looked it. He wore black velvet and leather of exquisite quality and cut; a scarlet rampant lion clawed its way across the black silken overtunic belted with heavy gold. Hands, hooked into the belt, were strong, long-fingered, callused, the hands of a soldier; no Cheysuli, he. The eyes were a clear, piercing gray. Black hair was frosted silver.

Neither young nor old. Aidan thought him fifty. But something he could not name whispered of agelessness.

It would do no good to wonder when he knew the man lied. "Who are you?" he repeated.

Gray eyes narrowed. "I have said: the Mujhar."

It was too much. Aidan, frowning, glanced around the ruins, trying briefly to place himself. And then the arrogance of the tone—and the claim—restored his attention to the stranger.

Who is he *to say such a thing?* And then he nearly laughed. *And to* me, *when it comes to that; I know the truth.*

"Mujhar, you say?" Aidan sat back on his heels. "And *I* say you are lying."

Well-cut lips tightened. "That is punishable by death."

"Oh?" Aidan smiled. "Then kill me, Mujhar . . . kill the man who *will* hold the Lion when the proper time is come."

"You?" Black brows swept up again. "*You* will hold the Lion?"

Aidan spoke lightly. "So I have been told. It has to do with my birth—I am Brennan's son, and grandson to Niall."

"Ah." It was succinct, yet brimming with comprehension. "Where I am, there is no time . . . and I did not realize so much had already passed." He smiled consideringly. "Are we to Niall already?"

This man is mad. And I am mad for listening.

He adopted a coolly condescending tone. "You will forgive me, I hope, if I fail to display the deference due a Mujhar—I show it to my grandsire, who is deserving of it. You I do not know."

"Oh, I think you do." The gray eyes were oddly lambent. "The history of the Cheysuli is full of my name and title."

Aidan held on to his patience. "Then why not give me both."

"You have the title: Mujhar. The name I am called is Shaine."

Shaine. Shaine? *Shaine?*

He wanted to laugh, but could not. This man touched his pride, as well as heritage. "I will thank you to keep your mouth from the name of my ancestor."

Gray eyes glinted. "But it is *my* name."

"Shaine is dead," he said flatly.

The stranger merely nodded. "A long time ago. Would you like to hear how?"

"I know how. I was taught. All of us were taught." Aidan did not smile. "Shaine killed himself when he voided Ihlini wards set to keep Cheysuli from Homana-Mujhar."

"A painful death, and somewhat unexpected," agreed the other. "But by then it no longer mattered . . . Finn would have killed me once he walked the hall. It was what he came to do." Briefly the eyes smoldered. "Hale's shapechanger son . . . gods, but I hated them. And Alix was the worst, coming before me like Lindir, but dark instead of fair." Lips writhed briefly. "Carillon would have wed her, and made her Queen of Homana. I could see it in his eyes."

Dumbstruck, Aidan stared. The words came very slowly. "She married Duncan instead."

"Duncan. Your great-great-*great*-grandsire." Gray eyes narrowed. "A long history. I weary of it all."

This cannot be happening. None of this is real. Aidan stared at the man. He filled his eyes with the man, stretching lids wide, then swallowed back the sour taste filling his mouth. *Am I dead?* he wondered. *Could this all be real?*

The knots in his belly tightened. Aidan felt numb. "If you are Shaine . . ." he mumbled. "If you *are* Shaine . . ." He twitched the thought away. "Am I dead?" he asked flatly. "Oh, gods, am I dead? Is this what it is to die?

"Dead? You?" White teeth parted the beard. "No, not yet. There is time still left to you."

Fleetingly, Aidan wondered how much; he forbore to ask. Relief was too overwhelming, until he considered again the circumstances.

He wiped one sweaty hand on a legging-clad thigh. His only chance was to focus on something, anything, to keep himself from losing control. "If you are Shaine the Mujhar, you *are* dead."

The man did not reply.

Aidan felt sick. He wanted to spew out the contents of his belly across the fallen altar, or onto leaf-thickened floor. Sweat bathed his flesh. His head began to ache. Worst of all was the fear.

I HAVE gone mad.

And then, *Gods, where is Teel? What has become of my* lir?

Still kneeling, he shuddered. Hands clenched on the links.

This is a new dream . . . gods, let it BE a dream—

Shaine the Mujhar stared back. "We are not discussing me. We have come to speak of you."

"Me?" Aidan blurted. "What have you to do with me?"

"Stand up," he was told.

Aidan slowly rose. Links in his hand chimed.

The man examined him. "Cheysuli," he said in disgust. "I should have known Carillon would lift my curse as soon as he claimed the Lion . . . well, it took him five years to win it back from Bellam, and longer still to end the extermination." The line of the mouth was bitter. "*Qu'mahlin*, you shapechangers call it? Aye, well, nothing lasts, not even the Cheysuli . . ." Gray eyes narrowed. "Red hair, fair skin . . . is it merely you mimic the fashion?"

Sickness was unabated. His belly writhed within. But he focused on something else so as to ignore his discomfort.

"Mimic the fashion—?" Abruptly, Aidan understood. It made him angry, very angry; it gave him courage again. "These *lir*-bands and the earring are mine, gained in the usual way, and properly bestowed during my Ceremony of Honors. There is no *fashion* to them; nor to me, my lord apparition: I am Cheysuli and heir to Homana."

Shaine the Mujhar smiled. "Are you so certain of that?"

Aidan struggled with himself. *I am mad—I must be mad—why else am I standing here arguing with a fetch?* He glanced around for Teel. *Where is my lir?*

Shaine the Mujhar still smiled. "Are you so certain?"

The derision snared Aidan's attention. "Of course I am certain," he snapped. "I have told you who I am, and you say I am not dead; how would I *not* be heir?"

"By never accepting the throne."

Aidan swallowed a shout. Quietly, he said, "I was born to accept the throne. The Lion will be mine."

Shaine lifted a hand and pointed to the chain dangling from Aidan's hand. "Men are but links," he said. "Links in a chain of the gods, who play at the forge as a child plays at his toys. Make a link, and solder it here—solder another there . . . rearrange the order to better please the eye." The arrogance had faded, replaced by intensity. "Some links are strong and never yield, bound to one another . . . others are flawed, and break, replaced by those who are stronger so the chain is never destroyed. It is a game of the gods, Aidan, to forge a flawless link, then join it to the other. One by one by one, making the chain strong. Making the chain perfect. Disposing of weakened links so as not to harm the whole."

Holding the broken chain, Aidan said nothing.

Shaine did not smile. "The weak link has a name: Aidan of Homana."

Anger rose, was suppressed. It would do no good to argue with a man who did not exist. "You are in my dream," Aidan rasped. "Dreams have no substance. This *chain* has no substance. Nothing you say is real."

"Then why did you summon me?"

Aidan shook his head. "I did not summon you. A man cannot summon a dream . . . nor can he raise the dead."

"But I am there, in your hand." Shaine pointed precisely. "The chain, Aidan; that link. I explained it all to you once; must I explain it all again?"

Aidan looked at the link clutched in his hand. His fingers tightened on it. If, in his twisted dream, this link was Shaine, who were the others?

But he banished the question at once; Shaine was his concern. "Begone," he said tautly. "I want none of you."

Gray eyes glittered. "But I am *in* you, Aidan. All of us are."

Aidan threw down the chain. Shaine disappeared.

The tremor ran through his body. It convulsed legs, arms, neck, then snatched at lax control. He felt the spasm, the jerk, then the sudden cessation of movement. He lay limply on the ground, sprawled in broken foliage now compressed beneath his body.

What—? he asked vaguely, numb with disorientation.

"Shansu," a voice said quietly. "Let the world settle."

Aidan had little choice. For the moment he knew nothing of who he was or where he was, or what had happened to him. Only that somehow—*how?*—he had come to be lying on his back on the ground.

"Shansu," the voice repeated. "I would be the last to harm you."

Who—? Aidan forced open eyes. Dazzled, he stared blindly up at the pewter-gray sky screened by a lattice of limbs, and recalled he was in the wood.

Not inside a ruined chapel with a dead Mujhar standing before him.

Consciousness solidified. "Teel," he managed aloud, groping through the link for familiar reassurance.

There was nothing. Nothing. No Teel. No link. Only the absence of everything, as if he had been emptied.

"Teel!"

The spasm returned in full force, this time prompted by the frantic flailing of his limbs. He still had no control, but this time he was the cause.

A hand touched his brow and pressed him gently against the ground. *"Shansu."* A third time. "Your *lir* is safe, I promise. I only sent him ahead. Clankeep is not so far . . . unless, of course, I have misreckoned the distance." The tone was wry. "That is possible, I suppose; I am not accustomed to human time divisions, or distances reckoned as leagues. Still, as the raven flies . . ." Now the tone was amused.

"Who—?" Aidan squinted.

The hand was cool on his brow. "For now, it makes no difference. I have a name, aye, but we do not bestow them on men, who cannot deal with the power held in a true name. If you like, you may call me the Hunter; it will do as well as my real one, which means very much the same."

Another one, Aidan thought dimly. *First the one calls himself Shaine, and now* this *one* . . . It drifted away on a wisp of disbelief. He would not allow himself. Self-possession was the key, if he was to survive.

Aidan licked dry lips. "I came off my horse."

"Most dramatically. Unlike you, the horse is unhurt." The voice was amused.

Aidan focused with effort. Now he could see someone. A man, kneeling by his side. A *brown* man: hair, skin, eyes, leathers, all degrees of peat-brown, as if he hid himself in the wood—or, Aidan thought dimly, as if he was *of* the wood. Not old, not young, but in between; a score of years older than Aidan, a score younger than Niall. Dark eyes were kind, but compelling.

Something in Aidan answered. "You are Cheysuli—?" But he broke it off almost at once. "No—no, of course not . . . how could I think such a thing?"

The Hunter smiled. "There is Cheysuli in me. Or, to be precise: there is *me* in Cheysuli."

For a man only recently revived from unconsciousness—and with an aching head—it was much too confusing. Very like his meeting with Shaine, which, Aidan was certain, came as reaction to the fall. "Let me sit—*aghh*—"

"Perhaps not," the Hunter said mildly.

Aidan was appalled by the pain. His head hurt, aye, but not so much as his chest. A demon was kicking his ribs. "Am I broken?" he asked faintly.

"Bruised, a little. Repairable, certainly. I would do it for you, but that is not my gift. I Hunt; I do not Heal."

That won Aidan's attention. "Hunt—" he muttered blankly. "What is it you hunt?"

"Men."

Something jumped inside painful ribs. "But—" He stopped. "No—I think not . . . you could not be—"

"—hunting you?" the brown man finished. "Oh, indeed I could be . . . in fact, I am certain I *am.*"

Sweat sheened Aidan's face. He felt it under his arms; in the hollow of his belly, beneath aching ribs. "What have you done with my *lir?*"

"Sent him ahead, as I said. Do you think I could hurt a *lir?*" The tone changed to shock. "No more than harm *you,* who are true-born of the Cheysuli . . ." The Hunter's voice faded. His face registered concern. "I have little experience with humans, even with those of my blood . . . perhaps I would have done better to come in another guise." He frowned thoughtfully. "But this one has always served me . . . it has always been so *benign* . . ."

Aidan lost fear and patience. "Who exactly *are* you? And why are you hunting me?"

The dark face creased in a smile. "To discover what you have learned."

"Have—learned—?" It was incongruous to Aidan that any of what he saw was real. That what he heard was real; the fall had addled his wits. First Shaine, and now the Hunter. "Am I supposed to have learned anything in particular? Or anything at all?"

"Oh, I think something. You have been alive for twenty-three years . . . I think you *must* have learned something." The smile was undiminished, though irony laced the tone.

And yet another time, as if repeated asking would eventually win him an answer: "What have you done with my *lir?*"

The brown man's smile vanished. Ruefully, he rubbed his jaw. "I see the link is even stronger than we expected . . . we might have done better to lessen it, to make *lir* and warrior less dependent upon one another, but without the strength of that bond, there could be repercussions. And we could not afford those." He shook his head. "No, I think it is as well."

Patience frayed. "*What* is as well?"

"The bond," the Hunter answered equably. "The thing you call the *lir*-link. The thing that sets you apart from all the others we made . . . except, of course, the Ihlini." He sighed. "We do not succeed in everything. Imparting free will was a risk we decided to take . . . the Ihlini were the result." He paused. A trace of grimness entered his tone. "And, now, the *a'saii.*"

Aidan gritted his teeth. "You have not answered my question."

"About your *lir?* But I have. I sent him ahead, to Clankeep."

Response was immediate. "Teel does no man's bidding! Teel can be *sent* nowhere, unless I do the sending!"

"Ah, but the *lir* answer to a higher power than that of the Cheysuli. They can be sent wherever we say."

"There is only one other power—" Aidan broke it off. He stared hard at the man, daring him to repeat the oblique claim, but nothing was forthcoming.

The wind, for a moment, rose, then died away to nothing. Storm clouds peeled away, leaving behind a clear sky. It was, abruptly, *spring*, not summer; grass grew, trees budded, the air was warm and light. Even as Aidan sat there, braced against the ground, a flower grew up between the fingers of one hand. And blossomed.

The Hunter's smile was mild. "Perhaps you begin to see."

Aidan snatched his hand away. The denial was absolute. "No."

The Hunter nodded in silence.

I am mad. I am. I must be. Or sick in the head; the fall—it was the fall . . . I landed on my head, and everything is a dream—yet another *dream . . . first Shaine, now this Hunter*—Aidan squinted fiercely. *If I look at things more closely—*

What he looked at was a man who claimed he was a god.

Spring dissolved itself. It grew cooler as Aidan stared, until he began to shiver. It was cold, too cold; in winter he wore fur-lined leathers, forsaking the linens of summer. But now he was caught, bathed by winter's breath. The ground around him hardened. The trees sloughed leaves. The grass beneath was dead, and all the flowers gone.

But a moment ago it was spring . . . Aidan shivered. And then it was warm again.

When he could, he cleared his throat. Perhaps if he proceeded with extreme caution . . . "*Why* did you send Teel away? If he is of your making—"

"Oh, not of *mine*—I do not do the making. That is a task for others, though all of us, of course, have some say in the matter." The Hunter's expression was kind, as if he understood all too well what Aidan was thinking. Which perhaps he did, if he was what he claimed. "As to why I sent him away, the answer is simple enough. This is a thing between you and I, Aidan, not among you and I and the raven. Even the *lir* are not privy to all we do."

The seasons, without fanfare, continued changing. Grass grew, then died; flowers bloomed, then died; trees changed their shapes; the sky was day, then night; then night and day again. And all without a word from the brown man watching Aidan. Without a single *gesture* to say he realized what he did was not done—could *not* be done—by anyone but a god.

Think about something else . . .

Aidan stirred, then ventured another question. "Why are the *lir* not privy to all you do?"

"Oh, they are quite arrogant enough without requiring another reason. They are familiars, not gods—they cannot know everything, or they become quite insufferable."

"No," Aidan said faintly, letting it sink in. "Teel needs no more cause for any additional arrogance. He has quite enough as it is."

White teeth gleamed. "I thought you might agree. I think any warrior would, faced with such a course." The Hunter rose, stretched legs, moved to a shattered tree stump. As he sat down, a tiny sapling sprouted at the base of the broken stump. "Teel is— different. I thought him well suited to you."

Aidan sat upright carefully, holding himself very straight. *I will say nothing of this to him—all these* wonders *he performs. Perhaps I am not meant to notice.*

But that seemed incongruous. How could he not notice?

Once more, Aidan focused. "Why? Why is Teel suited to *me?* Why not another warrior?"

"Because you also are different." There was no sting in the quiet words; from a god, they were revelation. "You will spend much of your time questioning things; that is the way of you. Many men act first with little thought for result—rashness is sometimes a curse, sometimes a virtue—but your gift is to think things through before acting." The Hunter smiled. "You will make mistakes, of course—you are man, Aidan, not god—but you are also exceedingly cautious. Some might call you reluctant, others will name you afraid, but cowardice is not your curse."

Aidan wet drying lips. "What *is* my curse?"

The god looked down at the sapling trying mightily to be a tree. He bent, cupped its crown in his fingers, murmured something quietly in a tongue foreign to Aidan. Then, in clear Homanan, "Not so quickly, small one . . . there is time for you to grow. For now you must wait on men." He took his fingers away and looked again at Aidan. "You are simply you. Try to be no one else. Let no one force you to be.

"But—" Aidan, staring at the tiny tree, did not finish, forgoing the question he meant to ask in a flood of others like it. "Is that all?"

"All?" Brown eyebrows arched. "Trying to be himself—or *her*self, as Keely learned—is one of the most difficult tasks a human can face."

Aidan waited a moment. "But I have to be Mujhar."

The Hunter was very solemn. "That, too, is a task. Not every man succeeds." He shifted on the stump. "I am here to tell you nothing more than I have. It is not the nature of gods to tell their children everything—man does not learn by being told; he must *do*. So, you will do." One leather-clad shoulder lifted and fell in a casual shrug.

Aidan, who felt in no way enlightened *or* casual, scowled at the Hunter. "Are you really here?"

"Are *you?*"

In spite of himself, he smiled. "With this pounding in my head, I could not begin to say."

Brown eyes glinted. "Horses are made for riding, not for falling off of. Now you must pay the price." He paused. "You might have flown, you know."

"I might have," Aidan agreed. "There is nothing so free as flying . . . but riding a good horse has its own brand of magic."

The Hunter laughed. "Aye, well, we gave you free will . . . choosing to ride instead of fly is one of the smaller freedoms."

Aidan shifted restlessly, then surpressed a wince. "That is all—? You came merely to say I must be myself?"

"Enough of a task, for now. But since I am here, you may as well tell me about your dream."

Ice encased his flesh. "You know about my dream? You know about the chain?"

The answer was oblique. "I mean the dream you dreamed just now, before coming to yourself. Your eyes were wide open, but you saw nothing of the day. Only inside yourself."

Aidan felt moved to protest. "But you are a *god*."

The Hunter looked annoyed. "You are a man," he said plainly. "We made you deliberately impulsive and idiosyncratic, and gave you minds with which to dream . . . do you think we also put thoughts in your heads? Why would we want to do *that* when it defeats the purpose of living?"

"My heads hurts," Aidan replied. "That is my only thought."

The Hunter displayed white teeth. "We gave you the freedom to rule yourselves, Aidan, because we wanted children, not minions. Devotion is appreciated; respect we honor highly. But we do not want fanatics and zealots. That is not why we made men." He paused, then softened his tone. "Now, tell me of the dream."

He did not want to, any more than tell Niall. But he had spoken to the Mujhar. Surely he could find it within himself to divulge the dream to a *god*.

He drew in a trembling breath. "Shaine," Aidan said, and told him the whole of it.

He thought, at the end, the Hunter would disparage him for it, saying he was too fanciful, or blame it on the fall. But the Hunter did no such thing.

"It was not false," he said quietly. "Who calls it so is a blind man, with no soul to use as eyes. Those in your head can play you false; those of your soul cannot."

"But Shaine has been *dead* for nearly one hundred years!"

Frowning, the Hunter nodded.

It frightened Aidan badly. "Have *you* no explanation?"

"There are tests," the Hunter replied absently. "I am only one among many; I cannot tell you what others plan for you. There are tests, and tasks . . . no *tahlmorra* is fulfilled without pain, or there can be no growth. Without growth or evolution, there can be no change. Without change, the world dies."

"Evolution?" Aidan echoed.

The Hunter's smile was sanguine. "A mechanism for change. For the *betterment* of a world."

Aidan, lacking reply, merely stared at the god.

"So." The Hunter rose. "I have said what I came to say. There remains only this." He reached into his belt-pouch. "This is for you, and only you. When you have learned both use and meaning, you will be closer to finding the answers to all those questions you ask aloud in the darkness of the night."

Something arced through the air. Aidan, scrambling forward painfully, caught it. And knew it instantly by touch. By the texture of the gold, formed into a seamless, flawless link big enough for a man's wrist.

"You *do* know—" he began, but found the Hunter gone.

In his place reared a tree, in full-blown majesty.

Chapter Five

Aidan made his way through Clankeep and rode straight to the blue pavilion bedecked with a painted black mountain cat. It was not his own; he had none. It was his father's pavilion, though Brennan rarely came. Its use had fallen to Aidan, though he also spent most of his time in Homana-Mujhar.

He reined in the dun before the laced doorflap. And scowled up at his *lir*, perched in perfect indolence atop the pavilion ridgepole.

You knew, he charged, sending annoyance through the link.

Teel fluffed feathers.

"You *knew*," he said aloud, as if the dual challenge carried more weight than one or the other.

I knew nothing, the raven retorted.

Aidan's brows shot upward. His tone dripped sarcasm. "Oh? Is this the first crack in your vaunted self-assurance? You admit to ignorance?"

Teel thought it over. *I knew what he was,* he conceded at last. *But not what he wanted.*

It was, Aidan thought, a compromise. Something Teel rarely did. "Why?" he asked aloud. "Why did he come to me?"

Teel turned around twice on the ridgepole, then stared down at his irritated *lir. You are angry.*

"Aye," Aidan snapped. "Should I not be? I have just spent a portion of my life—I'm not even knowing how much!—talking with dead men and gods."

Ah. Black eyes were bright. *Anger is good.*

Aidan glared. "Why?"

Because it is better than fear. If you give in to the fear, it can overwhelm you.

"For now the only thing overwhelming me is frustration," Aidan retorted. He scowled blackly at the raven. "You did not answer my question. Why did he come to me? This *god*."

Teel fluffed feathers. *I am quite certain he told you.*

"Something of something," Aidan agreed. "Not enough to make sense, merely to confuse."

Teel cocked his head. *Gods are often like that.*

Aidan drew breath for waning patience, caught it on a hiss as the pain of bruised ribs renewed itself. "Then I am to assume you will give me no answers to the questions I still have."

We are not put here to answer all *your questions,* Teel said brusquely. *Only some of them.*

"With you choosing which ones."

We answer what we can, if the questions are in your best interests. Teel dug briefly under a wing, then looked down at Aidan once more. *You will know what you must know when the time to know is come.*

Aidan gritted teeth. "Obscurity," he said grimly, "is a game I do not care for."

The raven's tone was amused. *But it is the one I am* best *at.*

Giving up, Aidan kicked free of stirrups and carefully let himself down from the saddle. It was a painful exercise and one he regretted immensely, clutching impotently at ribs. Likely he needed them strapped, which meant admitting to the accident. His father would be amused; Brennan *never* came off a horse.

Or, if he had, his son had never known of it.

"Hungry," he muttered aloud. "But chewing will hurt my head."

Out of sorts, are we?

Aidan went into the link. *Out of sorts and out of patience; I am here for the* shar tahl. *Perhaps* he *will have my answers, even if you do not.*

Teel eyed him archly. *Oh, he may have them . . . but are you worthy of them?*

Aidan looped the reins over a post set into dirt before the pavilion. *Surely a warrior with you for a lir is worthy of anything.*

It was sufficiently double-edged that Teel did not respond.

The *shar tahl's* pavilion was larger than most, since he required additional room for storage of clan birthlines and assorted ritualistic items. It was customary to wait no farther inside a *shar tahl's* or clan-leader's pavilion than a single pace; Aidan therefore sat very precisely near the open doorflap on a gray-blue ice bear pelt brought from the Northern Wastes. The *shar tahl* was not yet present, although word had been carried throughout Clankeep the Mujhar's grandson had arrived.

Even though Aidan was well-accustomed to the immense size and overwhelming presence of Homana-Mujhar, he felt daunted by the pavilion. It was here the history of the clan was kept, rolled tightly in soft leathers and tucked away inside strong chests. His own history resided somewhere in the pavilion, reduced to a single rune-sign on pale, bleached doeskin. A rune, no more than that, yet he felt small because of it. Small because of doubts; was he doing the right thing? The Hunter had not admonished him against displaying the golden link, merely said it was *for* him. He could not imagine anything to do with gods could be denied a *shar tahl*. Such men served those gods with steadfast loyalty.

He waited, legs folded beneath him, with the link clutched in two hands. Teel was not with him, leaving his *lir*, with some trepidation, to find his own way. Aidan was alone, and feeling immensely lonely.

He will say I am mad. Or, if he does not say it, he will think it . . . and soon even the clans will say I mimic Gisella—

Aidan cut it off.

I should look at another side . . . perhaps he will have my answers and share them willingly. Perhaps he will know what this is and what I should do with it—

Aidan gritted teeth. "Why does this happen to me? First all those dreams, now this nonsense of dead Mujhars and gods—" He clenched fingers around the link. Fear was unavoidable, no matter what Teel said. "What if I *am* mad?"

"Aidan."

He stiffened, then bowed, showing homage, and was startled when a hand touched the crown of his head.

"No, Aidan—not from you." The hand was removed. The *shar tahl* came more fully into the pavilion and moved around to face his guest. He was surprisingly young for his place, still blackhaired and firm of flesh. He was, Aidan thought, perhaps thirty-five or thirty-six.

But the *shar tahl*'s physical appearance was not the matter at hand. "Why not?" Aidan asked, glad to think of something else. "Honor is your due."

"And I do not disparage it. I only resent the time it wastes when there is distress to be addressed." The *shar tahl* sat down in front of Aidan. It seemed somehow incongruous to see a *shar tahl* in leathers; Aidan was accustomed to linen or woolen robes, though neither was required. But this particular man, displaying armbands and earring—his absent *lir* was a fox—was different from the others. Aidan knew it at once.

It is not merely age . . . the fire in him is different. It burns a little brighter—Inwardly, he frowned. *I have only known old* shar tahls *. . . this one is not old. This one is more like a warrior. Perhaps that is the difference.*

The *shar tahl*'s tone was mild. "You come so rarely, or so I have heard, that the reason must be quite important."

Guilt pinched Aidan's belly. He answered more brusquely than intended. "Aye, it is. This." He set down the link on the fur between them, then took his hands away.

The *shar tahl* did not at once look at the object. He looked only at Aidan, who felt years stripped away until he was a boy, staring guiltily but defiantly into the face of authority. Yellow eyes were kind, but also very attentive. "You do not know who I am."

Aidan maintained a blank expression. "The *shar tahl,* of course."

"I mean, which one."

He debated answers. This *shar tahl,* a stranger to Aidan, was as odd as the brown man who called himself the Hunter, who called himself a god. Aidan decided to avoid possible problems by stating the obvious. "The *shar tahl* of Clankeep."

The other smiled. "You take the easy road. That is not your reputation."

Aidan's answering smile was twisted. "My reputation is founded on many things, and so there are many reputations. Which one do *you* know?"

"The one I heard up north across the Bluetooth, in my home Keep." The *shar tahl* crossed his legs and linked dark fingers. "My name is Burr. I am but newly come to Clankeep—I thought it might be worthwhile for me to live nearer the Lion."

Something pricked at Aidan's awareness. Something sounded a faint alarm. "*How* nearer?" he asked. Then, very quietly, "As near as Teirnan might like?"

Burr's eyes narrowed, if only minutely. And then he smiled. "Teirnan, as you know, has been proscribed by all clan councils. He forgoes the teachings of the *shar tahls;* therefore he forgoes my own. And, undoubtedly, anything else I might say to him."

Certainty firmed Aidan's tone. "But you know him, my proscribed kinsman."

"Everyone knows of him."

Aidan spoke very precisely, so no mistake could be made. "I did not say *of* him. I said you knew *him*."

Quiet reassessment. Burr altered manner and tone, as if casting off prevarication and the habitual obliqueness of *shar tahl*. "I know him. I knew him. I *met* him, once." The tone was uninflected, shielded behind self-assurance.

Oddly, it rankled. "But you did not see fit to send word to the Mujhar."

"Teirnan has more to concern himself with than what the Mujhar might say, or do."

Aidan felt a flicker of irritation. For a fleeting instant it shocked him—this man was a *shar tahl*, due honor and respect—but it passed. What they spoke of—prince and priest-historian—could affect Homana's future, as well as the prophecy.

"What 'more' is there?" Aidan demanded. "You know what he has done."

"And paid the price for it." Burr's eyes did not waver. "Teirnan has lost his *lir*."

"Lost his—" It brought him up short. Aidan spread a hand, made the gesture denoting *tahlmorra*. "Then Teirnan is dead. We need not concern ourselves with him further."

"I did not say he was dead."

"But he *must* be—he lost his *lir*."

Burr's smile was very faint. "The death-ritual is voluntary. It is, to my knowledge, undertaken when a warrior truly believes in such binding clan custom."

Aidan nodded impatiently. "Of course. It is always done—" And then he understood. "You are saying Teirnan rejected *that*, too?" It was impossible to believe. "But that means he is mad. *No* Cheysuli warrior will countenance that. He has to die. The loss of control, the awareness of loss of balance, drives him to it. There is no other choice."

Burr did not answer. Aidan, staring, heard the echo of his own words inside his skull.

Am I mad, too? he wondered with a new insight. *Am I bound for Teirnan's course, to throw myself away? Is that why Shaine— or whatever he was—tells me I will not rule?*

It nearly overwhelmed him. *Lir*-bonded or not, was he meant to give up his life to keep the blood free of taint?

Numbly, he echoed, "There is no other choice."

The *shar tahl* spoke quietly. "He does choose, Aidan. Every warrior *chooses*. He dies if he wants to die. But that is not Teirnan's way."

Teirnan, not *Aidan.* He pushed away thoughts of himself and focused on his kinsman.

More than bruised ribs ached. Also family pride; the awareness of a betrayal he had never experienced. He had been told all about Teirnan's defection from the clan, his rejection of the prophecy and betrayal of heritage, but Aidan had been conscious of it with a pronounced sense of detachment. He had been too young to know Teirnan, to comprehend the issues.

But he was no longer too young. Now he began to understand why all his kin hated Teirnan.

Speculation took precedence over fear of his own ends. "He wants the Lion," Aidan said flatly. "He has always wanted the Lion."

"Aye, well, men want many things . . ." Burr neatly turned the subject. "What is it *you* want?"

Aidan was no longer certain he cared to continue the discussion with Burr. The man was different. He was unlike any *shar tahl* Aidan had ever known. That he thought differently was obvious. And what he might do with such thoughts—

Abruptly, Aidan laughed. *Is this what they say of me?*

Burr's smile lapsed. The eyes, so like Aidan's own, were fixed and uncannily feral. The voice was very quiet; the tone a whiplash of sound. "If you question my own commitment to my race, let me reassure you. My belief in the gods is unshakable. It has been since I was quite young—I knew as clearly as I knew my *lir* what I was meant to be. It was my *tahlmorra:* I could be nothing else. No man, no woman, no warrior—proscribed or otherwise—could ever turn me from that, any more than Teirnan or anyone else could turn you from the Lion. I am a Cheysuli *shar tahl*, fully cognizant of my service." Intensity dispersed abruptly, as if no longer needed. The calm smile returned. "What service may I do you?"

Something in Aidan answered. His distrust of Burr faded, replaced with an odd recognition. *This man is very like me*—He smiled back slowly, though its twist was decidedly wry. "I have many questions." He pointed at the link. "What do I do with that?"

Burr, for the first time, looked at the link. Aidan knew what it looked like, what it *felt* like; he had carried it by hand all the way to Clankeep, unable to hide it away. It was nothing and everything, all bound into the gold and runes, and he dared not let it go.

For Burr, he had let it go. It waited on the pelt, glinting dully in wan light.

Abruptly, the man was *shar tahl*. Aidan was startled by the sudden transformation. It was, he thought, merely his own perspective, somehow altered; this Burr was no different from the Burr of a moment before, in appearance or manner. And yet Aidan felt the change, the slow comprehension, that flooded the man with an eerie exaltation.

Burr unlaced his hands and reached out, as if to pick up the link. But he refrained. Fingertips trembled a moment. Then quieted into stillness. He did not touch the link. He looked searchingly at Aidan. Then abruptly looked away.

Aidan frowned. "What is it?"

Burr quickly rose to his feet and went directly to the open doorflap. The gesture was blatant: Aidan was to leave. "I cannot help you," he said. "You must find your own way."

Unquestionably dismissal, in tone and posture. Part of Aidan responded instinctively—a Cheysuli warrior was carefully tutored to honor a *shar tahl*—until he recalled his other self. The self meant for the Lion.

"No," he said quietly, still kneeling on the pelt. "I came to you with questions. You promised answers." Slowly he twisted his head and glanced over a shoulder at the *shar tahl*. "Are you the kind of man who can refuse to give them?"

Burr did not hesitate. "You ask too much."

Aidan was deliberate. "As warrior? Or as a prince?"

Burr drew in a breath, then released it audibly. His expression was peculiar. "We spoke of choices, my lord. We spoke of a warrior's *tahlmorra*. No Cheysuli is truly *forced* to accept his *tahlmorra*—he does have free will—but if he is truly commited to his people, to the prophecy, to his belief in the afterworld, he never refuses it. So we are taught: so I believe." The phrasing was deliberate; Aidan understood. "I came to my own arrangement with the gods when I was very young. Now you must come to yours."

"I know my *tahlmorra,*" Aidan declared. "I came to you for this."

Burr did not look at the link. "I have no answer for you."

Anger flickered dully. He had come for help, as advised by his grandsire, and this was what he got. More obscurity. His belly was full of it.

"Tell me," he said quietly. "You see something in this. You know what this is. Why will you not tell me?"

"I am not meant to tell you."

Control slipped askew. "*Gods,*" Aidan rasped, "will anyone speak plainly? My *lir* practices obscurity; now so do you. Tell me, *shar tahl*: am I to live, or die?"

"The gods will decide that."

Aidan's laughter was a sharp bark of blurted sound. "The Hunter tells me differently. *He* speaks of choices, even as you do."

Burr's eyes glittered. "I do not know everything."

"Neither do I," Aidan gritted. "I'm knowing nothing at *all*— d'ye think this is pleasant?" He sat rigidly on the pelt. "I came to you for help, because grandsire suggested it. Because I think I am going mad."

There, it was said. The silence was very loud.

Burr swallowed tightly. For a brief moment there was war in his face, a battle that underscored, to Aidan, the great need for him to know. Then the *shar tahl* muttered a brief, sibilant petition and pulled aside the doorflap.

Aidan was filled with emptiness. He was six years old once more, faced with adult betrayal; the inability of anyone—even those who should—to understand the pain that drove him so desperately. "Nothing," he murmured numbly. "You give me nothing at all."

Burr's jaw was clenched. "If I could, I would. But if your *lir* will not, who am I to do it?" He gazed at the link, glowing wanly in the light. "I only know part of it."

Aidan scooped up the link and rose, turning to face the *shar tahl*. Contempt shaded his tone. "What *do* you have for me?"

The yellow eyes were kind. "My lord, my sympathy."

Chapter Six

It was dark when Aidan rode into Mujhara, well after sunset. He had come close to staying one more night at Clankeep, but judged three enough; it was time he tested his newfound "knowledge" regarding links, Mujhars, and himself.

He rode in through the massive gates of Homana-Mujhar, only vaguely acknowledging salutes and greetings—he was too weary to offer more—and gave the dun into the keeping of the horseboy who came running. Brief instructions passed on, Aidan then went into the palace by way of the kitchens, studiously avoiding his kinfolk, who would no doubt ask him questions he did not wish to address. He was not yet in the mood. First things first.

Word of his return would not be carried to the Mujhar or his parents once they had retired for the night. Aidan kept himself to the kitchens, cadging meat, ale, and bread from servants startled by his presence, until well after bedtime. Then he sent Teel to his perch in private chambers, and went by himself to the Great Hall.

Bootsteps echoed as he walked the length of the firepit, dividing the hall in half from dais steps nearly to the doors. As always, he took no lamp or candle; this was better done in dimness, with only the summer-banked coals for light.

He silenced his steps, and stopped. In the darkness, Aidan laughed: bitter irony. Speaking with the Hunter had changed nothing for the better. Now the dream was real even when he did not sleep.

He stood, as he had stood so often, before the Lion Throne. In its seat was the chain.

Aidan linked hands behind his waist. "No *lir*," he declared. "Is that what makes the difference? You want me to come alone?"

Nothing answered him.

The challenge faded away. Aidan sighed, smearing one palm against his brow hard enough to stretch flesh. He was twitching from exhaustion, both mental and physical; he had not slept very well in the three nights at Clankeep. "—tired," he said aloud. "Will you never let me rest?"

In dim light, gold gleamed.

Go, he told himself. *Just go, go to bed—turn your back on this idiocy. Think of something else. Dream of something else. Imagine yourself with a woman—*

But the chain transfixed his eyes, washing him free of all thought except the need to touch it. To hold it in his hands.

I think I begin to hate you—

But nothing could make him ignore it.

Wearily Aidan mounted the dais steps. He halted briefly before the Lion, rubbing absently at gritty eyes, then slowly knelt. The motion was awkward and painful; his ribs still ached. He placed both hands upon the curving, carved armrests and gripped the Lion's paws. The throne was dead to him. A thing of wood; no more. He sensed none of its power or the ambience of its age.

Burning eyes locked on the chain coiled against dark velvet. "So," he said unevenly, "I shall put out my hand to touch it, and the gold will crumble to dust."

Aidan put out his hand. Fingertips touched gold. He waited for it to crumble, but the chain remained whole.

"Something," he breathed, "is different."

Nothing answered him. Silence was very loud.

He waited. He knew what had to happen. It happened without fail. It had *always* happened.

He clung one-handed to the Lion. "This time, something is *different.*"

The hissed declaration filled the hall. He heard himself breathing; the uneven rasping of air sucked through a throat nearly closed off by emotions. He could not name them all, only two: a slowly rising despair and a burgeoning exhilaration.

They were, he thought, contradictory emotions, even as he felt them. How could a man experience exhilaration and despair, both at the same time? From the same cause?

He allowed his fingers to move. Now the palm touched the chain.

Cool, rune-scribed metal. No different from that on his arms. Solid, substantial gold.

"I know you," Aidan challenged. "You entice me, you seduce

me, promising fidelity—the moment I pick you up, there will be nothing left but dust."

Nothing answered him.

Sweat prickled flesh. He ached, yet felt no pain, only a brittle intensity. A growing, obsessive hunger.

Aidan dared to close his fingers. The chain remained solid.

He laughed softly into the darkness. "Such a sweet, subtle seduction . . . if I but pick you up—" He suited action to words.

Links rang softly, chiming one against another.

Aidan knelt before the Lion. One hand steadied himself. The other held up the chain. It dangled in the dimness, one perfect link clutched in rigid, trembling fingers.

Jubilation crept closer, hand in hand with apprehension. Aidan stared, waiting. The hair stood up on his arms, tickled the back of his neck. He drew in a tenuous breath, taking care to make no sound. "What now?" he whispered.

In answer, the link parted. Half of the chain fell, spilling across crimson velvet.

Oh, gods—oh, no—not AGAIN—

A blurt of sound escaped him: forlorn, futile protest. Sweat ran down his temples, tracing the line of his jaw. "So," he rasped hoarsely, "you tease me a little *more*—"

Intrusion. He heard the scrape of silver on marble, the step of booted feet. Humiliation bathed him. If his father found him like this, or even the Mujhar—

Aidan set his teeth and turned, still kneeling, still clutching the remaining links against his bare chest. That much he had gotten, he had *won* . . . if he showed his father—if he displayed it to the Mujhar, or to anyone who asked—

Halfway breathed, breath stopped. The man was no one he knew.

And yet, somehow, he did. He knew that face; had *seen* that face. The same tawny hair, now silvered. The same blue eyes, but no patch; both eyes were whole. Even the same remarkable physical presence, though this man, Aidan thought, was a trifle taller than the Mujhar. The breadth of shoulder was startling; that, and his expression.

No, Aidan mouthed. And then, almost laughing: *Aye. First Shaine, now—this. Now HIM—*

Transfixed, he stared at the man. At the slow transformation in the features. First a quiet acceptance of his presence in a place not quite expected. Then the realization of what that place, and his presence, meant. Lastly the quiet joy, the subtle recognition of a man returned to his home after too many years—and deaths—away.

It was not an old face, not as old as the Mujhar's, though the lines were similar. But there was an odd awareness of age, an eerie aura of knowledge far greater than Aidan's own, so well-tutored in heritage. This man was not Cheysuli, but clearly he knew the Great Hall. Clearly he knew the Lion.

Unlike Shaine in his velvets, he wore plain soldiers' garb: ringmail over leather. Ringmail stained with blood; leather scuffed from usage. On his hand glinted the ring Aidan's grandsire wore.

Ringmail in place of velvets.

Aidan stared blankly, recalling Shaine, whose arrogance dominated. This man was as proud, but less of himself than of things that had occurred in a realm once his own.

Aidan's lips were dry. *A different kind of Mujhar—*

The length of the hall, he came. Then stopped before the dais, before the throne, before the prince still kneeling in rigid silence, pale Erinnish flesh stretched nearly to cracking over unmistakable Cheysuli bones.

"So *long*," the man whispered. "I thought never to see it again."

Numbly, Aidan murmured, "This is Homana-Mujhar."

The other man's jubilant smile was brilliant. "I know where I am. I know who you are. Do you know who *I* am?"

Aidan wet dry lips. "I can make a guess."

The stranger laughed aloud, in eerie exultation. "Then let me save you the trouble: my name is Carillon. That throne once belonged to me." He paused delicately. "And are you kneeling to me, or to your own *tahlmorra?*"

Aidan did not move. "Carillon was Homanan. He knew nothing of *tahlmorras.*"

Tawny eyebrows rose. "Nothing? Nothing at all? When it was *my* doing that the Lion Throne of Homana was given back into Cheysuli hands?" Blue eyes were assessive. "Ah, Aidan, have they neglected your history? Or are you merely being perverse?"

"Homanans have no *tahlmorras.*"

"Oh, I think they do. I think they simply lack the imagination to accept them." Carillon's voice was kind, pitched to a tone of quiet compassion. "It hurts to kneel on marble. If I were you, I would not."

Aidan put out a groping hand and caught at the Lion, dragging himself from the dais. He stared at his kinsman. His great-great-grandsire, with no Cheysuli in him.

I am so tired—so confused—

He sighed gustily, trying to summon respect for a man dead so many years even though the pragmatic part of him suggested he might be so tired and sore he was merely dreaming the whole thing. "I suppose you have come with a message, much like Shaine. I suppose you are here to talk about this chain, much like Shaine." He held it up; it dangled. "The rest of it is in the throne . . . I am only worth half of it." He grimaced, shoving away the acknowledgment of pain. "But more than I was before."

Carillon said nothing.

Aidan looked down at his kinsman, taller than Carillon only because of the dais. He lacked the height of his father or the Mujhar; certainly that of the man—or fetch—he faced now. "Shaine mouthed nonsense. Have you come to do the same?"

Now Carillon smiled. "I did not come: I was *brought.* By you, whether or not you know it. There is a certain need . . ." But he did not finish. "As for Shaine, he often mouthed nonsense. My uncle—my *su'fali,* as you might say—was a hard man to know, and a harder man to like. Respect, honor, even admire, aye—"

"Admire!" Aidan's astonishment echoed. "The *ku'reshtin* began the *qu'mahlin!* He nearly extinguished my race!"

Some of the fire dimmed in old/ageless blue eyes. "Aye, he did that. But I was speaking of the man before the madness. The man who was Mujhar, was *Homana,* before the fool who began a purge." Carillon sighed. Wan light glinted on ringmail, "He was a man of great loves and stronger hatreds. I will excuse him for neither; I did not understand him, save to serve him as an heir. And, as you know, even that was never intended; I was not raised to be Mujhar."

"No," Aidan agreed, giving up the last vestige of disbelief. It seemed he was meant to have discourse with all manner of men and gods.

"I was raised to be a soldier, and to inherit my father's title. Never my uncle's—that only became *my* place when Lindir ran away with Hale, and Shaine got no other heirs." Carillon glanced down at a lifted hand: blood-red ruby glowed. "So, I was made heir to Homana . . . and heir to travesty—" Abruptly he broke it off, smiling ruefully. "But you know all of this . . . I will bore you with old stories." Now the smile was twisted. "Finn would say it is my habit, to prate about history."

"Finn," Aidan echoed. "Could he come here? Could I summon him, if what you say is true?" He paused. "Finn—and *Hale?*"

After a momentary stillness, Carillon shook his head. "They were never Mujhars."

"Mujhars," Aidan murmured. He looked at the chain in his hand. Realization was swift. "Mujhars—and links. Is that what this is about? Is that what the dreams are for?" He held out the portion to Carillon. His voice shook, even as his hand. "Is that *it*, my lord? Each of those links—"

"—is a man." Carillon's voice was steady. "A man caught up in the game of the gods. But you should know that, Aidan. You should know very well."

I know nothing at all . . . Aidan strung out the chain, touching individual links. "You. Donal. Niall. Here: my *jehan.*" The chain ended abruptly.

Suspicion blossomed painfully. So did fear.

White-faced, Aidan swallowed. Looked at the Lion. Reached down and picked up the two halves of the broken link. They chimed in his hand. "And Aidan?" he asked softly, looking back at Carillon.

His kinsman's gaze did not waver. "You know what you know. Now you must deal with other things: acknowledgment and acceptance. Knowing is not enough."

Bitterness rose; engulfed. "I have been very well tutored. Do you truly think I would not acknowledge nor accept? Do you think I *could* not?"

Now Carillon's eyes were bleak. "We have each of us, in your birthline, done things we did not desire. Become what we did not want. We each of us chose our road, always cognizant of the choice . . . but none of it was easy. The gods gave us free will. Regardless of tutoring, refusal is always an alternative. The gods do not strike us dead, unless our time is done."

The response was automatic: "If we say no to our *tahlmorras*, the afterworld is denied us."

Carillion's tone was steady.. "That is a choice, too. Teirnan made it; will you?"

Aidan met the eyes of a dead Mujhar, only dimly surprised he could. Such miracles, now, were expected; they had, each of them, beaten belief into him. "I have to be what I am."

Slowly, Carillon smiled. "Then the gods will be satisfied."

In Aidan's hand, gold melted. At last he opened fingers. The chain flowed out of his hands and into nothingness.

He looked up to ask Carillon why. He found himself alone.

Chapter Seven

Aileen slammed down her goblet. Cider splashed over tne rim. "Not so soon!" she cried, astonishing them all. "I'll not be letting you do it!"

It stilled the room instantly. Servants with trays of food and pitchers of cider stopped dead in their tracks, staring at their angry princess, then cast furtive glances at one another to see what should or should not be done.

The outburst came in the midst of the midday meal. It had, heretofore, been an entirely normal gathering uneventful in the extreme. The Mujhar and all his family—excepting the absent Aidan—were halfway through the meal.

Now it appeared one of them would not finish. Or possibly *two* of them; it was at Brennan she had shouted.

The Prince of Homana, frozen in the act of lifting his own goblet to his mouth, also stared at Aileen. His astonishment rivaled that of the servants who, upon a subtle signal from Deirdre, melted out of the room. Food and drink could wait until the storm had blown over.

Brennan, thawing at last, quietly put down his goblet. He did not spill his cider. "I only meant—"

"I *know* what you meant!" Aileen's green eyes blazed. "D'ye think I'll sit here all mealy-mouthed and listen to such drivel?"

Brennan's face tightened. "What 'drivel' do you mean? I was discussing our son's future."

"Discussing his *marriage*, ye *skilfin!*" Aileen flattened her hands on the table and leaned down on braced arms. "I'll not allow it so soon. The boy deserves some time."

"The 'boy,' as you call him, is twenty-three years old." Brennan very carefully did not look in Ian's direction.

"Twenty-three years *young*," Aileen snapped. "The House of

Homana is long-lived—he'll be having time for marriage. Let him have time for himself."

Now Brennan did cast a sharp glance around the table. He saw three carefully neutral expressions, which did not particularly please him. He had expected support—except from Ian; clearly, they offered none. "*Jehan*," he appealed.

Niall lifted both hands in a gesture of abdication. "I married off four of my five children. This is for you to do."

Inwardly Brennan sighed. He looked again at Aileen. "This can be discussed another time—"

"You brought it up," she charged. "Oh, Brennan, d'ye not know what you're doing? Can ye not see what might happen? D'ye want him to be like us?"

Brennan lost his temper. "By all the gods, I love you! I have never kept it a secret!"

The admission was not precisely what any of them had anticipated, least of all Aileen. She had expected a different issue.

White-faced, she glanced at the tactfully averted faces of the Mujhar, his *meijha*, his *rujholli*. Only Brennan looked at her; no, he *glared* at her, with an angry, defiant expression. It belied the words he had shouted.

"Not now," she said weakly, turning toward the door. "Not now; not *here*—"

Brennan rounded the table and met her at the door, jerking it open. "Now," he said grimly. "But I will agree with the 'not here.' Shall we retire to our apartments and discuss this issue in private?"

Color set her afire. What she thought was obvious.

Brennan grasped her arm and steered her out of the room, lowering his tone. "That is not what I meant. I meant to discuss it; nothing less, nothing more. You know very well I would never shame you that way in front of kin and servants—that is not my way. . . ."

Aileen was not placated. "You are a fool!" she snapped, gathering heavy skirts as he pushed her up the stairs. "You see only whatever it is you *want* to see, being blind to people's feelings."

"I am not being blind to anyone or anything," he retorted, ascending rapidly to keep up with his angry wife. "What I am is being careful."

"What you *are* is being a *skilfin*, as always. You've lost whatever sense—*and* diplomacy—you might once have had."

"Oh? I have never believed thinking about the future of one's realm—"

" 'Tisn't your realm *yet*—here, will this do?" Aileen shoved open a door and watched it slam against the wall. "Is this sufficiently private?"

Brennan advanced through the doorway. "It was a topic of discussion. It was not a royal decree. I was merely suggesting it might be time we thought of Aidan's future."

"Aidan's future is Aidan's *future*. Let it remain so, Brennan." Aileen swung to face the doorway. "Give the boy—" She stopped. "Oh," she said weakly. "Have you heard everything?"

Brennan turned abruptly. Their son stood in the corridor.

"Enough," Aidan said calmly, folding hands behind his back.

Brennan frowned. "When did you come home?"

"Last night. Late." Aidan's crooked smile was private. "There was something I had to do . . . something to he resolved."

"And was it?" Aileen asked.

The smile became a scowl. "Not entirely," he muttered then flicked dismissive fingers as he altered tone and topic. "Am I to be married, then?"

Brennan swung back jerkily and walked directly across the chamber. It was a small room, no more; a nook for private withdrawal. Not unlike Deirdre's solar, though lacking amenities. It was little more than a cell, or an awkward, forgotten corner.

A bench was against the wall. Brennan sat down on it. "Your *jehana* and I were discussing it."

Aidan arched one eyebrow. "It was a loud—discussion. The servants were talking about it."

Aileen's face flamed. "Your father is being a fool."

Brennan sounded tired. "At least I know that word. You have never translated *skilfin*."

She had the grace to look abashed. " 'Tisn't a polite term."

"I had gathered that." Brennan looked at his son. Aidan did not, he thought, appear particularly disturbed by the topic. He was, as usual, keeping himself detached from the emotions he and Aileen battled, as if he feared to share them. "Well? Will you come in and give us your opinion? It *is* your future, as the Princess of Homana has taken great—*and* loud—pains to point out."

Aidan smiled lopsidedly. He came through the doorway, lingered idly a moment near his mother, then drifted farther into the chamber. Brennan thought his expression odd. There was distance in his eyes; and an eerie *otherwhereness* that Brennan found unsettling.

"Come back," Brennan snapped impatiently. "You had best attend this."

Aidan glanced sidelong at his father. "I fell off my horse," he said inconsequentially. Then, smiling wryly, "No—I was *swept* off. It does somewhat make a difference."

Aileen made a sound and moved as if to go to him, but a lifted hand kept her back. She contented herself with a question. "Are ye hurt, then? I thought it was dirt; 'tis a *bruise*, then, there on the side of your face."

Aidan briefly touched a cheekbone. "A bruise, aye—so it should be." Then, as if shaking himself, he looked more clearly at his father. "Do you want me married, then?"

There was only the slightest hint of Erinn in the inflection. It made Brennan smile; his son sounded, on occasion, very like his mother. "I want you content, though undoubtedly your *jehana* will not agree that I would consider your feelings."

" 'Tisn't sounding like it," she muttered.

Brennan cleared his throat. "I want you content, Aidan. I want you settled. I want you less disturbed by whatever it is that disturbs you."

Aidan laughed. "And marriage is the answer? With yours as the example?"

Brennan nearly gaped. The question had been so *blatant*—and so keenly on the mark. *As if he reads my thoughts* . . .

Aileen's face flamed red. "D'ye not care?" she demanded. "He'd have you wedded and bedded before nightfall, if he could—and all for the Lion, he says."

"Well, perhaps it is." Aidan went over to the bench occupied by his father and sat down at the other end. He looked tired, worn through, clearly thinking of something else. "I have no objection."

The negligent tone and manner set Aileen's eyes to blazing again. "No objection, have you? To being pushed this way and that? For being made to take a wife?"

Aidan scowled briefly, then wiped it away instantly. His tone, usually circumspect and polite, was pitched to cut through them both, as if he knew just where to aim. "I am not you, *jehana*. I am not and never have been in love with the wrong person. Nor am I my *jehan*, so badly hurt by an Ihlini witch's meddling." He cast a glance at Brennan, mouth twisted, as if to ask his pardon for speaking of private things. "I am not in love at all, so it really makes no difference.

His parents, stunned, stared. Aileen roused first. "It *should!*" she snapped. "The woman you'll be taking will share your bed for the rest of your life. D'ye think *that* makes no difference?"

Aidan sighed wearily, murmuring beneath his breath. Then, more clearly, "After the events of four days ago—when I got this bruise—I think debating the merits of marriage is the least of my concerns." He slumped against the wall and yawned, then straightened as if the position hurt. Indifferently, he asked, "Have you a woman in mind?"

Aileen stared at her son. Dark red hair tumbled into his face, until he flung it out of his eyes like a horse tossing his mane. It was, as usual, badly in need of cutting; he was lazy about such things. Thick lashes screened his eyes, but that did not disturb her. His eyes were like his father's; she could not read *his*, either. Aidan was a trifle paler than usual, and the bluish bruise was temporarily disfiguring, and he acted as if his ribs hurt; all that aside, he seemed perfectly normal, she thought—except for a sharper, more pronounced detachment that was, even when weighed against Aidan's customary feyness, something out of the ordinary.

"What events?" she asked suspiciously.

Aidan shrugged slightly. "Nothing worth the telling." He scratched gingerly at the bruise. "*Have* you a woman in mind—or are you simply wanting to argue?"

It was Brennan's turn to stare, albeit from a more awkward position. He frowned, marking the bruise, the pallor, the unfeigned detachment that spoke, to him, of boredom. Aidan was often detached, but rarely ever bored.

Brennan glanced at Aileen, seeking an explanation. Clearly she was as baffled by Aidan's demeanor. In that they always agreed. "No," he answered finally. "It had only just come up."

"*Brought* up by your father." But Aileen's tone was less than hostile. "D'ye really not care?"

Aidan smiled at her. "You cared because you loved Corin. *Jehan* cared because he knew it, and because he thought you might be worth the loving." He glanced briefly at his father, then back at his mother. "It makes no difference to me. There have been women in my bed, but none I want to keep there. If you have a candidate for eternity, I am willing to listen."

Aileen glanced at Brennan. "Hart has four daughters."

"And Keely, one." Brennan pulled at a lobeless ear, reaching for a long-absent earring. "Maeve has a daughter. Maeve has *two*."

Aileen's tone was odd. "Legitimate, if you please."

Brennan scowled; Maeve was his favorite. "Maeve's daughters *are* legitimate. She and Rory are married."

Aidan's tone was amused. "She wants a princess for me."

Aileen folded her arms. " 'Tis better for a prince."

He grinned, laughing in silence. "Very well, five princesses to pick from. Unless you take bids from other kingdoms, such as Ellas and Caledon."

"No," Brennan said thoughtfully. "There is the prophecy to think of. We now know the four realms mentioned . . . we need add no other blood."

"No," Aidan agreed. "Only the Ihlini."

Brennan looked at him sharply. "No son of mine—"

"Of course not, *jehan*." Aidan's tone was dryly deferential as he stretched out booted feet and planted both heels. "So, am I to choose sight unseen?"

Aileen frowned. " 'Twas what was done for us, your father and I. We saw naught of each other."

"And look at the result." Aidan's smile was so charmingly disarming, neither of them could respond immediately. "You are both of you fools—or *skilfins*," he continued, ignoring their stricken stares. "The Prince of Homana at least has the courage to admit he loves the Princess . . . she might do as well. Old wounds do heal— if you give them the time." He looked straight at his mother. "Twenty-four years is a long time. I'm thinking the two of you might be happier if you started all over again."

"How can you—" Aileen cut it off. Color waned in her face. "Oh, no," she whispered dazedly. "Deirdre said it might be true— she did say it might show itself . . ." Even her lips were white. "How long have you known how I feel? How your father feels?"

Aidan frowned. "I have always known how you feel. How either of you feel. How *everybody* feels."

"Always?" she echoed blankly.

Brennan sat erect. "What are you talking about?"

Aileen's hand was on her throat. "*Kivarna*," she murmured. "Oh, Aidan, after all this time . . . and none of us knowing—none of us *thinking*—"

"Knowing *what*?" Brennan asked testily. "What are you talking about?"

"*Kivarna*," she repeated. "Oh, gods, Aidan—is that what it is? All this time—is *that* what this is?"

Her son and husband stared.

Aileen pressed rigid fingers against her face. "All those things we've felt, the both of us, and you knowing them all—" She squeezed shut her eyes. "And you not knowing *why*—"

"Aileen!" Brennan said sharply. "What are you talking about?"

"Aye" Aidan agreed, detachment shredding abruptly. "*Jehana*—"

Aileen's face was white. Hands shook as she clasped them tightly in her lap. She tried to smile at Brennan, but it faltered. "*Kivarna*," she said only. "Your son is *Erinnish*, too." And with that she went out of the room.

Brennan stared after her. He had not seen her so distraught in years. Not since Aidan was young, and troubled by the dreams.

Frowning, he turned to his son. Aidan put up his hands. "A word, nothing more. But I am Erinnish, aye; I have been all my life." He grinned. " 'Twas her doing, I'm thinking. "

"But what is it—?" And then he gave it up. "Agh, gods—" Brennan collapsed once more against the wall. "Perhaps I *should* give you more time—sharing your life with a woman is never an easy thing."

Aidan, like his father, leaned against the wall, but took more care to settle still-sore ribs. "She really does love you. She always has, in her way. But she has never admitted it to herself; certainly not to you. She thinks of Corin, and feels guilty. She believes you deserve better, and so she blames herself."

Brennan sat in silence. Something pinched deep in his belly. Something that whispered of dread; of a thing left unattended to fester in someone's spirit, shaping a life for too many years.

He swallowed tightly and rolled his head against the wall to look at his son. "This is what she meant? This—*kivarna?*"

Aidan shrugged. "The word is as foreign to me. I have never heard it before."

Brennan, tensing, sat up a little. Very carefully. "But—you can do this? Always? This reading of people's thoughts?"

"Not thoughts. Feelings. And only bits of them. I thought everyone did." Aidan carefully felt his discolored cheekbone. His tone, now, was deliberate: he wanted to change the subject. "Have you ever come off your horse?"

"Many times." Brennan's thoughts were not on enforced dis-mountings. "Aidan—" He frowned. "You have been able to do this since childhood?"

Aidan lifted a single shoulder. "It began very young. I cannot say precisely when."

Gods, he can be cold— "—young," Brennan echoed. "Such as a night in the Great Hall, with the Lion . . . and a chain."

Aidan turned his head deliberately and looked into his father's eyes. What Brennan saw made him cringe. "I thought everyone felt it. That it required no explanation."

"I should have listened," Brennan rasped. "I should have listened then. Even Ian sees it."

"*Jehan*—"

"How is a child to trust when his parents give him no chance to say what troubles him most?" Brennan shut his eyes. "Gods, I have been a fool . . . and I have made you this way."

Aidan's tone was tight. "What way, *jehan?* What 'way' *am* I?"

"Different." The answer was prompt. "Private. Withdrawn. Guarded. As if you trust none of us." The pain tore at his vitals. "I did that to you."

"If you are concerned that I know everything you think, everything you *feel*—"

"No." Brennan cut him off. "What you know, you know; how much does not matter. What matters now is that you have this ability . . . and that you dream dreams."

Aidan's smile was wintry. "Everyone dreams."

"*Gods*—" But he let it get no farther. His mind was racing, running back over the years, over the memories, drawing from the deepest part of the well the things that glittered most brightly, like the keen edge of a new blade. "You were ill so often, and for so long . . ." It was not an explanation. It was not a just excuse. It was nothing more than a father's plea for understanding from a child he has turned away through misinterpretation. "You spoke to the Mujhar."

Aidan's tone was closed. "I spoke to my grandsire."

"But not to me, nor your *jehana*." Brennan's jaws clenched. "I suppose we deserved it, your meticulous privacy. But it was so long ago—did you never think to try again?"

Aidan's gaze was unflinching. "I sense *feelings*. At first, I knew you were only frightened, worried for my welfare. But you changed, even as I did. You began to realize a child's fancies were being carried over into adulthood." Aidan's expression was taut.

"Your feelings were all too blatant: you questioned my sanity. My worthiness for the Lion." His mouth warped a little. "How many children, even those in a man's body, care to discuss it with a *jehan* who wonders such things?"

Brennan's face was ravaged. "If you had told us of this ability—"

Aidan's tone sharpened. "I did not know what it was."

"If you had said *anything*—"

"You gave me no leave to try." Unsteadily, Aidan straightened. "But now you have, and I have said something of it. Enough. It has a name, now . . . better we leave it at that."

"How? There are things to be settled . . ."

"Such as marriage?" Aidan smiled. "Perhaps it is not such a bad idea."

Again, he changes the subject. And perhaps I should let him. Brennan made a dismissive gesture. His tone was conciliatory. "Perhaps your *jehana* has the right of it. Perhaps I *do* move too soon, pushing you this way and that—" He broke off, sighing, to look at his son. "There are times I think too much about what will become of the Lion, when the throne is not even mine. I look back at our history and see how tenuous is our claim—how vulnerable our race. We are still badly outnumbered . . . if the Homanans ever turned against us again . . ." But he let it trail off. Aidan was not listening. "Aidan . . ." He waited. "Aidan, I want to do right by you. If now is not the time—"

Aidan's response was detached. "It makes no difference."

Brennan held onto his equable tone with effort, knowing instinctively that to press his son now was to lose him. "Marriage is a large step for any man. For a prince—"

"It makes no difference." Aidan insinuated careful fingers into the folds of his jerkin, as if testing for soreness. "Perhaps a change such as this is precisely what I need, after everything else."

Concerned, Brennan frowned. "Aidan—"

His son smiled lopsidedly and raised a preemptive finger. "First you suggest I marry, now you attempt to talk me out of it. Which do you want?"

Brennan stirred restlessly; Aidan was, as usual, cutting too close to the bone. "I want you content."

Aidan's smile faded. He stared blankly at the door, distance in his gaze. "Perhaps that is not my *tahlmorra*. Perhaps, instead—"

But he waved it off without finishing. Detachment faded, replaced by dry irony. "A wedding will change many things."

If he wants to let it go . . . Brennan forced a smile. "A wedding usually does."

The tone altered oddly. "And if it changes *everything*—" Yet again Aidan did not finish, but his expression was intense.

Brennan's smile faded. Something cold touched the base of his spine. "Are you all right? Is there something troubling you?"

Aidan did not answer, staring fixedly into the distance.

He is not here, Brennan thought. *In the flesh, perhaps but not in the mind. He goes somewhere—else.* "Aidan," he said aloud. Then, more urgently, "*Ai*dan!"

His son stirred, clearly startled. And then he sighed, scrubbing at a wan, discolored face. "I am—confused. Forgive me . . . I have not been paying attention."

Brennan leaned forward. "Then tell me. Share it with me. Let me be the *jehan* I should have been years ago."

Aidan weighed his words, then sighed in resignation. His crooked smile was, Brennan thought, oddly vulnerable. "More than confused—*irritated.* There are things in my life I cannot understand, and no answers are forthcoming. No matter *who* I ask—" He sighed heavily, fingering the bruise. "Have you ever spoken with a god?"

It was an odd tack. "*To* them; many times."

"One particular god?"

He strived for lightness; to keep his head above water. "No. I generally address my comments—or petitions—to as many as possible, just to improve my chances." Brennan waited for laughter. When he heard no response at all, he dismissed forced levity. His son was revealing more of himself than ever before. This time the *jehan* would listen. "Why? Do you speak only to one?"

Aidan sighed. "I had never thought it necessary—like you, I spoke to them all. But now—" Abruptly he broke it off and rose, heading toward the door. "If there are five princesses to be considered, perhaps I should go to see them."

He is gone—I have lost him—

Nonplussed by the abrupt change in subject and his son's implicit dismissal, Brennan rose hastily. "But none of them are here."

Aidan paused in the doorway, arching ruddy brows. "Then perhaps I should go where they *are*."

Chapter Eight

The fire had died to coals. The horses, a few long paces away, were hobbled for the night, tearing contentedly at the now-sparse grass surrounding their plots. Food was packed away, bedrolls unfurled, skins of wine unplugged. Sprawled loose-limbed against saddles, two Cheysuli warriors stared up into star-peppered darkness and shared the companionable silence.

Eventually, Aidan broke it. "Tomorrow," he mused idly, scratching an itching eyelid. "Solinde in place of Homana."

His companion grunted absently, fingers stroking the huddle of chestnut fur slumped across most of one leg.

"It will feel good to leave Homana behind a while. It will give me a chance to start over again," Aidan mused. Then, thinking he had given too much away, he sighed and rolled his head to grin at his great-uncle. "Escort enough, I'm thinking . . . Teel, you, and Tasha."

"Certainly more comfortable; I prefer it this way, myself." Ian's answering smile was wry. "But Aileen nearly won the battle."

Aidan swallowed wine, mopped up a few spilled drops dampening his chin, then shook his head in detached irritation. "Why do women insist on so much ceremony? There is no need to send me into Solinde trailing a hundred men in my wake . . . and as for that chatter about protection, I say it is nonsense. We are at peace with Solinde—we *have* been for tens of years—Teirnan's *a'saii* have disappeared, and even the Ihlini are silent. What is there to protect me *from?*"

Ian's smile faded. The tone was carefully neutral as he stroked the huge cat at his side, chin resting on his thigh. "From yourself, perhaps?"

Aidan's contentment spilled away. The aftertaste in his mouth turned sour. "She wasted no time, did she? Or was it *jehan*, instead?" He shifted irritably against the saddle. "I should have said nothing of it. It is private, personal . . . it should make no difference—"

"That you know what others feel?" Ian tipped his head. "You must admit, *harani*, it is a powerful gift—"

"Is it?" Scowling, Aidan cut him off. "I did not choose to have it. I do not choose to use it. I only know what I know, what I *feel*—"

"—and what others feel." Ian's tone remained affable. "I only remark on it because it may be an explanation—"

"—for why I am so different?" Aidan twisted his mouth. "No man is like another."

"No." Ian drank from his wineskin with less spillage than Aidan; he had had much more practice. "And that very differentness is something all Cheysuli must deal with, when faced with an unblessed Homanan trying to comprehend how we can shapechange. We are *alien* to them, trading flesh and bone for fur . . . but this Erinnish gift you apparently have augments even that. And so I begin to see why we confuse the unblessed; you confuse *me*. You confuse us all."

Aidan's hand stole to his belt. Fingers touched the heavy link looped over leather next to his buckle. He stroked the gold absently. *I confuse myself.*

"But it does not matter." Ian settled more deeply into his blanket pallet, adjusting to Tasha's weight. "You are you, and I am I; we are what the gods decree."

Something thrummed across the *lir*-link: a feather-touch of amusement. Aidan glared hard through the darkness at Teel, perched upon a pack slumped on the other side of the fire. The raven said nothing, but Aidan translated the silence. He had had years of practice.

Gods, indeed— Abruptly, he was restless. He sat upright, slinging aside the stoppered skin, and swung on his knees to face his kinsman. "I *am* different," he said intently. "But no one knows how much. No one knows who I am. No one knows *what* I am . . ."

The light from the coals was dim. But Ian's expression was visible: Aidan's vehement outburst had clearly startled him. "Aidan—"

Everyone says I should speak, to divulge what I think; that it will do me good . . .

He did not necessarily think so, but was willing to try. There was too much pressure inside, too much apprehension. He needed to share it with someone other than a *lir* who couched so much truth in obscurity.

If only they could *listen*—

"I talk to gods, *su'fali*. To gods—and to the dead."

Ian's hand stilled on Tasha's head.

Aidan smiled a little. There was no amusement in it. "Ten nights ago, I met with Carillon. Before that, it was Shaine."

"Shaine," Ian echoed.

"The father of the *qu'mahlin*." Aidan shifted slightly, relaxing the tautness of bunched thighs. "Then, of course, there was the Hunter, the god himself . . ." He let it go unfinished. "But you could argue that it was the fall I took—that it addled my wits, and I merely *dreamed* all of it." Aidan's tone was elaborately dry. "But how would that explain seeing Carillon? I did not dream that. He was as real as you, standing before the Lion. He made the Great Hall his own, even with me in it. Even dead so many years . . . however many it is."

"Sixty-six," Ian murmured. "Have you learned nothing at all?"

Aidan looked at him sharply. Ian still lay stretched out against his saddle, one side engulfed by Tasha. His expression now was calm, but the mouth smiled a little. The eyes, so eerie a yellow, gazed serenely into the heavens.

"You *believe* me?"

"I have never known you to lie."

Now he distrusted the truth, certain no one could understand so easily, or in such a calm frame of mind. "But it was *Carillon* I saw! Carillon I *spoke* with!"

"And what did he have to say?"

Aidan frowned. He had expected startled reassessment, the mention of possible madness. Even though Ian had always given him the latitude to be himself, Aidan had not believed it could remain so. Not in light of his revelation.

But now something else caught his attention. "You knew him," Aidan said. "You knew him personally."

"Carillon?" Ian grunted amusement. "In a manner of speaking. I was four years old when he died."

"He was killed."

"In battle, aye. Actually, *after* a battle; the Atvian king killed him. Osric himself." Ian drank again. His tone was meditative. "A long time ago."

Aidan reached out and recaptured the skin he had tossed aside, dragging it across grassy ground. "What was he like?"

Ian quirked an eyebrow. "I thought you said you met him your-self ten nights ago."

Aidan waved a hand. "Aye, aye—I did . . . but how am I to know if he was real or not? *You* met the real man. The warrior Muj-har who won Homana back from Solinde and the Ihlini."

"Your great-great-grandsire." Ian smiled, tugging Tasha's tufted ears in absentminded affection. "I remember little enough. I was three the last time I saw him . . . to me he was little more than a huge man dressed in leather and ringmail, glinting and creaking when he moved. He was entirely Homanan, in appearance as well as habits . . . to me, that was what counted. Carillon the Homanan: my *jehana* made it so. He was Mujhar, aye—but I was taught to be aware his blood was different from mine."

"But you were kin to him."

Ian shrugged. "My granddam was his cousin . . . aye, we were kin, but the link was never explored. There was something else that took precedence—" He shifted against his saddle, resettling Tasha's weight. "I was the bastard son of Donal's Cheysuli light woman. I was not entirely *approved* of by the Homanans, who knew Donal was pledged to marry Carillon's daughter."

"Aislinn," Aidan murmured.

"Aislinn of Homana." Ian sighed and thrust one arm beneath his head. Gray-white hair, in the darkness, was silvered by the moon. "My *jehana* was half Homanan herself, but she hated it. I remember her petitioning the gods to let her spill out the Homanan in her blood many times—whenever my *jehan* left the Keep for Homana-Mujhar." Ian was silent a moment. "Eventually, she did . . . in the Keep across the Bluetooth, she spilled *all* of her blood. Homanan as well as Cheysuli."

Aidan made no comment. The history was his own, and well-learned in now-distant boyhood, but hearing it from Ian made it come alive. His great-uncle had known those people. Carillon, Finn, Donal—even Alix herself, who had proven to be the catalyst for the resurgence of the Old Blood. Others carried it, aye, but it was Alix who, by bearing a son to Duncan, breathed new life into the prophecy.

Who put new blood into the stable— Grimly, Aidan smiled. *When the old blood grows too weak, the new blood makes it strong.*

But his thoughts did not linger there. From his great-uncle, as with others, the emotions were tangible things. Aidan sensed shame, regret, grief; a tinge of bitterness. He put aside his own.

"*Su'fali*," he said softly, "has it followed you so long?"

Startled, Ian glanced over. His eyes asked the question.

Aidan answered it. "She killed herself, your *jehana*. She brought dishonor to her name, expunged her rune-sign from the birthlines . . . but that does not destroy the memory of the mother in the mind of her son."

"No." Ian's tone was rough.

With care, Aidan proceeded. "Once a year you carry out *i'toshaa-ni*—"

Ian cut him off. "That is my concern."

Aidan drew breath and tried again. "I think it is wrong for one man—one warrior—to assume responsibility for things he had nothing to do with."

"And you think that is why I carry out *i'toshaa-ni?*" Ian's eyes in the darkness were black, save for the rim of feral yellow. "You do not know everything, regardless of your 'gift.' "

Aidan gestured placation. "No, perhaps not—but I think that is a part of it. As for the rest, there is also the knowledge of what Lillith did to you, and what your child on her became."

Ian plugged the wineskin abruptly, squeaking the stopper home. "These are personal, private things."

"So is what *I* feel. Yet everyone wants to know."

Ian's motion to toss down the wineskin was arrested. Then, in silence, he set it carefully by his saddle. "Aye," he said finally, "everyone wants to know."

Aidan wet dry lips. "And yet when the taboo topic is raised, everyone turns away."

Ian's silence was loud.

"Taboo," Aidan repeated. "Even mere *contemplation* that a Cheysuli warrior might lie with an Ihlini woman."

Ian was, if nothing else, a man of much compassion. Yet now the emotions Aidan sensed were anger and bitterness. "We have little reason to consider such a bedding a benevolent thing," Ian declared. "Look at Lillith—daughter to Tynstar himself, half-sister to Strahan . . . servant of the Seker." He sighed, rubbing at tired eyes; age, all of a sudden, sat heavily on him. "Lovely, lethal Lillith—who, holding my *lir*, ensorcelled me so well I had little choice in the matter . . . and then bore me abomination."

"Who then bore *my* father a daughter." Aidan stroked back hair.

"You see, *su'fali*, it has been done before. And children have been born."

"But children who are not Firstborn." Ian's voice was emphatic. "Now, more than ever, we must be vigilant. The Ihlini have proved we can be tricked, even into bed . . . they have proved they have the power to alter the prophecy. It is only our good fortune the bloodlines were not whole . . ." Abruptly, his tone altered. "Aidan, if ever a child of the Lion sires a child for the Seker, everything is undone. *Everything* is undone."

Tension was palpable. Aidan sought to break it. "Do not fret about me, *su'fali*. I may be bound for my wedding, but she will not be an Ihlini."

Ian's face was taut. "There is danger in complacency."

"Aye," Aidan agreed. "But even if I should fail, the gods will tend to the outcome."

"Do not—" But Ian broke it off.

Aidan nearly laughed. "You were intending to suggest I not trust so much to the gods? But that is heresy, *su'fali*. And you a devout believer."

Ian fought to retain his composure. "This is not a topic for jest and mummery. We have dedicated our lives to the prophecy, devoted all honor and commitment to the gods—"

"—with whom I speak." Aidan shrugged correction. "Or, at least, with one."

"Aidan—"

"Fate," Aidan declared. "The Homanan word for *tahlmorra*. If it is meant to be, surely it will be. And nothing I do can change it."

Desperation underscored Ian's tone. "But it *can* be changed. By me, by you, by—"

"—Ihlini?" Aidan nodded. "Certainly they may try. And perhaps they can *win*—the gods gave us all free choice."

Staring in dismay, Ian slowly shook his head. "Does it make no difference to you? Does any of it matter?"

Aidan sighed. Weariness swept up out of the darkness and threatened to swallow him whole. "*Su'fali*, I do not mean to be contentious or perverse. But I have these thoughts, these *feelings*—" He shook his head, dismissing it. "I promise—all of it matters to me. But as for making a difference . . ." He collapsed against his saddle, too tired to stay upright. Through a yawn, he said, "—we shall have to wait and see."

* * *

The day dawned bright and warm, with no hint of rain in the air. They rode in companionable silence, taking comfort in mere presence, and lost themselves in the season. It was very nearly midday when Ian pulled his gray to a halt atop a hillock. "There," he said. "Solinde."

Aidan, reining in his dun, squinted across the distance. "How can you tell?" he asked. "It looks the same as Homana."

"There speaks ignorance." Ian grinned. "Is this land the same as the land around Mujhara?"

"No, of course not—"

"Is this land the same as that we left yesterday?"

"No, no—of course not—"

"And while there *are* similarities between this patch of ground and that, there are also differences." Ian resettled reins, unthreading tangled gray horsehair from red-dyed braided leather. "Just as there are in people."

Aidan forbore to answer. His great-uncle was being obscure.

No more than you, reminded Teel. The raven was a black blot against blue sky, swinging back from the border to return to his *lir.*

Aidan scowled into air. "How much longer to Lestra?"

Ian shrugged. "A six-day or so . . . I am not certain. The only time I went there was in *lir*-shape. It changes the measure of distance."

Aidan nodded vaguely. He sat quietly a long moment, soaking up the sun, then relaxed into the saddle. The depth of his relief was unexpected as well as welcome. Then he sat rigidly upright, thrusting arms into the air to cloak himself in the day. "Gods—I can *breathe* again!"

Ian's question was quiet. "Has it been so very bad?"

Aidan shrugged, lowering his arms. He was unwilling to discuss it. Not now. Not *here;* he did not want to destroy the new freedom he was feeling. "Not all of the time. But now it does not matter. I am no longer in Homana, hounded by gods and fetches, but in a new realm. And beginning a new life—complete with a *cheysula.*" He grinned at his kinsman. "Four daughters," he laughed. "Hart must be hungry for sons."

"Hart is hungry for nothing except the means to wager." Ian's tone was dryly affectionate.

Aidan laughed. "*Jehan* said I will like him."

Ian nodded agreement. "Everyone likes Hart . . . until he wins their coin."

Lir. It was Teel. *Lir, there comes a storm.*

"Storm?" Aidan spoke aloud. "The sky is blue as can be—"

Look behind you, lir. There the sky is black.

Aidan, sighing, twisted in his saddle to glance back the way they had come. "Teel says there is a storm . . ." He stopped speaking to gape inelegantly. "Where did *that* come from?"

"Tasha, too—" Ian also broke off. Then, with exceeding mildness, "I think we had better run."

Behind them the world was dark. Aidan glanced back toward Solinde—summer-clad Solinde—then back again to Homana, wearing wind-torn robes of black and gray, edged with a hem of lightning. "How do we outrun *that?*"

"By trying," Ian suggested, setting heels to his horse.

Aidan wasted a moment staring at the storm sweeping inexorably toward them both, rolling out of Homana like a wave of brackish ocean. It was impossible to believe; where they were it was warm, bright, still.

Then stillness began to move. Brightness began to fade.

By trying, Aidan agreed, then followed Ian's lead, sending his dun after the gray. Above him the rising wind buffeted Teel, who cried his displeasure.

"There is no cover!" Aidan shouted ahead to his kinsman. "The border is too barren . . . there is no place we can go!"

"Just run!" came Ian's reply, tossed back over a shoulder.

Aidan hunched down over the dun's neck, recalling the last storm-flight he and the gelding had shared. Then it had proved disastrous; he feared now might be the same. There were no trees with which to collide, but the scrubby grass of the borderlands could hide all manner of holes. A horse, falling in flight, could easily break his neck.

Or the head of the man who rides it—

He chanced a glance over a shoulder, squinting back stinging hair. The sky was indigo-black. He could not see the horizon. "Teel!" he shouted. *Lir—*

Here, the raven answered. *This wind disturbs my feathers.*

Aidan peered upward, reassured to see the raven. Teel was battling wind and winning, though his pattern was erratic.

We need trees, Aidan sent. *Trees—or better, a croft—*

Too late— Teel cried.

The curtain of darkness caught up, then settled its folds about them. It turned the day to night.

The dun was laboring. Fear dotted a line of sweat across summer-slick shoulders, brown in place of dun. Cold, clammy wind bathed exposed flesh. "*Su'fali*—" Aidan shouted. "We cannot run them forever!"

The first bolt of lightning broke free from the sky and struck the ground in front of them, blasting apart the earth in a rain of dirt and grass. The brilliance blinded Aidan. The explosion of thunder was deafening, buffeting his skull.

The dun gelding screamed, then tried to bolt. That he did not was only because Aidan used all the strength and skill he had to hold the horse in place; a blind man tipped off a frightened horse was surely bound for death. He fought even as the horse fought, spitting dirt from a gritty mouth, and blinked burning eyes repeatedly, trying to banish blackness.

—not blind—I am not—

"Teel!" he shouted. "*Su'fali*—" In thunder-bruised ears it was merely noise.

No rain, only wind. The darkness was absolute. It muffled the world around him like swaddling cloths on a corpse.

Teel— Through the link.

Lightning plunged into earth before him. The air stank and sizzled, raising the hair on his arms. Silhouetted against the brilliance was the shape of a man on horseback.

"*Ian*—" Aidan screamed. "Oh, gods—no—not *him* . . ."

The gelding thrashed and reared, as blinded and deafened as Aidan.

"Wait—*wait,* you thrice-cursed nag from the netherworld—"

But the dun chose not to wait. He shed Aidan easily and galloped off into keening darkness.

Aidan landed hard, one arm crooked awkwardly, but scrambled up without thinking about his own discomfort. Somewhere before him was his great-uncle and the gray horse who had fallen.

Teel, he sent frenziedly. Lir—*where is he . . . ask Tasha*—

Through the link came the familiar tone, naked of customary bite. *Six paces ahead, no more.*

Six paces . . . Aidan counted. And nearly tripped over Tasha, huddled by Ian's side.

"*Su'fali*—? *Su'fali*—"

Ian offered no answer.

"Oh, gods, not like this . . . please, do not be dead—"

Eyelids twitched. "No," Ian blurted. "No—not like this . . . agh, gods, *harani* . . ." The voice was tight with pain. "How—is the horse?"

Aidan looked, scraping hair out of his face. The wind was merciless. "Where—oh." The gray stood exhausted on three legs; a shattered foreleg dangled. Aidan looked back to his kinsman. "Broken leg," he answered tersely. "*Su'fali*—what of you?"

Ian's smile was faint, then spilled away. "Broken, too . . ." he gasped. "But I think hip in place of leg . . ." One hand hovered over a hip. "The horse fell, and rolled . . . gods, I will shame myself—"

"Because it hurts?" Aidan loosened Ian's belt gently. "You can *cry*, if you like—do you think I will complain?"

Ian's face was gray. His bottom lip bled from where teeth had broken through. "First, tend the horse. He has been a good mount."

Aidan did not answer, squinting against the wind and grit and hair as he peeled the waistband from Ian's abdomen.

The weak voice gained authority. "*Harani,* I will wait. The horse deserves a good death."

"And you, none at all." But Aidan knew his kinsman; he went to tend the horse.

It was not an easy task. He cared for horses as his father cared: with every bit of brain and body. But a broken leg was a death sentence, requiring immediate action. Aidan, with his Erinnish gift, sensed bewilderment and pain as the gray attempted to walk.

In Erinnish, he tried to soothe; the language was made for horses. He eased saddle and packs from the mount, then stroked the sweating neck. "*Shansu,*" he whispered gently, sliding long-bladed knife from sheath. "The gods will look after his own."

He went back to his kinsman wet with blood, then knelt at Ian's side. Tasha growled a warning. "*Shansu,*" Aidan repeated, one hand brushing her shoulders. Tasha growled again, ears flattening.

Ian's eyes were closed. In lightning, his years showed clearly, sharp bones protruding beneath aging flesh changed from bronze to linen white. Blood smeared his chin. Thunder boomed distantly.

"How can I move you?" Aidan pleaded, mostly of himself. "The pain alone could kill you. And if not that, what is to say the movement itself will not?" Wind whipped gray-white hair across Ian's face. Aidan peeled it back. "*Su'fali*, what do I do?"

Ian's eyes opened. From pain, they were nearly black. "Bones grow brittle with age," he remarked. "Take ten years away, and I would only have bruised."

Aidan tried to smile, because Ian wanted him to. "*Su'faili*, what can I do?"

"Be true to yourself," Ian murmured. "Be true to the blood in your veins."

"Earth magic," Aidan said numbly. "But—I have never required it. I have never even *attempted*—" Futility was painful. "I'm not knowing how to do it!"

"Ask," Ian said raggedly. "You are Cheysuli—*ask*—"

Aidan flung back his head, searching black sky for a smaller blackness. *Lir*— he appealed. *Teel*—

Would I tell you any different? Use what you have been given!

Beside her *lir*, Tasha wailed.

"—time—" Aidan muttered. "Gods—give me the *time*—"

You waste it! Teel told him. *What are you waiting for?*

Aidan did not know. Courage, he thought dimly; assurances of success.

Tasha's wail increased.

The raven's voice intruded. *Old men die of this!*

Old men, Aidan echoed. And looked again at his kinsman, who once had known Carillon.

Tasha's tail beat the ground. Angry eyes glowed dimly. The storm raged unabated, buffeting them with wind. It keened across the land, spitting dirt and grass and dampness.

"Now—" Aidan murmured, digging fingers into soil. "Let us see who is Cheysuli—let us *see* what gods can do—"

The lightning came down a third time and blasted him apart.

Chapter Nine

He stood before a door. The door swung silently open.

"Come in," the woman invited, and put her hand on his arm.

She drew him into the croft, where no croft had existed before. It was small, thatched, lime-washed white, smelling of warmth and wool. He saw three cats: the black on the hearth, the brown on a stool, the white-booted silver tabby curled in the tangle of color-less yarns piled in haphazard fashion on the floor. In the center of the room stood a loom.

She shut the door behind him. And, when he tried to speak, closed his mouth with her hand. "No," she said quietly. "Ian will be well. There is no need to fear." She gestured toward a chair.

He did not intend to sit, but found himself obeying. And staring at her in wonder.

She was unremarkable. A small, fragile woman with callused hands, graying hair snugged back in a knot pinned against her head. She wore a woolen skirt of many patches, as if she added a swatch of weaving each time the skirt wore thin. Over it was a tunic the color of winter grass: dull and lacking luster. A single col-orless stone shone on her buckle: lone, unwinking eye. Her own eyes were blue, faded with time, and the flesh of her face was worn.

Aidan stirred sluggishly, coming out of disorientation. Urgency made him curt. "Lady, I have no time—"

"You have as much time as I give you."

Her serene certainty filled him with trepidation. Aidan tried again, exerting more authority. "There is the storm, and my kinsman—"

Her composure remained unruffled. "Ian will be well. The storm is of my sending."

"*Your* sending—" He stopped, banished shock, summoned anger on Ian's behalf. "Lady, he is *harmed*—"

"He can be healed." Quietly she lifted the cat from her stool and sat down before the loom. The cat found a home in her lap, collapsing once more into sleep. She reached out and took up the shuttle.

Aidan, staring at her, knew it was the only answer he would get until she chose to give another. Nothing he said would shake her. She was not the kind touched by emotions; her concerns lay in other directions.

Impatience will not serve . . . With effort, Aidan banished it. He turned instead to the quiet courtesy Homana-Mujhar had taught him. "What do I call you, Lady? The first one was the Hunter."

"You may call me the Weaver." Her smile was luminous. "Come to my work, Aidan. Come and look upon the colors."

He did as he was bidden, dragging himself from the chair. A part of him denied what was happening, recalling the blast of lightning; a part of him counseled patience. He had met Shaine, Carillon, a god; now he met a goddess.

"Teel," he murmured dully. The link was empty of *lir.*

"Teel is very patient . . . come look upon the colors."

Aidan moved to stand before the loom. He was aware only dimly of the warmth of the croft, the purring of the cats, the scent of fresh-spun wool. She was gray, gray and dun, weaving gray and dun homespun—and then he looked at the loom. He looked upon her colors.

He could not name them all. He had never seen such brilliance.

The Weaver worked the shuttle. Back and forth, to and fro, feeding dullness into the pattern. Aidan thought it sacrilege—until he saw the truth.

The colors came from her. As she carried the shuttle through, each strand took on a hue.

"There is a thing you must do," she said quietly. "A task to be undertaken, but one you will deny. It is a task of great importance, of great *necessity*, but we cannot be certain you will do it. We gave humankind the gift of self-rule, and even gods cannot sway those who choose not to hear." In renewed silence, she worked the shuttle. "We make things easy; we make things hard. Humankind makes the choices." She stilled the shuttle, and held it. "Look into the colors. Tell me what you see."

He swallowed to wet his throat, "A man," he said huskily, "and a chain. The chain binds him, binds his soul . . . but it is not made of iron—" Aidan shut his eyes. When he looked again, afraid, the colors were brighter yet. "Gold," he said hoarsely. "Gold of the gods, and blessed . . . but there is a weakness in it. One of the links will break."

The Weaver's smile was sweet. "There is sometimes strength in weakness."

He fought down the urge to run. "Am I to fail, then? Am I the weak link?"

"Not all men succeed in what they desire most. As for you, I cannot say; your road still lies before you."

"And my—task?"

"The time has not come for you to make your decision."

"But—this—?"

"This is only a prelude to it."

Aidan shivered. "Why did you send the storm? Why did you send him pain?"

The Weaver looked at him. Her eyes were no longer kind. "If a man will not listen, we must make ourselves be heard."

"It was not necessary to harm *him*—"

Her voice was a whiplash of sound. "You are meant to go alone."

"By the gods—" he began, then stopped. Incongruously, he laughed. "Aye, well, so it is . . ." Aidan rubbed a stiff face. "You will forgive me, I hope, if I consider your actions unnecessary. He is a devout, committed Cheysuli—"

"One who will be rewarded." The Weaver's tone was gentle. "This is your journey, Aidan. Your task. You are meant to go alone."

"You might have *asked*—"

"Gods often ask. Too often, we are ignored." She gestured again to the loom. "Tell me what you see."

Wearily, Aidan looked. The colors, oddly, had faded, except for the chain of wool. Its hue was still brilliant gold, the gold of purest refining, glinting in firelight.

As he always did, Aidan put out his hand. He knew he would touch wool; when he touched metal, he promptly dropped it.

The link fell. It rang dully against beaten earth, then lost part of itself in wool. Dull, colorless wool.

Slowly Aidan bent down and peeled back the strands. The link was real, and whole.

He rose, clutching the link. Then fumbled at his belt, undoing leather and buckle, threaded the belt through. He slid the new link to the old. They clinked in harmony, riding his right hip. Aidan rebuckled his belt.

He looked at the tapestry. The colors, for him, were faded. "What *tahlmorra* do you weave me?"

The Weaver smiled: small, gray-haired woman with magic in her eyes. "You will weave your own, Aidan. That I promise you."

He opened his mouth, closed it. Then opened it again. "Am I worthy of this?"

"Perhaps. Perhaps not."

Aidan closed one hand around the links. Edges bit into his palm. It was all he could do to keep the frustration from his tone. "Is this how I am to spend my life?" Control frayed raggedly: now the frustration was plain. "Jerked out of the day or night to trade obscurity with gods—*and* goddesses—who play a private game? Am I to do your bidding like a tame little Cheysuli, never questioning this unknown task?" Anger replaced frustration. He shouted aloud in the croft. "Do you know what it is like having everyone think you are mad?"

Silence as the shout died. For a moment, he was ashamed. Then knew it had been required. Too much more locked away would make him lose the balance, and what would he be then?

The gods made us this way. They gave us the gift of the shapechange as much as the curse of knowing the loss of balance is loss of self.

"Do you know?" he repeated, because he needed an answer.

Tears glistened in the Weaver's eyes. "Do you know what it is like having to ignore petitions and prayers? To let a child die even though others beg for its life?"

Aidan was dumbfounded. "Why *do* you ignore such things?"

"Because sometimes the greatest strength comes out of the greatest pain."

"But a *child*—"

"There is reason for everything."

Aidan's tone slashed through her words. "What reason in the death of a child? What reason in the destruction of a race?"

The Weaver set down her shuttle, the cat, and slowly rose to face him. Aidan was much taller; it did not diminish her. "The world is complex," she told him. "The bits and pieces of it are very hard to see, even if you have eyes. The eyes of humans are blind."

It was not enough for Aidan, full to choking on obscurity. "I think—"

She did not allow him to finish, silencing him with calm. "Some see more than most. *You* see more than most; it is why we gave you the task. But if you saw it all, if you saw *every piece,* surely you would be mad."

He felt helplessness gathering. "Then a *tahlmorra* has no bearing on how we live our lives."

"There is a fate in everything. People choose not to see it. They see only the immediacy; they demand gratification even in their grief." The Weaver drew a breath. "If no one ever died, the Wheel of Life would stop. It would catch on the hordes of people, and eventually it would fail."

Aidan's tone was bitter. "Blood greases it."

"The Wheel of Life must turn."

"If it stopped, would *you* die? Would the gods disappear?"

The Weaver's eyes were bleak. "We disappear every day."

Helplessness crashed down. Aidan stretched out his hands, angered by impotence. "What am I to do? How am I to serve? You tell me you kill children, yet you expect me to do this task, which you then refuse to divulge. Is this how the Wheel turns? Is this how our worth is judged?"

Her expression altered. The eyes now were masked. "Is it cruel to keep the child from jumping off the wall because she believes she can fly?"

Irreverence bubbled forth. "If the child is Cheysuli, perhaps she *can* fly . . ." But the irony spilled away. "You make it black and white."

"Choices often are."

"But what of the *gray* choices? What of the subtleties?"

Her voice was implacable. "To a man who does not care, there are no subtleties. But there is no compassion, either. There is no empathy."

He let his hands fall slack. "I cannot deal with this."

"Every man deals with this. The result is not always pretty; the result is often bloody. But every man deals with this. Every man makes his choice."

It was too much, too *much;* he was incapable of comprehension. He smelled wool, cats, himself; he tasted futility.

Aidan scrubbed his face, warping syllables. "I have to go— there is Ian . . . I have to go from here—"

The door swung open in silence. "Then go," the Weaver said.

* * *

Aidan lay sprawled on the ground, stunned by the force of the lightning. His head rang with noise, filled up with tight-packed wool. Vision was nonexistent. Flesh writhed on his bones; all the hairs on his body rose.

He blurted something and thrust himself up, clawing into the daylight. Blood and dirt was spat out; he sucked in lungfuls of air. Links chimed at his belt.

Links—? Aidan caught them. And then he looked at Ian.

The aging face was wasted. "I saw it," Ian gasped. "I saw the lightning *strike*—"

"No. No—*su'fali*—"

"I *saw it*—" Ian repeated. "You lit up like a pyre, and when it died you were gone. When it died, you were *gone*—"

Aidan began to tremble. Shock and fatigue were overwhelming. "You would not—you would not believe—" Dazedly, he laughed. "You would never believe what happened—"

"Aidan, you were *struck*—"

"You would never believe what I saw—"

Ian's hand clutched Tasha's neck. "You would never believe what *I* saw!"

Aidan tried to stifle the laughter. He knew very well he walked much too close to the edge. "What I saw—what *I* saw—" He smothered his face with both hands, stretching the skin out of shape. "Oh, gods—" More laughter. "Oh, *su'fali*, if only I could tell you—" Abruptly he cut it off. "She said you would be well. She *promised* you would be well."

"Who—?" Ian's eyes widened. His silence was absolute.

Aidan, on hands and knees, moved to crouch by his kinsman. He ignored the cat's snarl. "Then *I* am meant to do it—she left this task for me . . ."

Ian still said nothing.

"She said you would be well, so I will have to do it." Grimly, Aidan smiled. "But I'm *still* not knowing how."

"Oh, gods," Ian murmured. "No wonder they whisper about you—"

"You will have to go back, *su'fali*. I am to go alone."

Ian shut his eyes. The *lir* by his side growled.

Teel? Aidan appealed.

The raven's tone was amused. *All one must do is ask.*

Aidan asked, and was given.

PART II

Chapter One

The city of Lestra, unlike Mujhara, was situated on a series of hills. None rose much higher than its brother or sister, but there were distinct prominences scattered throughout the city, each capped with clusters of buildings like curds of souring milk.

It gave Lestra a scalloped look, Aidan decided, as he wound his way through the warren of cobbled streets, each turn more confusing than the last. He asked directions to the palace several times, each time receiving an answer distinctly different from the last, and despaired of ever finding his way to his *su'fali*'s home.

Teel's contempt was dry. *Shall I find you the way?*

It was, of course, the simplest method of all, except Aidan preferred, at this point, to find the palace himself. He disliked giving Teel any more reason to feel superior than was absolutely necessary, as the raven took especial care to point out Aidan's human shortcomings all too often as it was.

Except they seemed to be lost—or *he* seemed to be lost—and he saw no help for it.

Aidan sighed and shifted in the saddle. *All right. I give in. Go find us the palace.*

Teel, perched on the saddlebow, did not leave at once. *You might find it yourself, if you gave up this useless horse. Why you persist in riding when you have the means to fly . . .* In the link, Teel sighed.

I persist in riding because, as I explained to the Hunter, there is a marvelous freedom in such things. I persist in riding this particular horse because, if you will recall, Ian refused to accept him in place of his own.

Teel ruffled one wing. *Because he went home in lir-shape, instead. Like any sensible Cheysuli.*

Aidan smiled grimly. *I am what you have made me.*

The raven demurred. *I made nothing. I bonded, no more, in*

order to give you the aid all warriors require—though you do, I will admit, require more than most. Teel's eye was bright. *Moreover, you are much too stubborn to accept anyone's guidance, god's or otherwise. You have made yourself.*

Aloud, Aidan suggested: "Then render me aid, *lir:* go find the palace."

The raven did, taking much less time than Aidan had hoped, and reported explicit directions that led Aidan—and his horse—directly to the front gate. Aidan tried to give his name and title to the guards, but they merely waved him through. He then tried to find the duty captain—who would, of course, carry word into the palace, then return with the proper summons—but was yet again waved along. Bemused, he rode through the outer bailey into the inner one without being challenged at all. And when, in growing frustration, he tried to pay a horseboy to carry word into the palace, the boy merely grinned and bowed his head, then took his horse away after nodding at the front door.

Teel, on the nearest wall, suggested Aidan go in. *They seem a welcoming sort, these Solindish.*

After an aimless hesitation, Aidan approached the massive front door. *My* su'fali *is not Solindish, as you well know.* He climbed the first flight of steps. *Could you at least send word through the link to Rael? I think it would be best if someone knew we were coming.*

Why?

Common courtesy. Aidan climbed the second flight. *As well as a proper defense . . . if I were an enemy, I need only walk through the door.*

You are not, and there is the door.

Aidan paused, glancing back. *Are you not coming in?*

Later. For now, I prefer the sun.

So Aidan left Teel upon the wall, in the warmth of a summer day, and entered, unannounced, his *su'fali*'s unguarded front door.

It was not, Aidan soon discovered, guarded any better inside than out. He stopped inside the front door, lingered politely a moment as he waited for servants to come running; when no one at all came, even walking, Aidan at last gave up. He headed down the first hall he could find.

No one appeared to ask him who he was or what he wanted. Disgruntled, he began opening heavy carved doors. All the rooms were empty. *If I were bent on assassination, surely I would suc-*

ceed. He boomed shut yet another door and turned again into the hall. *Then again, perhaps not—I cannot find anyone to kill!*

Sound interrupted disgust. Aidan stopped walking at once, listening expectantly, hoping for someone at last who might be able to guide him to living bodies, or at least tell him the way.

Echoes threaded corridors. Over Aidan's head arched wooden spans in scalloped, elaborate beamwork, drooping from ancient stone. The immensity of the palace dwarfed and warped the sound, distorting clarity.

I could die in here, Aidan thought in wry disgust. *I could starve to death on this very spot, and all anyone would find would be my dessicated corpse—*

A voice. A young, childish voice, raised to a note of possessive authority. He could not make out the words, but recognized the tone. Someone was put out.

And then the words came clear. "It was *me* he made eyes at, Cluna! Not you! He did not even *look* at you!"

"You!" scoffed a second voice, very like the first. "Why would he look at you when *I* am there? You only *wish* he would look at you!"

Aidan, smiling, folded arms across his chest, found the nearest pillar to lean against, and waited.

"It is *me* he likes, not you! He gives me sweets whenever he can."

"Sweets are no way to judge a man. *Words* are how you judge—"

"But *you* never give him a chance to speak, Cluna! How would you know what he says?"

"Oh, Jennet, just because he was polite to you does not mean he really cares. He was only being kind—"

"Kind to *you*," Jennet rejoined. "While, as for me—"

But they came around the corner and into Aidan's hall. Seeing him, they stopped.

"Oh," said one.

"Ummm," said the other.

Aidan merely smiled.

They scutinized him closely, marking clothing and ornamentation, especially the *lir*-gold on his arms. Clearly he was more than a servant, while something less than what he was, if using Homanan rank. They had learned, even as he had, how to judge others by subtleties, trained not to jump to conclusions when the conclusion might offend.

Which told him who they were, even though he already knew. "Cluna and Jennet," he said. "Which of you is which?"

Two sets of blue eyes glinted. "Whichever we choose to be."

"Ah." Aidan nodded. "A riddle, then, is it? I am to guess?"

Two heads nodded. Expectantly, they waited.

They were identical. Both fair-haired, blue-eyed, a little plump, with a sturdy femininity. One wore violet-dyed skirts and tunic, pale hair tied back in a matching ribbon with gem-weighted ends now straggling down her back much as loosened hair did; the other similar garments—and tattered ribbon—in pale blue, but the colors told him nothing. He did not know the girls and therefore could not judge the small things, such as a lift of the chin, a tilt of the head, the level set of small shoulders, but there was no need to judge. For the first time in his life, Aidan used his Erinnish *kivarna* to answer specific needs.

"You," he said to the one in violet, "are Jennet. And you, of course, are Cluna."

Identical mouths dropped open. It was Cluna, in blue, who spoke. "*No one* has gotten us right. Not on first meeting!"

Jennet assessed him closely. "How did you do it?"

"Easily," he answered. "To the stranger, you look very much the same. But two people are never truly one. You think differently, feel differently . . . you want different things."

They stared. First at him, then at one another. Then once more at him. Cluna shook her head. "No one else thinks so."

Aidan shrugged. "Because no one else is truly twin-born, not as you are. Even your *jehan* is different—twin-born, aye, but he and my *jehan* are quite dissimiliar in appearance and temperament. No one *expects* them to be the same. But they do expect it of you, and so neither of you is given the leave to be individual."

"He *knows!*" Cluna gasped.

Jennet reassessed him. "Your *lir* is telling you that."

Aidan laughed. "No, my *lir* is at this moment perched outside in the sun."

Blue eyes narrowed as she absently tugged her tangled ribbon. "Then how *can* you know?"

He forbore to explain the gift. "I understand feelings," he said, thinking it enough. "Now, as for you—"

"Are you *Aidan?*" Cluna asked.

Jennet cut off his answer. "He *cannot* be Aidan," she declared, flipping violet ribbon behind a shoulder. "Aidan is very sickly. Everyone says. He is not expected to live."

It was a sobering summation. Aidan eyed both girls a moment, then sighed faintly. "There was a time I was sickly," he agreed. "There was even a time they feared I might die. But not anymore."

Jennet lifted pale, inquisitive brows. "Well, then," she began, "who are you going to marry?"

Cluna was horrified. "Jennet, you cannot ask him that!"

"Why not? It is a fair question, I think." Jennet twined a lock of fallen hair around one finger. "We are thirteen now, and there has been talk of betrothing us into this kingdom or that. Even Homana has been mentioned."

"Oh, has it?" Aidan's tone was bland. "I'm thinking I might yet have something to say on that order."

Jennet was speculative. "I doubt they will let you. It makes them feel important to decide how we should live."

"*Jen*net!" Cluna wailed.

Her sister did not respond. "*Have* you come for a wife?"

Aidan smiled. "Perhaps."

Cluna's face was burning. "He will never have *you*," she asserted. "A queen must know her place—"

"I *do* know my place!" Jennet snapped. "As any fool can see, we are of marriageable age and excellent family."

A new voice intruded. "But *not* of excellent manners." A young woman advanced on them quickly, yellow skirts gathered in both hands. "I could hear you screeching all the way to my chambers. That is *not* how our lady mother desires you to behave . . . you are princesses, not street urchins—though you look more like the latter with your hair all pulled awry." She glanced briefly at Aidan, then back to the girls. "Jennet, have you no sense at all? You tax a stranger with inappropriate talk . . ." She cast a polite smile at Aidan, smoothing yellow skirts and the amber-studded girdle binding a narrow waist. "You will forgive them, I hope, if they spoke too plainly. Jennet has cost herself more than one friend by such bold talk."

"Not Tevis," Jennet declared. "He *likes* such talk."

Cluna disagreed. "Tevis is merely polite. He has no wish to offend our father."

"Enough," the woman chided. "Have you no sense of decorum? This man is a stranger!"

"Cousin," Janet supplied.

It stopped the other at once. For the first time she gave Aidan all her attention. She was as unlike her sisters as she could be, but by color and age he knew her. The oldest of all Hart's brood: Blythe, only months younger than he himself.

She was, he thought, magnificent. The heavy velvet gown, dyed a rich, warm yellow, set off her dusky Cheysuli coloring, though the eyes were blue instead of yellow. Her face was much like the faces of the Cheysuli women in Clankeep, formed of arresting planes and angles. There was little Solindish in her; that was Cluna's and Jennet's province. Blythe's black hair had been twisted and looped against the back of her head, showing off an elegant neck.

She was worth coming for— Aidan cut it off. He had spent too much time with women of lower rank, who encouraged his attention. He had become adept at dealing with them, and at judging their worth very quickly. *But this woman is not like them . . .*

Blythe's gaze was level. "Are you truly Aidan?"

He gazed back at her. *SHE could make me forget. All the dreams, the chain*— Again he cut himself off. "Aye," he offered calmly. "I was not expected, so I hope you will forgive me for arriving without a warning. My *jehan* did not think Hart would turn me away."

"Of course not. You are well come to Lestra." Blythe's Homanan was accented with the nuances of Solinde. Aidan found it attractive. "But you must promise me you forgive these little magpies, croaking about private things."

Both magpies glared at their sister, then turned their attention to Aidan. Summoning gallantry, he assured them he would.

Jennet banished contrition. "*Have* you come for a wife?"

Blythe's eyebrows rose. "What has possessed your tongue to be so heedless? Do you think Aidan came all the way from Homana simply to look for a wife?"

Aidan opened his mouth, shut it, scratched eloquently at his scalp.

"See?" Jennet challenged.

Blythe's eyes widened. "*Have* you, then?"

"See?" Jennet repeated. "You want to know as much as we do."

Aidan maintained a neutral tone. "There is some possibility—"

"Queen of Homana," Jennet considered.

Cluna glared at her. "Not for years and years. First there is *Princess* of Homana—"

Blythe's turn. "And *that* not for years," she declared. "There is one of those already: Aidan's mother, Aileen."

Cluna smiled shyly. "Jennet may be older, but I am nicer."

Jennet eyed her askance. "And Blythe the oldest of all. *She* comes first in everything."

"Enough!" Blythe cried, before full-scale war was begun. "All of you, come with me. Aidan must meet *jehan*."

Jennet twitched at skirts. "He is playing Bezat with Tevis. He sent us out when Cluna knocked over the bowl and scattered all the pieces."

"It was an accident!" Cluna cried. "And it was *really* your fault—if you had not left the bowl so close to the edge of the table—"

"And if *you* had kept your sticky fingers out of it—"

"Never mind," Blythe said ominously. "I know where Tevis is. I know where *both* of them are. And I know where you are going." Blythe locked a hand over Jennet's shoulder and steered her down the hall. "Cluna, you also. And Aidan—" Blythe's smile was both beautiful and beseeching. "Will you come with us?"

Aidan was a man who had grown up with no sisters. He liked women very much, but the ones he had spent most of his time with had been quite different. Looking at his kin, allied against refusal, he doubted he could do otherwise. Not in the face of so many females bent on a single thing that had nothing to do with bed.

Chapter Two

The round room was tiny but comfortable, lime-washed white for brightness, and tucked into a corner tower of the castle. A handful of casement slits let in the light of a fading day, painting the room in muted stripes. There were stools, chairs, tripod candle stands; one low table. At the table were two men: a Cheysuli in indigo leathers, gold gleaming on dark arms, and a younger, more elegant man dressed in russet velvet doublet over brown hunting leggings.

Aidan knew the elder, though they had never met. He was very like his own father.

Lost within their game, neither man looked up. Blythe sighed, exchanging an amused glance with her newly-arrived cousin, then silenced Cluna and Jennet with a raised finger. With eloquent, purposeful gravity, Blythe made the introduction.

A pair of heads lifted and turned, displaying startled expressions. Hart stared, then abruptly suspended movement in the midst of drawing a bone-colored stone from a rune-wrought silver bowl. Blue eyes at first were stunned; then disbelief entered. "No," he said only.

Aidan, amused, grinned. "Aye."

Hart frowned. His eyes were shrewdly attentive as he made a brief, alert assessment, marking hair, eyes, gold; the shape of facial bones. Then the frown faded. Doubt shaded his tone. "Aidan of *Homana?*"

"Not Aidan of Falia." Aidan's tone was dry. "Am I to spend the rest of my life reassuring my kinfolk I am well and truly alive?"

"Brennan's son," Hart murmured, the slow smile stretching his mouth. And then he was on his feet, dropping the forgotten Bezat stone. "By all the gods, *Aidan!*"

The fleeting thought was ironic. *By all the gods indeed—* But then Hart was hugging him, pulling him into a kinman's proud embrace, and Aidan had no more time for thought.

Hart said something in the Old Tongue, something to do with prayers answered for his *rujholli*, then released Aidan. Blue eyes were very bright. "You must forgive my doubt . . . all those years everyone feared for your welfare, and now you stride into my castle every inch the warrior!"

Aidan indicated his hair. "Except, I think, for this."

Hart waved a dismissive hand. "Aye, well . . . you have noted, I am sure, two of my own children lack the Cheysuli color." He grinned at his fair-haired daughters. "It comes from outmarriage. First Aileen, then Ilsa. If we are not careful, we will lose the coloring."

But he did not sound particularly concerned by the dilution of true Cheysuli characteristics. Aidan, looking at Hart's face, saw the same bones his father had, and hair equally black—or once equally black; now equally threaded with silver—but Hart's eyes were blue. Blythe looked very like him.

Blythe. Aidan glanced at her. Upon making the introduction, she had crossed the room to stand beside the young man in russet velvet. He waited in polite silence, displaying only a profile, and idly stirred the stones. Blythe reached down and took the wine cup by his elbow, murmuring in a low tone.

Aidan felt a flicker of unexpected apprehension. He was very accustomed to seeing approval or invitation in the eyes of attractive women. Blythe was different, but he found he wanted the same reaction. Yet her thoughts, clearly, were with another man. And Aidan, for all his experience, knew the rules were different. He had come looking for a wife, not a bedpartner of brief duration.

Apprehension mounted. *Am I too late for Blythe?*

Hart's ebullient voice overruled thinking. "How is my royal *rujho*? And *jehan*? Is Mujhara the same, or has it grown? Has Deirdre—"

But Jennet and Cluna, freed now of requested silence, began chattering at their father.

"Not now," he said above the high-pitched din that was, to Aidan, indecipherable. "There are too many things I have to ask of Aidan—" Then, in affectionate. exasperation, "Not *now;* I have said. You will have Aidan thinking I spoil you."

Aidan, who had already seen he did, smiled privately. Across the room Blythe glanced up, caught his expression and smiled back. They shared the tiny moment of acknowledgment, then Blythe set down the cup and came away from the table.

"Jennet," she said, "enough. *And* you, Cluna. There will be time for your chatter later . . . for now we must host our kinsman and treat him with Solindish honor." She flicked eloquent fingers. "You know where the kitchens are. Send for food and wine."

Jennet's mouth pursed, mutinously. "If he has come to find a wife, it concerns me. I should be allowed to stay."

At the low table, the young man stopped stirring stones.

"A wife?" Hart echoed.

"Not *now*," Blythe told Jennet. "Settling a marriage is something done by adults, and *you* have yet to prove you are anything more than a child. Go, and take your sister."

Brief rebellion from quieter Cluna. "But he might choose *me*."

Blythe pointedly opened the door. "He might even choose Dulcie."

Two mouths dropped open. Two voices chorused, "But Dulcie is only a *baby*."

"All the better," Blythe told them briskly. "Babies are easier to train." She smiled at Aidan, then motioned her sisters out. Eventually, they went.

"A wife?" Hart repeated. "But Brennan has said nothing of that in any of his letters."

His father and Hart corresponded often, Aidan knew, trying to compensate for the separation. Too distant even for the *lir*-link, the twin-born princes took what solace they could from parchment.

Aidan shook his head. "It came up of a sudden. They discovered, *jehan* and *jehana,* that I was twenty-three . . . apparently there is some significance attached to the age." He smiled at Blythe, not so much younger than he. "It must be a family custom than no man or woman be allowed to reach twenty-four without having married."

Blythe's color darkened. She turned jerkily to her father. "Perhaps I should go . . . perhaps I should accompany Cluna and Jennet—"

"Cluna and Jennet will do very well without you." Hart waved her back, then glanced across at the table. "No, Tevis—sit down. There is no need for you to go."

"But—my lord—" The young man was standing. He was tall, dark-haired, handsome, filling out leather and velvet with an elegance edged with power. Aidan recalled Cluna and Jennet were quite enamored of him. "If you truly intend to discuss a royal marriage—"

"Not now," Hart declared. "By the gods, not now. I am a man with four daughters . . . there will be time aplenty for that. And time aplenty to speak of family matters." He kicked another stool over toward the table, looking expectantly at Aidan. "Do you play?"

"Not that. I have heard of Bezat; I thought it best to avoid it. It carries—consequences."

"*All* games carry consequences." Hart reseated himself. "If you mean my missing hand, that had little to do with Bezat. It had to do with being a great fool . . . since then, I have learned better." He motioned impatiently. "Sit down, Aidan. Talk of marriages can wait . . . there is a game to learn!"

Aidan hesitated. "I was warned about you."

"All true," Hart agreed cheerfully. "Shall we add to the stories?"

"*Jehan,*" Blythe said warningly. "You know what *jehana* will say if you stay up all night again."

"Your *jehana*, at the moment, has more to concern herself with than what time I come to bed. She would more likely prefer me *out* of it . . ." Hart's eyes were bright as he grinned at Aidan. "Sit you down, *harani*. How best do we meet one another save over wine and a game?"

The gaming continued until dawn. Tevis, yawning, gave up at last and excused himself, pushing all of his coin across the table to Hart. His bloodshot eyes were red-rimmed.

"No more," he murmured sleepily. "You have all my wits and now my coin . . . I am for bed, my lord. You promised me one last night."

Hart leaned back on his stool, rolling a stiffened neck. Black hair touched his shoulders; the silver was in his forelock. "There is always a bed for you . . . if I refused, all four of my daughters would ply my name with curses." He grinned, working shoulders. "Even Dulcie adores you."

"She has excellent taste." Tevis rose, rubbing absently at thick hair. It was so brown as to verge on black, cut closely to his head. Equally dark brows arched smoothly over ale-brown eyes, defining the bone of the forehead. "Of course, at all of two, her allegiance is easily won." He yawned, stretched briefly, looked down at Aidan. "My lord. If you yet have the wits to think, you might consider ending this travesty. He will have all of *your* coin, too."

Aidan grunted and reached for wine, then thought better of it. "I am a careful man."

"So was I, once." Tevis bowed briefly in Hart's direction, then headed for the door.

Hart waited until it was closed. "He is here to marry Blythe."

Wandering wits snapped back at once. Aidan blinked. "Ah."

"Of course, nothing has yet been settled—nothing has been *said* . . . but it is why he came." Hart rose and walked stiffly to the nearest casement and shoved the shutter open to let in pale pink dawn. "He is of one of the oldest and finest families of Solinde . . . a *jehan*, prince or no, could ask for no better match."

Aidan recalled Blythe's subtle intimacies, the expression in Tevis' eyes when the subject of marriage had come up. He had suspected as much, though he wished it were otherwise. "You must do what is best, *su'fali*."

"No." Hart strode to another casement, pushed open another shutter. "No, I must do as my daughter desires." Aidan watched in startled silence as Hart opened shutters at two more casements, then swung to face his audience of one. "*You* should understand the need."

"I?"

"Of course." Hart's nostalgic smile was lopsided. "Aileen and Brennan married out of duty, and out of honor for a betrothal made without their consent. Before they were born."

"Ah," Aidan said.

"I was the middle son, the son whose disposition was not so important as Brennan's . . . no one linked me to anyone. Ilsa and I married for the sake of Solinde, but by then the point was moot. We were already bound." Hart leaned against the sill, folding arms across his chest. *Lir*-bands gleamed. "Given the choice, Aileen never would have married Brennan. She wanted Corin. But he left for Atvia, so Brennan got his *cheysula*." Hart's expression was blank, his tone carefully bland. "I will give my daughter the choice."

Aidan sighed, staring blankly at the bowl of bone-colored stones. "A man come to sell his horse would list its obvious assets. I am to be Mujhar, one day . . ." Aidan lifted his head. "But that makes no difference, does it? Not to you. The stories I have heard say you were always the least impressed by titles and rank."

Hart shrugged. "The only thing that impressed me was a man's willingness to wager." But he said it without smiling. Wearily, he threaded the fingers of his remaining hand through fallen hair and scooped it back from his brow. The gesture displayed a dual circlet of lines graven deeply into the flesh. Age sat lightly on him, as lightly as on Aidan's father, but nonetheless it encroached. "You have my permission to ask her, if you choose—that much I can give you . . . but it will be Blythe's decision."

Aidan lifted one shoulder in self-conscious concession; they both knew what she would say.

Hart's voice was neutral. "If it is kin you want, to keep the bloodlines whole—I have three other daughters."

Aidan shrugged again. "By now, the blood is everything we need to fulfill the prophecy, except . . ." He let it trail off; the ending was implicit.

Hart said it anyway. "Except Ihlini." He sighed and rubbed absently at the flesh of his left forearm where the leather cuff bound the stump. "Aye, there is that . . . but who of us will take on the distasteful task?" Black brows arched curiously. "You are the likeliest one."

Aidan shook his head. "Not I, *su'fali*. I am not my *jehan*."

Hart's expression stilled. "Brennan was tricked."

He did not like being reminded. He protects my jehan *as much as* jehan *protects him. Even now.* Aidan made his tone light. "Aye, so he was; I do not hate him for it, or think him due less respect. He was not the first . . . it happened even to Ian."

"And Ian still pays the price . . . . I think my *rujho* does, too." Hart stopped kneading his arm, changing the topic abruptly. "There are the other girls. Young, I know . . . but such things are not uncommon when House marries House."

Aidan thought of Cluna and Jennet. Thirteen-year-old hellions. The other was Dulcie, age two. He was a man who wanted a woman, not a child to raise. Not girls who thought they were grown, not knowing what else was expected. While it was true he would not inherit the Lion for many years yet, he wanted those years spent properly, not waiting for a girl-wife to discover she was a woman.

There is one last thing . . . He rubbed gritty eyes. "You have no son," he said softly. "What will you do for an heir?"

Hart did not smile. "Are you promising me one in exchange for persuading Blythe?"

Aidan sighed. "No."

Hart pressed himself off the sill and came to the table. He

poured himself fresh wine, lifted his cup and sipped. Then set down the cup again. "Ilsa is in bed because she is very near to term. In a week, possibly two, I may yet have an heir.

The words rose unbidden: "*Ru'shalla-tu, su'fali. Tahlmorra lujhalla mei wiccan, cheysu.*"

"You sound like a *shar tahl*." Hart smiled. "*Leijhana tu'sai, harani.* I, too, hope it is so."

"So." Aidan rose, kicking back his stool. "There is yet a princess left—an *older* princess—Keely's daughter, Shona. She is—nineteen? Twenty? Perhaps I should go at once, to set Blythe's mind at ease. She knows why I am here, as does Tevis. It would discomfit them to think I mean to come between them."

"Stay," Hart said. "There is no need to go in such haste. If Blythe and Tevis cannot survive your presence, they cannot survive a marriage. Stay at least until the birth. You can give the kinsman's blessing."

Aidan grinned. "And keep the hellions busy?"

"They will keep *you* busy." Hart eyed him consideringly. "Are you awake enough to ride?"

Aidan blinked. "Now?"

"Dawn is my favorite time, and Rael will be glad of flight. Will you come with me?"

He had been thinking of bed. But the morning air would refresh him after a night spent in a game, so he agreed readily. Teel would approve, also.

"Good. Mounts are always waiting; the privilege of rank." Hart swung open the door. "I will show you Lestra as Lestra should be seen."

Chapter Three

Hart led Aidan back through empty halls and corridors, striding purposefully without pause, and out into the bailey. He waited, smiling faintly, and after only a moment horseboys came running from the stable block. A tall black stallion was brought to Hart, saddled and waiting; a bay was given to Aidan.

"I have a horse," he said.

Hart's voice was bland. "Undoubtedly weary from the journey. Try this one instead." He swung up and gathered reins into the only hand he had, looking down patiently at Aidan. "What is it?"

Aidan sighed and gave in. "The way you keep your castle . . . *su'fali*, you know I mean no disrespect, but when I came here no one seemed perturbed by a stranger's presence. No one even asked if I was here to see *you*, or merely a tradesman come for business." He stroked the bay's nose. "And when I went into the castle—"

"—no one even bothered to ask who you were," Hart finished. "Aye, is it not soothing? No servants underfoot, no 'my lord' this, 'my lord' that before you can even think." He smiled down on Aidan. "I am not much like the Mujhar, drowning in too-helpful servants, and little like my *rujho*, so weighed down by responsibility that he can barely breathe. Protocol I find tedious . . . oh, I do what I must when I must—Ilsa sees to that—but I am happiest with my children and the freedom to be what I am." He swung the stallion gateward. "Do you plan to wait all day? Dawn only lasts so long."

Hastily Aidan mounted, settling into the bay. The stallion had a fiery eye, but his manners were excellent. Aidan smiled with pleasure and turned him after the black.

Hart led him through the winding streets without apparent confusion—Aidan expected none—and up toward the line of hills on the western outskirts of the city. When at last they climbed to the summit, Aidan was suitably impressed. Whitewashed buildings damp with dew glittered in the sunrise, pale pink and silver-gilt. Skeins of woodsmoke drifted from gray stone chimneys, knotting and tearing apart; Aidan was abruptly reminded of the Weaver's colorless yarns and the brilliant tapestry.

He shivered. One hand touched the two heavy links depending from his belt. Still there. Still real. He had dreamed none of it.

"There," Hart said.

With effort, Aidan took his hand away from the links. His palm was damp, but oddly warm, as if the metal had warmed it. The sensation was unsettling. Surreptitiously he wiped his hand against a leather-clad thigh, and looked for what Hart indicated.

At first he saw nothing; then a blot against the dawn. He squinted, trying to distinguish pale blot from new daylight. White wings clove the air in powerful, graceful sweeps, then flattened gently to soar.

"Rael," he murmured aloud.

The dark-eyed hawk was magnificent. White edged with jet, each feather delineated. He swept through the air with deceptive ease and grace, riding the currents of dawn.

Through the link there came a sardonic whisper. Aidan smiled, tilting his head. "*And* there."

Frowning, Hart glanced over. "Where?"

"There." Aidan pointed. "Not so large as Rael, perhaps, but feathered nonetheless. His name is Teel."

Hart looked, smiling. "Brennan wrote me when you received him . . . somewhat out of the ordinary, I think—there has not been a raven *lir* for more than one hundred years. They tell stories about him."

"Lorcha," Aidan agreed. "His *lir* died in the *qu'mahlin*. And as for stories, well . . ." He grinned. "I think Teel will inspire more. If not, he will make his own."

Hart tipped his head back as Teel, following Rael, sliced through the air. Then he looked at Aidan. "How is my *rujho?*"

"Very well—" Aidan began dutifully, then dismissed the platitudes. Hart knew Brennan better than any. "Settled," he said quietly. "The rank is heavy, aye, but he likes the responsibility. You know how he is . . . it makes him feel needed."

Hart's smile was faint. "He would make a good shepherd."

At first he was astounded. Then Aidan laughed out loud; he had never heard his father's competence phrased in quite that way. "Aye, so he would . . . and the flock would prosper for it." He shifted in the saddle, leaning forward on braced arms. "I know what you ask, without asking it." He did. "How does the marriage go? Is my *jehan* happy? Is he content within himself?"

"All of that, and more." Hart sighed, hooking reins over the pommel. The leather cuff rested on one indigo-clad thigh. "He writes, of course, and often—but it is not the same. There was always a private place in Brennan, a place where he went away from everyone."

Aidan was startled. "Even away from you?"

"I think he believed I could not—or *would* not, more likely— understand what he felt." Hart's expression was momentarily ashamed. "And I admit, I was not the most perceptive of *rujholli*. Twin-born, I understood him *better*—but not everything. Brennan and I are different. He was always the shepherd—" briefly, he grinned "—and I always the black lamb wandering too far from the flock."

"And Corin was the dog?"

Hart laughed. "Corin? No, not the *dog* . . . more like the fox in the henyard, making trouble for the cook."

Aidan shrugged. "Well, Kiri *is* a fox."

Hart's tone was solemn, though his eyes glinted amusement. "The gods are always wise."

Aidan looked for Teel, found him; the raven still circled, even as Rael. *Are they?* he asked intently.

Teel's tone was bland. *You know them better than I.*

"So," Hart said, "he and Aileen have made their peace at last."

Pulled back out of the link, Aidan shrugged. "They were never at war."

"No, but—"

"But?" He raised ruddy brows. "Do you want me to tell you things my own father has not told you?"

Hart was unabashed. "If you know those things."

To delay, Aidan plaited mane. He felt odd discussing his parents, even with his uncle. The thing he now knew as *kivarna* made him far more perceptive than anyone else, yet also more intrusive. And now Hart wanted answers to questions Aidan found discomfiting.

"They are content enough," he said finally. "*Jehana* would be happier if there was another son, or two . . . but I am in no danger of dying—at least, not as I used to be—and I think Council is no longer so vocal about the Prince of Homana looking to another princess."

Hart was aghast. "They would have asked it of him?"

"They did. When I was young, and ill for the thousandth time." Aidan sighed and looked across Lestra, frowning in recollection. "No one meant her disrespect, of course . . . they promised a courtesy title and a generous yearly pension, and all the honor due her. I think they hoped she would take herself back to Erinn, so things would not be so awkward—"

Hart's laugh was a curt bark of sound. "Brennan would never stand for that."

"No. Nor did he. And now they know better." Aidan shrugged. "But I know it troubles her. There are things other than a sickly childhood to threaten the Prince's heir. Niall had *three* sons; everyone, I think, would be happier with that."

Hart said nothing for a long moment. The morning was loud with silence. Then, quietly, "It must be especially difficult for you."

Aidan looked at him sharply.

Hart shrugged. "To know so many people crowded around your cradle, fearing you would die . . . and even when you outgrew that, they still attached the *question*—" He sighed and rubbed at red-rimmed eyes. "When they discussed your *jehana*, did no one think of you?"

It was an odd thought. "Why should they think of me?"

Hart looked squarely at him. "I grew up without a *jehana*—a true blood *jehana*—because she was sent away. But it was made clear, at an early age, that Gisella was quite mad. That she had done the unspeakable and tried to give her sons to Strahan. Exiling her was just."

Uncomfortable, Aidan waited.

Hart's voice was very quiet. "But you grew up differently. You had a *jehana*—a true blood *jehana*—more than fit to claim the name. Yet they thought to send her away because she bore only one son. And that devalued you. Surely you must have known it— must have *felt* it."

Surely he had.

Aidan looked away, staring down into the city. After a moment, he cleared his throat. "No one knew I knew. No one thought about the servants, talking among themselves. I was very young . . . no one knew I was there."

"Did you ever say anything to Brennan?"

"No." Aidan unplaited the mane. "No. What was there to say?"

"To Aileen?"

"No. To no one." *Except to the Lion. And, later, of course, to Teel.*

"No, neither would I." Hart smiled at Aidan's startled glance. "We all of us have our secrets. I will leave yours to you." He shifted in the saddle, resettling himself. "For all they may have believed in the need for more princes, they overlooked the obvious. Niall had two other realms to portion out to extra sons. Brennan lacks the luxury, now that Solinde and Atvia *have* Cheysuli on the thrones. He would find it much harder if there were more boys than you to place, like a hound keeper with a litter much larger than expected.

Aidan smiled back. "As hard as you do, with four girls to marry off?"

It hit home. Hart grimaced with a wry twist of his mouth. "Blythe would have been enough . . . but after her there were the twins who died in the summer of sweating fever—both girls—and then Cluna and Jennet. Next, Dulcie." Hart smiled as a wisp of wind ruffled hair. "I would trade none of them—but how *does* a man deal with four marriageable girls?"

"Well, Dulcie is a *bit* young to count as marriageable."

"Not when it comes to royal fledglings." Hart sighed. "You have been very fortunate. The eldest son—the heir—is always the most important in the scheme of who marries whom. My poor *rujho* was betrothed to Aileen before either of them were born."

"And Keely to Sean." Aidan nodded. "There was never any pressure . . . never any discussion—at least where I could hear. Until now." He grinned. "But I am amenable. They have let me have my freedom with never a whisper of duty. Perhaps the time is right."

Hart's stallion stomped and pawed at damp turf. He caught up loose reins with his hand and quieted the horse with a single spoken admonishment. "Well, regardless of common practice, I will not offer Cluna and Jennet even to Homana. They are too young." He laughed at Aidan's expression, part guilt and part relief. "Even if they *were* older, They are hideously willful girls."

Aidan's tone was elaborately mournful. "Which leaves only Blythe, and she is already promised."

"Not promised," Hart said quietly. "As I said, nothing is settled—"

Aidan shrugged, dismissing levity. "It does not have to be. You can see it in their eyes."

Hart sorted out reins, resettled his weight, stroked the black satin neck. Then stared down at his city and sighed his resignation. "It would go far toward healing old wounds."

It startled Aidan. "Why? I thought them all healed with your marriage to Ilsa."

"There was a man," Hart said quietly. "A proud, strong man, dedicated to Solinde. He disliked Homanan usurpers. He wanted the throne for Ilsa, so he could be Consort. So his son could become king. The first Solindish king since Carillon killed Bellam."

Old history. Older enmity. "A patriot," Aidan said.

"A true-born Solindishman of one of the oldest lines." Hart shifted again in his saddle. "I had him executed."

Aidan, who sensed old grief in his uncle as well as a trace of shame, looked at Hart's cuffed stump. "Do you mean the man who cost you your hand?"

"Dar of High Crags; aye. Tevis is his nephew. Son to Dar's youngest sister."

Astonishment overrode caution. "And do you mean to say you will give Tevis Blythe to pay him for Dar's *death?* To wash your guilt away, even though none is deserved?"

"Aidan—"

"The man cost you your *hand* . . . and very nearly your life! It was Dar who gave you to Strahan—do you think my *jehan* has said nothing of it?" Aidan, appalled, shook his head. "He told me all about it. Dar deserved to die. It was the only thing you could do."

Hart's face was tight. "Do you think that is the only reason for this marriage? It is politically expedient, aye—I have learned *something* of kingcraft—but it is not the sole concern. There is Blythe and Tevis also . . . and you have seen that yourself."

Aye, so he had. He had even said so to Hart. "Aye. Aye, *su'fali* . . ." Aidan sighed. "But my marriage is politcally expedient also . . . Blythe is my age, and half Cheysuli, and everything else as well—except Erinnish, but *I* have that." He scraped hair back from his face. "I left Homana to find a bride. One who would serve the role as well as the prophecy." He slanted a glance at Hart. "Do you blame me, *su'fali?* Your daughter is beautiful."

Unease evaporated. Hart's grin was brilliant. "I *thought* it might come to that!"

"She is." Aidan felt no shame. "What man alive would be blind to a comely woman . . . especially when he needs to put a *cheysula* in his bed?" He paused. "*And* on a throne."

Hart frowned a little. "You did not come *expecting* to win her, did you?"

"I thought my chances good." Aidan smiled disarmingly. "I am your twin-born *rujho*'s only son, the only one there can be, and heir to the Lion Throne. Part of the prophecy."

White teeth shone in a dark face. "Stooping to kinship pressure, are we? Thinking to convince me through bloodlink alone?"

Aidan arched brows. "It was certainly worth the try. And there had been nothing said of this Tevis of High Crags in your letters to my *jehan* . . . how was I to know?"

"Aye, well . . . Tevis only came to Lestra four months ago. He grew up in northern Solinde, high in the mountains . . . the mountain Solindish are different from the rest of us. They keep themselves isolated."

"'Us'?" Aidan echoed.

Hart made an acknowledging gesture. "I am their lord, after all. And different enough already, as I am often reminded. There is no sense in rousing old griefs . . . this is my *tahlmorra*, Aidan. And there is Solindish in me as well as all the other bloodlines."

"Not *all* of them." Aidan grinned, then felt the amusement die. "I thought you told me Tevis *came* to marry Blythe. If he did not know her already—"

"*You* did not."

"No." He refused to be turned aside, "But you made it sound as if they had known one another for years."

Hart reined in a restless stallion, pulling the fine black head away from the bay Aidan rode. "Did you know this is Bane's son? I sent the mare to Brennan four years ago for breeding, and this is the result. I am quite pleased . . . he is a willful young lad, but worth it."

Aidan liked and respected his kinsman, but something inside would not allow him to hide from the knowledge Hart was all too human. Although Aidan was, by everyone's reckoning, fully an adult, in his eyes his older kin were above reproach. Yet the *ki-varna* showed him reproach was due his elders as much as anyone else.

The *kivarna*, Aidan thought, showed him entirely too much.

Quietly, he said, "You are avoiding the issue, *su'fali*."

Hart glanced at Aidan, then sighed in surrender. "Tevis' *jehan* died ten months ago in a fall. Ilsa, being distant kin as well as queen, sent a letter of personal condolence to the widow. They began to correspond, and soon they traded news of various children, including Tevis and Blythe." Hart shrugged. "It is what *jehanas* do."

Aidan nodded. "And so eventually Tevis was sent in person to win the hand of the princess."

"There was no reason for him not to come. He had bided for many years in the fastness of High Crags . . . he was due a visit to Lestra to see his lord—"

"—*and* his lord's eldest daughter."

Hart's tone was even. "There is nothing to stand in their way."

And you do not want me *to.* Aidan laughed at Hart, lifting hands in surrender. "Aye, aye, I understand . . . no more said of it." He covered a yawn with one hand. "Dawn is done, *su'fali*. Time for me to sleep, before I fall off my horse. "

"You are too good a rider, and he too good a mount. You have that of Brennan; the horse has it of me." Hart looked for Rael. "There. Shall we go?"

Aidan nodded after a moment, turning the bay southward to wind back down the hills. Pleasure in the morning was now tinged with empathy. He had seen the brief wistful expression on his uncle's face, the subtle tensing of flesh by blue eyes as Hart looked for and found his *lir*. But he sensed more than wistfulness. He felt more than relief.

Hart wanted to fly with every ounce of his being.

With every fiber of the missing hand that denied him the chance.

Chapter Four

Aidan rolled over in bed. Sheets were tangled around him; with effort, he stripped them away. He frowned into unexpected daylight, blinking still-gritty eyes clear. *What am I doing in bed at this time of day?*

And then he remembered. A full night spent over the game, the dawn upon a hilltop. He vaguely recalled falling at last into bed when everyone else was waking.

How long—? He looked at the hour-glass. Four hours abed; barely time to recall his name.

A long, elaborate stretch succeeded in reminding his body it had a purpose other than lying sprawled in bed. Then something moved upon the canopy. Aidan glanced roofward quickly, momentarily startled, then grinned relief and self-derision and relaxed into the mattress once more, rubbing a stubbled jaw. On the canopy frame perched the raven.

So, Teel remarked. *Half a day gone already.*

Aidan yawned noisily. *Not quite half . . . half of a half, perhaps . . .* Yet another yawn. A growl from his belly stopped it; he clapped one hand to flesh. *How long since—?* he began, then remembered the cheese he had eaten while drinking Solindish wine.

And the wine remembers me . . . He rolled out of bed and stood, scrubbing a sleep-creased face. He wondered what he most needed: bath, food, more sleep. And in which order.

No time, Teel mentioned. *The lady has sent for you.*

For one irrational moment Aidan thought his *lir* referred to the Weaver. Then realized what he meant. "Now?" he asked aloud.

The raven contemplated. *Perhaps later,* he suggested, which told Aidan how badly he looked.

He promptly ordered a bath, and food to go with it. Then he would see the lady; likely she would thank him.

* * *

Ilsa of Solinde.

Aidan had heard all the stories, the songs and verses extolling her beauty, but such things, he had learned young, were often exaggerated. And when it came to feminine beauty, he knew very well what one man believed was beautiful was often not to another.

Ilsa was beautiful.

Ilsa was *glorious.*

One unwavering glance out of long-lidded, ice-blue eyes, and he was half in love with the woman wed to his uncle. The other half of him felt awkward as a boy in the first flush of young manhood only just discovering women, and what they could do to a body.

Inwardly, he reminded himself, *She is forty years old, or more.*

Ilsa's luminous smile mocked him, as did the fine-boned features. "Aileen had nothing to fear."

Aidan blinked, gathering wits with effort. He was not thinking of his mother, though Aileen and Ilsa were very close in age. Ilsa was not his mother, any more than he her son.

This woman could not be old enough to have borne Blythe or the twins.

Her Homanan was flavored with the delicate Solindish accent he had first heard in Blythe. He had liked it in Blythe, finding it attractive. Now he heard the same in the mother. "Wasted years, the worry. The crop stands tall in the field."

He understood her then. "But the harvest not yet begun." He smiled, inclined his ruddy head, gave her the honor rank and beauty were due. *"Cheysuli i'halla shansu."*

"Resh'ta-ni," she answered, though the accent was bad. Ilsa laughed at his expression, much as he sought to hide it. "Hart taught me some of the Old Tongue, but nothing of the accent. Forgive my poor attempt."

He would, as any man, forgive her anything. He very nearly said so, then swallowed it back. It was, he assumed, something she had heard all too often. He wished, for once, he had a gift for eloquent phrases, the ability to flatter with a smile, a gesture, a word. But he was not a courtier, disliking much of the game. His *kivarna* made him wary of false words when he understood most of the feelings.

Ilsa, still smiling, stroked back a stray wisp of hair from the winged arch of one brow. Her hair, he knew, had always been white-blonde, because they told stories about it. The pearlescent sheen was unchanged, and likely would remain that way. No one would be able to tell the difference, once she dulled into true white. It was a boon others would kill for; she accepted it gracefully. She wore it in two heavy braids bound with thin gold wire. It glistened in the daylight.

That she was abed, he had known; this close to labor, Ilsa took no chances. Hart had said her delivery of Dulcie was not easy, and she was no longer young enough to carry easily. No one wanted to risk the child who might yet be an heir, or the woman who was queen.

The chamber was flooded with daylight. No shuttered casements for Ilsa; she welcomed in the midday sun and granted it the freedom to go where it would. The curtains on the bed were drawn back and tied to testers, looped with gold cord.

Ilsa eyed him critically. "He kept you up all night."

Aidan laughed, smoothing fingers across his jaw. The bath had worked its miracle, as had a shave and food. But Ilsa was too discerning; she had had years of practice. "Aye. But I slept earlier." He did not tell her a lifetime of troubling dreams had accustomed him to less sleep.

Slender, elegant hands stroked the pearl-studded blue coverlet mounded over her belly. Padded bolsters sheathed in satin braced her upright. "I have told him, time and time again, not everyone is as suited to days without sleep," she said, sighing resignation. "Even *he* is not . . . but I have given up remonstrating with him. He does what he will do. I should have known better than to think he would ever change."

There was no bitterness in tone or words. Not even faint resentment. No matter what she said, he knew what she thought. Even without the *kivarna*, Aidan understood very well how strong was the bond that made Hart and Ilsa one.

"But you have," he countered. "I have heard how bad he was as a young man . . . how he refused all responsibility to lose himself in the game. I have seen him with his daughters. I have heard him speak of duty. Regardless of the cause, he is not the same man."

Ilsa smiled. Delicate color crept into her face. "In many ways, he is. And I would have it that way. Why banish what you love?"

He thought of his grandsire and Deirdre. What they shared was as strong, in different ways, as the thing between Hart and Ilsa. As a child he had been nebulously aware of something intangible linking Niall and Deirdre. Once older, having lain with a woman, he understood more of it. Lust was one thing, love another; the warmth and underlying respect Niall and Deirdre shared made the relationship invulnerable to outside influences. He sensed the same thing in Ilsa and Hart. But never between his parents. That they cared for each other, he knew. And were afraid to admit it.

"Why indeed?" he agreed, thinking of himself. *Who will share my life? Will it be as good as this?*

Ilsa's skin was translucent, pale as a lily. The eyes were luminous. In her he saw the twins, fair-haired Jennet and Cluna; and Blythe, who lacked the fairness, but had the slender, tensile strength with its powerful allure. How had Hart felt the first time he had seen her?

How did I feel the first time I saw Blythe?

One day before. Inwardly, he grimaced; a lifebond took more time. He had grown too accustomed to winning a bedpartner with a warm smile or a gesture. The women of Homana-Mujhar and the city responded readily to the title as well as himself, hoping for various rewards. Before coming to Solinde he had thought of women as pleasant diversions, or an escape from harrowing dreams. This circumstance was different. It was foolish to expect anything more than the first stirrings of attraction.

Although those I admit to freely. Blythe is magnificent . . . but I think Tevis' presence will make things difficult.

Ilsa gestured. "Will you sit?"

Aidan glanced at the indicated chair near the bed, then shook his head. "My regrets, but no. I have no wish to tire you."

She waved a gently dismissive hand. "They have kept me in bed a month. Listening to you speak will not prove onerous."

He glanced at the mound of bedclothes over her belly. She had borne six children, though only four survived. And now bore another to give her lord an heir.

It came out unexpectedly. "What if it is a girl?"

He had not meant it. He had barely even *thought* it. Embarrassment burned his face.

Ilsa's laughter cut off the beginnings of an apology. "No, no— do you think you are the first to ask it? You are only the most recent . . . just last evening one of my ladies asked the same."

"It is none of my concern . . ."

"It is everyone's concern," she corrected gently. "It has been from the beginning . . . this will be my last child."

He opened his mouth. Then shut it.

"Hart's decision," she said. "And perhaps a little of mine. It was difficult with Dulcie, though I was in no danger. The physicians suggest precautions, so I have taken myself to bed." She spread eloquent hands, then let them rest again on the bedclothes. "Boy or no: the last. And perhaps it is time." Ilsa tilted her head and smiled. "Instead of having children I would rather have *grand*children."

His answering smile was vague. "Blythe."

"And the others, eventually." The light in her eyes faded. "Hart spoke to me earlier. I am sorry, Aidan . . . I wish we had known a half-year ago. Then we might have looked to Homana instead of northern Solinde."

Aidan shrugged. "Hart explained it all."

"But if I do *not* bear a son . . ." A turn of her hand was eloquent. "A grandson could inherit."

Aidan thought of Dar, looking to marry Ilsa to put his son on the throne. Now that son could be born to Blythe instead. And the nephew of Dar of High Crags would rule in place of Cheysuli.

He shifted weight self-consciously. "Lady, I will go. I have been asked to stay until the child is born, to bestow the kinsman's blessing. After that, I am for Erinn." There was no sense in staying. Here, Blythe was the only option; now there was none at all unless he looked to Erinn.

Ilsa's smile was kind. "Keely's girl is older than my two fair-haired halflings. And undoubtedly more polite. I think you will do well."

He sensed relief in her, that he did not protest the marriage between Tevis and Blythe. He knew very well a match between Homana and Solinde would solidify the two realms and undoubtedly please the Homanans, while displeasing the Solindish. Hart had been Prince of Solinde in truth as well as title for more than twenty years, and yet it was all too obvious he was not fully certain Solinde wanted him. Ilsa was their queen. For her, they suffered Hart.

Her son they would accept, for her sake. He will have acceptable blood, if tainted with Cheysuli. I wonder if they think to get the throne back someday, when Hart is in the ground and his son—Ilsa's son—sits in the father's place?

Ilsa was Solindish. He did not really blame her for wanting a Solindishman for Blythe—he might desire the same for *his* daughter, were he a Solindishman—but he wished blood might play a less important role. His own life was ruled by merging the proper bloodlines, and now it also entangled Blythe, who should be free of it. Solinde was *Solinde*—and yet now they made it Cheysuli.

He closed his hand on the two links dangling from his belt. *Perhaps that is the reason for this service. By merging the blood and begetting the Firstborn again, there no longer is any need for dividing up the realms. Four realms become one; six races the same.* Something cold stroked his spine. *And the lir for none of us?*

"Aidan—?" Ilsa began, but the opening of the door cut off the rest of her words.

Cluna and Jennet, of course. Crowding into the room to plead for their mother's attention. Behind them came Hart with a small girl in his arms: black-haired, yellow-eyed Dulcie, Cheysuli to the bone.

Aidan smiled at the girl. Something in him answered the fey look in her eyes. *Blood calling to blood?* He took a step closer. "A lovely girl, *su'fali.*"

"My little Cheysuli," Hart declared, pausing a moment to let Aidan look at her, then moving past to Ilsa. "The gods finally condescended to let one of us look the part."

Cluna and Jennet were chattering at their mother, both mindful not to press too close. Pale hair, as before, straggled; Ilsa was gently chiding. Hart too stood close, then sat to bring Dulcie down where Ilsa could touch her, stroking fine black hair into neatness.

Aidan found the chamber crowded. He was not accustomed to children, and as unaccustomed to kin. A twitch from deep inside told him what he wanted: the freedom to fly the skies.

Hart, he knew, would understand, requiring no explanation. The others mostly ignored him, but something was due Ilsa.

Aidan paused at the door and looked back at her. Her bed was full of daughters, except for her oldest one. The one he most wanted to see. "May the gods grant you a son."

Ilsa glanced up from her crowded bedside. Her lovely face was alight. "*Leijhana tu'sai*, kinsman. May your words carry weight with the gods."

As Aidan stepped into the hall, he wondered if they could.

Chapter Five

He was waiting for her, as she had asked. In shadow, in a chair, hands resting unquietly on the downward sweep of each armrest. A ring glittered on one finger: sapphire set in silver. On yet another, jet, rimmed with delicate gold.

Blythe shut the door quietly, looking at him in concern. The flesh was drawn too tautly over the bones of his face. It made him look almost feral. "It may be nothing," she said. She had already said it twice, on the way to meet him in private.

He did not move at all, not even to agree, or to shake his head. He was angry, frightened, confused, but afraid to admit it. Afraid he had no right. She saw it in his eyes.

She walked slowly across the chamber to stand in front of the chair. The man seated in it did not look into her eyes, but stared as if transfixed at the girdle spanning her waist. Silver chimed as she moved, swinging with her skirts. It stopped even as she did; the silver sang no more.

She could hardly bear to look at him without touching him. It had been so from the beginning, from the very first time they had met. She had put no credence in such tales, consigning them to silly serving-girls dreaming away the hours, but then Tevis had come down from his mountain exile bearing an invitation from Ilsa to spend as much time as he liked. They were of an age, she and Tevis, and like-minded about many things. The instant attraction had flared into something far more physical; and yet the knowledge they dared not fulfill what they most desired increased the tension tenfold. That her parents approved was implicit in Ilsa's invitation; it was, Blythe knew, their way of telling her Tevis was suitable in all the ways that counted for kings and queens.

The last way was hers to decide: could she love and live with the man?

He filled her days and nights. She judged every man against

him, comparing the shape of facial bones, the set of eyes, the line
of chin and jaw. Even the way hair grew; in Tevis, easy to see because he cropped it short. She thought him everything a man
should be to light up a woman's world. The chatter among the
serving-girls and court women told her she was correct; he lighted
more worlds than her own, or would, had he the chance to stray.

But Tevis had never strayed.

He was a man, even as men judged one another. And yet sensi-
tive as a woman. It was the contradictions in him that appealed to
her most: the quietude that spoke of privacy and deep thought; the
understated power of personality that, allowed to flare, might consume them all.

Blythe drew in a breath and released it carefully. She put out
both hands and locked them into his hair, palms pressing against
his head as she threaded fingers tightly. Near-black hair was
cropped short, displaying the elegant shape of his head. At the
back of his neck it was longer, trying to curl; thick springy waves
seduced her.

Slowly she drew him forward. It was a measure of her own apprehension and anguish that she touched him as she did, forcing
the intimacy they wanted so badly, but had not shared. Neither of
them had dared. Now, she knew, they had to.

His breath caressed the girdle; she pressed him closer yet, turning his face against her pelvis. The arch of his cheek, through the
velvet, was hard.

She fought to keep her voice even. "We cannot be certain—"

Lean, long-fingered hands clasped her hips. His words were
muffled by skirts, but she heard them. "Aye, I think we can." The
hoarse tone was firm, but underscored with despair. "He has made
no secret of it: the heir to Homana has come to Solinde to find a
wife."

She felt the flutter of trepidation in her breast. Her hands in his
hair tightened. "If you were to go to my father—"

"He already knows."

Desperation rose. "And have you spoken to him? Have you actually *told* him you want to marry me?"

He withdrew from her sharply, taking his hands from her. A
spasm twisted his face. "No. Of course not. How can I? He is the
Prince of Solinde, and I am—"

"—kin," she finished flatly, "—to the *Queen* of Solinde."

It was a tangled sovereignty. Hart still used his Homanan title, forgoing the loftier Solindish ranking until his father died, when he would inherit fully. But Ilsa was Solindish, the highest of the high-born, and the Solindish Council had bequeathed her the title when she married Hart. Their petty revenge, Blythe knew; she knew also it did not matter. Her father did not care.

Just now, it might help.

He rose and moved away from her. The room was her own, a private sitting chamber adjoining her personal apartments, and they both knew it unwise. She was allowed great freedom, but only because of trust. She wondered if they would betray it.

He turned. In the dullness of late afternoon, ale-brown eyes were dark. His face was expressionless, but she knew how to peel back the mask and look at the man beneath.

Steadily, he said, "He will make you Queen of Homana."

Blythe lifted her head. "*Will* he, then? Even without my permission?"

The flesh by his eyes twitched. "What woman would not want—"

She did not let him finish. "The woman who would rather live in Solinde, in the high northern fastness of High Crags."

He shut his eyes briefly. Fleeting pain ruined his brow; it smoothed almost instantly. "You are Cheysuli," he rasped. "I have heard of the prophecy."

For a moment, all she could do was stare. Her heritage everyone knew—they had only to look at her father—but it had never been an issue. Not with Tevis. He had come down out of his mountains knowing nothing of her race, and had no reason to fear it.

Nor to remind her of her duty.

She controlled her emotions with effort. "I was born in *Solinde*. I am *of* Solinde. I would rather serve my home than a collection of foreign words."

For a moment, he only stared. And then laughed aloud. "A 'collection of foreign words'!" Tevis laughed again. Blue and black glinted on his hands; the two rings were his only vanity. "Do you know what your father would do if he heard you blaspheme so?"

She felt strangely calm. "I imagine he would be somewhat put out with me. I imagine he might even take it into his head to instruct me in Cheysuli history; certainly I would be told yet again about the *tahlmorra* in us all." Briefly, Blythe grimaced. "But it has nothing to do with me. I am much more than merely Cheysuli."

Brown eyes were black in the shadows. "Much more," he agreed softly, reaching out to touch her face. The fingers barely brushed the curve of her chin. Another step, and he touched her mouth; a third, the sweep of temple meeting cheekbone with a caress that burned her flesh.

Blythe leaned into it. Tension sang between them.

Abruptly he let her go. "I know what I am. Do you?"

She did not soften it. "The nephew of a traitor."

The curves of his face hardened. "They will say it is my revenge."

Blythe smiled. "Perhaps it is."

"You are the eldest," he said, "and there is no male heir."

"Within a week, that could change—"

"And if it does not," he persisted. "If the child is another girl, and the queen bears no more—"

"There will be no more."

It stopped him instantly.

"No more," she repeated. "It has been decided. This is the last, boy or girl . . . if it is a boy, Solinde has an heir."

"And, if not—?"

A bubble of laughter broke. "You said it yourself, did you not? I am the eldest. From me will come the next."

Bitterness pinched his tone. "They will say I *planned* it."

"Does it matter?" she asked. "I must marry someone."

"Then why not Aidan?"

"Because, you *ku'reshtin*, he is not the one I fancy."

Tevis did not smile. "They could force you."

She shook her head.

"If Aidan demanded it—"

"He is too proud to do it."

"Pride has little to do with marriage when a prince desires a wife."

She smiled. "You know nothing about his life. The last thing Aidan would want is a wife who loves another. Believe me, I *know.*"

His hands closed over her shoulders. "If I lost you now—if they took you from me—"

"No." She shook her head.

"But they *could*. Blythe, have you no wits? You are too valuable to waste on a crude mountain lordling when there is a prince in the offing!"

Blythe unclasped her girdle. Silver dripped from her hand, then spilled onto the floor. "Then I will rid myself of value. No prince can afford to marry a woman whose virtue no longer exists."

He caught her hands and held them so tightly she gasped in pain. "Not like this!" he hissed.

"I want it. *You* want it; you would not dare deny it!"

"No," he rasped. "No. You know better than that."

Blythe pulled her hands free and cupped his jaw in her palms. "Then forget everything else. Set everything else aside. Let this merely be *us*, because we want it so much."

"They can execute me for this!"

One wild laugh escaped her. "In this, I will be Cheysuli. I will invoke my heritage."

"Blythe—"

"Clan-rights!" she hissed. "I give them freely to you. Now let them argue with *that!*"

Aidan shed himself and flew. Each time he exulted, as he exulted now, in the magic that gave him another form and the chance to ride the sky. He could not comprehend what it was like to be earthbound, tied to the ground with so much freedom all around, and no chance to know it. Even the other warriors, gods-gifted all, were trapped by earthbound *lir.*

He had asked his father, once, what it was to be a mountain cat, trying to understand that a *lir* was a *lir* and none of them better than another. But he had failed. Brennan's explanation had been salient enough—only another Cheysuli could fully comprehend the all-encompassing joy of *lir*-shape—but somehow lacking. No man, Aidan believed, could truly experience freedom without the ability to fly.

What was it like for Hart? Once lord of the air, even as Rael: now trapped forever by the loss of the hand that destroyed his raptor's balance. In human form, merely hindrance; in *lir*-shape, absolute prevention. Too much of him was missing.

Was it one reason, Aidan wondered, he loved Ilsa so? Did he compensate the loss by turning to wife and children?

The denial was emphatic, much as he longed for its absence. Deep in his soul he knew nothing could compensate a warrior for losing the gift of *lir*-shape. Rael lived, and therefore Hart was in no danger of going mad, but the inability to fly must come close to causing madness. He was whole, and yet not. Aidan could not begin to imagine what such torture would be like.

Be grateful, Teel said. *Do not take for granted what the gods give you.*

The raven, he knew, could be referring to Hart's loss and Aidan's wholeness. But he might also be referring to the task set for him, mentioned by the Weaver. A task he could yet refuse.

He had not, since arrival, been troubled by dreams of the chain. He wondered if it had anything to do with holding two of the links. They were real now, tangible evidence of gods; their presence could mean he did have a task, or that he was going mad. Even with a *lir.*

Air caressed his wings. He adjusted them slightly, dropping down through sky to enter another layer of the air that carried him. Tiny muscles twitched and flexed, altering his flight. Beside him, Teel followed.

If I could share this with Blythe—

He cut it off instantly.

Tevis cannot give her this.

He twitched in irritation. Neither could he.

Why would you want a cheysula who wants another man?

Why did his father?

It hurt. It hurt so sharply he stopped breathing. *Lir*-shape, abruptly, was threatened; with effort, he found his balance.

Down, he told Teel.

Aidan stumbled on landing because he took back human form more quickly than usual. Booted feet struck earth and he fell, digging an elbow into turf. For a moment he held his position, awkward though it was, then rolled over onto his back. The day was temperate and bright, the turf immensely comfortable. He was sleepy and disinclined to get up quite yet. So he linked hands across his abdomen and stayed where he was, casually crossing ankles.

"I am a fool," he said aloud. "I set out to look for a wife, and decide I want the first woman I see. I think nothing of asking, because I have never needed to ask: I am, everyone tells me, destined to be the Mujhar of Homana."

Teel perched on Aidan's boot toe, saying nothing.

"She is beautiful rather than plain, which only sweetens the cookpot. I look at her and see a woman I would like to take to bed, which makes her more attractive. And then, in addition, she is a woman I could *like* . . . a woman I *do* like . . ." Aidan sighed deeply. "It is too much to hope for a *cheysula* I could like and love, and a woman who pleasures my bed. Princes and kings only rarely find such things . . . Hart did, with Ilsa, and I assume Keely as well, from what they say of her . . . but what room is there for me? Blythe loves Tevis."

"Blythe loves Tevis." He realized, as he said the words, the pain was already less. It had been foolish of him to care so much, even though that care had been more for finding a woman whose *potential* suited him. Blythe would have been perfect, but Blythe was no longer free. And that, he realized unhappily, had made him want her so much. Had she been free of Tevis, it might not have been the same.

He had wanted the unattainable, which had made him want her the more.

Some men, he knew, would hunt her nonetheless, counting the game much sweeter for her unwillingness to be caught, and the fillip of competition. But that was not Aidan's way.

To Teel, he grinned sardonic amusement. "I want it simple," he said. "Of all the royal fledglings hatched in fifty years, *I* may be the most suited to an arranged marriage. And yet I am left free to choose." He laughed aloud. "How many of my kin would have traded places with me?"

But the amusement faded quickly. He knew at least one: his mother. Left to her own devices, she would have married Corin. And he, born to them, would have been heir to Atvia instead of heir to the Lion.

But I would not have been me. I would have been different— *and therefore my* tahlmorra, *and the prophecy as well.*

It sobered him. Unsettled, Aidan sat up even as Teel lifted from his boot toe. He had managed, in contemplation, to remind himself of things too great for him to ignore.

Of Hunters in the woodlands and Weavers at the loom. And gold links on his belt, growing heavier by the day.

Aidan pressed himself up from the ground. Time he went back to Lestra.

He blurred into *lir*-shape. *Time the baby was born, so I can go on to Erinn.*

Chapter Six

Aidan knew it the moment he saw them. *Kivarna* or no, he knew. They gave it away in the tiny intimacies of bedmates: a brief, burning glance exchanged, a lingering touch, the small alterations in movement. In Tevis he saw a muted victory, the pride and satisfaction of a man who has won the woman he wanted; in Blythe, the languid, sensual movements of a woman now truly a woman, and the soft new warmth in her eyes.

He sat down at the common table, troubled, and looked at once to Hart. This was no time to speak of it—all kin, save for Ilsa and Dulcie, were present at the meal—but then he was not entirely convinced it was his place to speak of it at all. Nothing official had been said regarding his potential suit, and therefore Blythe's virginity did not really concern him as a successor to the Lion. But as a kinsman, it did.

With a flicker of disgust, he reached for cider. Even as a kinsman it was not his concern; Blythe was a free woman unbound by betrothals and arrangements, as well as a Cheysuli. It was her parents' place to determine the rightness or wrongness of her actions, and even then she remained Cheysuli. Hart would be denying one of the foremost tenets of the clans—that of free choice in bedpartners—if he protested. And Ilsa had made it plain Tevis met the requirements for marriage into royalty. They had done nothing wrong, only precipitated the ceremony.

Cluna and Jennet sat down on either side of Aidan. Warily, he kept an eye on both; they giggled, paid him elaborate courtesies, attempted to play the part—albeit shared—of chatelaine in lieu of Ilsa, whose place it properly was. In Ilsa's absence the role fell to Blythe, but her attention to duties was sorely preempted by Tevis.

Hart seemed oblivious to it all, and there was reason. "Ilsa believes the child could be born tonight or tomorrow—she should know, after six children—so I have set in motion the preparations for a proper celebration. The gods willing, we will be swearing homage to a new prince of Solinde before the week is out."

Aidan raised his cup. "Gods willing, *su'fali.*"

Tevis and Blythe, most conspicuously, did not look at one another.

Aidan cleared his throat. "Where is Dulcie?"

It was Jennet who answered for her father. "Oh, *she* cannot come to meals yet. She makes too much of a mess."

"So do you," Hart said mildly. "You have just spilled jam on your tunic."

Jennet, undismayed, scooped it off with a finger. "When are we going hawking?" she asked. "I heard you speaking about it last night."

Hart sipped cider. "I thought after the meal. I have already ordered the horses and hawks prepared." He glanced at his eldest. "I do not mean to rob you of the day, but perhaps it is best if you stayed with your *jehana.* She may have need of you."

Blythe opened her mouth as if to protest, but closed it almost immediately. Aidan saw the glance at Tevis, the dusky color in her face. Had she thought to spend the day in bed with the man?

"Not fair," Cluna put in. "Rael *always* sees the game first, and *always* makes the first kill."

Hart smiled, eyes bright. "Then I will tell Rael not to stoop, and let the rest of you compete."

Tevis, who sat directly across from Aidan, smiled. It was a strangely triumphant smile, full of subtle nuances and knowledge, but Aidan understood it. As Tevis met his eyes, he understood it all too well. The competition for Blythe, though unacknowledged, was over. Whose hawk killed first was of no importance to Tevis, who had already won the hunt.

In silence, Aidan lifted his tankard and slightly inclined his head. Something flickered briefly in Tevis' eyes—surprise? disbelief?—and then he smiled, lifted his own tankard and acknowledged the salute. Beneath the table, Aidan knew, fingers touched, then linked.

In Cheysuli leathers, leggings, and linen tunics, Cluna and Jennet were towheaded warriors riding out of the Keep; in this case, the Keep was Lestra. Outdoors, well free of the confines of the castle—and the preferences of their mother—they could lose themselves in the freedom of the Cheysuli half of their blood. Both girls reveled in it, shouting aloud their excitement. Both rode spirited horses, managing them with ease.

Hart, looking after them with Dulcie perched in the saddle before him, smiled as they rode by Tevis to fall into the lead.

"They chafe at walls," Aidan remarked, "though they may not know it yet."

Hart nodded. "The Cheysuli in them. Ilsa often forgets—no one thinks of my shapechanger blood with blue eyes and Ilsa's hair—but I never do. They are as Cheysuli as I ever was; they only lack the color."

Tevis rode abreast. "Will they have any *lir* of their own?"

Hart shook his head. "Unlikely. It is mostly a gift given to warriors, though occasionally a woman can speak with the *lir*, or shift shape. My *rujholla*, Keely, can, but it has yet to show itself in my line."

Tevis' eyes were on Dulcie. "What of the smallest one? She, of all your children, most resembles a true Cheysuli."

Hart laughed. "Aye, she does—even more than Aidan or me. As for the *lir*-gifts, who can say? She is too young yet to show them, even if they are hers."

"Would it matter?" Aidan asked Tevis. "What if Blythe were blessed?"

Tevis did not hesitate. "I do not care what she can do, or what her blood is made of. I do not care who she *is*, only that she be mine." He paused. "Should the Prince of Solinde be willing."

Well, Aidan reflected, *now it is out in the open.*

Hart's left arm was wound around Dulcie, holding her against his chest. Right-handed, he guided his mount. Not Bane's black son, but a quieter, more mannered bay mare. Faintly, he smiled. "It is for Blythe to say."

"But—my lord—"

"For Blythe," Hart repeated. "If you were not worthy of her, you would not be sharing her roof."

Or her bed? But Aidan shook that off; Hart could not know. *And now it is official. If Tevis has been waiting for some sure sign of parental approval, he need not doubt anymore.*

Shrieking, Cluna and Jennet went tearing across the meadow. Aidan nearly winced. "They will scare the game that way."

"Did you come expecting to catch some?" Hart asked in surprise. "No . . . we will see little enough with *those* two riding free. But it is an excuse to get away. No one begrudges it."

Aidan nearly laughed. "Then the walls chafe *you*."

"Aye, Hart agreed fervently. "I have never become accustomed . . . a holdover, I think, from the days we lived in Keeps. Walls bind our souls He looked at Tevis, riding quietly beside Aidan. "Do the mountains ever chafe you? High Crags is so isolated . . . do you ever wish for something else?"

Something indefinable flared in brown eyes. Then Tevis looked at the hooded hawk riding quietly on his saddlebow. "Always," he said quietly.

For one moment Aidan's *kivarna* came to life. And then died away to ash, telling him nothing of the man. Tevis was closed to him.

Why not? he wondered sourly. *He has what he wants. What else is there to read?*

"There," Hart said urgently. "Rael has seen something."

The hawk spiraled lazily, then drifted downward. Aidan was about to remind Hart that the hawk was not to hunt first, but a piercing scream broke the air as Rael abruptly stooped.

"Cluna!" Hart cried. He caught Dulcie against his chest in one firm arm and set his heels to the mare.

Teel took to the air as Aidan went after Hart. Tevis brought up the rear, though the hawk he carried on his saddlebow screeched and rang jess-bells in protest. They could hear Jennet shouting.

Cluna was huddled against the ground, crying. Close by, Rael drove again and again at the speckled snake, dodging the reptile's deadly strikes. The hawk was too large to be maneuverable, but his attempts distracted the snake from Cluna.

Hart tried to dismount, cursing, but Dulcie's clutching arms tangled his efforts. Jennet, silent now and white-faced, stood nearby with the horses, too frightened to go closer.

Cluna wailed something in Solindish Aidan did not understand. But he could tell by the way she held her left arm cradled against her chest the snake had bitten her. If they did not kill it and reach her quickly, it could be too late to save her.

Teel, he said through the link, swinging off his mount even as Hart finished dismounting. Tevis, too, was on the ground, saying something in Solindish.

"Wait!" Aidan snagged Hart's arm and pulled him back. "Let our *lir* do the work . . . too many of us might spoil their chance. And there is Dulcie to think of—"

Jennet wailed something, still clutching reins. Hart's head

snapped in her direction. "Did it strike you? Jennet—did the snake bite you also?"

Wordlessly she shook her head. Tears streaked her face. "No-no—only Cluna—"

Teel danced around the snake, seducing it this way and that. From behind came Rael, snatching at the place behind its head. Talons sank deeply, locking, and then Rael rose to fly clear of them all, dangling the writhing snake.

"Here—" Hart thrust Dulcie into Aidan's arms.

Even as he did so, Tevis was at Cluna's side. The knife flashed in his hand as he cut into the soft underflesh of her forearm, bisecting fang marks already swollen and discolored. Cluna whimpered but otherwise held her silence, and Tevis set his mouth over the cuts to suck the venom from her arm. The knife, forgotten, fell to the grass.

Jennet deserted her post with the horses and came to Aidan, reaching out to clutch a hand in hers. He felt her trembling through his own flesh; through his *kivarna* he sensed shock, anguish, shame, and a spirit full of fear.

In Solindish, she said something. Aidan put a gentle hand on her blonde head. Hair, as always, straggled out of its braid. "I have a poor grasp of your tongue, *meijhana.* I am sorry."

She gulped a swallow and tried again in Homanan. "I am *afraid*—"

"No need," he told her quietly. "Your *jehan* is Cheysuli, remember? He need only call on the earth magic."

Her face was very pale. "But he only has one hand—"

"*Shansu, meijhana*—I promise, it makes no difference. Your *jehan* is not crippled."

"But he cannot be a warrior. Not a real one, because of his hand. He *said* so."

In the daughter he heard a measure of the father's shame and anguish. Aidan's hand tightened briefly on her head, then slipped to cup a shoulder tightly. "Your *jehan* is as much a warrior as any Cheysuli I know. He is denied clan rights through old-fashioned ignorance, not a failure on his part. I promise you, *meijhana*, your *rujholla* will be well."

Cluna, crying silently, reached for Hart as he knelt to her. Tevis moved away as the father scooped up his daughter. "Bleeding—" she quavered.

"For the best," Hart told her. "Come, *meijhana*—I will take you back to the castle. There I can summon the earth magic."

"Why not here?" Aidan asked. "I can give you whatever help you need."

"My thanks, but no. It will be frightening enough for her, even as it heals. It will be better done in her own room, where she will feel safer. Tevis has bled her quickly enough . . . the rest can wait that long." He approached the horses, cradling Cluna in both arms. "Jennet?"

She broke away from Aidan, twisting hands into tunic. "My fault," she whispered. "The horse was afraid of the snake. Cluna fell when he sprang aside, and the snake bit her—" She lost her Homanan entirely and slipped again into Solindish, speaking too quickly for Aidan to decipher. But he saw Hart's compassion as he paused briefly by her side.

"No, *meijhana*, it is not your fault. Now mount your horse— you will come back with us." He glanced at Aidan. "Can you and Tevis bring Dulcie?"

"Of course, *su'fali*." Aidan smiled as the girl twisted in his arms to reach a fist in her father's direction. "I would not give her up when I have only just met her."

Tevis rose from where he had knelt to bleed Cluna. "I will bring her horse."

Distracted, Hart nodded and turned to his own mount. He set Cluna up into the saddle and hastily mounted, gathering her in against him as he hooked the cuffed stump around her abdomen. Her head tipped back against his shoulder, displaying a too-pale face. Dulcie, who had held the place first, protested in Aidan's arms.

Hart looked at Jennet. "Hurry," he told her, sending her flying to her mount. In a moment both horses and the great hawk were gone.

Aidan looked at Tevis. "No doubt he will remember to thank you when Cluna is settled. Until then, accept *my* gratitude."

Tevis' smile was faint. "For Cluna, if not for Blythe?"

Aidan sighed. "Aye, well . . . I will not contest it. You know as well as I that if I did, it would make no difference. I am neither blind nor a fool . . . you have won, Tevis. Be proud, but not *too* proud; she is still my kinswoman, and Cheysuli. When you marry one of us, you marry us all."

"If I wanted a red-haired Cheysuli as my kinsman, I would have bedded *you*."

Holding Dulcie, Aidan froze. And then he heard the quiet irony in Tevis' tone as the High Crags lord turned to gather up the reins of Cluna's mount, patiently cropping grass.

He smiled crookedly. *Once I rid myself of regret over Blythe, I may even like the man—*

Something glinted in the grass. "Wait." Aidan bent to pick up Tevis' knife. "Here—you have forgotten." He held it out.

Tevis felt at his sheath, found it empty, put out his hand with a murmured word of thanks. Aidan set the knife into Tevis' outstretched hand, and in that brief moment of contact the *kivarna* flared to life. Tevis was open to him.

Hostility. Pride. Barely suppressed ambition. Impatience that he must wait, when so much was his for the taking.

Aidan nearly gaped. "You *do* want the throne! The throne and everything else!"

Ale-brown eyes were smoky. Tevis did not even bother to ask Aidan how he knew. "Aye," he said harshly. "I want it back. I want *everything* back."

"Back," Aidan echoed. "But it was never yours—"

Tevis cut him off. "Not mine, but it would have been Dar's. *He* was heir to Solinde, even heir to Ilsa . . . but the shapechanger came here and took it, took her, took it all—"

"He *inherited*," Aidan declared, "from his father, the Mujhar, who inherited it from *his* father, who was bequeathed it by Carillon."

"Do you think I care about Homanan history? Cheysuli history?" Tevis stepped close. His hand gripped the knife. "By all the gods of Solinde, shapechanger, what do you think I am? A young boy content to sit in silence while his homeland is given over to the usurper? We are not so different as that, shapechanger blood or no . . . I know you well enough to say with complete conviction that you would do the same."

Aidan thought it best to ignore the latter, since he was grimly aware how closely Tevis came to the truth. Instead, he focused on what he knew to be patently false. "It was hardly usurped, Solindish. Carillon won it in battle. It was his to bequeath as he wished, and it was to *my* kin it came. Solinde is ours, now."

"Mine," Tevis said flatly. "Or, more like, my son's." He smiled as he saw Aidan's start. "What—did you think I meant to do murder? Do you think I want Blythe merely to serve my own ends?

No, shapechanger . . . I want Blythe for Blythe's sake, *and* for the sake of Solinde. The throne is not meant to be mine—I honor my ancestor-kings too much to count *myself* worthy of it—but if the shapechanger gets no son on the queen, then the task falls to me. *I* will sire the heir . . . and in my lifetime, if not Dar's, I will see a High Crags man on the throne."

Aidan held Dulcie more tightly as she squirmed. "And if the queen bears a son? What then, Tevis? Your plan is in disarray."

Lips parted as if Tevis intended a blistering retort. But instead he smiled. It was a crooked, twisted smile, altering his intensity into rueful acknowledgment. "If there is a son born to Ilsa, then my hopes are vanquished. All my ambitions fail." His eyes did not waver. "My lord of Homana, I am neither a fool, nor ignorant. I want what is best for Solinde. So did Dar, even if he was unfortunate enough to go about it the wrong way—"

Aidan's tone was vicious. "He cut off my uncle's hand and then gave him to the Ihlini. To Strahan himself, who nearly destroyed him."

Tevis gestured acknowledgment. "Aye, well . . . that was Dar. I have been told he was impetuous and obsessed—"

"And you are not?"

Muscles flexed briefly in Tevis's face. "I mean no harm to you, or to the man who calls himself Prince of Solinde. There is such a thing as a peaceful revolution, my lord . . . if I marry Blythe and sire a son, the revolution is accomplished without bloodshed. *That* is how I fight."

Aidan shifted Dulcie against his shoulder, focus fragmented by her presence and her pettish discomfort. She wanted her father, not him; Aidan did not blame her.

He sighed. "Then you fight more wisely than your kinsman."

Tevis smiled faintly. "Then perhaps I will succeed where he failed."

Resentment boiled up. Aidan wanted to hit him. He did not. "Did you come here for this? Did you come down from your mountain fastness to seduce a king's daughter?"

And realized, as he asked it, he might ask it of himself, while changing the words a little. It had all been so simple: he would go to Solinde, setting aside the desperation, and find himself a wife. It would satisfy everything: rank, title, body, even the need for escape.

But there was Tevis to be faced. "Did you?" he repeated, more intensely than before. Now it applied to them both.

Tevis turned his back. Fluidly he swung up into the saddle, then looked down on Aidan. "The seduction was accomplished long before I came. It was done in writing, my lord of Homana . . . a courtship between two mothers desiring the best for their eldest children. They made it easy for me . . . I saw my chance, and I took it. Only a fool would have refused."

Aidan felt impotent. "If Blythe suffers for this—"

Tevis gathered reins, then bent to catch Cluna's horse. "She will not," he said flatly. "I am a patriot, Homanan . . . a loyal Solindish-man. But I am also a *man*. What man, looking at her, would ever want to hurt her? What man, sharing her bed, would want to drive her from it?"

Aidan could offer no answer. Holding Dulcie, bereft of speech, he watched Tevis ride away towing Cluna's horse behind him.

When he was gone, Aidan sighed and pressed a cheek against Dulcie's head. "Oh, Dulcie-*meijhana*, what do we do now?"

Overhead, Teel croaked. *Go back to the castle*, he said. *There is nothing* to *do' here*.

Disgruntled, Aidan went to his horse and mounted, taking extra care with Dulcie. Then he turned back toward Lestra.

There was nothing *to* do, here. But plenty to do, there.

Chapter Seven

Aidan found the castle in an uproar when he rode in with Dulcie. He believed at first it was because of Cluna; he discovered almost at once Ilsa was in labor. .

A nursemaid came immediately for Dulcie, releasing him from his unexpected duty. The girl was glad to go, but not before she latched onto a handful of ruddy hair and tugged; Aidan, wincing, carefully peeled fingers away and freed himself, then bent and kissed Dulcie briefly on the forehead.

The nursemaid, smiling, told him he was to go at once to the prince's private solar, where the rest of the family gathered. Aidan took his leave, giving Teel his freedom to do as he wished, and went to find the others.

Hart was in a chair, perched stiffly on the edge with braced legs spread, elbows resting on thighs. Absently he massaged the skin of his forearm at the edge of the leather cuff. He hardly glanced up as Aidan entered. His dark Cheysuli face was taut and biscut-gray.

"What of Cluna?" Aidan asked. Only Blythe, Hart, and Tevis were present.

Hart shifted slightly. "In bed. The healing is done. There is a slight fever, but it will pass."

Aidan closed the door. Though he asked the question of Hart, he looked directly at Tevis. "And the queen?"

Tevis, seated with Blythe standing next to him, said nothing.

Hart abruptly thrust himself deep into the chair, stretching one side of his face out of shape as he scrubbed at it one-handed. "It will be hours, always hours. Blythe was an easy birth—" He glanced briefly at his eldest, smiling absently, then shifted in the chair as if he could find no favored position, "—but the others have been more difficult."

Quietly, Tevis unwound himself from his chair and leaned forward to pour wine. He rose, brought the cup to Aidan, handed it to him. He said nothing, but his gaze was direct and unwavering.

He wonders if I will say anything to Hart. Aidan accepted the cup. "*Leijhana tu'sai.*"

If Tevis understood the Old Tongue, he made no indication. He merely waited.

Inwardly, Aidan sighed. Much as he disliked the situation, he saw no reason to add to Hart's concerns at the moment. Imperceptibly, he shook his head at Tevis. Once more he surrendered the war.

Something indefinable entered clear brown eyes. For a moment there was a reassessment, then an odd respect. Tevis smiled faintly. The sunlight slanting through the casements fell fully on his face, limning good bones and fine skin, shining in thick dark hair. He would, Aidan thought, sire handsome sons; the daughters, with Blythe as mother, would be beautiful.

As imperceptibly, Tevis inclined his head in thanks. Then abruptly swung on his heel and went directly to Hart. "My lord, there is something I must say."

Aidan, frowning, watched him closely. He heard the subtle deference in the High Crags dialect. He had never heard it before. Tevis was, he realized, a man of eloquent charm. Aidan began to believe he was capable of anything.

Hart merely glanced at him in distraction. "Let it wait."

"No, my lord. It cannot."

"Tevis?" Even Blythe was nonplussed.

He lifted a silencing finger without looking at her. His eyes were locked on Hart. "My lord, I must admit to you I have not been the man you believed I was. And while it is quite true I love and honor your daughter and wish only to make her happy, there is something more. I will not lie any longer."

Aidan stood very still. *He plays a dangerous game.*

Hart's eyes were steady as he looked into the taut face. "You mean to tell me you covet the throne of Solinde."

Color drained from Tevis. "My lord . . . you knew—?"

From Blythe, a blurt of shock.

Hart merely shrugged. "I have known it for some time." He glanced briefly at Aidan, then straightened in the chair. His voice was perfectly even. "You are not the first, and will not be the last. I have three other daughters."

"My lord—if you *knew*—?"

"—why did I allow you to remain?" Hart looked at Blythe. "Because my daughter loves you. And you, in your way, love her. What sense is there in ending something desired by you both, merely because you are ambitious?"

Tevis smoothed the velvet of his doublet over one arm. "Even if those ambitions could threaten your sovereignty?"

Hart stroked his bottom lip with a finger, contemplating the young man standing before him. Eventually, he smiled. "When you are young, it is quite easy to believe in personal convictions. It is quite easy to be completely committed to a thing, as you are to Solinde. A zealot blinds himself, as he must, in order to succeed. But in that blinding, he cuts off a part of himself that makes the difference between success and failure."

"My lord—?"

Hart smiled. "The key to your strength lies in my daughter. But if you should come against me, she will turn on you. And you will then have nothing, even as Dar did." He paused delicately. "With the same result."

Blythe's face was white. Tevis said nothing.

Hart smiled again. "You can have what you want *without* forcing the issue . . . if the queen bears me no son."

Tevis still said nothing.

Hart sighed. "Do you think I want Solinde to stay mired in internal bickering? I know very well there are still factions who desire me ousted, and who might turn to violence to accomplish it. Executing Dar of High Crags—a known traitor—silenced his followers for a time, but it will not last forever. The peace of this realm rests entirely with Ilsa—unless it rests with you."

"Me," Tevis said numbly.

"A son out of Ilsa is of Bellam's line. *That* line has more claim than any you can muster . . . High Crags is, after all, an isolated mountain domain with geographically limited power." Hart tilted his head. "If she gives me that son, the factions are undone. But if she does *not*, then the succession falls to another. To Blythe, as you well know—through the son she could bear." Hart smiled. "It will not put you on the throne any more than it would have put Dar there . . . but then fathers often gain power through the manipulation of their children."

Blythe was looking at Tevis. Brief hope flickered in Aidan. *If he has lost her with this . . .*

Hart's voice was soft. "If you marry her, you stay here. You give up your claim on High Crags and become a vassal to *me*."

Tevis shut his eyes. Then opened them and quietly knelt before the Prince of Solinde. "My lord, I have wronged you."

Hart smiled. "You underestimated me."

The tone was heartfelt. "*Aye.*"

"Ah, well, I have spent the last twenty-two years of my life being underestimated by the Solindish. Someday perhaps they will look past the gold I wear—and the hawk who answers my bidding—and see the man instead."

"Aye, my lord. I have no doubt they will . . . if they have not blinded themselves completely."

The dry irony surprised Aidan. But then it was not in Tevis to be completely undone; he was, if nothing else, a survivor. For all his thwarted ambitions, he probably *would* make a loyal vassal.

And a good example for the others. Aidan smiled. Su'fali, *I, too, underestimated you. Perhaps one day your kin will look past the follies of your youth to the king you have become.*

Hart flicked a hand. "Go. There will be another time for the oath. Take my daughter and go . . . I think there are things you have to say to one another—in private."

Tevis wet dry lips and rose, turning to look at Blythe. For a long moment he said nothing. Then, very quietly, "Will you come?"

Color flared in her face. "I am, if nothing else, daughter to my father. Do you think I would allow you to harm him in any way? Do you think I would let you *dare?*"

"No," he answered quietly. "That I have always known."

"Then be reminded of it!" she snapped. Blythe looked at her father, then briefly at Aidan. Color stained her face: shame, embarrassment; Tevis had been unmasked before the man most likely to gloat. She glanced back at Tevis. "Indeed, I will come. And we *will* talk, my lord of High Crags. About *everything.*"

Aidan moved aside as Blythe swept out of the chamber. Tevis followed after a brief bow in Hart's direction. The door thumped closed behind them.

Hart looked at his nephew. "I have had him watched from the beginning. The reason Dar nearly succeeded was because I did not take him seriously, and because I did not know what he was doing. This way, Tevis does nothing without my knowledge."

"Commendable, *su'fali.*"

Hart smiled faintly. "But you think I am wasting my daughter when there could be another man more suited to her . . . a man more suitable for the throne."

Aidan moved to the nearest chair and sat down, sipping at last from the wine Tevis had given him. He shrugged. "I will have a throne, *su'fali*. Do I need another?"

Hart laughed. "The Lion has proved most selfish in the past. I doubt it would change now."

In companionable silence, they took up the Bezat bowl set on the table between them and began to play. There was nothing to do, but wait.

Aidan looked at his uncle, whose bowed head as he studied the game pieces hid much of his expression. *We wait,* he reflected apprehensively, *on the future of Solinde.* And then, as Hart drew from the bowl, *Was it this difficult for my parents, waiting to see if I would live or die? If the Lion would have an heir?*

Hart turned over the piece. It was blank on either side.

"Bezat," Hart said quietly. "You are dead."

Aidan put down the winecup. His taste for the game was gone.

He was very nearly asleep when at last the servant came. The hours, as Hart had promised, were many; it was evening, well past dinner, and they had drunk too much wine. Aidan did not have a head for so much, and wanted no more than to go to bed. But Hart had desired company to pass the time, and they had shared the hours in discussion of all manner of things. Aidan could only remember part of them.

He was jerked into wakefulness as the servant opened the door and murmured something to Hart, who was less circumspect. The Prince of Solinde leaped to his feet, moved to buffet Aidan's muzzy head in an excess of joy and emotion, and told him there was a son.

"A son," Aidan echoed dutifully, but by then Hart was gone. "A *son*," he said again, brightening with comprehension, and pushed himself out of the chair.

Most of the family and a few servants gathered in an antechamber near Ilsa's royal apartments. Tevis waited by a deep casement, leaning into the sill, as if trying to hide himself in shadow. Blythe, uncharacteristically, was not with him; instead, she waited nervously by the door even as Aidan entered. Cluna was not present— probably sleeping out the fever—but Jennet was. She, like Tevis, stood very quietly out of the way, half lost in the shadows. Her bedrobe was clutched in two rigid fists.

Aidan knew at once. He crossed the chamber to her. "Come," he said gently, and led her to a chair. She sat down as he asked, then stared blindly at him as he pulled over a stool for himself. Aidan took her hands into his own. "Speaking of it will help."

There was none of the pert forwardness in her manner he had come to expect. Fair hair was loose for sleeping, shining palely in candlelight. She wore a white linen nightrail and rich blue woolen bedrobe, tangled around her ankles. Her hands in his were cold.

Jennet drew in a very deep breath. "I am glad there is a son. A prince for Solinde."

Aidan nodded, "But you believe his coming will make your *jehan* blind to you."

Jennet's mouth trembled. "It will." Another breath. "He has Blythe. She was always his favorite. And now he has a son, and there will be no more room for Cluna and me."

"You have asked him this, of course."

Blue eyes widened. "No!"

He affected mild surprise. "Then how can you know?"

"I just do."

She was not Erinnish. There was no *kivarna* in her, only fear and loneliness. Aidan squeezed her hands. "It is better you do not put words in his mouth or feelings in his heart, unless you know them for fact. It would hurt him deeply if he knew you felt this way."

"But—what if he does?"

"I promise you, he does not. On the life of my *lir*, Jennet—and you know how binding an oath that is."

Clearly, she did. But her misery was unabated.

Aidan squeezed again. "You yourself are a princess, *meijhana*. You are old enough to understand that a realm needs a king, and the king an heir to follow. For too long Solinde has been without that heir. But princesses are important as well. Solinde has need of them also."

Jennet's mouth flattened. "Only because *jehan* can marry us off to men he wants to please."

The bitterness far surpassed her years. Aidan looked at her with renewed attention. "Has someone told you that?"

She shrugged. "I heard Blythe say something like to Tevis earlier." Blue eyes flickered. "She was angry."

Aidan did not smile. "Aye, so she was."

Jennet's worried expression came back. "I do not understand. Blythe has always wanted to marry Tevis. From the beginning."

Aidan could not help himself. "Does she not anymore?"

Jennet shrugged; Blythe was not, at the moment, her concern.

"She told him she would . . . that between them they had made certain she would have to." She frowned. "I did not understand that."

"No," Aidan agreed, thinking it was best. "I think you need not worry about such things yet. And I think, when the time comes, you will have even less to worry about—I think *no one* could force you to marry a man you did not wish to." He smiled. "Now, as to the new prince . . . I will not lie to you, Jennet. It may *seem* your father has forgotten you at first, in the newness of having a son, but it will pass. Your *jehan* will never replace you with anyone. He could not; no one else is Jennet."

She studied him solemnly, judging the worth of his words. "Do you promise that on the life of your *lir?*"

She was, he thought, a true daughter of royalty, seeking assurances in everything. He smiled, released her hands, touched her head briefly as he rose. "I promise."

Hart came into the chamber from the adjoining apartments. As he saw them he smiled, eyes alight. "Solinde has a prince," he announced with quiet pride, "*and* a healthy queen."

Jennet threw herself across the chamber and climbed into his arms as he caught her. He laughed aloud; so did Jennet. She shed the burgeoning maturity Aidan had seen and was merely a child again, at peace in her father's arms.

Aidan looked at Tevis and found him looking back. The young lord of High Crags wore an odd expression, and once again Aidan found his feelings masked. The *kivarna* was silent.

Tevis smiled. It was a smile of bittersweet defeat; of comprehension and acceptance. Something glittered in his eyes. A brief, eloquent gesture told Aidan Tevis fully understood the import of the boy's birth; his hopes for the throne, through *his* son, were extinguished. All Blythe could give him now was a nephew, much as he was himself. A royal nephew, perhaps, but absent from the line of succession.

Aidan looked at Blythe. She also watched Tevis, as if judging him even as Aidan did. Her expression was unreadable.

Reflexively, Aidan went into the link to Teel. *Do you think there may yet be a chance?*

But then Blythe crossed the chamber to Tevis, who cupped her face in his hand.

Aidan sighed. *No.*

From Teel there was nothing, who undoubtedly had known.

Chapter Eight

In three days' time, Hart called for an official naming ceremony. Cheysuli custom decreed the father must examine the naked infant for physical flaws, after the ancient ways mandating wholeness in a warrior; then, finding him unblemished, name him aloud to the gods and those kin assembled.

But for the newborn prince there was more: according to Solindish custom there must be named a second-father, a man bound to keep the child from harm should anything befall the natural parents. So Hart assembled everyone in a private audience chamber to appease both halves of the child's heritage.

Hart, with Ilsa beside him, stood on a low dais. On a polished perch behind them was Rael, jet-and-white in sunlight. The infant boy was cradled against his father's leatherclad chest in strong, dark arms shining with *lir*-gold. Hart had never looked happier, Aidan thought, as he smiled down into the baby's sleeping face. His pride was manifest, and yet Aidan wondered if the Cheysuli portion of the ceremony would bring unexpected anguish. Hart would be required to examine his son for physical flaws before he could name him, yet he himself was *kinwrecked*, expelled from the clans because of his missing hand. It was a harsh reality once required in times of hardship, yet no longer necessary. Brennan had tried to have the custom changed by appealing to Clan Council, but had failed to sway the men who declared too many of the old ways already had been lost.

It is Ilsa who keeps the pain at bay, Aidan reflected, gazing at the woman who stood at Hart's left side.

One pale, slender hand gently rested on his arm. The trace of fatigue in her face was tempered by a transcendent joy illuminating her already considerable beauty. There was an elegance in the woman unmatched by any Aidan had seen. He was, as always, taken aback by it. Even the glittering jeweled clasps fastening the coils of pale hair to her head could not compete with the brilliance of her eyes as she gazed out upon the people called to witness the naming of her son.

Blythe stood quietly with Tevis; Cluna, mostly recovered, stood with Jennet. Dulcie resided in Aidan's arms, though a nursemaid waited nearby to release him from the duty should the child prove tiresome. For the moment she was fascinated by the torque around his neck; smiling, Aidan unwound thin fingers from it and tried to bribe her with a coin so she would not tug quite so firmly.

Hart smiled brilliantly at them all. "This child is a child of two realms and two heritages, and both should be honored. No man should turn his back on any part of himself, for it is the sum of those parts that makes him what he is. So we have assembled you today to name this child after the fashion of Solinde *and* Homana, so no gods may be offended, and no race be overlooked."

Aidan glanced at Tevis, standing quietly to one side, and wondered how much it chafed the young lord of High Crags to see his hopes dashed so publicly. Tevis' face was expressionless, save for a brightness of his eyes as he looked at his liege lord and newborn prince. He gave nothing away of his thoughts.

Hart's voice jerked Aidan's attention back to the dais. "A Solindish child—and particularly a royal one—must have a second-father. It is not so different from the Cheysuli custom of a liege man in Homana, set to ward the Mujhar from physical threat . . . a second-father also tends the welfare of the child."

Hart settled the infant into the crook of his left arm and carefully peeled back the linen wrappings, unfolding the child from his cocoon. When he was free of the wrappings and entirely naked, Hart counted aloud the fingers and toes, looked into the tiny, flat ears, examined the unfocused eyes and made certain the small manhood was intact. Then he displayed the child to all of them.

"Before the gods of Homana, who are everywhere, I declare this child whole and free of blemish, acceptable to kin and clan. There is no taint in flesh or blood. By this naming he becomes a true Cheysuli, destined for a *lir* and loyal service to the prophecy." He drew in a breath and steadied his voice; even across the chamber, Aidan felt the upsurge of emotion. "I name this child Owain, son of Hart and Ilsa; now known as Prince Owain, heir to the throne of Solinde. I do this with the full blessing of the gods, and can only hope they gift him with a worthy *tahlmorra*." Briefly, he looked at Aidan. "No man may choose his, and certainly not a child."

Aidan turned as the nursemaid came forward and settled Dulcie into her arms. Then he stepped forward to bow his head in brief homage to Hart. Carefully he took up Owain's tiny right hand and kissed it. In his heart he murmured the words of a private kinsman's blessing, wishing health and happiness on the child; aloud he spoke similar words in the Old Tongue, feeling the weight of two gold links at his belt as he did so.

Finished, he inclined his head once again, made the Cheysuli gesture of *tahlmorra*, and turned to face the others.

"This child is a child of the gods. His *tahlmorra* is theirs to impart; their service is his to perform. *Tahlmorra lujhala mei wiccan, cheysu.* May the gods grant this child a perfect service to the prophecy of the Firstborn, and to the people of Solinde, whom one day he will rule."

He waited. The expected response came from those who knew it: *"Ru'shalla-tu."* May it be so.

Aidan smiled. His part in the ceremony was done. He returned to his place, took Dulcie back, waited.

"Leijhana tu'sai," Hart said quietly, eyes aglint, then rewrapped the newly-named Prince Owain. He left one hand and arm free. "It is a second-father's duty to care for this child, should something befall the natural parents. It is his duty to raise this child as his own, treating him as his own, sparing him nothing he would not spare children of his own body, giving him no more or less than he would give children of his own body.

"Upon reaching manhood the child shall go out of the second-father's house and make his own. But he will forever honor that man as his true-father—his *jehan*—with all the honor he would also give to the gods." Hart's face was solemn, but something lurked in his eyes. "The choosing of a second-father is never undertaken lightly. It is an honor bestowed a man who has proven himself strong and loyal. It is a mark of respect and trust, and is never undertaken without the full understanding of its responsibilities."

Hart's eyes rested briefly on Aidan. "A kinsman is often chosen, because there is like blood flowing in the veins and blood binds a man to another man more firmly than anything else. But others are honored as well." Hart smiled. "Tevis, Lord of High Crags."

Clear brown eyes widened almost imperceptibly. "My lord."

"Will you, as second-father, swear to raise Prince Owain as your own? Will you take an oath to serve this child as you would serve the Prince of Solinde, and any child of your body? Will you accept him as your liege lord, caring for his needs as he requires it, never failing this trust?"

Tevis, oddly, was pale. "My lord—you have spoken of a kinsman . . . what of Prince Aidan?"

Hart did not look at his nephew. "Aidan's *tahlmorra* takes him in another direction. We would have you for our son's second-father."

Next to Tevis, Blythe's face was alight. Aidan understood very well why Hart did as he did; it was, he thought, very clever. And undoubtedly would prove extremely fortuitous.

Tevis drew a deep, slow breath. "My lord . . . my lord, I will do anything you require. It will be my honor to serve Prince Owain as second-father."

Ilsa's smile was luminous. "We are honored by your oath."

Blythe pressed Tevis' arm. He approached slowly, head bowed in homage. When he stood before the dais, he knelt so as not to lift his head above that of the infant.

"Rise," Hart said. "Take his hand in yours."

Dazed, Tevis rose and reached out for the tiny hand. He stared at the baby's silk-smooth, fragile skin; the crumpled, sleep-creased face. "I swear," he said quietly. "I swear to raise you as a child of my own body. I swear to serve you. I accept you as my liege lord. I will care for your needs as you require it, and I swear I will never fail your trust." Tevis bent his head and kissed the tiny hand.

Blythe, Aidan saw, had tears in her eyes. Cluna and Jennet were solemn-faced, big-eyed; they understood full well the gravity of the ceremony. Ilsa, still clasping Hart's arm, looked on Tevis with great pride shining in her lovely face; Hart himself wore an expression of many things, not the least of them satisfaction and a quiet, contented triumph.

Inwardly, Aidan laughed. *Oh, aye,* su'fali, *you know exactly what you have done.*

Hart looked over Tevis' bowed head. His gaze met Aidan's. A new peace entered his eyes.

Aidan nodded acknowledgment. *He has his son . . . his future . . . and his immortality . . .*

Tevis stepped away. He bowed briefly, then returned to Blythe's side. His eyes were strange. He appeared singularly moved, but Aidan sensed no specific emotion through the *kivarna*. The gift, as always, was fickle. It would not be manipulated.

But Tevis, as if sensing Aidan's look, turned. For a moment his face was quite still, and then he smiled a genuine smile.

Aidan smiled back blandly, but inwardly he felt a tremendous sense of relief. *Perhaps, after all, he will be content with this.*

It was evening, in Hart's solar. The light was gone from the day, but candles filled the lack and set the chamber alight. They had succeeded in chasing the women from the room so they could forget the talk of new babies and turn their minds to other things, such as good wine, tall tales, and wagering.

Hart laughed aloud and leaned forward to scoop the winnings into his already impressive pile. Tevis swore mildly, counted what he had left, glanced to Aidan on his left. "Someone will have to stop him, before he robs us all."

Aidan grunted. "Not I. You see how little is left to me—*you* have more than I."

Tevis looked again at his stack of red-gold Solindish coins. It was much diminished, but he did have more than Aidan. He nodded to himself, took up his goblet of wine, drank half down.

Hart pointed. "There is that."

Aidan put a shielding hand over his heavy topaz ring. "This is my signet ring."

"Aye, well . . . it never stopped *me*. A man true to the game does not let such petty things as personal possessions stand in the way of a good wager."

Ruddy brows shot up. " 'A man true to the game'? Do you mean a man who has lost control?"

Hart scowled. "No."

Aidan could not resist it. "A man true to *himself* wagers nothing of importance."

Hart's scowl deepened. "Then what of those links on your belt? They serve no useful purpose."

Tevis nodded briefly. "I had wondered myself."

A hand locked over the links. "No."

"Why do you wear them, *harani*? Not for ornamentation—"

Aidan waved a hand. "I wear them because I want to. Here, if you are so hungry for a wager . . ." He pushed out the few remaining coins he had. "There. That will do. Small, perhaps, but a wager."

Hart sighed and rattled the Bezat bowl. The game was run through; the result, this time, was different.

"Hah!" Tevis cried. "You see? The face of fortune turns at last to one more deserving."

Glowering at the young man, Hart pushed the proper amount of coin back across the table. The sapphire ring on his finger glittered with icy fire; beside it rested the fiery ruby signet of the kings of Solinde. Save for the gold on his arms and in his left ear, the rings were the only jewelry Hart affected. The sapphire's setting matched that of Aidan's topaz, worked with tiny runes, and he recalled with a start that Hart was still considered a prince in Homana.

Aidan glanced at Tevis as he reached out to gather the coin. Like Hart, he wore a sapphire ring; were they fashionable this year? But his was not so massive, and the setting very new. The jet ring looked far older, set firmly in ancient gold.

Hart looked at Aidan intently. "You will have to play again."

"But I lost, *su'fali* . . . and that was the last of my coin."

Hart grunted. "Brennan gives you a light purse."

Aidan laughed and poured more wine. "He gives me all I need. I am not a profligate spender."

"Well?" Tevis asked. "How many in this game?"

"All three," Hart declared. "I will stake Aidan to more gold."

"Just so I can play? *Su'fali*, I swear, it is not that important to me—"

"You are my guest, and you will play." Hart's smile was charming. "I refuse to be the sole loser on my son's naming day."

Aidan dutifully lifted his cup. "To Prince Owain, may the gods grant him a good *tahlmorra*."

Hastily, Tevis raised his as well. "Prince Owain," he echoed absently, looking into the Bezat bowl. "Shall you stir?" He passed the bowl to Aidan.

Thus invited, he stuck two long fingers into the bowl and stirred the contents, rattling etched ivory against the rim. The game had mostly lost its appeal, since he now risked another man's coin, but it was good manners to continue when his uncle had been so generous. He only hoped he could win back enough to cover the loaned coin, since he hated being in debt.

"Here." Hart waited for Aidan to set down the bowl, then dipped in to draw out a piece.

They played mostly in silence, commenting briefly on the draws, or muttering dissatisfaction. Tevis' gaze was fixed on the bowl, but Aidan thought he did not really see it; his eyes had the dazed look of a man lost in thought elsewhere, no longer aware of his actions or surroundings. The skin of his face seemed tauter than ever, as if he was ill or under strain, but there was no other indication of his inattention.

"Tevis?" Hart said.

Tevis twitched on his stool. "My lord?"

"Yours is the next draw. For Aidan."

"Ah." He reached in, dug out the stone, turned it from one side to the other. "Bezat," he said blankly. "The deathstone."

Hart laughed at Aidan's resigned expression. "You lose! Now Tevis and I must play this out—"

The door was flung open. Dulcie's nursemaid stripped loose hair from her eyes. "My lord—you must come at once—"

Frowning, Hart pushed his stool away and rose. "Helda, what is it?"

"Oh, my lord—the *baby*—"

Hart threw down his winecup. It rang against the table even as it spilled a blood-red puddle onto polished wood. Aidan stood up so abruptly he overset his stool, and went after Hart; Tevis, white-faced, dropped the death-stone into the spreading wine and followed.

Aidan arrived in the nursery but a moment after Hart pushed his way through the crowding women. Ilsa was on her knees next to the cradle, clasping the linen-swathed infant to her breast. Her eyes were empty of everything save a harsh, horrible grief.

"Not again," Hart murmured, and then swung frenziedly on them all. "Out!" he shouted to the women. "All of you, *out*. At once."

Aidan and Tevis moved aside as the women departed raggedly. Night-clad Blythe arrived even as they left. "What is it?" she cried. Then, looking past to her mother, "Oh, gods—not *Owain*—"

Ilsa murmured down into the still bundle, seemingly unaware of Hart's presence. It was not until he knelt down and touched her that she raised her eyes.

"*Meijhana*—"

"Dead," she said only.

With trembling fingers, Hart peeled back the wrappings. He touched the face. "Cold," he murmured blankly. "Cold and white as death—"

Blythe's face was as white. "But he was well . . . earlier, at the ceremony . . . he was *well*—"

Hart's hand shook as he cupped Ilsa's head. "Oh, *meijhana*, there is nothing I can say to make the pain softer for you . . ."

What of you? Aidan wondered numbly. *What of your pain, su'fali . . . a son and heir, born and unborn in the space of three days . . .*

Tevis murmured something. Then, more loudly, "He was my son. Mine, too . . . I was second-father."

Blythe reached for his arm, but he withdrew it. Slowly he moved toward the huddled, grieving queen and the Cheysuli who knelt with bowed head, one large hand grasping the tiny fingers of the son who would never rule in his father's palace.

"Oh, no," Blythe said brokenly. "He should not . . . he is not Cheysuli, and does not understand about private grief—"

Aidan did. He moved at once to intercept the Solindishman. "Tevis, no. Let it wait. Come away, for now—" He put his hand on Tevis' arm. "Let the first grief pass—"

Fingers closed, then spasmed. It ran through Aidan like fire, setting bones ablaze even as his blood turned to ice, still and dark and cold, so *cold*—

"You," he croaked. "*You*—"

Tevis' eyes were black. "Put no hand on me."

"You—" Aidan choked.

Even Hart was drawn from his grief by the sound of Aidan's horror. He turned, rising, clearly distracted.

The *kivarna* was blazing within him like a pyre. In that moment Tevis' intentions were clear. "*You* killed the child!"

Blythe's voice was shrill. "Are you mad? Why would *Tevis*—?"

Hart grabbed Aidan's arm and jerked him around. "What are you saying?"

"It was Tevis," Aidan declared. The truth was so clear to him—could none of them see it? Feel it, as he did? "It was *Tevis*—"

The Solindishman's face was white. "I am his second-father. I am sworn to him, to protect him—and you say I *killed* him?"

Hart's voice was harsh. "Aidan, this is nonsense . . . Tevis has been with us for hours."

Aidan was shaking. "I know it. I know it. I *feel* it—" The final

shred of disbelief dissolved the remaining vestige of Tevis' shield.
"By the gods—*Ihlini*—"

"Are you *mad?*" Blythe cried.

The barriers were gone. Aidan sensed the seething ambition and
raw power in the man, the tremendous upsurge of *so much* power,
barely bridled; and hatred, so much hatred; *too much* hatred and
power and absolute dedication to the service of a god no one else
dared worship.

Tevis lifted a hand. Around his fingers danced the faintest glow
of flame, cold purple flame; *godfire* at his fingertips, revealing all
too clearly what he was. As, now, he intended.

"Wait," he said softly.

Perversely, Aidan wanted to laugh. "Ihlini," he said again, wondering at his blindness. How could he not have known? How could
the Cheysuli blood in him not know, or the Erinnish *kivarna?* He
of all people—

"Aye," Tevis spat between his teeth. "Child of the gods; child
of prophecy—*like you!*"

"He was a baby!" Hart shouted. "A helpless infant! What purpose does it serve to end *his* life?"

"Because I must end *all* the lives," Tevis snapped. "Each and
every life I can find—each and every seed—"

"Tevis," Blythe whispered.

"—until there are no seeds left, save ours." Tevis cast a malignant glance at Hart. "Had you left this son unborn, you would not
now know this grief. It is your fault, my lord of Solinde . . . to save
the lady this pain, you had only to do one thing."

Aidan heard the sluggish distraction in Hart's voice. Shock was
starting to distance him from a reality he could not face. "One
thing—?"

Tevis smiled. "Name me your heir, my lord. Put me on the
throne after you—"

"No!" Blythe cried. "Oh, gods—*no—NO*—"

"Ah," Tevis remarked. "She has only just realized the man she
slept with is Ihlini. A Cheysuli and Ihlini, in carnal congress . . .
just as the prophecy warned."

Ilsa, forgotten, rose slowly. Her face was ravaged by grief, but
it diminished none of her intensity. "Your war has been with
adults, Ihlini—always. Why now do you turn to a child? What
harm could he do you?"

An elegant shrug. "Now, very little. But it is important to me that no seed survive. Asar-Suti has made it quite clear that if the Ihlini are to regain dominion over the world, we must first destroy the Cheysuli and anyone who serves them."

"How?" Aidan asked. "You were with *us*. How could we not know? How could you touch this child from afar?"

Tevis displayed the sapphire. "A token from your father, my lord of Homana . . . something he gave my aunt many years ago. It has served us very well in the meantime. Anything once worn by man or woman contains an essence of that person—combined with Ihlini arts, we make a shield, so we may walk freely among you and the *lir*. As for touching him from afar, a simple thing to do with an infant. I merely thought on a tiny heart, quite still, and wished it into truth." He smiled. "A fortunate thing, this ring—Brennan should have known better than to give it to Rhiannon."

"Your aunt," Hart echoed. "*Rhiannon?*"

The smooth, urbane expression of a Solindish nobleman faded. Aidan heard Blythe's stifled denial; saw the draining of Hart's face. Tevis was no longer precisely *Tevis*. His features were much the same, but more refined, more feral. In his mind's eye, Aidan made the eyes a lighter brown, almost yellow; the hair a shade darker, now black.

"Oh, gods," Aidan blurted. "Strahan had a *son*."

Blythe's voice was a travesty. "Where is Tevis, then? *Was* there a Tevis?"

"Most certainly," Strahan's son agreed. "I killed him." He displayed the black ring on his other hand. "I killed Tevis and his father in High Crags, when I knew he was coming here. The father's body I left—there was no need of it—but Tevis' I required in order to arrange the proper glamour." He smiled. "Those who knew Tevis, *saw* Tevis when they looked at me. Those who did not, saw me. So, aye, *meijhana*, it was also Tevis you lay down with . . . at least, as much Tevis as remains of him, in this ring."

Blythe, trembling, pressed both hand against her mouth. Her face was ashen with comprehension.

Ilsa took a single step, then stopped. Against her breast she still cradled the murdered child. "I curse you," she said simply. "I am of the oldest House in this realm, Ihlini. With all that I was, I am, and will be—I curse you."

Tevis smiled at her, gently inclining his head. Then he looked at Hart. "I have killed the son," he said. "Now I must kill the father."

Something glittered in his hand. Silver, not purple; the *godfire* was gone. Not a knife, but its edge as deadly. Aidan had heard of the slender silver wafers with curving, elegant spikes. He had also heard the name: Sorcerer's Tooth. It flashed from the man they had known as Tevis and sliced across the room.

"Lochiel," he said softly, "so you will know me as you die."

Without thought, Aidan moved. He meant to knock down the Tooth; to block Hart from the lethal wafer. But he knew, even as he thrust out the hand to catch it, he had made a deadly mistake.

The entry was painless. It sliced into his palm, then through it, severing muscle, bone and vessel as the spikes rotated through the fine bones of his hand and exited the other side. Fingers closed once, spasming, and then vision turned inside out.

Hart caught him as he fell. And as he fell, he recalled the Ihlini forged their Teeth in poison.

Blythe screamed. And then she stopped.

Or he did.

Chapter Nine

Where he was, it was cold. So cold he ached with it. He could not move; could not see; could not hear or speak, but his awareness flickered with something akin to life even though he knew he was dead.

Someone had placed him on a barge. He lay on a bier, covered with a silken shroud, and his flesh was dead on his bones.

He floated in perfect silence on a lake of glass so clear he could see the darkness of the depths. He was alone. No one steered the barge. No one held the vigil at his side. No one wailed or keened or grieved, as if his death made absolutely no difference at all to anyone, even to his *lir.*

Teel.

He was alone. He felt a vague distress that his life could have so little meaning that his death would hold even less. He was prince, warrior, child of the prophecy, in line for the Lion; it was as if he had never been. The barge floated silently upon the waters of the glass-black lake, and he was still alone.

Teel.

He heard the ripple in the water. It was faint, so faint he believed it imagination, but the rippling slowly increased until he became convinced it was real. Someone—or something—approached him through the water.

Teel?

He struggled to open dead eyes. And again, this time to move an arm; neither answered. His flesh was still and cold and heavy, so heavy; Aidan began to understand death, and to know the futility and helplessness of a live spirit trapped within dead flesh.

The rippling became a splashing. Aidan, blind still, heard something grasp the edge of the barge. He felt no fear—he was *dead*—but curiosity overrode helplessness. With all the power remaining to him, he snapped open his eyes and looked.

A man. A warrior: Cheysuli. He wore leather and gold, clan-worked all, and his coloring was true. In his planed, feral face was a strange, eloquent sorrow. Softly he pulled himself out of water he did not displace, and then stood upon the barge. Aidan saw he was dry.

Lips and throat answered him. "Did you not swim?"

The other smiled. "I swam. But where I am, water cannot touch me."

Aidan, staring, saw the sword in his left hand. A true, two-handed broadsword of steel and gold, with a massive hilt bearing the rampant lion of Homana. In its heavy pommel, to balance the heavy blade, was a blood-red ruby. Down the length of the blade walked runes.

Two links Aidan possessed. Two Mujhars: Shaine, and Carillon. And now the third before him.

"Donal," he breathed.

The warrior smiled. "Aye."

Aidan looked again at the ruby. Huge and brilliant and red; the Mujhar's Eye, he knew . . . and no longer in existence.

Donal saw his expression. "Niall returned it to me."

"But—you were dead. And he threw the sword away . . . he went into the Womb of the Earth and threw it down the oubliette."

The voice was very gentle. "The sword was made for me, by Hale, my grandsire. When I have need of it, it answers."

Aidan wet dry lips; a thing he had believed impossible, on a dead man. With great deliberation he pushed himself into a sitting position. Silken shroud—crimson and black, the colors of Homana—slid down to his hips. He shivered, for he was naked beneath the fine silk. "There was no chain," he said. "I did not dream of a chain. Always before it has been the chain first, and then the Mujhar."

Donal's austere face softened. "Are you so certain?"

Aidan looked. Gold glittered in silk. At his feet, upon the bier, lay the chain. The links, as always, were solid, perfect . . . deadly.

He very nearly laughed. He knew the pattern now. "What have *you* come to tell me?"

"Do I have to tell you something?" Donal gazed across the lake into the setting sun. "No. I will let the others speak for me. The gods have set me a different task."

Aidan shivered, though he was not cold. "What task?"

"You may call me a steersman, for now." Donal moved to one

end of the barge and lifted the sword as a man would hold a staff. Long brown fingers closed on steel; by rights, it should cut.

Astonished, Aidan saw the sword reshape itself. The steel and gold flowed in either direction until it stretched, lengthening, and when it stopped he saw it was no longer a sword, but a golden pole, a steersman's pole, and as Donal slid it into the water Aidan saw the ruby send forth a starburst of brilliant light.

"To ward off the Darkness," Donal explained.

Aidan looked at the setting sun. He believed, in that moment, that his life or death would be decided by what he agreed—or refused—to do.

Quietly, Donal steered. "Your journey has been interrupted. I am here to put you back on the proper path."

"Then—I am not yet dead."

"Not as I know death. But neither are you alive, as the living know it. It is best to simply say you are *elsewhere* for the moment."

Aidan said nothing.

"Men die," Donal said. "Even Cheysuli die. But occasionally the gods see to it that a certain man—or woman—does not, because they have a use for him."

"Use," Aidan echoed. "A weighty word, I'm thinking."

"Most words are." Water splashed softly. "They sent me; therefore I am assuming they have some use for you."

Aidan thought about it. He recalled the things he had been told by the Hunter, by the Weaver, and by the two Mujhars. "And have they given you leave to tell me what this use is, or am I to guess?"

Donal looked at him. The setting sun illuminated his face. It was a face similar to his own, Aidan realized, though the color was much darker and all the angles sharper. The Erinnish in him had softened hue and hardness, redefining the wildness into something more civilized. It was easy to see why the Homanans, seeing a clan-born Cheysuli, had been so willing to name them alien.

This is what I might have been, instead of what I am. Had my line not looked to outmarriage . . .

He touched a strand of ruddy hair. The eyes in his head were right, but certainly not the hair. He did not know whether to be grateful or sorry for it.

Donal's tone was muted. "It would do little good for me to tell you all the answers, Aidan. Men are men, not gods; they often shun the knowledge of a better way. Men are willful, but the willfulness is what the gods gave them. And so the gods bide their time, waiting to see if the man will follow his proper *tahlmorra*, or turn away from it." Yellow eyes were strangely calm. "What of you, kinsman? Which path do you choose?"

"All Cheysuli follow their *tahlmorras*," Aidan answered automatically, and then knew how foolish it sounded in view of Teirnan's actions, and those of the other *a'saii*. Quickly he asserted, "I intend to follow *mine*."

"Freely, or because you are constrained by blood and heritage?"

"Freely, of course." Aidan spread his hands. "But the choice is hardly a true one . . . what other path is open to me?"

"Many paths are open to you. Any number of them will seem easier than the true path awaiting you. Your life is very young, Aidan . . . do not judge what has gone before as the measure of what will come. You may despise the gods before your time on earth is done."

Aidan disagreed politely. "I think not, kinsman."

Donal arched black brows. "Innocence speaks hastily."

Disgusted, Aidan scowled at him—this meeting with yet another dead kinsman was as obscure as all the others—then marveled that he dared. Donal had been dead for many years. "I have been properly raised, my lord Mujhar. You need have no fear your son has failed in his duty, nor *his* son . . . I will do whatever the gods ask of me."

"And if they ask your life?"

"They asked *yours*," Aidan retorted. "And you gave it."

Sorrow altered Donal's face. He briefly touched a *lir*-band—wrought gold depicting wolf and falcon—then let the hand fall away. "I gave it. But my *lir* were dead . . . I wanted no empty life, no madness. Better to die whole, knowing, than die a *lir*less madman."

Aidan shivered, though he was not cold. Out of habit he moved to pull the shroud to cover his nakedness, and as he did so he heard the chiming of links falling. He stopped himself from touching the chain.

He looked squarely at Donal. "You are my great-grandsire."

"Aye."

"Then I ask a kinsman's boon." Aidan took a deep breath. "Tell me what I must do. Tell me what I must become."

Donal, backlighted now by sunlight, though the barge had not turned, was only a silhouette. Aidan could no longer see his features. But he saw the pole shrink, swallowing itself, until it was a sword in the hand of its master. The point was set through one of the links; lifted, the chain dangled. Aidan stared, transfixed, as the chain was carried closer.

Donal tipped the sword. The chain slid off steel and landed in Aidan's silk-swathed lap. "I cannot tell you what to do. The gods constrain me from that. But I *can* tell you what you must become."

Aidan wrenched his gaze from the chain so close to his manhood to the shadowed face of his kinsman. "Tell me, then."

Donal's eyes were oddly serene. "You must become Aidan," he said gently. "Not Aidan of Homana; Aidan the prince; Aidan, son of Brennan, grandson of Niall, great-grandson of Donal." He smiled. "You must simply become yourself."

"But I *am* all those things! How can I not be?"

"That is your choice."

Aidan put out a shaking hand and touched the chain in his lap. "Is it?" he asked. "Is it my choice . . . or the gods'?"

But when he looked up, hoping for an answer, a word, anything, Donal—and the sword—was gone.

He jerked awake with a gasp. His chest felt heavy, empty, as if it had been sat upon for a very long time. He shuddered once, gulping air spasmodically, then opened his eyes and saw Hart's haggard face.

Breath flowed slowly back into his body, filling his chest until he thought he might burst. Then he swallowed forcibly, working his flaccid mouth, and managed to ask a question.

At first, Hart only stared. And then he muttered several things, including a *leijhana tu'sai* Aidan understood was for the gods, rather than for him, which he found oddly amusing. Quietly, he waited.

"Do you know," Hart said shakily, "I had composed it in my head? But the idea of putting it down on paper . . ." He shook his head, then abstractedly pushed silvering hair out of his eyes. "How could I tell Brennan? How could I make the words?"

Aidan smiled faintly. "No need now." He swallowed. "How long, *su'fali?*"

"Four days," Hart answered raggedly. "I thought we had lost you. I thought *both* of you—" He wiped his hand across his face, older now than before. "How could we have been so blind to him? To bring him into our home, into my daughter's *bed*—" He stood abruptly and turned rigidly away, as if he could not face Aidan. His voice was muffled. "Blythe swears she will kill herself."

Shock and revulsion turned Aidan cold. Suicide was taboo.

The dignity was stripped from Hart's voice, leaving behind a father's fear and anguish. "She swears the only way to undo her transgression is to destroy the body itself."

Aidan sighed wearily. "Then she is a fool indeed, and not fit to be Cheysuli."

It jerked Hart around. "How can you say—?" But he understood at once. "Oh. Aye. Perhaps if she looked at it that way . . ." He resumed his seat once more. "I think—I *hope*—once the shock has passed she will be more rational After all, both Ian and Brennan survived—"

"—and Keely." Aidan was oddly light-headed. "*Su'fali*—four days?" It felt like only an hour. It felt like four years.

Hart nodded. "At first I thought the earth magic too weak to destroy the poison. But this morning the fever broke."

Aidan reached for an itchy face and felt stubble. He grimaced in distaste; he detested his propensity for growing a beard. It felt oddly unclean. Or perhaps merely too foreign, evoking his other bloodlines.

Hart's smile was strained. "The Homanan in you. Brennan and I are smooth as a baby—" He broke it off. Only the closed eyes gave away his grief, and then he opened them again. New lines etched his flesh.

Aiden glanced around. He was in the guest chamber allotted to him. The room was empty save for Hart, who sat in a heavy chair beside the bed.

Teel.

Here. The raven briefly fluttered wings; he perched, as always, on the canopy. *Rest yourself,* lir . . . *I am here.*

Awareness reasserted itself; Aidan looked sharply at Hart. "The Ihlini?"

"Gone. Blythe's scream brought servants . . . Tevis—no, *Lochiel*—dared not remain. Too many Cheysuli." Hart's tone was grim. "He took his leave as so many of them do: in smoke and purple fire."

Aidan was, abruptly, in the audience chamber, holding a tiny infant only barely named. He recalled the insignificant weight; the crumpled, sleeping face; the hope for continuity.

He recalled also the look of pride and peace in Hart's face as he had named Tevis second-father.

The pain was greater than expected, because it was two-fold. The *kivarna* gave him that; he experienced his own grief while also echoing Hart's.

Aidan drew in a deep breath. He could think of no words worth the saying. So he said the obvious ones. "I am sorry, *su'fali.*"

"I know." A slight gesture closed the topic. A right-handed gesture, since he had no left.

And suddenly Aidan's fear and anguish was for himself. He thrust his left hand into the air, staring at it fixedly. It was swathed in bandages. He remembered, with unwanted clarity, the vision of steel piercing flesh, slicing too easily through skin and blood and muscle, dividing even bone.

"Is it whole? Oh, gods, *su'fali*—is it whole?"

Hart drew in a deep breath. "Whole," he said, "but damaged."

"How damaged?" All he could see was the old pain in Hart's eyes whenever he spoke of a clan no longer his. Would he share it, now? "Will I have the use of it?"

"I cannot say."

Aidan struggled upright. "Cannot, or will not? Are you trying to save me grief? Trying to save me the realization—?"

Hart's face hardened. "I told you the truth, Aidan. No one knows. The hand is whole, but damaged. You may or may not recover the use of it. I promise you nothing at all."

"A maimed warrior has no place in the clans," Aidan quoted numbly.

Pain and anguish flared afresh in Hart, with such virulence that it smashed through Aidan's awareness like a mangonel stone. "No," he agreed.

Aidan slumped back against bolsters. Strength and fear and comprehension spilled out of him like a bag of grain emptied. He had not wanted to pass the pain to Hart yet again. Ihlini poison had left him weak. "But," he said quietly, "I am still a prince, as you are, with a place at the Lion's side, with a hand or without."

When he could, Hart smiled. "Aye."

"The gods will have to be content with me as I am—*they* gave me the burden." Aidan's eyes drifted closed. "Where are my links?"

"Your links?"

Eyes remained closed. "The links on my belt." He was naked beneath the coverlet, as he had been on the bier.

"They were put away. Do you want them?"

"No. Just to know they are safe." *Because there will be a third to come. There must be; I met Donal.*

"Aidan."

All he could do was grunt.

"Shall I arrange to send you home once you are feeling stronger?

It made sense. He wanted to go. He had very nearly died—he would like to see home again, and all of his kinfolk—

—but his great-grandsire Donal had come to set him back on the proper path.

"No," he managed to whisper. "There is Erinn yet to see."

So, Teel observed, *you did not lose* all *of your wits.*

Sluggish irritation. *Only the use of a hand.*

Teel, to do him credit, did not respond to that. He merely tucked his head under a wing.

Blythe came, as he expected. She came as he put the last of his possessions into his saddle-packs, and stood just inside the door. Even in her bleakness, he thought her beautiful.

Right-handed, he closed the flap on the saddle-pack and looped the thong loosely through the buckle. Then he looked at Blythe.

Her hands, in skirts, were rigid. He wished he could do the same. "They said—" She stopped. "They said it does not move."

"The *hand* moves," he corrected. "Even the thumb, a little. But the fingers are mostly useless." Aidan forbore to look. He knew what it was, under the bandages. He had examined it most carefully when it was clear the healing was done.

She lifted her head a little. "Will it make you *kin-wrecked?*"

It took everything he had to answer casually, so as not to display the fear. "Probably."

Color flared in her face. "How can you sound like that—as if it makes no difference? As if you hardly care? You have only to look at my father to know what it means . . . the pain he has to live with—all because of a gods-cursed ancient custom in a race too blind to see that a man can be a man even *if* he lacks a hand—"

"I know," he said tightly.

"Then how can you stand there and shrug so elegantly, wearing all your gold, when you *know* what they might do—and to the man who will be Mujhar!"

"I know," he said again.

Tears glittered. "Know *what?*"

"How badly it hurts."

Blythe had cut her hair. She clawed at it now; it barely touched her shoulders. "He told me what you said. That I was not fit to be a Cheysuli. Not worthy of the taboo."

"No. Only a *lir*less man can accept the death-ritual, or there is no honor in the death."

"Honor!" she snapped. "What honor is left to me? I have been *defiled*—"

Aidan shook his head. "All you were, was tricked."

"I lay with an Ihlini!"

"Do you know who he is?"

Blythe blinked. "What?"

"Do you know who he is? The man you believed was Tevis?"

Clearly, she did not have the slightest idea what he meant. "Of course I know who he is. He told us: Lochiel."

"Strahan's son," Aidan said, "who is nephew to Rhiannon, who is our great-uncle's daughter."

"What?" Blythe snapped. "What has this to do with anything?"

Aidan shrugged. "I thought I spoke clearly enough."

"But none of this makes *sense*—"

"Does it not?" He shrugged again. "I thought I had just named off a generation or two of our birthlines."

"Aidan—"

Sympathy dissipated. "By the gods, Blythe, you are not the first Cheysuli—*or* the first of our line—to lay with an Ihlini! Ian did it first. Then Brennan, my father . . . then Keely, my aunt. And *all of them tricked*, Blythe. D'ye hear what I'm telling you?"

She shouted back at him. "Do you expect me to *like* it? Do you expect me to be *proud?* Do you expect me *not to care?*"

"No," he said softly. "I expect you to survive."

She swallowed painfully. "He wanted me for the throne."

"And for a son," he told her. "I know, Blythe—I know it hurts to realize you have been tricked, been *used* . . . but it could have been much worse."

"Worse?" She was aghast. "He killed a three-day-old baby!"

"But not you. Not Dulcie, or the twins. Not your mother or father. Think again, Blythe . . . it could have been much worse."

"He would have killed us all. You were there. He wanted my father first—"

"Because he was discovered." Aidan sighed; he still tired easily. "Had I not uncovered who he was, Owain's death would have been remarked as a sad, tragic thing—no true-born heir for Solinde. But Hart made it clear there was an alternative—*your* child, Blythe . . . your son by Tevis of High Crags. Lochiel did not come here planning to murder everyone for the throne, but to marry for the throne."

Her lips were pressed flat. "Is that supposed to please me?"

Aidan picked up the saddle-pack. "Perhaps not, just now. Perhaps all you can see is the humiliation you feel because you bedded an Ihlini."

Anger flared forth. "Save your compassion, Aidan. You do not know what it was like."

"What it was like?" He threw down the saddle-pack. "I'll tell you, then, so we'll *both* be knowing about it: you bedded him willingly. It was probably your idea, so you could be putting an end to the unwanted suit of an unwanted kinsman come from Homana to find a bride. And *that*, my highborn Solindish, is why you're so angry now!"

Color peeled away. White-faced, Blythe stared as the tears ran down her face. Her chin trembled minutely. "I am ashamed," she whispered. "Oh, gods—so *ashamed!*"

For the first time since he had arrived, Aidan touched Blythe. And the *kivarna* remained silent.

"I know," he said as softly, as she moved into his arms. "*Shansu, meijhana*—I know."

"I want to die," she whispered. "Oh, gods—I want to *die*—"

He stroked her ragged hair. "Your parents have lost three children. Are you wanting to steal another?"

A shudder wracked her body. "I want it back the way it was. The way it was before he came."

"The Wheel of Life has turned."

With a quiet, deadly vehemence, "Then the gods are very cruel."

Aidan looked over her shoulder at the hand that would not work. "Sometimes," he agreed sadly.

Thinking of the Weaver, who let so many die so the Wheel could turn again.

PART III

PART III

Chapter One

He rode westward, bound for Andemir on the wild coast of Solinde battered by the Idrian Ocean. There he would take ship to Kilore, where the Aerie of Eagles perched upon the white chalk cliffs of Erinn, overlooking the Dragon's Tail. He had heard much about Kilore from his mother and from Deirdre; he wondered if it would fit.

Teel flew overhead. *Will you not marry the girl?*

Aidan frowned skyward, but thick trees screened the raven. The plains were far behind; all he could see was forest and the track stretching before him, sheltered by foliage. *Blythe? No. At least, not just now. There is the possibility of a child . . . all of us agreed it would be best to wait.* He paused, thinking of Blythe as she had been, alive with love for Tevis, and the Blythe he had seen at the last, devastated by Lochiel. *She needs time. The worst thing for her would be to enter into a marriage just now. She associates me with Lochiel. Once I am back from Erinn, and if there is no child, then we might think of marriage.*

Are children not desired?

Aidan wondered how he might explain things to a raven, whose understanding of human things was not always perfect. The *lir* were very wise, but not omniscient.

Finally he gave him an answer. *Preferably my own.*

There is the prophecy, Teel said lightly. *Two magic races united . . .*

Ruddy eyebrows ran up under hair. *Are you saying I should marry Blythe, even if she bears an Ihlini halfling?* It was the last thing he expected a *lir* to advocate.

Should, or should not, Teel said, *is your choice to make.*

As always. Aidan scowled in the raven's general direction. *Why should that change now?*

Teel made no answer to his *lir*'s irritation, though smugness thrummed through the link.

Aidan thought about it. Two magic races, indeed. How else to merge the bloodlines than by bedding an Ihlini?

Inwardly, he quailed. For all he had offered solace to a frightened, angry cousin, he did not wish what had happened to her to be a thing *he* faced.

"That gods-cursed ring," he said suddenly. "I should have gotten it from him. Somehow. Some way. That gods-cursed ring of my *jehan*'s has been the bane of us all."

He looked down at his left hand. He wore no rings on it, because he saw no sense in ornamenting a useless finger. No longer bandaged, the hand was obviously a hindrance rather than a helpmeet. The fingers had begun to curl as severed tendons died, but not all equally. The Tooth had sliced through vertically, so that the cut ran across his palm from fingers to heel. He had partial use of his thumb, and a bit in the smallest finger, but the other three were too damaged. Each day they twisted more tightly. Eventually what had been a hand would become an awkward claw.

Aidan tucked the hand into one thigh, trying to ignore it. But his belly squirmed unpleasantly. The fear he had fought back since learning of his injury rapped yet again at tightly sealed shields.

I am not so brave, he thought hollowly. *All my studied nonchalance when Blythe shouted at me was nothing but affectation. I do care, almost too much—I do not want to be* kin-wrecked. *I do not want to be Hart, left outside the clans. I lack his kind of courage—*

Almost against his will, he tried to fist the hand. All it did was spasm and send pain the length of his arm.

"I cannot go home," he said aloud. "If I do, they will know— *everyone* will know . . . and then they will take my name off the birthlines in Clankeep. A *kin-wrecked* man, I'd be—what kind of Mujhar is that?"

Lir, Teel asked, *do you ever plan to stop? Or will you ride through the night?*

"Through the night!" Aidan snapped, then cursed himself for a fool. What good would it do to rail at his *lir?* Teel knew as well as he how helpless he felt, how frightened he was of being *kin-wrecked.*

Lir. Teel again. *The sun is going down.*

So it was. The woods were alight with sunset, gilding trunks and trappings. If he did not stop soon, he would lose all of the light and be left to make camp in the darkness, in a wood he did not know.

Aidan sighed. "All right, *lir.* Your point has been made. Go off and catch your meal—I will make a camp."

But once he had settled on a sheltering thicket of saplings, Aidan discovered how he had taken for granted things such as two whole hands. It was nearly impossible to unsaddle his horse, and he realized it was the first of many things he would be unable to do well one-handed. The acknowledgment came painfully. At first he tried to ignore it and go on as he always did; in the end, completely defeated, he swore at intricate buckles done up for him in Lestra, cursing thoughtless horseboys; then humiliation followed. So much depended on *two* hands, on *eight* fingers and two thumbs; he offered one of the latter and only four of the former.

He could not undo the final buckle. Frustration welled up. Its power stunned even Aidan. "Is this some kind of test?" he shouted, staring up at the tree-screened sky. "Or merely ironic coincidence, something worth laughing about?"

There was no answer save the clattering of gear from a horse only half unpacked. Aidan's ruined hand dropped away from the trappings as he leaned against the horse, brow pressed into saddle. Frustration and fear and futility were suddenly overwhelming. He felt very much as he had facing the Lion as a child, railing at a chain that existed only in dreams.

"Why?" he murmured into leather. "Why did it happen to *me?* What did I do to deserve this?" He knew, even as he asked them, the questions were unworthy. They were also selfish and petulant, but at that moment he did not care. He was angry and very frightened, and very much a child.

Aidan squeezed his eyes closed. "Oh, gods—I will be *kin-wrecked* . . . I will have to go before Clan Council and tell them what happened, and display my infirmity . . ." Humiliation writhed deep in the pit of his belly. "They will do all the things they did to Hart—" He sucked in a deep, noisy breath, trying to ward away panic. "Unless—unless I *insist* . . . I am not Hart, who was meant for Solinde . . . I will be Prince of Homana, and one day Mujhar—if I *insist* they change the custom—" Aidan pressed himself from the horse, new resolve hardening. "I will insist. I *will.* How can they deny me? One day I will be *Mujhar*—"

But even as he said it, Aidan felt the infant resolve waver. To stand before Clan Council and denounce one of the oldest tradi-

tions of his race was not a thing he wanted to do. His father had
asked, had petitioned; had even, he had been told, shouted at Clan
Council, but it had changed nothing. Even for the Mujhar's middle
son, the tradition could not be altered. Too many things had been
changed. Now the older warriors, abetted by *shar tahls*, hung on to
the old customs to keep new ones at bay.

"Fools," Aidan said aloud. "Blind, arrogant fools . . . what use
is it to waste a warrior now? We are no longer hunted, no longer at
war . . . they would do better, all those *shar tahls*, to look to the future instead of to the past."

The horse shook his head. Still saddled, he was unhappy. It renewed Aidan's anger. "Fools, all of them . . . had I any influence,
I would change things."

Teel's tone was severe. *Questioning your* tahlmorra?

Was hunting so bad you are back already? Aidan abruptly drew
his long-knife and cut the strap in two. "Why not question?" he
asked aloud. "If they did not mean us to, they would not have
given us words with which to ask them."

Cutting that will not help you when you pack the gear tomorrow.

No. Anger spilled away. "Too late," Aidan muttered, dragging
saddle and packs free. Teel was right, of course. Teel was usually
right.

But then if you went in lir-*shape, buckles would not matter.*

Aidan stopped moving. He had been afraid to ask; now he knew
he had to. "Do I still have recourse to *lir*-shape?"

You did not lose *the hand. It merely changed its shape.*

The answer made him weak with realization. He released a
gusty breath, mixing laughter with heartfelt relief. "*Leijhana
tu'sai*, for that."

Teel uttered a croak. *And for other things as well.*

Aidan grinned and settled the gear, then tended to the horse. He
felt better already, knowing he still could fly. Being *kin-wrecked*
was bad enough, but not being able to fly—

Aidan put it out of his mind. Instead he thought of his grandsire, Niall, who lacked an eye. He bore scars worse than Aidan's.
No one called *him* half-man, or a failure. All knew better.

If he could become like Niall—

"So," he said aloud, "if I do not think myself crippled, I will not
be crippled."

Much better, Teel remarked. *You are bearable now.*

Aidan knelt to lay a fire. "*Leijhana tu'sai,* again." Couched in exquisite dryness.

Fix enough for two.

Aidan stopped moving stones, peering through twilight at the raven-shaped shadow perched in a nearby tree. "Was hunting *that* bad?"

Not for me—for him.

Aidan dropped the rock and spun, moving from knees to feet in one quick motion. His hand was on his long-knife, but he forbore to draw it.

"Wise," the man applauded. "At least you are not overhasty."

The prickles died from his flesh. "If you do this often, *someone* will be."

"Oh, no . . . I think not. The others do not hear me as a man. They hear me as the wind, or an animal, or something else offering no threat. You see?"

The stranger moved out of the sheltering trees. His gait was awkward, ungainly; he leaned upon a crutch thrust under an arm. His right leg was missing from below the knee, yet he moved almost noiselessly. He sounded nothing like a man.

Aidan took his hand away from the knife. "I have enough for two."

"You see? Being crippled is not so bad . . . it softens another man's soul."

Aidan stared as the stranger made his way out of darkness. He was old, though not truly ancient, with a fringe of white hair curling around his ears. The top of his head was bald. The rest of it was a face comprising the map of Homana; Aidan cut off the impulse of looking for landmarks he knew. The stranger deserved better, and *he* was better mannered.

Dark brown eyes glinted from under bushy white brows. "A fine young man," he said. "Well-mannered . . . and well-born?" He nodded to himself before Aidan could give him an answer. "There is the look of a fox about you: red hair and yellow eyes . . . would a fox be your *lir?*"

Only a flicker of surprise; Cheysuli were no longer strangers. "No," he said, "a raven." He thought of his other uncle. "Though a kinsman claims a vixen."

"Oh, aye; of course." He wore rough woolen homespun tunic belted over equally rough-made trews, and a single brogan shoe. The half-trew on his right leg was knotted beneath the stump.

Uneasily, Aidan thought of Tevis who was not Tevis at all, but Lochiel in disguise, using subterfuge to bring down a king. This was Solinde, after all; the homeland of the Ihlini. But his *kivarna* told him nothing, and neither did his *lir*.

The stranger levered himself down and sat beside the fire that was not, yet, a fire. He smiled up at Aidan. "You did say food, did you not?"

"Aye," Aidan knelt to resume his work. When the ring was built and kindling laid, he drew out flint and steel.

And realized almost at once it would take two hands to light.

The heat of shame set his face ablaze. He gritted his teeth tightly and refused to look at the man. He thought briefly of asking him—the stranger had two hands—but then realized it was folly. He would not always have someone to help. He needed to learn what to do.

Eventually, he managed. A twist of useless hand, pressure from new sources, careful concentration. The fire was lighted at last. Sighing, Aidan turned, wiping dampness from his forehead, and saw the stranger nodding.

"The patience will come," he said gently. "So will the acceptance." He gestured to his stump.

Helplessness spasmed. "When?" Aidan blurted. "All I can think of now is what I was before!"

"Natural, that. I have done it, myself." The old man slapped the palm of his hand against one thigh. "The bitterness will fade, along with the helplessness. There are worse things in this world than lacking a bit of flesh."

Aidan's grunt was politely noncommittal as he added fuel to the fire.

Dark eyes glittered. "Do you count yourself less than a man?"

Aidan, piling on wood, wanted not to answer. There was no way he could fully explain what it was to a man like himself, warrior-born and bred. But a glance at the stranger told him the man wanted an answer.

Do not blame him . . . do not punish him, either. Aidan sighed and schooled his tone into patience and tolerance. "You are not Cheysuli . . . it is difficult to explain, but our law forbids a maimed man from remaining part of the clan. The warrior is expelled, cast out . . . in Old Tongue, he is *kin-wrecked*."

"Why?" the stranger rasped. "Why throw away a warrior because he lacks a useful hand?"

Aye, Aidan agreed. But retreated from bitterness into an explanation. "In the old days, when we were hunted, it was necessary that each warrior be able to fight. If he could not, he could not protect his kin, or his clan . . . he ate food better given to someone who could."

The stranger scratched at his stump. "A harsh law, that. But there are times in a man's life—or in the life of his people—that hard decisions must be made. When it comes to survival . . ." Again he gestured at the stump.

Aidan's mouth twisted. "I am less sanguine than you. This is but two weeks old."

"Then I will ask it again: do you count yourself less than a man?"

He was, at first, angry: who was this old man, this stranger, to ask him such a thing? But then anger spilled away. He knew he spoke the truth, though part of him tried to deny it. "No. *This* is not me. Not a hand. Not a leg. What I am comes from somewhere else . . . somewhere in here." Aidan touched his breast.

The stranger nodded. "But you would rather have it back."

Aidan thought of Hart, and quailed. "Who would not want it back?"

"And what would you give up to have it?"

Aidan looked into the eyes. They were expressionless in the darkness, but oddly purposeful. He no longer doubted the stranger was more than merely a stranger, come upon him by coincidence.

Not here. Not in Solinde. Not where Lochiel yet roams.

His hand went to his knife. He thought again of Hart, offered reattachment of his still-whole hand at the Gate of Asar-Suti, in the depths of Strahan's fortress. He had heard the story. The cost was service to Strahan. The cost was the weight of his soul.

Resentment faded. So did bitterness. Certainty replaced both, and an unexpected resolve. "It is only a hand," he said clearly. "Not worth the price you want."

"But to be whole again . . . a true warrior . . . not to be *kin-wrecked*—"

Aidan laughed at the man. "Not for any price will I risk my *tahlmorra.*"

Firelight made the old man young. His eyes were dark as pits. He sat upon his rock with his good leg stretched before him and the crutch at his side. He rubbed the knotted stump. "Think again," he suggested. "Think twice, or thrice, or more."

Aidan shook his head.

The old man smiled. Once more he touched his stump, save now the leg was whole. "Come here," he said.

Aidan knelt down before him.

"Give me your ruined hand."

Aidan offered the god his hand. "What are you called?"

"In this guise, I am the Cripple." He studied Aidan's hand, examining curled fingers, the two-sided scar. "He struck well, the Ihlini. But it was not at you he struck."

"No."

"You took what was meant for someone else."

"He was a kinsman. And a king."

"Kings are men, too. Men die; kings die. How do you know it was not his *tahlmorra* to die?"

He had not thought of that. "But—I had to. I could not let him be struck down. I *had* to. There was no choice."

"Perhaps it was *tahlmorra*. Perhaps it was *yours,* Aidan."

He dared a glance at pit-black eyes. "Was it you who sent Donal?"

"I sent him. I could not allow you to die just yet, even as you could not allow your kinsman to be struck down. And so you live." He shrugged. "For now."

Aidan shivered. He tried to suppress it; could not. "Can you tell me what you intend for me? Am I always to travel blind? I will serve you willingly, if you only give me the chance."

"No. " The Cripple's tone was cold. "No man accepts everything willingly. Sacrifices must be made. Too often a man *knowing* the sacrifice would never be willing to make it, just as you were unwilling to let the Ihlini kill your kinsman."

"But—"

"You will know what you must when the time is come. Now, as for this . . ."

Aidan looked down. The twisted hand was still cradled in the hands of the god, but liquid spilled out. At first he feared it was blood, but it was rich and gold and heavy.

"Open your hand, Aidan."

A part of him wanted to laugh. But he knew better, now. He no longer thought to question.

The fingers, tendons reknitted, answered his bidding. The liquid congealed, then formed itself into a shape. Across his unscarred palm lay a heavy rune-worked link perfectly matched to the other two.

The god smiled on him. "You sacrificed no portion of your *tahlmorra*. The price for your hand was honesty; that, you gave tenfold."

"Donal," Aidan said, staring at the link.

The god did not answer. The Cripple, with his crutch, was gone.

Aidan laughed. He wanted to cry. But he thought the laughter best. When he was done, he looked at the link. Then he looked at his hand, perfect and whole and unblemished.

"Why?" he asked of Teel.

The shadow that was his *lir* fluttered feathers briefly. *He asked you questions. You answered them. I think you might be wise to assume you said what he wanted to hear.*

"But what do they *want* from me?"

They are gods. Who can say?

Futility possessed him. "Teel—please—help—"

When at last the raven spoke, his tone was more gentle than Aidan had ever heard from him. *I do what I can. It is all a* lir *can do, certainly all I can do . . . the gods made us, too. And even the* lir *cannot predict or explain a* tahlmorra *that is still on the loom.*

Aidan gripped the link. "Why me, Teel? What do they see in me? Why do they come to *me?*"

Through the *lir*-link he heard a sigh. *I cannot say,* Teel answered. *No one has told* me, *either.*

Chapter Two

Crying out, Aidan awoke abruptly, thrusting himself upright into the dawn. For a long moment he did not know where he was, only that he was *somewhere* . . . and then he realized he was not in the Great Hall of Homana-Mujhar, trying to touch a chain in the lap of the Lion; nor was he in Lestra, staring in shock at a hand sliced nearly in two by poisoned Ihlini steel.

"Agh," he said aloud, "they *are* starting again!"

Teel, in a tree, fluttered. *What are starting again?*

"The dreams." Aidan rubbed his face, stripping dew-dampened hair out of gritty eyes and being glad all over again he could use both hands for the motion. He lowered his recovered hand and examined it critically again, as he had every morning since meeting the Cripple. Five days, now. The relief had not passed.

Neither had the dreams.

He wore three links at his belt, rather than two. They chimed as he rode, reminding him constantly of dreams and gods and tasks. He slept poorly and woke too often during the night, trying to banish the dream-chain long enough to get a proper night's sleep. He could not recall a time when he had felt so confused, so disoriented. At least before the gods had come to him, he had believed himself merely fanciful. Now he believed himself mad.

Sighing, Aidan peeled back blankets and kicked legs free. "Time to go, *lir.* Erinn gets no closer while I lie here in skins and wool, thinking about dreams."

It gets no farther, either.

Aidan forbore to answer and commenced packing his horse. He had long since learned commenting on Teel's remarks made no difference. The raven was cleverer than he; his best wager was to ignore him altogether, because then there was no clear-cut victory.

Of course, it meant the contest continued.

But it was better than nothing at all.

*   *   *

When he came across the wagon with its bright-painted canvas canopy, Aidan gave it a wide berth. He was ready to pass it by and forget about it, as travelers usually did on the road; often, it was safest. But the woman on the seat was so vivid she caught his eye and turned his head quite literally; Aidan nearly stared.

Her answering smile was so warm and guileless he could not simply ignore it—not if he desired to name himself a man for he rest of his life. He slowed his horse at once and waited for her team to catch up, then fell in beside her. His greeting was in accented Solindish; hers in the same tongue, though flawless. Much as he had expected.

Black hair fell in tight, tangled ringlets all the way to a narrow waist. She wore a chaplet of bright gilt dangling with false pearls that framed a heart-shaped face, and copper hoops in both ears. Black eyes were bold but also shy, as if she longed to be a bawd but had not yet learned how to do it properly. She was not truly beautiful, not as Ilsa was, but she had a burning liveliness of spirit that put Aidan in mind of his mother and Deirdre.

He glanced beyond her shoulder to the closed canvas canopy. "You should not be traveling the road alone."

"No," she agreed gravely, though her eyes were bright with mirth. "It would be a very bad thing. And it is why I do not do it." Her hand parted the bright canopy, baring the face of a young man so remarkably beautiful Aidan thought it might do better on a woman.

"A very bad thing," the young man said, crawling through the canopy to take his place on the seat beside the woman. "But then we know better than to allow Ashra to go anywhere alone . . . there are men who would stoop to stealing her to share more than she might care to."

And men who would steal you . . . But Aidan's manners would not allow him to say it.

Like Ashra, the young man had black hair, though he lacked her length or ringlets. The bones of his face were truly beautiful, and the skin smooth and dark and unblemished. Something in his expression and the assemblage of bones reminded Aidan of his own race, though he had never seen a Cheysuli with such magnificent purity of features, or green eyes. And yet there was something else as well. He was most like Ilsa, Aidan decided finally, though dark instead of light. His suppleness bespoke exceptional grace, and his speaking voice was firm, yet melodious.

Green eyes assessed Aidan. "I am Tye, singer by trade. Ashra dances. And the old man, Siglyn, is a magician." He gestured toward the canopy. "Travel is harsh on old bones; he will be well enough, but he requires rest." Briefly he eyed Aidan's saddle-packs, the travel-stained brown cloak drawn over both shoulders. "Where are you bound?"

"Westward to Andemir."

Ashra laughed. Her voice was low and, to Aidan, attractive. "Andemir for us, also. Perhaps we shall be road-partners."

"Ashra," Tye said quietly, with a quick warning gesture from one hand.

She laughed again, tossing back ringlets and shrugged a supple shoulder. "Your turn to drive, Tye. I will question this stranger, since you are so mistrustful."

"With reason," Tye said grimly, as she handed over the reins. "Which you know as well as I."

Obligingly, Aidan gave them his name, though omitting his rank. He had learned if a man truly wanted to know what others thought, he would do well to keep quiet about heritage and titles. People spoke more freely if they believed themselves of a kind.

He meant to ask them more about themselves, but Teel interrupted by alighting on Aidan's left shoulder. Ashra cried out in delight. "A tame raven!"

Aidan grinned. "Only sometimes."

"And other times?" she challenged.

Tye flicked her a warning glance, which she did not see. Aidan frowned. "For a troupe of players making a living off the road, you seem uncommonly wary."

Tye's austere expression—far too restrictive for the fluid lines of his face—relaxed, but only slightly. "With good reason, stranger—we were accosted three days back by a band of brigands who took what little coin we had. The old man was injured—struck on the head—and I have since learned to be suspicious of everyone." He looked at the raven. "But none of *them* had a bird, or the likelihood of wanting one, so I doubt you are one of them. Forgive my bad manners."

A line knitted Ashra's black brows. They were heavy and oddly straight, but Aidan found the look exotically attractive. "If the raven is tame only *some* of the time, as you say, what of the other times?"

"The other times he is most annoying," Aidan answered truthfully. "But to be fair, he is not tame . . . Teel is a *lir.*"

Black eyes widened. *"Lir* are blessed of the gods . . ." She looked more sharply at Aidan. "But you are not Cheysuli. What are you doing with one?"

He felt a brief flicker of surprise that she should know anything about who did and did not consort with the *lir*, but answered her question easily enough by throwing the cloak back from his shoulders to display the gold weighting bare arms. A hooking of hair behind left ear brought the raven-shaped ornament into daylight.

Even Tye frowned. "A *red*-haired Cheysuli?"

Aidan smiled. "My mother is Erinnish. This is her legacy . . . left to my own devices, I might have preferred black." He affected a negligent shrug. "But I do have my father's eyes."

For confirmation, Tye looked. And nodded, patently unimpressed. "Yellow as a beast's—" He grinned. "Aye, aye . . . no insult intended. I only tease, shapechanger."

Ashra raised level brows. "He would make a most handsome beast."

Tye grunted. "You are a woman. Women are often overly imaginative."

She stroked back a ringlet, retucking it under the chaplet. "Solinde is ruled by a Cheysuli."

"The usurper," Tye agreed, then laughed as Aidan stiffened. "Have you no sense of humor? I *tease*, shapechanger . . . does the animal in your blood keep you from enjoying the quips and jests of others?"

"When they are at my expense." Aidan smiled blandly. "Too often such words are meant, Solindish . . . do you mean yours?"

Tye sighed. "If I meant them, I would not now allow you to ride with us to Andemir." He paused. "If you desire to ride with us."

"He might if you sang," Ashra suggested.

Tye flicked her a quelling glance. Aidan began to wonder if they were brother and sister, or husband and wife. He hoped it was the former.

"When do we stop?" called a querulous voice from within the canopy. "Or will you rattle my bones into dust?"

Teel departed Aidan's shoulder, slapping his face with one wing. Aidan, muttering, rubbed at a stinging eye as Ashra laughed.

Tye nodded. "We stop, old man. Soon." He shot a quick glance at Aidan. "Will you share our food?"

He blinked the sting away and nodded. "My thanks. I have wine."

Ashsra's boldly charming smile flashed out again. "So have *we*."

Camp was established off the road in a cluster of sheltering trees. The sun, sliding down the line of horizon, painted slats of light and shadow across the canvas canopy. Aidan thought it much like the pavilions at Clankeep, bright blue painted with equally vivid figures: a dancer dressed in red and green and gold; a singer with wooden lute; a magician conjuring smoke and fire from the air. The wagon itself was of dark wood, but its wheels were painted red, lined with yellow on inner rims and spokes. Altogether it provided a most tempting—and visible—target to brigands.

Tye tended the horses as Ashra assisted the old magician from the wagon and escorted him to the patchwork cushion by the fire Aidan had laid. He was a very old man dressed in gray wool robe over time-faded indigo linen draperies. A plain leather belt with tarnished silver buckle snugged a narrow waist. The robe hung loosely, swirling a half-torn hem about swollen ankles. His feet were shod in crushed leather slippers. He scuffed through turf and fallen leaves as if movement were very painful.

Aidan went to him at once, offering a second arm. A pair of rheumy blue eyes fixed themselves on his face, weighing him against some inner measurement. But they were proud eyes, and freely disdained Aidan's arm. The thin mouth tightened as his grip on Ashra increased.

Aidan relinquished his offer at once, stepping away with a slight inclination of his head. Ashra helped the old man sit down on the cushion, then pulled his robe closed.

"Siglyn," she said softly, "his name is Aidan. He is bound for Andemir, as we are."

"What is that on his arms?" the old man asked harshly. "He carries enough wealth to bribe all the brigands in the world away from us."

"Hush," she chided gently. "He is Cheysuli, from Homana. That is the *lir*-gold a warrior receives when he becomes a man." Black eyes flicked in Aidan's direction, silently apologizing. "He is not a brigand come to rob us, or a man offering unwanted charity. Look at him again; you will see what he is, merely by looking into his eyes."

"Faugh!" The old man glowered as she bent to make certain he was comfortable on his cushion. His hair was white, very thin, very long. A matching beard straggled down the front of his robe. But his eyes, for all their agedness, were sharp as he glared at Aidan. "Come, boy," he ordered brusquely.

Aidan bit his tongue. Never in his life had he been treated so rudely or disrespectfully. Nevertheless he did as ordered and moved closer. He stood quietly, unwilling quite yet to bow, though undoubtedly it was what the old man wanted.

Siglyn eyed him. "Shapechanger, are you?" The flesh of his face creased. "Aye, perhaps you are, for all the fire on your head . . . you have the look in your eyes."

Aidan blinked. "The—look?"

"The wildness, boy! The feyness. Arrogant as an eagle, in its aerie above the world . . . and a wolf at bay betimes, mistrusting the selfsame world." Siglyn bared yellowed teeth. His fingernails were clean, but cracked; idly, he chewed them. "I've lived a long time, boy. I've seen many things. Not so long ago your race and mine were at war."

Aidan smiled; the old so often shortened time. "Long enough."

Siglyn frowned and removed fingers from mouth. "I fought in the wars with Carillon . . . you lack the accent, boy."

Ruddy brows rose. "Which one?"

"The one I heard, when we took prisoners." Nastily, the old man grinned. "You speak it differently."

Aidan shrugged. "I am from Mujhara. There are dialects—"

"Hah! Mujhara is the king's city." Siglyn sighed thoughtfully. "Never been there . . . never been out of Solinde. Been to Lestra, though, and *she's* a king's city." Blue eyes sharpened once more. "Why are you come to Solinde?"

Inwardly, Aidan sighed. But he had been taught to treat the elderly with great respect, regardless of the treatment received in return. "I am on my way to Erinn. To Kilore. I will take ship from Andemir."

Siglyn gifted him with a malignant stare. "You could have done *that* from Hondarth. Why are you come to Solinde?"

Aidan cleared his throat, maintaining a neutral tone. "I have kin in Lestra."

Tye came back from hobbling and graining horses. He pushed an arm through thick black hair and dropped down to tend the fire Aidan had been called away from. "Lestra," he said lightly, as if tasting the word. "*Shapechanger* kin in Lestra." He fed in a length of wood, then slanted a glance at Ashra and the old man. "Not many can claim that."

"A few." Aidan, glad to turn from Siglyn, knelt also and added wood.

The old man had not given up. He raised his voice preemptorily. "How is the *Mujhar?*"

Aidan laughed and dropped another faggot on the flames. "The last time I saw him, he was quite well. But you will not trap me like that, old man . . . I am not in hiding. You have only to *ask*, instead of wasting your time—and mine . . . hinting."

The magician laughed unpleasantly. "I *like* hinting," he said. "Not much left for an old man's nights."

Ashra knelt down next to Aidan and put a hand on his arm. "Who are you?" she asked. "Siglyn is not usually so bad . . . are you someone he knows?"

Aidan laughed once. "Only someone he thinks he knows, because he is a busybody." He looked at Ashra. In firelight, her bold features were softened. "I am grandson to the Mujhar."

Her mouth slackened slightly. Then she threw back ringlets with a toss of her head. The hand was gone from his arm.

Tye grunted. "I thought you looked too soft for a man of honest blood . . . and yet you ride with no servants."

Aidan sighed in resignation. "We do not *all* move about the countryside with great trains of servants in our wakes." Although his mother would have liked it. "It is not a Cheysuli custom to be dependent on others."

Tye laughed, one winged black brow rising. "Is that so? Well, I am surprised. I had thought all of royal birth had blood so thin they required propping up by the labor of others considerably less blessed."

Aidan grunted. "There speaks ignorance. Had you met your own lord, you would never say that."

Tye's tone was dry. "People such as we only rarely meet his like."

Aidan's tolerance was gone. He rose, wrapping the cloak around his arms. "I offered you wine; you may have it. But perhaps you would be more content without my company."

Ashra was at his side instantly. "Oh, no!" she cried. "Forgive him, my lord . . . Tye is often overhasty when he speaks, but never when he sings. Only wait, and you will hear." She cast a glance at the magician. "As for Siglyn, he is old. He forgets what he says. Bide with us the night."

The old man, thus invoked, stirred testily. "Don't speak for me when I have a tongue yet in my head! I say what I wish, and to *whom* I wish, no matter what they like."

Ashra grimaced, then smiled tentatively at Aidan. "Will you stay? You would be safer with a group . . . and we would no doubt be considerably safer with a Cheysuli."

Tye grinned. "Prove to us I am wrong. Show us you are worthy of our respect."

Aidan opened his mouth to refuse, but Teel was in the link. *Why not?* he asked. *It might prove less tedious than a night without argument.*

I have you *for that.*

One bright eye glinted. *A* lir *is many things, but a* lir *is not a woman.*

Aidan very nearly laughed aloud, but good manners kept him from it. It was discourteous to stay in the link any longer than was necessary, with the unblessed around.

He looked at Ashra. He thought about Teel's comment. And smiled. "I will stay."

When Aidan discovered the Solindish entertainers had little enough to eat, he offered to share his own rations in addition to his wine. The offer was accepted only after a brief discussion—in Solindish—that Aidan barely followed because of the dialect: Tye was uncertain they should place themselves so heavily in a stranger's debt, while Siglyn muttered about brigands who starved an old man by stealing food from his mouth; Ashra, who was hungry, said both of them were fools and *she* would eat shapechanger food even if they would not.

Scowling, Tye gave her leave to accept the offer. Ashra thanked Aidan prettily, black eyes flashing beneath lowered lashes as she dipped a graceful, if unstudied, curtsy, but it was Siglyn who ate more and faster than any of them. Aidan wondered idly where it showed itself on the old man, for he was thin and stringy almost to the point of emaciation.

When the food was gone, the wineskins were passed more frequently. Siglyn had his own and was disinclined to share, saying the vintage was a personal favorite, but Tye was companionable enough as he handed his skin to Aidan. Ashra drank sparingly, but high color came into her face as she stared transfixed at the fire.

Tye settled himself more comfortably against a rolled blanket thrust beneath his neck. "What is it like?" he asked, when he was done swallowing wine. "What is it like to take on the shape of an *animal?*"

Having done his share of damage to a wineskin, Aidan was not irritated by Tye's disrespect. He lay propped against his saddle and smiled. "You are asking the wrong man. There are others better suited to explaining the *lir*-shape, which is very personal—and others better suited to understanding."

For a long moment only the crackle of flames broke the heavy silence as Tye considered the irony. Then he smiled, lifted a wineskin in wry tribute, nodded his head at Teel, perched atop the wagon canopy. "Try to explain. I will *try* to understand."

Aidan shrugged, vaguely discomfited. He did not quite know where to start.

Tye frowned. "Do you not change? Do you not become *him?*"

Answering was easier. "No, not *him.* I become another."

"But a raven."

"Aye, a raven. That is how you know the shape we become: by the *lir* who accompanies us." He shrugged. "No matter what the stories say, we are not free to become anything—or any*one*—we desire. We are not monsters, or creatures of darkness. The gods made us, Tye . . . and they made the *lir.*"

Ashra's tone was detached as she stared transfixed into the flames. "Why did you choose a raven?"

"The choosing was not mine. It is never the warrior's choosing . . . there is more to it than that." Aidan squirmed into a more comfortable position, hugging wineskin between elbow and ribs. "When I was fourteen I fell sick—the *lir*-sickness, we call it—and knew only a great and terrible need. There is no cure for the sickness, no relief for the need, except to go out into the forest and find a *lir.* And so I did."

Tye's doubt was manifest. "Alone?"

Brief irritation flickered. "Of course alone . . . it is not a thing for another to share."

"They let a fourteen-year-old boy—one who would one day be king—go out alone into the forest?"

" 'They,' as you call them, are also Cheysuli. No one would stand in my way, least of all Cheysuli kin."

Tye frowned thoughtfully. "And so you found *him*."

Aidan shrugged. "Teel and I found each other. For the *lir* it is much the same: they know a need, and they fill it. A Cheysuli with no *lir*—and a *lir* with no warrior—is incomplete. Once linked, we are whole."

"With the ability to shift your shape."

Aidan nodded. "But only into whatever shape the *lir* represents. If I had two *lir*, as did my great-grandsire, Donal, I would then be able to assume two different forms. But I have only Teel . . . the gods are sparing with gifts."

Tye's laughter mocked. "The gods, when they do anything at all, are sparing with everything. Especially good fortune. Only the bad flows generously."

Aidan grunted mild disapproval. "They will hear you."

Tye made a derisive sound of dismissal. "The gods hear nothing. Why should they? Do you think they care? Do you think they pay the slightest attention to any of us?"

Ashra stirred. "Hush," she said quietly. "You offer offense to our guest."

The singer put out a hand to touch Ashra's arm. She sat close by his side, and Aidan had decided, with regret, they were not brother and sister. "You have already told him I am overhasty when I speak," Tye reminded her. "Why should I hide it now?"

She slanted him a glance from the corners of her eyes. "Offense should never be given a guest. Think what you like in private . . . there is no need to speak it."

Aidan waved a hand. "No need to bother yourself, Ashra—I think Tye and I will never be reconciled about much of anything."

Siglyn spoke for the first time since the meal. "Do you think only you are right, then, in what you believe? Because of your birth?"

Aidan sighed heavily. "My birth means nothing at all. Why do you dwell on it? In the clans only the blood matters, and its continuation, not in what flesh it flows. Do you see? I am Cheysuli first: child of the gods. I am then a warrior, and I honor my *tahlmorra*. I am a prince last of all."

"That," Tye declared, "is not possible."

Aidan, sliding into an Erinnish cadence, fixed him with a baleful eye. "I'd be venturing, my pretty lad, 'twould be far easier for me to shed my royalty than for the likes of you to gain it."

Ashra laughed, not in the least taken aback by Aidan's verbal attack on Tye. "Well said!"

"Indeed," Siglyn agreed morosely.

Tye, unaffronted, merely grunted. "Most probably. But I have no wish to be a prince."

Aidan nearly laughed; his *kivarna* bespoke the lie. "No man *never* wishes he were a prince, Solindishman. Had you the chance—"

"—he would accept it instantly," Ashra finished. "And you *would*, Tye."

Tye grunted again. "But it is bootless. There will be no chance for me to find out. I am only a singer, and a poor one."

Ashra was instantly outraged. "Poor! You are the best I have ever heard!"

Tye grinned at her. "And how many have you heard?"

Color stained her cheeks. "Enough," she said softly, touching fingers to his face. "Enough—and more—to know."

The old man tightened his robe around thin shoulders. "What magic do *you* claim, shapechanger?"

Aidan, considering, recalled Siglyn's trade was in magic, and fashioned his answer to suit it. "Nothing to rival yours, old man." He smiled disarmingly. "All I claim is *lir*-shape."

Siglyn grunted. "Nothing more? No more than that?"

Aidan shrugged, making light of his answer. "We can heal, when required."

Rheumy blue eyes narrowed. "And?"

Aidan put off answering by unplugging the wineskin and drinking, then carefully squeaking the cork home. "Some say there is a third gift," he admitted frankly. "But it is only rarely used. We do not care for what it does to a man's soul."

The old man smiled. It was not a pleasant smile. "And what does it do to a man's soul, that you would quail from it?"

Aidan's gaze did not waver. "It takes," he answered flatly. "It overpowers. It sucks away a man's will and leaves him with nothing at all save what the other tells him."

Siglyn's eyes shone. He grunted approval, as if vindicated. "I thought so. I've heard it said many a time the Cheysuli have he power to be demons, if they choose."

Aidan's tone was clipped. "We do *not* choose," he declared. "We understand too well what compulsion can do to a man, and we choose otherwise. The power to be demons is reserved by the Ihlini. It is what they practice."

Tufted white brows jerked upward. "*Do* we?" Siglyn asked. "Is that what we practice?"

Even as the purple flame shrouded the old man's fingers, Aidan was on his feet. The knife was in his hand, but Ashra was at his side instantly, touching his wrist.

"No," she said softly.

Siglyn laughed. It had a rusty, creaking sound, as if only rarely used. "I have taken you by surprise."

Aidan, whose immediate testing of the *lir*-link told him there was no interference, frowned at the old man. "Aye," he said abstractedly. "But—I can reach my *lir*. And he said nothing—"

"Does it matter?" Ashra asked.

"He should have warned me. A *lir* always gives warning of an enemy."

Her fingers turned the knife downward. "That should tell you something."

Aidan barely heard her. He stared across the fire at Tye, whose green eyes were odd in the flickering light. "And you?"

Tye smiled. "I am, as you are, many things. Solindish: aye. Ihlini as well. But also a singer. My teacher was Taliesin."

"Taliesin has been dead for more than twenty years!"

"I am older than I look." Tye sat upright, setting aside his wineskin. "You are not a fool, Aidan of Homana. Why act like one now?"

Bitterness welled up. "Am I a fool to be wary of the enemy?"

Siglyn glared. "How quick you are to assume the worst of us. Aye, you are a fool! You have not wit enough to *ask* your bird if we mean you any harm. And yet only moments before you condescended to inform us a prince is no different from any other."

Teel? Aidan asked. *Why was I not warned? You should have told me . . . and I should have sensed the interference in the link*— His belly tightened. —*unless they also have something of a Cheysuli for use in making shields*—

Teel sounded disgusted. *Are you so blind as that? Or have you become a lackwit?*

I am no lackwit because I prefer to know *who my enemies are*— Aidan broke it off laggardly, belatedly comprehending. *Is that it? Solindish, Ihlini, or no—they are not my enemy?*

In the link, Teel sighed. *There is hope for you yet.*

Irritated, Aidan glared again at the old man. "Do you blame me for being dubious? Our blood has been at war for centuries. You *yourself* fought—" He frowned. "And if you fought Carillon, it means you fought *with* Bellam."

"Of course it does," the old man snapped. "I was a loyal Solindishman—"

"—a loyal *Ihlini*—"

"—and dedicated to my land." Siglyn glared. "You are rude. You have no respect for the aged—"

"You have no respect for *me*—"

"Because we fooled you?" Siglyn grinned, baring old teeth. "You fooled yourself. Because *we* did not declare our race, as you do with all your barbaric, ostentatious gold—" he made a rude gesture all too dismissive of the *lir*-gold "—then we are obviously tricksters out to spill your blood." Siglyn indicated the knife still clutched in Aidan's hand. "Of course, *you* have the weapon . . ." He sighed, glancing at Tye. "The Cheysuli spend much of their time telling gullible Homanans that we are all demons and servants of Asar-Suti, the Seker—without once considering our feelings."

"Your *feelings!*" Aidan was astounded. "You are the enemy— at least, some of you are . . ." He scowled blackly at the old man, disliking the morass he was, from all appearances, walking into on his own. "*Too many* of you are. Do you know how many of my race—of my *kin*—your kind have killed? Do you know that Strahan's son only weeks ago murdered a helpless infant, and then tried to kill your lord?"

"What baby?" Ashra asked. "We have been long on the road, and news travels slowly . . ." A vertical line drew heavy brows together. "What baby, Aidan?"

"My cousin," he answered curtly. "Lochiel murdered him in his bed without even so much as touching him."

She exchanged a glance with Tye. Neither of them spoke, but Aidan sense they were not pleased by the news. Ashra squeezed his wrist briefly in a gesture he interpreted as sympathy.

Siglyn shifted on his cushion, clearly annoyed. "Strahan was a puffed-up, arrogant fool with delusions of godhood . . . must you judge us all by him?"

"It is a bit difficult *not* to, when he has been so dedicated to destroying my race. And now his son as well—"

"But we are not his sons, or his daughter," Ashra said quietly. "We are merely Solindish-born Ihlini, trying to make a living in a land gone mad from war." She sighed, removing her hand from Aidan's wrist. "Strahan has done more damage to his race than any other, save for Tynstar. It was he who *began* it all."

Siglyn grunted. "You know nothing about Tynstar, girl. I knew him personally—" But he broke it off, waving a hand at Aidan. "Sit down, sit down. If you are to hear the truth, you should do it with cloth beneath your rump and good wine close to hand." Tufted brows rose. "Sit *down,* boy!"

In the link, Teel suggested it might be wise. No sense in standing when one could sit and be more comfortable.

Aidan sat. But was not comfortable.

Chapter Three

"First," Aiden said, before any of them could speak, "I want to know how. *And* why."

Ashra, who added fuel to the fire, cast him a puzzled glance across one slender shoulder. Ringlets writhed, "What do you mean?"

"I should have known you. All my life I have been told a Cheysuli can tell when an Ihlini is near, because of the interference in the *lir*-link. And the *lir* always forewarns—" Aidan grimaced, not looking at Teel, "—*usually* forewarns." He sighed, shifting the wineskin in his lap. "None of us knew Lochiel because he had a ring once worn by my father. It has been bespelled for years, ever since he gave it, unknowing, to an Ihlini witch. Rhiannon." He dismissed her with a gesture. "Lochiel has the ring now, and he used it. Is that how Teel and I did not know you? Have you a like item?"

Tye shook his head as he settled down against his rolled blanket. "Have you met none of us before?"

Aidan nearly smiled. "No Ihlini has come into Mujhara—or Clankeep—for many, many years."

Ashra was clearly startled. "And you have been nowhere else?"

Her unfeigned astonishment at first puzzled him, until he realized she had most likely spent her life on the road, and could not comprehend a man who lived only in two places.

And then he considered how that sounded, even to him: he had been nowhere in the world save Mujhara and Clankeep. Even though one day he would rule a realm it took weeks to ride across.

Tye grinned. "All unknowing, she strikes true." He squirted wine into his throat, swallowed, then plugged the opening. "You did not know us because there was nothing to know."

"You are Ihlini—"

"—and kin." Tye's green eyes were odd in the light. "Without your gold and your *lir*, would another Cheysuli know you as Cheysuli?"

Aidan gestured. "I may lack the color, but—"

Siglyn cut him off. "Answer the question."

Aidan waited a moment, marshaling his courtesy, then did as Siglyn ordered. "Without my gold and my *lir*, it is possible he would not . . . but if you knew how to look for other things—"

Tye sighed in disgust. "He will not cooperate."

"Aidan." Ashra's voice was soft. "You did not know we are Ihlini because we are kin. It is true all Cheysuli bear certain similarities in color and shape of bones, but past that there is only what resides in here." She touched one breast. "We are less obvious than Cheysuli, lacking a uniform color and the *lir*, but our hearts are the same, and our blood."

Aidan avoided her eyes, looking instead at his healed hand. There was no scar, but he remembered all too well the pain, the shock, the acknowledgment of Lochiel's intent.

Siglyn's voice was harsh. "It's an easy enough answer, boy: we did not drink of the cup. We are uncommitted Ihlini—save to our land—and therefore Asar-Suti is not in us. Our blood is ours, not his . . . have you or any of your kin ever known a hostile Ihlini who was not one of the Seker's?"

Aidan, who had known none at all, could only think on the stories he had heard. His uncles had known Ihlini, but all had served Asar-Suti. Keely's contact had been with Strahan and his minions, all sworn to the Seker. There was Rhiannon, but she, too, belonged to the Seker. Every Ihlini, save for one, had meant his kin harm.

Then he stirred, recalling. "There was Taliesin."

Tye shook his head. "Taliesin repudiated the Seker. It was why Tynstar made him drink of the blood, so he would live forever knowing what had been done in the name of his race . . . and it was why Strahan destroyed his hands."

Aidan stared into flames. "Then I have never known—or known *of*—a hostile Ihlini who did not serve the Seker."

"To drink of the blood is to bind yourself to Asar-Suti," Siglyn said. "The bond, once forged, cannot be broken, save by death. Taliesin eventually was cast out—but an uncommitted Ihlini always knows one of the Seker's, just as a Cheysuli does."

Tye's lips peeled back. "There is a stench," he said clearly, "that clings to everything they touch."

Aidan drew in a breath. "And so you are saying they are different from you?"

Ashra smiled. "They have always been different."

He found breathing difficult. He wanted to laugh, but there was nothing to laugh *at*, save the memories of lessons taught so carefully in Clankeep. Lessons all Cheysuli learned, believing implicitly, because the *shar tahls* said so. If it was said by a *shar tahl*, it was so: everyone knew that. The *shar tahls* were the guardians of the prophecy, of the old ways, making certain tradition remained untainted and the service continued unbroken.

"Untainted," Aidan murmured, "by such things as the altering of a custom called *kin-wrecking*, even though the need is gone."

"What?" Siglyn snapped; the old man, regardless of revelation, was unchanged.

Aidan swallowed painfully. "What if they are wrong? What if, after too many years, it has become *habit* to hate Ihlini—*habit* to name them enemy, suitable only for killing? Do you see? We are taught it very young: to hate, and fear, and kill . . ." He shut his eyes and rubbed wearily at his face. "The prophecy says we must unite two magic races, and yet the *shar tahls* tell us time and time again we should have no congress with Ihlini, because Ihlini want to destroy us."

"*They* do," Ashra explained. "Those of the Seker *do*—but not the rest of us."

Tye's tone was oddly gentle. "Teachings can become twisted. There may be no intent, but it occurs . . . and eventually the twisting becomes unchanging tradition."

Aidan stared at them all. "Are we wrong? Are all the teachings twisted?"

A glint showed in Tye's eyes. "Why ask us? We are Ihlini. The enemy. And this is merely a clever game played to cause you grief, confusion—and doubt." He smiled crookedly. "Ask your *lir*, Cheysuli. Ask your other self."

Aidan did it through the *lir*-link, because there was no interference. Because he could, in spite of Ihlini presence. Because he was afraid not to, as if asking aloud cheapened the *lir*-bond his kind revered so much.

Tell me, he said. *Are all the teachings wrong?*

Teel did not answer.

Tell me, Aidan repeated. *Are we blinded by the very thing that all Cheysuli serve?*

The *lir*-link quivered briefly. Teel's reluctance to answer was manifest.

Aidan forsook the link. "Tell me!" he shouted. "I have conversed with *gods* . . . do I not deserve an answer from the *lir* they gave me?"

Teel's tone lacked his customary acerbity. *The times demand harsh truths,* he said at last. *And sometimes harsher falsehoods.*

Falsehoods. Aidan clamped his teeth shut. *Are you saying all of it is a lie?*

They have taught what had to be taught.

Why did it have *to be taught?*

Ignorant men do ignorant things.

Such as ignoring prophecies.

After a moment: *Aye.*

And ignoring the prophecy results in no Firstborn.

Feathers were fluffed. *Aye.*

You have us, Aidan said intently. *You have us, and the Ihlini. Are we not enough? Why must there be the Firstborn?*

Because they were firstborn . . . and the gods want them back.

Suspicion roused itself. *Firstborn—bestborn? Is that what it is? The gods gave us self-rule, and the bloodlines fragmented because of Ihlini ambition. So the only way of restoring the balance—of regaining the bestborn children—is to make them out of the bits and pieces culled from all the lands.*

Not all. Teel sounded himself again. *Not all—only four. Four realms and two races.*

Aidan felt rage building. With effort, he damped it down. *If they want them so badly, why not simply* make *them? It was what they did in the first place!*

Teel sighed faintly. *They gave their children self-rule. Self-rule perpetuates itself . . . none of you are what you once were, and the gods can force nothing. They can only ask, and suggest, and guide—*

Gods are gods! Aidan cried. *Gods can do anything!*

Even create a being greater than themselves.

Greater—?

There is nothing a god can do that you cannot do.

But there is—

All that a god can do can be done by the children. Only the ways and means are different.

Teel—

The raven sighed. *There is intellect, and freedom, and skills beyond belief. They gave you everything. They made you what you were*—you *made you what you are.*

I do not know what I am, anymore.

Amusement touched the link. *Child of the gods. What more is there to be?*

It was too much to contemplate. Aidan withdrew from the link and sat motionless near the fire, staring sightlessly into flames. Light burned first into his eyes, then into his brain.

"Times have changed," he murmured. "Everything has changed."

No one said anything.

"It was a means." Aidan stirred a little. "A means, nothing more. A way of communicating. Too often one man will not listen to another, no matter how wise he is . . . but if a *god* says it—" *Oh, gods.* "—if a god says it, one or two may listen. Then one or two more. Until eventually a grouping becomes a clan, and a clan becomes a people." He sighed heavily. "We serve a collection of words. And the words have become twisted."

Ashra's voice was soft. "Then set them straight," she said. "You have it in you, Aidan."

His laughter was bittersweet. "I have nothing inside me now save a profound emptiness."

Green eyes glinted. "Fill it," Tye suggested.

Aidan sighed and slung aside the wineskin, "I need sleep. I need a true sleep, not this pale mockery filled with too many dreams . . ."

"Everyone dreams," Tye said.

"Not like this. Not as I do." Aidan spread his skins. "Not so vividly, or so unsettlingly."

Ashra was very calm. "Siglyn speaks dreams."

"He *speaks*—?" But Aidan shook his head. "No insult intended, but I do not need a road magician's tricks—"

"And I'll give you none," snapped Siglyn. "I speak truths, not falsehoods."

Truths and falsehoods. Much as Teel had mentioned. Aidan looked across the fire at the old man. Shadows and firelight warred in his face, making planes and hollows and creases. The rheumy eyes were bright. The challenge in them implicit.

Aidan nodded once. "Speak my dreams," he said. "Divide the falsehoods from the truths."

The old man smiled. "First there is Tye, and Ashra. Then I will speak your dreams."

Chapter Four

Tye brought his lute from the wagon and seated himself on his blanket across the fire from Aidan. The instrument was delicate, of a pale blond wood with ivory pegs and inlay. In firelight, fragile sinew strings glowed gold.

Slender hands caressed the wood and strings though no sound was emitted. The lute waited. "Will you hear me, Homanan?"

Not Cheysuli. Frowning, Aidan nodded.

"Will you *listen*, Homanan?"

He wanted to protest; did not. He nodded yet again.

Notes ran from the lute like water, clear and cool and sweet. It sang of tenderness and joy, love and dark hatred, astonishment and acceptance. The sounds pinned Aidan to his skins, then flayed him until his spirit vibrated with the richness of its song. And then the lute-song, dying away, became nothing more than accompaniment to the human instrument.

Tye sang in a true baritone almost at odds with his beauty, for Aidan had expected a tenor. But the baritone was clear and effortlessly eloquent, swinging down to caress the top range of a skilled bass, then soaring upward to drift across the sweet register of the finest tenor. Tye's magic was manifest.

Aidan stared into the fire until it burned away his sight. He saw colors inside his head. And then a shadow crossed his vision, blotting out the fire, and he saw Ashra begin to dance.

She wore bright layered skirts of green and red and gold, and a snug black leather jerkin that displayed full breasts and narrow, curving waist. She knotted slender hands in tangled ringlets and lifted them until they cascaded down her shoulders and back. She tipped back her head, baring an exquisite throat, and Tye's song abruptly turned from the grace of illusion to the driving notes of seduction. When Ashra danced, the Wheel of Life stopped turning.

Aidan found he could not breathe. A brief, warning tickle

touched the back of his consciousness, reminding him Ashra was
Tye's woman, but he was vividly aware of a new and perverse
side of his nature promising him he could brush Tye aside like a
gnat. He had been intrigued by Ashra from the first, from the *very*
first; he had respected the bond between singer and dancer, but
that respect was coming undone as he watched her now. He could
not help himself: he wanted Ashra badly.

She came to him. Hair hung to her waist, tumbling as she
moved, clinging to breasts and hips. She bent, touched him, took
his hands into hers. Her touch set him afire.

Black eyes promised him all he wanted and more. Ashra's smile
was for him, for him alone; Tye no longer mattered. And when she
drew him up, first to his knees, then to his feet, he allowed it; he
wanted it; *needed* it.

"Come," Ashra whispered.

She led him from his pallet of skins to the bare earth before the
old magician. Dully, Aidan stared down at him; he wanted, at this
moment, nothing to do with Siglyn or his dream speaking. He
wanted only Ashra.

"Come," she said again, and took him to the ground. He knelt
there willingly, because she requested it.

The old man's eyes were very bright. "Sit you there," he said.
"Do nothing, save what I tell you."

Aidan, still lost in lute-song and lust, merely nodded.

Ashra withdrew. The old man put his hands on Aidan's head,
cradling his jaw as one might a child's, or a woman's. The palms
were rough-textured from age, but the wiry fingers were strong.
Aidan stared into rheumy blue eyes, because he had no other
choice.

"Son of the forests, son of the cities, son of the sunlight and
darkness," Siglyn said softly. "Warrior and prince, skeptic and
adept. You are more than many, and less than what you must be.
And you dream . . ."

Aidan, sucked in a sudden breath, because he had forgotten. He
was aware the music had died, and Ashra no longer danced. She
stood behind him, while Tye sat silent as stone upon his blanket,
holding the moon-bleached lute.

"You dream of chains," Siglyn said. "Chains that bind a man;
chains that set him free. Bound, the life continues; broken, it is
freed. Which do you seek?"

"It breaks," Aidan blurted. "Always. I have only to touch it—"

"Do you wish it to break?"

"Wishing makes no difference. It simply *breaks*—"

Siglyn's hands tightened. "Chained warrior; chained prince; chained raven. That is what I see."

Aidan swallowed painfully. "If I broke it . . . if I broke the chain, would I be free?"

"That is not for me to say."

"But you said the life is freed if the chain is broken."

Siglyn removed his hands. "Did I say such a thing? Or did you perceive it?"

Aidan's blurted laugh was hollow. "I could not even begin to tell you."

"But I can begin to show you. And if you wish it, I will."

Aidan's head came up. "What is the cost?" he demanded. "There always must be a price."

"Of course there is," Siglyn agreed. "Nothing is gained without risk; nothing is learned without cost; nothing is given without a price. The gods exact a heavy toll."

"And you, old man? What do you expect?"

The old man laughed. "Paying the price without knowing the cost is a part of learning. The choice—and the risk—is yours."

Aidan knelt in dirt with the fire—and Ashra—at his back, conscious of an almost overpowering sense of futility. He could not deal with this; could not comprehend the riddles he was expected to anticipate and answer. He could only sit helplessly before an old Ihlini magician and shake his head.

"Tell me," he rasped. "Show me. I will accept the cost."

Blue eyes narrowed. "Willingly?"

He drew in a deep breath and blew it out as quickly. "It is a part of my *tahlmorra*. I am required to do it willingly."

"Tye," Siglyn said, but his eyes never left Aidan's face.

Tye rose, set down his lute, and crossed the fire's shadow. He knelt at Aidan's side. Briefly he worked at his belt, a snake of hammered links lying flat against his hips, gilded by firelight. He gave it into Siglyn's hands.

The belt was of poor workmanship. Aidan, looking at it, saw where the hammer had crushed a link too flat, beveled another too crooked, crimped the gilt entirely. Even its gilding was false, shedding itself in Siglyn's hands.

But the old man smiled. He lifted the belt and threw it into the fire. "Fetch it out," he said.

Aidan blinked. "Out of *there?*"

"You agreed to do as I said, no matter what the cost."

"And this is the price? I am to burn the flesh from my bones?"

"Do as I say."

The vestiges of distrust rekindled. "How do I know this is not an Ihlini trick?"

Siglyn's teeth showed. "You do not."

Aidan glanced at Tye, who knelt next to him. The smooth dark face was expressionless, the green eyes averted. Tye merely waited.

Ashra moved from behind Aidan and walked to Siglyn's side. Like Tye's, her face was curiously blank, but her eyes were not averted. They bored into Aidan's. They did not beseech, but he knew himself seduced.

Briefly, he considered *lir*-shape. A raven might slip into the flames quickly and retrieve an object without risking much of himself, but Aidan knew the belt was too heavy. The only way he could fetch it out, as Siglyn required, was to reach into the flames and lift it.

He turned, and knelt on one knee by the fire. It was not so large a fire that it might threaten his life, but nonetheless it would hurt. If he were quick enough, he might singe only the hair on his hand and arm, but the hot metal would surely sear his hand. And he had only recently gotten back the use of both.

I was told there was a task. Perhaps this is it.

Aidan set his jaw so hard his teeth ached. Then he reached into the fire.

He plunged his left hand down through the flames into coals, grabbing for the belt. His fingers found the heated links and caught them up, dragging the belt from the fire. He spun around and dropped it in the dirt in front of Siglyn, nursing his hand against his chest.

"Are you burned?" the old man asked.

Aidan opened his mouth to shout of course he was burned—and then realized there was no pain. He held out his hand and saw unblemished flesh. He had not singed a single hair.

Siglyn nodded, "You put your hand into the flames, fully expecting it to be burned. It matters little the flames were not real . . . only that you *believed* them real—and still performed the task." He nodded again. "There is some hope for you yet."

Aidan stared at Tye's belt in the dirt. The cheap gilt paint had burned away, leaving base metal bared. It was, he thought bitterly, analagous to himself.

Siglyn reached down and lifted the belt. He took an end into either hand, stretching it, then snapped the links flat. Metal cracked, then flaked away. In silence, the old man tied knots in the cheap metal belt. Four of them. And as he snapped the knotted belt a second time, the knots became joined links of purest, flawless gold.

Aidan nodded. Of course.

"Chained warrior; chained prince; chained raven." Siglyn smiled. "Your choice. To break it, or make it whole."

Aidan unbuckled his leather belt and slid the three matching links into his hands. A brief examination told him they were of the same making as the joined links in Siglyn's hands.

"How?" he asked. "How do I make it whole?"

"That is your choice?" Siglyn asked.

"Aye: to have it whole."

"Be certain of it."

He smiled. "I am. I would have it whole."

Siglyn's eyes were very still. "Give one link to Tye. One to Ashra. The last to me."

Aidan did so.

"Name them."

Aidan looked at the link in Tye's hand. "Shaine," he said quietly. "Shaine the Mujhar."

"And?"

"Carillon." He looked into Ashra's emotionless face. "Carillon of Homana."

The link glittered in Siglyn's hand. "The last?"

"Donal, who was Cheysuli."

Siglyn nodded once. "The links are distributed. The chain is for you. The joining is for you."

Slowly Aidan knelt in front of the old man. From him he took the chain of four joined links. He touched the one he had named Donal to the single link Siglyn held, and in the snapping flash he squinted, knowing the joining complete.

He repeated the ritual with Ashra, then Tye. Four links were joined to three: the chain at last was whole.

Aidan waited, staring fixedly at the fifth link. Waiting. When it remained unbroken, he smiled joyously at Siglyn. "Whole," he exulted. "*Not* shattered. *Not* broken. Its name is not Aidan!"

Relief was overwhelming. Aidan cast a glance at Tye, at Ashra, looking for some sign of acknowledgment, but they gave him nothing more than silence. It did not matter. Aidan laughed at them all, then yawned a tremendous yawn into Siglyn's face.

"Forgive me," he said, when he could. "I did not mean to do that."

"Magic does tire a man," the old Ihlini said gravely. "But not so much as dealing with gods." His hand was on Aidan's head. "Sleep, child of the Firstborn . . . and dream your dreams in peace."

He slept dreamlessly, knowing peace for the first time in too long. When he awoke he fully expected to be alone. But the wagon still stood by the tree, and Ashra sat by the fire.

Memory rushed back. Aidan sat up, pushing a hand through tangled hair. "I thought—" But he broke it off raggedly, no longer certain what he thought.

Ashra smiled. "You thought you would be deserted. No. Not yet."

He looked beyond her and saw Tye with the horses, hitching them to the wagon. Siglyn was absent; probably *in* in the wagon. Teel, perched on the canopy, croaked a morning greeting.

Aidan looked back at the girl. "Why?" he asked roughly. "What was all of it for?"

"You should know, by now. " Ashra tossed her head and sent ringlets flying. Copper hoops in her ears flashed. "It is because of you we are here."

Certainty increased. "But you are not gods."

"No." Her smile was sweet. "We are what you see: Singer, Dancer, Magician, But we are servants of the gods, as you witnessed last night. We do their bidding."

Aidan recalled too well what had occurred the night before. "Are you real?"

"As real as can be, as the gods made us." Ashra's bold eyes were bright, full of unselfconscious awareness of what her body had promised. "We are as you wish us to be. It remains for you to decide."

The image of her dancing rose before his eyes. He recalled her supple, seductive movements; the bright promise of her eyes. And the burning of his flesh as she put her hands upon him. "Real," he said hoarsely. "I want you to be real."

Her smile enveloped him. "Then I am."

His traitor's body betrayed him. "And if I said I no longer wanted you to share Tye's bed?"

Ashra laughed aloud. "I have shared Tye's bed since before you were born. Since before your father was born, and his. I think it very likely I will go on sharing his bed."

It hurt. "Then there is no hope for *us*—"

"No," she agreed solemnly. "That is what dreams are: wishes, and the illusion of reality. And truth. If you lay with me, you would never know if it were real or false. And that would not satisfy you."

A dry irony shaped his tone. "For a while, it might."

She laughed again and rose with the supple motion of a born dancer. The chaplet in her hair gleamed against black ringlets.

"Wait." He put out a hand to delay her. "If none of this is real, why did you let it go so far? Last night . . ." Shrugging, he let it go. "I am not a celibate man, nor a boy misinterpreting a woman's intent. I have seduced women myself, and I have been seduced. You lured me last night with promises of coupling. Why, if you meant nothing of it?"

A graceful hand swept across breasts, then down to touch curving hips. So easily she seduced him, though her eyes were serious. "Because you *are* a man," she said, "and a man must recognize his own mortality, his own weaknesses and flaws, before he can set them all aside. Desire is one of the strongest of all emotions. A man cannot always control it. He cannot always set it aside when it must be."

He thought of countless times he had allowed himself to lose control. Much of it had been genuine desire. But as much had been the need to lose himself in something to forget what drove him so.

"I have slept with many women . . ." It was a statement of truth, not a boast. He had never been that kind. Women to him were special, because of the *kivarna*. He knew what they felt in his bed. It deepened his own pleasure, to know what it was for the woman. But he had *used* the women . . . though very considerate, he had not looked for anything more.

Ashra's exotic face softened. "I did not tease you out of cruel perversity. I did it so you would see how easily it is done, so it would not lead you into misfortune. You are a man, not a god, and you must know it always. Even when you might believe yourself more gods-blessed than most."

He grunted skepticism. "Am I?"

Her smile was slow, serene. "You are many things, Aidan. But you must be only *one*, before you understand."

Tye came up beside her, slipping an arm around her waist. "How fares the lesson?"

She smiled and squeezed him briefly. "He does not yet understand."

Tye nodded. "The learning will come of its own time and place. We have done as much as we dare . . . it is time we moved on."

"Siglyn?" she asked.

"In the wagon." Tye kissed her on top of her head. "Go and see to his comfort, while I bid our prince farewell."

Ashra moved away. Aidan looked at Tye, bitterness lacing his tone. "Have I amused you?"

Tye's face was solemn and inexpressibly lovely. It was not womanish after all, Aidan decided, merely the work of a master's hand. "The struggles of a man never amuse me," Tye said quietly. "I have seen too much to laugh at anything. Ashra, Siglyn, and I have been about this for a very long time . . . you are not the first, and certainly not the last. But for now, as you travel toward your *tahlmorra*, you will feel yourself quite alone. Quite apart from the rest. But never think yourself *better*." His green eyes were level. "Do you understand?"

"I think I understand nothing," Aidan admitted truthfully.

Tye laughed. "It will come." He briefly inclined his head. "Nothing is done without purpose. Remember that, Aidan."

Aidan watched the singer walk toward the wagon. Tye climbed up onto the wide seat and took up the reins. Beside him sat Ashra, chaplet glinting in the dawn. The wagon jolted into motion as Teel lifted from the canopy. As it trundled away, the mists closed around, muting the canopy's brilliant colors. In a moment the wagon was gone.

Aidan looked down at his pallet of skins and wool. The chain lay there. A whole, unbroken chain, as he had made it the night before.

He knelt down and touched it. Took it into his hands. And knew, for the first time, the journey he undertook would lead him to different roads, and to choices rarely offered.

It was up to him to make them.

Chapter Five

The first thing Aidan noticed about Kilore was the scalloped line of chalk cliffs thrusting upward out of the seashore like a mailed, white-gloved fist. Atop the fist, he knew, perched the Aerie of Erinn, where all the proud eagles were hatched. His own mother had been. It seemed odd to think of it, so far from Homana. But this was Aileen's home. Homana was his.

The second thing Aidan noticed about Kilore was the pungent smell of fish. Its pervasiveness was oppressive; he grimaced quiet distaste as the ship was carefully docked. He deserted it at once, walking hastily onto the dock, and promptly tripped over a tangle of net and kelp as he twisted his head from side to side in a bid to see everything.

He made an effort to recover his balance with some show of aplomb; nevertheless, he was embarrassed. He was half Erinnish himself, with sea-blood in his veins. Surely it meant something.

But no one seemed to have noticed; if they had, no one cared. The day was nearly done. Fishing boats were coming in brimming with the day's catch. No one had time for him.

Aidan left the docks and went into the city proper, a tumbled collection of buildings clustered between ocean and cliffs, meticulously avoiding dray-carts and baskets full of fish and effluvia. He soon found himself in the markets where the catch was fully displayed. Here the stench was worse.

"I come from this stock," he muttered. "I had best get used to it."

Why? Teel asked. *Are you planning to live here?*

Aidan laughed. *Not if I can help it.* He paused, looking around. *How do I find the road to the castle?*

Easier done from up here.

Aidan glanced up. Teel, in a flock of seabirds, was black

against cream and white. *Where do I go?* he asked. *Your view is better than mine.*

Teel agreed benignly. *You might try going up.*

Aye, but I meant which road— Aidan grinned, comprehending. Aye, lir; "*up.*"

He went up, and up again, reveling in *lir*-shape and the ability to fly. He might have stayed an hour or two longer, drifting about the fortress, but it made no sense to do so when his business was within. Regretfully, Aidan took back his human shape at the head of the cliff path, and walked the rest of the way across dampened ruts to the massive gates of Kilore.

Unlike Hart's castle, Sean's was properly guarded. Aidan was required to show his signet as proof of identity, then was taken at once through the baileys into the fortress itself. Dark stone was wind-scoured smooth, even on the corners, giving the blocky fortress a soft, rounded appearance Aidan knew was deceptive. No one had ever taken Kilore. The fortress was unbreechable, perched on its clifftop aerie all warded about with stone. The walls were spiked with iron.

A servant escorted him to a private chamber and gave him leave to enter. Aidan at first thought it odd that he would be so summarily sent in to face his aunt and the lord of Erinn—Liam, Aidan's grandfather, had died four years before—but the servant merely smiled and opened the door. Aidan stepped in.

A man stood just inside of the door. His broad back was to Aidan; he leaned on a longsword, nodding from time to time. As he heard the door shut he glanced back briefly, showing a strong-featured face, then returned his attention to the other occupants.

It was a practice chamber, Aidan saw in surprise. Not the private chambers of a lord and his lady, but a chamber reserved for learning the use of weapons. Racks filled the walls, full of swords, spears, pikes, halberds, and other deadly things. The room itself was plain, with no illumination save for torch brackets set high in the walls, spilling light into the chamber. On steel, it ran like water.

Two people sparred in the chamber, scuffing across smooth stone. Aidan paid them little notice as he quietly shut the door, then stepped up next to the man just before him and made the mental adjustment to change languages. He had learned his Erinnish from Aileen and Deirdre and spoke it passingly well, but with a Homanan accent,

"My lord?" he began diffidently.

The other barely glanced at him. "A moment," he said briefly. "They'll be done soon enough."

Aidan looked. A man and a woman. To himself, he smiled: he knew without even asking who the woman was. Only Keely knew the sword, and was so steadfast in its art.

But nothing in their sparring led him to believe she and her teacher would be done any time soon. They seemed well matched, and neither in any hurry to end the bout. They led one another into traps, parried expertly, patiently began again. Faces were flushed and breathing was loud, but both were obviously supremely fit and not in the least winded.

This might last all day . . . Except the man at his side—Sean, he assumed—had said it was nearly done. Aidan glanced sideways at the big man by his side. "How can you tell?"

The other smiled. "I'm the sword-master. I'm supposed to be knowing these things."

Surprise stole diffidence. "*You* are the sword-master?"

The man grinned, showing a gap in one side of his upper teeth; an eyetooth was missing. "Aye. Did you think I was the lord?"

Aidan slanted him a glance. No, now that he knew better. He was too rough, too worn for lordship. And certainly too old; Sean was, he knew, closer to fifty than to forty. This man was older yet.

Intently, he glanced back at the couple. "Then *that*, I take it, is Sean."

"Aye. And yon woman the lady." The sword-master grinned. "If he's not careful, she'll have him. And then we'll be hearing all about it for at least a seven-day."

"He's too big," Aidan protested instantly, with no prick of reproval for discounting Keely so quickly. "*Much* too big—how could a woman beat him?"

The older man cast Aidan a considering glance. "You're not from Erinn, lad, in spite of your Erinnish—or you'd be knowing the answer."

It stung. "I am *of* Erinn. That woman is my aunt—your lord is my uncle."

The sword-master grunted. "The House is a large one . . . I'm not knowing which one you are."

Aidan blinked. "Homana," he answered. "Grandson to the Mujhar."

It earned him another glance, but this one was equally unimpressed. "There's another of those here."

Aye, so there was: Keely's son, Riordan, if Aidan recalled correctly. "Aye, but—" He broke off, staring. "She *will* beat him!"

"Aye. She has before." The sword-master grinned. " 'Twill be a noisy meal."

Aidan was astonished. He had heard of Sean's legendary size and prowess from his mother and others. He had expected to find Sean smaller in fact, since stories were often wrong, but this time it was the truth. Sean of Erinn was a very large man of very obvious strength . . . and yet Keely was beating him.

Until Sean hooked her foot and dropped her like a stone.

"You *ku'reshtin!*" She glared up at him from the floor. "It was to be a true bout, not a wrestling match!"

Sean grinned down at her. "I wanted to win, lass. To do it, I'll be doing whatever I must. So will any man with a bit of a brain in his head."

"*Ku'reshtin,*" she muttered, more quietly. She hitched herself up on elbows, wincing elaborately. "I would have had you, and you know it."

"I know it," Sean agreed cheerfully, leaning on his sword. "Why d'ye think I cheated?"

"A Cheysuli would never have done—"

"A Cheysuli most likely wouldn't have a sword in his hand in the first place." Sean reached down. "Here, lass, catch hold—I'll not leave you on the floor."

"But you'll *throw* me there." Keely caught his hand and let him pull her up. She wore snug Cheysuli leathers and soft, supple boots mostly suited for household use. Blond hair was braided back from a face no longer young, but striking for its spirit. She was tall, slender, fit. She was also past forty, but age sat lightly on her. She moved like a young woman as she bent to pick up the fallen sword. "So," she said, "you win. Next time will be different."

" 'Twill always be different—next time." Sean cast a glance at Aidan, thick eyebrows sliding up beneath a tangle of curly hair. He was blond, bearded, brown-eyed, with shoulders fit for a plow. "So, lad, you're here. Are we to know who you are, coming so freely into our home?"

Aidan smiled faintly, displaying his heavy signet. "I was brought here properly. And I did pass the test."

Keely studied him. A frown knitted brows. "You have the look and the eyes . . . but that is *not* Cheysuli hair."

"Erinnish," he agreed with resignation, wondering how often

he would have to explain himself. "Aileen's hair, though darker; Brennan gave me something."

Keely's eyes widened. Aidan found it briefly amusing that she should remark on color; she was fair-haired, fair-skinned, and blue-eyed, and no gold on her arms. He more than she had the right to invoke their race.

"Not *Aidan*," she said. "You were a sickly child . . . Aileen said you had outgrown it, but I did not expect this!"

Aidan nodded gravely. "I am better now. Instead of dying today, I will wait until tomorrow."

Sean laughed aloud, sliding his sword back into a rack. Keely did not smile, though a spark in her eyes kindled. She studied Aidan closely, much as she would, he thought, a horse. "Brennan's son," she mused. "Are you as stuffy and pompous as he is?"

Aidan sighed aloud, though inwardly he laughed. She was everything they said; probably more. He was looking forward to it. "He was hoping marriage had forced you to grow up . . . I'll be telling him the truth: you're obviously as bad as you ever were."

Keely scowled. "Don't be giving *me* that Erinnish cant, my lad . . . you've never been here, boyo, and I've lived here very nearly longer than you've been alive."

She had gained her own share of the cant. Aidan, grinning, offered her the courteous bow she would, he knew, scorn. It was why he did it. "They tell stories of you," he said. "Would you like to hear them now?"

Sean's big hand closed on Keely's shoulder. "Not now, lad— we'll be due some wine and ale. Come into the hall with us; Keely will mind her tongue."

"Then I will be disappointed."

"*Ku'reshtin*," she said calmly, handing her sword to the man still waiting by the door. "Well? He beat me."

"He cheated," the big sword-master said equably. " 'Tis the only way he can win. I've taught you that much, lass, in the years since you've come."

Keely laughed and slapped a corded arm. "Aye, so you have— but perhaps you should look to a new lesson that teaches *me* how to cheat."

Sean shoved open the door. " 'Tisn't in you, lass . . . you've too much Cheysuli honor." He waved her through impatiently, eyeing Aidan with great good cheer. "Have ye come for long, lad?"

Aidan followed Keely. "Long enough to find a wife."

His aunt stopped dead in her tracks, swinging to face him abruptly. "A wife," she said softly. "And would you be meaning my girl?"

Aidan smiled blandly. "I wouldn't be meaning your boy."

It was not, perhaps, the best way to put himself in Keely's favor, but then he had not come to give her the kindnesses and false courtesies she had, from all reports, always despised. He knew enough of her history to be fully aware she would be less inclined to consider his suit than Sean, who was, his sister said, a reasonable, intelligent man. Aileen had also said Keely was much the same, but could be difficult. Aidan did not yet know if marriage to Shona would be suitable, but there was no sense in lying about the reason he had come. Especially to Keely.

Even now, as Sean led the way into the central hall and waved him into a chair and handed down a cup of Erinnish liquor, Keely's expression was stiff. "Does Brennan want this?"

Aidan sipped, blinked surprise at the bite of the liquor, then raised the cup in tribute to Sean. All as he looked at Keely. "Not this *particularly*," he said, "but he wants me married, aye."

A faint line etched itself between her brows. " 'Not this particularly,' " she quoted. "An odd thing to say. Does that mean my oldest *rujholli* argues against my daughter?"

Sean snorted. "I doubt he'd be such a fool. 'Twould be a good match." He ignored the black glance Keely cast him and contented himself with settling his large body into a rough, iron-bound chair. Blond beard parted slightly to exhibit white teeth. "You married into Erinn, and Erinn into Homana. He'd hardly be a man for saying the lass isn't worthy of it."

Keely, who remained standing very near Aidan's chair, tapped a booted right foot briefly. "No," she conceded. "All right, then, kinsman—what is your meaning?"

Aidan did not answer at once, distracted by his surroundings. Kilore was not a place of much refinement. Certainly nothing like Homana-Mujhar, or even Hart's castle in Lestra. It was, first and foremost, a fortress. The casements were tall but very narrow, more like arrow-loups than windows, and the cavernous ceiling was broken up only by greenish, studded beams as big around as a man. Illumination was negligible, save for the blazing fire in the massive fireplace.

"Well?" Keely prodded.

Recalling her question, Aidan smiled. "He merely said he wants me married." The smile stretched into an ironic downward hook. "It is suggested the Lion might be happier with one more male in line to plant a rump in the wooden lap."

Keely's mouth twisted. "How like him," she said lightly, then turned away from Aidan. She took up from a nearby table the cup Sean had poured her, then perched herself on the edge. "And does Aileen say the same?"

"She says I should have more time." Aidan shrugged. "I doubt it will make a difference. The Mujhar is in good health, and my *jehan* is young enough to rule for decades after. If I take a *cheysula* now and get a son on her, or wait ten more years, I doubt the Lion would notice."

Keely's gaze was steady. Pointedly, she said. "And yet you are here."

Sean stirred in his chair. "Lass, the lad's not a child. Could be he's *ready* for a wife." Brown eyes warmed. "Though perhaps he'll think better of it once he's met our lass."

Aidan smiled back. He liked Sean very much. "Is she much like her *jehana?*"

Sean's brows rose. "Like us both, lad . . . a full plate, you might say."

"She has a mind of her own," Keely declared. "No daughter of mine will ever sit behind a man when her place is *beside* him."

Sean nodded blandly. "No daughter of yours would dare such a thing, with you to set her straight."

Aidan laughed into his cup. "Aye, well . . . I did not set out for Shona. I went to Solinde first—"

"Blythe," Keely said at once. She nodded consideringly. "There has been a Solindish-born Queen of Homana before . . . but very long ago." She frowned faintly. "Though there was grief of it— Electra betrayed Carillon by becoming Tynstar's light woman."

"*And* bore him a child. Strahan." Aidan sighed, thinking of Strahan's son. "It does not matter so much any more . . . Blythe is not at the moment ready for marriage, to me or to anyone else." He frowned consideringly into his cup, then sorted out his words. Quietly he told them the story of what had happened.

Softly, yet with a great malignancy, Keely cursed Lochiel when Aidan was done. And the man who had sired him.

"So," she said viciously, "this time they strike at *Solinde*. If they cannot take Homana directly, they will try another way." She slammed down the cup. Wine sloshed over the rim. "To murder a helpless infant . . ." Three long, stiff strides carried her toward the fireplace. All Aidan saw was her back, and its eloquent rigidity. After a moment she turned. "It will be worse for Blythe."

Neither man spoke, transfixed by her intensity.

"Worse," Keely repeated. "For me, it was force. But Blythe bedded him *willingly*—" Keely's face spasmed. "She will hate herself for that."

Sean stirred, stretching out a hand. "Lass—"

Keely shook her head. "You were right to leave her, Aidan. She will want nothing to do with marriage for now. Perhaps for some time to come. And if there is a child—" The lines of her face altered. She looked older, and tired. "She will have to make her choice, just as I did. Although, in the end, the gods saw to it themselves . . ." Keely sighed and thrust splayed fingers into her hair, stripping loosened loops back from her cheeks. "If Hart has any sense, he will show her the proper way of performing *i'toshaa-ni*."

Aiden smiled faintly. "Hart has sense." He shifted forward in his chair. "Aye, I came to speak of Shona and marriage; even so, I am not *convinced* she is the only alternative . . . if we do not suit, I will not insist on it." He thought of his parents. "I know better."

Keely's expression was odd. "I thought that long finished. In her letters, Aileen says they do well enough—"

Aidan, who had no desire to bog himself down in a convoluted discussion of the feelings between his parents, interrupted smoothly. "Let us say I would prefer a match well-suited from the beginning. As yours was."

Keely and Sean exchanged glances. Sean grinned crookedly, but swallowed more liquor rather than say anything. Keely's manner was brusque. "Aye, well . . . it speaks well of you that you are willing to consider Shona's feelings instead of politics. Aileen's doing, I'd wager; Brennan thinks too much of the Lion."

"A common curse, among our kin." Aidan relaxed back into the big copper-bound chair, hooking the foot of his goblet over his belt buckle. He was weary from the journey, but it was a good weariness. What he felt most was a deep, abiding contentment. It came, he sensed, from Kilore herself . . . and the couple who lived with her.

Keely smiled for the first time since he had met her. "You look more suited to Kilore than Homana-Mujhar, or even Clankeep. There may be more of Erinn in your blood than Homana."

He smiled back, unoffended. "My *jehana* has said that once or twice . . . until I come back from Clankeep, and *then* she says I am naught but Cheysuli, prickly pride and all."

Sean grunted. "I am in a better place to judge, I'm thinking, not being biased." He ignored Keely's skeptical grunt. "And 'tis too soon to know . . . how long d'ye plan to stay?"

Aidan opened his mouth to answer—he thought to stay until he and Shona knew if there was a chance, or no—but was interrupted by a treble voice piercing the hall as the big door, opened by a servant, disgorged an angry boy.

" 'Tisn't *fair!*" he cried, marching across to hall to stop in front of his father. " 'Tisn't fair *at all*. She hasn't the right to be ordering me around, this way and that—and *no right at all* to take the bow away!"

He was blond, like both his parents, and his eyes were Keely's blue. His skin was very fair, as Sean's must have been before wind and time had weathered it. If there was any Cheysuli in him, Aidan could not see it.

"The bow," Sean said blankly.

"*My* bow," the boy declared, and then had the grace to look abashed. "At least, 'twould be my bow if you saw fit to let me have one." He slanted a blue-eyed glance at his mother. "Shona has a bow."

Keely nodded gravely. "Shona is somewhat older."

"But she's a *girl*," Riordan declared.

Sean grinned. "A lad with eyes in his head, is it?" He sat forward in his chair, shifting a body much larger than that of his son's. Aidan wondered fleetingly which branch of the Houses Riordan would emulate: the broad bulk of his father's, or the slender fitness of his mother's. "When you're a mite older, lad, you'll be having your own bow. If Shona's told you no, 'tis because she tends your welfare."

" 'Tisn't," Riordan retorted. " 'Tis because she thinks she's *better.*"

Keely sighed. It was, somewhat obviously, an old argument. "A Cheysuli warbow is not something a boy should play with, Riordan—"

"I wasn't playing with it," he declared. "I was trying to shoot at a target, just as Shona does—just as *you* do—but she caught me at it and took the bow away." He sighed aggrievedly. " 'Tis bad enough already . . . now they'll be saying I'm a coward afraid of his sister."

"*Who* will?" Sean asked.

The small face was downcast. "All the other boys."

Sean and Keely exchanged a glance. The interplay was subtle: Sean's arched brow, Keely's lifted shoulder.

"'Tis something we should be tending to, then, I'm thinking," Sean said quietly. "Tomorrow we'll see to finding you a bow—a boy's bow, Riordan, not a Cheysuli warbow—and we'll set out to learn the proper way. I'll not be having them say you're a coward, but neither will I be having a boy too small for a warbow chance hurting someone else."

Riordan, who had been all set to argue, saw he would lose even that much if he protested. So he did not. He merely grinned at both his parents, slanted a briefly curious glance at Aidan, then headed out of the room. His posture was one of irrepressible exuberance.

"Nine," Keely said, before Aidan could ask. "And spoiled near to rotting by a much too permissive *jehan*."

Sean sat back in his chair, smiling blandly. "Aye, well . . . I *am* the Lord of Erinn. Who is there to stop me?"

Aidan watched the door thump closed. "Nine," he mused. "Too young yet for *lir*-sickness, or any signs of it."

Keely's mouth twisted. "He may never require a *lir*. The Erinnish blood, I have discovered, is thicker than our own . . . Shona has none of my gifts, and Riordan may miss as well." She flicked an unreadable glance at Sean. "But as it is Erinn he will inherit, there may be no need."

Aidan did not answer. Keely had schooled her tone into a negligent matter-of-factness, but his *kivarna* told him the truth. She had hoped Shona would share her own unique gifts, thereby asserting the Cheysuli portion of her heritage. The girl had not; now Keely hoped—and probably prayed—Riordan would make up the difference. It was true that in Erinn the need was not so great as in Homana—Aidan's grandsire, Niall, had gained a *lir* so late it made his claim to the Lion tenuous in the eyes of the clans—but undoubtedly Keely wanted to leave the mark of their race in Erinn's history. It was a natural desire; he felt it in himself. But for Keely, the need was stronger.

She recalls too clearly what Strahan did to her . . . and the child she might have borne him. Dishonored, as Ian was—giving Erinn a Cheysuli lord will mitigate her guilt—

He broke it off. It was not his place to delve into Keely's feelings. They were private. *Kivarna* or no, he should respect them.

Sean combed his beard with two fingers. "Shona is out on the headlands, with the dogs. 'Twould not be a bad thing to see her alone, rather than cluttered up by a household."

Keely shot him a sharp glance. "She is not a woman for games." She turned the gaze on Aidan. "Tell her the truth of why you have come."

Aidan smiled blandly. "If you like, I will wear a placard."

His aunt scowled darkly. "I have good reason for what I say. Too many men tease and twist a woman. I'll not have it done with Shona."

Aidan set down the goblet. "*Su'fala*, the last thing I would do is tease and twist a woman. I promise, I will be honest with Shona—I see no reason to play games with a woman I might marry—but I will not blurt out my reason for coming before the proper moment. What chance would I have then? If she is anything like you, she prefers honesty to lies, but there is room for diplomacy. Also courtesy."

Keely's eyes narrowed. "Brennan taught you that."

Aidan smiled calmly. "My *jehan* has taught me many things, aye . . . but I am no more my father than you are your mother."

It was a telling stroke, as he meant it to be. Keely's mother—his granddame, Mad Gisella—had earned only contempt by her conduct with the Ihlini. The last thing Keely wanted was to be thought anything like her.

Keely raked him with a sulfurous glare. Then her mouth twitched. "*Ku'reshtin*," she said calmly, flicking a hand toward the door. "Go. I will let Shona deal with you—you will find her a worthy match." Another dismissive flick. "On the headlands, as he said. Amidst a pack of hounds."

Chapter Six

The turf was lush, thickly webbed, excessively green. None of the nubby rugs in Homana-Mujhar approached its thick texture, nor even the bear pelts in his own chamber, so far away. Erinn was much damper than Homana, and its flora responded with a vigorous, unrestrained growth. Everywhere he looked was *green;* even as he glanced back at Kilore, falling behind, he thought the mottled gray stones acquired a greenish hue, as if to blend in with the turf and trees and storm-gray skies.

So far from home, he thought vaguely, feeling the brief pang of regret flutter deep in his belly. He had not, as he had so belatedly realized in Ashra's company, ever been anywhere. It had never seemed odd to him—he was sufficiently satisfied with life in Mujhara and Clankeep—but now he knew himself incomplete. There were places in the world he could not go, and therefore places in himself he would never know. A man who chained himself to his home drew a curtain over his eyes, blinding himself to all the majesty of the world.

And yet he proposed, one day, to chain himself to a beast. The Lion of Homana, acrouch in Homana-Mujhar.

Is that so bad? Teel's croak emanated from overhead; Aidan glanced up. *A man could have a worse* tahlmorra *than to be Mujhar.*

Aidan was not disposed to argue. *He could.*

Are you wanting dogs?

He frowned briefly, momentarily nonplussed, then followed the raven's change of topic. *More to the point: do I want the woman with them?*

Teel angled back toward Kilore. *Meet her and find out.*

The raven departed swiftly. Aidan, laughing quietly, looked ahead. The headlands were flat, a green flood of turf edging toward the sea—except that the edge was sharp as a blade, dropping off to a chalky cliff. Somewhere along here, Aidan recalled, his grandsire had ridden a horse off the edge of the world, intent on escape. Deirdre had bidden Niall do it, to keep his honor intact; he had broken another part of his honor as he had broken his parole to Shea, Lord of Erinn, but the circumstances had required it. Had he not gone . . .

Aidan smiled. *Had he not gone, he would never have married Gisella of Atvia, nor sired four children on her, including my own jehan—*

In the distance, something barked. And again. And Aidan, knowing how to read the nuances of such sounds, stopped walking and held his ground.

The river, in full spate, poured across the turf. Ash-gray, smoke-gray, storm-gray, even palest silver. A handful of hounds—no, *more*—nine or ten; he could not count them all. But they clearly counted him, ranging themselves around him. None of them barked, now; the warning had been given. They waited.

Bitches, most of them. Two or three half-grown males, still pups, awkward and gangly. And one huge male who stood hip-high to Aidan, massive shoulders tensed. Hackles bristled on neck, shoulders, rump; deep in his chest, he rumbled.

How many men would test that? Aidan wondered in detachment. *How many men would dare?*

Not he. He was no fool.

The pups, he saw, were less interested in domination than in seeing who he was. But the big male—their sire, undoubtedly—was in no mood to allow anyone closer to Aidan, or Aidan closer to them. And the bitches—how many were there, again?—would not allow a stranger to harm their young.

Impasse. Aidan sighed, wondering how long it would take Shona to release them. He *could* take *lir*-shape and escape this travesty, but he wanted to meet her as a man, on her terms; taking *lir*-shape would lend him an advantage he did not, just yet, want to display.

Then he saw her. Distant yet, but approaching, striding along the edge of the cliffs with no apparent thought for her nearness to danger; hummocky turf curling over the edge could give and send her to her death. But Shona strode on easily, smoothly, without haste; could she not call to them? Or whistle?

No. He realized that as she came closer yet. She was blatantly unconcerned with any discomfort or anxiety engendered by the wolfhounds. What concerned her were the hounds themselves.

She came into their midst as one of them, a hand touching here, there; thick long tails waved. But none of the hounds moved, save to flick an ear, or thump her hip with a tail.

Her language was Erinnish, as expected. Her tone cool, quiet, unhurried. *He* could wait as long as it took. He saw it in her eyes.

Aidan assessed her. Tall. *Very* tall; she was, he thought in shock, at least as tall as himself. While he did not match the elegant height of most Cheysuli, he was easily six feet. So was Shona.

And big-boned to match her height, with broad, level shoulders. There was no delicacy in her, or fragility, or anything approaching femininity. She was, quite clearly, Sean's daughter. Keely, next to Shona, would be shorter, slighter, leaner.

A true-born Erinnish, big of bone and stature . . .

Incongruously, he thought of Blythe. Slender, elegant Blythe, very much a woman. And while there was no doubting Shona's gender—no man would dare—there was nothing at all in her reminiscent of feminine Blythe. Whom Aidan had thought beautiful.

No, he thought wryly, *that is not in Shona's purvue.*

But something was. In movement, in posture, in expression, Shona's gift was *presence.*

She was blonde, like Keely and Sean. A wild, unruly blonde, had she worn her hair cut short. But she did not, and so the curls were tamed. The long, heavy braid—thick around as his forearm—hung over her left shoulder, dangling to her hip. She had tied it off with a leather thong ornamented with amber beads. Their color matched her tunic; her trews were dusty ocher.

Sean's daughter indeed: brown eyes observed him calmly. Her features, though perfectly regular, were not those he might have chosen, given leave. They lacked the elegant aquilinity of Blythe's. There was no delicacy. It was a strong, almost masculine face, devoid of beauty or elegance. Its statement was one of strength. And of unremitting power.

Something tickled his belly. *This woman was born for a throne . . . it shines out of her like a beacon—*

He wondered what Teel would say.

He wondered what Shona would say.

"Enough," she said softly in a low, smoky voice.

For one odd moment he thought she meant him; that she knew why he had come and was giving him his dismissal. But he saw the hackles go down; the male wolfhound's tail waved.

The growling stopped. Aidan blinked. The sound had been so

low, so infinitely soft, he had not truly heard it. But with its absence, the silence was absolute. The threat was dissipated; he felt himself relax.

"So," she said, "you're here. What are ye wanting from me?"

To marry you, he said. But only to himself.

Blonde brows arched. "Are ye mute?" she asked.

Until this moment, no. Aidan cleared his throat. "Handsome dogs," he said; the inanity amazed him.

Shona considered him, "They'll do," she allowed gently. " 'Tis what I do, d'ye see? I bred the boyo myself, and all the lads and lasses . . . but not *all* the bitches, of course. The line must not get too tight, or the blood will ruin itself."

Aye, he agreed fervently. *Much like our own.*

Shona gestured briefly. "That one, d'ye see, came from over-island. And that one from Atvia . . ." She shrugged. "They're not known for their wolfhounds, there, but 'twas a line I admired. I brought the bitch in to shore up what was *here.*"

Why are we discussing dogs? Aidan smiled weakly. "I like that one there."

Shona glanced briefly at his choice. Her contempt, though fleeting, was manifest. Her smile was barely polite. " 'Tis a judge of wolfhounds, is it?"

"No," he demurred.

Eyes crinkled. "Good; the man admits it. He's the worst of the litter, that lad. A bit crooked in the rear to run down a pack . . . but you'll be knowing that, I'm sure."

"No," he said again. "I know nothing about wolfhounds." *And less about myself; this is not a woman I would* look *at, in Homana—*

Shona laughed aloud. It was a full, hearty laugh, more like a man's than a woman's. "So, it knows what it doesn't know—not so many men will admit such a thing, and fewer to a woman. You must be worth the knowing." She tilted her head a little. "*Are* you worth the knowing?"

"Some days," he agreed.

Shona smiled. It set her face alight. And then she turned to the wolfhounds, said a single word, and Aidan was engulfed.

"There," she said, "they're free. And so are you, if you like; they'll none of them harm you now."

Not intentionally, perhaps, but ten or twelve wolfhounds—even

some only half grown—were enough to drag down a man even in
polite greeting.

The pups, of course, were uncontrollable, but the others were
only slightly more reserved. Aidan found his elbows trapped in
gently insistent mouths, and his manhood endangered by whipping
tails thick as treelimbs. He did what he could to protect himself—
something deep inside laughed to consider Homana's future unmanned by a pack of dogs—then one of the hounds reared up and
put both front paws on Aidan's chest.

Off-guard, Aidan stepped back, felt the paw beneath his boot
and heard the anguished yelp; sought to move, and did: landing
full-length on the turf.

"Agh, get off the man . . . let the man *breathe*, d'ye hear—?"
Shona waded in, slapping at hips and shoulders. Eventually the
knot parted; Aidan saw sky again, instead of a forest of legs.

He was laughing. He could not help himself. He had grown up
with only cursory attendance by dogs—Cheysuli, having *lir*, did
not keep pets—and knew little enough about the subtleties of unblessed animals kept as companions. He had known Homanans
who trained dogs for hunting, or kept cats to kill the vermin, but
he had never thought about what it was like. There had been Serri
and Tasha in his childhood, and eventually Teel. *Lir* were very different. A man could *reason* with *lir;* now, in this moment, all he
could do was laugh and fend off exuberant hounds.

Shona urged them back, giving Aidan room. Eventually he sat
up. He did not at once stand, thinking it might be easier to keep his
balance on the ground. The dogs milled around him, snuffling at
ears and neck. Noses were cold, damp, insistent; Aidan pulled up
his cloak and snugged it around his neck.

Shona laughed. "They're meaning you no harm. 'Tis their way
of welcoming you."

Incongruously, he thought of another welcome. The welcome
of a woman for a man, home from hunting, or war. He saw Shona
standing before a rude hillcroft, wild hair and homespun skirts ravaged by the wind, waiting for his return. He saw Shona bedecked
as a queen, receiving foreign envoys who were agog at the height
and bearing of Homana's queen; at the overwhelming strength that
blazed within her spirit. And he saw Shona kneeling in soiled bedding, sweat- and blood-smeared, gently aiding a wolfhound bitch
as she strained to pass a leggy pup into the world.

He took no note of the milling wolfhounds. Only of Shona, in their midst; of the sudden excruciating acknowledgment that pinned him to the turf.

This is what it is to recognize a tahlmorra—

Smiling, Shona reached down a hand. "You'd best come up from there, or they'll be making a rug out of you."

Fingers linked, then hands. And Aidan, moving to rise, felt the power blaze up between them.

Deaf. Blind. Mute. Flesh rolled back from his bones, baring the Aidan within. His body pulsed with a tangle of emotions so alien he felt ill.

Shock . . . astonishment . . . denial . . . anger . . . fear . . . an odd recognition—

—awareness, sharp and abrupt, of intense, painful arousal—

And comprehension so acute it cut like a knife.

Shona.

And then she tore her hand from his. The contact was broken. The clarity, the empathy, the comprehension was cut off, leaving him sweating and shaking and ill, bereft of understanding. All he knew was an unpleasant incompleteness.

Much like a *lir*less warrior.

Vision cleared. He found himself still half-kneeling on the turf, splayed fingers rigid. His breathing was ragged, noisy, as if he had fought a war and lost.

Shona's face was white as the chalk cliffs. Like Aidan, she shook. "Who—?" she blurted. "Who *are* you—?"

He tried to speak and could not. Unwittingly, his free hand groped for hers.

Shona lurched back a step. "*No*—"

The wolfhounds growled.

"Wait—" he managed to croak.

Three more steps. Then she whirled, braid flying, and ran.

Chapter Seven

He lay supine, heels, buttocks, and shoulder blades pressed into cool turf. A mounded hummock pillowed his head. Wind blew down the headlands, rippling the folds of the cloak he had snugged across his chest. Hair teased his eyes, but he let it alone, ignoring it, until it crept between lashes. Then he stripped it away limply and tucked the hand back into woolen cloak.

He did not know why he lay on Erinnish turf so close to the chalk cliffs, defying the vigorous wind, except that it brought him an odd sort of numbness. Not a true peace, for that required a contentment in spirit, but a certain detachment, a distance that allowed him to push away the acknowledgment of what had happened.

He smelled salt, sea, fish, and a pervasive dampness. The rich earth of Erinn, supporting webby turf. But most of all he smelled emptiness, albeit in his mind. And a blatant futility.

"I should go home," he said aloud.

He had thought it several times since Shona had left him. But he had not said it, until now; now it took on the trappings of resolve. He *would* go home—

"Lad."

It took Aidan a moment. Then he realized the voice was quite real, not a figment of his currently turbulent thoughts, and he sat up. He intended to stand, but Sean waved him back down. The Lord of Erinn, wind-blown, wind-chafed, joined Aidan on the spongy green turf and, as Aidan, stared out into the sky beyond the edge of the cliffs. Sean had changed out of the plain woolens worn for swordplay into more formal tunic and trews of very deep red. Silver bands the width of Aidan's forearms clasped formidable wrists, worked with intricate knots of wire and thumb-sized bosses.

Aidan drew in a breath, then sighed. "She told you."

Sean continued to stare into the sky. His voice was a rusty baritone. "She told us a stranger came, giving her no name. And that when he touched her—when she put out her hand to help him up— the world fell into pieces."

Aidan gritted teeth. "Not so much the world, for me. *I* fell into pieces."

Silently, Sean put a hand to the turf and uprooted a plot with gentle violence. Then, as if realizing what he had done, he replaced it and tamped it down with broad, deft fingers. And laughed softly, acknowledging the fruitlessness of his repair.

Aidan waited. He still felt empty, and numb, and bereft of something he had only briefly begun to understand, in that instant of physical contact.

Sean's laughter died. His face was a good face, full of strength and character undimmed by nearly fifty years. The gods had been kind to him, gifting him with strong but well-made bones, and a spirit to match them. Aidan had heard stories of how Sean had come from Erinn to win Keely's regard, knowing full well if he lost he lost everything. He had won, in the end, but the battle had been duplicitous and dangerous. He was not, Aidan knew, a stupid man, or a fool; Sean of Erinn was an ally well worth having. And Aidan had hoped, for a very short span, Sean would also become a father.

It was Shona's face, Shona's eyes, Shona's hair, underscored by masculinity. And it hurt with an intensity he had not believed possible.

Sean frowned. "There is a thing of Erinn, my lad, very hard to explain. 'Tis a thing of the blood, much as your *lir*-gifts are . . . with something of the same price to be paid, in certain circumstances."

Recognition flickered sluggishly. "Do you mean the *kivarna?*"

Sean's eyes sharpened. "What are you knowing about it?"

He shrugged. "Only that it exists, and that it gives some people the ability to understand how others feel." He paused. "And that I *have* it."

Sean sighed heavily. "How long have you known?"

"That it had a name?—a few months, no more. My *jehana* told me when she realized I had the ability . . ." Aidan's mouth twisted. "I thought it was something everyone had. I never even *asked*."

Sean shook his head. "Not everyone, lad, 'Tisn't so prevalent as it once was—even then, 'twas mostly limited to the Aerie. We intermarried too much, in younger days . . ." He squinted into the sky. "Shona has it from me."

Aidan frowned. "But even if she *does*, what difference does it make? Why does the *kivarna* have anything to do with what happened when we touched?"

Sean did not look at him. He stared down at his hands, assiduously pulling up turf and shredding it. "When I came to manhood," he began, "I was no better than a rutting boar. What woman I wanted, I took, if she was willing . . . and she was. She *always* was: I was the Prince of Erinn." He looked at Aidan briefly, sharing the common knowledge of rank and title. "I was taught very young about *kivarna*, so I understood why I found it distasteful to pursue an unwilling woman, and why I was not a bully, and why it hurt me when someone else's feelings were hurt. 'Twas a difficult thing, as a child—but then, you'd be knowing that." His smile was crooked. "They say I sired half the bastards on this island, but no. There was the Redbeard, too . . . perhaps *between* the two of us, we accounted for half."

Aidan, frowning, wondered why Sean was telling him the story of his youth. It was none of Aidan's business how many bastards Sean had sired, or that he had sired any; and it had nothing whatsoever to do with his *kivarna*.

"My lord—"

Sean lifted a silencing hand. "What I'm saying, lad, is I was very lucky, because I took care to be so. I knew I would one day be marrying the Princess Royal of Homana, and that if I was *not* very careful, I alone could turn the future of Erinn—and possibly Homana—into a travesty."

Aidan's frown deepened.

"*Kivarna*," Sean said softly, "has its own sort of price."

Aidan reined in impatience. "My lord—"

"A man who has *kivarna* is blessed in bed," Sean said bluntly, "because he knows what the woman feels. But that same man, lying with a *woman* who has the gift, seals himself to her forever. As she seals herself to him."

Aidan stared at him, recalling all too clearly the results when he and Shona had touched.

Sean drew in a breath. "Had I lain with a woman who had *kivarna*, I could never have lain with Keely. D'ye see? 'Tis a *mutual* binding . . . you may know up here you should lie with another woman, a woman who lacks the gift—" he tapped his head "—but the body says otherwise. The body refuses."

"Refuses?" Aidan echoed.

Sean's expression was odd. "There are more ways to geld a man than with a knife."

"But—" Aidan stared at him blankly. "Are you saying so long as I lie with women who lack *kivarna*, I am in no danger?"

"Aye, lad. And I'm assuming you've found that out already." One of Sean's brows arched sardonically. "Have you not?"

Impatiently, Aidan waved a hand. "Aye, aye . . . I was never a rutting boar—" He stopped. "Perhaps I was, a little—but the *reasons* were different . . ." He saw Sean's private smile; he scowled and went on. "So, you are saying that Shona and I share this *kivarna*, and if we slept together we would be bound to one another."

"Forever," Sean affirmed.

"But you do not share this with Keely."

The Lord of Erinn grinned. "'Tis your way of asking if I'm faithful, is it?" Then, as Aidan tried to protest, Sean shook his head. "'Twas never an issue, lad. She has no Erinnish, and no *kivarna*, but it doesn't matter. Keely is more than woman enough for any man, even a reformed boar." Then the humor faded. "D'ye understand what I'm saying?"

"Aye." Oddly, jubilation welled up. Now he understood. Now it had a name. Now it had a *purpose*. Aidan smiled. "What is the problem? I came to Erinn to see if Shona and I would suit one another. Obviously, we do."

Sean's expression was solemn. "Do you?"

"Aye! Even this *kivarna* says we do."

Sean nodded after a moment. "Aye. But there's something you're forgetting."

Aidan spread his hands. "What?"

"Shona. She's wanting no part of you."

She paced, because she could not stand still. Back and forth, back and forth—until the dogs began to whine. Until her mother, rather more calmly than expected, told her to stop.

Shona swung around. "Stop!" she cried. "You tell me to stop? 'Tis the only thing keeping me whole—"

Keely's contempt, though subtle, displayed itself nonetheless. "There is no sense in allowing yourself to become so overwrought."

Shona's eyes blazed. "And would *you* not be overwrought?"

Looking at her daughter, Keely sighed. She had bequeathed the girl her own stubbornness and outspokenness—Shona disdained such things as polite diplomacy when bluntness would do, and she had little patience for convoluted courtesies. She was, Keely reflected, exactly as she had made her . . . and now her mother must live with it.

But so must Shona. And just now it was impossible.

They were in the central hall, where Shona had announced her arrival by slamming open the door before the startled servant could do it for her, with less drama. Shona's flamboyant arrival, complete with eleven wolfhounds, nonetheless was quickly forgotten in the shock of seeing brown eyes gone black in confusion and shock, and the pallor of her face. She had blurted out what had happened. Sean had at once dispatched himself to find Aidan; Keely dismissed gathering servants and shut the door personally, telling her daughter of Aidan's reason for his visit.

Now the girl paced before the fireplace. The hounds, sprawled here and there as living, breathing carpets, watched her worriedly. Keely, lacking *kivarna*, nonetheless shared a portion of their anxiety. But she would not let her daughter see it.

Shona turned on her heel and paced back the other way. "Married, is it? They might have warned me. They might have *written*. Even *he* might have; was he thinking I'd welcome him?"

"Undoubtedly," Keely answered. "We give welcome to all our guests."

Shona cast her an impatient scowl. " 'Twasn't what I meant . . . I *meant* he might have been thinking how I'd react, meeting him like that."

"I doubt he anticipated the *kivarna*," Keely said dryly. "Aileen said nothing of it to me in any of her letters, and it was the last thing I expected. We all forget he is half Erinnish . . ." She sighed and chewed idly at a thumb. "And for all you were taken by surprise, I'm thinking he was, too. Are you so selfish to think only of yourself?"

Shona had the grace to look abashed. She stopped pacing and threw herself down into a chair. It was her father's favorite, and engulfed her. Her expression altered slowly from fierce outrage to something akin to compassion. She smiled lopsidedly. "He was no more prepared for it than me. You should have seen his face . . ." Shona slung one muscled leg over the chair arm, settling into its depths. "I felt everything he felt, when we touched—it mirrored what I felt, throwing it back at me . . ." She frowned, squirming uncomfortably. "'Twas not something I'm wanting to repeat . . . gods, but he was so *open*—" Shona laced fingers into her braid and tugged, as if to distract herself. "And I knew, when he touched me, he was wanting me—*needing* me—"

She broke off with a muttered curse, clearly embarrassed as well as frustrated. Keely waited, trying to sort out her own welter of emotions.

Shona sat upright abruptly, unhooking the dangling leg and planting both booted feet on the floor. She leaned into her elbows and hid her face behind both hands. Her words were muffled, but the raw helplessness of the tone was undisguised. "Gods help me, but 'twas what *I* was wanting too—every bit of it, I wanted . . . I could not *help* myself—" She drew her hands away and cast an anguished plea at her mother. "What was I to do? I couldn't bear it, all that nakedness of feelings, all the knowing what he wanted, and me . . . all I could do was run away! Like a child, a wee bairn fleeing—" Self-contempt was plain. "And me knowing all the while if I gave in, it was over . . . if I even *wavered*—" She shut her eyes. "Gods, I feel so helpless . . . it made me feel so *helpless*—"

Keely drew in a deep breath, trying to still her voice. "It was the *kivarna*—"

Shona rubbed violently at her brow. "I'm knowing *that*, well enough . . . I just never thought—" She broke it off, rose, began to pace again. "How can I marry him? We're strangers to one another, knowing nothing about our habits and interests . . . how could he think I might be willing?"

Keely lifted one shoulder in a shrug. "The way anyone thinks a man might be willing, or a woman, when they first meet."

Shona stared blankly at the dogs, sprawled on the stone floor. Eventually she sat down by one of the bitches and began to stroke the narrow, wiry head. One of the pups came over and collapsed as near to Shona as possible, burrowing her head into her lap. Absently, Shona petted both hounds.

"'Twasn't that way for you and father."

Keely grunted. "You know that story. I've told you."

"So has he." Briefly, Shona grinned. "But you loved one another before you married. You've *both* said so."

"Your *jehan* and I had less in common when we met than you and Aidan. There was no *kivarna* for us."

Shona's cheeks reddened. "I'm wanting more than what we felt. That was little more than two children setting a broomstick alight—and having the rafters catch!"

Keely smiled. "Aye, well . . . there is something to be said for passion, and something to be said for peace. Sometimes one outdistances the other, but eventually they catch up."

Troubled, Shona continued to stroke the wolfhounds. "But I know the cost of *kivarna*. I'm knowing what it means. If we married, Aidan and I, and he died, I'd be left alone. Forever. With no man to love, or love me back." She looked at her mother. "What would you do if father died?"

Keely drew in a long, painful breath, then released it. "Go on," she answered quietly. "He would expect it of me."

Shona's eyes were steady. She was too much like her father; Keely found it difficult to answer that face. "What would you expect of yourself?"

After a moment, Keely smiled. It was ironic and bittersweet. "Once, I would have told you no man is worth the loyalty of a woman, or her soul. That no man is so important his passing would leave a woman bereft; she has strength of her own, and worth, and should go on very well without him." She stroked a strand of hair back from her face. "But I have learned that a woman need not subjugate herself to live with a man, nor give up any part of her beliefs. A woman is free to love as she will, and therefore free to grieve." She looked at her daughter's intent face. "If your father ever asked me to do something I was adamantly opposed to, I would refuse. No one has the right to expect another to compromise personal beliefs simply to accommodate the other. If he asked me not to grieve, I would laugh into his face. But if I thought he expected me to end my life when he died, I would leave him instantly."

"Even if you loved him?"

"I will always love your father. But I would leave him. And he knows it."

Shona's face was grim. "It would be more difficult if there was *kivarna* between you."

Keely gestured. "Perhaps. But *because* we had it between us, it might never come to that. Perhaps if more men and women shared a mutual *kivarna*, there would be less contention between them."

The tone was argumentative. "So, you think I *should* marry him."

Keely smiled calmly. "I think you should make the choice for yourself, and then live with it."

Shona scowled. "That is easy for you to say."

Keely laughed aloud, "Is it? Oh, my foolish lass, you're knowing nothing about it. Nothing at *all* about it."

Shona looked affronted. "How can you say that? You're not in my position—"

Keely stood up, tugging her jerkin back into place. "We all make choices," she said, "Man, woman, and child. And then we must live with them."

Shona's voice rose as Keely approached the door. "But your choice isn't like mine. It never was. You *loved* my father. You're not knowing what this is like."

Keely was at once swept back years to the bleakest portion of her life. To the hardest decision she had ever faced. To the knowledge that the child she carried was a child of rape, both physical and emotional, and the product of her most hated enemy. Knowing the child, if born, might have equal access to magics more powerful than any presently known, and that he or she might use them for evil.

Swept back to the decision that she could not, would not bear the abomination, and would do whatever she could to miscarry it. Because it was, to her, the only answer. The only alternative.

Keely drew in a breath. "There are people in this world who want to make decisions for you. Some of them even do it out of misintentioned goodness, of well-meant kindness. They believe wholeheartedly they are doing you a service when they take away your freedom of choice, in the name of their morality. Who am I to take away *your* right to choose?" She spread her hands. "I will answer any question you have, and I will give you all the advice you want, but I will not make the decision for you. That is for you to do."

Shona opened her mouth to protest. But she did not, and after a moment, she smiled. "Aye, so it is. And for that freedom, I should be grateful."

"Aye," Keely agreed, thinking of Brennan and Aileen, who had known no freedom.

And of their son, and her daughter, whose unexpected "gifts" might rob them of their share.

Chapter Eight

Aidan stood beside his borrowed bed, contemplating his baggage. One set of saddle-pouches, carrying changes of clothing, preserved food, a few other oddments. A servant had been sent to unpack for him, but Aidan had thanked him and dismissed him. He was not yet certain he was staying long enough to unpack anything.

Teel, perched upon a bedpost, fluttered blue-black wings. *The least you can do is stay to the evening meal. Why run away on an empty belly?*

Aidan grimaced. *I am not running away. Why stay where I am most obviously not welcome?*

The woman is the daughter, not the lady . . . let the others determine your welcome.

He had left the door open. Someone stepped through. He knew before she spoke exactly who it was; the *kivarna* told him plainly. "So," she said coolly, "I'm thinking there's something to be settled."

Aidan did not turn. "Aye. And I am settling it this moment."

The smoky voice was curt; she did not understand his reference. "What?"

He turned. She was everything he recalled: long of limb, broad of shoulder, impossibly strong of will. She blazed with determination. "Am I to go, or stay?" He gestured idly toward the unpacked saddle-pouches. "I have only to throw them over my shoulder and walk back down to the city. There will be a ship. And I can go home."

Shona's assessive eyes narrowed. "You give in easily."

"Give in?" He loaded the words with elaborate surprise. "I did not know we had even gotten *that* far."

Now her tone was glacial. "We got nowhere at all, *I'm* thinking, except to recognize the *kivarna*." Her feet were spread, legs braced; she was poised for war, Aidan thought, in one way or another. Her jaw was tightly set. "Did you know what would happen?"

He made a sound of disgust. "I know as much about *kivarna* as you do about having a *lir.*" Abruptly he paused, thinking of Keely. If Shona were like her mother, his last comment bore no meaning at all. "You have no *lir*, have you? Or recourse to *lir*-shape?"

Muscles flexed in her jaw. "No."

The *kivarna* flared briefly. He had touched a nerve. It was plain to him: Shona displayed no physical characteristics of her mother's race, nor the magic of the Cheysuli. What she was, most obviously, was Erinnish, complete with Erinnish *kivarna.*

And she feels diminished because of it.

Aidan shook his head, answering her more kindly. "No, I knew I had it, but not what it was. Nor what it could do."

It seemed to mollify her. And he realized, with an unpleasant jolt, that the extra sense he relied on to tell him what people felt was *her* gift as well. Shona could read him as well as he read her.

He was not certain he liked that.

Unexpectedly, Shona laughed. "Aye," she agreed, "unpleasant. Unsettling, I'm thinking—*and* you. D'ye see what we'd be dealing with, day in and day out?"

Rebellion flickered. "There is more to it than that."

Derision was blatant. "Oh, aye. There's this, too. I'm thinking." And she strode across the room to catch both of his hands in hers, grasping tightly. "This, too, my boyo. D'ye think we can deal with *this?*"

It flared up between them as strongly as before, but the emphasis was different. There was less of pure, driving need and more of anticipation, of promised pleasure, of warmth and exhilaration; of a certainty of completeness. There were layers, Aidan realized, even to physical need, buttressed by the spiritual and emotional. What lay between them was far more than a desire for mere physical gratification. With Shona, there was a future beyond a single night—or hour—in bed.

Once, it might have frightened him. But now it was what he wanted.

This time, Aidan broke contact, to show her that he could. Even as she tensed, intending to release him, he pulled his hands from her grasp.

Aidan pointed at the bed. "There is more to life than that. And I *want* more."

Color stood high on her face. This time there was no fear, no flight, no denial. This time there was comprehension, and control.

And yet clearly she was as shaken as he by the *kivarna*. "I want—" Her voice was hoarse. She swallowed heavily. "I want the freedom to choose."

"You have it."

"Have I?" In the light, her features were harsh. "If we face *this* every time we touch, what choice is that? That, my lad, is helplessness—"

He cut her off. "The first time you sat upon a horse and it ran away with you, that was helplessness. The first time one of your wolfhound bitches whelped you a dead puppy, that was helplessness. But you still ride, do you not? And you still breed dogs."

Her face was very white. "I'll not be bound by this. I'll not give up my freedom to a whim of the gods, who no doubt find this amusing."

Aidan very nearly smiled, thinking of the Hunter, the Weaver, the Cripple, but she would not understand. Instead, he appealed to her taste for confrontation. "Then prove yourself stronger. Vanquish it." Aidan turned to face her squarely. "If we believe a falsehood, it gains strength. So challenge this *kivarna* to a duel. Find out which of you is stronger."

Level brows knit. "Why?" she asked. "You saw me but hours ago, and now you argue a commitment to something that could well destroy us. We're not *required* to marry . . . we're neither of us betrothed. 'Tisn't like your parents, or mine. We're bound to nothing at all." She shook her head. "How can you be so willing to set aside personal desires and chain yourself to a stranger in the name of *kivarna?*"

He shrugged. "Because this *kivarna* may well be linked to my *tahlmorra*. Which is part of the prophecy . . ." Aidan sighed, scratching idly at his neck. "I am somewhat accustomed to doing what is expected, by gods and by parents."

Shona grimaced. "*Tahlmorras*, prophecies—" She looked harshly at Teel, still perched upon the bedpost, then shook her head with an expression of impatient tolerance. "Oh, aye, my mother told me all about such things . . ." Tolerance faded abruptly. Shona turned away and took two paces toward the door before swinging back. "D'ye really believe such blather? I know my mother does; do *you?*"

Aidan's right hand closed around the chain threaded onto his belt. "Aye," he said. "I do."

She stared at him, judging his commitment. When she saw he

meant it, her tone was incredulous. "And because of these beliefs, you're willing to pay the price of the *kivarna?* That if one of us should die, the other is sentenced to a life of abstinence and loneliness?"

Aidan shrugged. "Considering the cost of the *lir*-bond, I find the *kivarna*'s demands rather tame."

Her tone was venomous. "And you're a liar, my lad."

"Am I? I?" Aidan laughed at her. "You should know, my lass. Use your accursed *kivarna*."

Brown eyes were nearly black. Her strong chin was thrust upward in challenge. "How am I to know you can't lie with it? 'Tis only a matter of *feelings,* not words. And even then I'm not knowing *everything* you feel—"

"Words lie," he told her. "Feelings, even those well-hidden, tell only the truth."

Shona swore. "Full of sweet words, are you? Forgive me if I don't swoon, but I'm not that weak a woman."

"Good," he said flatly. "I am a man who wants a companion, not a serving-girl."

Shona's contempt was plain. "Don't forget whose daughter I am. They neither of them raised a fool."

Aidan scooped up his pouches. "Not a fool, " he agreed. "Just a stubborn, blinkered mule." He slung the pouches over his shoulder and walked by her through the door.

Lir. Are you coming?

Teel's tone was amused. *I will go out the casement. The air is clearer, out of doors.* He flew from bed to casement sill, then slipped out the narrow slit and into the sky beyond.

Aidan turned to the right, heading toward the spiral stair leading down to the bottom floor.

"Aidan. *Aidan!*"

He continued walking.

"Come back here, you *skilfin.* D'ye think I'd be letting you walk out of here like this?"

His pace did not slow.

She came up behind him. "What would my parents say if they thought *I* was the cause of you leaving without a proper welcome or guest-gift?"

"You are," he answered briefly, into the corridor. "You may as well face them with the truth . . . or are you a coward?"

"I'm not afraid of them. They give me no cause."

"No. What you're afraid of is the *kivarna* itself." Aidan went down the winding staircase, attuned to her nearness. Her steps did not flag as Shona followed him down.

For several moments all he heard were her footsteps, echoing his own. And then strong fingers caught in the wool of his cloak, clenching through to the leather jerkin. *"Stop,"* she commanded.

He stopped, even as she jerked her hand away, and turned. She stood two steps above, which made her tower over him. She braced either hand against the staircase walls, as if to hold herself in place. Loose cuffs fell away from her arms, baring strong wrists and sinewy forearms more suited to warrior that woman. The thick braid fell across one shoulder, dangling past her breast, her waist, and hip to brush the top of her wool-clad thigh. In the dimness of the narrow staircase much of her expression was muted, but he saw the set of her jaw; the fierceness of her eyes; the upward slant of cheekbones too blunt for Cheysuli elegance, yet striking all the same. The sheer power of her personality, reflected in expression, stature, spirit, stripped the words from his mouth; all he could do was stare.

Shona came down one step. Palms scraped against the walls. "I *am* afraid," she admitted. "But you're knowing that. You have only to use what *I* use, when I want to know the truth of a person." One more step; her head was level with his. "I know the sword and the bow and the knife. I am more content with men's things than with women's—I have that of my mother . . ." Briefly, Shona smiled. "But there's more to me than that. There's another woman inside me, one who wants a man the way other women do . . . the way they dream about. The one who wants a man to love her, and to love him back—" She lifted a staying hand as he opened his mouth to speak. "No. D'ye hear? D'ye *feel?* What I'm saying is the truth: I want all of it, Aidan, the way the stories promise. A man and a woman meet, and they fall in love, and they marry . . ." Her mouth jerked briefly. "You give it to me twisted. You give it to me empty."

After a long moment he nodded. "I never meant it to happen this way. I came so we could meet, to see if we suited one another, as friends first. I never meant to pressure you, or make you feel trapped. I promise you that. But when you reached out and took my hand, the choice was taken from me. The time the stories promise was stolen from us both—"

"I know." Shona drew in a deep breath and released it heavily. " 'Tis a capricious thing, the *kivarna;* you're knowing that as well as I." She caught hold of the braid and flipped it behind her shoulder.

"D'ye see? 'Tisn't right for either of us. You'd do better with a woman not so bound up by *Erinnish* magic—a Cheysuli woman, perhaps, or a Homanan—and I'm thinking I'd do better with an Erinnishman, a big, brawling islander who has no *kivarna* at all, so we neither of us will suffer."

Which us? he wondered. *You and your brawling islander? Or you and me?*

"Aidan."

It was not Shona, who stared past him in open curiosity, but her father, who waited at the foot of the stair. Aidan turned. "Aye, my lord?"

Sean's face was solemn. "You'd best be coming with me."

How could they know already I intend to leave? He frowned faintly, trying to find the proper words. "My lord—"

"Aidan, come with me. It has to do with Gisella."

For a moment, the name was alien. Aidan stared at Sean. "Gisella—?" And then he knew. "My granddame?"

Sean nodded. "Corin has sent word from Atvia. Gisella is dying."

Keely's face was a travesty, a mask made of stone. Only the eyes were alive: blue and bright as glass, glittering with emotions. There was anger, shock, resentment, even hatred. But mostly there was a cold and abiding commitment to feel nothing at all, no matter how much she wanted to.

No matter how much she *had* to.

She waited as they came into the hall: Sean, Aidan, Shona. She stood rigidly by one of the chairs, but did not sit; nor did her posture indicate any intention to sit. A folded, crumpled parchment lay discarded on a nearby table. In her hands she gripped a silver goblet. The pressure of her fingers against the metal turned them white.

"So," she said, "it comes. Too many years too late, but at last it comes."

Sean did not go directly to her. Instead he moved by her as if to sit down in the chair she disdained, and then paused. One big hand settled upon her right shoulder. A moment later the other shoulder was also engulfed. Very gently, he squeezed, and Aidan saw the tension of Keely's fingers relax almost imperceptibly. Now the goblet shook.

Aidan looked at her face. *Is it comfort he offers her? Or restraint?*

"So," Keely repeated. "Gisella is dying, and wants to see her kin."

It startled him. Slowly Aidan sat down, conscious of Shona drifting toward the fireplace. His senses chafed at the distance, but he
studiously ignored them. If this was what *kivarna* was, this strong
physical tie, he was not certain he wanted to obligate himself to it.
Understanding the feelings of others was bad enough.

Aidan cleared his throat. "Will you go?"

Keely's astonishment was blatant. "I?"

"Aye. She is your *jehana*. If she wants her kinfolk, surely she
means you."

Keely laughed once, mirthlessly. She gulped from the goblet,
then thunked it down upon the table. "Whether she means me or not
makes no difference. She gave up any claim to me more than forty
years ago, when she tried to hand my *rujholli* over to Strahan."
Keely's face hardened. "I renounced her in life. Now I renounce her
in death."

Sean's hands remained on her, gently working the taut tendons
stretched between neck and shoulders. "Lass, 'tis Corin you should
be thinking of. 'Twill dishonor him if no one goes."

"Corin will understand." Keely's eyes were hard as stone. "I
thought perhaps Aidan might go."

"Me!" He stared at her in surprise. "I have never even seen her.
Gisella is nothing to me . . . *Deirdre* is my granddame, if only in
name." He shrugged, feeling uncomfortable. "I have no desire to see
a dying old woman."

"Her blood is in your veins," Keely said. "It is what makes you
a part of the prophecy, Aidan—" But she pulled free of Sean and
strode away from them all, turning back awkwardly when she had
gone three paces. "I cannot go. I cannot *make* myself go, even if I
should. I have spent a lifetime hating that woman . . . she is old and
sick and dying, and *mad* . . ." Wearily she rubbed her brow, stretching the flesh out of shape. "Someone should go, for Corin's sake if
nothing else . . . and for Gisella's. But not me. I would look at her,
and see the woman whose actions nearly destroyed me, and I would
hate her. And no one, dying, deserves hatred. She deserves
forgiveness—" Keely's face was frozen. Tears glittered briefly.
"There is none of that in me."

Sean's voice was quiet rustiness as he looked at Aidan. "She's
seen none of her grandchildren, lad, I've no doubt she's a lonely old
woman, now—it might ease her passing if she saw you."

"I know, but . . ." Aidan sighed, giving up. "Aye. I understand. If
nothing else, I can carry word home to my grandsire that the Queen

of Homana is dead . . . it might be best from a kinsman, rather than a messenger." He pulled himself out of his chair. "I will go."

"Wait." It was Keely. "If you go, there is something you must do."

Aidan nodded, willing.

Her gaze remained steady. "You must leave your *lir* behind."

"Leave Teel! Why? How can you even ask it?"

Sean's voice was placatory. "There is reason, lad."

"I cannot leave my *lir* behind."

Keely shook her head. "You must, Aidan, or risk losing him. In Atvia, ravens are death-omens. They shoot them whenever they can, so the birds cannot bear tidings of death to the next one meant to die."

It was unbelieveable. "But *Corin* rules. He is Cheysuli. Surely he has taught them what a *lir* is."

"They understand," Keely told him. "But Kiri is the only one they know, and she is a fox. For centuries the Atvians have killed ravens. That sort of habit is not easily overturned, even by a king— especially a foreign one . . ." She sighed. "Is it worth taking the chance? Leave Teel here."

He shook his heat. "If he remains here, I have no recourse to the *lir*-gifts. No shapechange, no healing—"

"Will you need either, there?" Keely put her hand on his arm. "Stay a week. A ten-day, at the most. Then come back—" she cast an enigmatic glance at her daughter "—and do whatever you must do to settle your affairs."

Aidan looked at Shona. For a long moment their gazes locked. Then she turned her head, staring into the fire resolutely, and his reluctance to go to Atvia evaporated. Perhaps the best thing for them at this moment was to part, to put things in perspective. To better understand precisely what the *kivarna* meant, without feeling its presence so tangibly.

Aidan looked back at Keely. "First I will speak to Teel, then I will go."

Sean's smile was faint. "No need to *run*, lad . . . stay the night while we feast you. I'll see you fetched across the Dragon's Tail first thing in the morning."

Aidan nodded. Shona turned on her heel and strode out of the hall.

Chapter Nine

Clearly, the Atvians had expected Keely, or someone of her household. When only Aidan arrived, a stranger unattended by even a single servant, or a message from the Lord and his Lady, they displayed polite bewilderment, then belatedly mustered the appropriate courtesy and ushered him into a chamber. To wait, he was told, for a proper personage.

Aidan, left to ponder the wisdom of his coming, idly walked the room. Rondule was, much like Kilore, a fortress built to defend Atvia, not a dwelling designed to offer excessive comfort. There were chairs, tables, benches; three pelt rugs; a newly lighted fire. The beamwork was roughhewn, hacked out of massive timbers, and left purposely crude. Not much like Homana-Mujhar's fine, silk-smooth beams, arching in graceful waves beneath the dark stone groins.

Aidan sighed and halted by the fireplace, warming morning-chilled hands. The brief voyage across the Dragon's Tail had been accomplished with speed and skill, but he had a landsman's belly. He was pleased to be aground again.

Over the mantel hung a massive wooden shield bossed with brass. The shield was obviously quite old, with an honor all its own; gouges pocked the dark wood and the brass was dented in places. Pieces were missing here and there, displaying the dark outlines of the original ornamentation beneath. Aidan knew better than to believe it a keepsake brought by Corin from Homana; more likely it was left over from the wars between Atvia and Erinn.

It seemed odd now to think of it. But the enmity between the two island realms, separated only by a narrow channel, had forged a bitter rivalry into ongoing hostility, so that two peoples who might otherwise be much alike had spent generations killing one another. Now they were united in a peace forced by Corin's assumption of the Atvian throne and a treaty first with Liam, then with Sean, but Aidan knew better. People did not change their ways so quickly. Only twenty years or so before Alaric had ruled, pure Atvian of the old line, a man dedicated to making Erinn part of his domain. Corin, his grandson by Gisella, had ended that ambition by inheriting on Alaric's death; Sean, married to Corin's sister, had no wish to continue the battles that had, until Liam's time, stolen away a portion of Erinn's manhood every year.

The door swung open. Aidan turned, expecting Corin; instead, it was a woman.

She paused, then entered the room and shut the door behind her. Small hands were clasped together in the folds of her deep russet gown. The color was most flattering against dusky skin. Dark brown hair was braided neatly back from delicate face and slender neck, then netted in gold and pinned to the back of her head. A rope of dark garnets bound her waist, then dripped down to the hem of her skirts. The dyed brown toes of slippers peeped under the hem as she moved toward him, smiling exquisite welcome.

She was, most obviously, not a serving-girl. Aidan revised his greeting instantly and offered a courteous inclination of his head, explaining who he was and why he had come in place of Keely or Sean.

Huge eyes reflected momentary surprise. Then, still smiling, she gathered swirling skirts in deft, graceful hands and swept into a curtsy. Garnets rattled briefly; then she rose and placed one flattened hand over her heart, dipping her head in eloquent acknowledgment. Beneath lowered lashes, Aidan saw brown eyes rich and expressive. The mouth, curving slightly in a delicate, fragile face of quiet loveliness, made no move to speak.

She was thin, very thin, but with a tensile grace that belied the fragility of her body. The long, slender neck, set off by the netted hair, was exquisitely elegant. He thought of Shona, so tall and broad and strong, and realized next to this woman the Erinnish princess would resemble a sturdy kitchen wench, albeit one with a royal pedigree. But this woman's strength did not require a body so much as it required eyes; looking at her, Aidan found himself understanding her disability, and why it made no difference.

The door swung open again. The woman turned, skirts swinging out, and Aidan realized she was only mute, not deaf. He saw her delicate face light up as the man entered, and then she went to him and took his hand, drawing him through. Her smile was luminous as she turned to Aidan, still grasping the man's hand; she put out her own, gesturing gracefully, and seemed to say everything necessary with that single motion.

It was, of course, Corin. Aidan knew it at once. There were few men in the world who so strongly resembled the Mujhar, though Niall's stamp was somewhat diluted by the other blood in Corin's veins, and the Lord of Atvia was much younger. He was tawny-haired and blue-eyed, but bearded, like Sean. He also lacked Niall's tremendous height and weight, built shorter and slighter, though no one would name him small. He was, Aidan thought, at least as tall as Brennan and Hart, perhaps even a bit taller. He wore traditional Cheysuli leathers, which Aidan found unexpected in light of Corin's realm. There was gold on his arms and in his left ear, glinting through thick hair. He was nothing at all like his brothers, Aidan realized. But like his sister, aye. Keely was in his face and smile.

Corin nodded thoughtfully, assessing Aidan rapidly. His tone was very dry. "Not so much of a weakling after all, are you? Was it Brennan's righteousness, or Aileen's stubbornness that made you defy all the doomsayers who predicted your death?"

Aidan smiled politely. "And were you one of them?"

White teeth flashed. "Hardly! You forget, *harani*—I know your *jehana*. I never believed for a moment a son with Aileen of Erinn in him would give up so easily."

Aidan had expected more. Sadness. Resentment. Perhaps bitterness, even after so many years. Instead what he sensed was pride, and an undercurrent of approval. It was almost as if Corin looked on Aidan as his own son, and was pleased with what he saw. It was not the reception Aidan had expected.

"She is well," he offered quietly, looking for reaction. "She sends her greetings."

"So does Brennan, no doubt." Laughter glinted in Corin's eyes. "I know what you do, *harani*. Doubtless all the servants fed you the tales . . . well, I imagine the follies of our youth *do* make good telling. He shrugged, smiling warmly down at the woman at his side. "But old wounds heal, Aidan. I loved her once, very much; now it is a pleasant, if bittersweet, memory." One hand guided the slender woman forward. "Pay your respects, *harani*. This woman is Atvia's queen." Corin's brows arched slightly. "In the Old Tongue, my *cheysula*. Her name is Glyn."

Aidan opened his mouth, then shut it. He wanted to protest that of course the woman was not Corin's wife, because no message had ever arrived announcing the wedding. But who was he to argue? And why? It was well within Corin's power to marry whomever he chose, publicly or privately—and yet Aidan was left feeling oddly flat. After so many years and so many stories, he had come to believe Corin would never marry, because Aileen had married Brennan. It was almost as if Corin had betrayed his mother.

He swallowed heavily and stepped forward, accepting the woman's fragile hand and bestowing the kiss of homage. Her warm smile and eloquent eyes soothed him immediately, dissolving the remaining resentment, until he smiled back at her.

"Had I known, I would have brought a bride-gift." Delicately, he offered Corin reproach, and a chance to explain himself.

Corin, unruffled and unrepentant, shrugged. "It was a private thing. I did not wish to share Glyn with anyone." His tone was very quiet as the woman returned to his side. "Few would have understood the Lord of Atvia taking a woman who could not speak."

Perhaps not at first. But Aidan felt Glyn's muteness beside the point. One had only to look at her expression, as she gazed at Corin, to know what her world was made of.

Corin's beard hid much of his crooked smile. "When a man stops railing at his *tahlmorra*, often the gods repay him with more than he deserves. After too many years of solitude, they sent Glyn to me. I have learned to leave the past behind, living instead in the present." A gesture dismissed the subject. "Now, I am assuming Keely refused to come."

Aidan nodded. "She said you would understand."

Corin grimaced. "I do. I wish she did . . ." The dismissive gesture was repeated. "Do you know, I think if Gisella had tried to give her daughter to Strahan as well as her three sons, Keely would be less bitter. But Gisella did not. Keely was dismissed as entirely unimportant, because she was a girl." He smiled faintly. "That is the definition of Keely, *harani*: she would rather be caught in the midst of some Ihlini vileness than be left *out* of it merely because of her sex."

"And Shona is very like her," Aidan sighed ruefully, then set the topic aside. "You sent word Gisella wishes to see her kinfolk. Will I do?"

Corin's expression was odd. His tone odder still. "That is the wrong question. It is not simply will you *do*, but whether you will

survive with your dignity intact." He gestured toward the door.
"Come with me."

The room lay deep in shadow, for the casement slits were shuttered and only a handful of candles illuminated the bedchamber.
The commingled scent of beeswax and death filled his nose as he
entered. The door thumped shut behind him as the serving-woman
went out, leaving him alone inside the chamber. Corin had said
Gisella was not strong enough for more than one visitor at a time.
Aidan, lingering uneasily by the door, was not certain *he* was
strong enough to visit.

He had never been so close to death before. He had learned to
fight, as he was expected of a man who would be Mujhar, but he
had never been to battle. His kin were vigorous and strong; he had
never watched the aged wither away until their spirits left them.

He had not anticipated the smell. He had not expected the emotions. He faced the dying woman with a horrified fear of what he
would see and feel, because he thought his *kivarna* might be the
undoing of him.

When his eyes grew accustomed to the gloom, he saw the faint
outline of her body beneath the silken coverlet of the canopied bed.
The fabric was a deep, heavy indigo, nearly inseparable from the
dimness. Only after a moment of concentration could Aidan see
the differentiation between coverlet and shadows. Gisella seemed
to wear it like a shroud.

She was propped up by bolsters and pillows. At first he could
only barely see her face, blending with the dimness, then he saw
the shine of eyes. Pale, feral eyes, like his own, fixed on him—on
the intruder—with a fierce intensity.

*Gods—I see now why the unblessed fear us so much when they
see us for the first time—* Aidan swallowed painfully and wet
dry lips.

Her hair was mostly gray, dark, mottled gray, but her face was
outlined by silver-white. She wore it loose over thin shoulders;
twin ropes of cord against indigo silk. Her skin, once Cheysuli-
dark, had yellowed with age and illness, her face was all of hollows. Aidan, unsettled, wondered what illness would take her to
the grave. Mere age only rarely ravaged a Cheysuli so virulently.
Generally his race died gracefully.

Aidan stopped at the foot of the bed. *She is mad,* he reminded
himself. *A sick, dying, mad old woman—*

The pale eyes did not so much as flicker. "Which one are you?"

The flat tone was colorless. Aidan did what he could to put life into his own. "Aidan," he told her. "Aidan of Homana; Brennan's son."

Gisella smiled. Her teeth were displayed in a feral clenching. "Yet another son I have not seen."

He was careful. "You have Corin."

Her voice rasped. "Who?"

"Corin." Aidan drew in a breath. "Your third-born son. Corin, now Lord of Atvia—"

"My father is Lord of Atvia. Is Corin my father?"

Oh, gods—"Corin is your son."

Querulous, now. "Who are you?"

"Aidan." He began it yet again. "Aidan of Homana—"

"Brennan's son; I *know*." Teeth showed briefly. "They tell me things, all of them . . . and then tell me again and again and *again*—do they think I am a fool?"

"No." Aidan briefly sought a chair out of the corner of his eyes, then dismissed the impulse immediately. He did not wish to remain with Gisella that long. He wanted to leave as soon as he decently could.

"And will *you* be Mujhar?"

It snapped his attention back. "Aye. One day."

Pale eyes glittered. "But Niall still lives. Still rules. *Niall* still rules . . ." Gisella put thin fingers to her mouth and stroked withered lips, as if recalling all too graphically once she had shared a man's bed. "Niall," she said softly.

"My grandsire." Aidan surreptitiously glanced back toward the door. "Perhaps I should come back another time—"

"Come here. Come *here*. Come closer. Come *here*."

Against his will, he responded.

Gisella stared up at him. He stood there, letting her look and fought down the impulse to run. His *kivarna* was afire with the confused welter of her emotions, so tangled and black and incomprehensible. She was mad, all too obviously mad, but there was more to her than that. Underneath the layers of confusion was the girl she might have been, once, had Lillith not twisted her. A childlike, innocent girl, trapped in a woman's body, but nonetheless innocent. She was not and never had been fit to be queen. But neither had she deserved the meticulous, deliberate reshaping of her spirit. Lillith had destroyed the innocence. Lillith had destroyed Gisella in a quest to destroy Homana.

Gisella pointed to him. "You."

He waited.

"Cheysuli," she said. "They told me. Lillith. My father. They *told* me—" She smiled. "Cheysuli, Atvian. Erinnish, Solindish, Homanan. All necessary to complete the prophecy."

She was, uncannily, lucid. Aidan stared at her.

"They bind the Houses and mingle the blood—my blood, *your* blood, *their* blood . . . to make the proper child. *The child.* The boy who will become king over all the lands; a man combining the blood of two magical races and—and—" She tilted her head, frowning faintly. "Peace."

Aidan nodded, "The prophecy, granddame. Two magical races and four warring realms, united in peace."

"Tahlmorra," she murmured.

Again Aidan nodded. "We each of us have one."

Her eyes sharpened. "Do you?"

"Of course."

Slowly, she shook her head. "No. No. No."

"Granddame—"

Gisella glared at him. "Lillith told me about it . . . a *tahlmorra* is nothing more than a binding made up long ago by men calling themselves the Firstborn so they could make people think them greater than everyone else."

"Granddame, Lillith lied—"

"Give them a prophecy, she said. Give them a fate and call it *tahlmorra,* something to bind them so strongly they will never break away . . . something to turn them into nothing more than servants, but leave them their pride so they will believe themselves better, *better* . . . better than everyone else so they will *keep* themselves bound—"

"No granddame—"

"Lillith told me," she said plainly. "She told me the truth of it: the Cheysuli have been made what they are by the connivance of the Firstborn, who saw the power of the Ihlini and feared it. So they fashioned themselves an army—Lillith *said*—but called it a race, to use the Cheysuli as their weapons. They turned warrior against sorcerer; child against child—"

Aidan overrode her. "Granddame, *she lied.*" He waited until she stared at him, outraged. More quietly, he went on. "You are ill and angry and confused . . . granddame, Lillith did naught but lie to you, all these years ago—"

"You are lying to me now."

"No." Aidan sighed. "Granddame, I have a task, and a *tahlmorra*. Repeating lies Lillith told you will not turn me away from what I have to do."

"The throne will never be yours."

It stopped him in his tracks.

Gisella smiled, tilting her head to one side. "Never."

"Granddame—"

"It denies you." She saw his shock, his recoil. "The Lion. I *know*, Aidan." She gathered the coverlet in thin, sharp fingers and leaned forward. Her voice was very soft; in its quietude, Aidan heard conviction, and the cant of prophecy. "Throneless Mujhar. Uncrowned king. A *child*, buffeted by fates he cannot understand . . ." She slumped back against the bolsters. "Touched by the gods, but ignorant . . . a man so touched, so claimed as one of their own, can never know peace as a king." Gisella smiled warmly, yellow eyes alight. "You will never rule Homana."

Aidan blurted the first thing that came into his head. "Are you saying I will die? Granddame? Am I to *die?*"

In a tiny, girlish voice, Gisella began to sing.

Chapter Ten

He awoke near dawn, haggard and shaking and frightened. His chambers were cold with the light of false dawn, but even yanking the covers up in a convulsive gesture did not warm him. Aidan sat upright and cursed, rubbing viciously at grainy, burning eyes.

Teel?

But almost at once he recalled the raven was not with him. Teel waited for him in Erinn, near Shona; a sick, uneasy loneliness curled deeply in Aidan's belly. He was quite alone, *too* alone, even though his own kinsman slept within the fortress.

So did his grandmother.

"Another dream," he muttered in disgust, but this one had been much different.

He recalled only bits and pieces: himself, seated on the Lion Throne in the Great Hall of Homana-Mujhar; himself, dead in the Lion, with blood running from mouth and throat; himself, mourned as a throneless Mujhar, an uncrowned king. No proper monarch, Aidan of Homana; merely a nameless prince all too soon forgotten.

He stripped tangled hair back from his face, purposely pulling too hard, as if the discomfort might alter his memories. It did not. "A witch," he muttered. "An Atvian witch, trained to treachery by an Ihlini . . ."

He was empty. Unwhole. Teel was too far even for the *lir*-link. And Shona too far for the *kivarna*.

He needed one or both of them. He knew it with perfect clarity as he sat huddled in bed, shivering. Teel for the *lir*-link and all its gifts; Shona for the physical, the spiritual, the emotional. They were each of them tied into his *tahlmorra*, into his life; if he neglected either, or dismissed either, he destroyed a part of himself.

Into his head came Gisella's declaration. He heard it again so clearly as if she stood beside his bed, bending over him as a mother over a child; as a grandmother over a grandson badly frightened by nightmares.

But Gisella offered no comfort. Gisella offered fear and self-doubt. *"You will never rule Homana."*

Aidan tore back the covers and climbed out of bed hastily, finding and pulling on fresh leathers, boots, his belt, a dark blue cloak. Then he paused by the saddle-pouches, reaching into one to draw out the chain of gold. The links were massive, perfect, heavy. Six of them he could name: Shaine, Carillon, Donal, Niall, Brennan, himself. But the others he could not. Undoubtedly one belonged to his son, and the others to the Mujhars after him.

Aidan put a finger on the sixth link, his own, and wondered what sort of king he would be.

And then wondered if he would be a king at all.

Almost viciously, Aidan whipped off his belt. He threaded the leather through the links and put it on again. He could feel the weight and curvature of each link. A man would kill for such a fortune; Aidan pulled his cloak over the belt and left the chamber, pausing in the corridor just long enough to tell a servant he was well, but required air. He had sat up late with Corin the night before, trading news, drinking wine. No one would question a morning ride; likely he needed one.

Without Teel, he was half a man, a shadow. He felt his spirit cut free from his body like a boat loosed from its moorings. It made him snappish and impatient; the horseboy, startled out of sleep, hastened to ready a mount even as Aidan apologized. When the horse was ready, he swung up quickly and rode clattering out of the bailey, intent on shedding the residual unease and bad temper as soon as possible. It was the dream, of course; he knew it. Since the chain had been made whole in Solinde, he had suffered none, sleeping soundly each night. But the nightmare he had experienced but a half hour before filled him with a nameless, increasing dread.

Aidan left the city as soon as possible and rode up into the hills, skirting the headlands overlooking the Dragon's Tail. Below him the city was quiet. Smoke threaded its way from chimneys and spread a thin haze over the rooftops, but he could see little other activity. Just before dawn, he was truly alone atop the ramparts of the city, riding the backbone of Atvia. The castle itself perched atop a jagged, upthrust stone formation. The knobby dome was called the Dragon's Skull.

He saw the crumbled headland tower in the distance. It stood alone at the edge of a cliff, sentinel to the sea. Morning mist wrapped itself around damp gray stone, but the rising sun changed silver beading to saffron, altering the pitted, grainy texture to smooth ocher-gold.

Aidan contemplated it, then shrugged. *I have nothing better to do . . .*

He thought it a shell, until he rode closer; then saw the bench by the low door and the windows shutters latched back to let light into the tower. It was a curious dwelling. Once it had served as a vanguard against the Erinnish enemy's approach; now it was little more than a crofter's incongruous hut. Aidan, hungry, dismounted and threw reins over his mount's head. He left the horse to graze and went across the hummocky turf to the tower, hoping its inhabitant would share his morning meal.

The door stood open, much as the shutters did. Aidan called out but received no answer; after an indecisive moment he ducked beneath the low lintel stone and went in. He had coin. He did not know a crofter alive who spurned good money, even from a stranger too hungry and impatient to wait for an invitation.

The tower was round. So was the room. The walls were bare of tapestries, but whitewashed. Kindling had been laid in the rude fireplace, but the fire had gone out. Aidan, with flint and steel in his belt-pouch, knelt to tend it properly.

In the gray light of dawn there was an air of desertion in the tower, and yet signs of habitation belied the feeling. A narrow cot was pushed against the curving wall. A table with only the merest slant to its legs stood in the center of the room. A stool was tucked under it. A rickety bench leaned against the wall by the door; on the other side was a twist of stairway, leading toward the upper floor, and the roof.

Aidan heard a step in the doorway. Still kneeling, he turned. He thought the posture less threatening to the man who lived in the tower, especially with flint and steel in his hands rather than knife or sword. But the anticipated man resolved himself into a woman, Aidan rose anyway, hastily, and tucked the implements away.

Mist was behind her, and sunlight. It clung to her roughspun gray cloak, shredding as she moved, dissipating as she smiled. Her unbound hair, snugged beneath the cloak, was black and glossy as a raven's wing. Something about her reminded Aidan of someone—black hair, wide black eyes; a vivid, alluring beauty.

The thought came unbidden, shredding the residue of his fear. *She could give me escape. She could give me release.*

So many women had. And this one expected it. He had learned to judge the eyes, the subtleties of movement.

She can give me ease . . .

He smiled as she came into the tower, and took the bucket of water from her hands. Their fingers touched briefly.

Kivarna—and other things—told him the truth. *She wants it as much as I.*

He set the bucket on the table, hoping the weight did not prove too much. The table held. So did her gaze, locked on his face. Her own was enigmatic. She did not question his presence in her tower; she did not appear frightened or dismayed by finding a stranger in her dwelling. She merely dropped the cloak from her shoulders and tossed it across the table, next to the bucket, and smiled.

Her gown, incongrously, was crimson, bright as new-spilled blood. It was cut loose at the shoulders, loose at narrow waist. He saw that her hair, now freed of cloak, was completely unbound, falling nearly to ankles. Loose gown, loose hair; moist, smiling mouth. Aidan, drawing a difficult breath, felt the powerful response deep in his belly.

He thought of Shona. Of Ashra. Of Blythe. Of women he had bedded, and women he had wanted to. Before *this* woman, all of them paled to insignificance.

She will give me heart's ease, and banish Gisella's words.

Black lashes were long, and eloquent. She knew how to use her eyes, her face, her body. Her tone was langourous. "Were you sent?" She paused, stroking back a strand of hair with a negligent, silver-tipped nail. "Or did you come?"

"I—came."

"Ah." She moved past him to the fire, loose grown swirling, loose hair swinging, and put out elegant hands. A curtain of silken hair fell forward across her right shoulder and hid her face from him. "My thanks for the fire, my lord."

The earring was hidden by hair, the *lir*-bands by his cloak, as was his belt. There was nothing about him, he thought, worthy of attaching rank to him."Why do you call me that?"

Still her face was hidden. "You wear it like a crown." She turned, black eyes alight. "Do you know who I am?"

Mutely, he shook his head. He did not really care.

She laughed softly: a husky, seductive sound. "I am a woman

and you a man. Perhaps that is all you need to know." Her smile was enigmatic. "I am a whore, my lord—or so *they* would have you believe."

His voice was rusty. " 'They'?"

"The castle folk." She waved a graceful hand, indicating the distances beyond the door, the mist, the morning. "Your kind, my lord."

"Are they? Are you?" He knew he did not care. Not in that moment. She was the most striking woman he had ever seen. She burned with a flame so bright he could feel it in his own flesh, creeping through to bones.

She lifted both hands and threaded fingers into hair, pulling it up from shoulders, from neck, from face. It cascaded through slender fingers, defining the shape of her face and the elegant line of her spine. "Do you want me, my lord?"

Aidan wanted to laugh, but could not. She was blatant in her actions, but he found he did not care. "If I lay with you, lady, it would mean what the castle folk say is true."

More hair slipped through her fingers. "Do you care?"

No. No and no. "What payment, lady?"

Black eyes narrowed. As she took her hands away, hair curtained the sides of her face. "You could not pay it, my lord. And you might be grateful for it."

He thought not. He also thought she lied. A glance at the narrow bed, too narrow for two people, confirmed it. He did not know what she played at, or why, but he was tired of it. "I came in because I was hungry. I hoped to bargain for food . . . but I will leave, if you prefer it."

It was the hardest thing he had done, when he wanted to stay so badly.

She laughed. "No. I prefer no such thing. Your cloak, my lord . . . and I will give you food."

He slipped it and gave it to her. Her eyes, marking *lir*-bands, widened briefly. Something else came into her eyes as he saw the links threaded through his belt. Something akin to avarice, and comprehension. Uneasily, Aidan began to wonder if she were a whore after all, and counting her price in advance.

She fed him on barley bread and eggs, and when he asked where were her chickens she smiled and said she required none. He drank milk but forbore to ask about the cow, because he feared she might say she had none. She seemed to have very little, and yet gave it all to him.

When he was done she took his hand and let him to the narrow stair behind the door, and took him up to her bedroom.

No narrow cot was shoved against the curving wall. In the center of the chamber stood a wide bed draped with fine linens and lush pelts. There was nothing else in the room. Slanted light from a single wide casement illuminated the bed.

He looked at her. He could not call her whore. Something in her eyes kept him from it, though he understood her now. She needed no cow, no chickens, no stock. She needed nothing but the continued attentions of any man who could pay her price.

Surely *he* could. He would be Mujhar of Homana.

"Can you banish dreams?" he asked. Then, more intensely, "No—can you banish nightmares?"

The woman's smile gave him his answer. He put out his hand, and she took it.

He awoke to the chime of gold. It rang repeatedly, as if someone counted coin; as he listened more closely he realized it was not coin at all, but links. And he sat upright in the bed.

She was wrapped in his cloak. Bare feet and ankles showed at the hem; the rest was flung carelessly around the slender, magnificent body he had so thoroughly enjoyed. Her hair flowed to the pelt coverlets and pooled, blue-black on indigo.

"Where is your *lir?*" she asked.

He stared at her. Then her eyes moved from the chain to his face. Very softly, she repeated her question.

"In Erinn," he said at last. "Does it matter?"

Her lips parted in a glorious smile. "I think it might." She dangled the chain from one hand. It glowed in slanting sunlight. "How did you come by *this?*"

He did not care for her manner. He altered his own to match it, hoping the answer might startle away her arrogance. "A gift," he said, "from the gods."

"Ah." She nodded musingly. "I thought so." Once again the chain flowed back and forth from hand to hand, chiming. "Indeed, I thought so."

Frowning, he asked her the question he was beginning to think he should have asked at the very beginning. "Who are you?"

Something moved in her eyes. Something dark and dangerous

and infinitely *amused.* "Lillith," she told him gently. "Lillith of the Ihlini."

He felt his belly cramp, and something much deeper. Fear. Denial. Disgust. And comprehension. A terrible comprehension.

Lillith's black eyes glinted. "I could not believe it would be so *easy.* I thought surely you must know me. I thought it was why you had come, to vanquish the sorceress . . ." She smiled. "Corin banished me, of course, and for a while I went . . . but Valgaard grows tedious without my brother, and Lochiel saw fit to go to Solinde to try his own workings . . ." She shrugged an elegant shoulder. The cloak slipped, baring satiny flesh. "So I came back here, to Atvia. For a while. To see, from afar, how Corin dealt with Gisella." Lillith smiled. "Poor, addled Gisella—has she begun to plague *you,* yet?"

He could manage one sentence. "Gisella is dying."

"Is she?" Lillith considered it. "Ah, well, it is the price of remaining entirely human . . . I, of course, serve Asar-Suti, and have an advantage." Her eloquent eyes assessed him. "Do you know how old I am?"

Aidan drew in a tight breath. "Old enough to know better."

Lillith laughed. The sound was free, unconfined, and it frightened him. "Aye," she agreed. "But how old am I *really?*"

He had heard stories, of course. Lillith was Tynstar's daughter. Tynstar had been dead nearly a hundred years, and had sired Lillith hundreds of years before his death. And yet, looking at her, Aidan knew very well he could not believe the stories. She was young, beautiful, and infinitely deadly.

He ignored the question, and asked one of his own. "What do you want from me?"

Lillith thought about it. "Oh, a child, I think."

Aidan recoiled.

She nodded. "A child, such as the one I bore Ian. Rhiannon. To be used for Ihlini purposes." She looked at him consideringly. "Your prophecy rushes you toward reestablishment of the Firstborn. The Cheysuli may even succeed in accomplishing it . . ." Frowning slightly, she tapped a silver-tipped nail against one link. "We have, heretofore, failed to stop you. Perhaps it might be best if we *aided* you—only with a twist." Lillith's smile widened as she made a fluid gesture of explanation. "If we control the Firstborn, we control everything. One way to control them is to make our own." The faint smile dropped away. Her eyes bored into his.

"You, my lord, are very important to me, and to all of us. *You*, my lord, have the proper blood. You are everything: Cheysuli, Homanan, Solindish, Atvian, Erinnish. All you lack is the required *Ihlini* blood." Tilting her head, she made another graceful gesture. "Do you see? A child conceived between Aidan of Homana and Lillith of the Ihlini would *be* a Firstborn. The prophecy would be complete . . . only it would be on *Ihlini terms*."

For a long moment all he could do was stare. Her explanation was so clear, so precise. With unsettling matter-of-factness, she spelled out the doom of his race.

Worst of all, for him, was the knowledge she could do it. In part, it *had* been done; first Ian, by siring Rhiannon; then Brennan, by siring gods knew what on Rhiannon.

And what might *he* sire?

A shudder wracked Aidan's body. "You make me vomit," he declared, knowing he as much as she was to blame for this situation.

Lillith smiled. She put out a hand, drew a rune, and a chamber pot appeared on the floor beside the bed. "There, my lord. You need not soil the covers."

The hollowness in his belly began to knot painfully. He knew very well she could do whatever she threatened. But he would not admit it to her. "Will you resort to rape?"

Lillith laughed. "Rape, my lord? You only recently proved yourself more than capable of responding to me . . . and as for repeating the act, need I remind you your *lir* is in Erinn? You are, as Ian was, *lir*less and therefore powerless. You will do or say whatever I require." She shifted forward onto her knees, moving close to him. The cloak slipped, pooling across her heels. "You are quite helpless, Aidan—need I prove it?"

She said the last against his mouth. He tried to pull away, to strip her arms from his body, but something kept him from it. She was pulling him down onto the bed, rousing him, taking away his control and sanity.

She made him respond, taking him to the edge but no farther, even as he hated it, and then withdrew, laughing as he cursed himself, and her. She lifted the chain before his face, letting it drip from both hands. "*Lir*less man," she taunted. "Child of the gods, are you? More like child of the earth, of *me*—"

His eyes fixed on the chain. Heavy links gleamed as she cradled it. He thought of the Hunter, the Weaver, the Cripple. He thought of himself, on his knees before the Lion, sobbing aloud as he put out his hands for a nonexistent chain. And yet here it was before him, whole, unbroken, untarnished, joined by his own hands in the ceremony presided over by Siglyn, witnessed by Tye and Ashra.

Ashra, who had warned him a man might lose control of himself if a woman's arms proved too beguiling.

I am a child of the gods . . .

"No," he said aloud.

Lillith laughed. "Ian said the same thing, many times. But that spell is weak. The binding always fails."

"I said NO—"

The chain moved in her hands. Aidan, transfixed, watched it coil upon itself. Lillith uttered a single cry of shock and tried to throw down the chain, but it clung to her arms like shackles.

Godfire leaped from the tips of her fingers, then sputtered out. The chain wound itself around her right arm and began to work its way toward her shoulder.

"Stop it!" Lillith hissed. "*Stop* it!"

Aidan lunged from the bed and stumbled against the wall, feeling cold stone scrape against bare buttocks.

"Aidan!" she cried. "Make it *stop*—"

The chain crawled beyond her elbow. In the light from the casement, it glowed.

"*Aidan!*"

The chain burrowed through hair and wrapped itself around her throat.

Lillith gave up her entreaty of Aidan and resorted to a tongue he did not know. She shouted, hissed, chanted; calling, no doubt, on the noxious god she had served for so long. But the chain ignored her grasping, desperate fingers and settled snuggly around her throat, cutting off her voice entirely. All Aidan heard was a throttled inhalation.

White teeth showed in a rictus grin. Lillith staggered up from the bed, clad only in hair and gold, and turned toward Aidan, pleading soundlessly. Her color was deepening. Black eyes protruded slightly.

Aidan, unmoving, stood next to the casement. Lillith stumbled toward him, still wrenching at the chain, clutching at hair and flesh and metal.

She saw the answer in his eyes. Comprehension convulsed her

briefly. Then she turned from him, took two steps, and flung herself through the casement into the skies beyond.

When he could move again, he dressed. Slowly, because he still shook. He waited, sitting slumped on the wide bed, and when his strength began to return he thought he could manage the stairs. Carefully he went down, taking up his cloak from the crooked table, and went out to find her.

She lay sprawled on thick green turf, awkward in death as she had never been in life. He had thought she might have aged in death, showing her true features. But she was still Lillith. Still young, still beautiful—and still very dead.

Her hands were locked around the chain. Distaste stirred sluggishly, but numbness replaced it. Aidan pulled her hands away and freed the chain, then unwound it from throat and black hair. He set it aside and shook out his cloak.

When she was covered, save for the curtain of hair fanned out against the turf, Aidan walked out to the edge of the cliff. The chain dangled from one hand. He considered, for an angry moment, throwing it into the sea so far below, but did not. The anger dissipated. The chain was his, fashioned expressly for him by the gods themselves. It was so infinitely a part of him it even answered his wishes.

Or did the gods?

Aidan stared blindly across the turbulent Dragon's Tail to the clifftop Aerie of Erinn. And nodded his acceptance.

"*Resh'ta-ni*," he murmured. "*Tahlmorra lujhala mei wiccan, cheysu. Y'ja'hai.*"

Chapter Eleven

When Aidan, still somewhat shaken, returned to the castle he was met by a servant who said he must go to Gisella's chamber at once. Foreboding swept in from the distance he had built brick by brick in his soul as he rode down from the headlands, and he realized the delicately nurtured equanimity was nothing more than a sham. He understood the gods—or himself—no more than he had *before* Lillith's death, and now Gisella commanded his presence yet again.

Corin met him just outside the chamber. His face, beneath the blond beard, was excessively stiff. Only the eyes gave him away. "She wants you," he said harshly. The physicians say there is very little time . . ." He passed a hand over bloodshot eyes. "I think they have the right of it, no matter what she believes." His mouth flattened as he took his hand away. "She said she could sing to herself until you came."

"Gods," Aidan blurted. "How have you stood it so long? She is mad, completely mad—how can you bear to look at her and know she is your *jehana?*"

Corin shrugged awkwardly. "I learned years ago it was easier if I thought of her as someone else. Deirdre has always been my *jehana*—" He saw the expression on Aidan's face, the concurrence, and sighed, nodding. "Deirdre has been many things to very many of us. While Gisella has been—Gisella." He gestured. "Go in, Aidan. It will be the last time." A muscle twitched high on his cheek, beneath an eye. "This time I come, too."

Aidan went in. He was aware of Glyn's presence almost at once, which somehow soothed him. She sat very still in a chair beside the door, keeping vigil. A queen, even cast off, deserved whatever honor could be offered at her death. And word must be sent to the man she had married so many years before.

Glyn did not smile, though she looked up at him. Her eyes, so large and eloquent, seemed to offer strength, which he needed. He nodded gratitude almost imperceptibly, the moved slowly toward the bed.

Gisella's breathing was audible. It caught, was throttled, then rasped raggedly in her throat, as if expelled from lungs too tired to function. Her color was a sickly grayish yellow. Her eyes were closed, but as Aidan stepped noiselessly to her bedside, they opened.

Gisella smiled. "Do you know the story?"

Wary, he said nothing.

"The story," she repeated. "How I came to be mad."

Oh, gods . . . Aidan swallowed tightly. "I have heard it."

Her voice was thready, but unyielding. "She was a raven, my mother . . . not knowing it was a bad thing. Not knowing here, in Atvia, ravens are killed whenever they can be. They are a death-omen, you see." The cords stood out in her throat, like knotted wire. "My father saw her—saw a raven—and shot her out of the sky, Not knowing it was Bronwyn in *lir*-shape. Not knowing she fled him, meaning to go back to Homana . . . he shot her down. And as she died, she bore me." The yellow eyes were unflinching, untouched by the tale. "They say it is why I am mad."

She did not sound it. She sounded perfectly lucid. Perfectly normal. And Aidan, looking at the fading old woman, wondered if Lillith's death had somehow broken through Gisella's addled wits to another woman beneath. To the *real* Gisella, sane as anyone else, and worthy of wearing a crown.

Gisella's breath rasped. "The chain is broken."

He twitched. "What?"

"The chain. Lillith told me about it. She said she would break it. Destroy it. So the prophecy would die."

Aidan frowned. "When did Lillith tell you this?"

Gisella's face folded upon itself as she thought. "Days? Weeks? Perhaps months." She looked past him to Corin, who approached quietly. She forestalled his question. "*He* said he sent her away, but she came back. Lillith always came back. She *loved* me."

Aidan nodded perfunctorily, unwilling to argue that Lillith's attentiveness had nothing at all to do with love. "Granddame—"

"She broke it."

The chain again. Aidan reached for patience. "No."

"She *said* she would."

"The chain is not broken." He put his hand on one of the links. "Do you see?"

Feral eyes stared at the gleaming links. Gisella attempted to push herself up in the bed, but failed. And Aidan, much as he longed to help her, could not bring himself to touch her.

Gisella's mouth opened. "She said she would break it! She *promised!*"

"She failed." Aidan glanced sidelong at Corin. "Lillith is dead."

Gisella's eyes stretched wide. "*No—*"

"All of them are dead. Tynstar. Strahan. Now Lillith. Do you see, granddame? Their time is finished. The prophecy is nearly complete. Everything Lillith told you was a lie. The chain is whole. I am alive. And the prophecy *will* be completed."

"No." She glared up at him, trembling. "Throneless Mujhar. Uncrowned king—"

"Granddame, it is over."

"I talk to gods," she whispered.

Aidan's belly knotted.

"I talk to *gods,*" she repeated.

Corin murmured something beneath his breath. Something to do with madness, and dying. But Aidan knew better. Perhaps she *did* talk to gods.

He drew a careful breath. "What did they tell you? That I am to die?"

Her eyes lost their focus. "You are not to be Mujhar. The Lion wants someone else."

It chilled him clear to bone. Aidan suppressed a shudder, shutting one hand around a link. For all he knew, it was his own; for a moment, it did not matter. "Granddame . . ." It took all his strength to sound very calm. "Lady, if that is true, then surely the gods will tell *me.*"

Gisella gazed at him. "The broken link . . ." she whispered.

Aidan marked the bluish tint of her tips, the weakening of her voice. "Granddame—"

But she no longer looked at him. Her grandson was forgotten. Now it was her son she tried to reach, third-born of Niall's children. "Strahan never would have slain you," she said in a poignant appeal. "He only wanted to *use* you. He needed you. He needed me. He needed all of us," The cords of her neck tautened. "I needed to be needed. What I did was not so bad."

Corin's posture was impossibly rigid. "What you did cursed you in the eyes of your children forever," he said hoarsely. "You must decide if it was worth the sacrifice."

Her eyes were fixed on his face. As the last breath rattled in her throat, she whispered something no one in the chamber could hear.

When it was certain she was dead, Corin called in a servant from the corridor and ordered arrangements for the news to be carried throughout Atvia. Then, as the servant departed at once, Corin walked slowly back to the bed. He leaned down, shut the withered lids, then sat down upon the edge. From the bedside table he picked up a twisted gold torque.

He gazed at it steadily, turning it over in his hands. Aidan, looking at it, recognized the workmanship as Cheysuli. He had several similar torques of his own, though none such as this. It was, he knew, a Cheysuli wedding torque, signifying the bond between warrior and wife.

Corin's voice was odd. "He gave it to her before he had a *lir.* Before he knew what she was, and what she meant to do." He sighed heavily, frowning. Aidan sensed anguish, regret, sorrow, and more than a little confusion. No doubt Corin had expected to feel relief. But relief was slow in coming; what he felt mostly was grief. "She was Cheysuli, once. But they never gave her the chance to know what it meant."

Aidan damped the *kivarna* purposely, giving Corin privacy. "I would not presume to speak for Hart and my *jehan,* to say if they would or would not have forgiven her. I know Keely did not." He paused. "What of you?"

Corin's mouth twisted painfully. "She never asked. I doubt she knew how."

"And if she had?"

Corin looked at Glyn for a long moment. Tears stood in his eyes. "I think," he said finally. "I would have, had she asked. Had she *tried.*"

Aidan looked a final time on the woman in the bed, then turned to go. But Glyn, rising from her chair, stopped him at the door. Her hands were on his bare left arm, delaying him. He glanced at her in surprise and saw a deep compassion in her eyes. She did not have *kivarna,* perhaps, but her own measure of empathy was plain.

"Wait," Corin said. He rose from the bed.

Aidan wanted nothing more than to leave. Glyn's hands on his arm seemed to burn into his flesh, reminding him how easily he had succumbed to Lillith's power. He had wanted the Ihlini woman the moment he saw her, and while he believed any man, in his position, might feel the same, it grated within his soul to know he had been so malleable.

"Come into the corridor." Corin's hand on his shoulder guided Aidan out of the room as Glyn pulled open the door. She shut it behind them, staying within, throwing up a barrier between the dead woman in the bed and two men who owed their lives to her, if not respect and honor and love.

Aidan, dreading the question, stared resolutely down the corridor, as if his express *dis*interest might dissuade Corin's interest.

But if Corin saw the unspoken wish, he did not honor it. His voice was harsh. "You said Lillith was dead."

Aidan shut his teeth. "She is."

"We have been fooled before, *harani,* and to our detriment. Are you certain—"

Aidan's tone was clipped. "Quite certain."

Corin's expression was grim. "I hope you will understand if I insist on knowing how. Lillith has plagued us at all too many years—"

"I killed her."

"*You*—" But Corin broke it off. No doubt he was recalling his own sister had been responsible for Strahan's death. He relaxed. "Then we all owe you our gratitude. *Leijhana tu'sai, harani.*"

Aidan shrugged. What had happened was too personal, too unsettling for him to share with anyone. He recalled too clearly the power that had risen at *his* command. While he himself had not laid hands upon her, it had been at his behest that the gods had come to his aid. She was as dead as if he himself had twisted the chain around her throat and thrown her from the tower.

That sort of power, that sort of *influence,* terrified him.

"Aidan—"

"You would not understand."

"I might." Corin sighed. "I know very well what that woman was. But let it go. What matters is that she is dead." His gaze went to Aidan's waist, to the gold threaded through by leather. "Gisella spoke of this. She said Lillith meant to break it."

"She said a great many things." Foreboding made him curt. "*Su'fali,* forgive me . . . there are things too personal to speak of. Let it suffice that Lillith is dead, and Gisella, and the chain is whole."

"And what Gisella said of you?" Corin's hand clasped a bare arm briefly. "You know better than to give credence to a madwoman on her deathbed. She was babbling—talking to gods?" He shook his head, "Let us go down to the hall. There are preparations to be made—"

"No." Aidan felt the apprehension rising. He recalled with distressing clarity that Gisella had not been the first or only one to tell him he would never hold the throne. There had been Shaine, then Carillon. Even the gods themselves seemed to be preparing him for something else, something *more*. And the Lion, time and time again, had repudiated him.

He knuckled dampness from his brow. The biting edges of comprehension made him queasy. "I have to go." He heard himself: a half-choked, unsteady voice. "Teel is in Erinn. I have been too long without my *lir*."

"Aidan." Corin's hand closed on him again. Now his tone was commanding, granting no room for compassion. "Gisella was mad, and a tool of the Ihlini. Whatever she said to you, whatever her babbling meant, let none of it bear fruit. She was *mad*."

Aidan looked into the steady blue eyes so much like his grandsire's single one. He wanted to give in and agree, to laugh and jest and suggest they go to the hall, as Corin wanted, but he could do none of those things. He could find no words to tell Corin that Gisella had not been babbling.

That she was not the first to warn him of his ending.

That he was very much afraid.

Chapter Twelve

Wolfhounds gathered around her. Muscles tensed, tails waved, dark eyes brightened expectantly. Shona held the stick: the dogs were prepared to chase it until she forfeited the game.

It was a good throwing stick: long as her arm, gnarled and rounded, bent just enough in the middle to distribute the weight properly. It was their favorite, and hers; toothmarks scored in the wood dated back five generations. Shona pulled it behind her head and hurled it with all of her strength. An ocean of dogs gave chase.

It was a game she generally enjoyed, laughing aloud and calling encouragement as the winner then fought off a pack of usurpers, intent on snatching the stick from his jaws. But today, this morning, she neither laughed nor called out. She simply threw the stick again and again, methodically, until at last even the strongest of the pack retired to sprawl on the turf, huge tongue lolling freely. The stick lay at her feet, where the big male had spat it out.

She felt no worse, nor better. Perhaps she should have chased the stick.

"Shona."

Her mother. Shona shut her eyes a moment, then turned. "Aye?"

Keely's faint smile was neutral. "I thought you would be *glad* to see him go."

Shona bent and picked up the stick. "I am."

"Are you?"

"Of course. We said what there was to say, I'm thinking . . . what good in beating a dying horse?"

Keely sighed. The wind snatched at braided hair, trying to undo the plait that dangled over one shoulder. Like her daughter, she wore woolen tunic and trews, belted with Erinnish copper. "There is something to be said for speaking your mind honestly, instead of hiding behind diplomatic falsehoods. You are much like me: you say what you think. But there is a price for such openness, Shona. That sort of forthrightness makes it difficult to hide your feelings even when you most want to."

Shona hurled the stick. The dogs, still sprawled on turf, merely watched it fly, then fall. None of them went to fetch it.

She made a gesture of futility encompassing dogs and herself. "What am I to do? I meant to send him from me, brideless . . . then Corin's summons saved me from explaining more than I already had: that I'm refusing to surrender control of my life to something so binding as the *kivarna*. 'Tisn't *fair*." She broke it off, grimacing bleakly. "But it gives me no choice, now. 'Tis in my blood, and his . . . and we've had a taste of it." Glumly, she stared at the dogs. "Like a newborn pup on a nipple: give me more—and more—and *more*."

Keely sighed heavily. "Gods—how could we have foreseen? Your *jehan* and I put off having a child immediately, because of many things . . . and when at last we knew I had conceived I made him promise, if you were a girl, you would have all the advantages a boy has, growing up—if you wanted them. Among them was free choice in marriage partner . . ." Keely's bleak expression mirrored her daughter's. "And now because of this, that choice is stripped from you."

Shona shrugged. "I could still refuse. 'Tis difficult now, but once he's gone and the memory of the *kivarna* dies away . . ." She laughed abruptly. "Perhaps what I'm needing is to find an islander with *kivarna* . . ." But that, too, trailed into silence. "No. 'Tis too late. I'm lying if I deny it." She pressed both hands against her face and scrubbed violently at her brow. "Agh, what I *should* have done was go to bed with someone. If I knew what it was already, perhaps I could fight off this *kivarna*." She took her hands away and smiled ruefully at her mother. "But right now all I'm thinking about is how I felt when Aidan touched me. And how I'm wanting *more*."

"Like a newborn pup on a nipple." Keely smiled crookedly. "I come from a race ruled by *tahlmorra*. I am perhaps not the best person to offer advice. But it seems to me if the gods touched his blood *and* yours with this 'gift'—and then brought you together— perhaps there was a reason."

Shona snorted inelegantly. "The easy way, I'm thinking—let the gods make the choice."

Keely shook her head. "*You* must make the choice. And then you must live with it."

Shona shook her head. "No. 'Tisn't a question of living with the choice. 'Tis living with the *man*."

Keely looked past her daughter to the wolfhounds, rousing from their rest to fetch the stick once more. "There are worse to be had than Aidan."

"And he *is* half Erinnish." Shona grinned lopsidedly as she took the stick from the big male. "'Tis something in his favor—that, and the hounds like him."

Keely sighed resignation. "I suppose there are worse ways to judge a man."

"None better," Shona said, and hurled the stick skyward.

Aidan stepped off the ship onto the docks at Kilore and stopped dead in his tracks. The *lir*-link meshed even as he sent the preemptory call to Teel.

Relief as the link flared anew washed through him with such abrupt violence he nearly fell. Trembling, he draped himself against the nearest stack of crates and lost himself in the reaffirmation, conscious of odd looks from strangers and not caring in the least. All that mattered was Teel. Only Teel.

Lir.

Eyes snapped open. *Where are you?*

Here.

Aidan looked up intently and saw the dark speck in the sky, rising over the fortress atop chalky palisades. The smile hooked one corner of his mouth and then both, widening to a transfixed expression of relief and exhilaration.

Slowly the speck enlarged, and wings became visible. Aidan sighed deep contentment. Muttering his thanks over and over again, he gripped the crate and waited for the physical contact. As Teel settled onto his left shoulder, Aidan grinned fatuously into the sunlight.

After a moment, he laughed. *Has it been like this for you?*

Teel did not answer at once. When he did, the characteristic acerbity was missing. *We belong together. They made us for one another, you and I.*

You *were* the one who said I should go.

But I did not say we would enjoy it. Teel paused. *Will you fly?*

Aye, Aidan said fervently. *I have been too long on the ground.*

Teel lifted off the shoulder and flew. Aidan, not caring one whit who saw the shapechange, with or without warning, lifted both arms, snapped up hands, give himself over to the change.

The void was swift and powerful, filling him with familiar exultation. As always, he walked the edge of pain, but it was a sweet, comforting pain, filling every portion of his being with triumph. He would not trade this for anything, anything at all.

Muscles knotted. Bones reknitted. The heart, pumping blood, sought and found new avenues. Aidan, shouting aloud, heard the human voice altered even as he cried out, and knew the change complete.

He did not go at once to the fortress, but lingered over Kilore with Teel, sweeping across the ocean, then angling back again. He was not a hawk, to soar, or a falcon to plunge in stoop, but a raven. He flew as a raven flies, glorying in the freedom, but knew it only delayed what lay before him. So he flew to the fortress gates, took back his human form, and gave polite greeting to the astonished guard contingent.

Aidan smiled blandly. "Surely you have seen the Lady do similar things."

One of the men cleared his throat. "Aye. But she always warns us, first."

That did not sound like Keely. But then perhaps she had changed, during her years in Erinn; after all, he had not known her at all. She had sailed from Homana when he was but a few months beyond a year. He did her a disservice if he gave credence to *all* the tales.

He was admitted at once and went immediately into the fortress, looking for Sean and Keely. He found them in the central hall, occupied by guests. He paused in the doorway, thinking another time might be better; Keely saw him, put something down, rose and called him in. Sean, bent over a gameboard with another man, looked up, saw him, pushed away his stool.

Aidan acceded to Keely's invitation solemnly, the peace regained in *lir*-shape dissipating too quickly. He felt the eyes on him, all of them, and glanced briefly at the visitors as he made his way to Keely. And realized, as he looked at the man with Sean, he was among kinfolk. There was only one man in the world who claimed all of Sean's size and more, as well as the flaming red beard.

"Well?" Keely's voice was sharp.

He saw no reason to soften the truth, or belabor it. "The Queen of Homana is dead."

She was very still. Then she drew in a deep breath, released it, nodded once. "*Leijhana tu'sai.*"

Aidan felt a flicker of unaccustomed hostility. "Are you giving me thanks for the news, or to the gods for answering your petition?"

Keely's mouth opened. Blue eyes were wide and astonished, outraged by his presumption, and then he saw the flinch of comprehension. Keely turned from him rigidly and sought her chair, sitting down with exceptional care. She took from the table the thing she had held as he entered; he saw it was a sword. Now it rested across her knees, as if she meant to continue polishing it, but she made no move to pick up the cloth. Both hands were on the blade, dulling the shine; he saw the tension in her fingers as she closed them, and he wondered if she intended to cut herself so the physical pain would keep the emotional at bay.

"*Jehana,*" Keely said numbly. No one made a sound, not even Sean, who watched her compassionately, or the blonde woman nearest her with a young child in her lap.

The moment lasted a year. Then, with renewed resolution, Keely shook her head. "No. That was Deirdre—" She looked at Aidan, blinking away unshed tears. "There are kinfolk for you to meet."

Aidan smiled. "I know. Rory Redbeard, is it not?" He nodded a greeting, glancing at the huge man.

"And your *su'fala,*" Keely continued steadfastly, as if introductions might delay the acknowledgment of Gisella's passing. "Maeve. And four of five cousins."

Courtesy kept him in the hall. He greeted all of them—the blonde, green-eyed woman very much like Deirdre, her mother; the red-haired boy of sixteen, so obviously Rory's; the blonde girl of fourteen or so, and another perhaps ten, both sweet-faced and shy; the last a very young child in Maeve's arms—but he wanted only to find Shona. There were things he needed to say to her.

"Where is—"

Sean was the one who answered. "Outside, with Riordan. And Blais." His brown eyes were steady. "On the south side of the wall, shooting arrows."

Aidan nodded absently and turned to go at once, only vaguely aware he should stay to talk, to exchange news, but to do so would drive him mad. He had renewed his link with Teel; now there was Shona.

"Aidan."

Irritated, he turned back. Keely rose, holding the sword. "I want you to have this. I had it made—'tis a woman's blade."

The Erinnish lilt nearly made him smile. "I thank you for your generosity, *su'fala*, but what use is a woman's blade to me?"

"Not for you. For your daughter, For Shona's—" Keely broke it off, scowling fiercely at the blade. "I want no milk-mouthed granddaughter in Homana-Mujhar. Give her a sword, Aidan—and give her the means to use it."

Keely set the sword into his hands. He appraised it carefully, marking its superior balance, the perfect weight, and excellent quality, and grieved that he would dishonor the giving as well as hurt Keely. But there was nothing else for it. He would not lie to her.

Aidan handed back the sword. "Keep it," he said softly. "And give it to *Shona's* daughter."

The emphasis was deliberate. As he turned away he heard her indrawn breath of shock, and knew she understood what he intended to tell her daughter.

He found them, as Sean had said, on the south side of the fortress wall. Three of them: Riordan, Shona, and a stranger. Their backs were to him as he approached. Shona's thick blonde braid divided her back in half, dangling to her thighs, and Riordan's unruly shoulder-length hair tumbled in the wind. But the stranger's hair was very black, also long—though not nearly as long as Shona's—and also braided. For a moment Aidan believed the stranger a woman, until he looked beyond the hair and saw height, shoulders, stature.

He wore Erinnish clothing: long-sleeved wool tunic, dyed dark green, with copper-bossed leather bracers snugged halfway up his forearms; leather over-tunic, belted with copper platelets hooked together by copper rings; and green woolen trews tucked into low-heeled calfboots. Although most Erinnish were light- or red-haired, Aidan had seen some with near-black hair. But there was no doubting the stranger's heritage, regardless of where he was or what he wore. His eyes, when he turned, were pure Cheysuli yellow.

Aidan's *kivarna* tingled. Recognition, acknowledgment; his blood knew perfectly well even if *he* did not.

The stranger smiled. The hair, though braided back in an Erin-nishman's warrior plait, looped through with cord, was also held from his face by a slender leather thong.

This man looks more Cheysuli than I do, even without the gold . . . It was an unsettling thought. Aidan did not know him. Neither did his *kivarna*.

But then Shona turned, and Aidan forgot all about strange Cheysuli warriors. So, clearly, did she; her color drained away, leaving her gray as death, then rushed back to splotch her cheeks and set brown eyes to glittering with a vibrant intensity. In loud silence, she held the bow. A compact Cheysuli warbow once refused to her brother.

Now apparently not. Riordan, deaf and blind to the sudden tension—which betrayed the absence of *kivarna* in Sean's son—impatiently tapped the bow. "Shoot it, Shona—or let *me* shoot it!"

Aidan approached steadily, taking care with each step. He was not purposely delaying the moment, but his nerves screamed with acknowledgment of her nearness. He refused to give into emotion, or physical sensation, merely to please a gift he did not fully understand. His *kivarna* needed training. He was prepared to instruct it.

Riordan now tugged at the bow, but Shona was unmoved. She clung to the weapon with steadfast determination, ignoring her young brother's muttered threats. She was as intense as Aidan; he wondered if she, too, fought the silent battle with her senses.

He meant to speak to Shona. But the stranger, standing beside her, beat him to it. "Aidan, it is?" he asked. "They said you'd be coming—but not so soon, I'm thinking . . . unless Gisella died."

Distracted, Aidan spared only a quelling glance for the stranger. His world was alive with Shona's nearness, and yet something about the stranger snared his attention as well. It was more than a little astonishing to hear a Cheysuli warrior speaking pure, fluent Erinnish with a broad Erinnish accent. His command of the tongue and its nuances was expert enough to mark him islander-born, except that he was so blatantly Cheysuli.

And then Aidan knew. Not islander-born, but almost. As close as one could come, while drawing first-breath in Homana. "Blais?" he asked tentatively, recalling Sean's brief mention.

The other nodded, grinning. "Half-cousins, we are. Maeve is my mother. And the Redbeard, well . . ." Blais shrugged, gesturing oddly. "In spirit if not in blood, Rory is my father."

In spirit *only*. Aidan recalled, with unsettling clarity, precisely who Blais was.

Yellow eyes narrowed assessively. "If you're not minding, cousin, I'll be sailing back with you."

"Back?"

"To Homana." The faint smile was ironic. For all his accent was Erinnish, Blais' attitude was Cheysuli. "You *will* be going back, I'm thinking . . . who would turn his back on a throne like the Lion?"

Who indeed? Certainly not Teirnan, Blais' true father. Teirnan still fought *for* the throne, with his treacherous followers.

Blais' eyes glinted. In fluent Old Tongue, he said, "I think it is past time I met my *jehan*. I have a *lir*, but no gold, no Ceremony of Honors, no proper *shu'maii*. I am as Cheysuli as you, cousin . . . do you not think I am due what other warriors are given?" He paused delicately, then added in Homanan, "A warrior should know his own bloodline. It is easier for the gods to keep track of us."

A well-schooled tongue . . . But Aidan, looking from Blais to Shona, forgot his kinsman almost at once.

"Now, then." Blais, smiling privately, switched back into Erinnish as he took the warbow from Shona. "We'll be letting *me* show the boy, while you two take a walk."

Shona made no protest. She walked to Aidan, then by him toward the headlands, out beyond Kilore.

She stopped at last, pausing on an overlook above the Dragon's Tail. Wind whipped them both, dragging at Aidan's hair, but Shona's was safely confined in a network of complex braids, small ones wrapped around big ones, then joined into a single thick plait that hung like rope from her head. She still wore trews and tunic, but the wool was very fine, the pale yellow dye very good, the embroidery exquisite. Her throat was naked of ornaments. Aidan longed to touch it, to put a torque upon it in the shape of his own *lir*.

Or one perhaps incorporating a wolfhound as well, to show they *shared* the bond.

Shona's voice was tight. "I thought you would stay there longer."

It was not quite what he had hoped for. "She died yesterday, at midday."

Shona shrugged slightly. "I thought you might stay with Corin, for whatever ceremony is due her." She paused. "She was my granddame, too."

He had not thought of it. "Did you ever see her?"

Shona's laugh was a blurted, breathy exhalation. "My mother would never let me. But then, I never asked." At last, she looked at him. Something flickered in her eyes. "'Tis sorry I am, Aidan. For you, if not for her . . . my mother never allowed me to think of Gisella without thinking of what she did, but 'twas probably different for you. Your father likely didn't hate her so much."

"My father only rarely spoke of her. There was no hatred of her—just an absence of thought." Discomfited, Aidan shrugged. "Deirdre was there. No one wanted to dishonor her. So no one mentioned Gisella."

"And now the Mujhar is free . . ." Shona smiled a little. "D'ye think he'll marry her now, and make her a queen at last?"

Aidan laughed. "The moment he hears the news, the Mujhar will summon a priest." Then the humor died. "No, perhaps not— Gisella *was* the queen, and there are proprieties . . ." He sighed. "Deirdre will have to wait. But she has already waited so long, I doubt this will disturb her."

"And Maeve will be a princess, true-born and legitimate." Shona laughed. "A bit too late for my mother . . . she said she resented Maeve's bastardy for a very long time, since it made Keely of Homana something to be prized for other than she was. She told me if Maeve had been trueborn, *she* would have had more freedom."

"And likely she would not have married your father, and you would not be here." Aidan paused. "I am going home to Homana."

Shona nodded. "I know."

"Alone."

Her color drained. "*Why?*"

"Because I am going to die."

Anger. Resentment. Her *kivarna*, and his, was ablaze. "How can you know?" she snapped. "How can you think such a thing? And how can you be such a *fool* as to think I will believe you?"

"Shona—"

"If you're not wanting me, say it. Stow this blather about dying, and say it. I'm not needing lies made up to hide the truth, merely to spare my feelings." Her brown eyes were nearly black. "D'ye think I can't tell, with the *kivarna*? D'ye think—" And then she broke off, eyes widening. "By the gods of all the oldfolk, you *do* believe you're to die!"

Aidan turned from her. He could not bear to look into her eyes and see the shock, the comprehension, that reinforced his own.

Shona more than any might understand how he felt, and that doubled comprehension frightened him even more. He could, when he tried, ignore it, shunting aside the gnawing fear, but Shona brought it back. Shona deepened it.

"Aidan."

He walked rigidly to the edge of the cliff and stared down at the turbulent sea.

"Aidan—" And then she broke off, muttering in swift, disgusted gutter Erinnish he could only barely understand, because his mother had never taught him.

"Go back," he said roughly. "Blais might suit you better."

The muttering stopped. Shona's voice was dry. "Blais is sailing with you." She came up and stood beside him. Wind whistled across the headlands, curling over the lip of the cliff. "Why are you dying?" she asked.

Deep inside, something knotted. "Because I think I have to."

"*Have* to! Why? What man *has* to die, except when he's grown old?"

He did not know how to start. "There is this prophecy."

"I'm knowing *that*."

"And there are gods."

"That, too."

"And then there is *this*." He gripped the chain on his belt.

Shona did not answer.

Aidan clamped folded arms across his chest, to hold himself together. From head to foot, a shudder wracked him. "I killed a woman," he hissed, "without even touching her!"

She reached out to him. This time it was Aidan who pulled back, warding away intimacy.

"No." Shona closed cool fingers around his forearm. "You're needing it, Aidan. Who am I to look away? I'm selfish betimes, when I like, but I'm not cruel. You *need* me, just now . . . who am I to shut my eyes to your pain? What reason is good enough?"

He could think of one: *kivarna*.

But then she touched him and the *kivarna* blazed to life, shocking them both with its intensity, and he was babbling, telling her what had happened and how, except he did not *know* how, only that it had; only that *he* had, in his idiocy, in his maleness, allowed himself to be lured and seduced by an Ihlini witch who had done it before, even though he had been warned against it; an Ihlini sorceress who had seen him, seen his lust, seen a way to additional power through him, through his body, and through the child he would give her. He had been warned by Ashra, who was a tool of the gods almost but not entirely human; had been warned by Carillon himself, and Shaine; had been warned by Gisella—mad, dying Gisella, claiming she talked to gods—and who was *he* to argue? *He also* talked to gods, and with them, face-to-face. They told him things, he said, clinging to her hands so tightly he feared he might crush them. They told him things, and expected things of him, and he did not think he had the strength to do what they wanted him to.

Shona's voice was uneven. "And what is it you're thinking they want?"

"*Me to die.*" He expelled it spasmodically. Then squeezed his eyes tight shut. "Gods, Shona, d'ye see? Do you see what I am? I lay with her even though I had been warned, without even giving it thought, and when I knew what she was and what she could do— what she *intended* to do—I killed her. I called on the gods, and they answered. Because *I asked them to.*" He could not stop shaking.

Shona stepped closer. He tried to back away, but she held him, slipping close, wrapping arms around him in a hug intended to offer comfort. And it did, but something more; something he hoped she would not recognize.

Her smoky voice was soothing. "Hush, my lad, my boyo— you're not knowing what you're saying . . . you're all bound up inside and out, knotted to death with gods and dreams and uncertainties . . . 'tis no wonder you hurt so. D'ye think I can't feel it, with or without the *kivarna?*" She sighed heavily. "And you not knowing a thing at all, I'm thinking . . . ah, Aidan, how can you be so foolish as to think it's *death* they want? How can you know they don't mean you for something else?"

He gave way and hugged her hard, glad of her closeness, grateful to her for staying with him, for touching, for talking, for simply being *there*, so he was not so terribly alone.

He had been very alone for most of his life, even when in a throng.

But not with her. Not with her. *Never alone with Shona.*

Aidan clung to her with all his transitory strength. This moment, he needed her very badly. "Why not for something else?" He threaded fingers into the complex weavings of her braid. "Because of the dreams, and the things I have been told . . ." He was aware, suddenly, how close to the edge of the blade they walked, so tantalizingly near. If they slipped, if they allowed their attention to wander, they could be cut. Even killed. "Gods, Shona—don't—"

"D'ye think it matters?"

He was lost, and knew it. "I cannot take the chance. I will not punish you . . . I will not sentence you to a life of loneliness and abstinence . . . I will not marry a woman only to die, and make her a prisoner of the *kivarna*—" He pressed her against him, rocking, rocking, trying to assuage the pain, the longing, the need. "I will not do this to you."

"Aidan—"

He set her back, lifting a staying hand between them. He pressed air again and again, keeping her from touching him. "No. No. I am going back. Alone. If I am to die, I will do it without hurting you."

"And if you're *not?*" she shouted. "What *then*, ye *skilfin?*"

"No," he said. "No." And then turned from her stiffly, striding back toward Kilore.

Chapter Thirteen

She came as he lay awake in the darkness, wracked by self-doubts and contempt. Who was he to think he was an instrument of the gods, carefully selected for some specific purpose? Who was *he* to think himself different from everyone else, when each man and woman alive knew doubts and fears and confusion?

But who was he to deny it when he had proof in the form of a chain of flawless gold, heavy and substantial?

Who was he at *all?*

She came, pulling aside the bed hangings, and he knew her instantly.

He heard the robe slipped off her shoulders. He slept, as always, with no candle lighted; he required no illumination. In daylight or in darkness, he would know her anywhere.

Deep inside, he quivered. And then the *kivarna* awoke.

She climbed up into the bed. Her hair, free of plaited braids, rippled over shoulders to twine against the bed pelts. She was naked, but for hair; save for anguish, so was he.

The pain was exquisite; the knowledge bittersweet. Shona knelt beside him, then slowly placed a cool hand upon his chest. Beneath flesh and bone beat his heart. His breathing ran ragged.

"Ah, no," she whispered. "Don't let it be in fear. Let it be in joy."

His voice sounded rusty. "You know the truth, *meijhana*."

"Do I?" The hand drifted upward to touch his throat, his chin, his mouth. "Do you?"

Every sense was alive as she touched him. His body rang with it.

Shona's smoky voice was soft. "If 'tis myth, we'll have shared naught but a night's pleasure. If 'tis truth, then we'll by sharing *more* of these nights, I'm thinking."

Against his will, he smiled. And took her into his arms.

*   *   *

Two months later, at dockside, Keely put a sheathed sword into Aidan's hands. "There," she said firmly. "What excuse do you offer *this* time?"

He laughed. "No excuse at all. Aye, *su'fala,* I will see to it you have no milk-mouthed granddaughter in the halls of Homana-Mujhar. She will have this sword, and the means to learn its use."

Keely looked beyond him to the ship. Then turned abruptly away, as if she could not bear to look at the vessel that would carry away her daughter. Fiercely, she stared back toward the cliffs. "Where is Shona?"

"Bringing the dogs," Aidan said dryly.

Even Keely was startled. "*All* of them?"

Aidan smiled crookedly. "The big boyo himself, as well as the bitch from over-island, and the one from Atvia, and the two in whelp, and the one she got last year from the fawn bitch who died, and the pups from the last litter . . ." He sighed. "Ten or twelve, at least. We will repopulate Homana-Mujhar."

Keely inspected his expression. "Do you mind? She is head-strong, aye—I made her so—but she knows what she is doing. She loves those hounds . . ." She sighed. "I think it is compensation for having no *lir*-gifts."

"Or perhaps she simply loves dogs." Aidan grinned. "Here she comes now—and Sean. And Blais."

"And dogs," Keely muttered. "There will be no room on the ship."

"Not once those two bitches have whelped. Ah—here is Riordan, also."

They made their way to the dock, trailing hounds and servants with baggage. Blais strode down the dock first, accompanied by his ruddy wolf, who walked unconcernedly ahead of the pack of hounds bred to kill her kind. She had, as *lir* were required, made her peace with unblessed animals. Or else she had put the big male in his place, and he the rest in theirs.

Aidan glanced at the ship. High in the rigging, perched upon a spar, Teel preened himself.

Sean himself directed the loading of Shona's baggage, calling out orders in his rusty voice. The hounds milled around, getting in everyone's way; Shona's remonstrations did nothing in the midst of such confusion, for half the dogs were too young to have learned proper manners. But when at last the loading was done,

Shona sent the dogs up the plank onto the ship—and discovered none of them would go.

"Agh, gods," Sean muttered, and scooped up one of the bitches. Without further delay he carried her up the plank and onto the deck.

"There," Shona said, "d'ye see? Will you walk on all your legs, or be carried like a meal sack?"

The huge dark male, eyeing the ship balefully, leaned against her hip. Shona staggered and nearly fell.

Aidan fished her out of the pack and pulled her away from the water. "He will go when you go. Get the others on board—we can tend him later."

One by one the rest of the dogs were led up the plank and onto the deck. When at last only the big male remained, Sean himself knelt down to look him in the eye. "'Tis a fine, bright boyo you are, my lad, and 'tis sorry I am to see you go. But we've others here—though none as fine as you—and the lass will be needing you. Tend her well, my braw, bright lad, and come back whenever you like. The lasses will be mourning."

So was Sean. Shona went to him and hugged him, clinging to his big frame, then let go and turned away, putting her hand on the hound's neck. With no more urging required, he climbed the plank to his pack.

Aidan, looking at Sean and Keely, felt inadequate. He was taking Shona away from a warm, loving family who had instilled her with courage, spirit, and determination, along with pride and a powerful loyalty. He could not predict if she would find the same in Homana, or even if they could make it. For one horrible moment he believed he was taking her to a doomed future.

Sean shook his head as Aidan glanced at him. "'Tis something every man feels," he said, "and something every woman faces." His brown eyes were warm and bracing, and Aidan realized the *ki-varna* lived in Sean as strongly as in his daughter. "You'll do well enough, my lad. And so will my lass."

Blais came out on deck, leaning against the rail. "Are we sailing *today?*"

"*Skilfin,*" Shona muttered, then turned abruptly to embrace her mother.

Aidan climbed up the plank. The big male wolfhound greeted him with a whine. "She will be here in a moment." He patted the narrow head.

"Or two days from now," Blais amended.

Aidan glared at his cousin. "She has every right to take as long as she likes. Erinn is her home . . . *and* yours, I'm thinking."

Blais grinned. "An Erinnishman, is it? Aye, well—let her take her time. 'Tis indeed her home she's leaving . . . while I'm going to mine."

Aidan was surprised. "You intend to stay in Homana?"

Blais shrugged. " 'Twill depend on many things."

"Such as your father?"

Yellow eyes flickered. "A man has every right to seek out his *jehan*."

Aidan smiled coolly. "A Cheysuli, is it? After all this time?"

Blais sighed. "Aye. It is. And you should walk in my boots, cousin . . ." He thrust out one booted foot. "I have the hair, the eyes, the color, the *lir*—but no one in Erinn truly understands."

"Keely might."

"Keely does. 'Twas she who suggested I go."

Aidan frowned his doubt. "Even knowing—"

"—what my father is?" Blais shrugged. "She said that while *she* bore no affection for Teirnan of the *a'saii*, she was not blaming a son for desiring to know his *jehan*."

Perhaps because she never desired to know her jehana, *and felt guilty because of it.* Aidan nodded. "A man has a right to know his father. But he may not like what he meets."

Blais' expression was serious. "My mother never lied to me. I know what he did. I know what he wants to do. But I'm thinking 'tis only fair I hear *his* side of the story."

Aidan granted him that. But he did not think it would last.

Shona at last broke away from her kinfolk, hugging Riordan a final time, and walked straight-spined up the plank. Her expression belied nothing of what she was feeling, but Aidan knew. For all they promised to return as soon as was decently possible, such plans often changed. Keely herself had been home twice in twenty-two years, and not for the last fifteen of them. She knew as well as any the likelihood of seeing Shona any time soon was negligible.

Blais still leaned against the rail. Like Shona, he stared down at the dock. Rory and Maeve and their children stood beyond Sean and Keely, with Rory dwarfing all but Sean; both sisters were crying. Of all the women, only Maeve's eyes were dry.

Blais' jaw was taut. "She's not wanting me to go."

Shona shrugged as the ship was secured to sail. "None of them *wants* us to go."

"She less than most. She thinks I'll be joining my father."

Shona's tone was hard. "'Tis your decision, I'm thinking. To be a fool, or not."

Blais looked at her. "He's not softened your tongue, has he?"

Shona displayed her teeth. "He knows better than to try."

Aidan lifted a hand as the ship slipped her mooring. On the dock, the eagles waved, from the shadow of their aerie.

PART IV

Chapter One

By the time the ship reached Homanan waters, eleven wolfhounds had become twenty-four. Blais spent much of his time secluded with his *lir*, locked away in private thoughts. And Shona and Aidan, reveling in the wind and the freedom and the magic of the *kivarna*, were almost sorry to see the end of the voyage draw near. They had come to prize the isolation of the vessel, knowing all too soon Aidan would face the increasing responsibilities of his title. They had spent weeks learning one another's likes and dislikes, in bed and out of it, and were not quite prepared to lose the privacy.

And yet as the ship sailed into the harbor, it was Shona who clung to the rail and pointed to the mist-wreathed island so close to Hondarth. "Is that it?"

"The Crystal Isle? Aye." Aidan leaned close to her. "The *shar tahls* teach us it is the birthplace of the Cheysuli; that the Firstborn appeared there, then went to Homana."

Shona's expression was intent. " 'Tis where he took her."

"Where who took—? Oh." Aidan clasped a rigid hand. "Aye. And where she killed him."

Restless, Shona pulled away and paced two steps, then turned back, braid swinging, toward the island. "Strahan made this place over into an Ihlini domain. She said so."

"For a time. No one lives there now . . . it was and always has been, save for two brief occupations, a significantly Cheysuli place."

"Significantly," Shona muttered. "That's something I'm not knowing, with so much Erinnish blood . . ." She sighed, transfixed again by the mist-wreathed bump of land. "For so many years I prayed to be as my mother, able to talk to *lir* and take on any shape . . . but there was nothing. All I had was the *kivarna*."

Aidan laughed. " 'Tis enough, I'm thinking."

She flicked him an impatient glance, though a tiny smile acknowledged his purposeful lilt. "Could we go?"

It startled him. "Now? But we are so close to the mainland—"

"I'd like to go, Aidan. I know so much of what happened to my mother . . . and yet I've never seen any of the places I've heard so much about."

Blais appeared from the bow of the ship, flanked by his ruddy wolf. Like Shona, he stared hard at the island. "If 'twas here we were born, as the *shar tahls* say, we *all* should see the place. 'Tis history, and tradition . . ." He flicked an ironic glance at Aidan. "Or are you so secure in your heritage you're needing no reminding?"

Aidan understood very well the pointed jibe. Of them all, Blais had less reason to see the island. His Cheysuli father had turned his back on such things as tradition and heritage, forging his own renegade clan out of malcontents disturbed by too much change within the existing clans; yet if Blais wanted to go to the Crystal Isle, it indicated he at least wanted to weigh matters before deciding on a side.

Something to be said for our arrogant kinsman . . .

Aidan, giving in, turned to call the order to the captain, who in turn passed the orders along to his men. The ship heeled off of Hondarth and sailed toward the island instead.

Curving white beaches stretched in either direction, blinding the eye in sunlight. Shona, Aidan, and Blais, accompanied by adult wolfhounds and appropriate *lir*, strode off the ship onto the crushed white shells. A path wound away from the beach toward the wooded interior. Through the trees they could see the glint of white stone here and there, bleached brilliant by sunlight.

Shona directed the dogs up the beach, laughing as they romped, but then turned her attention to the path and its destination. "Where does it go?"

"Undoubtedly to the palace." Aidan gestured toward the white mass only vaguely visible behind foliage and forest. "It was a true palace for decades, serving the Firstborn, but later fell into disuse. Carillon restored it as a prison-palace for his exiled queen, Electra, and then Strahan lived in it for a time, in hiding . . . but other than that it has not been truly inhabited for many years."

"Why wait?" Blais asked lightly, and headed up the path toward the palace.

Shona looked back to the hounds. All but the two bitches with litters and the new pups were present, splashing through surf and leaping upon one another. Seawater glistened on wiry coats, silver-gilt in the sunlight.

"They have noses," Aidan reminded her. "They will find us if they get lonely."

She gifted him with a sour scowl. "They were bred for sight, not smell."

"Does it matter? If you like, I will have Teel keep an eye on them."

She gave the pack of hounds another judicious look, considering, then struck out after Blais, leaving Aidan to catch up.

The path to the palace was mostly overgrown, since it had been more than twenty years since anyone had tended the island, but Aidan and Shona found it less tedious than expected. Here and there a vine or branch was broken, testimony to Blais' earlier passage, and the white shell-and-stone path was layered with years of dirt, deadfall, and the unintended scatterings of animals. But it was easy enough to follow, and led directly to the big wooden gates in the bailey wall.

"Here," Shona breathed. "She said she climbed up the gate, and over . . ." Slowly she walked through the opening left by a yawning gate leaf. "D'ye see? She said the iron studs allowed her purchase for bare feet."

Aidan, following, looked at the gate. He would not want to climb it, himself. That Keely had, in the midst of a raging storm, to escape Strahan only underscored her determination.

"And somewhere here is where Taliesin died. He got her free of the palace, and used his sorcery to keep Strahan at bay for a little . . ." Shona glanced around. "They must have come from there. D'ye see? A side door, mostly hidden . . ."

Aidan, distracted, nodded. Something was impinging on his awareness. Something *tugged* at him, like a child on his father's tunic, trying to get his attention.

"And then across here, to the gate . . . she got over and ran into the trees."

Again he nodded. He was only vaguely aware of Shona's observations.

"Do we go in here? Or in the front?"

Aidan twitched shoulders. Something cool tapped his spine. "Wherever you like, *meijhana.*"

"Here, then. The way she came, with Taliesin." She paused. "Are ye coming, then?"

Troubled, Aidan nodded and followed her across the cobbles to the narrow side door, little more than a wooden slat in the thick stone wall. Its hinges were rusted stiff, but Shona simply grasped the latch and tugged, undeterred by anything so tame as twenty years of disuse and neglect.

Rust crumbled. So did hinges. The door fell away from the wall.

"Agh—" Shona caught it, then grinned as Aidan swore and sucked at the ball of his thumb. His instinctive grab for the falling door had resulted in a shallow slice. "Wounded, are you?"

He shrugged it away and levered the door against the wall as Shona peered into the interior. She sniffed. "I smell sorcery."

"You smell mold and dust and dampness—and perhaps a cousin somewhat interested in annoying us."

" 'Twasn't through here he came. The door was whole . . . besides, d'ye think he'd ever go in the side when there's a *front* way all the grander?"

Aidan looked inside the entrance. "Probably not."

"Go," she suggested, fisting him high on the shoulder.

Teel? Aidan appealed.

The raven's tone was amused. *Mold and dust and dampness. And, somewhere, a cousin.*

But nothing more?

Not here.

It was not nearly as comforting as Aidan anticipated. "Not *here?*" What did that mean?

"Will you go?" Shona asked. "Or d'ye want me to go first?"

Aidan sneezed. Mold and dust and dampness. "No," he muttered glumly, and went into the narrow corridor.

It intersected with a wider corridor running in either direction. The floors were floured with dust. Heading deeper into the palace were two sets of footprints: man's boots, and a wolf's pawprints.

"This way," Aidan suggested, and followed the marks in the dust.

Eventually they reached a wide doorway that opened into a massive hall. The ceiling arched high overhead, intricately fan-vaulted, pale, and delicately textured like an elaborate spun-sugar cake. The hall itself was rectangular, with arched windows cut through white stone high in the walls. Below each arched embrasure hung a faded banner. Window upon window, banner upon banner, dripping down lime-washed walls. The colors were muted by time, but the patterns remained discernible. Aidan, who knew his clan history, realized the banners were not of Cheysuli making, but of a much later time.

"Carillon," he murmured. "He must have had them put here."

"But would Strahan *leave* them here?"

"As reminders of his victory? I think so." Aidan moved further into the hall, abreast of Shona, who walked with her head tipped back, throat stretched, so she could see the vaulted ceiling.

Then she stopped. "Look at the columns!" Her voice echoed oddly. "All twisted into spirals—and the *runes*—"

Aidan looked as she touched the nearest column. It was, as she said, twisted, spiraling up to the fan-vaulting. On either side of the ridge that marked the upward sweep of the spiral, runes had been chiseled deep into stone.

"Can you read them?" she asked.

Aidan studied the nearest chain of glyphs winding its way from floor to ceiling, higher than he could see. "Some of them," he said at last, reluctant to admit he knew too few of the symbols. "Something to do with asking the blessing of the gods, and the birth of the Firstborn—" Aidan, broke off, shivering. The flesh stood up on his arms.

" '*Tis* cold, " she agreed. "All this stone, and no fires—"

"Not that," he muttered, then moved farther into the hall. "I imagine there were pelts, and furniture—" He broke off yet again, staring.

"*Aidan,*" Shona gasped.

They had moved from behind a column, angling into the hall. Now the dais came into sight. They stood far to one side of it, nearly behind it; from their view all they could see was one side of dark wood, sweeping forward like haunches, and the upward curve of the back. It arched up, then over, forming a wooden canopy.

"The Lion," Aidan blurted. And then, in relief, "No. No. This one is smaller, less elaborate . . ." He drew in a deep breath of relief. "Even the head is different. The jaws are not open—" He laughed, moving closer. "How could I—"

And then he stopped dead, for there was movement in the throne.

He thought, improbably, of yet another dead Mujhar, come to take him to task, to upbraid him for his failings. But there were none left. He had met with all he knew, those in his immediate ancestry. Those before Shaine did not matter, save for knowing their histories. Shaine had been the one most responsible for the plight of the Cheysuli, and for furthering the prophecy by *forcing* the Cheysuli to act.

Shona laughed. The sound rang in the hall and blotted out the darkness. " 'Tis *Blais*—oh, gods, we should have known." And she took Aidan's hand and pulled him around the side of the dais.

Blais, stumping negligently against the scrolled back, hooked a muscled, trew-clad leg over an armrest to dangle a boot. He arched one raven brow. "It suites me, I'm thinking."

Shona made a derisive sound. "No more than *me*, ye *skilfin*."

Aidan loosed his hand from Shona's and took two paces closer. The dark stone dais was low, barely raised above the floor, and the throne itself a much smaller version of the Lion in Homana-Mujhar, but it spoke to him nonetheless of majesty and magnificence; of power too long forgotten. Of things he needed to know, while knowing none of them.

"D'ye want it?" Blais asked lightly. "Will you fight me for it?"

Dimly, Aidan knew his cousin only jested. Blais was, for all his arrogance, a decent man, if uncommitted. Undoubtedly he jibed for the fun of it, no more; but to Aidan, transfixed by the throne, it whispered of heresy.

He climbed the dais. Blais, so casually ensconced with his *lir* at his other foot, did not move. Not even when Aidan paused and put out a hand to touch the armrest.

Its shape was a lion's foreleg, with a downward-curling paw forming the place for a hand. It was very like the Lion Throne in Homana-Mujhar in appearance, and yet Aidan was conscious of an entirely different presence. *That* throne had repudiated him. This one, somehow, did not.

Blais uncoiled himself and stood. "There. 'Tis yours. You've more right than I, I'm thinking—at least, until I settle things with my father."

Distantly: "Your *jehan* is a traitor. A heretic. He is *kin-wrecked*; do you wish to become tainted yourself?"

Blais' tone hardened. He spoke in Old Tongue to match Aidan's unexpected change of languages. "My *jehan, leijhana tu'sai,* does not even know I exist. My *jehana* never saw fit to tell him she had conceived, *or* that she had borne me, before sailing off to Erinn with Rory Redbeard." He slipped back into Erinnish. "I'll do whatever I choose, *kin-wrecked* or no. 'Tis due the both of us."

The wood was satiny. Aidan's *kivarna* spoke to him of tasks yet undone; of knowledge yet unlearned; of a people yet unborn. "Aye," he said quietly, answering Blais, and then took his hand away. He turned to face Shona. "Will you stay here? There is something I must do."

She stared. "Now? Here? But—"

"Will you stay?"

Shona and Blais exchanged glances. Eventually she nodded. "I'll wait. Blais and I can argue about which chamber was used for what . . ." Her voice trailed off. "Are you well, Aidan?"

"I have to go," he said.

Shona pointed. "There is the door. And that way lies the ship— if you take too long, I'll be there."

Grinning, Blais resettled himself in the throne. "And I'll be *here*. This beastie suits me well."

"*Skilfin*," Shona muttered, but Aidan walked away from them both and heard nothing more of their wrangling.

Chapter Two

Aidan walked out of the palace through the front doors though hardly conscious of it. And then directly across the cobbled bailey to the open gates, thinking nothing of Keely's escape or Taliesin's death or even Strahan's defeat. Instead he thought of the flicker of awareness that guided him. It was not precisely *kivarna*, nor was it the *lir*-bond that gave him access to the earth magic. It was something older, something stronger . . . something rooted more deeply in the fabric of his life—and countless lives before him—that drew him out of the old Cheysuli palace, where another lion crouched, into the forested depths of the Crystal Isle.

He heard a fluttering in the trees and glanced up to see Teel settling onto a branch. The raven's tone was almost too quiet for Teel. Too *gentle*.

Are you certain this is the way you wish to go?

Aidan stopped. *This is the way I have to go.* Something skittered out of his awareness, whispering of apprehension. He appealed to Teel at once. *Should I go back?*

I did not say that, nor did I suggest it. I merely asked: are you certain this is the way you wish to go?

Aidan drew a steadying breath and looked around. A path lay before him, though little more than a twisted, narrow passage through the trees and thick foliage. No one had passed for decades, and yet he made his way easily enough, even through snagging creepers and sweeping boughs. But he saw no reason not to go. He had felt no premonition of danger, and surely Teel would warn him if what he did might prove deadly.

He released the breath evenly. *It seems the thing to do. A thing I should do.*

The raven studied him a lengthy moment, as if weighing his worth. His eyes were bright and black. *Well enough,* Teel said finally, and flew away into shadows.

Aidan went on. He rounded a curve in the twisted path and saw the ruins before him: tumbled, rectangular stones that once had stood upright in a meticulous circle, warding a chapel. The stones leaned haphazardly upon one another, or lay fallen in the dirt. The doorway was shallow and lopsided, its lintel stone cracked. The stones themselves had once been a uniform gray; now they were pocked and stained with age, wearing green lichen cloaks to hide blackened pits and scars.

He approached slowly, peeling aside foliage. He was very much alone. Teel was gone, the link suspiciously empty. Aidan knew the raven was within calling distance if he chose to summon him, but obviously he was intended to go on without benefit of company. Not even that of a *lir.*

A single stone stood three paces from the door. Aidan passed it, paused, then ducked beneath the cracked lintel and went in.

The interior of the chapel was even worse than the exterior. Rotted beamwork had fallen like tossed rune-sticks in a fortune-game, hiding much of the floor. The place was little more than a shell, but Aidan felt the power. It was a tangible presence.

The altar leaned crazily to one side like a drunken man, propped up by fallen brothers. Sunlight penetrated the gaps between the standing stones and slanted deep inside, stripping the altar gold and gray. Worn runes were dark against the stone, nearly indecipherable, but they snared Aidan's attention and drew him to the cracked plinth and tilted altar like an infant to the breast.

He found himself on his knees. He could not recall when he had knelt, or if he had fallen; he knew only he felt dampness seeping through his leathers. His hands were pressed against the altar stone as if he worshiped it; he began to think he did. Or that he must.

"Gods," he whispered hollowly.

Did he pray? Or did he merely express awe, as so many did, not thinking at all of gods? Aidan could not answer. He only knew he hurt deep inside. Wracked with doubt, contempt, confusion, he was exquisitely certain he was insignificance personified.

He knelt before the altar of his ancestors, and cried. Because of anguish, of doubt, of uncertainty. Because he was so unworthy. Because his color was so dull within the tapestry of the gods; his link so weak, so fragile, so very sure to break. He was Aidan, and he was nothing.

"You are what you wish to be."

Aidan jerked upright and spun on his knees, one hand slipping instinctively to his knife. But the hand fell away as he saw the man. The Hunter.

He tingled unpleasantly from subsiding shock. With effort, he managed to speak. "Will you give me my answers now?"

"If you ask the proper questions." The Hunter came into the chapel and found a stone on which to seat himself. The incongruity struck Aidan; here was a god for whom the chapel had been built, perched upon the wreckage with perfect equanimity.

Aidan shook his head. "How do I even begin?"

The Hunter smiled warmly. "You began quite some time ago. As a boy, in fact. The dreams, Aidan . . . all those turbulent dreams that troubled your sleep."

"I have them no longer. Not since I sailed from Erinn."

The Hunter's mouth quirked. "Aye, well . . . women often have the ability to make a man think of things other than troubling dreams." The smile widened. "Enjoy your peace—and sleep— while you may. You have spent much of your life with neither." He paused. "Are your knees not growing numb?"

They were. Aidan took the question as an invitation to rise. He stood slowly, unsticking damp leather from knees, and fixed the Hunter with what he hoped was a compelling gaze. "Why are you here? Did I summon you?"

"In a way, but not through any prayer or muttered invocation." The Hunter's tone was dry. "I came here because it is time for you to know more. To answer all those questions you have had, and no one of whom to ask them."

"Good," Aidan said, before he thought about it.

The Hunter—the god—laughed. "Men believe we move in mysterious ways merely to confuse the issue. No. We have reason for what we do. If we wrote it in stone, most men would forget to read. If we showed ourselves to everyone the way we have to you, we would therefore become commonplace, and consequently of no importance. Gods must maintain some portion of mystery here and there, or the awe and honor recedes, and nothing is ever done."

Aidan had never thought about it that way.

The Hunter picked a daub of mud from his leathers. "There are men and women in the world who consider the gods little more than figments of imagination—for we gave you that, as well—and little more than a mechanism by which some—those quicker of wit and large of ambition—control others. It is a simple explanation, and effective. There are also people in the world who lay everything at the feet of a natural progression, denying our power, our presence, our *existence*." He shrugged. "They are welcome to disbelief."

"But that is heresy," Aidan protested.

"Ignorance," the god corrected. "They are afraid. Puffed up with self-importance because they believe strength lies in *not* requiring gods. They believe they have discovered Truth, and that it lies elsewhere. Not in the palm of the gods. " Smiling, the Hunter made the Cheysuli gesture denoting *tahlmorra*. "But it was we ourselves—gods, Aidan—who *gave* man self-rule and the ability to think for himself; therefore we also allow him his petty heresies. It is an individual's personal decision which afterworld he prefers— or none at all."

Aidan felt battered. "But I have always believed."

"We know that. And now you will benefit from it." The Hunter glanced away from Aidan a moment, then smiled. A woman came through the low doorway: a small gray-haired woman with magical eyes and a weaver's callused hands.

"Aidan," she said kindly, "you have been patient far beyond most men's capabilities."

Shame flared. "I have not. I have doubted, and feared, and railed. I have questioned."

The Weaver was unruffled by his admission. "Naturally," she agreed calmly. "Men must always question. We gave them curiosity, and impatience, and anger, and the need to know. You are a man; you are no different. But you still have been very patient."

Aidan felt on the verge of a great discovery. And he felt afraid. "So—now you will tell me everything?"

"We will give you the means with which to make your decision."

The response was swift. "There is no need. I will do whatever you ask."

She smiled, hands folded in a multicolored skirt woven of colorless yarn. "We do not require blind obedience, though often it seems that way . . . and some would go so far as to argue we do." She shook her head. "No. We require sacrifice and hardship, but given and undertaken freely, because learning is not accomplished without either."

"Have I learned anything? Or nothing?"

There was a sound at the tumbled entryway. "Surely you have learned *something*," remarked the Cripple as he crutched into the chapel. "You have learned how easily a man can be steered from the proper path by a woman."

Aidan stared fixedly at the old man, marking again the creviced face, the shiny pate, but mostly the missing right leg. It was as if the god had chosen to show himself in the guise Aidan had seen first.

He swallowed heavily, pulling himself back with effort. "Do you mean Shona?" Dread rose up like a wave. "Are you saying I should *not* marry her?"

The Cripple's dark eyes glinted. "We are saying no such thing. She has the blood your House requires."

"Then who do you—?" Heat bathed him. "Lillith."

The old man leaned on his crutch. "Ashra warned you," he chided gently. "She gave you good warning, and you chose not to heed it."

The response was swift. "I was *lir*less."

"An excuse."

"But the *truth*. She used sorcery."

"No. You *believed* she did, because you stopped believing in yourself." The Cripple shook his head. "Lillith, though indeed powerful, used nothing more than herself. With you, it was sufficient."

Shame suffused him. He was hot and cold at once, unable to look any of them in the eye.

The Cripple's tone softened. "But I will warrant you learned something from it."

"*Aye.*" The single word was heartfelt. "You answered me. When I called. When I asked your intercession. The chain." He filled his hands with heavy gold. "You answered my petition."

The Cripple was silent. The Weaver also said nothing. Aidan looked sharply at the Hunter, trying to suppress apprehension so violent it knotted muscles and belly.

The brown man's tone was infinitely quiet. "Think what it means," he suggested, "when a man can say he summons the gods at will."

Aidan had no answer.

The Hunter's eyes were steady. "Does it make *him* a god?"

"No!"

"Think, Aidan. Surely it means something."

"It means—" Sweat dampened his temples. Aidan wet dry lips. "It means they have chosen him for something."

"And does that make him better than anyone else?"

"No."

"Perhaps—different."

Resentment shaped his tone. "You *want* me to claim myself different, so you can shame me. So you can enforce humility."

The Hunter laughed. "We are not *that* cruel, Aidan. Answer truthfully."

"Do I think myself different?" Aidan looked from one to the other, to the other. "Aye. Because I *am*."

The Hunter idly inspected a cracked thumbnail. "And what will you do with your difference?"

Suddenly infinitely weary, Aidan sat down on a fallen stone. He could think of nothing to say that would please them, or satisfy their convoluted examination, and so he said nothing at all.

The Weaver's blue eyes were bright. "At least you do not speak before you know how," she observed dryly. "That is something."

"Something," the Cripple echoed. "I think he has become weary of us. I think he is exercising his impatience."

"What do you expect?" Aidan snapped. "You batter me with words and innuendos, hinting at tasks and undertakings . . . do you think I will sit meekly by waiting *forever* while you decide if I am worthy for whatever new game you have developed since the last time we spoke?" He glared at them. "What is the sense in bestowing self-rule upon us, and curiosity, if we are not to use either?"

"Some people do sit meekly by forever." The Cripple said mildly. "Everyone—and everything—has its place in the Wheel of Life."

Aidan, who had had this conversation with the Weaver, glanced at her. She did not smile.

"Chained warrior," the Hunter murmured.

"Chained prince," added the Weaver.

"Chained raven," ended the Cripple.

The Hunter took it up. "Chains that bind a man; chains that free a man."

The Weaver nodded once. "Bound, the life goes on. Broken, it is free."

The Cripple smiled. "Which do *you* seek?"

Aidan touched the chain. "I made it whole."

Dark eyes were fathomless. "The choice was made freely?"

"Aye. I chose it."

"Who are you?" asked the Weaver intently.

"Aidan of Homana." He looked at each of them. "Prince of Homana, after my *jehan*, who will be Mujhar. A warrior of the clan. Cheysuli." He paused. "And very, very confused."

The Hunter laughed. "The last is obvious. As for the others . . . well, your road yet lies before you. You have not come as far down it as we had hoped."

Fear flickered to life. "Not—?"

The Weaver's voice was gentle. "There is still the task to be done."

Aidan was on his feet, "*What task?*" he shouted.

"And the sacrifice to be made," agreed the Cripple, ignoring the outburst. "But I think, when the time comes, he will make it freely."

Aidan, angry and afraid, opened his mouth to ask another question. But he was all alone in the chapel.

And no wiser at all.

Chapter Three

In Hondarth they had purchased horses for themselves, and made arrangements for Shona's baggage train to follow at a more sedate pace. Now, having covered the distance between the port city and the crossroads near Mujhara, Blais looked at Aidan.

"Which way?"

"East. That way." Aidan gestured. "Mujhara is west, but a few leagues up the road. Clankeep, from here, will take you half a day."

Blais shrugged. "I've waited twenty-two years to see it. Half a day won't tax me."

Shona shook her head. Around her mount, wolfhounds milled. "You should come with us to Homana-Mujhar. There are kinfolk, and the Lion . . . can't you wait a day or two before haring off to look for Teirnan?"

" 'Tisn't just that," Blais said quietly. "There's the Ceremony of Honors, first, to celebrate my *lir* and warriorhood Cheysuli fashion, and to receive the gold I'm due." He slanted a smile at Aidan. "*Then* I'll be 'haring off' to look for my father."

Aidan frowned. "Forgive me if I offend, but who will be your *shu'maii?* You know no one in the clans . . . unless you mean to name me."

"No." Blais grinned cheerfully. "And I do know someone—a *shar tahl*, in fact. His name is Burr."

It took Aidan a moment to remember. When he did, he stared hard at Blais. "Burr is from the north, across the Bluetooth. I have spoken with him . . . how do *you* know him?"

"I wrote to Clankeep." Blais' patience was exaggerated for Aidan's benefit. "Burr wrote back, telling me what he could of my father, since no one else would." His face hardened. "Is it they're afraid I'll do the same? Without even knowing me?"

The question made Aidan uncomfortable. "I cannot answer for Clankeep . . . I only know that Teirnan's rune was erased from the birthlines. He was *kin-wrecked*, Blais—that means he no longer exists in the eyes of the clans."

The feral set of Blais' facial bones was more pronounced as he stared back at Aidan. "*Kin-wrecking* one warrior should not be passed on to his son, if he's done nothing. They're not knowing anything about me, least of all whether I'll be following my father. Why not judge me for me?"

Aidan shifted in the saddle. "He repudiated everything. The clans, the prophecy, the Lion—*everything*. He took with him warriors, *lir*, women, and children. Do you expect Clan Council to look kindly on a man who turns his back on everything our race stands for?"

Blais slipped into Old Tongue. "No. I expect them to look kindly on a son who is not guilty of the *jehan*'s crime."

Aidan looked at his cousin. He could not really blame Blais for his bitterness. He was not certain *he* would feel so sanguine if he were judged by the actions of a kinsman he had never seen. It was unfair, he thought; but then he had come to believe there were several things about Cheysuli tradition that were unfair.

"Go," he said quietly. "Burr is a good man—a *shar tahl* with insight—and he will aid you. He will make a good *shu'maii*. But if you need me, send your *lir*. Or come yourself. You will be welcomed in Homana-Mujhar."

Blais laughed. "That is something, I'm thinking." He glanced at Shona. "Be careful with the boyo, lass. Homanans are more fragile than Erinnish."

"Blais—" She steadied her horse. "Blais, give thought to whatever you do. 'Tisn't always your greatest strength—" she smiled "—and sometimes your greatest failure. Take the *time*, my lad, to be certain of what you do."

"Did you?" Blais inquired. " 'Twas *you* who brought all those wolfhounds." And then, as Shona glared, he lifted his arm in a farewell wave and took the eastern road. His wolf loped beside him.

Outlying crofts, cradled in troughs between hills, soon gave way to villages and then at last to the proper outskirts of Mujhara herself, until Aidan and Shona clattered through narrow cobbled streets toward the rose-hued stones of Homana-Mujhar, deep in the heart of the city. Shona spent much of her time whistling and calling back her wolfhounds, who wanted to investigate—or challenge—everyone, and Aidan was much relieved when the massive bronze-and-timber gates finally jutted before them.

"Homana-Mujhar?" Shona asked, leaving off remonstrating with the big dark male.

"The front gates." Aidan drew rein and leaned slightly downward, offering his signet ring as identification, but the men on the gates knew him and called out vulgar greetings, until they spied Shona and found a better use for their tongues.

Aidan, laughing, waved her through, counting wolfhounds, and was relieved as the last of the great dogs slunk through. The two bitches with litters had been left with the baggage train, so that he and Shona had not been slowed by puppies.

First the outer bailey, then under the portcullis that gave entry into the inner bailey and to the palace itself. Shona muttered something beneath her breath, staring in awe at the curtain wall, parapets, and ramparts. Homana-Mujhar lacked the crude, overt strength of Kilore, Aidan thought, but its sprawling magnificence could be denied no more than its defenses.

" 'Tis no wonder it never fell," Shona breathed.

"But it did," he told her. "Once, to Bellam of Solinde—with the help of Tynstar the Ihlini." He jumped off his horse and threw the reins to a horseboy, then turned to lift Shona down.

She was having none of it. Trews precluded the encumbrance of skirts and she jumped down herself, slanting him a scornful, amused glance, then gathered her hounds, close. "What of the lads and lasses?"

"We have kennels, of course."

She nodded pensively. "But—now? Can they not come in with us first?"

He blanched, envisioning giant wolfhounds racing through the corridors of Homana-Mujhar. "All of them?"

"We can put them in our chamber."

"It will not be 'our' chamber, not at first. The Homanans are somewhat bound up in proprieties . . . we will have to have separate chambers until after the ceremony."

Shona's eyes widened. "We've been sharing a bed for months! We've never kept it a secret."

"The Homanans—"

"—are *skilfins*," she muttered. "Well, then, if we're to have separate chambers, I'll be putting the hounds in mine." She turned on her heel and marched toward the steps, thick braid swinging.

Aidan, following, tried to compromise. "It does not mean we have to sleep alone, Shona—only *live* in separate chambers. No one has to know who sleeps where . . ." Except they would. Everyone knew such things. Common gossip had a nefarious power when it came to making the rounds. "Never mind," he said. "Put them wherever you will . . . but if any of them bites me when I come in at night, 'tis out to the kennels for them all."

Shona slanted him a glance. "Perhaps."

"Or you could come to *my* chamber."

She arched a brow as they reached the top step. "If the Homanans are so persnickerty—I'd be thinking *you'd* have more right to be sneaking about the castle at night than me."

"But I do not keep fourteen dogs on my bed."

"Eleven," Shona corrected pointedly. "And for now there are only *nine*, until the two bitches and the puppies arrive."

Aidan sighed. "Does it matter?" And then signaled the door to be opened. "This is the formal entrance. There are other, less conspicuous ways in—"

"My lord." A servant bowed briefly. "My lord, you are to go at once to the Mujhar's chambers. By order of the Prince of Homana."

"Go to—why?"

The servant was not forthcoming, except to repeat the need for haste. "At once, my lord."

Blankly, Aidan turned to Shona. But before he could say anything, she spoke to the wolfhounds, dropping each with a gesture. A command to hold kept them in place; Shona turned back to Aidan. "They'll not move to trouble anyone."

Another time he might have argued with her—his experience with dogs did not lead him to believe they would stay where they were put—but just now he was not even slightly concerned with whether the wolfhounds stayed or wandered. He merely nodded absently and led Shona through torchlighted corridors and up two winding staircases to the Mujhar's sprawling apartments on the third floor.

Two men in the crimson tabard of the Mujharan Guard flanked the largest entrance. The door itself stood open. As Aidan arrived with Shona, both guardsmen bowed. He nodded absently at them, then went in with Shona at his side.

He knew the truth when he saw Deirdre. She sat in a chair at

Niall's bedside, very still and pale. Her eyes were fixed on the bed's occupant.

Ian stood at one of the casements, his back to the doorway. All Aidan could see was his silhouette, but nothing more was required. The rigidity of Ian's posture bespoke the measure of his grief.

It was Brennan who came across the room to Aidan. His gaze rested briefly on Shona's stricken face, then he turned to his son. "He will wish to see you. Come."

Aidan was cold. Cold and sick. He did not want to be present. He wanted to turn and walk out immediately, to go somewhere no one could find him, because if he was gone the dying could not be accomplished.

But he did not turn and walk out. Slowly, numbly, Aidan moved toward the canopied bed. Aileen was there as well, seated on a stool near Deirdre. Curled at Niall's side was the ruddy-brown wolf, Serri.

Niall lay beneath silken bedclothes. But his face was uncovered still, displaying the ravages of the thing that would claim his life. The patch over his eye did not hide the loose downward slant of the right side of his face, or the drooping of his mouth. His flaccid flesh was waxen.

"*Jehan,*" Brennan said quietly. "Aidan has come home."

For one horrible moment Aidan feared his grandfather was already dead, but then he heard the ragged, shallow breathing and saw the single eye crack open. It was clear, unclouded by pain; Aidan's *kivarna* abruptly flared to life, bringing him the unwelcome and painful awareness that Niall knew precisely what had happened and precisely how long he had.

Niall's right arm lay slackly across the wolf, not hugging Serri because he could not, but touching him, maintaining the physical contact as well as the mental. Serri's head rested very gently on Niall's chest. Incongruously, Aidan thought of Shona's wolf-hounds. And then was ashamed.

A lir is nothing like a dog . . .

He was, oddly, perfectly calm. He stood beside the bed, beside his father, and looked down on the wreckage of his grandfather.

"Take his hand," Brennan said softly. "He cannot reach for it himself—and he would want it."

Dully, Aidan knelt down and reached for Niall's hand. The flesh was cold and lifeless. "Grandsire. I am come home."

The single eye remained open. The lips twitched, then twisted.

Niall's speech was slow and halting, but he made himself understood. "The girl?"

Aidan nodded, turning slightly to stretch out a hand to Shona. "I have brought her home, grandsire. All the way from Erinn. Keely's girl, grandsire . . . and Sean's."

Shona moved across the bedchamber slowly, lacking her natural grace. Aidan sensed her grief and shock and abiding regret: she looked on her grandsire the Mujhar for the first and last time, for it was quite clear Niall would not live to see the sun rise.

She stopped beside Aidan, but did not kneel. She was very tall in a chamber full of tall men, and incredibly dominating through sheer force of personality. Aidan, sensitized to her, still felt the tingle of her strength, and smiled in bittersweet acknowledgment as he saw the recognition in Niall's eye.

Shona wore, as usual, Erinnish tunic and trews, belted and booted. The heavy braid of intricate double and triple plaiting hung over her shoulder, dangling against the bedclothes. There was nothing even remotely feminine about her, or subdued. She burned like a beacon.

"Keely's girl," Niall slurred. "Ah, gods, but I knew she would bear one worthy of the blood and trust and truth . . ." He swallowed with difficulty. "You must wait your turn, my bright, brave Erinnish lass, but one day you will grace the halls even as my Deirdre . . ."

Aidan twitched. "Grandsire—"

Brennan touched his shoulder. "Not now, Aidan. Later."

But Aidan knew better: there would not be a later.

"Grandsire, I bring news from Atvia." He cast a glance at Deirdre, so white and still in her chair. "What would you most desire in the world?"

Niall was visibly weakening. "I have what I most desire."

"No . . ." Aidan caught Deirdre's hand and pulled her from the chair, onto her knees beside the bed, then placed her hand atop the Mujhar's. "No, there is more. There has always been more."

The dimming eye flared. "Is it true? Gisella—?"

Aidan swallowed down the painful lump. "Aye. In my presence." Then, knowing it would require a formal declaration in front of kinfolk as witnesses before being accepted by the Homanan Council, he raised his voice. "The Queen of Homana is dead."

The cold fingers twitched. Aidan took his own hand away and

left Deirdre and Niall to share the handclasp. Niall's voice was deteriorating, but he managed to give the order. "Have the priest fetched at once."

Deirdre was shocked. "Niall—*no* . . . let it wait—"

He summoned waning strength. "If I do nothing else before I die, my proud Erinnish princess, I will make you a queen."

Aidan, at the doorway, dispatched one of the guards for a priest. Then he waited beside the door, not wanting to intrude on the Mujhar and his *meijha.*

The marriage ceremony was necessarily brief. Niall struggled to say his vows. Deirdre answered quietly but firmly, and when it was done she bent to kiss his ravaged mouth.

"Queen of Homana," he whispered. "It should have been yours from the first."

Deirdre, dry-eyed, shook her head. "I never was wanting it," she answered. "All I ever wanted was you. The gods were kind enough to allow it . . . but oh, my braw boyo, the years have been so short . . ."

Niall's eye did not waver as he gazed at Deirdre of Erinn, now Queen of Hornana. "Better than none . . ." he whispered. "Better than none at all . . ."

She was queen for the space of a breath. As Niall ceased to live, the title passed to Aileen, and Brennan became Mujhar in his father's place.

It was Ian who executed the custom. Slowly he went to the bed and took Niall's hand in his, easing the heavy black seal ring from the still hand, and then he turned. To Brennan.

"My lord," he said formally, "you are the Mujhar. Will you accept this ring; and with it, my fealty?"

Brennan's mouth barely moved. "*J'hai-na,*" he said, "*Tu'halla dei, y'ja'hai . . . Tahlmorra lujhala mei wiccan, cheysu. Cheysuli i'halla shansu.*"

Ian waited until Brennan put out his hand, and then he stripped from it the glowing ruby signet of the Prince of Homana. He replaced it with the black ring etched with a rampant lion.

Brennan, stark-faced, nodded. "*Y'ja'hai.*" He took back the ruby ring from Ian, and turned.

Aidan, still standing by the door, abruptly realized the ceremony included him. Panicking, he backed up a step, met the wall with his heel, and stopped.

Brennan took Aidan's cold hand into his and eased the topaz

ring from his right forefinger. The ruby went on in its place. *"Tu'jhalla dei,"* Brennan said formally. "I declare you Prince of Homana, heir to the Lion Throne."

Aidan felt empty. He stared at his father, seeing a stranger; feeling a stranger himself, defined by a single sentence that did not, he felt, accurately sum up anyone, least of all himself.

"Tu'jhalla dei," Brennan repeated. Lord to liege man; they all of them were liege men now, if by definition different from the Cheysuli custom. That had been Ian's place. And Brennan did not, Aidan realized in shock, have a true liege man.

He swallowed heavily. *"Ja-hai-na,"* he whispered. *"Y'ja'hai, jehan. Leijhana tu'sai. Cheysuli i'halla shansu."*

He heard Aileen's quiet tears. Saw Deirdre's bone-white, bone-dry face. Saw the rigidity of Ian's posture; the grief and comprehension in his father's eyes. Sensed Shona's tangled emotions as painful as his own.

Something moved. He looked to the bed. Serri sat up, amber-eyed in the shadows. Then he jumped down and trotted out of the chamber.

Aidan moved.

"Let him go," Brennan murmured.

"But—*Serri*—"

"Serri is a *lir.*"

It was, Aidan knew, enough. Sufficient to explanation. And as he nodded, acknowledging, he heard, as they all did, the single distant mournful wail keening through the corridors.

In chorus, the wolfhounds answered.

Chapter Four

In the pale, still hours of dawn, Aidan found himself in the Great Hall. The firepit coals were banked. Only the merest tracery of first light crept into the hall through stained glass, muting the colors into unaccustomed pastel softness. The dawn did not yet illuminate anything below the intricate beamwork of the high ceiling, losing itself in scrollwork.

Aidan stood for a moment just inside the silver doors, listening to the silence, and then he began to walk.

He looked at the walls as he walked: at the faded tapestries generations old; at the brighter, richer ones worked by Deirdre and her ladies. He looked at the intricate patterns of weapons displayed on the walls: whorls of knives and lances, brass bubbles of bossed shields, the gleaming patina of blades. Even the floors now were not so stark; carpets imported from foreign lands softened the hard bleakness of stone. Once Homana-Mujhar had been little more than a fortress, a stone shell; now it was the cynosure in all its magnificent splendor, the seat of Homana's power. And the font of that power was the Lion itself.

Aidan at last looked at the throne, thinking of the smaller version on the Crystal Isle. But this one was different. This one was filled. This one housed a Mujhar.

Aidan stopped dead. He felt betrayed, his intention usurped. It did not matter that he knew the man, or that he was flesh of the man's own flesh, only that he had come to summon his grandsire, and his father had stolen the chance.

Brennan watched him with eyes devoid of expression. He sat slumped in the throne haphazardly, arms and legs askew. He wore black, as was his custom, and faded into the dim hollowness of the crouching Lion.

Kivarna flared. Aidan sensed grief and anger and sorrow and pain; the acknowledgment of a new task. And the desire to abjure it altogether, if it would change the present.

Aidan walked. And then stopped. He stood before the Lion and the Mujhar it now protected.

Brennan did not stir, except to move his mouth. "Men covet thrones," he said quietly. "Men conspire and kill and start wars and destroy cities, all for the winning of a throne. But rarely do they think of what it means to *sit* in one . . . or to acknowledge the consequences, the cause of the change in power."

Aidan said nothing.

"The firstborn sons of kings know they will inherit, one day," Brennan continued, "but they never think about how they will get it. They consider only what they will do when they are kings in their fathers' places, and what changes *they* might make, and how they will conduct themselves . . . but never do they consider how thrones pass into their hands."

It seemed to require a response. "How?" Aidan asked softly.

"A man *dies,*" Brennan said, "to make another king in his place."

Aidan purposely damped down the blazing of his *kivarna.* He had no desire to intrude on his father's anguish; and even less to let it intrude on his. "He would not have wanted to live forever," he said evenly. "Especially like that. You know that, *jehan.* His time was done. Yours was come."

"Too glib, Aidan."

"But the truth." Aidan glanced behind, judging the coals, then sat down on the rim of the firepit, balancing carefully. "When did it happen?"

"Two days ago. At midday." Brennan scrubbed a hand across his weary face. "He was with Deirdre, in her solar . . . they were discussing the need for refurbishing guest chambers. Nothing of any consequence . . ." He sighed, expression bleak. "One moment he was fine, the next—as you saw him."

Aidan nodded. He had heard of it before, though he had never seen the results.

"We were not at war," Brennan said. "And most likely never to go to war again, so that he could die in battle . . . but somehow I always thought it would come upon him another way."

Aidan thought of something he had heard once, and repeated it, hoping to soothe his father. " 'A warrior can predict his death no more than his *tahlmorra.' "*

Brennan grimaced. "Too glib, again. But then you have always had smooth words when everyone else had nothing." He moved, putting order to his limbs. "Why did *you* come?"

Aidan, hunched on the rim of the firepit, stared blindly at the dais through eyes full of unshed tears. "I wanted to bring him back."

Brennan said nothing at first. And then he released an uneven sigh that bespoke the grief and understanding. "I wish there were a way—"

"There is." Aidan's face spasmed. "I have done it before . . . with other dead Mujhars."

"Oh, Aidan—"

"I *have*."

Brennan hooked rigid hands over the clawed handrests and pulled himself forward, from under the Lion's maw. "Now is neither the time nor the place to speak of dreams—"

Aidan was on his feet. "But I *do* speak of them—because they are more than dreams!" He took two long strides forward, stopping at the first of three dais steps. "*Jehan*, you have no idea how it is for me—how it has *been* for me—"

"I have every idea!" Brennan cried. "By the gods, do you think we have not stayed awake at nights? Your *jehana* and I have spent countless days and nights discussing you and your dreams, trying to make sense of seemingly senseless things . . . Aidan, have you any idea how it has been for us?" He clutched the dark wooden throne. "And now you come on the night of your grandsire's death to say you can *summon* him!"

"*I can*," Aidan whispered.

Silence. Brennan's eyes were ablaze with grief and something akin to frustration. "We all loved him. We all would like him back. But none of us concocts a story—"

" 'Tis *not a story!*" Aidan shouted. "I have spoken with dead Mujhars: Shaine, Carillon, Donal—why not with *Niall* now?"

Brennan's face was ashen. His hands shook on the throne.

"I can," Aidan repeated.

Brennan closed his eyes.

I will prove it to him. I will prove me to him—Aidan clutched the links on his belt. *If I cannot prove this to him, he will never trust me again. This is necessary.*

"No," Brennan croaked.

Aidan twitched, staring. He had begun to concentrate.

"No," Brennan repeated. "You will not do this thing."

"If I do not—"

"He is dead. Let him be dead."

"The others have come, *jehan*—"

"I said *let him be dead!*" Brennan leaned forward. "I do not know what—or *who*—you are . . . for the moment I would like you simply to be my son." His face worked a moment. "I need you to be my son."

Stricken mute by the magnitude of his father's emotions, Aidan could only stare. And then, when he could, he nodded. He took his hands from the links.

Eventually, Brennan eased himself back in the throne. His posture was less rigid, his tone less intense. He smoothed the fit of his jerkin with a deft, yet eloquent gesture. "So, you have settled on Keely's girl."

Aidan understood very well what Brennan did. The change in topic was intended to change also the knowledge of what they had only just shared regarding Aidan's congress with dead Mujhars. Neither would ever forget it, but Brennan wanted it set aside so he need not deal with it.

Aidan shrugged. "Neither of us 'settled' on one another. The gods took an interest . . . there was no other choice."

"She is not much like Keely . . . more like Sean."

Aidan smiled faintly. "She is very like Keely on the inside. On the outside—well, there is Keely there as well. Once you get past the Erinnish height and stature, and Sean's coloring . . ." He smiled more broadly, "Shona is mostly Shona."

"You realize the wedding will have to wait," Brennan warned. "There is the Homanan mourning custom for a deceased Mujhar . . . they would look askance on any wedding, even a royal one, so close to the Mujhar's passing."

Aidan shrugged. "Then we will wait. It does not matter. Shona is not a woman much taken by ceremony . . . it will hardly blight her life if we wait a while longer to have a priest mumble the words."

"A woman with sense." Brennan smiled faintly. "Of course Aileen will attempt to change her mind . . ." He let the words trail off. He could not avoid the topic he had tried diligently to close. "Those things you said to me . . . things you have said before."

Aidan waited.

"Are they true?"

He was tired, confused, grieving. But no less than his father. "Did Ian say anything when he came back from the Solindish-Homanan border?"

Brennan frowned. "Say anything?"

"About me." Too clearly he recalled the Weaver's storm and Ian's shattered hip. "About anything that happened."

"Only that you and he felt it best you go on alone." Brennan shrugged. "I did not argue. Ian would never have left you had he believed there might be danger, and you have never been the sort to seek it out." He paused. "Why? Is there something he should have said?"

"No. He left it to me." Aidan scrubbed wearily at gritty eyes. He had tried to sleep, but could not. "*Jehan*—I told you once before about speaking with gods."

The recoil was faint, but present. "Aye." Brennan's tone was guarded.

"What if I said there was more to it than that? That I met with them personally?"

Delicate objectivity; *kivarna* stripped it bare. "As you have with the Mujhars."

"Aye. With all of them."

Brennan sighed deeply, giving in. "I would say perhaps you are putting too much weight in the things you dream."

Aidan smiled. "I have always dreamed. I have never dreamed about talking to gods, or with meeting them."

Clearly unsettled, Brennan shifted in the throne, looking infinitely older. "Men do not talk *with* gods, Aidan. They talk *to* them, through petitions and prayers. For the *shar tahls*, it may be different . . . but even the Homanan priests say they serve out of faith and belief, not because of personal contact."

Aidan's mouth hooked down in irony. "I am not a priest, *jehan* . . . I cannot say *what* I am, other than to agree the circumstances are quite unusual."

Brennan's black brows met. "Aidan, this is not possible—"

He said it matter-of-factly. "Then I must be mad."

It stopped Brennan cold. He stared fixedly at his son, trying to read the truth. "But—with *gods*, Aidan?"

"Only three of them. They assumed human form for it, so as not to frighten me senseless. And they spoke—they speak—in riddles, telling me there is a task I must perform, and sacrifices, and the fashioning of a chain." He paused. "That much I have done."

Brennan stared blankly at the heavy chain depending from Aidan's belt. What he thought was clear: Aidan could have bought it, or had it made. That was the only explanation.

Aidan sighed. "The task remains. But I wanted you to know, so you and *jehana* could stop worrying about me."

"*Stop* worrying!"

"I am not cursed after all; rather, I am blessed. Chosen for some specific purpose."

"*What* specific purpose?"

Aidan shrugged. "They have not shown or told me yet."

Brennan struggled with comprehension. Objectivity lost. "You will be Mujhar one day," he growled. "That, I should think, is task—and blessing—enough. As for a special purpose, how many men are born to inherit a throne, least of all the Lion?"

Aidan shook his head. "There is more. They know very well I am in line for the Lion—they made it so, did they not?—and yet they have made it very plain there is something else I must do."

Slowly Brennan shook his head. "How can a Mujhar rule a realm when he converses with the gods as if they were mortal men?"

"I would think it is something far out of anyone's ken," Aidan answered. "And perhaps a beneficial thing. If a man *knew* he acted with the blessings of the gods . . ." He shrugged, scratching an eyebrow, dismissing implications to increasing weariness. "It is so vague a thing . . ."

"*Aye,*" Brennan agreed heartily. He stared pensively at his son, clearly concerned as well as baffled. "How is it Aileen and I got you? You were never what we expected, not from the very first."

Deep inside, something twisted. "And are you disappointed?"

Brennan sat bolt upright. "No! Never *that,* Aidan—you are everything a man and woman could desire in a son. But you *are*—"

"—different?" Aidan smiled, thinking of the last discussion with gods he had had. "But I have been clearly advised that it does not make me *better.*"

Brennan sighed and sat back in the Lion. He rubbed both eyes wearily, stretching the flesh out of shape. When he looked at Aidan again, dawn etched lines and shadows where there had been none before. "There will be more responsibility for you now. You are Prince of Homana. Men will seek you out, asking your opinions on all manner of things, and asking you to plead their cause before me. They will hound you night and day . . ." He smiled crookedly,

"All the honor will be yours, but also the weight of it. And there are times it grows so heavy . . ." His hand closed over the massive black ring he now wore. "You will never again know the peace you have experienced up till today."

Aidan thought about the "peace."

"Things will never be the same. Prepare as best you can."

Aidan stared hard at the ring glowing bloody on his hand. "*Tahlmorra lujhala mei wiccan, cheysu.*"

Brennan shook his head. "*Cheysuli i'halla shansu.*"

Chapter Five

With meticulous precision, Aidan crossed his bedchamber to the chair beside the bed and sat down, settling himself slowly. The candle on the table was too bright; squinting, he leaned over and pinched it out.

Shona closed the door. Mutely she went to him and reached down two-handed to remove the gold circlet he wore. "Here," she said calmly. " 'Twill ease the ache, I'm thinking."

It did help. With the tight metal band gone, the tension lessened slightly. He sighed, slumping against the chair; sighed again as Shona set the circlet on the table and began to rub his temples. "A long two months," he murmured.

" 'Tis over now," she said. "Niall has been laid to rest with all due ceremony . . . 'tis time the rest of you were able to breathe again."

He had not thought of it like that. He had known only that the Homanans required daily Ceremonies of Passing for a full sixty days to honor the dead Mujhar; duly honored, Niall was formally interred in Homana-Mujhar's mausoleum, his dressed-stone sarcophogus resting beside Carillon's. There was none for Donal, who had given himself over to the Cheysuli death-ritual following the deaths of his *lir*, but Niall's passing had not required adherence to the stringent Cheysuli custom. His had required only multitudinous ceremonies designed to honor his memory, after the fashion of Homanans.

But it was done. The sixty days, save for several hours, were now passed. And he could breathe again.

Already his head felt better. Smiling, Aidan reached up and caught Shona's competent hands. "Now perhaps we can think about *our* ceremony."

Shona shrugged, turning to perch on the arm of the chair. Because of the ceremony, she wore skirts instead of trews, and a gem-encrusted girdle spanning the width of her hips. "I'm not needing one of *those* to know we're bound."

"No. But the Homanans prefer such things." He threaded idle fingers into the weave of her braid. "And it will give Deirdre something to do."

The archness left Shona's tone. "Aye. Poor Deirdre . . . gods, what grief she feels, and yet she tends to everyone else. First to Brennan, who is a ship without a rudder; then to Ian, who tries to close himself off to what we're *both* of us knowing is a horrible emptiness."

"He was the Mujhar's liege man."

"Liege man, brother, boon companion—d'ye think the titles matter?" She pulled herself up and sat instead on the bed, but three paces away, tugging at the fit of her loose-cut gown. "He has spent his life serving our grandsire, according to love and to custom, and now that service is ended. What d'ye think he'll be doing?"

Aidan rubbed a temple. The headache was receding, but a residue remained. "We have been his whole life. He has neither *cheysula* nor *meijha* . . . I think he will stay with us, to give us whatever help he can."

"And himself, as well." Shona sighed pensively, idly resettling the girdle. "But there is Deirdre, still. Will she stay? Or will she go?"

"Back to Erinn?" Aidan shook his head. "Homana is her home. She has been here most of her life."

"But Niall is dead, and her only daughter—and all of her grandchildren—live in Erinn."

"Except for Blais." Aidan frowned. "I wish he had come. The Mujhar was *his* grandsire, also . . . and yet he did not come to any of the ceremonies. You *know* he must have heard—word has been carried throughout all of Homana."

Shona's mouth hooked down sardonically. "Blais is not a man to do what others expect, or desire. 'Tis a stubborn *skilfin* he is— likely he heard, but chose not to come."

"He would have been welcomed."

"Would he? He is the traitor's son."

Aidan shifted restlessly. "Likely he would find less welcome among the Cheysuli than the Homanans. The Homanans care little enough about Teirnan—what did he do to them? His heresy has to do with his own race. It is a Cheysuli concern."

"Aye, well . . . likely Blais had his reasons." Shona eyed him attentively. "Your head is better."

"Aye."

"Good. Then you won't be minding a walk."

"A walk?" Aidan frowned. "It is late. I thought we would go to bed."

"We'll do that after," she said. "There's something I want to see. Before, I didn't ask because 'twasn't fitting, in light of Niall's death. But now there's nothing to hinder it." She stood expectantly, tugging at rucked up skirts and the binding of the girdle. "I want to see the Womb."

Aidan's brows rose. "The Womb of the Earth?"

Shona nodded. "I've heard all about it. My mother told me, and others . . . about the oubliette beneath the floor of the Great Hall, and all the marble *lir*."

Aidan looked at the bed a moment, thinking about sweet oblivion and an end to a nagging headache. But Shona was due an introduction to her heritage on any terms she liked, and he saw no reason to refuse. His head *was* better; nodding, he rose and gestured her out of the room.

"No dogs," he warned.

She cast him a dark look. "I've left them all in my chamber."

"Good. If you want to meet the *lir*, you can do it without dogs."

Shona shouldered open the door. " 'Tis only because they like *me* better that you resent them."

"I do not resent your dogs. Only that there are so many—do you know how little room there is left to me when they try to sleep on my bed?"

Shona preceded him out the door, kicking skirts aside. The change in attire did nothing to hide long-legged strides. "They sleep on *my* bed, boyo, since you've banished them from your chamber."

"They come anyway, whenever they can. Just yesterday four of them had nested—"

" 'Tis because they smell me there. But if you like, I can sleep in my own bed." Shona headed down the staircase, yanking skirts out of the way.

"No. But we do have kennels."

"They'll fight with your hounds."

"I have no hounds. They belong to Homana-Mujhar." Aidan

followed a step behind, taking care not to step on her heels or the hem of her skirts. "I know you love them, *meijhana*—"

"Aye." Her tone was final.

"—but could you perhaps treat them as dogs? The servants are complaining about the hair, and bones always underfoot, and the *other* things underfoot."

"The pups are near to broken."

"And do you intend to keep them all?"

Shona continued down the stairs in silence. When she reached the bottom, she stopped, waiting for Aidan. "No," she said at last. "But 'tis hard to give them up."

"I know, but—"

"They'll go," she said fiercely. "Not all, but some of them. 'Tis what I breed them for . . . to improve the lines, and to sell them. Already I have offers."

"For all of them?" he asked hopefully.

Shona's scowl was black. "For *some* of them," she said. "Some of them I'm keeping."

It was a beginning. Aidan let it pass and gestured her to continue. "The Great Hall," he said. "The entrance is there."

When they reached the silver doors, Aidan took a torch down from one of the corridor brackets and carried it within, spilling haphazard illumination across the floor. Only hours before, the hall had been full of kin and high-ranking Homanans, all gathered in Niall's name; now the hall was emptied of life entirely, except for themselves.

Shona paused inside as the door swung shut. " 'Tis different." She glanced upward. "They've taken down all the black banners— all the wreaths." Slowly she turned in a circle. "They've taken away *everything* of the mourning ceremonies."

"The mourning is concluded." Aidan fell silent, then amended the declaration. "The *official* mourning is concluded; now begins the reign of a new Mujhar."

Shona peered the length of the hall. "In this light, the Lion is malevolent."

"In any light," Aidan muttered, then carried the torch toward the firepit. "The one on the Crystal Isle was much more *ben*evolent."

"D'ye think so?" Shona followed. "Blais and I decided it was naught but a bit of wood, fashioned for vanity. There was no life to it." She watched as Aidan mounted the rim of the firepit and began kicking aside coals. When he handed her the torch, she took it amenably and held it so he could see. "Do you know, they might have made it a *bit* more easy to reach the stairs . . . why did they bury the opening *here?*"

Aidan continued to rearrange the contents of the firepit, waving his hands at drifting ash. "Originally the firepit did not extend so far. Cheysuli built Homana-Mujhar centuries ago—at that time there was no need for hiding anything. But when they decided to give the Lion back to the Homanans, the firepit was extended to cover the opening to the staircase." He paused, modulating his tone carefully. "It was thought wisest to obscure the *Jehana's* Womb, so no defilement was possible."

"D'ye think—?" She broke it off. "Aye. They would have. My mother has told me how bloodthirsty were the Homanans in the days of the *qu'mahlin*." She moved as Aidan gestured her aside, then marveled as he caught hold of the iron ring attached to the hinged plate set almost flush in the floor. " 'Tis no wonder they never found it, is it? Buried like this . . ."

Aidan gathered every ounce of his strength and levered the plate up, then eased it down against the firepit rim. Stale air rushed out of the opening, causing the torchlight to gutter and dance. But after a moment it stilled, and flame bloomed afresh.

"Safe," he murmured, and took the torch back from Shona. "Stay close behind me, *meijhana*. If the stairs are damp, they can be dangerous."

Shona's tone was dry. "Aye. I'd not be knowing aught of such a thing, island-born as I am."

"I meant because of your skirts. You're not knowing much about *them*." Aidan cast her a bright glance, then started down the shallow stairs, thrusting the torch before him. The staircase was cut directly out of solid stone, pitched steep and narrow. He had been told the stairs numbered one hundred and two; for the first time in his life, he counted.

"Gods," Shona breathed "how deep do we go?"

Her voice echoed oddly from behind. "Not so deep," he answered. "Not so deep as the Womb itself."

Shona said nothing else until they reached the bottom. The ending was abrupt and without warning, in a small closet, until Aidan found the proper keystone and pressed. A portion of the wall grated on edge, turning; blackness gaped before them.

Torchlight spilled into the vault, caressing veins of gold and the smooth ivory silk of polished marble. From out of the shadows *lir* leaped, breaking free of marble bonds, tearing wings and beaks and claws out of stone. Wolf, bear, mountain cat; hawk, falcon, eagle. And countless other *lir*, twisted this way and that, as if once they had lived to walk the earth or ride the skies.

"Gods—" Shona breathed.

"*Lir*," Aidan responded.

"Look at all of them . . ." Shona leaned forward, edging toward the vault. "Can we go in?"

"Aye. Beware the oubliette."

She looked. In the center of the vault, half-shrouded in distorted torchlight, spread the nothingness of the Womb. A flawlessly rounded hole, rimmed with rune-scribed marble, dropping straight down into the depths of the earth itself. The oubliette was three paces equidistant from the four *lir*-worked walls.

She was in awe, but not fear. Shona took two steps inside the vault, then turned back. He saw comprehension in her eyes, and a vast, abiding acknowledgment. She was, as he was, Cheysuli, child of the gods, born of the earth and the wind and the sky; born to pride and power and magic.

Shona smiled. She put out her hand, and he took it. Two steps and he was beside her, within the vault housing the Womb; together they gazed on the *lir*, marveling at the artistry that made them so alive, so vibrant within the stone. Even the ceiling was worked with *lir* of all shapes and sizes, struggling to burst free. In the distorting torchlight, all of them seemed to lean toward the open door, as if longing to exit the vault. As if they *could*, given leave. Given the power to do so.

Aidan shivered. Shona laughed softly and squeezed his hand. "Aye. I feel it, too. D'ye see? Each of them means to go."

He felt curiously distant. "One day, each of them will."

"What?"

He shook himself. "What?"

"What you said, Aidan. 'One day, each of them will.' " Shona stared at him. "What were you meaning by that?"

"I said that?"

"Just now." She frowned. "Have you forgotten already?"

He shivered again, glancing around. "It is this place. I feel it in my bones. A cold, deep darkness . . ." He peered over the edge of the oubliette without moving so much as a toe. "There is a story that one of our kinsmen threw himself into the Womb."

She was properly horrified. "Down *there?*"

"Aye, Carillon."

"But—Carillon was Mujhar." Shona's tone was puzzled. "If he threw himself into the Womb, how did he become Mujhar? Did he not die?"

"Not then. Supposedly he became Mujhar *because* he threw himself into the Womb." Aidan frowned, peering around the vault. "They say at one time it was how a true Mujhar was judged worthy. He went in a child and came out a man; went in a prince, came out a king. He was born of the *Jehan*." Aidan looked at her, marking her expression. "It is one of the *stories*, Shona. I doubt there is truth to it."

"My mother never told me *that*."

"Aye, well . . ." He shrugged. "There are hundreds of stories about our ancestors, *meijhana*—and doubtless one day there will be as many about us."

Shona arched a brow. "And children to tell them to?"

He grinned. "One day."

She touched the knotted girdle. "Sooner than that, I'm thinking."

He opened his mouth to question her, but the *kivarna* flared up even as she laughed. While he could not sense the presence of the child, he knew the truth without a doubt. Shona's emotions were to easy to read.

"Gods," he blurted, "*when?*"

She smoothed a hand over the girdle, rattling its weight of gems. In the torchlight, colors flashed. "Did you truly not guess?"

"*No.*" He looked. "Not even now. Are you certain?"

"Oh, aye." She made a face. "To me, I'm showing—see how the gown barely fits? And how short the girdle is tied?" She sighed, twisting her mouth. "I meant to hide it so I could tell you closer to my lying-in . . . but Aileen and Deirdre saw it too soon. They sent the midwife to me." She grinned. "Three months, my lord . . . and we'll have us a wee bairn of our own."

"*Three months—*"

She nodded. "I'm so tall and wide the babe is spread all over. If I were a smaller woman, there'd be more bairn here." She put a hand to her belly.

He was not thinking of that. "But that would mean . . ." He paused, counting back. "That would mean we were still in Erinn."

Shona nodded. "And, by the days, 'twas that first night together." She laughed. "You're a potent one, I'm thinking."

Aidan frowned. "I thought it was the Homanan food."

"So, you *did* notice!" She scowled fiercely, though without much sincerity. "Too polite to mention you thought I was getting fat?"

He colored. "There are more flattering things to discuss."

"Aye, well . . ." Shona grinned. "Does it matter? 'Tis a bairn, not too much Homanan food—will it be a lad, d'ye think?"

"How am *I* to know?" Aidan slid the torch into a bracket by the door and turned to pull her close. "And does it matter? If not, there will time for us to make a lad."

"Six or seven," she agreed, and then blurted out a garbled sound of shock. "Aidan—*look*—"

He swung from her, alerted by the very real alarm in her tone, and saw the shadow stretching down into the door. And then the man who wore it, stepping into guttering torchlight to stare blindly at them both.

Silvering black hair was long and unkempt, tangling on his shoulders; leathers were stained and tattered, fitting his frame too loosely; bare arms were naked of *lir*-gold. But the marks of armbands remained, graven into flesh. As much as the loss of them—and his *lir*—were graven into his spirit. Teirnan of the *a'saii* was well and truly mad.

Foreboding swept in. Aidan touched the hilt of his knife. "What do you want?"

Teirnan stood framed in the doorway. His tone was an odd amalgam of detachment and intensity. "What I have always wanted."

He felt rather than heard Shona's movement behind him. Instinctively he put out a shielding hand, thinking of the unborn child. "How did you get in?"

Teirnan's smile was a travesty. "Such a thing to ask a Cheysuli."

Aidan swallowed back increasing trepidation. He had never met the man, knowing him only by reputation; that reputation made him an enemy. "Your *lir* is dead," he said. "Spin me no tale of *lir*-shape, kinsman. You are *kin-wrecked* and *lir*less, and you have no place here."

Torchlight limned his intensity. "But you have just called me kinsman. And I *am*." He stared past Aidan to Shona. "Are you Keely's daughter?"

Her voice was level. "Aye."

He nodded. "Blais described you. And the others . . . but none of them matter. Even *you* do not; you are not of my flesh. You are not of my bone." Yellow eyes burned fiercely in the torchlight. "And most certainly not of my spirit."

There was Blais in him. Aidan could see it, even beyond the harshness of age and privation. They were of a like height and stature, in addition to coloring. Maeve had given her son nothing. *Unless it be her good sense.* Aidan drew in a breath. "Very few are of your spirit," he retorted. He looked more closely at the warrior, looking again for Blais, or something of Maeve, and marked the lines etched so deeply into the flesh beside his eyes, the hollows below arched cheekbones. Teirnan's self-exile had not been an easy one. But Aidan thought the emptiness of his spirit had more to do with *lir*lessness than with a life of privation. "So, you have met Blais. What do you think of your son?"

Muscles ticked in the ravaged face. "He is not my son. He is *hers* . . . Maeve made a Homanan out of him—an *Erinnish*—" Teeth showed briefly in a feral clenching. "Left to me, he would have been a warrior. Left to *her* he is nothing, a shadow-man, a soulless halfling with no understanding of the truth."

"Ah," Aidan said. "He repudiated you."

"Wise man," breathed Shona.

"He came to me and said he was my son—*my* son, whom she kept from me all these years . . ." Again the feral grimace. "She should have left him to me."

"So you could twist him? So you could take him into the deepwood and feed him on lies?" Aidan shook his head. "Maeve knew what you would do. It is why she left Homana."

"He was *my* son, once—"

Aidan overrode him. "He is a warrior. Clan-born, bloodborn . . . no matter what you say, Teirnan, he is a true-born Cheysuli, with the right to choose. The gods gave us that right. Even you have profited from it—if you call the travesty of your life profitable." Aidan shook his head. "You were a fool, kinsman. There are other ways of undoing things. Quieter ways of accomplishing change."

Teirnan was too thin, too tense, too *unbalanced*. He had voluntarily shed the anchor of his life by renouncing the prophecy and everything it stood for; the death of his *lir* had stripped him of everything else. There was nothing left to Teirnan save the fanaticism that had driven him from the clans, and even that was stretched too fine. Without a *lir,* he was nothing. A void stood before Aidan clad in human flesh shaped in the likeness of a man.

"Why did you come?" Aidan asked.

"For the Lion," Teirnan rasped. "Niall is dead. Now it is mine."

Aidan shook his head. "The Lion has been claimed."

"By Brennan?" Teirnan laughed. "That is an old conflict, kinsman . . . it began even before you were born. Brennan and I are old enemies and older rivals, both pursuing the Lion." His smile was a rictus. "If he thinks it is for him, tell him to come down *here.*"

Aidan frowned. "What do you mean?"

"Tell him to come down here. *Here,* in this vault. With the door *shut,* and the Womb of the Earth to receive him."

Aidan felt Shona's nearness. Also her puzzlement; the unasked questions: what did Teirnan want? What did he expect?

Teirnan touched marble *lir.* "Tell him to come here before the Womb, and ask the blessing of the gods in the *old* way. The way Carillon did, wanting to be Mujhar."

Apprehension became fear. "Why?"

Teirnan's eyes burned. "Because he will not. Because he is *afraid;* do you not know the stories? Brennan of Homana is afraid of places like this. Because he *knows* the Womb will swallow him whole and never give him up."

"That has nothing to do with it." Aidan knew very well his father would not enter the vault, but it had nothing to do with fear of the Womb. It was a fear of enclosed places; it had always been Brennan's weakness. "He *is* Mujhar, Teirnan. The Homanan Council says so, Cheysuli Clan Council—"

"Only the gods matter."

Aidan nearly laughed. "I know something of that, kinsman. As for you? You turned your back. You took your *a'saii* and went away from everything, repudiating your heritage. How do you expect to convince anyone—even your own son—you are worthy to be Mujhar?"

"How?" Teirnan took one step into the vault, then another. "By being *born,* kinsman . . . as the old Mujhars were born."

Comprehension blossomed. "Teirnan—*no*—

He stood on the brink of the Womb. "She will give me back," he said. "She will. I am a child of the gods. Child of the *Jehana.* I will go in the man and come out the Mujhar."

"Teirnan—" Shona blurted.

"She will give me back," he repeated. "Hers is a fertile Womb.

She gave Carillon back. She will give me back a Mujhar, so my
son will not renounce me. So *no one* will renounce me. I will be
Mujhar, blessed in the old way, the way of our ancestors." He lingered on the edge. "I see it in your faces; you think she will not do
it. You think my way is madness."

"Don't," Shona whispered, one hand splayed across her belly.
"Gods, man, *don't*—"

Teirnan's face spasmed. "I must. It is the old way. Too much of
the old ways have been lost—too many of the customs discarded
in the name of the prophecy . . . do you not see? If I am made Mujhar, I can change things back. I can make us what we once were."

"Teirnan." Aidan took a single step toward the oubliette, and
the man. "This will not win back your son. This will not win you
the Lion."

It was a litany. "The *Jehana*'s Womb is fertile. She *will* make
me Mujhar, just as she did Carillon." Teirnan's laughter echoed. "*I,*
at least, am Cheysuli."

"No," Aidan said. Twofold denial: of the act, and of the claim.

Teiman smiled and stepped off the rim.

This time the Womb was barren.

Chapter Six

The assumption of power by a new king was done with very little fanfare. Brennan considered it unseemly under the circumstances; even though the two-month mourning period was over, sorrow lingered. Niall had ruled Homana for nearly fifty years. Neither his presence—nor the honor and affection—would fade immediately.

The new Mujhar received messages of condolence from other kingdoms with good grace, remarking privately to Aidan that no one was laggard in also wishing Niall's successor a lengthy, peaceful reign, and set about exerting his own power over the Homanan Council without delay. And though Brennan had spent most of his life preparing for the moment, Aidan knew he did not enjoy it.

Although the changes were not immediately evident, it became quite clear Brennan was arranging the governing of Homana to suit his personal tastes. His policies were more assertive, though not overtly aggressive, and the kings of Caledon, Falia, and Ellas found long-standing trade treaties in the throes of renegotiation. Brennan wrote long letters under official seal to Corin and Hart, informing them they now ruled their realms autonomously, as Niall had always intended they do once he was dead. But he involved them in his new plans for Homana as a way of insuring Solinde and Atvia followed suit. The prophecy would not be served if the realms remained divided by more than distance. If they were to insure four realms were to unite, politically the three brothers had to think as one.

That left Erinn, under Sean's rule. Though married to Keely, Sean was neither Homanan nor Cheysuli, with nothing owed to the prophecy. But he did owe the Mujhar; Niall had wisely forced a trade alliance that improved Erinn's economy so that separation would prove detrimental. With Keely's presence—and influence—Sean agreed to a new alliance that extended the old treaty. Erinn would not lose; neither would Homana.

Aidan watched his father's machinations with a sense of wonder tinged with amusement. He had always known Brennan was the most serious of his kinfolk; now he saw why. The Prince of Homana was never allowed to forget his place; never allowed to think of himself as independent of the Mujhar; never allowed to think for himself; never given the opportunity to know freedom from his future. The Prince of Homana, named Mujhar, stood the highest in three realms. And Aidan was next in line.

It was brought home with perfect clarity the day Brennan called him into his private chamber and said they should consider opportunities for betrothing Aidan's child.

Aidan, perched on a casement sill, stared. "It is not even *born* yet!"

Brennan, slumped deep in a chair, gestured impatiently. "We can discuss possibilities regardless of its gender."

"Why *should* we? Let the child be born."

The Mujhar sighed and rubbed a hand through silvering hair. "You know as well as I we none of us have the freedom to wait so long. *You* had more than most, but there was me between my *jehan* and you. Now I am Mujhar and you the Prince . . . we should look to insuring your hold on the succession."

Aidan sighed with forced tolerance. "No one is going to wrest my grasp from the succession, *jehan*. Teirnan is dead. There is no one else in all of Homana who wants to change the order now."

"We cannot be certain of that. Now that Teirnan is dead, the *a'saii* appear to have fallen into disarray—but how are we to be sure? There is Blais, after all."

"Blais repudiated him. That is one of the reasons Teirnan threw himself into the Womb." Aidan eased himself back into the deep-cut casement. "Just because Blais refuses to come to Homana-Mujhar does not mean he plots against the succession. Blais is *stubborn,* and he came to be a Cheysuli, not an ambitious kinsman desiring more than his due."

"We will discuss it anyway."

Aidan eyed his father. There was a new note of authority in Brennan's tone. Their dealings before had been courteous and circumspect with a mutual regard, but there had always been a generalized affection that lightened parental orders and commands. Now Brennan spoke as a king to his heir. Aidan began to see the taut web that the title wove around him.

Since his father had no intention of dismissing the topic, Aidan chose a diplomatic tone of voice. "Cousins have wed cousins for years, *jehan*. Is that what you desire? Or do you think we should look elsewhere?"

Brennan's scowl deepened, but it was not directed at any-thing—or anyone—in particular. "A part of me agrees with the first, for we have mixed linked bloodlines to form closer kin-ties. It was required to strengthen the gifts. But we are so *closely* tied . . ." He sighed. "Perhaps it *is* time we looked to other realms."

Aidan nodded thoughtfully. "We are now too close to Erinn. "

"And to Solinde."

"And Corin's Glyn is barren." As his father looked up sharply, Aidan shrugged. "He told me before he left. He does not care, he says—he did not marry her for children."

Brennan scowled thoughtfully. Then sighed, shrugging, "If we look to other lands, there is Ellas, Falia, and Caledon."

Aidan raised a single brow. "But Homana has never married into those realms. Finn's daughter came the closest by marrying the youngest son of Ellas' High King—" he paused "—how many generations back?"

Brennan waved a hand. "It does not matter. That is old history, and we are speaking of new."

"Aye, well . . ." Aidan thought it over. "I am not so certain I like the idea of marrying my daughter into foreign lands."

Brennan smiled. "But if she is a son, he will remain here. And the princess come to *him*."

"As Shona has?" Aidan arched a brow. "*While* we are speaking of weddings, what of mine?"

Brennan gestured. "I thought you might wish to wait. Even though official mourning is ended, it would not be seemly to hold a large wedding celebration within a year of the Mujhar's passing."

"Then we will hold a small one." Aidan shrugged. "As I have said before, Shona is not a woman for ceremony. And I myself do not care. I only thought it might be wise in view of the imminent birth. There are only two months left, *jehan*. And you know the Homanans."

"Aye, so I do." Brennan stroked a temple. "I could speak to Aileen. Together, she and Deirdre could fashion a ceremony. And it might be good for Deirdre."

"It might be good for us all." Aidan slipped off the sill. "I will speak to Shona. I promise, *jehan*, she cares little for ceremony. She will not insist on splendor." He grinned. "All she insists on is for the two months to pass, so she can rid herself of the burden."

"So did your *jehana*." Brennan smiled briefly. "I will speak to Aileen."

"There *is* one thing."

Brennan eyed him warily. "What is it?"

Aidan was amused; was he so unpredictable? "I want to take her to Clankeep. To bear the child there."

Raven brows rose. "Why? Would she not prefer Homana-Mujhar?"

Aidan shook his head slowly. "She has grown up ignorant of her heritage, except for what Keely taught her. Shona has a great need to know her ancestry, to understand the history of our people. She is empty of us, *jehan*. She is empty of the knowledge. There are *shar tahls* to learn from, and clansmen to meet." He shrugged. "I think she longs for a thing of which she has no understanding."

Brennan sighed. "*Lir*-sickness, in a way. After all, she is Keely's daughter. Who is to say what needs burn in her blood?" He looked at his son. "Take her wherever she wishes. She is Cheysuli, too. Nothing is closed to her."

Aidan nodded. "I will tell her to plan for a wedding. Then we will go to Clankeep."

"You might *ask*," Brennan suggested. "Telling is not always wise."

Aidan grinned. "You forget, *jehan*. There is the *kivarna* between us. She will know the truth of things the moment we see one another."

Something glimmered in Brennan's eyes. "Then I would say it is fortunate you are not a habitual liar."

"Nor *any* kind of liar." Aidan crossed to the door. "I think it is time I put up my own pavilion in Clankeep. As a gift to the child."

"No," Brennan said quietly, as his son swung open the door. "As a gift to yourself."

Aidan paused, staring. He sensed regret commingled with a desire to alter things of the past. "*Jehan?*"

"As a gift to yourself," Brennan repeated. "You will lose too much in the years to come. The Lion will swallow you up, as well as the Homanans. It is how things are, and not necessarily *bad* . . . but I might wish for another way, had I to do it again."

"What would you change?"

Brennan's gesture encompassed the chamber. "This. Walls bind me, Aidan . . . they bind every Cheysuli. But I cannot very well order the Lion taken out of the Great Hall and dragged off to Clan-keep, to crouch amidst the trees." Briefly, he smiled. "The Lion *is* Homana . . . but we are more than that. So, when you put up your pavilion, raise it for yourself. To honor your ancestry. To remind you of what we were."

In silence, Aidan nodded. And then he went out the door.

The family gathered in the Great Hall: Deirdre and Aileen in embroidered Erinnish gowns unearthed from their trunks; Ian and Brennan in soft, dyed leather and clanworked gold. Others were present as well, powerful Homanan nobles and others from the clans, but Aidan felt the absences of far too many people: Niall, Hart and his kin, Keely and Sean, Corin.

But there *was* Shona. And as she joined him at the silver doors to walk the length of the Hall, he knew the absences filled.

She wore green. Rich, Erinnish green, unadorned save for in-tricate stitching done in delicate gold; and bright Erinnish emer-alds spanning a burgeoning waist, laced into unbound hair that brushed the hem of her skirts.

He took her to the dais, where the priest waited for them. Aidan said his vows quietly, damping his *kivarna* so he could last the mo-ment, then listened with great pride as Shona also said the words. The priest was Homanan, the language was Homanan; in the Old Tongue, and then in Erinnish, Aidan repeated the vows. And then placed around her throat the torque of interlocking repeated fig-ures: a raven in liquid flight, a wolfhound leaping after.

Shona's eyes were bright. And then the moment was past; they were, in the eyes of gods and men, husband and wife, *cheysul* and *cheysula*, Prince and Princess of Homana.

Duly presented by the Mujhar of Homana, Aidan and Shona were free to mingle with the guests. Shona almost immediately de-clared her longing to be back in trews and boots so she could stride about the Great Hall like herself, instead of a mincing maiden; Aidan informed her he had yet to see her—or *anyone*—mince, and she was obviously no longer—and had not been for some time—a maiden. Shona flashed him a baleful glance, but it was ineffective. The *kivarna* told him the truth: she was as moved as he by the knowledge of their future, bound together forever by something far stronger than vows.

All too quickly the women dragged Shona away from him.

Aidan found himself momentarily alone, holding an untouched cup of wine someone had thrust into his hands. Smiling faintly, he looked across the hall and saw Deirdre, elegant in her gown, but hideously apart from the frivolity around her. Grief had aged her in the nearly three months since Niall had died, dulling her hair and etching shadows beneath her eyes. The flesh of her face was stretched taut over bones showing a new fragility.

Aidan was abruptly assailed by the fear she might soon follow Niall. He knew of men and women who, left alone after so many years of companionship, dwindled and died. He had always known her as a strong, spirited woman, conducting herself with becoming decorum in view of her unofficial status, yet knowing far better than most how to run a household as large and diverse as Niall's.

Apprehension increased. He could not sense her, could not *read* her; it was not a gift he could control. Aidan abruptly crossed the hall to intercept her as Deirdre moved from candlelight into shadows.

"Granddame." He presented her with the cup of wine, pressing it into rigid fingers. She thanked him and accepted it, but clutched the cup too tightly. He feared she might spill the wine. "Granddame," he repeated, "I have been remiss. I have not seen you lately."

Deirdre's smile was gentle. "You have had much to contend with of late. A new title, new honor, new wife . . . and soon a new child." Briefly green eyes brightened. "You'll be seeing what your grandsire and father have had to contend with all these years: a proud Erinnish woman with the freedom and facility to speak her own mind."

She had lost much of her Erinnish lilt over the years spent in Homana, but he heard the underlying echoes of Aileen and Shona in her tone. Suddenly he was fiercely proud of the island realm—and the Aerie—for rearing proud, strong women. And for sharing them with Cheysuli.

He took one of her hands and kissed it. "You outshine them all today."

She smiled again; this time it touched her eyes. "How gentle you are, Aidan . . . I forget how little you resemble Niall's children in temperament."

"Gentle!" It was not how he would characterize himself. He was not certain he liked it.

"I think it must be the *kivarna* in you. You understand too well how other people feel, how the slights can hurt. Brennan was always much more reticent to say anything without thinking it over—the diplomat in him!—but Hart and Corin and Keely always said whatever they wished *when*ever they wished to say it, and suffered the consequences." Deirdre smiled. " 'Tis a trait of Erinn, as well . . . Aileen and I both share it—*and* Shona, no doubt!—though not so much as Niall's children." Her eyes were very kind. "But you have always been different. From the very first. And I have always been grateful for it."

It was not what he had expected. "Why?"

"Because this House is made of warriors." Slender shoulders moved in a shrug. "I do not complain—the world is large enough for all manner of men. Niall raised his sons for a purpose: to be strong and fierce and determined, no matter what they faced, because they would face much." She smoothed back from his brow an errant auburn forelock. "You, too, are a warrior, Aidan . . . but there is more in you than that. You serve your prophecy with less fierceness and more dignity. You do not think of wars with the Ihlini or a treaty with Caledon or a betrothal with this land or that. You think about people, instead. They are *human* to you, instead of sticks in a fortune-game." Her gaze was intent. "That is important, Aidan. You are not so bound, so driven—be who you are, not what the others are."

After a moment, he smiled. "I think I am more bound by the prophecy than anyone here, granddame."

She sighed and removed her hand, cradling the cup once more. "There is more to life than that."

"It *is* life."

Deirdre looked away from him a moment, gazing across the crowded hall toward the Lion. "You are all of you so different."

"Granddame—?"

"You Cheysuli." She looked back. "There are times, I'm thinking, you lack any freedom at all."

"The gods gave us self-rule, granddame."

"Did they?" Her smile was bittersweet. "If that is true, follow your own intuition. Do not let the history of your ancestors warp you from your path."

She sounded uncommonly like the Hunter, or Ashra, or any of the oddities he had met in the past year. "What do you mean?"

"The Cheysuli are so supremely certain that their way is the true way that it is leaving little room for anyone else in the world. 'Tis an insular and arrogant race, because it has had to be." She raised a finger as he began to nod. "But no longer. Now you can loosen the shackles and *breathe*."

"Granddame—"

"D'ye think I judge too harshly because I am Erinnish? That I could not understand?" Deirdre shook her head. "But I do, Aidan. Far better than anyone thinks. I lived with a Cheysuli warrior for more than forty years. I helped raise three more of them—four, if you count Keely with her *lir*-gifts—and yet a fifth when you were born. Oh, I know, Aidan. I know you very well."

The summation hurt. "And do you find us lacking?"

Deirdre's tone was gentle. "Not lacking. Bound. Too bound by customs. There is so little change in the clans . . . change is *healthy*, Aidan!"

His hand dropped to the links at his belt. Change was within him, he knew. Why else would gods speak to him? Why else would they set him a task he had yet to understand? Everyone said he was different. Was he so different he would alter the traditions of his race?

The response was instinctive, denial as much as truth. "Too much change can hurt."

Deirdre's hand was cool on his arm. "Nothing is done well if it is done too quickly. But you are less inclined than most to act without thinking. Even Brennan sees himself bound by tradition . . . I think you will be a different kind of Mujhar when you ascend the Lion. And I think it will be good."

Aidan's smile was lopsided. "You give my *jehan* short shrift."

Deirdre laughed. "Brennan will do well enough; probably better than most. He has waited for this all of his life. And he is what Homana requires *now*, but not always." Her green eyes were very warm. "Your turn will come, Aidan. When it does, use it."

Chapter Seven

They knelt side by side upon the blue ice-bear pelt from across the Bluetooth River. The *shar tahl* looked back at them, black brows knitted. "Why did you come to *me?* I am only one . . . also the youngest and newest in Clankeep." He studied them both. "You have the right, of course—I am fully acknowledged as a *shar tahl*—but I thought you might go to another."

Aidan smiled. "It is precisely *because* you are not like the others that we came to you."

Shona nodded. "And because of Blais. You were the only one who wrote him of his father."

Burr sighed, smoothing a wrinkle from his leggings. The edge of winter was upon them; he, as they did, wore heavier leathers, thicker woolens, furred cloaks. "Aye. I thought the others unjust, in that. But they viewed Blais' request as unanswerable; Teirnan was *kin-wrecked*, his rune-sign expunged from the birthlines. In their minds, how could they tell him of a warrior who no longer existed?"

"But *you* answered," Aidan said.

Burr shrugged. "I had to. He was a man in need—a Cheysuli warrior requiring information of his heritage." Yellow eyes were very steady. "Had I refused him the information, I would have renounced one of the foremost responsibilities of my position, which is to serve all Cheysuli in matters of heritage, custom, tradition . . ." He smiled. "I am not saying the others *did*. I merely interpreted the custom differently. I no longer believe in the need for *kin-wrecking* at all; Blais' request, therefore, was one I had to answer."

Aidan gazed at him. He wondered anew at the man's commitment. Not its quality or depth, but at its ability to be flexible. Part of it, he believed, had to do with Burr's comparative youth. He was, Aidan had learned, thirty-seven, which made him nearly fifteen years junior to the youngest of the other *shar tahls*. But the rest of it had to do with a different kind of belief system. Burr saw things differently, and interpreted things accordingly. There was room in his world for change, just as Deirdre had suggested.

"So," Shona said, "we've asked it. Will you be giving us our answer?"

Burr grinned. "Of course you may set up a pavilion within Clankeep. Would I say no to you, after permitting Blais to do the same?"

"But he is not here," Aidan said.

"No. But he will return. There are things he must reconcile with himself . . . his *jehan*'s withdrawal from the clans is one of them, as well as Teirnan's death." Burr shifted, slipping a hand from his knee to the red dog fox curled by his side. "And have you permission of the clan-leader?"

Shona laughed. "He gave it instantly. Would he dare do otherwise to the son of the Mujhar?"

"Oh, he might." Burr's tone was mild. "Aidan is not well-known here, other than occasional visits. And there is talk of dreams, and nights he walks the corridors of Homana-Mujhar, conversing with the Lion." The *shar tahl*'s white teeth flashed as Aidan and Shona exchanged uneasy glances. "But it is thought mostly due to having his spirit chafed by too many walls and Homanan responsibilities. Surely here, in the heart of the land, he will learn what it is to be a warrior of the clans."

"Surely he will," Aidan agreed dryly.

"Just as he will surely learn more about his heritage if he studies with a *shar tahl*."

Aidan nodded. "And may I choose which one?"

"Done," Burr said. "Put up your pavilion, then come to me each day."

"Leijhana tu'sai." Aidan rose, reaching down to help an ungainly Shona to her feet. But before he turned away to open the doorflap, he paused. "There was a time you said I had your sympathy. Do I still?"

Burr's lids flickered minutely. "You have many things of me, my lord. Among them my sympathy."

To press him would be futile, Aidan knew. There was a core of quiet stubbornness in Burr he knew better than to test. It was, he believed, much like his own.

Sighing, he pulled aside the doorflap and gestured Shona to precede him into the chilly day.

For three days Aidan and Shona cut, dyed, and stitched the pavilion fabric until it resembled the proper shape. Then they designed and painted the black raven on the slate-gray sides, and with the help of three other warriors set up the frame and ridgepole and dragged the oiled fabric over it, pegging and tying it down as necessary. Finally it stood on its own, rippling in the breeze so that the raven's wings moved, and Shona stepped into Aidan's arms as the warriors faded away, tucking chilled hands into his furs.

" 'Tis *ours*."

Nodding, he gazed at the pavilion as he slung an arm around her waist.

"Ours," she repeated. " 'Twasn't something I moved into when we married, but something we built together."

With the *kivarna*, he knew very well what she meant. He shared it. "Aye. Kilore and Homana-Mujhar have housed many kings, many children . . . but *this* place is ours."

She sighed as a chilly breeze tugged at braided hair. "There is such peace about Clankeep—I'm thinking I could stay here forever."

Aidan smiled. "Forever is a long time, my lass . . . and you not properly knowing what it *is* to be Cheysuli."

"Yet," she clarified. "And I'm knowing *something* of it. D'ye think I'm lying when I tell you how I feel, surrounded by such history? Such security in tradition?" She hooked a thumb into his belt. "I know what you say about change, my lad, but can it wait? I've only just got here. I'd like to see what being Cheysuli is all about before you begin changing everything."

"Only some things," he said distantly. "Things such as the abomination called *kin-wrecking*—" He cut it off. "Enough. I am only a prince, not Mujhar—and even *that* bears no certainty of power. The Cheysuli have always been subject to the power of gods, not of kings . . . it would require more than Aidan the Mujhar to convince the clans to change."

"Then *be* more," she said simply. "Make yourself more, my lad . . . you have it in you, I'm thinking."

"Aye. Perhaps." Aidan turned to her, sliding hands down to splay across the mound of her belly. She had given up trews in favor of loose skirts weeks before, for the child had become intrusive. Aidan felt the tautness of her flesh stretched so tightly under the soft wool skirt and loose tunic. He laughed. "We have put up the pavilion just in time."

Shona cupped his elbows even as he cupped her belly. "He will be Cheysuli," she said fiercely. "Before anything else: *Cheysuli.*"

Aidan smiled. "Even before his Homanan rank? Or Erinnish?"

"Even before that." Her eyes were fixed on his in a strange, wild pride. "Gods, d'ye know what it is to come here? To *feel* so much in my heart? All those years in Erinn, cut off from the place I most belong . . ." She drew in a breath and released it slowly, audibly. "I have no *lir*-gifts, but I do have the blood . . . and it burns, Aidan. It burns so *much.*"

"I know," he said, "I know. Gods, Shona, how can I not? I feel it the same way."

"But you've *been* here," she protested. "You've had this all your life, since the time you were born; and *Teel*—" She broke off, looking at the ridgepole. "D'ye see? There he is."

He smiled. "I see."

"I'm not knowing how to say it, but you should be able to feel it. All my life I knew the freedom of Kilore, the freedom of the headlands, the freedom of the seas, for my father took me sailing . . . but 'tisn't the same! *Here* I feel free. *Here* I feel whole. *Here* is where I belong."

"But there is also Homana-Mujhar—"

"Oh, aye, I'm knowing we can't *always* live here. There will come a time . . . but for now? They've no need of you in the palace, nor the city . . . can we not stay here as long as possible?"

He smoothed back a lock of hair pulled loose from the braid. "We will stay as long as we can. Gods willing, we will give our child the foundation you lacked." He smiled. "And I, for that matter; I grew up in Homana-Mujhar."

Shona looked at the neat stacks of chests, rolled pelts, cairn stones, and kindling, set beside the pavilion. Keely's sword, scabbarded, leaned against the pile of stones. " 'Tis time we made it a home. All the gifts the clan and our kin gave us are worthy of being cherished."

Aidan smiled. Between them flared the powerful pleasure that was more than mere passion, mere physical satisfaction. It was a deep, abiding contentment akin to exultation; a burgeoning comprehension that what they shared could not be extinguished. He wanted to be inside the pavilion, sitting before the cairn. He wanted to share it with his woman. He wanted to be no one but himself: a warrior of the Cheysuli.

This pavilion has nothing to do with that, Teel chided. *You have been a warrior since we bonded.*

Aidan grinned. *Of course.*

The raven cocked his head. *You are uncommonly pleased with yourself.*

I am too happy to argue.

Because of the pavilion?

Partly. There is more.

Because of the woman?

That, too. But more.

Teel's eye was bright. *The child, then. Because there will be a child.*

All of those things, lir.

The raven fluffed wings. *Such simple things*, lir: *a home, a woman, a child.*

Aidan smiled. *Simple and magnificent. And sufficient unto my needs.*

Teel's tone was amused. *Not so much, I'm thinking.*

Laughing aloud, Aidan hugged Shona. "Let us begin with the cairn, and a fire. 'Tis cold out here, *I'm* thinking!"

Chapter Eight

He dreamed. The hammered silver doors of the Great Hall of Homana-Mujhar swung open, crashing against the walls, so that his view was unobstructed. The flames in the firepit died back, sucked away, until only coals glowed. Beyond the pit, crouched upon the dais, was the malevolent Lion Throne, carved of still-living wood. He knew the wood still lived, because he saw it breathe.

No. He saw the *Lion* breathe; in his sleep, Aidan twitched.

Wood creaked. Slowly the toes tightened, claws scraping against veined marble. Wooden flanks tautened, then gave, rippling with indrawn breath. The tail, carved snug against a wooden haunch, loosed itself and whipped, beating a staccato pattern against the marble dais.

The Lion rose from its crouch. It shook its head, and the great mane tumbled over massive shoulders. The Lion of Homana, no longer a wooden throne, stood upon the dais and surveyed its royal domain. Within it stood Aidan.

The Lion coughed. It blinked. And then it opened its mouth—

"*Aidan!* What is it? What is that noise?"

He awoke, sweating, aware of the dream and the not-dream; the echoes of Shona's voice and the outcry within the *lir*-link.

"Teel?" he asked numbly.

"*Lir—lir—Ihlini—*"

Shona was sitting upright. "Gods—all over, such *noise*—"

Lir—lir—Ihlini—

He scrambled up "Teel?"

Ihlini—Ihlini—

"Aidan?"

"Ihlini," he breathed. "Here? In *Clankeep?*"

Outside, there was screaming.

"Oh, gods," he blurted. "Ihlini—*in Clankeep*—"

Even as Shona hastily pulled on soft boots, Aidan was at the doorflap. He wanted to tear it open, but did not, instinctively knowing not to give their presence away. A part of him told him it probably did not matter; if Ihlini were in Clankeep, they would not search pavilions. They would simply destroy everything.

Aidan drew aside the flap far enough so he could peer out one-eyed. And saw the conflagration.

He spun at once. "We have to get out. Now. *Now,* Shona—they are burning everything."

Lir—lir—Ihlini—

Throughout Clankeep the *lir* cried their warnings, within the links and without. Aidan heard screaming.

Women and children, screaming.

"Shona—"

She was beside him, cradling belly. "Where do we go?"

"Out of Clankeep. Entirely away—" He had a knife, and somewhere a bow . . . hastily he caught up the warbow and the pitiful handful of arrows. "They are killing the children, *meijhana.*"

He saw it go home. Shona snatched up a cloak and dragged it around her shoulders. She wasted no time looking for anything else, or begging for this or that. She merely waited, grim-faced, as he nocked one of five arrows. Beyond her face, through the slit of the doorflap, he saw the flames lapping at the pavilion across the clearing, and shadows running in darkness.

"We must get beyond the wall," he told her. "We must go out toward the gates, then slip through."

"Or over the wall," she said calmly.

"You cannot climb—"

"I will."

Aidan tore aside the doorflap. A line of flame licked from the burning pavilion and crept across to theirs.

"This way—the back—" He caught her hand and dragged her.

They ducked out, shredding the laces with Aidan's knife. The night was ablaze with flame. The cold, lurid flame that came from the netherworld.

Their pavilion, but newly raised, stood six paces from the wall. Aidan had believed it a safe, cozy spot: shielded by wall at the back, by trees on either side. Only the front was unprotected; there had been no need in Clankeep.

"The children—" Shona whispered, as screams renewed themselves.

"To the wall." Aidan steadied her as best he could, while watching for Ihlini. *Teel?*

Above you . . . lir*, they are everywhere—Ihlini everywhere—*

Around them, trees caught fire; laces of purple flame danced along close-grown limbs, passing destruction from brother to brother. Burning sap dripped onto the new pavilion even as the lone streamer from the clearing touched their doorpole, and climbed.

Shona clawed at the wall. It was of natural, undressed stone, lacking mortar save for the moss and dirt of years sealing the joints together. In childhood, Aidan had scaled it; it was not difficult to climb because it was not sheer, but Shona was unbalanced by the child, lacking grace and control. He did not see a way for her to climb it normally, even as she thrust fingers into seams and dug a booted toe at joints.

"I will—" she murmured. "I *can*—"

Behind them, screams and fire, and the shrieking of a hawk.

"Climb, Shona—" He thrust a hand against her spine, trying to steady her.

Lir—lir—Ihlini—

The warning shrilled through the link. Aidan wrenched his head around and saw the horseman come riding.

"Shona—hold *on*—" He spun, raising the warbow, and sighted hastily. Loosed, but the arrow was wide.

He was dazzled by the flames. Throughout Clankeep pavilions burned, falling into charred heaps. Crown fires spread from tree to tree, leaping across the wall into the wood beyond. He saw people running: Cheysuli and Ihlini. He heard people shouting, women screaming, children crying in shock and fear.

The horseman still came on, bared blade gleaming.

Bared blade—a sword—

Aidan did not take the time to think. He ducked beneath the sweeping blade and nocked a second arrow. Behind him the raven-painted pavilion flared into flames, hissing and crackling as fabric was consumed. From all over Clankeep the smell of burning oil and paint hung in the air, as well as the stench of charred flesh. Smoke rolled through the clearings.

Renewed screaming and outcries became an underscore to the macabre dance he entered into with the horseman. The night was moonless and dark, which made the shadows thicker, and the Ihlini rode a black horse. The only thing Aidan saw was the pallor of a face and the glint of the naked blade.

No sorcery here, save godfire—he must use a conventional weapon—

It was something, Aidan thought. At least he had a chance.

Shona still clung to the wall. He saw her pale face turned toward the burning pavilion. The *lir*-torque at her throat glinted in the flames, throwing light into her eyes as she opened her mouth to shout.

The sword scythed by. Aidan, ducking once more, came up and loosed again.

It took the horse full in the throat and brought the animal to its knees, screaming as it died. The rider flung himself free and rolled, tossing off a dark cloak as he came up. Dark leathers polished shiny glistened in the *godfire*. The sword still sang in his hands.

"Shona—*climb*—"

"No purchase," she answered evenly, stepping back to level ground.

Aidan cursed. He could not afford to have his attention diverted by Shona, and yet he could hardly keep it from her. His *ki-varna* was shrieking at him: she was frightened, as he was, but also very angry. What he sensed most was rage. A cold, deadly rage engendered by the Ihlini.

They were killing *children.*

He had lost the other arrows. One remained to him. Aidan nocked even as the Ihlini ran toward him with the sword.

The face swam out of the flames. A cool, smooth face, underscored by upswept cheekbones and dark arched eyebrows; the chiseling of nose and mouth. Aidan had seen that face.

"*Tevis,*" he blurted.

The other smiled coolly. "Lochiel," he corrected.

Who had murdered Hart's son.

Aidan loosed. Lochiel sliced the arrow in half.

He cannot be so fast—

But Aidan believed it was possible he could be many things.

He threw down the useless bow and yanked his knife from the sheath, feeling a sickening tightness in his belly. A knife was no match for a sword.

The pavilion burned behind him. Aidan felt the heat, heard the crisping fabric, smelled the acrid stench of burning pelts. Another step, and he would be in the flames.

Shona ran by him, ducking into the burning pavilion. Even as he opened his mouth to shout, she was out from under the collapsing ridgepole. Keely's sword was in her hands.

He caught it as she offered him the hilt, and put his knife into her hands. "Go to the gate," he said swiftly. "Make your way into the wood—"

But it was all he could manage. Even as Shona nodded, turning to follow his orders, Lochiel came at him.

She ran. Awkward and ungainly, cursing the Ihlini, Shona did as he told her. And Aidan could breathe again.

The sword was a willow branch. It was ground to suit a woman, and then only in practice: the blade was stripped of weight and edge. Its hilt was finer and less heavy than that of his own weapon, and the pommel knot, for him, was unbalanced, hindering his grip. But still it was a sword.

Aidan blessed Keely. Trying not to think of her daughter.

Lochiel was swift and relentless. Aidan parried once, twice, a third time, countering the blows with strength born of rage and desperation. He heard the screaming, the killing, the shrieking. The roaring of the flames. The sound of his own breathing, through a raw and burning throat.

From the corner of his eye, he saw Shona stop running. Saw her swing around. Saw her come back toward him.

No, meijhana—no—

The *kivarna* told him the truth: she could not bear to leave him. She could not bear not to know.

"Run!" he shouted to her.

Irresolute, she slowed. Instinct warred: protect the child, aid the man. Defend what was hers.

A strong, proud woman. An eagle of the Aerie, undeterred by Ihlini. Knowing she could not flee when the man was left behind.

"Run!" Aidan shouted.

The blade broke in his hands.

Gods—

Lochiel laughed. The tip of his sword drifted down; deftly he turned, caught his knife out of his sheath, and threw.

It spun, arcing swiftly, and lodged itself hilt-deep in Shona's breast.

Aidan screamed. The *kivarna* between them shattered, destroyed in a single moment as the knife penetrated. The broken sword fell from his hands as Aidan lunged to grab Lochiel, but the Ihlini stepped neatly out of the way. The blade he had so negligently lowered to aid his knife throw came up with a snap of the wrist. The tip pricked into Aidan's left shoulder as he hurled himself forward, then drove through relentlessly.

Pain. Pain redoubled, and tripled; his *kivarna* reverberated with the outrage done to Shona. His own injury did not matter. What mattered to him was Shona—

But his legs would not work, nor his arms. He felt the blade grate on bone as Lochiel twisted the sword, jerking it from his shoulder, and then blood flowed swift and hot.

Shona.

He fell. To his knees. His left arm hung uselessly, twitching from shock and outrage.

Shona.

Lochiel walked by him. Away from him. He turned his back on him. He carried the bloodied sword lightly, easily, deft as a born swordsman. Aidan, twisting frenziedly to watch even as he tried to rise, thought the young Ihlini graceful as a dancer as he stepped across burning ridgepoles and deftly avoided drifting bits of burning fabric. The screams, now, were gone, replaced by a deadly silence.

Save for the crackle of flames.

Lochiel went to Shona. He knelt and pulled the knife from her breast. Her swollen belly pushed toward the sky. Lochiel tore tunic aside. The bloodied knife glistened.

Aidan knew what he meant to do. Instinctively, he *knew.*

In one rushing expulsion of breath and strength, Aidan lurched to his feet. He tried to run. Fell. Lurched up again, staggered, stumbled across the ground. Dripping blood hissed in ash.

Shona.

He had no knife. No sword. Only desperation, and the wild, killing rage.

"Put no hands on her—"

Lochiel, kneeling, slanted him a single glance across his shoulder. And then turned back to his work.

"Put—no—hands—"

Lochiel removed the baby, cut the cord, wrapped the child in Shona's cloak. Carefully he set the bundle on the ground beside the body. With a lithe, twisting turn, he rose to face Aidan.

"I want the seed," he said. "I will make the seed *mine*."

Legs failed him. Aidan fell awkwardly. "Sh-Sh-*Shona*—"

"No more time," Lochiel murmured.

From out of the burning darkness looped the glitter of a blade. The edge bit in, then turned. The skull beneath shattered.

Chapter Nine

Muddy ash fouled Brennan's boots. Blankly, he stared at them. How much of the ash was from wood? How much of the ash from bone?

He shuddered. The spasm took him unaware, rippling through from head to toe, stretching his scalp briefly until the flesh at last relaxed. And he knew, with sickening clarity, it was what his son now fought. But on a different level: Aidan had nearly died. Aidan still might die.

Clankeep lay in ruin. Most of the wall still stood, for stone does not die from fire, but nearly all of the pavilions were destroyed. Some lay in skeletal piles, ridgepoles charred black. Others were nothing but coals, or mounds of muddy ash.

Brennan, looking, felt sick.

A man nearby, bending to peel aside a charred husk of bedding pelt, let it fall from ash-smeared fingers. "My *lir*," he murmured rigidly. And then nodded, accepting; he had spent the morning looking, while Brennan inspected Clankeep. Now the man was freed. Now the warrior could go.

Brennan watched him. Deep in his belly the snake of futility writhed. *Lir*less, the warrior would die, though he had survived the attack.

"A waste," he murmured quietly, damning the tradition. Damning the need for it.

The *lir*less warrior stood over the bedding pelt and the remains that lay beneath it. Shoulders slumped briefly; then he made the fluid gesture Brennan knew so well. And walked out of the walls into the charred forest beyond.

So many already dead. And now one more.

Brennan sighed. He was weary, so very weary . . . drained of strength and answers. Here he was superfluous, with nothing to do but watch as the others tended their dead, their living, the remnants of their lives.

"So many dead," he murmured, "and all because Lochiel desired to send us a message. To assure us he *existed*."

"Brennan." It was Ian, walking slowly through ash-grayed mud and charred pavilions. His face was strained, and old. "They found her the day after, over there. She has been attended to. They gave her the Ceremony of Passing six days ago." Ian's gesture was aimless. "There is nothing we can do, save tell Aidan when he wakes."

His mouth was oddly stiff. "*If* Aidan wakes."

Ian hesitated a moment too long. "Given time—"

Brennan's tone was vicious. "Do you think time will make a difference? You have seen him—you have *heard* him! When the Ihlini cracked his skull, all the wits spilled out."

Ian drew in a quiet breath. "You do him an injustice."

"By the gods, *su'fali*—he is mad! You heard his babble! When you can understand a phrase, it makes no sense at all." Brennan's face spasmed. "I would be the first to declare him fit and the last to declare him mad . . . but I know what I have heard. I know what I have seen."

Ian's tone was patient. "I have seen men struck in the head do and say strange things—"

"And have they prophesied?" Eloquent irony.

Ian sighed. "No."

"Gods—" Brennan choked. "Why did they let us have him at all if they meant to take him from us?"

Ian offered no answer.

"So many times, as a child, he nearly died. We knew he would, Aileen and I—we tried to prepare ourselves for the night he would wake, coughing, and die before the dawn . . . the fever that would burn him . . . knowing we would lose him, and that there would be no more." Brennan balled impotent fists. "And now, when he is grown, when he is a strong, healthy man—they take him away from us!"

"*Harani*—"

"I should not have let them come. When he told me he meant to bring Shona here, to bear the child here—" Brennan's face spasmed. "I should have refused. I should have said it was better for her to bear it in Homana-Mujhar—"

"You could not have prevented him."

"—where there are physicians, and midwives—and protection from the Ihlini."

"There was nothing you could have done. Aidan is grown, Brennan . . . he makes his own decisions."

"I could have insisted."

"He—*and* Shona—had a perfect right to do as they wished. You had no right to stop them."

"But *look what happened*—"

"*Tahlmorra*," Ian said softly.

Brennan's shoulders trembled. His voice was a travesty. "Why did they give him to us if they meant to take him away?"

Ian put a hand on his nephew's shoulder. "Come, *harani*. It is time we went back. Aileen will need you . . . and, perhaps, your son."

Brennan shut his eyes. "They have destroyed my son," he whispered. "Even if he lives."

He became aware he had been shouting. His throat ached from it, but when he tried to form the words with his mouth, nothing happened. He felt separated from his body, drifting aimlessly, apart from the world and yet still a part of it. And when he opened his eyes, he stared out of the bed into faces he did not know, yet they knew him.

He sensed the violence in his body before it came, and as it came he understood it. His flesh crawled upon his bones, rippling and writhing. And then his limbs began to twitch. Slowly at first, then more quickly, until the convulsions took bones and muscles and made clay of them, molding them this way and that.

Fire was in his head.

He screamed. He heard himself screaming, though he could make no sense of it; he heard voices attempt to soothe him, though he could make no sense of it. He did not know the language.

He convulsed, head slamming back into the pillow on a rigid, arcing neck. Arms and legs contracted. His teeth bit bloody gashes in his tongue until someone forced a piece of padded wood into his clenched jaw. His teeth ground until gums bled, shredding the padding. Splintering the wood.

The seizures passed at last. He lay spent against the mattress, quivering in his weakness. No one spoke to him now. Perhaps they understood he had no means with which to answer.

Memory. It ran around inside his head like a ball set to spin-

ning; spinning and spinning and spinning until at last the momentum ended; then bouncing and rattling and rolling against the inside of his skull.

Memory: Flames. Screams. Stench.

Oil and paint and flesh.

Blood hissing in ash.

His jaws snapped open. His throat disgorged sound. But nothing was emitted, save the rasp of a dying breath.

Memory: Death.

Each day someone held a candle near his eyes. He could see it, but could not blink. Could not tell them it hurt. The words were garbled nonsense. When he tried to put up a hand to block the candle's light, the arm spasmed and jumped. They held it down for him. Some days the spasm passed. Others it spread and worsened. Then they held him *down, pinning arms and legs.*

Someone had cracked his head, like an egg against a rock.

He dreamed. Not of a golden chain. Not of a living Lion. Of a man. A young, magnificent man, strong and full of life. His vibrancy was tangible; his power as yet untapped.

A tall, lithe young man, striding like a mountain cat through the webwork of Aidan's dreams. His eyes were cool and gray, with a gaze so compelling it could stop a hardened assassin from unsheathing sword or knife. The hair was thick and black, framing a youthful face of austere, yet flawless beauty, bearing the stamp of authority far surpassing any monarch's. It was not a womanish face, even in all its beauty; a trace of ruthlessless in the mouth maintained its masculine line. Only rarely did it smile. When it did, power flickered; he could rule or seduce man and woman with equal facility.

Dreaming, Aidan twitched.

The man was not Cheysuli. The man was not Ihlini. The man was of all blood, forged from the heart of war, tempered on the anvil of peace. And his gifts were such that they surpassed all others.

Aidan whispered: Firstborn.

And knew what it meant.

Rebirth.

And death.

The ending of what he knew; the beginning of what he did not.

He cried out in fear, recoiling from the truth; from the man who prowled his dreams.

Deep inside, something roused. Something woke.

He spoke. He heard himself. Saw their frightened faces as they heard him. Saw the horror in their eyes; the comprehension of madness: surely he was mad? What else would make him so?

He spoke. He raved. He chanted. The convulsions came again. And passed.

Lips were bitten. Tongue and gums lacerated. Muscles shrieked with each dying spasm.

The broken head mended.

He thought perhaps he might, until the child of the prophecy strode through his dreams again.

He woke. He knelt on the floor. Shouting. They all came running, all of them, and this time he heard himself. This time he understood. The words of his dream spewed out.

"I am the sword!" he cried. "I am the sword and the bow and the knife. I am darkness and light. I am good and evil. I am the child and the elder; the girl and the boy; the wolf and the lamb."

He wavered on his knees, but none dared to touch him. Words poured forth. "Born of one prophecy, I am come to make another. To bind four realms into one; to bind eight into four. I am the child of the prophecy; child of darkness and light; of like breeding with like."

He sucked in a quivering breath. "I am Cynric. I am Cynric. I am the sword—and the bow—and the knife. I am the child of prophecy: the Firstborn come again."

He stopped. The words were gone. He was empty, and hollow, and purged.

Aidan tumbled downward, welcoming the darkness. But hands raised him up again, showing him the light.

The door was ajar, as they always left it now. Deirdre, who had ordered old hinges oiled so as not to disturb Aidan, slipped into the chamber. It smelled of herbs and an odd pungency. Aidan's wounds had been healed; even so, the smell was not of blood or body.

She frowned, pausing to draw air deep into her lungs. Exhaling abruptly, she knew. It was a thing she had not smelled since leaving Erinn.

She looked to the high-backed chair set so closely beside the bed. "By the gods, Aileen—are you summoning the *cileann?*"

Aileen started, crumpling the dried herbs she clutched in her hands. The pungency increased, then faded as she rose, scattering broken stems and leaves. As she saw her aunt, she dropped back into the chair. Color tinged her face. Defiantly, she raised her chin even as she brushed bits of herbs from her skirts. "Neither Homanan nor Cheysuli gods have answered all our petitions. I thought perhaps the *cileann*—"

"This is Homana," Deirdre said quietly. "The *cileann* have no dominion here. 'Tis too far from their halls."

Aileen's face crumpled. "I wanted to try *something!* Nothing else has worked!"

Deirdre crossed the room. A glance at Aidan's bruised, too-pale face told her his condition was unchanged. He had roused but three times since the attack, and only long enough to babble nonsense in three languages: Homanan, Cheysuli, Erinnish.

But now she turned her attention back to her niece. Aileen's red hair was unkempt, twisted into a haphazard plait. She had eaten little since Aidan had been brought to Homana-Mujhar, nor had she slept but an hour here and there.

Deirdre put a soothing hand on Aileen's head, stroking dull hair gently. What she said was inconsequential, much as the words a horseman uses to quiet a fretful colt, but at last it began to work. Aileen wiped away tears and managed to smile at her aunt. "My thanks, for that. But it has been so *hard*—"

"I know, Aileen, I know . . . and may be harder yet. But you cannot be squandering your strength now, when it does no good. He will need you when he wakes. You must eat, and sleep, so he'll be knowing you when he rouses. He will be expecting his *jehana*, not a hag-witch with greasy hair and ditches beneath her eyes."

As Deirdre had intended, Aileen pressed hands against her face. Vanity, in this case, would decoy her thoughts, even if only briefly.

It passed too quickly. Aileen took her hands away and stared steadfastly at her son. "What if he never wakes?"

"He may not," Deirdre said steadily. "I have heard of such things: men and women who, struck in the head, never rouse entirely. They sleep until they die. But Aidan is very strong, and very stubborn. I think if the gods meant him to die, he would not be alive now."

"Brennan says—" She checked.

Deirdre sighed quietly. "Brennan does not know everything. He is upset, as you are. And worried, as you are. And, like you, he has known too little of rest and food. Do you blame him for speaking nonsense?"

Aileen's tone was dull. "Is it nonsense to concern yourself with the succession of Homana? He must, Deirdre . . . he is Mujhar now, and cannot afford to set aside such things. If Aidan dies, or is mad, what is Homana to do? There must be an heir for the Lion."

"There will be an heir for the Lion."

Aileen's tone, abruptly, was filled with self-loathing. "But not from the Queen of Homana."

"There is no need," Deirdre declared. "She has already borne a son. The Lion is satisfied."

The fire died out of green eyes. Aileen looked at her son. "If he lives," she whispered.

He lived. He came awake with a throttled cry and this time remained awake.

The link thrummed within him. *Lir,* Teel said. *Lir, I am well. I sit above you on the bedframe.*

He did. Relief was all-consuming. Aidan, released, trembled. And wondered, as he trembled, if he would lose himself again. If the convusions would steal his body and twist it into knots.

It hurt to breathe. His body, wracked too often, ached from residual pain; from cramps now passed, but remembered with vivid intensity. With exquisite clarity.

His lips were swollen and bitten. His tongue much the same. But his wits were perfectly clear.

I am not mad, he declared. Then, in doubt, *Am I?*

The chambers were deeply shadowed. He lay in his own bed, cushioned by pillows and bolsters. But leather was firmly knotted around wrists and ankles, then fastened to the bedframe.

Aidan spasmed. *Gods—they have* tied *me—*

He stilled. *Am I mad?*

From the corner of an eye, he saw movement. Spasming, he looked, and saw his mother present. Propped in a chair, the Queen of Homana slept. He knew by looking at her she had known too little of it. The truth was in her face.

Memory rolled back: *Screaming. Fire. Dying.*

Aidan went very still.

The reek of burning pavilions, the stench of burning bodies. And blood hissing in ash as Lochiel cut the child free.

At wrists and ankles, leather tautened. "No!" Aidan shouted. "No—no—NO—"

Aileen came awake at once, lunging out of the chair. Her hands

came down on his shoulders—had he not been wounded in one?—
and pressed him back again, aiding the leather straps that bound
him to the bed.

"No!" he shouted. "*NO!*"

Aileen's green eyes were wide. "Aidan, stop!" she cried. "No
more of this—no *more*—"

"He killed her!" he shouted. "He killed her and cut her
open—"

"Aidan! Listen to me!" Aileen shot a frightened glance over her
shoulder toward the door standing.ajar and shouted for her husband. Then, turning back, she pressed against his writhing flesh.
"Stay still. You must remain still. Your poor head can stand no
more of this battering."

The pain came in waves. "Shona," he whispered.

Brennan came in, shoving the door open so hard it thudded
against the wall and echoed down the corridor. His face was gaunt
and strained.

"Awake," Aileen told him, "and remembering everything."

Brennan moved to the bed. The straps bound arms and legs;
hissing, Aidan fought them. "No," Brennan said. "No, let them be.
We put them there for a reason , . ." His voice trailed off as he
looked down on his son. "How much do you remember?"

Aidan wanted to answer. But he felt the ripple in his flesh that
presaged another seizure. No matter how hard he tried to retain it,
he was losing control of his limbs. His head arched back, thrusting
into the pillow.

Brennan forcibly set Aileen aside. He leaned over his son and
held him down against the mattress, pinning him tightly. "No," he
hissed. "No—you will *not*—"

Aidan's vision flickered. The light in his room changed. Something buzzed in his ears, distorting his father's voice.

"No," Brennan repeated. "Come *back* to us, Aidan—all of you,
and whole—not this crazed prophet—"

Jaws locked into place. He tried to say her name. Only the sibilant escaped, like the scrape of broom on stone.

Brennan's hands tightened. "I want you back!" he shouted. "Do
you hear me, Aidan?—*you.* For everyone who needs you. For
everyone who loves you."

Aidan forced it between his teeth. "Shh—shh-ona—"

Brennan's fingers tightened. The look in his eyes altered. "No,"
he said gently. "Aidan—I am sorry."

It was confirmation. Strength spilled out of him. With it went the spasms.

"Shona," Aidan whispered. In silence, Aileen cried.

Brennan unsheathed his knife. With precise care, he cut the leather straps binding his son. Mutely he peeled away the linen cuffs made to protect the flesh, then discarded everything. As Aidan lay slack on the bed, Brennan massaged his wrists.

"Clankeep?" Aidan croaked.

"Mostly destroyed," Brennan answered. "Much of the wall still stands, but little inside. And even outside . . ." He shrugged. "Had it not rained two days after, only the gods can say how much damage might have been done to the surrounding forest."

"How many people?"

Brennan's expression was grim. "The count is one hundred and four. Women and children, mostly."

"Lochiel," Aidan murmured.

"He sent a message. A *written* message, also; Clankeep was the first. That one in blood."

Distracted, Aidan frowned. "What message?"

"That he intends to do as his father—and *his* father—failed to do before him. Destroy the prophecy. Destroy *us.*"

"Strahan's son," Aidan murmured. "He was killing women and children. I heard them dying." Attention wandered. He frowned, remembering. "I had a sword wound."

"Healed with the earth magic," Aileen told him. "And the bones of your head—" She broke off, glancing at Brennan.

"But not the wits inside?" Aidan's lips twitched once. "Have I been so very odd?"

"Do you recall none of it?" Brennan asked.

"Nothing but Shona. Nothing but her . . ." Aidan stirred restlessly, ruthlessly pushing away the memory of Locheil's butchery. "He preys on children. First he kills Hart's son, then he turns to my child before it is even born."

"Lie still," Aileen chided. "You have been very ill. It would be best if you slept."

He rolled his head slightly in denial. He was afraid of sleep. He was afraid of what might come, sliding out of darkness into the light where he could see. And where he could be afraid.

His head ached unremittingly. The memory would not go. "He wanted it," he murmured. "He wanted it for a purpose."

Aileen's voice, so gentle. "Sleep, Aidan. Rest."

The pain was increasing. "Lochiel took my *child*."

"Butcher," Brennan murmured. "Even Strahan did not stoop to that."

"He took it," Aidan repeated. "He stole it from her body."

"Aidan, rest." His mother again, smoothing a pain-wracked brow.

He realized they did not understand. He needed them to. He *required* them to. "He took it. Lochiel took the child. He cut Shona open and *took* the child from her."

"Aidan." Brennan leaned down, hands pressing a warning against Aidan's shoulders. "Let it go. Shona is dead—and surely the child, after that. It has been weeks . . . the clan gave her a Ceremony of Passing along with all the others—" Briefly, Brennan broke off. "And I have written Keely."

"*No*—" He twitched away from the pain. "He took the child from Shona. *Alive.* He wanted it for some purpose."

Aileen was horrified, hands covering her mouth. Frowning, Brennan shook his head. "No child could survive that."

Aidan did not listen. "He wanted it. For himself. He said—he said—" Aidan squinted. "He said he would make the seed of the prophecy *his*."

"Aidan, no—"

Consciousness receded. "Lochiel took my child. I will have to get it back."

Chapter Ten

His recovery was slow, impeded by weakness and fits. The wounds themselves had been healed, but only outwardly. Inwardly Aidan was still very much aware of the edge he walked. If he lost his balance once, he would be tipped off into the void. It was very like the balance required in *lir*-shape; he chose to think of it as that, since he was accustomed to it, and tried to regain the man he had been before Lochiel.

Winter. Time had passed, too much time; the Cheysuli in Clan-keep worked to rebuild what they had lost, but most of the effort would have to wait until spring. And Aidan, walled up in Homana-Mujhar, chafed at the weather and weakness that kept him indoors, prisoner of unpredictablity.

Blinding headaches stole the wits from his head and sense from his tongue. From time to time he came out of a seizure to the echoes of a language he did not know, even though he spoke it. No longer bound to his bed by straps or debilitation, Aidan moved freely within Homana-Mujhar—but often found himself in odd portions of the vast palace without knowing how he got there. He dreamed when he was awake, losing himself even in the midst of conversation. The servants began discreetly eyeing him with pity or wariness, depending on his behavior of the particular moment, and Aidan found himself loathing them as well as himself.

At last he talked Ian into practicing the knife with him in a private chamber. He needed by spring to regain quickness and ability if he was to hunt Lochiel for his child, and only Ian would agree. But Aidan quickly discovered his reflexes had been destroyed. He was slow and awkward with a knife; what would it be like with a sword? And his vision was slightly askew; how would that affect his prowess with the warbow?

Finally, furious, he threw the bitter truth in Ian's austere face. "I will never be the same!"

Ian lowered the knife and regarded him in perfect stillness. "No," he said finally. "It is folly to harbor that hope."

It shocked him. Even knowing, it shocked. Aloud, the truth was so harsh.

His grip on the knife loosened. He shook, as he so often did, no matter how hard he fought it. "Then what am I, *su'fali?*"

Ian sheathed his knife. "A man who has been sorely hurt," he said gently, "in spirit as well as body. Aidan—you cannot expect to be what you once were. Not after that. Do not even hope for it."

Aidan clutched his knife. It shook. "At least you are honest," he rasped. "Everyone else tells me to give myself time; that of course all will be well. All will be as it was before." He clenched his teeth so hard his jaw ached. "It will never be the same."

"No." Ian's eyes were kind. "They lie because they love you, and because they want to lessen the pain. They know no other way, *harani* . . . honesty is difficult for people to deal with when it offers only sorrow. You want so *badly* to go after Lochiel, and yet they wonder how you can. You are not—what you were."

The word was ash. "No."

Ian smiled. "No one knows what to expect of you anymore, and it makes them nervous. There is someone else inside of you, someone else who speaks, someone who *prophesies*—" He sighed. "You always were different. Now it is worse."

Mutely, Aidan nodded.

Something moved in Ian's eyes. "Have you looked at yourself since the attack?"

Aidan shrugged. "My hand is not yet steady enough to shave myself. *Jehana* fears I will cut my throat . . ." Frustration tightened. "Someone shaves me, and I do not require a polished plate to dress."

"Then perhaps you should go and look." Ian smiled as Aidan tensed, eyes widening in horror. "No, no—it is not so bad as that. I promise. Save for one detail, you are much as you were. But it is the sort of thing others will remark on, particularly when they know the contents of your life."

Aidan shrugged again. "I will look." He scowled down at the knife in his hand. There were good days and bad days. On the good ones he dropped things only occasionally. On the bad, he would do well to touch nothing at all.

"*Harani.*" Ian's tone was gentle. "I know what you want to do.

I know how much you need it. But you cannot go alone. You must take someone with you."

"You?"

Ian shook his head. "I am too old now. But there is your *jehan*."

"He is Mujhar. He has no time."

"A man who has no time for his grandchild is not worthy of kingship." Ian shook his head. "You judge him too harshly. Do you think you were the only one hurt by Shona's death? Do you believe you are the only one who has suffered?"

Anger flared. "You were not there. *None* of you was there. None of you can know—"

"She is dead, Aidan." Ian's tone was level. "Guilt, rage, and recrimination will not bring her back."

Aidan gripped the knife. "You do not know—"

"I *do!*" Ian's eyes were alive with grief. "I watched Niall die, knowing there was nothing I could do. I watched my *jehana* die, able to do nothing as she cut open her own wrists. I watched my *jehan* walk out of Homana-Mujhar, knowing he left his kin to die a *lir*less warrior's death, alone and bereft in the forest." He drew in a shaking breath. "I know, Aidan. Better than you think."

Ian did. Aidan's *kivarna* told him that.

He turned away stiffly, shamed by his selfishness, yet feeling the painful uprush of anguish and helplessness as strongly as before.

And then came the odd little snap in his head that dropped him to his knees. The knife fell from his hands.

"Aidan!" Ian moved swiftly, kneeling to catch both rigid wrists in an attempt to shut off the spasms. "Aidan—fight it—"

"I am the sword," Aidan whispered. "The sword and the bow and the knife—"

"Aidan, *fight* it—"

"I am no one; I am everyone—"

"Aidan!"

"I am Cynric, I am Cynric—"

"Stop this, Aidan. Shut it away. Use the earth magic. Use compulsion. *Shut it away*—"

"Eight into four and four into one. I am the Firstborn come again, and from me will come the others—"

"*Aidan*—"

"I am Cynric. I am Cynric. The sword and the bow and the knife—"

"Stop this madness *now!*"

The spasming passed. Fingers uncurled. Distantly, he asked, "How can I be mad? I am the voice of the gods."

Ian released his wrists. He was ashen-faced, staring. "What have you become?"

Aidan, hanging yet on his knees, knew. He had survived the first sacrifice. He had undertaken the task.

"Their servant," he said softly. "Chosen among all others. Knowing no other master. Not even a *tahlmorra*."

"Aidan!"

"They want me," he told him simply. "They want all of me. There is no room for a wife. Or a child. Or a Lion—"

Ian caught an arm, jerking Aidan to his feet. "Come with me. I will take you to your chambers."

He went with his great-uncle willingly, too numb to do otherwise. As always after a fit, he had a headache, and yet his wits were exquisitely lucid. He knew what he had done, what he had said, and what he was meant to do.

Ian pushed open Aidan's door. "Go to bed. I will send Aileen."

Aidan winced. "No."

"Then go to bed."

Mutely, Aidan nodded. Ian put a hand on his shoulder and urged him through the door.

It thumped closed behind him. Irresolute, Aidan stood in his bedchamber. And at last, recalling what Ian had suggested, he went to the polished silver plate hanging on the wall.

His face was unchanged, save for an unusual pallor. But a wondering hand went to his left temple, fingering the thick new growth of hair that had come back at last after being cut away. At the corner of his eyebrow was a purplish line, a straight slash of a line that stretched across his temple. The end of it was hidden in his hair. Thick new hair. A wing of purest white.

Aidan smiled. It was a cold, deadly smile. "*Leijhana tu'sai,* Ihlini. Now I can never forget."

He shivered. He felt ill, weary, old. He went to bed, as advised.

And dreamed of a chain that shattered beneath his touch.

Chapter Eleven

The chamber lay mostly in shadow, save for a single fat candle in a stand near the bed. It cast a sickly light; the wick was half-drowned in wax, sputtering its death. But no one moved to tend it.

Aileen stood in the doorway, staring in consternation at her son. "You can't mean to *keep* them here!"

Aidan did not answer. He linked his hands behind his back and gazed steadfastly at his mother.

"But—you can't," she insisted. "Not so many. Aidan, they are too big—there are too *many* . . ." Aileen's brow creased. "The kennels are kept very clean. They will do well enough there."

Undoubtedly they would. But that was not where he wanted them.

Quietly, he said, "Forgive me, *jehana*. I want to be alone."

She started to gesture, to remonstrate gently, but with authority. "Aidan, those dogs . . ." But she let it trail off. The hand fell lax at her side. He was so *still* . . .

She glanced around the chamber—Shona's chamber, Shona's bed, Shona's belongings—marking the chests as yet unpacked. Aidan and his new *cheysula* had gone too quickly to Clankeep for all of her things to have been arranged. Now they mocked her absence.

Aileen looked back at her son: at the still, white face. "Very well," she murmured, and left him alone once more.

He waited. For a moment longer he stood in the precise center of the chamber, staring fixedly at the now-empty doorway. Then, abruptly, he strode decisively through the throng of gathered wolfhounds and quickly shut the door, dropping the latch with a firm click.

Behind him, dogs whined.

He turned to face them. The big dark male. The bitches. The half-grown adolescents and the gangly, colt-legged puppies. Bright eyes stared back at him, tails poised to wave. But they sensed his tension and turmoil, the cessation of his breathing. Uncertainty dominated.

Ears flattened slowly. Heads sank lower. One puppy soiled himself; another began to whimper.

Breath rushed out of lungs. "*Gods*—" Aidan choked. Grief stole everything else.

Trembling, he walked into the huddle of hounds and began to touch their heads. It hurt to breathe, but he managed; in gasps, and sobs, and spasms. Touching all the heads. Assuaging their confusion. Seeking his own release in contact with her hounds.

Tentative tails waved, then quickened as he spoke. The voice he did not himself recognize, but they comprehended the tone. He was naming all their names: that they understood.

One by one by one: Shona's litany. She believed each dog was born with a specific name, and it was a person's task to discover the proper one, not just tack on anything; they had spent days on the voyage from Erinn trying out names on the two litters, collecting and discarding, until each of the puppies was named. Aidan recalled them all clearly, and Shona's lilting, ritual recital each time she greeted the dogs.

He sat down on the floor and let them gather around him. The puppies climbed over his legs, staging mock battles to claim his lap. The adolescents, too big for such play, snuffled his ears insistently, tending the human hound. The bitches came to his hand and bestowed a lick or two.

Only the male held back, promising Aidan nothing.

It hurt. It was unanticipated, and it *hurt*. Aidan understood the male's reticence well enough—the hound had bonded to Shona in puppyhood, offering no one else anything more than cursory courtesy—but Aidan had believed the dog would be starved for attention, eagerly coming forward to any familiar scent in response to Shona's now-permanent absence.

But he did not. And *would* not, Aidan knew now, on any terms but his own.

The puppies, growing cramped in his lap and weary of dominance struggles, deserted. The others settled quietly, finding places on the floor. Aidan got up slowly and climbed into the bed. It was not night. He was not tired. But it seemed the best place to be.

He lay very still. He stared at the canopy. He remembered what

Sean had said: *"There are more ways to geld a man than with a knife."*

Shona.

—striding along the headlands at the edge of chalky cliffs—

—nocking and sighting a warbow with a small, towheaded brother—

—gathering a storm of hounds—

—climbing into his bed—

—gripping locks of his hair—

—winding her own around him—

—tracing the line of lips—

—taking him into her—

The sound escaped his mouth. A throttled desperation.

—other women—too many women—now none of them enough—

"Stop," Aidan gasped.

—none of them enough—none of them *ever* enough—

The sound was repeated: "Stop!"

—the first girl; the woman—

"STOP!" Aidan cried.

"There are more ways to geld a man than with a knife."

Shona. Shona.

Shona.

—everything slipping away—

—the sharpness, the brightness—

—memories of discovery, the exultation of the flesh—

All of it slipping away . . .

Dissolving as he reached, until nothing at all was left save a distant recollection of what he had been.

"Shona," he whispered.

Shona had come to his bed. Now he came to hers, seeking a rapport. A residue of her life in place of the memory of her death.

He floated in nothingness, a cork caught in the millrace, until the millwheel—no, the *Wheel*—trapped him at last and cast him down into the pond.

If I could drown myself . . . But the thought was driven away by the presence of a hound.

The male. He stood at the bedside, pressing his chest into the mattress as he stretched out long neck and head. Nostrils expanded, then closed as he whuffed softly, inspection completed.

Folded ears rose, then flattened. Chin resting on bedclothes, he gazed fixedly at Aidan.

Waiting. Deep in his throat, he whined.

Stiffly, Aidan reached out and touched the long muzzle with trembling, tentative fingers. Then traveled the stop between liquid dark eyes onto the dome of the skull itself. Hair was coarse and wiry, the bone beneath crested. A self-possessed, dignified dog of massive, powerful elegance and abiding loyalty.

Deep inside, Aidan ached. For the hound as well as himself. *He* knew what had happened; the wolfhound understood nothing save the woman no longer came.

The ache intensified. Aidan rolled closer and thrust a clutching hand into muscled shoulders, locking fingers into hair. "I know, my braw boyo . . . he has stolen her from us both." Grief narrowed his throat. "But 'tis for me to do *alone*, this buying back of my child. No matter what anyone says."

He took his *lir*, a knife, and a horse, packed with saddle-pouches. He did not yet trust himself to *lir*-shape for any length of time. Eventually, he felt, the strength and control needed for sustained *lir*-shape would return—he had already tested it in several short flights—but for now he could not rely on it. The journey was too important.

If the child still lives. If Lochiel sees fit to let *it*—

He shut off the thought at once.

Much of the harshness of winter had passed, leaving only a residue of frost and wind. He rode wrapped in furs, feeling the cold more; would he ever feel well again? Or was he destined to be different on the outside as well as the inside?

At long last he reached the Bluetooth and took the ferry across, clutching the wooden rails as the barge fought the current. The Bluetooth was the delineation between northern Homana and southern, although the division was not equal. The high north was not as large or as populated because of harsh winters, and was usually called the Wastes; somewhere there was a Keep, but Aidan was not disposed to seek it out. His path went to Solinde, not to northern Homana. Perhaps another time.

The Wastes gave way to mountains. Aidan rode ever higher, resting at night in frigid passes cut out of wolf-toothed peaks, until at last he crossed over the Molon and exchanged Homana for Solinde.

When finally they reached the narrow defile his father had described as the gateway to Valgaard, Aidan pulled up. Beyond lay the canyon housing Lochiel's fortress, and the wards set by him. He had heard the place described countless times: a field of glassy rock, pocked with smoking vents belching forth the breath of the Seker; huge, monstrous beasts shaped of stone by Ihlini testing their strength. All could be used against him.

He glanced skyward, seeking Teel. *You will have to remain here.*

The raven fluttered down to perch upon a wind-wracked tree. *Is this your choice?*

I have no choice.

Is this what you wish to do?

This is what I must *do.*

Teel's eye was bright. *The Ihlini could kill you.*

Aidan smiled. *He could. He might. He probably will—but not immediately. He will want to gloat, first. And that may buy me the time to do what I need to do.*

Teel made no answer for a very long moment. Then he fluffed black feathers. *Well. I have lived a long time.*

And will longer still, if I succeed.

The raven's echo was odd. *If you succeed.*

Aidan knew better than to ask for explanation.

He made his way through the defile, across the steaming field of beasts, around the rents in the earth that gave way to the netherworld. Never had he felt so vulnerable, so weak, and yet he knew it was required. It did not enter his mind to turn back, or even to think twice about what he intended to do.

Gates. And guards, of course. Aidan walked up the steam-bathed pathway and paused, pushing the hood from his head. In winter light, his earring gleamed. "Take me to Lochiel," he said. "Tell him my name: Aidan. He will be most anxious to see me."

They took him. Having stripped him of all save leathers and gold, they ushered him into a small tower chamber and left him there, alone, as he contemplated the comfort of a fire and other amenities. He sought none of them, neither chair nor warmth nor wine, and waited as they had left him, in the center of the chamber.

Lochiel came. In amber-dyed velvets and soft-worked suede, he was the same man with the same lithe movements and handsome looks Aidan had marked before, gaming with him in Lestra.

Pale, ale-brown eyes; short-cropped, thick dark hair; a clarity of feature that reminded Aidan of someone. Someone he should know.

Aidan forced a smile. And then it required no force; a cold self-possession took control of expression and tone. "Surely you knew I survived. You did not intend it, I know; I have come to save you the trouble of seeking me out."

Pale eyes weighed him. Aidan's *kivarna* told him his arrival had taken the Ihlini completely by surprise, who was not pleased by it. But Lochiel gave nothing away in expression, which remained austerely smooth, and nothing away in eyes, which marked in Aidan a certain pallor and gauntness of face in addition to the white wing in auburn hair.

Lids lowered, shielding eyes. His lashes were long, like a woman's; the smoothly defined forehead and arched brows tugged at Aidan's memory.

Lillith? No. Someone else . . .

Lochiel moved. He did not walk: he prowled. Aidan stood very still, waiting mutely, as the Ihlini paced slowly around him. It was unsettling to be so raptly observed, like a mouse beneath an owl, but he made no indication. It was important to show Lochiel a serenity he would not anticipate.

The Ihlini halted before Aidan at last, the heel of his left hand resting idly on his knife hilt. He wore, as always, a sapphire ring on his forefinger: Brennan's. On his right hand, a bloodstone, rimmed in rune-wrought gold.

Aidan watched him closely. Something about the suppleness of the Ihlini's body merged with the line of his brow, the set of his mouth, to tickle Aidan's awareness. He was not an easy man to decipher, even with *kivarna*. He was, Aidan reflected, a wound wire ready to snap.

The chiseled mouth moved. A muscle ticked high in the cheek. Ale-brown eyes, abruptly shielded again behind lowered lids, changed color in Aidan's mind.

Something clicked into place.

"Have you a son?" he asked.

Lids lifted. Lochiel appraised him intently. And then he smiled. "No. I have no son." He paused. "I have *yours.*"

Aidan tensed all over. He wanted nothing more at that moment than to rip Lochiel to pieces. But the reaction was what Lochiel waited for, and so Aidan, with great effort, damped down the impulse.

He smiled pleasantly. "Do you know a man called Cynric?"

The smooth brow tightened. "No. And if you hope to confuse me with such babblings, save your effort. I have heard reports you are mad . . . do you think I care?"

Aidan's certainty vanished. The brief likeness he had seen faded. He did not think again of the young man in his dreams, the young man so much like Lochiel, but of himself, of his child, and of the man before him.

Ihlini, he knew, did not fully come into their power until they reached puberty, much as a Cheysuli warrior gained a *lir*. There was a time of learning, of refining, just as there was in Cheysuli custom. And a time of complete assumption, when power was understood and properly wielded.

Lochiel was young, but well past puberty. He was, Aidan judged, of his own age. And in Valgaard, the very font of Ihlini power, Lochiel would have recourse to all the dark arts he needed.

Aidan inhaled a careful breath. "What did you do with my son?"

Lochiel smiled. Aidan, unsettled, was put in mind of the elegant young man who had so charmed Cluna and Jennet—and Blythe. "I intend him no harm. On the contrary: I took him for a purpose. I will raise him as my own. He will come to know his proper place in the prophecy, as all Cheysuli do, so that he can aid its destruction. I will turn him from his *tahlmorra* and make him work against it."

Aidan bit back the retort he longed to make. Quietly, he denied it. "That is not possible."

"Oh?" Dark brows arched. "There *was* a Cheysuli woman, a kinswoman of yours, named Gisella. She was turned, and used."

Aidan shrugged indolently. "I will prevent you."

"You?" Lochiel smiled. "With what? Power? You have none here . . . this is Valgaard, Aidan. The Gate is here, entry to the netherworld. Even if you could summon your *lir*, even if you could summon *lir*-shape, or compulsion—what could you do with either? This is *Valgaard*. I can snuff you out like a spark."

Aidan's sudden smile was brilliant. "Ask Lillith what I can do."

Lochiel recoiled.

There. That touched him. There are *weaknesses in him* . . . Aidan nodded intently, driving home the promise of power.

"Because of *me*," he whispered. "At *my* behest. Because the gods *answered* me."

The challenging gaze was unrelenting. Lochiel sought something in Aidan's eyes, in expression, in his tone. And then turned away abruptly, striding to a table, where he poured a cup of wine. None was offered Aidan; he drank it down himself. When he was done, he smiled. "This is *still* Valgaard."

Aidan smiled back. "Would you like to meet them now? *Right* now; *here?*"

Lochiel slammed down the cup. The footed stem bent. "I have sovereignty over this place!"

Aidan tilted his head. "Shall I test it for you?"

The Ihlini's smile was malignant. "*And* I hold your son."

He very nearly laughed. "My gods would never harm him."

"Ah, but *mine* would." Lochiel attempted to right the tipped cup; when he could not do it, he glanced down in distracted annoyance. When he saw the stem was bent, he cast the cup away with a negligent flick of dismissive fingers. He stared at Aidan again. "Do you wish me to summon my gods? They can duel, yours and mine: the gods of light and air against those of death and darkness."

Aidan made no reply.

Pale eyes widened. Lochiel's lips parted minutely. Even his posture was arrested, alert as a hound on a scent. His expression now was intensely compelling. "Is this why you came here? Hoping to set your gods on mine—or on *me!*—and win back your son that way?"

Aidan set his teeth. There was still a chance, he believed, no matter what Lochiel said.

A blurt of disbelief distorted Lochiel's mouth. "I understand, now . . . you thought you could come before me and threaten me— no, *frighten* me—into acquiescence—"

Aidan allowed a delicate tone of contempt to underscore his words. "How could a man do that? How could he dare? Are you *not* the Ihlini, and heir to all the arts?"

Lochiel still stared. "But you *did* . . ." A faint bemused frown tightened brows briefly as he reassessed his conclusion, then faded as he laughed aloud in discovery. "I understand, now—your weapon is *faith!* You believe your gods can win even here in Valgaard!"

Aidan began to wonder if perhaps he had misjudged. If perhaps he had made a mistake. He had been so certain. So determined. His conviction was absolute.

I trust them. I HAVE to. They answered me before. When I faced Lillith.

Lochiel's tone was a whiplash. "Do you think this is a game? Did you come expecting to play Bezat with me?" Pale eyes narrowed. "We are *all* at the mercy of our gods, Aidan. Certainly you and I. I am not so complacent as you. I know better. In the moment of their confrontation, they could well destroy us both. And that is not how I want to die."

Nor Aidan. He had come to threaten Lochiel with a weapon no one else had: divine retribution. He had tapped it once, facing Lillith—but he *had* been complacent. He had believed utterly in his gods, who would face only a single man. A man of great power, but still merely a *man;* now Lochiel threatened a gruesome retribution of his own conjuring, with a god that frightened Aidan much more than anticipated. Asar-Suti, the Seker, had always been an undefined threat, hosted only in vague references.

Now, in the heart of Valgaard, smelling the god's noxious breath, the threat became all too real. He took it more seriously.

As seriously, perhaps, as Lochiel takes MY gods.

Lochiel, face taut, snatched up the silver cup and displayed the ruined stem. "Do you see? This was nothing, I did it unaware. It required no power, no magic. Nothing more than anger." His gaze was unrelenting. "Do you understand? They are *gods*, Aidan! Your gods, my gods—do you think it matters? We are men, and flesh is weak . . . weaker by far than silver . . ." He shut both hands on the rim and crushed together the slender lips. Then displayed the result to Aidan. "I can think of more *comfortable* ways."

Inwardly, Aidan rejoiced. He had found a weakness in Lochiel. He was himself as afraid of a confrontation between the Ihlini's gods and his own, but he had the advantage. He *knew* Lochiel was afraid. And that fear could serve him.

With a serenity he did not entirely feel—Lochiel would call it complacency—Aidan merely shrugged. "I can think of no better way of settling what lies between us. Summon your gods, Ihlini. I will summon mine. We will let them decide this issue."

Lochiel threw down the ruined goblet. His smooth face was white and taut. And then, with infinite tenderness, he asked a single question: "Do you recall how easily I killed Hart's son from afar?"

Aidan was very still. Complacency dissolved. Conviction wavered profoundly.

Lochiel's gaze was unrelenting. "I could do the same now, with *your* son."

It burst free before he could stop it. "*No*—" And cursed himself desperately as he surrendered his advantage.

Lochiel smiled thinly, gracious in victory. "But I am remiss. Come with me, my lord. Come and see your precious son."

In an adjoining chamber, Aidan saw the wide, high-standing cradle carved out of satiny wood. For a single insane moment he could not comprehend such a normal and mundane thing being within an Ihlini household.

Lochiel gestured. "There. Alive, as promised. For now."

. Aidan stepped closer, then stopped abruptly. The cradle held *two* babies, not one; in infancy, identical.

Lochiel laughed. "You asked if I had a son. No. A daughter. But I invite you to tell me which seed is mine, and which yours."

Aidan stared at the babies. They were swaddled against the cold, hands, head, and feet hidden, with only small faces showing. Both slept, oblivious, depriving him of eye color, although even that was no proof. Shona's eyes had been brown; so were Lochiel's. And his *kivarna*, strangely, was silent.

Lochiel moved to the cradle. "Even as I cut the child from the belly of your dead Erinnish princess, my own woman bore me a daughter. Melusine has given suck to your son, so he would know the taste of mother's milk." He saw the spasm of shock in Aidan's face, and smiled. "They share the same breast, the same cradle, the same roof. Tell me again, Aidan, how it is impossible for a Cheysuli to be turned against his *tahlmorra*."

"No," Aidan said hoarsely.

Lochiel put both hands down and touched two heads, caressing each in an obscene parody of affection. "What do you say to knowing your son will think I am his father?" He paused. "Perhaps I should say: *jehan*."

"No." Yet again. Knowing it was futile.

Lochiel bent and whispered tenderly to the sleeping babies, though his gaze remained on Aidan. When he straightened it was with the fluid grace that once more called the dream-being, Cynric, to Aidan's mind.

The Ihlini's voice was hushed, mocking solicitude. "What shall

I do with them? Kill one, and let you wonder if it was your son—or my daughter? Or kill them both, so you *know?*"

Aidan nearly laughed. "Do you expect me to believe you would kill your own daughter?"

"I can make more. And if it gives you pain . . ."

The off-handedness hurt most. Desperation boiled up. "You *ku'reshtin!*"

Lochiel cut him off with a silencing slice of his hand. "Choose one, Aidan. Assume the role of a god and determine a child's fate."

It was a cruel twist on a conversation Aidan had had with the Weaver. "And if I say let both live? Would you honor that decision?"

Lochiel spread eloquent hands. "Both are mine regardless."

Aidan twitched. His head throbbed dully. He tried to set aside the discomfort, but failed. Weakness worked its way from head to neck to shoulders, then down to encompass the rest of his body. He knew what would happen if he did not control the weakness. He fought to suppress the trembling before it showed itself.

Lochiel saw it regardless. Dark brows arched slightly, the chiseled mouth pursed. He considered the white wing of hair. "The sword blow," he said softly.

Aidan suppressed the first spasm. "What of our bargain?"

Clearly Lochiel was distracted. "Our bargain?"

"You said I could choose."

But the Ihlini was beyond that. He smiled slowly, replete with comprehension as he watched the tremors in Aidan's hands. "You are pale, my lord. Have you a headache? Have you an illness?"

"Let me choose," Aidan grated. It was something on which he could focus.

Lochiel laughed: "In addition to your manhood, I have deprived you of your health." He saw Aidan's jerk of shock. "Oh, aye—I knew all about the bonding of mutual *kivarna*. I take pains to know such things." He studied Aidan more closely. "Why else do you think I killed her? And *where* I killed her: there, before your eyes. She was hardly a worthy opponent, and of no danger to me that night . . . but her loss would devastate you. Even in the moments before I killed you." His mouth twisted in a mocking moue of pity. "But you survived after all, and now the poor Prince of Homana is unmanned. *Castrate . . . gelding . . .* no more bedsport for *you!*" He paused, lingered a moment. "And no more heirs for Homana. *I* have the only one."

Aidan's head was pounding. Waves of pain poured down, distorting his vision so that Lochiel became a man of two heads and eight limbs. Teeth clenched convulsively. He had no time at all.

"What use *are* you?" Lochiel mused. "With empty head—*and* empty loins—what use are you to the Lion?"

The Ihlini blurred before him. Sweat broke from Aidan's flesh, followed by the first onset of spasms that would suck the strength from his limbs and drop him to the floor, a twisted wreck of a man. Humiliation bathed him.

Not before Lochiel—

Lochiel gazed at him intently. And then a smile began. "No," he said in discovery. "No, I will *not* kill you. What need? You can do more to harm the prophecy by living . . . gods, who would want *this* for a king?"

Please, do not let me fall . . . do not let me lose everything, not here, not now . . . not before this man—

Lochiel nodded. "Better to leave you alive."

Aidan stumbled forward, catching himself against the heavy cradle. Swaddled babies slept on; he wanted to touch them, to wake them, to learn which was his son, but his body failed him. His legs gave way beneath him and he knelt against his will, before Lochiel the Ihlini, whose smile was oddly triumphant.

"Choose," Lochiel commanded.

Trembling, Aidan clung to the cradle.

"Choose," he repeated intently. "This time it is not a game."

"W-why? Why not?"

"Because this time I will abide by it. Choose a child, Aidan. Then walk free of Valgaard."

"*Why?*"

"Because I want you to go back. I want you on the Lion. I want you where all can see you, so they can see what you are. A man who succumbs to fits . . . or a man who succumbs to demons?" Lochiel made a fluent gesture of multiple possibilities. "I want you *there*, not here. As you are, you will do much more damage to the power of the Lion. To the power of the Cheysuli. Do you think the Homanans will keep you? Do you think they will trust you?" Lochiel shook his head. "I want you *on* the throne, so they can throw you off. Turmoil eases my task . . ." He shrugged. "But you will not go without a child. You would sooner remain here and die of a fit—or my displeasure—than go back without a child." He paused. "So *choose.*"

Aidan still clung to the cradle. "I could choose your daughter—"

Lochiel lost his temper. "Do you think I care? If it is my daughter, you will still have to take her with you to Homana-Mujhar . . . an Ihlini witch raised in the bosom of the Lion." Pale eyes glittered. "To destroy the prophecy, I will risk a daughter. I will risk *ten* daughters. But will *you* risk a son in order to save her?"

Aidan pressed his forehead against the cradle, letting the rim bite in. He shut his teeth on his tongue, trying to deflect the pain gnawing at his limbs. With great effort he pulled himself to his feet, standing rigidly. "Is that all?" he rasped. "Or is there something more?"

"The chain," Lochiel declared.

The trembling died on the instant. Aidan clutched a link depending from his belt. "You want—*this*—?"

"Aye. Is it not worth the price of a child who could well be your son?"

"Why? What is this to you?"

"The embodiment of a man, and all the men before him." Lochiel's smile was wintry. "Give me the chain, Aidan. And you are free to go."

The Ihlini knew. He *knew*. "Will you break it?" Aidan asked.

"Only one link," Lochiel answered. "Only one is required. And the pattern will likewise be broken." He shrugged off-handedly. "This alone will not destroy the prophecy, but it *is* a beginning. If I remove that link from the pattern, small changes shall become large."

Aidan knew the answer. If he refused, Lochiel might well kill him anyway, thereby removing him from the pattern in flesh as well as link. If he stayed alive, there was always a chance he could undo things later. And there was the child; if he walked out of Valgaard with his son, he kept the seed of the prophecy alive. And the human link, he thought, was stronger than the other.

And if I choose the girl—? But Aidan knew that answer, also: choice was a risk everyone took. Choice, and risk, was required.

Aidan unbuckled his belt. Slowly he unthreaded the leather from the links, sliding them free until the chain lay in his hands. He gazed at it, head bowed, realizing in some distant portion of his mind that the weakness in his body had gone. He stood perfectly still before the Ihlini and pondered the ending of his *tahlmorra*.

There will be no afterworld . . . but without Shona, do I want one?

Shona. The Lion. The chain. So many broken links. So many turbulent dreams, harbingers of his fate. So very many *questions*, asked so many times.

But Aidan at last understood.

He pulled the chain taut in his hands. He recalled the binding before Siglyn and Tye and Ashra; how he had drawn the chain from the fire and made it whole again, merely because he believed it. Because it had been required.

Smiling contentedly, Aidan took a final grasp on either end of the chain and looked directly at Lochiel as he jerked the chain apart.

The weak link shattered. Remnants of it rang against stone as they fell, glittering, to scatter apart like dust. He held the dangling end of a sundered chain in either hand, knowing the name of the broken link was Aidan after all.

Lochiel's tone was dry. "Impressive," he remarked. "Now choose a child, and go."

He moved to the cradle. Under his feet crunched bits of broken link. He ignored it.

Two bundled babies. Aidan put down in the cradle the two halves of linked chain. He picked up one of the babies without bothering to rely on *kivarna*; it was as dead as the rest of him. He would take his plight to chance.

"Go," Lochiel said. "You have my leave to go."

Aidan turned and walked from the room, cradling against his chest the son who might rule Homana.

Or the daughter who might destroy it.

Epilogue

Wind whistled through the defile as Aidan walked out of the canyon. Beyond, the wailing stilled. Winter wastes were summer. Trees, once wracked by Ihlini malignancy, now displayed the dignity of smooth, young limbs. Buds sprouted leaves.

Smiling, Aidan nodded. With Teel and the horse waited the brown man called the Hunter.

The god matched his smile. "You looked at the child."

"Aye."

"What did you discover?"

"My son."

The brown eyes were wise and calm and very kind. "Do you think the milk he took from an Ihlini woman's breast will curdle his spirit?"

Aidan, turning a shoulder to the sun to protect the child tucked beneath his cloak, sighed. "I think not."

"Good." The Hunter gestured to a boulder near his own. "Sit you down, Aidan, and tell me what you have learned."

Aidan eyed the rock. "It will be too cold. I have a child to care for."

The Hunter said nothing. Lichen and grass crept up the rock, nestling into hollows, until the boulder was covered. A handful of violet clover blossoms bloomed. The throne was offered in silence.

After a moment Aidan sat down. He looked at the Hunter. "I have learned it is sheer folly for a man to try and discern what the gods intend for him," he began quietly. "I have spent my entire life trying to know what you wanted of me, attempting to interpret troubling dreams that denied me a throne and gave me a chain I could not keep whole, no matter how hard I tried." He smiled briefly. "And I have learned how helpless is a man when the gods choose to meddle in his life."

Brown brows arched. "Meddle? Do we meddle?"

"Aye." Aidan grinned, at him, "It is your way, I suppose . . . so I will not take you to task for it."

The brown eyes were assessive, the calm face devoid of familiar expression. After a moment the mouth moved into a faint smile. "You have also learned to hold us in some disregard, it seems—to judge from your tone."

Aidan laughed at him, pulling his son more closely against his chest and resettling the shielding cloak. "Not in *disregard*. I have simply surrendered, that is all. You will do with me as you will, regardless of what I want, so I will no longer cause you—*or* myself—any difficulties with my waywardness."

"We cannot *tell* you what to do. We never have."

Aidan's tone was abruptly cold. "No. But you remove impediments from my life. Like Shona."

The Hunter's expression was briefly sorrowful, and then it passed. "There is another way of looking at it."

Grief blazed up momentarily, overpowering in its strength. Then died away to ash, much as desire had. Aidan let it go. He could not, just now, lose control. "What way?" he asked. "Is she not *dead?*"

"She is dead. But do not in any way believe we considered her an 'impediment' to be removed from your life. She was not, nor did we remove her. Shona existed because of her singularly great worth. She was the catalyst. What we did was put her *into* your life . . . and give you such joy in her arms and bed you would not want to share it with another, ever." The eyes were steady. "Was she not worth it, Aidan? The submission of the heart . . . the sacrifice of the body. Even for so short a time?"

He had lost what men most treasured, though they perverted it to common lust too many times in the quest for mere gratification. He himself had done it, regardless of the reasons. But with Shona, he had not. Even knowing, Aidan had not believed the sacrifice of so much would be required of him. Now he understood why.

And did not hesitate. "She was worth everything."

After a moment, the Hunter nodded. "It remains, Aidan: we cannot tell you what to do."

"There is no need for that. I know what to do. *Now.*"

"Do you? And what is that?"

Aidan stared beyond the god a long moment, lost in thought, in memory. Then he stirred. Smiling, he stripped the glove from his right hand. The ruby ring glowed bloody in the whiteness of winter wastes only recently touched by summer.

He pulled it from his finger. "First," he murmured, "I rid myself of this, and the title that goes with it."

The Hunter was unmoving upon his rock. His eyes were very dark, and infinitely compelling. "By that, you renounce your rank."

"I do."

"It is a rank many men would kill for, craving the power for themselves, and the promise of more. It is an ancient and honorable title. Your *jehan* held it, and his *jehan*, and his before that . . . many men, Aidan. Very many men. I ask you: do you know what you do?"

"Oh, aye. I know what I'm doing, I'm thinking."

The lilt did not touch the Hunter. "Do you do it willingly, or merely because it seems the easiest thing?"

Aidan laughed. "Are we not done with testing *yet?*" He shook his head, gripping the ring in his palm. "Are you finally asking me the questions I wanted you to ask? Now will you give me my answers?"

"Answer *me*, Aidan."

Quelled for the moment, Aidan nodded. He wet his lips. "I surrender my rank and title willingly, knowing what I do."

"To what benefit?"

"To benefit the prophecy," Aidan answered firmly. "Which I have always served, unknowing; and continue to serve, now *knowing*."

"You remove yourself from the succession of Homana."

"Aye. Willingly."

"I repeat: to what benefit?"

Aidan, smiled, tucking the ring into his belt-pouch and tugging on his glove again. "There was a chain, god of dreams, that once was broken in my hands, and later rejoined. I believed the dreams ended and the task performed, as was intended. But as I stood before Lochiel, I realized that was not true. The joining of the chain, while not precisely *wrong*, was not the desired end."

He recalled Shaine, Carillon, Donal; Ashra, Tye, Siglyn. All who had aided him in his decision, though he had not known it then.

The Hunter's voice was soft. "What was the desired end?"

"To break it." Aidan's attention returned. "The chain was meant to be broken—and by me—to improve the next link." He

gazed down between the folds of his cloak on the bundle that was his son. "To provide *this* link with the strength he requires to complete the prophecy."

The god stirred upon his rock. "What else, Aidan?"

He considered it. The answer came easily. "Chained warrior," he said distantly. "Chained prince; chained raven. Bound, the life goes on. Broken, it is free." He gazed directly at the Hunter. "The chain is broken; the decision made. I wish to go free."

The Hunter's face was expressionless. "Freedom carries its own weight of responsibilities."

"I know that." And suddenly Aidan was laughing with the unhindered joy of realization. The sound rang in the rocks; he let the laughter go out of sheer exuberance and acknowledgment of the truth. He felt so *free* at last. For the first time in his life.

When the laughter died, he grinned at the god. "Lochiel has lost after all."

The Hunter smiled faintly. "What will you do?"

Aidan's answer was prompt. "Take my son to Homana-Mujhar and give him over to his *tahlmorra*. Mine lies elsewhere."

"Ah. Then you have realized you did *not* break it in Valgaard."

"Oh, no." Aidan shrugged. "I learned what it was, instead."

The Hunter nodded. "What of *you*, Aidan, when your son is made the heir?"

He looked down on the bundled child. "The Lion Throne was never meant for me. Gisella was right when she said I would be a throneless Mujhar and a crownless king." He smiled, recalling his fear. "I think I am bound for another realm and another lion . . . for an island floating on the breath of the gods, where lies a fallen altar and a deserted chapel. I think my task is to make it whole again, restoring it to its original purpose so that it may serve Cheysuli in need once more."

"They will call you priest," the Hunter warned. "Half-man. Shadow-man. Warrior without a heart." He paused. "Even coward and castrate."

For a moment only, it pinched. Then fell away into dust, as all desire had. He was content within himself; with the knowledge of what he was.

"Perhaps the Homanans will," Aidan agreed. "It is their nature to disparage what they cannot understand. As for the others—" he shrugged "—it makes little difference. It is time to bring light to the land again, to chase away the dark." He smiled dreamily, gloriously tired. "Names do not matter. And the Cheysuli will call me something else entirely."

"What is that, Aidan?"

"*Shar tahl.*" He grinned briefly. "Like Burr, only worse—I will teach them things they do not want to hear. I will untwist all the twists. I will show them there are new ways to be honored as deeply as the old." The smile fell away. "And I will prophesy."

"For whom?"

Aidan's breath was a plume. "Cynric."

"Who is Cynric?"

"Child of the prophecy. The sword and the bow and the knife. The Firstborn, come again."

The Hunter gestured. "Is that Cynric?"

Aidan glanced in surprise at the child in his arms. "This one? No. This is Kellin. Prince of Homana. The next link." He looked at the god. "Cynric comes later. Cynric comes after. Cynric is the beginning of a new chain."

"And who are *you?*"

He knew the answer, now. "Aidan," he said. "Just—Aidan."

The Hunter smiled. And then he rose, stepping off the rock.

Aidan stood up hastily, cradling the infant who would one day rule Homana. "Is there nothing else?"

"What else is there?" asked the god. "You have discovered your *tahlmorra*, and accepted. That is all that exists for any warrior." Briefly he put his hand against the lump of Kellin's head beneath the cloak. "Guard him well, *shar tahl*. He has yet to learn what sort of *tahlmorra* lies before *him*."

Aidan, overcome, nodded mutely.

The Hunter smiled. His eyes were very warm as he put his other hand on Aidan's head. "Safe flight, my raven. You are everything we hoped."

And Aidan was alone, save for his son.

Carefully, he peeled back the hooded wrappings shielding the tiny face. The Hunter had left the season warm; he did not fear the cold. In the bright sun of a summer day, Aidan looked upon his son. He touched the delicate forehead, traced the line of the brow, fingered the wispy black hair.

And smiled in a sorrowful wonder. "We made this," he murmured. "The bright, bold lass and I."

In her son, Shona lived on.

Aidan nodded tightly. *Better to have something* . . . Abruptly, he banished it. Kellin was more than something.

He inhaled deeply and blew out a streamer of breath. There was nothing left but to go.

Aidan mounted his horse with great care and arranged Kellin more comfortably in his arms. For now the baby slept; he could not hope for it all the way.

Or *could* he? Did he not converse with gods?

Laughing, Aidan glanced up at the thick-leafed tree on which Teel perched. And then the laughter stilled. "Have you always known?"

The silence between them was loud.

"Have you?" Aidan repeated. "The *lir*, you have always maintained, are privy to many things."

Teel offered no answer for a very long time. Then the raven stirred. *Including all the pain. All the fear.* The tone, unexpectedly, altered from tart gibe to tenderness. *It was necessary.*

"What was necessary?"

Obliqueness, Teel answered. *Obscurity of a purpose: to make you angry. To make you fight something, even a contentious* lir.

"Because otherwise I might have given in." Aidan nodded. "Otherwise I might have broken. The anger was a focus . . ."

Teel fluffed black wings. *A warrior who walks with dead men and converses with the gods does not have an easy road. I was meant to make you take it.*

"*Make* me?"

Teel reconsidered. *To suggest you take the road, with whatever means I had.*

Aidan considered that. After a moment he nodded. "Do not change, *lir.* I am used to contentiousness."

I had not thought to change. Why surrender preeminence?

Aidan laughed. The child in his arms squirmed, then settled once again.

He gathered reins and turned the horse southward. "Ah, well, what does it matter? The Wheel of Life has turned." He guided the horse one-handed, cradling Kellin with the other. "And the hounds will like the island."

The raven lifted and flew. Southward, toward Mujhara. Southward, toward an island where the standing stones lay fallen, waiting for the *shar tahl* to set them upright again.

A TAPESTRY
OF LIONS

Prologue

In thread, on cloth, against a rose-red stone wall gilt-washed by early light: Lions. Mujhars: Cheysuli, and Homanan; and the makings of the world in which the boy and his grand-uncle lived.

"Magic," the boy declared solemnly, more intent upon his declaration than most eight-year-olds; but then most eight-year-old boys do not discover magic within the walls of their homes.

The old man agreed easily without the hesitation of those who doubted, or wished to doubt, put off by magic's power; magic was no more alien to him than to the boy, in whose blood it lived as it lived in his own, and in others Cheysuli-born.

"Woman's magic," he said, "conjured from head and hands." His own long-fingered left hand, once darkly supple and eloquent, now stiffened bone beneath wrinkled, yellowing flesh, traced out the intricate stitchwork patterns of the massive embroidered arras hung behind the Lion Throne. "Do you see, Kellin? This is Shaine, whom the Homanans would call your five times great-grandfather. Cheysuli would call him *hosa'ana.*"

It was mid-morning in Shaine's own Great Hall. Moted light sliced through stained glass casements to paint the hall all colors, illuminating the vast expanse of ancient architecture that had housed a hundred kings long before Kellin—or Ian—was born.

The boy, undaunted by the immensity of history or the richness of the hammer-beamed hall and its multitude of trappings, nodded crisply, a little impatient, black brows drawn together in a frown old for his years; as if Kellin, Prince of Homana, knew very well who Shaine was, but did not count him important.

Ian smiled. *And well he might not; his history is more recent, and his youth concerned with now, not yesterday's old Mujhars.*

"Who is this?" A finger, too slender for the characteristic incomplete stubbiness of youth—Cheysuli hands, despite the other houses thickening his blood—transfixed a stitchwork lion made static by the precise skill of a woman's hands. "Is *this* my father?"

"No." The old man's lean, creased-leather face gave away nothing of his thoughts, nothing of his feelings, as he answered the poorly concealed hope in the boy's tone. "No, Kellin. This tapestry was completed before your father was born. It stops here—you see?—" he touched thread, "—with your grandsire."

A dirt-rimmed fingernail bitten off crookedly inserted itself imperatively between dusty threads, once-brilliant colors muted by time and long-set sunlight. "But he should be here. My father. *Somewhere.*"

The expression was abruptly fierce, no longer hopeful, no longer clay as yet unworked, but the taut arrogance of a young warrior as he looked up at the old man, who knew more than the boy what it was to be a warrior; he had even *been* in true war, and was not merely a construct of aging tales.

Ian smiled, new wrinkles replacing old between the thick curtains of snowy hair. "And so he would be, had it taken longer for Deirdre and her women to complete the Tapestry of Lions. Perhaps someday another woman will begin a new tapestry and put you and your father and your heir in it."

"Mujhars," Kellin said consideringly. "That's what all of them were." He glanced back at the huge tapestry filling the wall behind the dais, fixing a dispassionate gaze upon it. The murmured names were a litany as he moved his finger from one lion to another: "Shaine, Carillon, Donal, Niall, Brennan . . ." Abruptly the boy broke off and took his finger from the stitching. "But my father isn't Mujhar and never will be." He stared hard at the old man as if he longed to challenge but did not know how. "Never *will* be."

It did not discomfit Ian, who had heard it phrased one way or another for several years. The intent was identical despite differences in phraseology: Kellin desperately wanted his father, Aidan, whom he had never met. "No," Ian agreed. "You are next, after Brennan . . . they have told you why."

The boy nodded. "Because he left." He meant to sound matter-of-fact, but did not; the unexpected shine of tears in clear green eyes dissipated former fierceness. "He ran *away!*"

Ian tensed. *It would come, one day; now I must drive it back.* "No." He reached and caught one slight shoulder, squeezing slightly as he felt the suppressed, minute trembling. "Kellin—who

said such a monstrous thing? It is not true, as you well know ...
your father ran from nothing, but *to* his *tahlmorra*—"

"They said—" Kellin's lips were white as he compressed them.
"They said he left because he hated me."

"*Who* said this?"

Kellin bit into his bottom lip. "They said I wasn't the son he
wanted."

"Kellin—"

It was very nearly a wail though he worked to choke it off.
"What did I do to make him *hate* me so?"

"Your *jehan* does not hate you."

"Then why isn't he *here? Why* can't he come? Why can't I go
there?" Green eyes burned fiercely. "Have I done something
wrong?"

"No. No, Kellin—you have done nothing wrong."

The small face was pale. "Sometimes I think I must be a
bad son."

"In *no way*, Kellin—"

"Then, why?" he asked desperately. "Why can't he come?"

Why indeed? Ian asked himself. He did not in the least blame
the boy for voicing what all of them wondered, but Aidan was intransigent. The boy was not to come until he was summoned. Nor
would Aidan visit unless the gods indicated it was the proper time.
But will it ever be the proper time?

He looked at the boy, who tried so hard to give away none of
his anguish, to hide the blazing pain. *Homana-Mujhar begins to
put jesses on the fledgling.*

Strength waned. Ian desired to sit down upon the dais so as to
be on the boy's level and discuss things more equally, but he was
old, stiff, and weary; rising again would prove difficult. There was
so much he wanted to say that little of it suggested a way to be
said. Instead, he settled for a simple wisdom. "I think perhaps you
have spent too much time of late with the castle boys. You should
ask to go to Clankeep. The boys there know better."

It was not enough. It was no answer at all. Ian regretted it immediately when he saw Kellin's expression.

"Grandsire says I may not go. I am to stay *here,* he says—but
he won't tell me why. But I heard—I heard one of the servants
say—" He broke it off.

"What?" Ian asked gently. "What have the servants said?"

"That—that even in Clankeep, the Mujhar fears for my safety.

That because Lochiel went there once, he might again—and if he knew *I* was there . . ." Kellin shrugged small shoulders. "I'm to be kept here."

It is no wonder, then, he listens to castle boys. Ian sighed and attempted a smile. "There will always be boys who seek to hurt with words. You are a prince—they are not. It is resentment, Kellin. You must not put faith in what they say about your *jehan*. They none of them know what he is."

Kellin's tone was flat, utterly lifeless; his attempt to hide the hurt merely increased its poignancy. "They say he was a coward. And sick. And given to *fits*."

All this, and more . . . he has years yet before they stop, if any of them ever will stop; it may become a weapon meant to prick and goad first prince, then Mujhar. Ian felt a tightness in his chest. The winter had been cold, the coldest he recalled in several seasons, and hard on him. He had caught a cough, and it had not completely faded even with the onset of full-blown spring.

He drew in a carefully measured breath, seeking to lay waste to words meant to taunt the smallest of boys who would one day be the largest, in rank if not in height. "He is a *shar tahl*, Kellin, not a madman. Those who say so are ignorant, with no respect for Cheysuli customs." Inwardly he chided himself for speaking so baldly of Homanans to a young, impressionable boy, but Ian saw no reason to lie. Ignorance was ignorance regardless of its racial origins; he knew his share of stubborn Cheysuli, too. "We have explained many times why he went to the Crystal Isle."

"Can't he come to *visit*? That's all I want. Just a visit." The chin that promised adult intransigence was no less tolerant now. "Or can't I go *there*? Wouldn't I be safe *there*, with him?"

Ian coughed, pressing determinedly against the sunken breastbone hidden beneath Cheysuli jerkin as if to squeeze his lungs into compliance. "A *shar tahl* is not like everyone else, Kellin. He serves the gods . . . he cannot be expected to conduct himself according to the whims and desires of others." It was the simple truth, Ian knew, but doubted it offered enough weight to crush a boy's pain. "He answers to neither Mujhar nor clan-leader, but to the gods themselves. If you are to see your *jehan*, he will send for you."

"It isn't fair," Kellin blurted in newborn bitterness. "Everyone else has a father!"

"Everyone else does *not* have a father." Ian knew of several boys in Homana-Mujhar and Clankeep who lacked one or both parents. "*Jehans* and *jehanas* die, leaving children behind."

"My mother died." His face spasmed briefly. "They said I killed her."

"No—" No, Kellin had not killed Shona; Lochiel had. But the boy no longer listened.

"*She's* dead—but my father is *alive!* Can't he come?"

The cough broke free of Ian's wishes, wracking lungs and throat. He wanted very much to answer the boy, his long-dead brother's great-grandson, but he lacked the breath for it. "—Kellin—"

At last the boy was alarmed. "*Su'fali?*" Ian was many generations beyond uncle, but it was the Cheysuli term used in place of a more complex one involving multiple generations. "Are you sick still?"

"Winter lingers." He grinned briefly. "The bite of the Lion . . ."

"The Lion is *biting* you?" Kellin's eyes were enormous; clearly he believed there was truth in the imagery.

"No." Ian bent, trying to keep the pain from the boy. It felt as if a burning brand had been thrust deep into his chest. "Here—help me to sit . . ."

"Not there, not on the *Lion*—" Kellin grasped a trembling arm. "I won't let him bite you, *su'fali.*"

The breath of laughter wisped into wheezing. "Kellin—"

But the boy chattered on of a Cheysuli warrior's protection, far superior to that offered by others unblessed by *lir* or shapechanging arts and the earth magic, and guided Ian down toward the step. The throne's cushion would soften the harshness of old wood, but clearly the brief mention of the Lion had burned itself into Kellin's brain; the boy would not allow him to sit in the throne now, even now, and Ian had no strength to dissuade him of his false conviction.

"Here, *su'fali.*" The small, piquant face was a warrior's again, fierce and determined. The boy cast a sharp glance over his shoulder, as if to ward away the beast.

"Kellin—" But it hurt very badly to talk through the pain in his chest. His left arm felt tired and weak. Breathing was difficult. *Lir* . . . It was imperative, instinctive; through the *lir*-link Ian summoned Tasha from his chambers, where she lazed in a shaft of spring sunlight across the middlemost part of his bed. *Forgive my waking you—*

But the mountain cat was quite awake and moving, answering what she sensed more clearly than what she heard.

And more— With the boy's help Ian lowered himself to the top step of the dais, then bit back a grimace. Breathlessly, he said, "Kellin—fetch your grandsire."

The boy was all Cheysuli save for lighter-hued flesh and Erinnish eyes, wide-sprung eyes: dead Deirdre's eyes, who had begun the tapestry for her husband, Niall, Ian's half-brother, decades before . . . —*green as Aileen's eyes*— . . . the Queen of Homana, grandmother to the boy; sister to Sean of Erinn, married to Keely, mother of Kellin's dead mother. *So many bloodlines now . . . have we pleased the gods and the prophecy?*

The flesh of Kellin's Cheysuli face was pinched Homanan-pale beneath thick black hair. *"Su'fali—"*

Ian twitched a trembling finger in the direction of the massive silver doors gleaming dully at the far end of the Great Hall. "Do me this service, Kellin—"

And as the boy hastened away, crying out loudly of deadly lions, the dying Cheysuli warrior bid his mountain cat to run.

PART I

Chapter One

"Summerfair," Kellin whispered in his bedchamber, testing the sound of the word and all its implications. Then, in exultation, "*Summer*fair!"

He threw back the lid of a clothing trunk and fetched out an array of velvets and brocades, tossing all aside in favor of quieter leathers. He desired to present himself properly but without Homanan pretension, which he disliked, putting into its place the dignity of a Cheysuli.

Summerfair. He was to go, this year. Last year it had been forbidden, punishment as much for his stubborn insistence that he had been right as for the transgression itself, which he *still* believed necessary. They had misunderstood, his grandsire and granddame, and all the castle servants; they had *all* misunderstood, each and every one, regardless of rank, birth, or race.

Ian would have understood, but Kellin's *su'fali* was two years' dead. And it was *because* of Ian's death—and the means by which that death was delivered—that Kellin sought to destroy what he viewed as further threat to those he loved.

None of them understood. But his mind jumped ahead rapidly, discarding the painful memories of that unfortunate time as he dragged forth from the trunk a proper set of Cheysuli leathers: soft-tanned russet jerkin with matching leggings; a belt fastened with onyx and worked gold; soft, droopy boots with soles made for leaf-carpeted forest, not the hard bricks of the city.

"—still fit—?" Kellin dragged on one boot and discovered that no, it did not fit, which meant the other didn't either; which meant he had grown again and was likely in need of attention from Aileen's seamstresses with regard to Homanan clothing . . . He grimaced. He intensely disliked such attention. Perhaps he could put on the Cheysuli leathers and wear new Homanan boots; or was that sacrilege?

He stripped free of Homanan tunic and breeches and replaced them with preferred Cheysuli garb, discovering the leggings had shrunk; no, his legs had *lengthened,* which Kellin found pleasing. For a time he had been small, but it seemed he was at last making up for it. Perhaps now no one would believe him a mere eight-year-old, but would understand the increased maturity ten years brought.

Kellin sorted out the fit of his clothing and clasped the belt around slender hips, then turned to survey himself critically in the polished bronze plate hung upon the wall. Newly-washed hair was drying into accustomed curls—Kellin, frowning, instantly tried to mash them away—but his chin was smooth and childish, unmarred by the disfiguring hair Homanans called a beard. Such a thing marked a man less than Cheysuli, Kellin felt, for Cheysuli could not ordinarily grow beards—although some mixed-blood Cheysuli not only could but *did;* it was said Corin, in distant Atvia, wore a beard, as did Kellin's own Erinnish grandfather, Sean—but *he* would never do so. Kellin would never subscribe to a fashion that hid a man's heritage behind the hair on his face.

Kellin examined his hairless chin, then ran a finger up one soft-fleshed cheek, across to his nose, and explored the curve of imma-ture browbone above his eyes. Everyone *said* he was a true Cheysuli, save for his eyes—and skin tinted halfway between bronze and fair; though in summer he tanned dark enough to pass as a trueblood—but he could not replace his eyes, and his prayers in childhood that the gods do so had eventually been usurped by a growing determination to overlook the improper color of his eyes and concentrate on other matters, such as warrior skills, which he practiced diligently so as not to dishonor his heritage. And anyway, he was *not* solely Cheysuli; had they not, all of them, told him re-peatedly he was a mixture of nearly every bloodline there was—or of every one that *counted*—and that he alone could advance the prophecy of the Firstborn one step closer to completion?

They had. Kellin understood. He was Cheysuli, but also Homanan, Solindish, Atvian, and Erinnish. He was needed, he was important, he was *necessary.*

But sometimes he wondered if he himself, Kellin, were not so necessary as his blood. If he cut himself, and spilled it, would that satisfy them—and then make him unimportant?

Kellin grimaced at his reflection. "Sometimes they treat me like Gareth's prize stallion . . . I think he forgets what it is to be a *horse,* the way they all treat him. . . ." But Kellin let it go. The image in the polished plate stared back, green eyes transmuted by bronze to dark hazel. The familiarity of his features was momentarily blurred by imagination, and he became another boy, a strange boy, a boy with different powers promised one day.

"Ihlini," Kellin whispered. "What are you *really* like? Do you look like demons?"

"I think that unlikely," said a voice from the doorway: Rogan, his tutor. "I think they probably resemble you and me, rather than horrid specters of the netherworld. You've heard stories of Strahan and Lochiel. They look like everyone else."

Kellin could see Rogan's distorted reflection in the bronze. "Could *you* be Ihlini?"

"Certainly," Rogan replied. "I am an evil sorcerer sent here from Lochiel himself, to take you prisoner and carry you away to Valgaard, where you will doubtlessly be tortured and slain, then given over to Asar-Suti, the Seker—"

Kellin took it up with appropriate melodrama: "—the god of the netherworld, who made and dwells in darkness, and—"

"—who clothes himself in the noxious fumes of his slain victims," Rogan finished.

Kellin grinned his delight; it was an old game. "Grandsire would protect me."

"Aye, he would. That is what a Mujhar is for. He would never allow anyone, sorcerer or not, to steal his favorite grandson."

"I am his *only* grandson."

"And therefore all the more valuable." Rogan's reflection sighed. "I know it has been very difficult for you, being mewed up in Homana-Mujhar for so many years, but it was necessary. You know why."

Kellin knew why, but he did not entirely understand. Punishment had kept him from attending Summerfair for two years, but there was much more to it than that. He had *never* known any freedom to visit Mujhara as others did, or even Clankeep without constant protection.

Kellin turned from the polished plate and looked at Rogan. The Homanan was very tall and thin and was inclined to stoop when he was tired, as he stooped just now. His graying brown hair was damp from recent washing, and he had put on what Kellin called his "medium" clothes: not as plain as his usual somber apparel, but not so fine as those he wore when summoned to sup in the Great

Hall with the family, as occasionally happened. Plain black breeches and gray wool tunic over linen shirt, belted and clasped with bronze, replaced his customary attire.

"Why?" Kellin blurted. "Why do they let me go *now?* I heard some of the servants talking. They said grandsire and granddame were too frightened to let me go out."

The lines in Rogan's face etched themselves a little more deeply. "Even they understand they cannot keep you in jesses forever. You must be permitted to weather outside like a hawk on the blocks, or be unfit for the task. And so they have decided you may go this year, as you have improved your manners—and because it is time. I am put in charge . . . but there will be guards also."

Kellin nodded; there were always guards. "Because I'm Aidan's only son, and the only heir." He did not understand all of it. "Because—because if Lochiel killed me, there would be no more threat." He lifted his chin. "That's what they say in the baileys and kitchens."

Rogan's eyes flinched. "You listen entirely too much to gossip—but I suppose it is to be expected. Aye, you are a threat to the Ihlini. And that is why you are so closely guarded. With so many Cheysuli here Lochiel's sorcery cannot reach you, and so you are closely kept—but there *are* other ways, ways involving nothing so much as a greedy cook desiring Ihlini gold—" But Rogan waved it away with a sharply dismissive gesture. "Enough of a sad topic. There will be guards, as always, but your grandsire has decided to allow you this small freedom."

Summerfair was more than a freedom. It was renewal. Kellin forgot all about rumor and gossip. Grinning, he pointed at the purse depending from the belt. His grandfather had given Rogan coin for Summerfair. "Can we go? Now?"

"We can go. Now."

"Then put on your Summerfair face," Kellin ordered sternly. Rogan was a plain, soft-spoken man in his mid-forties only rarely given to laughter, but Kellin had always known a quiet, steady warmth from the Homanan. He enjoyed teasing Rogan out of his melancholy moods, and today was not a day for sad faces. "You will scare away the ladies with that sad scowl."

"What does my face have to do with the ladies?" Rogan asked suspiciously.

"It's *Summerfair*," Kellin declared. "Everyone will be happier than usual because of Summerfair. Even *you* will attract the ladies . . . if you put away that scowl."

"I am not scowling, and what do you know about ladies?"

"Enough," Kellin said airily, and strode out of the room.

Rogan followed. "How much is enough, my young lord?"

"*You* know." Kellin stopped in the corridor. "I heard Melora. She was talking to Belinda, who said it had been too long since you'd had a good woman in your bed." Rogan's face reddened immediately. It was the first time any of Kellin's sallies had provoked such a personal reaction, and the boy was fascinated. "Has it been?"

The man rubbed wearily at his scalp. "Aye, well, perhaps. Had I known Belinda and Melora were so concerned about it, I might have asked them for advice on how to change matters." He eyed his charge closely. "How much do you know about men and women?"

"Oh, everything. I know all about them." Kellin set off down the corridor with Rogan matching his longer strides to the boy's. "I was hoping I might find a likely lady during Summerfair."

A large hand descended upon Kellin's shoulder and stopped him in his tracks. "My lord," Rogan said formally, "would you be so good as to tell your ignorant tutor precisely what you are talking about?"

"If you mean how much do I know," Kellin began, "I *know.* I learned all about it last year. And now I would like to try it for myself."

"At ten?" Rogan murmured, as much for himself as for Kellin.

"How old were *you?*"

Rogan looked thoughtful. "They say Cheysuli grow up quickly, and there are stories about your grandsire and his brothers. . . ."

Kellin grinned. "This might be the best Summerfair of all."

"Better than last year, certainly." The understated amusement faded from Rogan's tone. "You do recall why you were refused permission to go."

Kellin shrugged it away. "Punishment."

"And why were you punished?"

Kellin sighed; it was very like Rogan to impose lessons upon a holiday, and reminders of other lessons. "Because I set fire to the tapestry."

"And the year before that?"

"Tried to chop the Lion to bits." Kellin nodded matter-of-factly. "I had to do it, Rogan. It was the Lion who killed Ian."

"Kellin—"

"It came alive, and it bit him. My *su'fali* said so."

Rogan was patient. "Then why did you try to burn down the tapestry?"

"Because *it's* made of lions, too. You know that." Kellin firmed his mouth; none of them understood, even when he explained. "I have to kill all the lions before they kill me."

Summer was Kellin's favorite season, and the fair the best part of it. Never searingly hot, Homana nonetheless warmed considerably during midsummer, and the freedom everyone felt was reflected in high spirits, habits, and clothing. Banished were the leathers and furs and coarse woolens of winter, replaced by linens and cambrics and silks, unless one was determinedly Cheysuli in habits at all times, as was Kellin, who wore jerkin and leggings whenever he could. Everyone put on Summerfair clothing, brightly dyed and embroidered, and went out into the streets to celebrate the season.

Doors stood open and families gathered before dwellings, trading news and stories, sharing food and drink. In Market Square Mujharan merchants and foreign traders gathered to hawk wares. The streets were choked with the music of laughter, jokes, tambors, pipes, and lutes, and the chime of coin exchanged. The air carried the aromas of spices and sweetmeats, and the tang of roasting beef, pork, mutton, and various delicacies.

"Sausage!" Kellin cried. Then, correcting himself—he had taken pains to learn the proper foreign word: "*Suhoqla!* Hurry, Rogan!"

Kellin's nose led him directly to the wagons at the outermost edge of Market Square, conspicuously far from the worst of the tangle in the center of the square. Already a small crowd gathered, Homanans nudging one another with elbows and murmuring pointed comments about the foreigners and foreign ways. That other traders were as foreign did not seem to occur to them; *these* foreigners were rarely seen, and therefore all the more fascinating.

Kellin did not care that they were foreign, save their foreignness promised *suhoqla*, which he adored, and other things as intriguing.

Rogan's voice was stern. "A more deliberate pace, if you

please—no darting through the crowd. You make it difficult for the
guard to keep up in such crowded streets—and if we lose them, we
must return to the palace at once. Is that what you wish to risk?"

Kellin glanced around. There they were, the guard: four men of
the Mujharan Guard, hand-picked to protect the Prince of Homana.
They were unobtrusive in habits and clothing generally, except
now they wore the crimson tabards of their station to mark them
for what they were: bodyguards to the boy in whom the future of
the Cheysuli—and Homana herself—resided.

"But it's *suhoqla* . . . you know how I love it, Rogan."

"Indeed, so you have said many times."

"And I haven't had it for almost two years!"

"Then by all means have some now. All I ask is that you recall
I am almost four decades older than you. Old men cannot keep up
with small—" he altered it in midsentence, "—young men."

Kellin grinned up at him. "A man as tall as you need only
stretch out prodigious legs, and he is in Ellas."

Rogan smiled faintly. "So I have often been told." He looked
beyond Kellin to the wagon. "*Suhoqla* it is, then. Though how your
belly can abide it . . ." He shook his head in despair. "You will
have none left by the time you are my great age."

"It isn't my belly I care about, it's my mouth." Kellin edged his
way more slowly through the throng with Rogan and the watchdogs following closely. "By the time it gets to my belly, it's
tamed."

"Ah. Well, here you are."

Here he was. Kellin stared at the three women kneeling around
the bowl-shaped frying surface. They had dug a hollow in the
sand, placed heated stones in the bottom, then the clay plank atop
the stones. The curling links of sausage were cooked slowly in
their own grease, absorbing spiced oil.

The women were black-haired and black-eyed, with skins the
color of old ivory. Two of them were little more than crones, but
the third was much younger. Her eyes, tilted in an oval face, were
bright and curious as she flicked a quick assessive glance across
the crowd, but only rarely did she look anyone in the eye. She and
her companions wore shapeless dark robes and bone jewelry—
necklaces, earrings, and bracelets. The old women wore cloth
head-coverings; the youngest had pulled her hair up high on the
back of her head, tying it so that it hung down her back in a series

of tight braids. Two yellow feathers fluttered from one braid as she moved.

"A harsh place, the Steppes," Rogan murmured. "You can see it in their faces."

"Not in *hers*," Kellin declared.

"She is young," Rogan said sadly. "In time, she'll grow to look like the others."

Kellin didn't like to think so, but filling his mouth was more important than concerning himself with a woman's vanishing youth. "Buy me some, Rogan, if you please."

Obligingly Rogan fished a coin out of the purse provided by the Mujhar, and handed it to one of the old women. The young one speared two links with a sharpened stick, then held it out to Kellin. "Ah," Rogan said, looking beyond. "It isn't merely the women, after all, that attract so many . . . Kellin, do you see the warrior?"

Tentatively testing the heat of the spiced sausages, Kellin peered beyond the women and saw the man Rogan indicated. He forgot his *suhoqla* almost at once; Steppes warriors only rarely showed themselves in Mujhara, preferring to watch their women-folk from the wagons. This one had altered custom to present himself in the flesh.

The warrior was nearly naked, clad only in a brief leather loin-kilt, an abundance of knives, and scars. He was not tall, but compactly muscled. Black hair was clubbed back and greased, with a straight fringe cut across his brow. He wore a plug of ivory on one nostril, and twin scars bisected each cheek, ridged and black, standing up like ropes from butter-smooth flesh.

Kellin lost count of the scars on the warrior's body; by their patterns and numbers, he began to wonder if perhaps they were to the Steppes warriors as much a badge of honor and manhood as *lir*-gold to a Cheysuli.

At the warrior's waist were belted three knives of differing lengths, and he wore another on his right forearm while yet another was hung about his throat. It depended from a narrow leather thong, sheathed, its greenish hilt glinting oddly in the sunlight of a Homanan summer. The warrior stood spread-legged, arms folded, seemingly deaf and blind to those who gaped and commented, but Kellin knew instinctively the Steppesman was prepared to defend the women—the young one, perhaps?—at a moment's notice.

Kellin looked up at his tutor. "Homana has never fought the Steppes, has she?"

Rogan sighed. "You recall your history, I see. No, Kellin, she has not. Homana has nothing to do with the Steppes, no treaties, no alliances, nothing at all. A few warriors and woman come occasionally to Summerfair, that is all."

"But—I remember *something*—"

"That speaks well of your learning," Rogan said dryly. "What you recall, I believe, is that one of your ancestors, exiled from Homana, went into the service of Caledon and fought against Steppes border raiders."

"Carillon." Kellin nodded. "And Finn, his Cheysuli liege man." He grinned. "I am kin to both."

"So you are." Rogan looked again at the scarred warrior. "A formidable foe, but then Carillon himself was a gifted soldier—"

"—and Finn was *Cheysuli*." Kellin's tone was definitive; nothing more need be said.

"Aye." Rogan was resigned. "Finn was indeed Cheysuli."

Kellin stared hard at the Steppes warrior. The forgotten *suhoqla* dripped spiced grease down the front of his jerkin. It was in his mind to make the warrior acknowledge the preeminence of the Cheysuli, to mark the presence of superiority; he wanted badly for the fierceness of the scarred man to pale to insignificance beside the power of his own race, men—and some women—who could assume the shape of animals at will. It was important that the man be made to look at him, to see him, to know he was Cheysuli, as was Finn, who had battled Steppes raiders a hundred years before.

At last the black, slanting eyes deigned to glance in his direction. Instinctively, Kellin raised his chin in challenge. "I am Cheysuli."

Rogan grunted. "I doubt he speaks Homanan."

"Then how does he know what anyone says?"

The young woman moved slightly, eyes downcast. "I speak." Her voice was very soft, the Homanan words heavily accented. "I speak, tell Tuqhoc what is said, Tuqhoc decides if speaker lives."

Kellin stared at her in astonishment. "*He* decides!"

"If insult is given, speaker must die." The young woman glanced at the warrior, Tuqhoc, whose eyes had lost their impassivity, and spoke rapidly in a strange tongue.

Kellin felt a foolhardy courage fill up his chest, driving him to further challenge. "Is he going to kill me now?"

The young woman's eyes remained downcast. "I told him you understand the custom."

"And if I insulted you?"

"Kellin," Rogan warned. "Play at no semantics with these people; such folly promises danger."

The young woman was matter-of-fact. "He would choose a knife, and you would die."

Kellin stared at the array of knives strapped against scarred flesh. "Which one?"

She considered it seriously a moment. "The king-knife. That one, one around his neck."

"That one?" Kellin looked at it. "Why?"

Her smile was fleeting, and aimed at the ground. "A king-knife for a king—or a king's son."

It was utterly unexpected. Heat filled Kellin's face. Everyone else *knew;* he was no longer required to explain. He had set aside such explanations years before. But now the young woman had stirred up the emotions again, and he found the words difficult. "My father is not a king."

"You walk with dogs."

"Dogs?" Baffled, Kellin glanced up at Rogan. "He is my tutor, not a dog. He teaches me things."

"I try to," Rogan remarked dryly.

She was undeterred by the irony. "Them." Her glance indicated the alerted Mujharan Guard, moving closer now that their charge conversed with strangers from the Steppes.

Kellin saw her gaze, saw her expression, and imagined what she thought. It diminished him. In her eyes, he was a boy guarded by dogs; in his, the son of a man who had renounced his rank and legacy, as well as the seed of his loins. In that moment Kellin lost his identity, stripped of it by foreigners, and it infuriated him.

He stared a challenge at the warrior. "*Show* me."

Rogan's hand came down on Kellin's shoulder. Fingers gripped firmly, pressing him to turn. "This is quite enough."

Kellin was wholly focused on the warrior as he twisted free of the tutor's grip. "*Show* me."

Rogan's voice was clipped. "Kellin, I said it was enough."

The watchdogs were there, *right* there, so close they blocked the sun. But Kellin ignored them. He stared at the young woman. "Tell him to show me. Now!"

The ivory-dark faced paled. "Tuqhoc never shows—Tuqhoc *does.*"

Kellin did not so much as blink even as the watchdogs crowded him. He pulled free of a hand: Rogan's. "Tell him what I said."

Tuqhoc, clearly disturbed by the change in tone and stance—and the free use of his own name—barked out a clipped question. The young woman answered reluctantly. Tuqhoc repeated himself, as if disbelieving, then laughed. For the first time emotion glinted in his eyes. Tuqhoc smiled at Kellin and made a declaration in the Steppes tongue.

Rogan's hands closed on both shoulders decisively. "We are leaving. I warned you, my lord."

"No," Kellin declared. To the young woman: "What did he say?"

"Tuqhoc says, if he shows, you die."

"Only a fool taunts a Steppes warrior—I thought you knew better." Rogan's hands forced Kellin to turn. "Away. Now."

Kellin tore free. "*Show* me!" Even as Rogan blurted an order, the watchdogs closed on the warrior, drawing swords. Kellin ducked around one man, then slid through two others. The dark Steppes eyes were fixed on the approaching men in fierce challenge. Kellin desperately wanted to regain that attention for himself. "Show me!" he shouted.

Tuqhoc slipped the guard easily, *so* easily—even as the challenge was accepted. In one quick, effortless motion Tuqhoc plucked the knife from the thong around his neck and threw.

For Kellin, the knife was all. He was only peripherally aware of the women crying out, the guttural invective of the warrior as the watchdogs pressed steel against his flesh.

Rogan reached for him—

Too late. The knife was in the air. And even as Rogan twisted, intending to protect his charge by using his own body as shield, Kellin stepped nimbly aside. *For ME*—

He saw the blade, watched it, judged its arc, its angle, anticipated its path. Then he reached out and slapped the blade to the ground.

"By the gods—" Rogan caught his shoulders and jerked him aside. "Have you any idea—?"

Kellin did. He could not help it. He stared at the warrior, at the Steppes women, at the knife in the street. He knew precisely what he had done, and why.

He wanted to shout his exultation, but knew better. He looked at the watchdogs and saw the fixed, almost feral set of jaws; the grimness in their faces; the acknowledgment in their eyes as they caged the Steppesman with steel.

It was not his place to gloat; Cheysuli warriors did not lower themselves to such unnecessary displays.

Kellin bent and picked up the knife. He noted the odd greenish color and oily texture of the blade. He looked at Rogan, then at the young woman whose eyes were astonished.

As much as for his tutor's benefit as for hers, Kellin said: "Tell Tuqhoc that I am Cheysuli."

Chapter Two

Rogan's hand shut more firmly on Kellin's shoulder and guided him away despite his burgeoning protest. Kellin was aware of the Mujharan Guard speaking to Tuqhoc and the young woman, of the tension in Rogan's body, and of the startled murmuring of the crowd.

"Wait—" He wanted to twist away from Rogan's grasp, to confront Tuqhoc of the Steppes and see the acknowledgment in *his* eyes, as it was in the woman's, that a Cheysuli, regardless of youth and size, was someone to be respected. But Rogan permitted no movement save that engineered by himself. *Doesn't he understand? Doesn't he know?*

Unerringly—and unsparing of his firmness—the Homanan guided Kellin away from the wagons to a quieter pocket in the square some distance away. His tone was flat, as if he squeezed out all emotion for fear of showing too much. "Let me see your hand."

Now that the moment had passed and he could no longer see the Steppes warrior, Kellin's elation died. He felt listless, robbed of his victory. Sullenly he extended his hand, allowing Rogan to see the slice across the fleshy part of three fingers and the blood running down his palm.

Tight-mouthed, Rogan muttered something about childish fancies; Kellin promptly snatched back his bleeding hand and pressed it against the sausage-stained jerkin. The uneaten *suhoqla* grasped in his other hand grew colder by the moment.

Rogan said crisply, "I will find something with which to bind these cuts."

Blood mingled with sausage grease as Kellin pressed the fingers against his jerkin. It stung badly enough to make the corners of his mouth crimp, but he would not speak of it. He would give away nothing. "Leave it be. It has already stopped," He fisted his hand so hard the knuckles turned white, then displayed it to Rogan. "You see?"

The tutor shook his head slowly, but he gave the hand only the merest contemplation; he looked mostly at Kellin's face, as if judging him.

I won't let him know. Kellin put up his chin. "I am a warrior. Such things do not trouble warriors."

Rogan shook his head again. Something broke in his eyes: an odd, twisted anguish. His breath hissed between white teeth. "While you are fixed wholly on comporting yourself as a warrior, neglecting to recall you are still but a *boy*—I realize it will do little if any good to point out that the knife could have *killed you.*" The teeth clamped themselves shut. "But I'll wager that was part of the reason you challenged him. Yet you should know that such folly could result in serious repercussions."

"But I could *see*—"

Rogan cut off the protest. "If not for yourself, for me and the guard! Do you realize what would become of us if you came to harm?"

Kellin had not considered that. He looked at Rogan more closely and saw the very real fear in his tutor's eyes. Shame goaded. "No," he admitted, then anxiousness usurped it, and the need to explain. "But I needed him to see. To *know*—"

"Know what? That you are a boy too accustomed to having his own way?"

"That I am Cheysuli." Kellin squeezed his cut hand more tightly closed. "I want them *all* to know. They have to know—they have to understand that I am not *he*—"

"Kellin—"

"Don't you see? I have to prove I am a *true* man, not a coward—that I will not turn my back on duty and my people—and—and—" he swallowed painfully, finishing his explanation quickly, unevenly, "—any sons *I* might sire."

Rogan's mouth loosened. After a moment it tightened again, and the muscles of his jaw rolled briefly. Quietly, he said, "Promise me *never* to do such a thoughtless thing again."

Feeling small, Kellin nodded , then essayed a final attempt at explanation. "I watched his eyes. Tuqhoc's. I knew when he would throw, and how, and what the knife would do. I had only to put out my hand, and the knife was *there.*" He shrugged self-consciously, seeing the arrested expression in Rogan's eyes. "I just knew. I *saw.*" Dismayed, he observed his congealing sausage as Rogan fixed him with a more penetrating assessment. Kellin extended the stick with its weight of greasy *suhoqla.* "Do you want this?"

The Homanan grimaced. "I cannot abide the foul taste of those things. *You* wanted it—eat it."

But Kellin's appetite was banished by aftermath. "It's cold." He glanced around, spied a likely looking dog, and approached to offer the sausage. The mongrel investigated the meat, wrinkled its nose and sneezed, then departed speedily.

"*That* says something for your taste," Rogan remarked dryly. He drew his own knife, cut a strip of fabric from the hem of his tunic, motioned a passing water-seller over and bought a cup. He dipped the cloth into the water and began to wipe the cut clean. "By the gods, the queen will have my hide for this . . . you are covered with grease and blood."

Rogan's ministrations hurt. No longer hungry, Kellin discarded the *suhoqla.* He bit into his lip as the watchdogs came up and resumed their places, though the distance between their charge and their persons was much smaller now.

Humiliation scorched his face; warriors did not, he believed, submit so easily to public nursing. "I want to see the market."

Rogan looped the fabric around the fingers and palm to make a bandage, then tied it off. "We are *in* the market; look around, and you will see it." He tightened the knot. "There. It will do until we return to the palace."

Kellin's mind was no longer on the stinging cut or its makeshift bandage. He frowned as a young boy passed by, calling out in singsong Homanan. "A fortune-teller!"

"No," Rogan said promptly.

"But *Rogan*—"

"Such things are a waste of good coin." Rogan shrugged. "You are Cheysuli. You already know your *tahlmorra.*"

"But you don't yet know yours." Grinning anticipation, Kellin locked his bandaged hand over Rogan's wrist. "Don't you want to find out if you'll share your bed with Melora or Belinda?"

Rogan coughed a laugh, glancing sidelong at the guards. "No mere fortune-teller can predict *that.* Women do what they choose to do; they do not depend on fate."

Kellin tugged his tutor in the direction the passing boy had indicated. "Let us go, Rogan. That boy says the fortune-teller can predict what becomes of me."

"That boy is a shill. He says what he's told to say, and the fortune-teller says what he's *paid* to say."

"*Ro*-gan!"

Rogan sighed. "If you desire it so much—"

"Aye!" Kellin tugged him on until they stood before a tent slumped halfheartedly against a wall. A black cat, small version of the Mujhar's *lir,* Sleeta, lay stretched out on a faded rug before the entrance, idly licking one paw; beside him curled a half-grown fawn-hued dog who barely lifted an eyelid. The tent itself was small, its once-glorious stripes faded gold against pale brown, so that it merged into the wall. "My grandsire gave you coin for such things," Kellin reminded his tutor. "Surely he could not count it ill-spent if we *enjoyed* it!"

Graying eyebrows arched. "A sound point. That much you have mastered, if not your history." Rogan gestured for the guardsmen to precede them into the tent.

"No!" Kellin cried.

"They must, Kellin. The Mujhar has given orders. And after what you provoked in the Steppes warrior, I *should* take you home immediately."

Kellin compromised immediately. "They may come wait *here.*" His gesture encompassed the rug and entrance. "But not inside the tent. A fortune is a private thing."

"I cannot allow the Prince of—"

"Say nothing of titles!" Kellin cried. "How will the fortune-teller give me the truth otherwise? If he knows what I am, it cheats the game."

"At least you admit it *is* a game, for which I thank the gods; you are not entirely gullible. But rules are rules; the Mujhar is my lord, not you." Rogan ordered one of the guardsmen into the tent. "He will see that it is safe."

Kellin waited impatiently until the guardsman came out again. When the man nodded his head, Rogan had him and his companions assume posts just outside the tent.

"Now?" Kellin asked, and as Rogan nodded he slipped through the doorflap.

Inside the tent, Kellin found the shadows stuffy and redolent of an acrid, spice-laden smoke that set his eyes to watering. He wiped at them hastily, wrinkling his nose at the smell very much as the street dog did to the *suhoqla,* and squinted to peer through the thready haze. A gauzy dark curtain merged with shadow to hide a portion of the tent; he and Rogan stood in what a castle-raised boy would call an antechamber, though the walls were fabric in place of stone.

Rogan bent slightly, resting a hand on Kellin's shoulder as he spoke in a low tone. "You must recall that he works for *coin*, Kellin. Put no faith in his words."

Kellin frowned. "Don't spoil it."

"I merely forewarn that what he says—"

"Don't *spoil* it!"

The gauzy curtain was parted. The fortune-teller was a nondescript, colorless foreign man of indeterminate features, wearing baggy saffron pantaloons and three silk vests over a plain tunic: one dyed blue, the next red, the third bright green. "Forgive an old man his vice: I smoke *husath*, which is not suitable for guests unless they also share the vice." He moved out of the shadowed curtain, bringing the sweet-sour aroma with him. "I do not believe either of you would care for it."

"What is it?" Kellin was fascinated.

Rogan stirred slightly. "Indeed, a vice. It puts dreams in a man's head."

Kellin shrugged. "Dreams are not so bad. I dream every night."

"*Husath* dreams are different. They can be dangerous when they make a man forget to eat or drink." Rogan stared hard at the man. "The boy wants his fortune told, nothing more. You need not initiate him into a curiosity that may prove dangerous."

"Of course." The man smiled faintly and gestured to a rug spread across the floor. "Be in comfort, and I will share with you your future, and a little of your past."

"He is all of ten; his past is short," Rogan said dryly. "This shouldn't take long."

"It will take as long as it must." The fortune-teller gestured again. "I promise you no tricks, no *husath*, no nonsense, only the truth."

Kellin turned and gazed up at Rogan. "You first."

The brows arched again. "We came for *you*."

"You *first*."

Rogan considered it, then surrendered gracefully, folding long legs to seat himself upon the rug just opposite the fortune-teller. "For the boy's sake, then."

"And nothing for yourself?" The fortune-teller's teeth were stained pale yellow. "Give me your hands."

Kellin dropped to his knees and waited eagerly. "Go on, Rogan. Give him your hands."

With a small, ironic smile, Rogan acquiesced. The fortune-teller merely looked at the tutor's hands for a long moment, examining the minute whorls and scars in his flesh, the length of fingers, the fit of nails, the color of the skin. Then he linked his fingers with Rogan's, held them lightly, and began to murmur steadily as if invoking the gods.

"No tricks," Rogan reminded.

"Shhh," Kellin said. "Don't spoil the magic."

"This isn't magic, Kellin . . . this is merely entertainment."

But the fortune-teller's tone altered, interrupting the debate. His voice dropped low into a singsong cadence that made the hair rise up on the back of Kellin's neck: *"Alone in the midst of many, even those whom you love . . . apart and separate, consumed by grief. She lives within you when she is dead, and you live through her, seeing her face when you sleep and wake, longing for the love she cannot offer. You live in the pasts of kings and queens and those who have gone before you, but you thrive upon your own. Your past is your present and will be your future, until you summon the strength to give her life again. Offered and spurned, it is offered again; spurned and offered a third time until, accepting, you free yourself from the misery of what is lost to you, and then live in the misery of what you have done. You will die knowing what you have done, and why, and the price of your reward. You will use and be used in turn, discarded at last when your use is passed."*

Rogan jerked his hands away with a choked, inarticulate protest. Kellin, astonished, stared at his tutor; what he saw made him afraid. The man's face was ashen, devoid of life, and his eyes swam with tears.

"Rogan?" Apprehension seized his bones and washed his flesh ice-cold. "*Rogan!*"

But Rogan offered no answer. He sat upon the rug and stared at nothingness as tears ran down his face.

"A harsh truth," the fortune-teller said quietly, exhaling *husath* fumes. "I promise no happiness."

"Rogan—" Kellin began, and then the fortune-teller reached out and caught at *his* hands, trapped the fingers in his own, and Kellin's speech was banished.

This time there were no gods to invoke. The words spilled free of the stranger's mouth as if he could not stop them. *"He is the sword,"* the hissing voice whispered. *"The sword and the bow and the knife. He is the weapon of every man who uses him for ill, and the strength of every man who uses him for good. Child of darkness, child of light; of like breeding with like, until the blood is one again. He is Cynric, he is Cynric: the sword and the bow and the knife, and all men shall name him evil until Man is made whole again."*

The voice stopped. Kellin stared, struggling to make an answer, any sort of answer, but the sound began again.

"The lion shall lie down with the witch; out of darkness shall come light; out of death: life; out of the old: the new. The lion shall lie down with the witch, and the witch-child born to rule what the lion must swallow. The lion shall devour the House of Homana and all of her children, so the newborn child shall sit upon the throne and know himself lord of all."

A shudder wracked Kellin from head to toe, and then he cried out and snatched his hands away. "The Lion!" he cried. "The Lion *will* eat me!"

He scrambled to his feet even as the guardsmen shredded canvas with steel to enter the tent. He saw their faces, saw their intent; he saw Rogan's tear-streaked face turning to him. Rogan's mouth moved; but Kellin heard nothing. One of the guards put his hand upon his prince's rigid shoulder, but Kellin did not feel it.

The Lion. The LION.

He knew in that instant they were unprepared, just as the Steppes warrior had been unprepared. *None* of them understood. No one at all knew him for what he was. They saw only the boy, the deserted son, and judged him worthless.

Aren't I worthless?

But the Lion wanted him.

Kellin caught his breath. *Would the Lion want to eat a worthless boy?*

Perhaps he *was* worthless, and that fact alone was why the Lion might want to eat him.

To save Homana from a worthless Mujhar.

With an inarticulate cry, Kellin tore free of the guardsman's hand and ran headlong from the tent. He ignored the shouts of the Mujharan Guard and the blurted outcry of his tutor. He tore free of them all, even of the tent, and clawed his way out of pale shadow into the brilliance of the day.

"Lion—" Kellin blurted, then darted into the crowd even as the man came after him.

Run—
He ran.
Where—?
He did not know.
Away from the Lion—
Away.
—won't let the Lion eat me— He tripped and fell, facedown, banging his chin into a cobble hard enough to make himself bite his lip. Blood filled his mouth; Kellin spat, lurched up to hands and knees, then pressed the back of one hand against his lower lip to stanch the bleeding. The hand bled, too; Rogan's bandage had come off. The cut palm and his cut mouth stung.

It smells— It did. He had landed full-force in a puddle of horse urine. His jerkin was soaked with it; the knees of his leggings, ground into cobbles as well, displayed the telltale color and damp texture of compressed horse droppings.

Aghast, Kellin scrambled to his feet. He was *filthy*. In addition to urine and droppings weighting his leathers, there was mud, grease, and blood; and he had lost his belt entirely somewhere in his mad rush to escape the Lion. No one, seeing him now, would predict his heritage or House.

"Rogan?" He turned, thinking of his tutor instead of the Lion; recalled the fortune-teller's words, and how Rogan had reacted. And the watchdogs; where were they? Had he left everyone behind? *Where am—*

Someone laughed. "Poor boy," said a woman's voice, "have you spoiled all your Summerfair finery?"

Startled, he gaped at her. She was blonde and pretty, in a coarse sort of way, overblown and overpainted. Blue eyes sparkled with laughter; a smile displayed crooked teeth.

Humiliated, Kellin stared hard at the ground and tried to uncurl his toes. *I don't want to be here. I want to go HOME.*

"What a pretty blush; as well as I could do, once." Skirts rustled faintly. "Come here."

Reluctantly Kellin glanced up slantwise, marking the garish colors of her multiple skirts. One hand beckoned. He ignored it, thinking to turn his back on her, to leave the woman behind, but the laughter now was muted, replaced with a gentler facade.

"Come," she said. "Has happened to others, too."

She wasn't his granddame, who welcomed him into her arms when he needed a woman's comfort, but she *was* a woman, and she spoke kindly enough now. This time when she beckoned, he answered. She slipped a hand beneath his bloodied chin, forcing him to look up into her own face. At closer range her age increased, yet her eyes seemed kind enough in an assessive sort of way. Her hair was not really blonde, he discovered by staring at exposed roots, and the faintest hint of dark fuzz smudged her upper lip.

The woman laughed. "Don't blush *quite* so much, boy. You'll have me thinking you've never seen a whore before."

He gaped. "You are a light woman?"

"A *light*—" She broke off, brows lifting. "Is that the genuine accent of aristrocracy?" She leaned closer, enveloping him in a powerful, musky scent. "Or are you like me: a very good mimic?"

She is NOT like granddame after all. Kellin tugged at his ruined jerkin, than blotted again at his split lip. She watched him do it, her smile less barbed, and at last she took her hand from his chin, which relieved him immeasurably. "Lady—"

"No, not that. Never that." Her hand strayed into his hair, lingered in languorous familiarity. Her touch did not now *in the least* remind him of his grandmother's. "Why is it," the woman began, "that boys and men have thicker hair and longer lashes? The gods have truly blessed you, my green-eyed little man." The other hand touched his leggings. "And how little *are* we in things that really matter?"

Kellin nearly squirmed. "I—I must go."

"Not, so soon, I pray you." She mocked the elaborate speech of highborn Homanans. "We hardly know one another."

That much Kellin knew; he'd heard the horseboys speaking of whores. "I have no money." Rogan had plenty, but he doubted the Mujhar would approve of it being spent on women.

The whore laughed. "Well, then, what *have* you? Youth. Spirit. Pretty eyes, and a prettier face—you'll have women killing over you, when you're grown." Her eyes lost their laughter. "Men would kill for you now." The smile fell off her face. "And innocence, which is something everyone in the Midden has lost. If I could get some back, *steal* it back, somehow—"

Kellin took a single step backward. Her hand latched itself into his filthy jerkin; she did not seem to notice her hand now was also soiled. "I must go," he tried again.

"No," she said intently. "No. Stay a while. Share with me youth and innocence—"

Kellin wrenched away from her. As he ran, he heard her curse.

This time when he fell, Kellin managed to avoid urine and droppings, landing instead against hard stone cobbles after his collision with a woman carrying a basket. He feared at first she might also be a whore, but she had none of the ways or coarse speech. She was angry, aye, because he had upset her basket; and then she was screaming something about a thief—

"No!" Kellin cried, thinking he could explain and set everything to rights—the Prince of Homana, a *thief?*—but the woman kept on shrieking, ignoring his denials, and he saw the men, big men all, hastening toward him.

He ran again, and was caught. The man grabbed him by one arm and hoisted him into the air so that one boot toe barely scraped the cobblestones. "Give over, boy. No more kicking and biting."

Kellin, who had not thought to bite, squirmed in the tight grasp. He intensely disliked being hung by one wrist like a side of venison. "I am not a boy, I'm a *prince*—"

"And I'm the Mujhar of Homana." The man waited until Kellin's struggles subsided. "Done, are we?"

"Let me *go!*"

"Not until I have the ropes on you."

Kellin stiffened. "Ropes!"

"I and others like me are sworn to keep the rabble off the streets during Summerfair," the big man explained. "That includes catching all the little thieves who prey on innocent people."

"I'm not a thief, you *ku'reshtin*—"

The big hand closed more tightly. "Round speech for a boy, by your tone."

"I am the Prince of Homana!"

The man sighed. He was very large, and redhaired; he was also patently unimpressed by Kellin's protests. "Save your breath, boy. It only means a night under a decent roof, instead of some alley or doorway. And you'll be fed, so don't be complaining so much when you're better off now than you were."

"But I'm—" Kellin broke off in astonishment as the men looped a rope around one wrist, then the other. Prince or no, he was snugged tight as a gamebird. "Wait!"

The man nodded patiently. "Come along, then, and I'll see to it you have a decent meal and a place to sleep. I'll free you first thing in the morning if anyone comes to fetch you."

The furious challenge was immediate. "If I had a *lir*—"

"What? Cheysuli, too?" The giant laughed, though not unkindly. "Well, I'm thinking not. I've never yet seen one with green eyes, nor leathers *quite* so filthy."

Chapter Three

Kellin did not know Mujhara well. In fact, he knew very little about the city he would one day rule, other than the historical implications Rogan had discussed so often; and even then he was ignorant of details because he had not listened well. He wanted to do something much more exciting than spend his days speaking of the past. The future attracted him more, even though Rogan explained again and again that the past affected that future; that a man learning from the past often avoided future difficulties.

Because he was so closely accompanied each time he left Homana-Mujhar, Kellin had come to rely on others to direct him. Left to his own devices, he would have been lost in a moment as he was lost now. The big red-haired man led him like a leashed dog through the winding closes, alleys, and streets, turning this way and that, until Kellin could not so much as tell which direction was which.

He felt the heat of shame as he was led unrelentingly. *Don't look at me—* But they did, all the people, the Summerfair crowds thronging the closes, alleys, and streets. Kellin thought at first if he called out to them and told them who he was, if he asked for their support, they would give it gladly. But the first time he tried, a man laughed at him and called him a fool for thinking they would believe such a lie; would the Prince of Homana wear horse piss on his clothing?

Don't look at me. But they looked. Inwardly, Kellin died a small, quiet death, the death of dignity. *I just want to go home.*

"Here," his captor said. "You'll spend the night inside." The giant opened the door, took Kellin inside, then handed over the "leash" to another man, this one brown-haired and brown-eyed, showing missing teeth. "Tried to steal a goodwife's basket of ribbons."

"No!" Kellin cried. "I did *not*. I fell against her, no more, and knocked it out of her hands. What would I want with ribbons?"

The gap-toothed man grinned. "To sell them, most like. At a profit, since you paid nothing for them in the first place."

Kellin was outraged. "I did not steal her ribbons!"

"Had no chance to," the redhead laughed. "She saw to that, with her shrieking."

Kellin drew himself up, depending on offended dignity and superior comportment to put an end to the intolerable situation. Plainly he declared, "I am the Prince of Homana."

He expected apologies, respect, and got neither. The two men exchanged amused glances. The gap-toothed Homanan nodded. "As good a liar as a thief, isn't he? Only that's not so good, is it, since you're *here?*"

Courage wavered; Kellin shored it up with a desperate condescension. "I am here with my tutor and four guardsman, four of the *Mujharan Guard*." He hoped it would make a suitable impression, invoking his grandfather's personal company. "Go and ask *them;* they will tell you."

"Wild goose chase," said the redhead. "Waste of time."

Desperation nearly engulfed injured pride. "Go and *ask*," Kellin directed. "Go to Homana-Mujhar. My grandsire will tell you the truth."

"Your grandsire. The Mujhar?" Gap-tooth laughed, slanting a bright glance at the giant.

Kellin bared his teeth, desiring very badly to prove the truth of his claims. But his leathers were smeared with filth, his bottom lip swollen, and his face, no doubt, as dirty. "My boots," he said sharply, sticking out one foot. "Would a thief have boots like these?"

The redhead grinned. "If he stole them."

"But they *fit*. Stolen boots would not fit."

Gap-tooth sighed. "Enough of your jabber, brat. You'll not be harmed, just kept until someone comes to fetch you."

"But no one knows where I am! How can they come?"

"If you're the Prince of Homana, they'll know." The giant's eyes were bright. "D'ye think I'm a fool? You've *my* eyes, boy, plain Homanan green, not the yellow of a Cheysuli. Next time you want to claim yourself royalty, you'd best think better of it."

Kellin gaped. "My granddame is Erinnish, with hair red as yours—redder! I have *her* eyes—"

"Your granddame—and your mother to boot—was likely a street whore, brat . . . no more chatter from you. Into the room. We're not here to harm you, just *keep* you." The red-haired giant pushed Kellin through another door as Gap-tooth unlocked it. He was dumped unceremoniously onto a thin pallet in a small, stuffy room, then the door was locked.

For a moment Kellin lay sprawled in shock, speechless in disbelief. Then he realized they'd stripped the rope from his wrists. He scrambled up and hammered at the door.

"They won't open it. They won't."

Kellin jerked around, seeing the boy in the corner for the first time. The light was poor, admitted only through a few holes high up in the walls. The boy slumped against the wall with the insouciance of a longtime scofflaw. His face was thin, grimy, and bruised. Lank blond hair hung into his eyes, but his grin was undiminished by Kellin's blatant surprise.

"Urchin," the boy said cheerfully, answering the unasked question.

Kellin was distracted by newborn pain in his cut hand, which now lacked Rogan's bandage. He frowned to see the slices were packed with dirt and other filth; wiping it against his jerkin merely caused the slices to sting worse. Scowling, he asked, "What kind of a name is that?"

"Isn't a name. Haven't got one. That's what they call me, *when* they call me." The boy shoved a wrist through his hair. His eyes were assessive far beyond his years. "Good leathers, beneath the dirt . . . good boots, too. No thief, are ye?"

Kellin spat on the cuts and wiped them again against his jerkin. "Tell *them* that."

Urchin grinned. "Won't listen. All they want is the copper."

"Copper?"

"Copper a head for all the thieves they catch."

Kellin frowned, giving up on his sore hand. "Who pays it?"

Urchin shrugged. "People. They're fed up wi' getting their belt-purses stolen and pockets picked." He waggled fingers. "Some o' them took up a collection, like . . . for each thief caught during Summerfair, they pay a copper a head. Keeps the streets clean of us, y'see, and *they* can walk out without fearing for pockets and purses." Urchin grinned. "But if you're good enough, nobody catches you."

"*You* got caught."

"Couldn't run fast enough with this." Urchin extended a swollen, discolored foot and puffy ankle. "Dog set on me." He was patently unconcerned by the condition of foot and ankle. "If you're not a thief, why're you here?"

Kellin grimaced. "I was running. They thought it was because I was stealing."

"Never run in Mujhara," the boy advised solemnly, then reconsidered. "Unless you be a fine Homanan lord, and then no one will bother you no matter *what* you do."

Kellin glanced around. On closer inspection, the room was no better than his first impression, a small imprisonment, empty save for them. "Not so many copper pieces today."

Urchin shrugged. "The other room is full. They'll put the new catches in here. You're the first, after me."

Kellin peeled a crust of blood from his chin. "How do we get out?"

"Wait till someone pays your copper. Otherwise we stay here till Summerfair is over, because then it won't matter."

"That's three days from now!"

Urchin shrugged, surveying his injured foot. "Be hard to steal with this."

Kellin stared at the swollen limb, marking the angry discoloration and the streaks beginning to make their way up Urchin's leg. It was a far worse injury than the few slices in his hand. "You need that healed."

Urchin's mouth hooked down. "Leeches cost coin."

Morbidly fascinated by the infected limb, Kellin knelt down to look more closely. "A Cheysuli could heal this, and he would cost nothing."

Urchin snorted.

"He *could*," Kellin insisted. "*I* could, had I a *lir*."

Urchin's eyes widened. "You say *you're* Cheysuli?"

"I am. But I can't heal yet." Kellin shrugged a little. "Until I have a *lir*, I'm just like you." The wound stank of early putrefaction. "My grandsire will heal you. He has a *lir;* he can." *And he will heal my wounds, too.*

Urchin grunted. "Will he come here to pay your copper?"

Kellin considered it. "No," he said finally, feeling small inside. "I think Rogan will do that, and I doubt he will like it."

"Few men like parting with coin."

"Oh, it is not the coin. He will not like *why* he has to do it, and it will give him fuel to use against me for months." Kellin cast a glance around the gloomy room. "He would say I deserved this, to teach me a lesson. But it was the *Lion*—" He looked quickly at Urchin, breaking off.

The Homanan boy frowned. "What lion?"

"Nothing." Kellin left Urchin's side and retreated to a pallet near the door. He pressed shoulder blades into the wall. "He will come for me."

"That tutor?" Urchin's mouth twisted. "I had a tutor, once. He taught me how to steal."

Kellin shrugged. "Then stop."

"Stop." Urchin stared. "D'ye think it's so easy? D'ye think I asked the gods for this life?"

"No one would ask it. But why do you stay *in* it?"

"No choice." Urchin picked at his threadbare tunic. His thin face was pinched as if his leg pained him. "No mother, no father, no kin." His expression hardened. "I'm a thief, and a good one." He looked at his swollen ankle. "Sometimes."

Kellin nodded. "Then I will have Rogan pay your copper, too, and you will come back with me."

Urchin's dirt-mottled face mocked. "With you."

"To Homana-Mujhar."

"Liar."

Kellin laughed. "As good a liar as a thief."

Urchin turned his shoulder: eloquent dismissal.

With his pallet nearest the door, Kellin awoke each time a new arrival was pushed into the room throughout the night. At first he had been intrigued by the number and their disparate "crimes," but soon enough boredom set in, and later weariness; he fell asleep not long after a plain supper of bread and thin gravy was served, and slept with many interruptions until dawn.

The commotion was distant at first, interesting only the few recently imprisoned souls who hoped for early release. That hope had faded in Kellin, who found himself reiterating to a dubious Urchin that indeed he was who he said he was, and was restored only when he heard the voice through the door: the red-haired man, clearly frightened as well as astonished.

Kellin grinned at the young thief through pale dawn. "Rogan. I *told* you, Urchin."

The door was opened and a man came in. It wasn't Rogan at all, but the Mujhar himself, followed by the giant.

Kellin scrambled hastily to his feet. "Grandsire! You?"

The giant was very pale. "My lord, how could we know? *Had* we known—"

Stung by the outrage, Kellin turned on the man. "You knew," he declared. "I told you. You just didn't *believe* me." He looked at his grandfather. "None of them believed me."

"Nor would I," Brennan said calmly. He arched a single eloquent brow. "Have you taken to swimming in the midden?" Yellow eyes brightened faintly, dispelling the barb. "Or was it an entirely *different* kind of Midden?"

Kellin recalled then the whore's words, her mention of the Midden. It basted his face with heat. Such *shame* before his grandsire! "My lord Mujhar . . .". He let it trail off. Part of him was overwhelmed to be safe at last; while the other part was mortified that his grandsire should see him so. "No," he said softly, squirming inside filthy leathers. "I fell . . . I did not mean to get so dirty."

"Nor so smelly." Brennan's gaze was steady. "Explain yourself, if you please."

Kellin looked at the giant. "Didn't *he* tell you?"

"He told me. So did the other man. Now it is for you."

Kellin was hideously aware of everyone else in the room, but especially of his grandfather, his tall, strong, *Cheysuli* grandfather, whose dignity, purpose, and sense of self was so powerful as to flatten everyone else, certainly a ten-year-old grandson. The Mujhar *himself,* not Rogan, standing in the doorway with the sunrise on his back, *lir*-gold gleaming brightly, silver in his hair, stern face even sterner. The wealth on his arms alone would keep Urchin and others like him alive for years.

In a small voice, Kellin suggested, "It would be better done in private."

"No doubt. I want it done here."

Kellin swallowed heavily. He told his grandsire the whole of it, even to the woman.

Brennan did not smile, but his mouth relaxed. Tension Kellin had been unaware of until that moment left the Mujhar's body. "And what have you learned from this?"

Kellin looked straight back. "Not to run in Mujhara."

After a moment of startled silence, the Mujhar laughed aloud, folding bare bronzed arms across his chest with no pretensions at maintaining a stern facade, even before the others. Kellin gaped in surprise; what was so amusing, that his grandsire would sacrifice his dignity before the others without hesitation?

"I had expected something else entirely," Brennan said at last, "but I cannot fault your statement. There is truth in it." Amusement faded. "But there is also Rogan."

Kellin's belly clenched. He nodded and stared at his boot toes. "Rogan," he echoed, "I meant not to make him worry."

"Tell him that."

"I will."

"Now."

Kellin looked up from the ground and saw Rogan in the doorway just behind his grandsire. The man's face was haggard and gray, his eyes reddened from sleeplessness. Kellin thought then of the aforementioned repercussions, Rogan's own question regarding what would become of him and the Mujharan Guard if harm came to Kellin.

"I am unharmed," Kellin said quickly, grasping the repercussions as he never had before. "I am whole, save for my lip, and that I got myself when I fell down."

"And your cut hand; Rogan told me." Brennan extended his own. "Let me see."

Kellin held out his hand and allowed his grandsire to examine the cuts. "Filthy," the Mujhar commented. "It will want a good cleaning when we return, but will heal of its own." His yellow eyes burned fiercely. "You must know not to test others, Kellin. No matter the provocation. If you had not been so quick—"

"But I knew I *was*," Kellin insisted; couldn't any of them see? "I watched him. I watched the knife. I *knew* what it would do."

Brennan's mouth crimped. "We will speak of this another time. For now, I charge you to recall that for such a serious transgression as this one, you endanger others as well as yourself."

Kellin looked again at Rogan. He tugged ineffectually at his ruined jerkin. "I am sorry."

The tutor nodded mutely, seemingly diminished by the tension of the night. Or was it the Lion, biting now at Rogan?

"Well." The Mujhar cast a glance around the room. "It is to be expected that you smell like the Midden, or *a* midden—though I suppose it is less your own contribution than that of everyone else."

Kellin nodded, scratching at the fleas that had vacated his pallet to take up residence in his clothing.

Brennan considered him. "I begin to think you are more like my *rujholli* than I had believed possible."

It astonished Kellin, who had never thought of such a thing. "I am?"

"Aye. Hart and Corin would have gotten themselves thrown into a room just like this, or worse, for about the same reason—or perhaps for a crime even worse than thievery—and then waited for me to fetch them out." He looked his grandson up and down. "Are you not young to begin?"

Ashamed again, Kellin stared hard at the ground. Softly, he said, "I did not expect *you* to come."

"Hart and Corin did. And they were right; I always came." Brennan sighed. "You did expect someone."

"What else?" It startled Kellin. "You would not *leave* me here!"

Brennan eyed him consideringly. "I did leave you here. I knew where you were last night."

"Last *night!*" It was preposterous. "You left me here all night?"

Brennan exchanged a glance with Rogan. "In hopes you might profit from it, albeit there were guardsmen—and a Cheysuli—just across the street." His eyes narrowed. "You said you have learned not to run in Mujhara . . . well, I suppose that is something." His tone was ironic. "Surely more than Hart or Corin learned."

"Grandsire—"

"But whether you learned anything is beside the point. Your granddame made it clear to me that if I did not fetch you out *at once* come dawn, she would have my head." He smiled slightly. "As you see, it is still attached."

Kellin nodded, not doubting that it was; nor his granddame's fiery Erinnish temper.

"So Rogan and I are here to fetch you, very much as you expected, and will now take you back to Homana-Mujhar, where I shall myself personally supervise the bath just to make certain the body in it *is* that of my grandson, and not some filthy street urchin masquerading as the Prince of Homana."

"Urchin!" Kellin cried, turning. "We have to take him with us!"

"Who?"

"Urchin. Him." Kellin pointed to the astonished boy. "I told him you would pay his copper and bring him with us—well, I said

Rogan would—" Kellin cast a glance at his tutor, "—so you could heal him."

"Volunteering my services, are you, you little wretch?" But Brennan crossed the room and knelt down by the boy thief. "How are you hurt? Ah, so I see. Here—"

"No!" Urchin jerked away the infected foot.

"There is no need to fear me," Brennan said quietly. "I will look, no more; if you are in need of healing, it shall be done in Homana-Mujhar."

"I can't go *there*!"

"Why not?" Brennan examined the infected bite. "Walls and a roof, no more . . . you are as welcome as Kellin."

"I am?"

"For now. Come. Trust me."

Kellin looked at his grandfather through Urchin's eyes: tall, dark warrior with silvered hair; yellow eyes clear and unwavering as a wolf's, with the same promised fierceness; *lir*-gold banding bared arms; the soft, black-dyed leathers clothing a powerful body. He was old in years to Kellin, but age sat lightly on Cheysuli; Brennan was still fit and graceful, with a cat's eloquent ease of movement.

"He won't hurt you," Kellin explained matter-of-factly. "He is my grandsire."

Brennan smiled. "The highest of compliments, and surety of my goodwill."

Urchin's eyes were wide. "But—I'm a *thief*."

"Former thief, I should hope. Come with me to Homana-Mujhar, and you need never steal again." The Mujhar grinned. "Where you may also shed forty layers of dirt, ten years' worth of fleas, and fill that hollow belly."

"No!" Urchin cried as Brennan made to pick him up. "You'll catch my fleas!"

"Then I shall bathe also."

"I am too heavy!"

"You are not heavy at all." Brennan turned toward the door, toward the red-haired giant. "I will have the fines paid for everyone in this room, and the other; you will see to it they are released at once. But I sympathize with those who fear for their purses; if any of these are caught again, keep them here till Surnmerfair is ended: in the name of the Mujhar." He smiled briefly at Kellin, slipping into the Old Tongue. "*Tu'halla dei.*" He cast a glance at gape-mouthed faces, then settled Urchin more firmly against his chest. "The Guard has horses waiting. You'll ride behind me."

"My lord," Rogan said quietly, following his lord from the room as Kellin slipped out. "There is the matter of the fortune-teller."

"Ah." Brennan's face assumed a grim mask. He glanced down at Kellin as he carried Urchin into the street. "What did he say to you, Kellin?"

Kellin shrugged. "I couldn't understand it all. They were just—*words.*"

"Tell me the words anyway."

Kellin squirmed self-consciously; he did not want to admit to his fear of the Lion. "Cynric."

Brennan's mask slipped, baring naked shock beneath. "Cynric? He said *that?*"

"A name." Kelolin frowned. "And a sword, and a bow, and a— knife?"

"Gods," Brennan whispered. "Not my grandson, *too.*"

It terrified Kellin to see his grandfather so stricken. "Not me?" he asked. "Why do you say that? Grandsire—what does it *mean?*"

"It means—" Brennan's mouth tightened into a thin, flat line. "It means we will go visit your fortune-teller—who speaks to you of Cynric—before we go home."

"Why? What did he mean?" Desperation crept in; did it have to do with the Lion? "What does 'Cynric' mean?"

" 'Cynric'?" The Mujhar sighed as he handed Urchin to a guardsman and ordered him put up on his own mount. "It is a name, Kellin . . . an old, familiar name I have not heard in ten years. Since your *jehan* first brought you to us—"

"Before he left." Kellin blurted it out all at once; bitterness encased it. "Before he *left!*"

"Aye." Brennan rubbed absently at the flesh of a face suddenly grown old. "Before he left." He looked at Rogan. "Can you direct us?"

Rogan glanced very briefly at Kellin before looking back to the Mujhar: a subtle question to which the boy was not blind, though adults believed he was. "My lord, perhaps later would be better."

"No." Brennan threaded reins through his hand, turning toward his mount. "No, I think *now.* He has spoken the name to Kellin without knowing who he was—or so you would have me believe. . . ." He patted Urchin's stiff thigh, then climbed up easily.

"And even if he *did* know who Kellin was, he also knew the name. I want to ask him how he came by it, and why he speaks of it now to a ten-year-old boy."

"Aye." Rogan moved like an old man toward his own mount. "Of course, my lord, I can direct you to him at once. Although I must warn you—" the tutor mounted with effort, as if his bones hurt, "—he smokes *husath*. It is possible . . ." He made a gesture with one hand that suggested such a man was unpredictable, and his employment.

Brennan's face was grim. "Aidan never did. But he knew the name, also."

"Grandsire?" Kellin stood in the street, staring up. It seemed to him Urchin had usurped his place. "Is there a horse for me?"

"Rogan's," his grandfather told him, "so you may say more privately how sorry you are for the worry you caused."

Ashamed, Kellin nodded. "Aye, grandsire. I will."

Summerfair revelers still gathered in the streets, making it difficult for a mounted party to pass through; Brennan gave orders that his presence not be cried, since he wanted to come upon the fortune-teller unaware, and so the Mujharan Guard merely *suggested* people move, rather than forcing it. The journey took longer than Kellin recalled to reach the faded, striped tent, but then he could not remember for how long he had run.

"Here," Rogan murmured.

The cat and the dog were gone. Flies sheathed the doorflap. "My lord." One of the guardsmen swung down and then another. Kellin watched as two of the crimson-tabarded men entered the tent while the other two stood very close to the Mujhar and his heir.

One of the men was back almost immediately, face set grimly. "My lord."

Brennan hooked his leg frontwise over the pommel to avoid Urchin and slid off, throwing glittering, gold-banded reins to Rogan. "Stay here with Kellin."

"Grandsire!"

The Mujhar spared barely a glance. "Stay here, Kellin."

It burst from Kellin's throat: *"Don't let the Lion eat you!"*

Brennan, at the doorflap, turned sharply. "What do you mean?"

Oh, gods, now it was too late; he had let it slip; he had *said* it; and his grandsire would laugh; *all* of them would laugh—

"Kellin."

Kellin pressed himself against Rogan's back. "Nothing," he whispered.

Rogan stirred. "A childhood tale, my lord. Nothing more."

Brennan nodded after a moment's hesitation, then went into the tent.

Don't let the Lion eat him—

"Kellin." Rogan's voice, very soft. "What is this lion?"

"Just—the Lion. You know. I told you."

"There is no lion in there."

"You don't *know* that. The fortune-teller said—"

"—too much," Rogan declared. "Entirely too much."

"Aye, but . . . Rogan, there really is a lion. The *Lion*—he wants to eat Homana."

"A dog bit my ankle," Urchin offered. "But that's not the same as a *lion* biting it."

Kellin stared at him. "The Lion bit my *su'fali*. And he died."

Rogan began quietly, "Kellin, I think—"

But he never finished because the Mujhar came out again, yellow eyes oddly feral as he stared at his grandson. "Kellin, you must tell me what the fortune-teller said. Everything."

"About Cynric?"

"Everything." The Mujhar's mouth was crimped tight at the corners. "About the lions, too."

It alarmed Kellin. "Why? *Was* it the Lion? Did it eat the fortune-teller?"

"Kellin—*wait*—"

But Kellin slid off over the horse's rump and darted between his grandfather and the doorflap. He stumbled over a rucked-up rug just inside, caught his precarious balance, then stopped short.

Sprawled on his back amid blood-soaked cushions and carpets lay the fortune-teller. A gaping, ragged hole usurped the place his throat had been.

Chapter Four

Torches illuminated the corridor. Kellin crept through it silently, taking care to make no sound; he wanted no one to discover him in the middle of the night, lest they send him off to bed before his task could be accomplished.

Ahead— He drew in a deep breath to fill his hollow chest, then turned the corner. Massive silver doors threw back redoubled torchlight, so bright he nearly squinted. *They must have polished them today.* But that was not important. Importance lay beyond, within the Great Hall itself.

Ten more steps, and he was there. Kellin filled his chest with air again, then leaned with all his weight against the nearest door. *Hinges oiled, too.* It cracked open mutely, then gave as he leaned harder, until he could slide through the space into the dimness of the Great Hall.

He paused there, just inside, and stared hard into darkness. Moonlight slanted through stained glass casements, providing dim but multicolored illumination. Kellin used it in place of torchlight, fixing his gaze upon the beast.

There— And it was, as always: crouched upon the dais as if in attack, rampant wood upon gold-veined marble, teeth bared in ferocity, gilt gleaming in mouth and eyes.

There— And him *here,* pressed against the silver doors, shoulder blades scraping.

Twice he had come, since Ian had died. First, to chop the Lion into bits; again to burn the tapestry hanging just behind, lest the Lion summon confederates in his bid to devour the Mujhar, the queen, and perhaps Kellin himself.

The fortune-teller said so— Kellin shivered. He came now with no ax, no torch to set flame to tapestry, but alone and unweaponed, intending no harm at all this time but warning in harm's place, to make the Lion *know.*

He sucked in a noisy breath, then set out on the long journey. Step by step by step, pacing out the firepit, until he reached the dais. Until he faced the beast.

Kellin balanced lightly, distributing weight as he had been taught: upon the balls of his feet, knees slightly bent, arms loose at his sides, so he could flee if required, or fight.

"You," he exhaled. "Lion."

The throne offered no answer. Kellin swallowed heavily, staring fixedly at the shadow-shrouded beast.

"Do you hear?" he asked. He disliked the quaver in his tone and altered it, improving volume also. "It is I: Kellin, who will be Mujhar one day. Kellin of Homana." He leaned forward slightly, to make certain the Lion heard. "I am not alone anymore."

Still there was no answer.

Kellin wet his lips, then expelled the final warning: "I have a *friend.*"

"Kellin?"

He twitched; was it the Lion? *No*— He spun. "Urchin!"

The Homanan boy squeezed his way through the doors just as Kellin had done. "Why are you—" He broke it off, staring beyond Kellin. "Is that the Lion Throne?"

Kellin was very aware of the weight crouched behind him. "Aye."

Urchin's steps were steady as he approached, showing no signs of limp. The Mujhar's healing a week before had proved efficient as always; once over the shock of being touched by legendary Cheysuli magic, Urchin had recovered his customary spirit. "What are you doing here? Talking to it?"

Before Urchin, Kellin did not feel defensive. "Warning it."

"About what?" Urchin arrived before the dais, brushing aside still-lank but now-clean hair. "Does it answer?"

"It eats people." Kellin slanted Urchin a glance. "It killed my *su'fali.*"

"Your what?"

"*Su'fali.* Uncle—well, great-uncle. It bit him, and he died." The pain squeezed a little, aching inside his chest. "Two springs ago."

"Oh." Urchin stared at the throne: wary fascination. "You mean—it comes alive?"

It was hard to explain. Others had told him not to speak such nonsense, and he had locked it all within. Now Urchin wanted the truth. It was easier to say nothing. "It wants my grandsire next."

"It does?" After a startled reassessment, Urchin frowned. "How do you know?"

"I just know. In here." Kellin touched his chest. "And the fortune-teller said so. It ate *him*, too."

"Rogan said—"

"Rogan said what the Mujhar told him to say." Kellin scowled. "They don't want to believe me. They didn't believe me when I told them about Ian, and they don't believe me now." He looked hard at Urchin. "Do you believe me?"

Urchin blinked. "I don't know. It's *wood*—"

"It's the Lion, and it wants to eat Homana." Kellin lifted his chin. "I told it I had a friend, now; that I wasn't alone anymore."

Urchin blinked. "You mean—me?"

"*Aren't* you my friend?"

"Well—aye. Aye, I am, but . . . you're the Prince of Homana."

"Princes need friends, too." Kellin tried to keep the plea out of his voice.

"But I'm only a *spit*-boy."

"Grandsire will give you better when you've learned things," Kellin explained. "He told me it's best if you start there, then move up, because a castle is strange to you."

"It is," Urchin agreed. He eyed the Lion again, then glanced back to Kellin. "Rogan doesn't teach the other spit-boys."

"No. I asked grandsire because I said we were friends."

Urchin nodded, looking around the massive Great Hall. "This will be yours, one day?"

"When grandsire dies."

"He's strong; he'll live a long time." Urchin slanted a sidelong glance at Kellin. "Why isn't your father here? Shouldn't he be next?"

Kellin's belly hurt, as it often did when someone mentioned his father. "He gave it up. He *renounced* his title." His spine was rigid. Words spilled out, and virulence; he had learned to say it first, before anyone else could. "He is mad. He lives on an island and talks about the gods."

Urchin blinked. "The priests do that all the time, and they're not mad."

"My father *sees* things. Visions. He has fits." Kellin shrugged, trying not to show how much it hurt. Urchin was his friend, but there were things Kellin could not share. "Grandsire says he is a *shar tahl*—that is Old Tongue for 'priest-historian'—but I say he is something else. Something *more:* part priest, part warrior, part fortune-teller—and all fool."

"He gave away *everything?*"

Kellin nodded mutely.

"He could have been Mujhar . . ." Urchin looked at the Lion again. "He could have been *Mujhar.*"

"A fool," Kellin declared. "And one day I will tell him. I will go to the Crystal Isle, and find him, and *tell* him."

Urchin grinned at him. "Can I go with you?"

Kellin smiled back. "You will be my captain of the guard. Commander of the *Mujharan* Guard, and I will take you everywhere."

Urchin nodded. "Good." He stared up at the Lion, studied it, then drew himself up before it. He slanted a grin at Kellin, then turned back to the throne. "I am Urchin, Lion! In the name of Kellin, I command the Mujharan Guard! And I say to you, Lion, you shall set no teeth to his flesh, nor spill royal blood!"

It echoed in the hall. Gilt eyes glinted faintly.

Kellin stared at the Lion. "You see? I am not alone anymore."

The Queen of Homana, in her solar, approved of them both. Kellin could tell. He had pleased her by working harder at his studies, and by being altogether less obdurate about learning his duties as Prince of Homana. When she was pleased, her green eyes kindled; just now, he felt the warmth redoubled as she smiled at him and Urchin. "Rogan says both of you are doing very well."

Kellin and Urchin exchanged glances. Urchin was stiff, as he always was before the queen or the Mujhar, but his smile was relaxed and genuine. Cleaned up, he was altogether presentable, even for a spit-boy. The weeks had improved him in many ways.

"In fact," the queen went on, "he told me yesterday he was quite impressed with both of you. Urchin is yet behind you, Kellin, but 'tis to be expected. He's had no proper lessons before now." Her expression softened as she glanced at the taller boy. "You are to be commended for your diligence."

Urchin's face reddened. "Kellin helps me."

"But he learns on his own," Kellin put in quickly. "I only point out a few things here and there. He does most of it himself."

"I know." Aileen of Homana had lost none of her vividness with the passage of time, though her color had dimmed a trifle from the brilliant red of youth to a rusted silver. But she was still Erinnish, born of an island kingdom, and she still boasted the tenacity and fiery outspokenness that had nearly caused a political incident between her realm and Homana when she had professed to love Niall's third-born son in place of the prince she was meant to wed; Corin himself had prevented it by taking up his *tahlmorra* in Atvia, and Aileen had married Brennan after all. "He's as quick at his learning as he is his duties at the spit; 'twill not be long before he outgrows the kitchens and enters into more personal service."

"With me?" Kellin blurted.

Aileen laughed. "In time, Kellin—first he must learn the house-hold. Then we'll be seeing if he's ready to become the Prince of Homana's personal squire."

"But he has to be," Kellin insisted. "I want to make him com-mander of the Mujharan Guard."

"Oh?" Rusty brows lifted. "I think Harlech might be wishing to keep his post."

"Oh, not *yet*." Kellin waved a hand. "When he is older. When I am Mujhar."

Aileen's mouth crimped only slightly. "Indeed." She looked at Urchin. "Do you feel yourself fit for such duty?"

"Not yet," Urchin replied promptly. "But—I will be." He cast a sidelong glance at Kellin. "I mean to guard him against the Lion."

Aileen's smiled faded. Her glance went beyond the boys to the man in the doorway.

"The Lion," echoed the Mujhar; both boys swung at once. "The Lion is no threat, as I have said many times. It is a throne, no more. Symbolic of Homana, the Cheysuli, and our *tahlmorra,* which is of no little import—" he smiled faintly, "—but assuredly it offers nothing more than the dusty odor of history and the burdensome weight of tradition."

Kellin knew better than to protest; let them believe as they would. He *knew* better.

Now, so did Urchin.

"I, too, am pleased," the Mujhar declared. "Rogan has brought good tidings of your progress." He glanced briefly at his wife, passing a silent message, then touched each boy on the shoulder. "Now, surely you can find better ways to spend your time than with women and women's things," he grinned at the queen to show he meant no gibe, "so I suggest you be about it. Rogan has the day to himself and has gone into the city; I suggest you see if Harlech has something to teach you of a commander's duties."

Urchin bowed quick acquiescence, then followed Kellin from the chamber.

"Wait." Kellin stepped rapidly aside to the wall beside the still-open door, catching Urchin's arm to halt him. "Listen," he whispered.

Urchin's expression was dubious; blue eyes flicked in alarm toward the door. "But—"

Kellin mashed a silencing hand into his friend's mouth. He barely moved his lips. "There is something he wants to tell her . . . something I am not to hear—" Kellin bit off his sentence as his grandmother began speaking.

" 'Tis Aidan, isn't it?" she asked tensely in the room beyond. "You've heard."

"A message." The Mujhar's tone was curiously flat, squashed all out of shape. Without seeing his grandsire, Kellin heard the layered emotions: resignation, impatience, a raw desperation. "Aidan says 'Not yet.' "

His granddame was not nearly so self-controlled. "Didn't ye *tell* him, then?"

"I did. In the strongest terms possible. 'Send for your son,' I said, 'Kellin needs his father.' "

"And?"

"And he says, 'Not yet.' "

Urchin's breath hissed. Kellin waved him into silence.

"Gods," Aileen breathed. "*Has* he gone mad, as they say?"

"I—want to think not. I want to disbelieve the rumors. I want very much to *believe* there is a reason for what he does."

"To keep himself isolate—"

"He is a *shar tahl*, Aileen. They are unlike other Cheysuli—"

Her tone was rough, as if she suppressed tears. "There's Erinnish in him, too, my braw boyo—or are you forgetting, that?"

"No." The Mujhar sighed. "He shapes others, Aidan says, to understand the old ways must be altered by the new."

"But to deny his own son a father—"

"He will send for Kellin, he says, when the time is right."

For a long moment there was silence. Then the Queen of Homana muttered an oath more appropriate to a soldier. "And when *will* it be right? When his son is a grown man, seated upon the Lion Throne Aidan *himself* should hold?"

The Mujhar answered merely, with great weariness, "I do not know."

Tension filled the silence. Then Kellin heard a long, breathy sigh cut off awkwardly.

"Aileen, no—"

"Why not?" The voice was thick, but fierce. "He is *my son,* Brennan—I'm permitted, I'm thinking, to cry if I wish to cry."

"Aileen—"

"I miss him," she said. "Gods, but I miss him! So many years—"

"Shansu, meijhana—"

"There is no peace!" she cried. "I bore him in my body. You're not knowing what it is."

"I am bonded in my own way—"

"With a *cat!*" she said. " 'Tisn't the same, Brennan. And even if it were, you have Sleeta *here.* I have nothing. Nothing but memories of the child I bore, and the boy I raised. . . ." Her voice thickened again. " 'Tisn't fair to any of us. Not to you, to me; and certainly not to Kellin." Her voice paused. "Is there no way to *make* him come? To compel him?"

"No," Brennan said. "He is more than our son, more than a *jehan.* He is also a *shar tahl.* I will not compel a man blessed by gods to serve a mortal desire. Not for me, nor for you—"

"For *his son?*"

"No. I will not interfere."

Taut silence, as Kellin spun tightly away. Urchin hesitated only a moment, then hastened to catch up. "Kellin—"

"You heard." It took effort not to shout. "You *heard* what he said. About my father—" It filled his throat, swelling tightly, until he wanted to choke, or scream, or cry. "He doesn't want me."

"That's not what the Mujhar said. He said your father would send when the time was right."

Kellin strode on stiffly. "The time will *never* be right!"

"But you don't *know* th—"

"I do." Venomously. "He renounced the throne, and renounced me. He renounced *everything!*"

"But he's a priest. Don't priests do those things?"

"Not *shar tahl*s. Not most of them. They have sons, and they love them." Kellin's tone thinned, then wavered. He clamped down on self-possession with every bit of strength he had. "Someday I will see him, whether he wants me or no, and I will tell him to his face that he is not a man."

"Kellin—"

"I *will*." Kellin stopped and stared fiercely at Urchin. "And you will come with me."

He dreamed of gods, and fathers, and islands; of demanding, impatient gods; of Lions who ate humans. He awoke with a cry as the door swung open, and moved to catch up the knife he kept on a bench beside his bed, with which he might slay lions.

"Kellin?" It was Rogan, bringing with him a cupped candle. "Are you awake?"

Kellin always woke easily, prepared for lions. "Aye." He scooched up in bed. "What is it?" His heart seized. *Not the Lion—*

There was tension in Rogan's tone as he came into the chamber, swinging shut the door behind him. He did not chide his charge for speaking of the Lion. " Kellin . . ." He came forward to the bed, bringing the light with him. It scribed deep lines in a haggard face. "There is something we must discuss."

"In the middle of the night?"

"I can think of no better time." A slight dryness altered the tension. Rogan put the candle cup on the bench beside the knife, then sat down on the edge of the huge tester bed. "My lord, I know you are troubled. I have known for some time. Urchin came to me earlier, but do not blame him; he cares for you, and wants you content."

"Urchin?" Kellin was confused.

"He told me what you both overheard today, when you eavesdropped on the Mujhar."

"Oh." Only the faintest flicker of remorse pinched, then was consumed by remembered bitterness. "Did he tell you—"

Rogan overrode. "Aye. And after much thought, I have decided to do what no one else will do." The tutor's eyes were blackened by shadows, caved in unreadable darkness. "I offer you the opportunity to go to your father."

"To—" Kellin sat bolt upright. "You?"

Rogan nodded. His mouth was tight. "I make no attempt to explain or excuse him, my lord . . . I merely offer to escort you to the Crystal Isle, where you may ask him yourself why he has done as he has."

"My father," Kellin whispered. "*Jehan*—" He stared hard into darkness. "When?"

"In the morning."

"How?"

"We will say we are going to Clankeep. You wish to take Urchin there, do you not?"

"Aye, but—"

"I shall tell the Mujhar you wish to introduce Urchin to Clankeep and the Cheysuli. He will not refuse you that. Only we shall go to Hondarth instead."

"But—the Mujharan Guard. They'll know."

"I have prevailed upon the Mujhar to allow us to go without guards. You are Cheysuli, after all—and I know how much close confinement chafes the Mujhar. He understands the need to allow you more freedom . . . and there has been no trouble for quite some time. If Clankeep were not so close, it would be different."

"But won't he know? Won't he find out? It is two weeks' ride to Hondarth."

"It is not unusual for a Cheysuli boy, regardless of rank, to desire to spend some time among his people."

Kellin understood at once. "But we will go to the Crystal Isle while he believes we are at Clankeep!"

The tutor's silence was eloquent.

Kellin drew in a breath. "You will have to send word."

"From Hondarth. By then it will be too late for the Mujhar to stop us."

Kellin looked into the beloved face. "Why?"

Rogan's smile was ghastly. "Because it is time."

Chapter Five

They left early, very early, with only a loaf of bread and a flagon of cider serving as breakfast. Kellin, Urchin, and Rogan made a very small party as they exited Homana-Mujhar before the Mujhar and the queen were even awake.

"Where is Clankeep?" Urchin asked.

Kellin flicked a glance at Rogan, then grinned at his Homanan friend. "We aren't going to Clankeep. We are going to the Crystal Isle. To my *jehan*."

Urchin absorbed the new information. "How far is the Crystal Isle?"

"Two weeks of riding," Kellin answered promptly. Then, evoking his Erinnish granddame, "And but a bit of a sail across the bay to the island." Inwardly, he said, *And to my jehan*.

"Two weeks?" Urchin scratched at his nose. "I didn't know Homana was so big."

"Aye." Kellin grinned. "One day all of it will be mine, and you will help me rule it."

Urchin was dubious. "I'm only a spit-boy."

"For now." Kellin looked at his tutor. "Once, Rogan was only a man who gambled too much."

Rogan's face grayed. Even his lips went pale. "Who told you that?"

Kellin stiffened, alarmed. "Was I not to know?"

The tutor was plainly discomfited. "You know what you know, my lord, but it is not a past of which to be proud. I thought it well behind me. When I married—" He broke it off, abruptly, nostrils pinched and white.

Alerted, Kellin answered the scent. "You are married?"

"I was." Rogan's face was stiff, and his spine. "She is dead. Long dead." He guided his mount with abrupt motions, which caused the gelding to protest the bit. "Before I married Tassia, I gambled away all my coin. She broke me of the habit, and made me use my wits for something other than wagering."

"And so you came to Homana-Mujhar." Kellin nodded approvingly. "I recall the day."

"So do I, my lord." Rogan's smile was twisted. "She was one month dead. You were all of eight, and grieving for your great-uncle."

"The Lion bit him," Kellin muttered. "He bit him, and Ian died."

"How far do we go today?" Urchin asked, oblivious to dead kinsmen and dead wives.

"There is a roadhouse some way out of Mujhara, on the Hondarth road," Rogan answered. "We will stay the night there."

The common room was dim, lighted only by a handful of greasy tallow candles set in clay cups. The room stank of spilled wine, skunky ale, burned meat, and unwashed humanity. It crossed Kellin's mind briefly, who was accustomed to better, that the roadhouse was unworthy of them, but he closed his mouth on a question. They were bound for the Crystal Isle in absolute secrecy, and for a boy to complain of his surroundings would draw the wrong sort of attention. Instead, he breathed through his mouth until the stench was bearable and kept a sharp eye on the purse hanging at Rogan's belt. He had learned that much from Urchin, who had grown up in the streets.

"Look." Kellin leaned close to Urchin and nudged him with an elbow as they slipped into the room behind Rogan. "See the one-eyed man?"

Urchin nodded. "I see him."

"You've been places I have not—what is he doing?"

Urchin grinned. "Dicing. See the cubes? He'll toss them out of the leather cup onto the table. The highest number wins."

Rogan halted at a table near the center of the room and glanced at his two young charges. His face was arranged in a curiously blank expression. "We will sit here."

Kellin nodded, paying little attention; he watched the one-eyed man as he shook the leather cup and rolled the dice out onto the table. The man shouted, laughed, then scooped up the few coins glinting dully in wan light.

"Look at the loser," Urchin whispered as he slipped onto a stool. "D'ye see the look? He's angry."

Kellin slid a glance at the other man. The loser made no physical motion that gave away his anger, but Kellin marked the tautness of his mouth, the bunched muscles along his jaw. Deliberately the loser tossed two more coins onto the table, matched by the one-eyed man. Each man tossed dice again.

A knife appeared, glinting dully in bad light. The one-eyed man, wary of the weapon displayed specifically for his benefit, did not immediately reach to gather up his winnings.

Urchin leaned close. "He thinks the one-eyed man is cheating."

It fascinated Kellin, who had never been so close to violence other than the Lion. "Will he kill him?"

Urchin shrugged. "I've seen men killed for less reason than a dice game."

Rogan's lips compressed. "I should not have brought you in here. We should go upstairs to our room and have a meal sent up."

"No!" Kellin said quickly. Then, as Rogan's brows arched, "I mean—should not the future Mujhar see all kinds of those he will rule?"

The taut mouth loosened a little. "Perhaps. And an astute one will recognize that to some Homanans, the man on the Lion Throne means less than nothing."

It was incomprehensible to Kellin who had been reared in a household steeped in honor and respect. "But how can they—"

A shadow fell across their table, distracting Kellin at once. A slender, well-formed hand—unlike the broad-palmed, spatulate hands of the one-eyed man and his angry companion—placed a wooden casket on the table. A subtle, muted rattle from the contents was loud in the sudden silence.

Kellin glanced up at once. The man smiled slightly, glancing at the two boys before turning his attention to Rogan. He was young, neatly dressed in good gray tunic and trews, and his blue eyes lacked the dull hostility Kellin had marked in the dicers. Shining russet hair fell in waves to his shoulders. "Will you play, sir?"

Rogan wet his lips. He moved his hands from the table top to his lap. "I—do not play."

"Ah, but it will take no time at all . . . and you may leave this table with good gold in your purse." An easy, mellifluous tone; a calm and beguiling smile.

Kellin glanced sharply at Rogan. *He would not—would he?* After all his dead wife had done?

But he could see the expression in the tutor's eyes: Rogan desired very badly to play. The older man's mouth parted slightly, then compressed again. Rogan's gaze met the stranger's. "Very well."

"But—" Kellin began.

The stranger overrode the protest easily, sliding onto a stool before Kellin could finish. "I am Corwyth, from Ellas. It is my good fortune that we are chance-met." He cast a brief glance around the room. "The others do not interest me, but you are obviously a man of good breeding." He spared a smile for Kellin and Urchin as he addressed Rogan. "Your sons?"

"Aye," Rogan said briefly; he did not so much as glance at Corwyth, but stared transfixed at the casket.

It fascinated Kellin also. A passing glance marked nothing more than plain dark wood polished smooth by time and handling, but a second glance—and a more intense examination—revealed the wood not smooth at all, but carved with a shallow frieze of intricate runes. *Inside*—? Kellin leaned forward to peer into the mouth of the casket and saw only blackness. "Where are the dice?"

Corwyth laughed softly. "Be certain they are there." He sat at Rogan's right hand, with Urchin on *his* right; Kellin's stool was directly across the table. "Have you played before?"

The Ellasian addressed him, not Rogan; he seemed to know all about Rogan. Kellin shook his head quickly, slanting a glance at his tutor. "My—father—does not allow it."

"Ah, well . . . when you are older, then." Corwyth ignored Urchin utterly as he turned his attention to Rogan. "Will you throw first, or shall I?"

Rogan's taut throat moved in a heavy swallow. "I must know the stakes first."

Corwyth's smile came easily, lighting his mobile face. "Those you know already."

A sheen of dampness filmed Rogan's brow. "Will I lose, then? Or do you play the game as if there might be a chance for me?"

The odd bitterness in the older man's tone snared Kellin's attention instantly. But Rogan said nothing more to explain himself, and Corwyth answered before Kellin could think of a proper question.

The Ellasian indicated the rune-carved casket with a flick of a fingernail. "A man makes his own fortune, regardless of the game."

Rogan scrubbed his face with a sleeve-sheathed forearm, then swore raggedly and caught up the casket. He upended it with a practiced twitch of his wrist. Six ivory cubes fell out, and six slender black sticks.

All of them were blank.

Urchin blurted surprise. Rogan stiffened on his bench, transfixed by the sticks and cubes. Breath rasped in his throat.

"Did you lose?" Kellin asked, alarmed by Rogan's glazed eyes.

Corwyth's tone was odd. "How would you like them to read?" he asked Rogan. "Tell me, and I shall do it."

Rogan's fingers gripped the edge of the table. "And if—if I requested the winning gambit?"

"Why, then I should lose." Corwyth grinned and glanced at Kellin and Urchin. "But, after all, it is my game, and I think I should still find a way to win." His gaze returned to Rogan's face. "Do you not agree?"

"Kellin—" Rogan's tone, was abruptly harsh. "Kellin, you and Urchin are to go upstairs at once."

"No," Corwyth said softly. A slender finger touched each of the blank ivory cubes and set them all to glowing with a livid purple flame.

"*Magic*—" Urchin whispered: dreadful fascination.

Kellin did not look at the cubes or the black sticks. He stared instead at Corwyth's face, into his eyes, and saw no soul.

He put out his small hand instantly and swept the cubes from the table, unheeding of the flame, then scattered all the sticks. "No," Kellin declared. "*No.*"

Corwyth's smile was undiminished; if anything, it increased to one of immense satisfaction. "Perceptive, my lord. My master has indeed done well to send me for you now, while you are yet *lir*less and therefore without power. But I think for all your perception you fail to recognize the extent of *his* power, or mine—" his tone altered from conversational, "—and that the game we initiated has already been played through." Smoothly he caught Rogan's arm in one hand, and the wristbones snapped.

Rogan cried out. Sweat ran from his face. His shattered wrist remained trapped in Corwyth's hand, who appeared to exert no pressure whatsoever with anything but his will.

Kellin leapt to his feet, thinking only that somehow he must get Rogan free; he must stop Rogan's pain. But the instinct was abruptly blunted, the attempt aborted, as Corwyth shook his head. *He will injure Rogan worse.* Kellin knew it at once. Slowly he resumed his seat, aware of a minute trembling seizing all his bones. "Who?" he asked. "*Who* is your master?"

"Lochiel, of course." Corwyth smiled. His cordial attitude was undiminished by the threat he exuded without effort, which made the moment worse. "Do you know of another man who would presume to steal a prince?"

"Steal—" Kellin stiffened. *Me? He wants—me?*

Urchin stirred on his stool. His thin face was white. "Are you— Ihlini?"

The dead cubes and sticks scattered on the floor came abruptly to life again, flying from the dirt-pack to land again upon the table and commence a spinning dervish-dance across the scarred surface. Purple *godfire* streamed from the cubes; the black sticks glistened blood-red.

Urchin sucked in an audible breath. Kellin, infuriated by Corwyth's audacity, smashed a small fist against the table top. "*No!*"

The cubes and sticks fell at once into disarray, rattling into silence as the dance abruptly collapsed.

"Too late," Corwyth chided. "Much too late, my lord." He looked at Rogan and smiled.

The awful tension in the Homanan's body was plain to see. "No," he whispered hoarsely. "Oh, gods, I cannot—I *cannot*—"

"Too late," Corwyth repeated.

Rogan looked at Kellin. "Run!" he cried. "*Run!*"

Chapter Six

Kellin lunged to his feet, grasping for and catching a fistful of Urchin's tunic. He saw the blue blaze in Corwyth's eyes, sensed the pain radiating from Rogan's shattered wrist. *I must do something.*

"Urchin—" He tugged on the boy's tunic, who needed no urging, then together they scrabbled their way across the room, jerked open the door, and fell out into the darkness.

"Did you see—" Urchin choked.

"We have to run. Rogan said *run.*" Kellin yanked at Urchin's tunic.

Urchin was clearly terrified. "H-horses—"

"They will lie in wait for us there—we must *run,* Urchin!"

They ran away from the roadhouse, away from the road itself, making for the trees. They shared no more physical contact; Urchin had at last mastered himself. The Homanan boy, accustomed to fleeing, darted through the wood without hesitation. City-reared Kellin now was less certain of his course and followed Urchin's lead.

A branch slapped Kellin across the eyes, blurring his vision. He tasted the sourness of resin in his mouth, spat once, then forgot about it in his flight. He could see little of the ground underfoot, trusting instinctively to the balance and reflexes of youth as well as the training begun in Homana-Mujhar.

"Urchin—?"

"Here—" Ahead still, and still running, crashing through deadfall and undergrowth.

Kellin winced as another branch clawed at his tunic, digging into the flesh of bare arms. And then he saw the glint of silver in the trees and slipped down into the creek before he could halt his flight. Kellin fell forward, flailing impotently as cold water closed over his head.

He kicked, found purchase, if treacherous, not far under his feet, and thrust himself upward to the surface. Kellin choked and spat, coughing, shivering from fright and cold.

"Kellin—" It was Urchin, bankside, reaching down. Kellin caught the hand, clung, and scrabbled out onto the creek bank. Urchin's face was seamed with branch-born welts. "We can't run all night! "

Kellin tried to catch his breath. "We—have to get as far—far from them as we can—"

"There was only that one. Corwyth."

"More." Kellin sucked air, filling his chest. "Kick over one rock and find a single Ihlini . . . kick over another and find a nest." He scraped a forearm across his face, shoving soaked hair from his eyes. "That's what everyone says."

Dry, Urchin nonetheless shivered. "But if they're *sorcerers*—

"We have to *try*—" Kellin began.

The forest around them exploded into a spectral purple glow. Out of the blinding light came two dark shadows, silhouetted against livid *godfire*.

Kellin grabbed at Urchin and swung him back the way they had come. "Run!"

But Corwyth himself stood on the other side of the creek. With him was Rogan.

Urchin blurted his shock even as Kellin stopped short. Breathing hard, Kellin nonetheless heard the soft susurration of men moving behind them. The hairs on the back of his neck stirred. "I taste it," he murmured blankly. "I can *taste* the magic."

Corwyth smiled. Rogan did not. The *godfire* painted them all an eerie lavender, but Kellin could see the pallor of his tutor's face. Rogan's eyes glistened with tears.

Pain—? Kellin wondered.

"My lord," Rogan said. "Oh, my lord . . . forgive me—"

Comprehension brought sickness. Sickness formed a stone in Kellin's belly. "Not *you!*" No, of course not; Rogan would deny it. Rogan would explain.

"My lord . . . there was nothing left for me. I had no choice."

Corwyth lifted a minatory hand. "There was choice," he reproved. "There is always choice. I may be, to you, an enemy, but I suggest you tell the truth to this boy, who is not: it was neither I nor my master who forced you to this."

Kellin's conviction was undiminished. *Rogan will deny it—he will tell me the truth.* After all, how many times had Kellin been told of the perfidiousness of Ihlini? *This is some kind of trick.* "He hurt you," Kellin declared. "He broke your wrist; what *else* can you say?"

"There was no threat," Corwyth countered quietly. "The wrist was merely to prove the need for care. I have no need of threats with Rogan. All I was required to do was promise him his dearest desire."

"Ihlini lie," Kellin declared, even as Urchin stirred in surprise beside him. "Ihlini lie all the time. You are the *enemy.*"

"To assure our survival, aye." Corwyth's young face looked older, less serene. "To Ihlini, *you* are the enemy."

It was an entirely new thought. Kellin rejected it. He looked instead at Rogan. "He's lying."

"No." Rogan's mouth warped briefly. "There was no threat, as he says. Only a promise."

It was utter betrayal. "*What* promise?" Kellin cried. "What could *he* promise you that the Mujhar could not offer?"

Rogan shut his eyes. His face was shiny with sweat.

"Tell him," Corwyth said.

"You would have me strip away *all* his innocence?"

The Ihlini shrugged. "He will lose it soon enough in Valgaard."

Urchin's face was a sickly white in fireglow. He breathed audibly. "Valgaard?"

"Rogan?" Kellin swallowed back the fear that formed a hard knot in his throat. "Rogan—this isn't *true?*"

The tutor broke. He spoke rapidly, disjointedly. "It was him . . . a year ago, he came—came and asked that I betray you to the Ihlini."

"*Me!*"

"Lochiel." Rogan shuddered. "Lochiel wants you." His entire body convulsed. "He could not reach you. He could get you no other way. Corwyth promised me you would be unharmed."

Kellin could not breathe. "You agreed?"

"My lord—if he had intended harm—"

"You *agreed!*"

"Kellin—"

It was the worst of all. "He is *Ihlini!*"

"Kellin—"

"How could you do this?" It was a refrain in Kellin's mind, in Kellin's mouth. "How could you do this?"

Rogan's face was wet with tears. "It was not—not of my devising . . . that I promise you. But *he* promised. Promised *me* . . . and I was weak, so weak. . . ."

Kellin shouted it. "*What* did he promise you?"

Rogan fell to his knees. "Forgive me—forgive—"

The stone in Kellin's belly grew. He felt it come to life. It pushed his heart aside then squeezed up into his throat. His body was filled with it.

And the stone had a name: rage.

Kellin heard his voice—*mine?*—come from a vast distance. It was an ordinary voice, shaped by normal inflections, with no hint at all of shock, or terror, or rage. "What did he promise you?"

"My wife!" Rogan cried.

It was incomprehensible. "You said she was *dead.*" And then Kellin understood.

"My wife," the tutor whispered, hands slack upon his knees. "You are too young to understand . . . but I loved her so much I thought I would die of it, and then *she* died—she died . . . because of the child I gave her—" He broke off. His gaze was fixed on Kellin. He gathered himself visibly, attempting to master his anguish. "I refused," Rogan said quietly. "Of course I refused. Nothing could make me betray you. I would have accepted death before that."

"Why didn't you?" Kellin shouted.

"But then this man, this Ihlini, promised me my wife."

Kellin shivered. He looked at Corwyth. "You can *raise the dead?*"

The Ihlini smiled. "I am capable of many things." He extended his right hand, palm up, as if to mock the Cheysuli gesture of *tahlmorra;* then a flaring column of white light filled his hand.

"Magic," Urchin murmured.

"Tricks," Kellin declared; he could not admit the Ihlini might offer a true threat, or fear would overwhelm him.

"Is it?" The light in Corwyth's hand coalesced, then began to move, to dance, and the column resolved itself into a human shape.

A tiny, naked woman.

"*Gods,*" Rogan blurted. Then, brokenly, "Tassia."

Kellin stared at the burning woman. She was a perfect embodiment of the Ihlini's power.

Corwyth smiled. The woman danced within his palm, twisting and writhing. She burned bright white and searing, spinning and spinning, so that flaming hair spun out from her body and shed brilliant sparks. Tiny breasts and slim hips were exposed, and the promise of her body.

Kellin, whose body was as yet too young to respond, looked at Rogan. The Homanan still knelt on the ground, eyes fixed in avid hunger on the tiny dancing woman.

"Do you want her?" Corwyth asked. "I did promise her to you. And I keep my promises."

"She isn't real!" Kellin cried.

"Not precisely," Corwyth agreed. "She is a summoning from my power; a conjured promise, nothing more. But I can make her real—real enough for Rogan." He smiled. "Look upon her, Kellin. Look at her perfection! It is such a simple thing to make Tassia from this."

The tiny, burning features were eloquent in their pleading. She was fully aware, Kellin saw; Tassia *knew*.

Rogan cried out. "I bargained my soul for this. Give me my payment for it!"

The light from the burning woman blanched Corwyth's face. "Your soul was mine the moment I asked for it. The promise of this woman was merely a kindness." He looked at Kellin though his words were meant for Rogan. "Speak it, prince's man. Aloud, where Kellin can hear. Renounce your service to the House of Homana. Deny your prince as he stands here before you. Do only these two things, and you will have your payment."

Rogan shuddered.

"Speak it," Corwyth said.

"Leave him alone!" Kellin cried.

"Kellin—" Rogan's expression was wracked. "Forgive—"

"Don't say it!" Kellin shouted. "Do not give in to him!"

"Speak," Corwyth said.

Tears ran down Rogan's face. "I renounce the House of Homana."

"Rogan!"

"I renounce my prince."

"No!"

"I submit to you, Ihlini . . . and now ask payment for my service!"

Corwyth smiled gently. He lifted his other hand as if in benevolent blessing. Rogan's head bowed as the hand came down, and then he was bathed in the same lurid light that shaped the tiny woman.

"Wait!" Kellin cried. "Rogan—*no*—"

Rogan's eyes stretched wide. *"This is not what you promised—"* But his body was engulfed.

Kellin fell back, coughing, even as Urchin did. The clearing was filled with smoke. Corwyth pursed his lips and blew a gentle exhalation, and the smoke dispersed completely.

"What did you do?" Kellin asked. "What did you do to Rogan?"

"I gave him what he desired, though of a decidedly different nature. He believed I intended to remake his dead wife. But even *I* cannot do that, so this will have to suffice." Corwyth's right hand supported the dancing woman, now rigidly still. In his other hand, outstretched, burned a second tiny figure.

Urchin cried out. Kellin stared, transfixed, as he saw the formless features resolve themselves into those he knew so well. *"Rogan."*

Corwyth brought his hands together. The man and woman met, embraced, then merged into a single livid flame. "I do assure you, this was what he wanted."

Kellin was horrified. "Not like *that!*"

"Perhaps not." Corwyth grinned. "A conceit, I confess; he did not have the wit to specify how he wanted payment made."

Kellin shuddered. And then the stone in chest and throat broke free at last. He vomited violently.

"No!" Urchin cried, then screamed Rogan's name.

Corwyth knelt down beside the creek.

"Wait!" Kellin shouted.

Corwyth dipped his hands into the water. "But let it never be said I am a man who knows no mercy. Death, you might argue, is better than this."

"Rogan!"

But the flames were extinguished as water snuffed them out.

Chapter Seven

Kellin found himself on hands and knees in clammy vegetation, hunched before the creek in bizarre obeisance to the sorcerer who knelt on the bank. His belly cramped painfully. His mouth formed a single word, though the lips were warped out of shape. *Rogan.*

And then the horrible thought: *Not Rogan any more.*

A hand was on his arm, fingers digging into flesh. "Kellin— *Kellin*—" Urchin, of course; Kellin twisted his head upward and saw the pale glint of Urchin's eyes, the sweaty sheen of shock-blanched face. Ashamed of his weakness, Kellin swabbed a trembling hand across his dry mouth and climbed to his feet. *Show the Ihlini no fear.*

But he thought it was too late; surely Corwyth had seen. Surely Corwyth *knew.*

The russet-haired Ihlini rose, shaking droplets from elegant hands with negligent flicks of his fingers. "Shall you come without protest, my lord?"

Kellin whirled and stiff-armed Urchin, shoving him back a full step before the Homanan boy could speak. *"Run!"*

He darted to the left even as Urchin spun, running away from Corwyth, away from the creek, away from the horror of what he had witnessed, the terrible quenching of a *man*—

He tore headlong through limbs and leaves, shredding underbrush and vines. In huge leaps Kellin spent himself, panting through a dry throat as he ran. He fastened on one thought— *Urchin*—but the Homanan boy was making his own way, making his own future, crashing through brush only paces away. Kellin longed to call out but dared not risk it. Besides, Urchin was better suited to flight than he, growing up a boy of the streets; best Kellin tend himself.

Corwyth's voice cut through the trees like a clarion. "I require only you, Kellin. Not him. Come back, and I will spare him."

"Don't listen!" Urchin hissed as he broke through tangled foliage near Kellin. "What can he—"

The Homanan boy stopped short, fully visible in a patch of moonlight. His chest rose and fell unevenly as his breath rattled in his throat.

Kellin staggered to a stiff-limbed halt, arms outflung. His breathing was as loud. "Urchin?"

The boy's blue eyes were fixed and dilated.

"Urchin—*run*—"

Urchin's eyes bulged in their sockets.

Even as Kellin reached for him, the boy's limbs jerked. Urchin's mouth dropped open, blurting inarticulate protest. Then something pushed out against the fabric of his tunic, as if it quested for exit from the confines of his chest.

"*Ur*—" Kellin saw the blood break from Urchin's breastbone. "No!" But Urchin was down, all asprawl, face buried in leaf mold and turf. Kellin grabbed handfuls of tunic and dragged him over onto his back. "Urchin—"

Kellin recoiled. A bloodied silver wafer extruded from Urchin's breastbone, shining wetly in the moonlight.

He mouthed it: *Sorcerer's Tooth.* Kellin had heard of them. The Ihlini weapons were often poisoned, though this one had done its work simply by slicing cleanly through the boy's chest from spine to breastbone.

Corwyth's voice sounded very close, *too* close, though Kellin could not see him. "A waste of life," the Ihlini said. "You threw it away, Kellin."

"No!"

"You had only to come to me."

"*No!*"

"And so now you are alone in the dark with an Ihlini." Corwyth's laughter was quiet. "Surely a nightmare all Cheysuli dread."

Urchin was dead. Muttering a prayer to the gods—and an apology to Urchin for the pain he could not feel—Kellin stripped hastily out of his jerkin, tucked it over the exposed spikes, then yanked the wafer from Urchin's chest.

He twisted his head. *Where is—?*

Just behind. "Kellin. Surrender. I promise you no harm."

Kellin lurched upward and spun. "I promise *you* harm!"

He heard Corwyth cry out as the glinting weapon, loosed, spun toward the Ihlini. Kellin did not tarry to see if the Tooth had bitten deeply enough to kill. He fled into darkness again.

Kellin ran until he could run no more, then dropped into a steady jogging trot. Though his breath fogged the air, the first terror had faded, replaced by a simple conviction that if he did not halt, not even to catch that breath, he could remain ahead of Corwyth.

He assumed the Ihlini lived. To believe otherwise was to court the kind of carelessness that might prove fatal. If he had learned one thing from his beloved Ian, it was never to assume one was safe when one could not know.

Deadfall snapped beneath booted feet, then died out gradually as Kellin learned to seek out the thicker shadows of softer, muffled ground. In six strides he learned stealth, reverting to simple instincts and the training of his race.

If I had a lir— But he did not, and wishing for one would gain him nothing save a tense uncertainty of his ability to survive.

At last even his trot collapsed into disarray. Kellin staggered, favoring his right side. Exhaustion robbed him of strength, of endurance; apprehension robbed him of grace. He stumbled once, twice, again. The final tumble sent him headfirst into a tangle of tall bracken, which spilled him into shadow. Kellin lay there, winded, sucking cold air scented heavily with mud, and resin, and fear.

Go on, his conscience told him. But the body did not respond. *Remember what happened to Rogan. Remember what happened to Urchin.*

Kellin squeezed shut his eyes. He had, until the moment of Urchin's death, believed himself inviolable. Ian had died, aye, because the Lion had bitten him, and the fortune-teller had died by the same violent means, but never had Kellin believed death could happen to *him.*

Rogan and Urchin, dead.

I could die, too.

Could the Ihlini's sorcery lead Corwyth directly to Kellin?

Run—

He stumbled to his feet yet again, hunching forward as a cramp bit into his side. He banished the pain, banished the memories of the deaths he had witnessed, and went on again.

—am a Cheysuli warrior . . . the forest is my home—and every creature in it—

He meant to go home, of course. All the way to Mujhara herself, and into Homana-Mujhar. There he would tell them all. There he would explain. There he would describe in bloody detail what Corwyth had accomplished.

The sound was a heavy cough. Not human. Clearly animal. A heavy, deep-throated cough.

Kellin froze. He sucked in a breath and held it, listening for the sound.

A cough. And then a growl.

—am Cheysuli—

So he was. But he was also a boy.

The growl rose in pitch, then altered into a roar.

He knew the sounds of the forest. This was not one of them. This was a sound Kellin recognized because it filled his dreams.

He did not cry out, but only because he could not. *Lion?*

"No," Kellin blurted. He denied it vigorously, as he had denied nothing before in his life. Urchin had come, and the Lion had been driven away. The daytime was safe. And only rarely did the Lion trouble his dreams now, since Urchin had come.

But Urchin was dead. And night replaced the day.

"No!" Kellin cried. *There can be no Lion. Everyone says.*

But it was dark, so dark. It was too easy to believe in such things as Lions when there was no light.

He fastened himself onto a single thought. "I am not a child anymore. I defeated the Steppesman and knocked down his knife. Lions do not exist."

But the Lion roared again. Kellin's defiance was swamped.

He ran without thought for silence or subterfuge. Outflung hands crushed aside foliage, but some of it sprang back and cut into the flesh of his naked torso, jerkinless in flight. It snagged hair, at eyes, at mouth; it dug deeply into his neck even as he ducked.

Lion!

He saw nothing but shadow and moonlight. *If I stop—*

From behind came the roar of a hungry, hunting lion, crashing through broken brush on the trail of Cheysuli prey.

Huge and tawny and golden, like the throne in Homana-Mujhar.

How can they say there isn't a Lion?

Blood ran into Kellin's mouth, then spilled over open lips; he had somehow bitten his tongue. He spat, swiped aside a snagging limb, then caught his breath painfully on a choked blurt of shock as the footing beneath crumbled.

Wait— He teetered. Then fell. The ground gave way and tumbled him into a narrow ravine.

Down and down and down, crashing through bracken and creepers, banging arms and legs into saplings, smacking skull against rocks and roots. And then at last the bottom, all of a sudden, *too* sudden, and he sprawled awkwardly onto his back, fetching up against a stump. Kellin heard whooping and gulping, and realized the noise was his own.

Lion?

He lurched upward, then scrambled to his feet. He ached from head to foot, as if all his bones were bruised.

Lion?

And the lion, abruptly, was *there*.

Kellin ran. He heard the panting grunts, smelled the meat-laden breath. And then the jaws snapped closed around his left ankle.

"No!"

The pain shot from ankle to skull. Jaws dug through leather boot into flesh, threatening the bone.

Kellin clawed at the iron teeth of the iron, bodiless beast that had caught boy instead of bear. Fingers scrabbled at the trap, trying to locate and trigger the mechanism that would spring the jaws open.

No lion— It was relief, but also terror; the beast could not be far behind.

Kellin had heard of bear traps. The Cheysuli disdained such tools, preferring to fight a beast on its own level rather than resorting to mechanical means. But some of the Homanans used the heavy iron traps to catch bear and other prey.

Now it's caught ME— Pain radiated from the ankle until it encompassed Kellin's entire body. He twitched and writhed against it, biting into his bloodied lip, then scrabbled for the chain that bound trap to tree. *it* was securely locked. Designed to withstand the running charge of a full-grown bear, it would surely defeat a boy.

Frenziedly, Kellin yanked until his palms shredded and bled. "Let go—*let go*—LET GO—"

The deep-chested cough sounded again. Through deadfall the

lion came, slinking out of shadow, tearing its way through vines and bracken.

Kellin leapt to his feet and ran, and was jerked down almost at once. Iron teeth bit through boot and compressed fragile flesh, scraping now on bone.

—*no*—*no*—

—no—*no*—NO—"

The lion, still coughing, broke out of shadow into moonlight. Kellin jerked at the chain again, but palms slipped in sticky blood. The weight of the trap was nothing as he tried to stand again, to meet his death like a man.

But then the lion roared. The boy who meant to die a man was reduced, by sheer terror, into nothing but a child screaming frenziedly for his father.

But his father would not come, because he never had.

Chapter Eight

Horseback. And yet he did not ride as a man but as a child, a small child, rump settled across the withers, legs dangling slackly upon one shoulder while the rest of him was cradled securely against a man's chest.

Kellin roused into terror. "Lion—" He was perfectly stiff, trying to flail his way to escape. Terror overwhelmed him. "Lion—LION—"

Arms tightened, stilling him. "There is no lion here."

"But—" He shut his mouth on the protest, the adamant denial of what the voice told him. Then another panic engulfed. "*Ihlini*—"

The man laughed softly, as if meaning no insult. "Not I, my lad. I've not the breeding for it."

Kellin subsided, though his strained breathing was audible. His eyes stretched painfully wide, but saw nothing in the darkness save the underside of a man's jaw and the oblique silhouette of a head. "Who—?" It faded at once. Pain reasserted itself. "My *leg*."

"I'm sorry for it, lad . . . but you'll have to wait for the healing."

It took effort to speak, to forced a single word through the rictus of his mouth. "—whole—?"

"Broken, I fear. But we'll be mending it for you."

Kellin ground his teeth. "—*hurts*—" And then wished he had said nothing, nothing at all; a Cheysuli did not speak of pain.

"Aye, one would think so." The grip shifted a little, sliding down Kellin's spine to accommodate the weight that was no longer quite so slack.

" 'Twas a trap for a bear, not a boy. You're fortunate it left the foot attached."

Kellin stiffened again, craning, as he tried to see for himself.

The other laughed softly. "Aye, lad, 'tis there. I promise you that. Now, settle yourself; you've a fever coming on. You'll do better to rest."

"Who—?" he began again.

The rider chuckled as Kellin tried to sit up. He turned his face downward. "There, now—better? I'm one of you after all."

"One of—me?" And then Kellin understood. Relief washed through him, then ebbed as quickly as it stole his strength away.

Indeed, one of him. The stranger was his grandsire, if stripped of forty years. His accent was Aileen's own. There was only one Cheysuli warrior in all the world who sounded like the Mujhar's Erinnish queen.

"Blais." Kellin murmured. Weakness and fever crept closer to awareness, nibbling at its edges.

The warrior grinned, displaying fine white teeth in a dark Cheysuli face. "Be still, little cousin. We've yet a ways to ride. You'll do better to pass it in sleep."

In sleep, or something like. Kellin slumped against his kinsman as consciousness departed.

He roused as Blais handed him down from the horse into someone else's care. Pain renewed itself, so strongly that Kellin whimpered before he could suppress it. And then he was more ashamed than ever because Blais himself was Cheysuli and knew a warrior did not voice his discomfort.

Sweating, Kellin bit again into a split lip and tasted fresh blood. It was all he could do not to moan aloud.

"My pavilion," Blais said briefly. "Send someone to Homana-Mujhar with word, and call others here for the healing."

The other warrior carried Kellin inside as Blais dismounted and carefully settled him onto a pallet of thick furs. Kellin opened his eyes and saw the shadowed interior of a Cheysuli pavilion. Then the stranger was gone, and Blais knelt down on one knee beside him. A callused palm touched Kellin's forehead.

"*Shansu*," Blais murmured. "I know it hurts, little cousin, no need to fight it so. I'll think none the less of you."

But Kellin would not give in, though he sweated and squirmed with pain. "Can't *you* heal me?"

Blais smiled. His face was kind in a stern sort of way. He was very like them all, though Erinn and Homana ran in his veins as well as Cheysuli blood. Physically the dilution did not show; Blais' features and coloring were purely Cheysuli, even if the accent was not. "Not without help, my lad. I was ill myself last year with the summer fever—well enough now, you'll see, but weak in the earth magic yet. I'd rather not risk the future of Homana to a halfling's meager gifts."

Halfling. Kellin shifted. *What am I, then?* "You have a *lir.* Tanni. I remember from when you visited Homana-Mujhar two years ago."

"Aye, but she came to me late. Don't be forgetting, lad—I was Erinn-raised. The magic there is different. I'm different because of it."

Fever-clad weakness proved pervasive. Kellin squinted at his cousin through a wave of fading vision. "I'm different, too, like you . . . will I get my *lir* late?"

" 'Tis between you and the gods." Blais' callused palm was gentle as he smoothed back dampened hair. "Hush, now, lad. Don't waste yourself on talking."

Kellin squirmed. "The Lion—"

" 'Twas a bear-trap, lad."

Kellin shut his eyes because it made him dizzy to keep them open. "An Ihlini Lion . . ." he asserted weakly, "and it was after me."

"Lad."

"—*was*—" Kellin insisted. "The Ihlini killed Urchin. And *Rogan.*"

"Kellin."

"They were my friends, and he *killed* them."

"Kellin!" Blais caught Kellin's head between two strong hands, cupping the dome of skull easily. "No more of this. The healing comes first, *then* we'll be talking of deaths. D'ye hear?"

"But—"

"Be still, my little prince. Homana has need of you whole."

"But—"

And then the others were there, crowding into the pavilion, and the wave of exhaustion that engulfed Kellin was as much induced by the earth magic as by his fever.

Voices intruded. The murmurs were quiet, but they nonetheless broke apart Kellin's tattered dreams and roused him to wakefulness.

"—harsh for any man to lose his closest companions," Blais was saying from outside as he pulled aside the doorflap. "For a lad, that much the harder."

Light penetrated the interior, turning the inside of Kellin's eyelids red. The answering voice was well-known and beloved.

"Kellin has always seemed older than his years," Brennan said as he entered the pavilion. "Sometimes I forget he is naught but a boy, and I try to make him into a man."

" 'Tis the risk any man takes with an heir, especially a prince." Blais let the doorflap, drop, dimming daylight again into a wan, saffron tint.

Brennan's voice was hollow. "He is more than that to me. I lost Aidan—" He checked. "So, now there is Kellin. In Aidan's place. In all things, in Aidan's place. He was made to be Prince of Homana before he was even a boy, still but an infant wetting his napkins."

Kellin cracked his lids slightly, only enough so he could see the two men through a fuzzy fringe of lashes. He did not want them to know he was awake. He had learned very young that adults over-heard divulged more information than when asked straight out.

Blais' laugh was soft as he settled himself near the pallet. "You had no choice but to invest him when you did. Aidan had re-nounced the title already, and *I* had come from Erinn. D'ye think I am deaf? I heard all the whispers, *su'fali* . . . had you delayed Kellin's investiture, my presence here in Homana might have given new heart to the *a'saii*. Your claim on the Lion would have been threatened again."

"I might have packed you off to Erinn," Brennan suggested mildly.

"Might have *tried*, my lord Mujhar." Blais' tone was amused as he gestured for his guest to seat himself. "When has a warrior been made to do anything he preferred not to do?"

Brennan sighed as he knelt down beside his grandson. "Even Kellin. Even a ten-year-old boy."

The humor was banished. "He spoke of a lion, and an Ihlini."

The line of Brennan's mouth tautened. "The lion is something Kellin made up years ago. It is an excuse for things he cannot ex-plain. He is fanciful; he conjures a beast from the lions in banners and signets, and the throne itself. And because he has been unfor-tunate to witness Ihini handiwork, he interprets all the violence as the doings of this lion."

"What handiwork?"

"The death of a fortune-teller. He was a foreigner and unknown to us, but his death stank of sorcery."

"Lochiel," Blais said grimly.

"He knows very well Kellin offers the greatest threat to the Ihlini."

"Like his father before him."

"But Aidan no longer matters. He sired the next link, and that link now is the one Lochiel must shatter." Brennan's fingertips gently touched Kellin's brow. "It all comes to Kellin. Centuries of planning all comes down to him."

Blais' tone was dry, for all it was serious. "Then we had best see he survives."

"I have done everything I could. The boy has been kept so closely it is no wonder he makes up stories about lions. Had my *jehan* kept me so tied to Homana-Mujhar, I would have gone mad. As it is, I am not in the least surprised he found a way to escape his imprisonment. But Urchin and Rogan are also missing; I can only surmise they, too, were lured away. No Ihlini could get in, and Kellin is too well-guarded within the palace itself. He would go nowhere without the Homanan boy, and Rogan would never permit Kellin to leave if he heard any whisper of it. So I believe we must look at a clever trap set with the kind of bait that would lure all of them out."

Blais' tone was grim. "An imaginary lion?"

Kellin could no longer hold himself back; his eyes popped open. "There *was* a Lion!"

"Cheysuli ears," Brennan said, brows arching, "hear more than they should."

"There was," Kellin insisted. "It chased me into the beartrap . . . after Urchin and Rogan died."

Brennan shut his eyes. "More deaths."

Blais shifted. He sat cross-legged, one thigh weighted down by the head of a ruddy wolf. His expression was oddly blank as he stroked the wide skull and scratched the base of the ears.

Brennan's momentary lapse was banished. He was calm, unperturbed. "Tell us what happened, Kellin. We must know everything."

Kellin delayed, testing his ankle. "It doesn't hurt any more."

"Earth magic," Blais said. "You've a scar, but the bones are whole."

"A scar?" Kellin peeled back the deerskin coverlet and saw the bared ankle. Indeed, there was a jagged ring of purplish "tooth" marks ringing his ankle. He wiggled his foot again. There was no pain.

" 'Twill fade," Blais told him. "I've more scars than I can count, but hardly any of them show."

Kellin did not care about the scar; if anything, it proved there *was* a Lion. He looked now at his grandsire, putting aside the Lion to speak of another grief. "It was Rogan," he said unsteadily. "*Rogan* betrayed me to the Ihlini."

The Mujhar did not so much as twitch an eyelid. The mildness of his tone was deceptive, but Kellin knew it well: Brennan wanted very badly to know the precise truth, without embellishments or suppositions. "You are certain it was he?"

"Aye." Kellin suppressed with effort the emotions to which he longed to surrender. He would be all Cheysuli in this. "He said he would take me to my *jehan*. That you knew we were to go, just the three of us, but that we meant to go to Clankeep. He said he would send true word to you where we were, but only after we were on our way to Hondarth."

Brennan's face grayed. "Such a simple plan, and certain to work. I was a fool. Lochiel has ways of suborning even those I most value."

"Not money," Kellin said. "So he could have his wife back. Only—" He checked himself, recalling all too clearly the tiny dancing woman and Rogan's horrible ending. "Corwyth killed him first. With sorcery. And then *Urchin*." Pain formed a knot in chest and throat. "Urchin's dead, too."

After a moment the Mujhar touched Kellin's head briefly. Gently, he said, "You must tell me everything you remember about how this was done, and the Ihlini himself. *Everything,* Kellin, so we may prepare for another attack."

"Another—?" Kellin stared hard at the Mujhar, turning over the words. Realization made him breathless. "They want to *catch* me. Corwyth said so. He said he was taking me to Lochiel, in Valgaard."

Brennan's expression was grim, but he did not avoid candor. "You are important to the Ihlini, Kellin, because of who you are, and the blood in your veins. You know about that."

He did. Very well. *Too* well; it was all anyone spoke of. "They won't stop, then." It seemed obvious.

"No."

Kellin nodded, understanding more with each moment. "That's why you set the dogs to guarding me."

"Dogs? Ah." Brennan smiled faintly. "We dared not allow you

to go anywhere alone. Not in Mujhara, not even to Clankeep." His jaw tightened. "Do you recall how you sickened after your Naming Day feast?"

Kellin nodded, recalling with vivid clarity how ill he had been after eating his meal. He had not wanted fish for a sixth-month, after.

"Lochiel had no recourse to sorcery in order to harm you, not so long as you remained in Homana-Mujhar, or at Clankeep, but coin buys people. He bribed a cook to poison the meal. We were forced to take serious steps to safeguard Homana's prince, and his freedom suffered for it." Brennan's words were stated with careful precision. "Rogan understood. Rogan knew why. He comprehended fully how you were to be protected."

That is why they were all so upset when I ran away from the fortune-teller. Guilt flickered. "It was after I heard you speaking with granddame. About how my *jehan* would not have me see him." Kellin swallowed heavily. "Rogan came and said he would take me to my *jehan*."

Brennan's expression was bleak as he exchanged a glance with Blais. "I have learned from this, too, though I believed myself wise in such matters." He sighed heavily. "Nearly every man has his price. Most will deny it, claiming themselves incorruptible, but there is always something that will lure them into betrayal. If they disbelieve it, it is because they have not been offered that which they most desire."

Rogan was offered his wife. Kellin wanted to protest it. It hurt him deeply that Rogan had betrayed him, but he understood his grandfather's words. Hadn't *he* been bought by the promise of his father?

"I would never submit to an Ihlini," he muttered. "Never."

"And that is why you are here." Brennan smiled faintly, tension easing from his features. "Tell us everything."

Kellin did. By the time he was done he felt tears in his eyes, and hated himself for them.

Blais shook his head. "There is no shame in honest grief."

Brennan's tone was gentle. "Rogan was everything to you for two years, and Urchin was your best friend. We think no less of you because you loved them."

Kellin let that go, thinking now of something else. "You said something about me. To Blais, earlier. That I offer the greatest threat to the Ihlini." He looked first at Blais, then at the Mujhar. "What harm can *I* do them?"

"You can bring down their House," Brennan said quietly, "merely by siring a son."

It was incomprehensible. "Me?"

The Mujhar laughed. "You are young yet to think of such things as sons, Kellin, but the day will come when you are a man. Lochiel knows this. With each passing year you become more dangerous."

"Because of my blood." Kellin looked at the scar ringing his ankle, recalling the warm wetness running down between his toes. "*That* blood."

Brennan took Kellin's wrist into his hand and raised it, spreading the fingers with the pressure of his thumb. "All the blood in here," he said. "In this hand, in this arm, in this body. And the seed in your loins, provided it quickens within the body of a particular woman. Lochiel cannot risk allowing you to sire that son."

"The prophecy," Kellin murmured, staring at his hand. He tried to look beneath the flesh to bone and muscle, and the blood that was so special.

"The Firstborn reborn," Blais said. "The bane of the Ihlini. The end of Asar-Suti."

Kellin looked at his grandfather. "They died because of me. Rogan. Urchin. The fortune-teller. Didn't they?"

Brennan closed the small hand inside his own adult one. "It is the heaviest burden a man can know. Men who are kings—and boys who are princes—carry more of them than most."

His chest was full of pain. "Will more die, grandsire? Just because of me?"

Brennan did not lie. He did not look away. "Almost certainly."

Chapter Nine

Kellin felt important and adult: Brennan had said he might have a small cup of honey brew, the powerful Cheysuli liquor. He knew it was his grandfather's way of making him feel safe and loved after his encounter with tragedy, so he sipped slowly, savoring the liquor *and* the intent, not wanting the moment to end because he felt for the first time as if they believed him grown, or nearly so. Nearly was better than not; he grinned into the clay cup.

The Mujhar was not present. When Brennan returned to the pavilion, he, Kellin, and Blais would depart for Homana-Mujhar, but for the moment Kellin was required to stay with his cousin. Brennan met with the clan-leader to discuss the kinds of things kings and clan-leaders discuss; Kellin had heard some of it before and found it tedious. He was much more interested in his kinsman, who was fascinating as a complex mixture of familiar and exotic.

An Erinnish Cheysuli with Homanan in his blood, Blais did not *look* anything but Cheysuli, yet his accent and attitude were different. The latter was most striking to Kellin. Blais seemed less concerned with excessive personal dignity than with being content within his spirit; if that spirit were more buoyant than most, he gave it free rein regardless.

At this moment Blais was working on a bow, replacing the worn leather handgrip with new. His head was bent over his work and a lock of thick black hair obscured part of his face. *Lir*-gold gleamed. Next to him sprawled sleeping Tanni, toes twitching in wolf dreams.

"It could be you," Kellin blurted. "Couldn't it?"

Blais did not look up from his handiwork. "What could, lad?"

"You," Kellin repeated. "The man in the prophecy. The man whose blood can do the things everyone wants it to do."

Now Blais raised his head. "My blood?"

"Aye. You are Cheysuli, Erinnish, and Homanan. You are halfway there."

"Ah, but you are *all* the way there, my lad. I've no Solindish or Atvian blood bubbling in my veins." Blais' face creased in a smile. "You've no fear of me usurping your place."

"But you're older. You are a warrior." Kellin looked at Tanni. "You have a *lir*."

"And so will you, in but a handful of years." Strong fingers moved skillfully as Blais rewrapped the leather.

"But I heard you," Kellin said quietly, grappling with new ideas. "You talked to grandsire about the *a'saii*."

The hands stilled abruptly. This time Blais' gaze was sharp. "I said something of it, aye. You see, lad—I have more cause to concern myself with *a'saii* than any warrior alive."

"They were traitors," Kellin declared. "Rogan told me—" He cut it off abruptly. "Grandsire said they wanted to overthrow the proper succession and replace it with another."

"So they did." Blais' tone was noncommittal. "They were Cheysuli who feared the completion of the prophecy would end their way of life."

"Will it?"

Blais shrugged. "Things will change, aye . . . but perhaps not so much as the *a'saii* fear."

"Do you?" Kellin needed to know. "Do you fear it, Blais?"

An odd expression crossed Blais' smooth, dark face. For only a moment, black brows pulled together. Then he smiled crookedly. "I fear losing what I have only just found," he admitted evenly. "I was born here, Kellin. Keep-born, but reared in Erinn a very long way away. Customs are different in Erinn. I was a part of them, but also longed for others. My *jehana* taught me what she could of the language and customs of Cheysuli, but she was half Erinnish herself, and now wed to an Errinishman. It was Keely who taught me more, who showed me what earth magic was, and what it could bring me." His smile was warmly reminiscent. "She suggested I come here, to find out who I was."

Kellin was fascinated. "Did you?"

"Oh, aye. Enough to know I belong here." Blais grinned, caressing Tanni's head. "I may not *sound* all Cheysuli, but in spirit I am."

"Why," Kellin began, "do you have more cause to concern yourself with *a'saii* than any warrior alive?"

Blais' brows arched. "You've a good ear to recall that so perfectly."

Kellin shrugged, dismissing it. "The *a'saii* are disbanded. Grandsire said so."

"Formally, aye. But convictions are hard to kill. There are those who still keep themselves apart from other clans."

"But *you* stay here."

"Clankeep is my home. I serve the prophecy as much as any warrior. As much as you will, once you are grown."

Kellin nodded absently. "But why do you have cause?"

Blais sighed, hands tightening on the bow. "Because it was my grandsire who began the *a'saii*, Kellin. Ceinn wanted to replace Niall's son—your grandsire, Brennan—with his own son, Teirnan. There was justification, Ceinn claimed, because Teirnan was the son of the Mujhar's sister."

"Isolde," Kellin put in; he recalled the names from lessons.

"Aye. Isolde. Niall's *rujholla.*"

"And Ian's."

Blais grinned. "And Ian's."

"But why *you?*"

Blais' grin faded. " Teirnan was my father. When I came here from Erinn, those who were *a'saii* thought I should be named Prince of Homana when your father renounced his title."

Kellin was astonished. "In my place?"

Blais nodded.

"In my place." It was incomprehensible to Kellin, who could not imagine anyone else in his own place. He had been Prince of Homana all his life. "But—*I* was named."

"Aye. As the Mujhar desired."

Something occurred. "What about you?" Kellin asked. "Did *you* want the title?"

Blais laughed aloud. "I was reared by a man who is the Lord of Erinn's bastard brother. I spent many years at Kilore—I know enough of royalty and the responsibilities of rank to want no part of it." He leaned forward slightly, placing the tip of his forefinger on Kellin's brow. "*You*, my young lad, will be the one to hold the Lion."

"Oh, no," Kellin blurted. "I have to kill it, first."

Blais stilled. "Kill it?"

Kellin was matter-of-fact. "Before it kills all of *us.*"

*   *   *

When Kellin—with grandfather, cousin, and numerous liveried and armored guardsmen—entered the inner bailey of Homana-Mujhar, he discovered it clogged to bursting with strange horses and servants. Horse-boys ran this way and that, grasping at baggage-train horses even as they gathered in the mounts of dismounting riders; servants shouted at one another regarding the unloading; while the bailey garrison, clad in Mujharan scarlet, did its best to sort things out.

The Mujhar himself, trapped in the center of the bailey as his horse restively rang shod hoofs off cobbles, finally ran out of patience. "By the blood of the Lion—" Brennan began, and then broke off abruptly as a tall man came out of the palace doorway to stand at the top of the steps.

"Have I made a mess of all your Mujharish majesty?" the man called over the din. "Well, doubtless you are in dire need of humbling anyway."

"Hart!" Brennan cried. "By the gods—*Hart!*"

Kellin watched in surprise as his grandsire hastily threw himself down from his mount and joined the throng, pushing through toward the steps. Brennan mounted them three at a time, then enfolded the other man in a huge, hard hug.

"*Su'fali,*" Kellin murmured, then grinned at Blais. "*Su'fali* to both of us. Hart, come from Solinde!"

"So I see." Blais squinted over the crowd. "They are two blooms from the same bush."

"But Hart has blue eyes. And only one hand; an enemy had the other one cut off." Kellin followed Brennan's lead, climbing down with less skill than his longer-legged grandfather, and then he, too, was swallowed up by the crowd. Kellin could see nothing, neither grandfather, great-uncle, nor steps.

He considered ducking under the bellies of all the horses, but reconsidered when he thought about the kicks he risked. Like Brennan before him, if with less success, Kellin shoved his way through the milling throng of baggage train and household attendants. Solindish, all of them; he recognized the accent.

His path was more difficult, but at last Kellin reached the steps and climbed to the top. His grandsire and great-uncle had left off hugging, but the warm glints in their eyes—one pair blue, the other yellow—were identical.

So is everything else, except for Hart's missing hand. Kellin looked at the leather-cuffed stump, wondering what it was like to be restricted to a single hand. And Hart had lost more than a hand; the old Cheysuli custom of *kin-wrecking* still held. He was, because of his maiming, no longer considered in the clans to be a warrior despite his blood and his *lir*, the great hawk known as Rael.

Kellin glanced up. Spiraling in a lazy circle over the palace rooftops was the massive raptor, black edging on each feather delineating wings against the blue of the sky. *I may have a hawk when I am a warrior—*

"Kellin!" Brennan's hand closed over a shoulder. "Kellin, here is your kinsman. You have never seen him, I know, but to know who Hart is a man need only look at me."

"But you *are* different," Kellin said after a brief inspection. "You seem older, grandsire."

It brought a shout of delighted laughter from Hart, who struck his twin-born *rujholli* a sharp blow with his only hand. "There. You see? I have said it myself—"

"Nonsense." Brennan arched a single brow. "You surely count more gray in your hair than I."

"No, " Kellin said doubtfully, which moved Hart to laughter again.

"Well, we *are* very like," the Mujhar's twin said. "If there are differences, it is because the Lion is a far more difficult taskmaster than my own Solinde."

"Has Solinde thrown you out?" Kellin asked. "Is that why you have come?"

Hart grinned. "And lose the best lord she ever had? No, I am not banished, nor am I toppled as Bellam was toppled by Carillon. The Solindish love me, now—or, if not love, they tolerate me well enough." He tapped the cuffed stump on top of Kellin's head. "Erinnish eyes, Kellin. Where is the Cheysuli in you?"

"*You* have Homanan eyes," Kellin retorted. "And now your hair is gray; *mine* is all over black."

"Sharp eyes, and a sharper wit," Brennan said dryly. "The Erinnish side, I think."

Hart nodded, smiling, as he assessed his young kinsman. "You are small for twelve, but your growth may come late. Corin's did."

"I am *ten*," Kellin corrected. "Tall enough for ten; grandsire says so."

"Ten." Hart shot a glance at Brennan. "I miscounted, then."

"Aging, are you?" Brennan's eyes were alight. "Forgetting things already?"

Hart demurred at once. "I merely lost track, no more. But I *did* think him older."

"Does it matter?" Brennan asked, laughing. "I am hardly infirm, *rujho*. The Lion will yet be mine a while. Kellin should be well-grown before he inherits."

"I was not thinking of thrones, *rujho*, but of weddings."

"Weddings! Kellin's? By the gods, Hart—"

"Wait you." Hart put up his hand to silence his brother. "Before you begin shouting at me, as you have always done—" he grinned, eyes alight, "—it is for you to say, of course. And now that I see he is so young, perhaps it is too soon."

"Too soon for what?" Kellin asked. "A wedding? Whose? Mine?"

Hart laughed. "So full of questions, *harani*."

"Mine?" Kellin repeated.

Hart sighed, scratching idly at his beardless chin. "I have a daughter—"

Brennan interrupted in mock asperity. "You have four of them. Which one do you mean?"

Hart's shrug was lopsided. "Dulcie is thirteen, which is closer to Kellin than the twins. And—" He shrugged again, letting go what he had begun. "There is reason for this, *rujho* . . . we will speak of it later."

"Too young," Brennan said.

Hart's eyes were speculative. "Too young to marry, perhaps, but not for a betrothal."

"This can wait," Brennan said. "Let us be *rujholli* again before we must be rulers."

Hart sighed heavily. "That may be difficult. I have all of them with me."

"Who?"

"They wanted to come," Hart continued. "All but Blythe. She carries her first child after all this time, so we thought it best she remain behind. It will be my first grandchild, after all."

Diverted, Brennan stared at him. "Is she wed? When? I thought Blythe intended never to marry."

"She did not, after Tevis—" Hart paused to correct himself, gritting the name through his teeth. "—after *Lochiel*." He forced himself to relax, blue eyes bright in remembered anger. "But she met a Solindishman of respectable family with whom she fell in love after much too long alone; she *is* past thirty." Hart grinned. "And she would be quite put out if she heard me say that. But she and her lordling married eight months ago, and now there will be a child."

"But the rest . . ." Brennan glanced around. "They are here?"

"All of them."

"Ilsa?"

"All of them. They insisted. My girls are—" he paused delicately, "—somewhat firm in their convictions."

Brennan eyed him. "You never were one for self-discipline, Hart. Why should I expect you to be capable of ruling your daughters when you never could rule yourself?"

"I understand discipline quite well, *leijhana tu'sai,*" Hart retorted. "But there are times when my girls make such things difficult."

Brennan studied Hart a moment. "You have not changed at all, have you?"

Hart grinned unrepentantly. "No."

"Good." Brennan clapped him on the back. "Now, come inside."

It was abrupt, if unintended, but dismissal nonetheless; they turned as one and strode into the palace without a word or a glance to the boy they knew as the Prince of Homana.

"Wait" But they were gone, and a hand was on Kellin's shoulder, pulling him back.

"Begrudge them nothing, lad." It was Blais, smiling faintly as he moved to stand beside Kellin.

"But what about me?" Kellin was aggrieved. "Grandsire dismissed the Lion, and now they dismiss *me.*"

"They were twin-born, my lad, linked by far more than a simple brother-bond. And they've not seen one another, I am told, for nearly twenty years."

"Twenty years!" Kellin gaped. "I could have been born twice over!"

Blais nodded. "When you are a king, 'tis not so easy to find the time—or the freedom—to go where you will. Hart and Brennan are halves of a whole, parted by title and realm for much too long a time." He briefly touched Kellin's shoulder. "Let them be whole again, lad. They'll be having time for you later."

Kellin scowled. "And weddings, too?"

"Weddings! What has this to do with weddings?" But as Blais stared after his vanished uncles, his expression changed. "Aye, it could be that. 'Tis a topic of much import in royal Houses." He grinned. "Thank the gods *I* am not in line for a throne, or surely they'd be disposing of me, too!"

"And me?" Kellin demanded. "Am I to be married off with no say in the matter?"

Blais did not appear unduly concerned. " 'Tis likely," he confirmed. "You're to be Mujhar of Homana, one day. I'll not doubt there've been letters about your future bride since you were formally invested."

"Cheysula," Kellin said darkly, proving to his cousin he knew the Old Tongue, too, "and I'll choose my own."

"Will you, now?" Blais ran a hand through thick black hair, mouth quirking in wry amusement. " 'Tis what Keely claimed of herself, when she chafed at her betrothal—but in the end she wed the man they promised her to."

"Sean." Kellin nodded. "I know all about that." He was not interested in his great-aunt, whom he had never met. He cast a speculative glance up at his kinsman. "Then you are not promised?"

Blais laughed. "Nor likely to be. I'm content to share my time with this woman, or that one, without benefit of betrothals."

Kellin understood. *"Meijhas,"* he said. "How many, Blais?"

"Many." Blais grinned. "Would I be admitting how many? A warrior does not dishonor his *meijhas* by discussing them casually."

"Many," Kellin murmured. He grinned back at his cousin. "Then I'll have many, too."

Blais sighed and clapped his hand upon a slender shoulder. "No doubt you will. No prince I ever knew lacked for company. Now— shall we go in? I'm for meeting these Solindish kin of ours."

Chapter Ten

In short order Blais and Kellin met all of the Solindish kin en masse in Aileen's sunny solar. The chamber seemed small of a sudden. Kellin duly took note of all his assorted kinfolk: Ilsa, the Lady of Solinde, with her profusion of white-blonde hair and gloriously expressive gray eyes; the middle daughters Cluna and Jennet, twins like Hart and Brennan, who reflected their mother's coloring and the beginnings of her beauty augmented by Cheysuli heritage; and Dulcie, the youngest—the girl whom Hart had said might become Kellin's *cheysula*.

To the latter daughter Kellin paid the most attention. His knowledge of weddings and marriages was slight, but he took it more personally now that his name had been linked with hers.

He was, however, briefly distracted. Blais, whom he had decided was everything a warrior should be—and his rescuer, to boot—was all of a sudden different. It was a subtle difference, Kellin could not name; he knew only that Blais' attention to his young cousin was oddly diverted, as if something else far more fascinating had caught his attention. Kellin understood none of it—Cluna and Jennet seemed silly girls to him, and not worth more time than was necessary to be polite—but Blais seemed most disposed to speak with both of them for a very long time.

Soon enough Blais offered to escort both Cluna and Jennet on a tour of Homana-Mujhar; and the adults suggested that what *they* had to say to one another was better said without Dulcie's and Kellin's presence. Kellin was instructed to do as Blais did: show his cousin every corner of the palace.

Outside in the corridor, Kellin glared mutinously at the closed door. *No one has time for me. The Lion nearly ate me, but no one thinks about THAT—*

Beside him, Dulcie laughed. "They set their traps for him."

Kellin scowled. "What do you mean?" He thought uncomfortably of the bear-trap, conjured by her words.

"Traps," she said succinctly. "They are frivolous women, both of them, only concerned with what is required to catch a handsome man." She gnmaced wryly. "I saw it; didn't you?"

Kellin had not. "Of course I did," he said forthrightly, denying his ignorance.

Dulcie eyed him. "He *is* a handsome man, as Cheysuli go; I see now we are all alike, save for some differences in color." She grinned. "Your eyes are green; mine at least are yellow, like a proper Cheysuli's should be."

And proper she was, black-haired and yellow-eyed with skin the same coppery hue as Blais' and every other Cheysuli Kellin had seen. Dulcie was young—*twelve?*—but clearly was Cheysuli in all respects.

Kellin felt a twinge of self-consciousness; just now, faced with Dulcie—and having met Blais—he wanted very much to be as Cheysuli as possible. "I will be Mujhar." He thought it a good offense.

Dulcie nodded. "One of the reasons they want us to marry." She twined a strand of black hair into fingers and began twisting it. "Do you want to?"

Kellin stared at her. How could she be so matter-of-fact about it? Importantly, he said, "That is something I will have to consider."

Dulcie burst out laughing. "*You* consider? They will no more abide by what you wish—*or* me—than a stud horse minds his rider when a mare in season is near."

Kellin had not thought of it that way. "But if I am to be Mujhar, they must listen to me."

Dulcie shook her head. Her brows were straight, serious bars across a sculpted brow. She wore black hair in dozens of braids tied into a single plait and beaded at the bottom. "They will listen to no one, only to the prophecy." Dulcie grimaced. "I have had it stuffed into my ears often enough. It is all about blood, Kellin, and the need to mix it correctly. Don't you see?"

Kellin did not, though once again he claimed he did. "I am the one who is to sire the Firstborn," he declared. "Everyone says so."

Dulcie grinned. "Not without a woman!"

Color stained Kellin's face. "Is that supposed to be you?"

She shrugged, twisting hair again. "What else do you suppose they talk about behind that door but inches in front of your face? They will have us betrothed by supper."

Kellin glared at her. "Why to you? Why not to Cluna, or Jennet?"

"They are too old for you," Dulcie said matter-of-factly, "and likely by now they have both set their caps for Blais. I think neither of them wants a boy for a husband."

It stung. "I am nearly eleven."

"And I nearly thirteen." Clearly, Dulcie was undismayed by his youth. "It has to do with the blood, as I said. There is only one bloodline left to get, Kellin—the one bloodline no Cheysuli desires to acknowledge. But how else do they expect to get the First-born? It wants Ihlini blood."

He was startled, recalling Corwyth, and Lochiel's designs. "Ihlini!"

"*Think* about it," Dulcie said impatiently. "They need it from somewhere, from someone who favors the prophecy."

"But not an *Ihlini*—"

"Kellin." Her tone was exasperated. "That is why my father is proposing you and I wed. To get the Ihlini blood."

"But—" It was preposterous. "You do not *have*—"

"Aye," Dulcie answered, "I do. We all of us do: Blythe, Cluna, Jennet, and me. Because of our mother."

"But she is *Solindish*."

Dulcie's tone was freighted with condescension. "Solinde was the birthplace of Ihlini, Kellin. Remember the stories of how they broke away from the Firstborn and left Homana?"

He did. He had not thought of those stories in years. "Then—" Kellin frowned. He did not like the implication. "Then the Ihlini are not so different from the *a'saii*."

Dulcie smiled. "Now you begin to understand."'

He eyed her assessively. "Can you conjure *godfire?*"

"Of course not. The Ihlini blood in us goes back more than two hundred years. No arts remain in our House." Dulcie shrugged. "Electra learned a few tricks, but nothing more. Tynstar did not share the Seker's blood with her."

He frowned. "Then why should it matter now?"

"Because no Cheysuli warrior would ever lie down with an Ihlini woman," Dulcie replied. "At least—not a *willing* one. So they will marry *us* off and hope for the best . . . if for no other reason than to keep the Ihlini from making their own through you."

"Through me?"

Dulcie sighed. "Are you stupid? If the Ihlini caught you and made you lie with an Ihlini woman, there could be a child. It would be *the* child." She laughed at his expression. "The Ihlini would use you, Kellin, like a prize Cheysuli stud."

Within hours he was full to bursting on kinfolk—and most of them female, at that, full of gossip and laughter—and so to escape, Kellin went to his own chamber and climbed up into his huge bed. He made mountains and hillocks of his coverlet, then planned his own campaigns as Carillon and Donal must have planned them years before, when Homana was at war.

"With Solinde," he muttered. He was not at the moment disposed to like Solinde, since she had managed to produce a twelve-year-old girl who believed he was stupid.

The knock at the door was soft, but persistent. Kellin, startled from his game, called out crossly for the person to enter.

Aileen came in, not a servant at all. Her hair, rust threaded with silver, was bound in braids around her head with pins that glittered in sunlight. Her green gown was simple but elegant. She wore around her throat a fortune in gold: the mountain cat torque that marked her Brennan's *cheysula*.

Is that what Dulcie expects from me? Kellin jerked flat his coverlet and slid out of the bed to stand politely. "Aye, granddame?"

"Sit." Aileen waved him back onto the bed, then sat down on the edge herself. "Kellin—"

Whenever he spoke with Aileen he unconsciously echoed the lilt of her accent. He blurted it out all at once before she could finish. " 'Tis done, isn't it? You've betrothed us."

Aileen arched reddish brows. "The idea doesn't please you, then?"

"No." He fidgeted, self-conscious; he liked his granddame very much and did not want to upset her, but he felt he had to tell the truth. "I want to choose for myself."

The faintest of creases deepened at the corner of Aileen's eyes. "Aye, of course you do. So did I. So did Brennan. But—"

"But I can't, can I?" he challenged forthrightly. " 'Tis like Dulcie said: you'll do whatever you want."

The Queen of Homana sighed. " 'Tis true those of royalty have little freedom in matters of marriage."

" 'Tisn't fair," Kellin asserted. "You tell me I will have power when I am grown, but then I am *told* whom I must marry. That is no power."

"No," she agreed quietly. "I had none, nor Corin, whom I wanted to marry in place of Brennan."

"In place of—grandsire?" It was a completely new thought. "You wanted to marry my *su'fali?*"

"Aye."

He blinked. "But you were already betrothed to grandsire."

"Aye, so I was. It did not lessen the wanting, Kellin; it was Corin I loved." Her green eyes were kind. "I know this may shock you, but I thought it fair to tell you. You are young, but not so young the truth should be kept from you, even those truths of men and woman."

"But you married grandsire."

"Aye. It was agreed upon before I was born: Niall's oldest son would marry Liam's daughter." She shrugged, mouth twisted awry. "And so I was *born* betrothed; it was only later, when Corin came to Erinn, that I realized how binding—and how wrong—the agreement was. I fell in love with Corin and he with me, but he was the stronger person. He said the betrothal must stand, and sailed away to Atvia."

"He married Glyn." He had never seen her—he had seen only Hart of his scattered kin—but he knew of the mute woman Corin had wed.

"Years later, aye. Then *I* was wed, and a mother, and my future was utterly settled."

Kellin digested all of it. "You are telling me that I should marry Dulcie."

Aileen smiled. "No."

It stilled him a moment. "No?"

"I told them to give you time, both of you time; to let you grow to adulthood. You've been kept close most of your life, Kellin, and we owe you some measure of freedom." An odd expression crossed her face. "The kind of freedom I had once, before coming to Homana."

Relief overflowed. "*Leiihana tu'sai,* granddame!"

Aileen laughed. "One day marriage will not be such a chore, my lad. That I promise."

"Was it a chore for you?"

The question stopped her. Aileen's eyes filled with memories he could not know, and were not shared with him. "For a very long time, it was," she answered finally. "But not any longer."

"Why?"

"Because when I allowed myself to stop resenting my marriage; when I stopped resenting the Cheysuli *tahlmorra* that dictated I sleep with Brennan instead of with Corin, I fell in love with your grandsire." Her smile was poignant. "And so now I have a new regret: that I wasted so much time in *not* loving him."

Kellin could only stare at his grandmother. There were no words for what he felt; he knew only that he was young, too young after all, to begin to understand the complexities of adulthood.

Something new came into his head. "Did my *jehana* love my *jehan?*"

Aileen's mouth softened. "Very much, Kellin. 'Twas a match few people experience."

He nodded dutifully, uncomprehending. "But she died when I was born." He looked searchingly at Aileen. "Is that why he hates me? Is that why he gave me up and went away—because I killed his *cheysula?*"

Aileen's face drained. "Oh, Kellin, *no!* Oh, gods, is that what you've been thinking all these years?" She murmured something more in Erinnish, then caught him into her arms and pulled him close. "I'll swear on anything you like that your birth did not kill her, nor did it drive your father away. He gave you up because it was his *tahlmorra* to do so."

"But you believe he was wrong."

She withdrew a little to look into his face. "Have you a touch of the *kivarna*, lad? Have you been hiding the truth from us?"

"No," he blurted, intrigued. "What is it?"

"D'ye know what people feel?" She touched her breast. "D'ye know what is in their hearts?"

Perplexed, he frowned. "No. I just saw it in your face."

Aileen relaxed, laughing a little. "Aye, well—'tis a gift and a curse, my lad. Aidan had it in full measure, and Shona—'twould come as no surprise if it manifested in you."

Kellin was bewildered. " 'Twas in your face, granddame—and your voice." *And what I heard you say to grandsire once before.* But that he would not admit.

Aileen hugged him again briefly, then surrendered him to the bed as she rose and shook out her skirts. "I think he was wrong," she said firmly. "I always have. But I'm a woman, Kellin—and though I'll not swear a man loves his child less, he's not borne that babe in his body. Aidan did as he believed he had to, to please the gods and his *tahlmorra.* And one day, I *promise,* you will ask him to his face how he could do such a thing."

He heard the underlying hostility in her tone. "But not yet."

Aileen's lips compressed. "Not yet."

After a moment Kellin nodded. It was a familiar refrain. "Well," he said easily, "once I have killed the Lion, he will *have* to let me see him."

"Oh, Kellin—"

"I will," he declared. "I *will* kill it. And then I shall go to the Crystal Isle and show *jehan* the head."

Aileen's mouth, he saw, was filled with all manner of protest. But she made none of them. With tears in her eyes, the Erinnish Queen of Homana left her grandson quite alone.

Chapter Eleven

Blais' door was ajar. Candlelight crept from the room into the corridor, slotted between door and jamb; Kellin peeked in carefully, not wanting to discover that Blais was not alone at all, but accompanied by Cluna, or Jennet, or Cluna *and* Jennet. They had taken up entirely too much of Blais' time, Kellin felt. It was his turn for his cousin's attention.

He paused there in the slot. He saw no female cousins. Only Blais himself, sprawled across the great tester bed with his *lir*, lovely Tanni, who lay upon her back with legs spread and underparts exposed in elaborate pleasure as Blais stroked belly fur. In that moment she was dog, not wolf; Kellin felt a pang of hope that perhaps he, too, would gain a wolf.

Then again, there was lovely black Sleeta, his grandsire's mountain cat, and Hart's magnificent Rael. There were so many wonderful *lir* in the world; surely the gods would see to it he gained the perfect one.

Blais' arm moved in slow repetition as he stroked Tanni. He lay on his belly, torso propped up on one elbow. Thick black hair fell forward over his shoulders. He wore no jerkin, only leggings; gold shone dully in candlelight against the bronzing of his flesh.

Someday I will have such gold. Kellin wet his lips. "Blais?"

Blais glanced up. Tanni flopped over on her side and bent her head around to inspect Kellin. "Aye?" Blais beckoned, smiling. "Come in, come in—we have no secrets, Tanni and I—and if I wanted privacy I would have shut the door."

Kellin slipped through the slot between door and jamb. Linked behind his back, both hands clutched an object. "I have a question."

His cousin's black brows arched. "Aye?"

He sucked in a deep breath. "Are you going back to Solinde with them?"

"Solinde!" Blais sat upright, shaking hair away from his face. "Why would I go to Solinde?"

"Because of—them." Abashed, Kellin stared at the floor.

"Who?" Blais began, and then he cut off the question. "Why do you ask, Kellin?"

Miserably, Kellin looked up to meet Blais' steady gaze. "I saw you," he whispered. "Earlier today, on the sentry-walk."

"Ah." Blais nodded.

"You were kissing Jennet."

"Cluna."

It stopped Kellin's attempt at explanation. "Cluna? But, I thought—"

Blais laughed. "You were thinking 'twas Jennet I wanted? Well, aye, and so it was—yesterday. Today 'twas Cluna." He shifted into a cross-legged position, one hand tugging gently at Tanni's ear. "You see, Cluna wanted to sample what her *rujholla* had tasted the day before. They compete in everything." He shrugged, grinning. "I accommodated them both."

Kellin was bewildered. "Then which one will you marry?"

"Marry!" Then Blais laughed. "Gods, Kellin—*neither.* Were you thinking I would? No. I'll not go to Solinde, and I'm doubting either of them could bear to live at Clankeep. There is too much of Solinde in them." He smiled more warmly at his cousin. "Were you thinking I meant to desert you?"

Without warning tears welled up. Kellin was astonished and ashamed, but there was a thing he had to say. "I have no one left," he explained unsteadily. "Only you. Urchin and Rogan—" He bit into his lip. "There is grandsire and granddame, but it isn't the same. 'Tisn't like true friends; they *have* to like me. But you . . . well—" he swallowed heavily, spilling it all at once. "I will be Mujhar one day. I would have need of a liege man."

Blais' face was still. Only his eyes were alive in the dark mask: fierce and bright and yellow.

Kellin felt all of his muscles knot up. *He'll refuse me—he will say no.* He wanted it so badly, and yet he knew it was unlikely. They were years and worlds apart, and very different in nature.

Blais' tone was muted. "I had not expected this."

Panic nearly overwhelmed. "Have I offended you?"

"Offended! That the Prince of Homana desires me to be his liege man?" Blais shook his head. "No, there is no offense in this—only honor. And I never believed myself worthy of such honor."

"But you are!" Kellin cried. "You saved me from the bear-trap, and the Lion. Your worth is proved. And—and there is no one else I would have."

Blais stared hard at Tanni, as if he feared to give away too much if he looked at Kellin. "There has been no liege man in Homana-Mujhar since Ian died."

"He would approve," Kellin said. "He would say you are worthy."

Blais smiled faintly. "Then how could I refuse?" Levity faded again. He was suddenly very solemn. "I will serve you gladly, my lord."

Kellin sighed. From behind his back he took the knife and showed it to Blais. It was gold and steel, with a rampant lion twisted about the hilt. Its eye was a single ruby. Softly, he said, "There is a ceremony."

Blais rose from the bed, knelt upon the floor, and drew his own Cheysuli long-knife. Without hesitation he placed the blade against the inside of his left wrist and cut into the flesh. "I swear," he said quietly, "by this blood; by my name and honor and *lir*, that I will serve as liege man to Kellin of Homana as long as he will have me." Blood ran from the knife cut and dripped crimson on the stone floor. "Will you have me, my lord?"

Wonder welled in Kellin's breast. "I will." And then, quoting the words he had learned long ago: *"Y'ja'hai. Tu'jhalla dei. Tahlmorra lujhala mei wiccan, cheysu."*

"Ja'hai-na," Blais responded. Then he offered his bloodied knife to his lord and took the other in return.

Kellin looked down upon the Cheysuli weapon with its wolf-head hilt. He felt the tears well up, but he did not care. *I am not alone any more.*

He awoke sweating near dawn, disoriented and fearful. He felt oppressed, squashed flat by dread.—*Lion*—

Kellin wanted to whimper. How could it come to pass? Blais was in the palace. Blais was his liege man. The Lion could not withstand a sworn Cheysuli liege man.

The flesh rose on his bones. "Lion," he murmured. And then, searching for strength, *"Tahlmorra lujhala mei wiccan, cheysu."*

But the sense of dread increased.

Kellin wanted Blais. Together they might vanquish the beast forever. But to summon Blais meant he had to get out of bed.

Kellin shuddered, biting into his bottom lip. He smelled the tang of fear on his flesh and hated himself for it. His scarred ankle ached, though he knew it completely healed.

"Cheysuli," he choked, squeezing his eyes tightly shut. "A *warrior*, someday." Warriors were brave. Warriors did what required doing.

From beneath his pillow he took the Cheysuli long-knife bestowed by his liege man. Stiffly, slowly, Kellin slid down from his bed. He wore only a sleeping tunic that reached to mid-thigh; bare toes dug into the stone floor as if he might take root. *You have a liege man. He will fend off the Lion.* He clutched the knife in both hands, then crept out of his room into the corridor beyond.

False dawn, he thought; even the servants still slept. An ideal time for a lion to stalk the halls.

Kellin chewed his lips painfully, then unclenched his teeth. With the knife as his ward, he moved slowly and deliberately toward the door that was Blais', so far down the corridor as to be a league away.

Kellin pushed open the door. Candlelight from the corridor cressets spilled inside, illuminating the chamber. Kellin saw tousled black hair, the gleam of a *lir*-band, and the glint of Tanni's eyes from the foot of the bed where she lay.

"Blais," he said. "Blais—the Lion is come."

Blais sat up at once, one hand reaching for the royal knife at his bedside. His eyes, pupils expanded in darkness, showed a ring of purest yellow around the edges. "Kellin?"

"The Lion," Kellin repeated. "Will you come? We have to kill it."

Blais ran a hand through his hair. He yawned. "The lion?" And then he came fully awake. "Kellin—" But he cut it off. His expression was masked. "Where is it?"

Kellin gestured with his knife. "Out there. Walking the corridors."

Blais grunted and slid out of bed. He was nude save for *lir*-gold, but paused long enough to slip on leggings. Barefoot, he patted Tanni and murmured a word in the Old Tongue. Then he smiled at Kellin. "A wolf is no match for a lion."

Kellin felt markedly better as Blais followed him out into the corridor. "A sword might be better," he said, "but I am not old enough yet. Grandsire said."

"Have you not begun swordplay?"

"Aye, a little—but the arms-master says it will be a long time before I have any skill. I am too small."

Blais nodded. "A Homanan skill. I am no good at it, myself, though the gods know Sean tried to teach me often enough." He shrugged. "I have no aptitude."

They went on. Torchlight glinted off the earring in Blais' hair. He looked fully awake and alert, Kellin thought in satisfaction. *This time the Lion will lose.*

When they neared the Great Hall, Kellin pressed himself against the wall. A shudder claimed his body from head to toe, stilling only as Blais closed a hand over one shoulder.

"I am your liege man," Blais told him. "I am with you, my lord."

Kellin grinned his relief. " 'Tis inside," he said. "I can feel it." To Blais, it was not difficult to explain; a liege man would know, would understand. "He has come to swallow Homana."

The tone was excessively neutral. "How do you know this?"

"The fortune-teller said so."

Blais seemed briefly dubious, but let it go. He smiled. "Then we shall have to see to it the lion swallows nothing but my knife blade."

Joy and wonder bubbled up in Kellin. *This is what it is to have a liege man!*

Blais pushed open one of the heavy silver doors, sliding effortlessly inside. Kellin slipped through behind him. "Here?" Blais whispered.

"Somewhere . . ." Kellin moved forward slowly, wishing he might have the courage to use the knife he clutched.

Blais stepped out into the center of the long hall and strode the length of the firepit. Coals glowed from its depths beneath an ashen cloak.

The alcove curtain near the massive throne billowed in the darkness. A single coal fell out of the pit and crumbled into ash. *"There!"* Kellin gasped.

Blais reacted instantly, running silently toward the alcove. He caught the curtain and tore it aside, knife glinting.

"Is it there?" Kellin cried. "Blais?"

Blais went rigid, then reeled back from the alcove. Kellin heard the slap of bare torso against the wall. The knife fell from a slack hand. "Tanni!" Blais cried. *"Tanni—"*

Kellin ran. By the time he reached Blais, his kinsman was slumped against wall and floor, body trembling convulsively. Yellow eyes were wide and crazed, turned inside out. Sweat filmed his face.

"Blais!"

Blais shuddered. Then he reached out and caught Kellin's thin arms, closing his taloned fingers into flesh. "Tanni—Tanni—*lir*—"

"*Blais!*"

"—gods—oh, gods . . . no—" Blais' face was the color of the ash in the firepit. "Tanni—" He let go of Kellin all at once and lurched to his feet.

"*Blais*—"

But Blais did not respond. He stumbled toward the end of the hall, seeking doors; his grace was utterly banished, leaving him reeling like a drunken man, or a sick one. He smashed into one of the doors and shoved it open.

Kellin gathered up the, fallen knife and ran after his liege man. Fear of the Lion was quite vanquished; what he feared now was that something terrible had befallen Blais. *Don't let him go, too!*

Blais ran even as Kellin caught up, but his body betrayed him. Only his outstretched hands, rebounding off walls, kept him upright. Ropes of muscles stood up in relief against naked flesh.

"Blais!"

And then they were in Blais' chamber, and there was blood everywhere, on the floor and across the bed; a lurid arc against the curtains. Blais tore them aside, then fell down onto the bed. "*Tanni*—"

People crowded in the door. Kellin heard the questions, the startled exclamations, but he answered none of them. He could only stare at the warrior who had been his cousin, his liege man, his friend; who now was a *lir*less Cheysuli.

"Blais—" This time it was a wail because he knew.

Brennan was behind him. "Kellin . . . Kellin, come away."

"*No.*"

Hart was with him, face shiny it was stretched so tautly across the bones of his cheeks. "Come away, Kellin. There is nothing you can do."

"No!" Kellin threw down the knives, then ripped himself out of Brennan's reaching hands. "Blais—Blais—you *cannot*. No! I need you. I need you! You are my liege man!" He fastened both hands around one of Blais' rigid arms and tugged, trying to pull his kinsman away from the gutted wolf. "Blais!"

Blais turned a ravaged face on them all. "Take him away . . . take him from here."

"No!" Kellin gulped back the fear. *"Tu'jalla dei—"*

Brennan caught Kellin's arms. "Come away."

"He can't go!" Kellin screamed. "I refuse him leave. I am the Prince of Homana and I *refuse* him leave to go!"

They were all of them in the chamber: Aileen, Ilsa, his Solindish cousins. Dulcie's yellow eyes were wide.

"Tu'jalla dei!" Kellin shrieked. "He has to stay if I say so. He swore. *Tell* him, grandsire! *Tu'jalla dei."*

Brennan's face was stark. "Such things are for gods to do, not men, not even princes and kings. This is the price, Kellin. Blais accepted it when he accepted his *lir*. So did I. So did we all. And so will you."

"I will not! I *will* not!"

Aileen's voice shook. "Kellin—"

"No! No! No!" He writhed in Brennan's grip. "He swore by blood and honor and his *lir*—" Kellin broke it off on a strangled gasp. Indeed, by his *lir*, and now that *lir* was dead. "Blais," Kellin choked. "Don't leave me."

Blais stared blindly. Blood smeared his chest. "I never knew," he said dazedly. "I never knew what pain there was in it."

Brennan looked old beyond his years. "No warrior can. Not before it happens."

Blais held up his bloodied hands. "I am—*empty*—" He shoved a forearm across his brow and left a bloodslick behind, shining in his hair.

"Tu'jalla dei," Kellin said brokenly.

But Blais seemed not to hear. He stripped off his *lir*-bands and the earring and put them on the blood-soaked bed. Then he gathered up Tanni's body into the cradle of naked arms and turned toward the door.

As one, they all moved aside. Blais went out of the chamber as wolf blood splashed on stone.

"Blais!" Kellin screamed.

Brennan lifted him from the ground, containing him easily. "Let him go. He is a walking dead man; let him go with dignity."

"But I *need* him."

"He needs his ending more." Brennan held him close. "I wish I could spare you this. But you, too, are Cheysuli, and the price shall be yours as well."

Kellin stopped struggling. He hung slackly in his grandfather's arms until Brennan set him down. "No," he said then, looking up into the face that looked so old in its grief. "No, there will be no price. I will have no *lir*."

Hart's voice was kind. "You cannot gainsay what the gods bestow."

"*I* will." Kellin's voice took on a hard bitterness. "I refuse to have one."

"Kellin." Now Aileen, moving forward.

He cut her off at once with an outflung hand. "I refuse it. Do you hear?" He looked at his kinfolk one by one. "They all leave. *All* of them. First my *jehan*. Then Rogan. Then Urchin ... and now *Blais*." His voice sounded alien even to Kellin. "They all go from me."

Brennan touched his shoulder. "This grief will pass, one day."

Kellin knocked the hand away. "No! From now on I walk alone. With no friends, no liege man, no *lir*." He looked at Brennan fiercely. "And I *will not care*."

Aileen was horrified. "*Kel*lin!"

He felt a roaring in his head; felt it rush up from his belly and engulf his chest, threatening his throat. If he opened his mouth, he would vomit.

He knew its name: rage. And a hatred so virulent he thought he might choke on it.

"No more," he said quietly, making it an oath. "The gods cannot take from me what I do not have."

Interval

Naked, the woman lay next to him in the darkness. She had not slept when he was done, for he had, as always, disturbed her with his intensity, and she could not tumble out of passion into sleep the way he could.

She lay very quiet next to him, not allowing her flesh to touch his. If she disturbed him, he would waken in ill humor, and she had learned to avoid his black moods by submitting everything to him: will, body, spirit. She had learned the trick long ago, when she had first become a whore.

She let his warmth warm her, driving away the chill of the winter night. Her dwelling was tiny, not so much more than a hovel, and she could not afford the endless supply of peat and wood that others bought or bargained for to get them through the Homanan winter. She hoarded what she had, although when *he* came she piled it all on the hearth. Even if it meant going without for days after.

He shifted, and she held her breath. One broad hand moved across her belly, then cradled her left breast. The fingers were slack and passionless. He had spent that passion earlier; though he was easily roused, she did not do it now.

She sighed shallowly, not daring to move his hand. He had bought her body, let him fondle it as he chose. It made no difference to her. At least he was a prince.

She had other lovers, of course, but none so fine as he. They were hard men, tough men, with little refinement and less imagination. He, at least, was clean, with a good man smell, lacking the stench of others who had no time for baths, nor the money to buy wood to heat water. It was no trouble to him to bathe whenever he wished; she was grateful for it. She was grateful for *him*.

That he had chosen her was a miracle in itself. She was young still, only seventeen, and her body had not yet coarsened with use, so she presented a better appearance than some of the other women. And she had high, firm breasts above a slim waist, with good hips below. She would lose it all, of course, with the first full-term pregnancy, but so far she had been able to rid herself of the seeds before any took root.

But what of *his* seed?

She laughed noiselessly, startled by the thought. Would she bear a prince's bastard? And if she did, would he provide for her? Perhaps she could leave this life behind and find a good, solid man who would forget about her past. Or would *he* take the child, claiming it his?

It was possible. It had happened in the past, she had heard; the bastards had been sent to Clankeep, to the shapechangers, to grow up with barren women. He would not risk leaving a halfling with a Homanan woman, lest someone attempt to use it for personal gain.

He called her *meijha* and *meijhana*, words she did not know. She had asked him if he had a wife, and he had laughed, correcting her: "*Cheysula*," he had said, and then "*No, I have no cheysula. They expect me to wed my Solindish cousin, but I will not do it.*"

She turned her head slightly to look at his face. In sleep he was so different, so young, so free of the tight-wound tension. It was a good face in sleep, more handsome than any she had welcomed in her bed, and she longed to touch it. But to do so would waken him, and he would change, and she would see the customary hardness of his mouth and eyes, and the anger in his soul.

She sighed. She did not love him. She was not permitted to love him; he had told her that plainly their first bedding three months before. But she did care. For all his black moods he was kind enough to her, even if it was an unschooled, rough kindness, as if he had forgotten how.

He had spoken harshly to her more often than she would choose, but he had only struck her once; and then he had turned away abruptly with a strange, sickened look in his eyes, and he had given her gold in place of silver. It had been worth the bruise, for she bought herself a new gown she wore the next time he came, and he had smiled at her for it.

Her smile came unbidden; a woman's, slow and smug. *In my bed lies the Prince of Homana.*

He moved. He stretched, flexing effortlessly, and then he sat up.

She saw the play of muscles beneath the flesh of his smooth back, the hint of supple spine, the tangle of black hair across the nape of his neck. She lay very still, wondering if she had spoken her thoughts aloud.

For a moment his profile was very clear in the dim light, outlined by the coals in the tiny hearth across the room. She saw the elegant brow and straight nose. He was yet groggy with sleep and soft from it; when the sleep fled, his bones would look older and harder, with black brows that drew down all too often and spoiled the youth of his face.

He slanted her a glance. "Did you dream of me?"

She smiled. "How could I not?"

It was his customary question and her customary answer, but this time neither appeared to please him. He scowled and got out of the narrow bed, then reached to pull on black breeches and boots. She admired as always the suppleness of his muscles, the lithe movements of his body. It was the Cheysuli in him, she knew, though he did not seem other than Homanan. She had seen a warrior up close once and still shivered when she recalled the strangeness of his eyes. Beast-eyes, some folk called them, and she agreed with them.

His were not bestial. They could be disconcertingly direct and nearly always challenging, but they were green, and a man's eyes. For that she was grateful.

He lifted the jug from the crooked table and poured wine, not bothering to don the shirt and fur-lined doublet on the floor beside the bed. She hunched herself up on one elbow. "Are you going?"

"I have had from you what I came for." He did not turn to look at her. "Unless you have discovered yet another position."

She, who believed she could no longer blush, burned with embarrassment. "No, my lord." She had displeased him; he would go, and this time he might not come back.

He swallowed down the wine and set the mug down with a thump. "This vintage is foul. Have you no better?"

"No, my lord."

Her flat tone roused something in him. He turned, and the thin gold torque around his throat glinted. "You reprove *me?*"

"No!" She sat up hastily, jerking the bedclothes over her breasts in an instinctive bid for a modesty she had surrendered years before. "Never!"

He scowled at her blackly. His mouth had taken on its familiar hard line. And then he smiled all unexpectedly, and she marveled again at the beauty of a man who could be cruel and kind at once. "I have frightened you again." He poured more wine and drank it, seemingly unaffected by its foul taste. "Do you fear I will turn into beast-shape here before you?" He laughed as she caught her breath, showing white teeth in a mocking grin. "Have no fear, *mei-jhana* . . . there is no *lir*-shape for this Cheysuli. I have renounced it. What you see before you is what I am." He still smiled, but she saw the anger in his eyes. "My arms are bare, and my ear. There is no shapechanger in this room."

She held her silence. He had shown her such moods before.

He swore beneath his breath in a language she did not know. He would not come to her bed again this night, to set her flesh afire with a longing she had believed well passed for her until *he* had come with no word of explanation for a prince's presence in a Midden whore's hovel.

A sudden thought intruded. *He might not come back ever.*

The fear made her voice a question she had sworn never to ask. "Will you leave me?"

His eyes narrowed. "Do you care?"

"Oh aye, my lord—very much!" She believed it would please him; it was nonetheless the truth.

A muscle jumped in his jaw. "Do I please you? Do you care for me?"

She breathed it softly. "More than any, my lord."

"Because I am a prince?"

She smiled, believing she had found the proper answer. "Oh no, my lord. Because you are you. I care for *you*."

He turned from her. Stunned, she watched as he put on his shirt and doublet, then swept up and pinned on the heavy green cloak. It was lined with rich dark fur, and worth more than the house she lived in. She saw the gold cloak-brooch glitter in firelight, ruby gemstone burning. The brooch was worth more than the entire block.

And then he strode across the room to her and caught her throat in his hands, bending over her. "No," he said. "You do not care for *me*. Say you do not."

She grasped at his hands. She wanted very badly to say the proper words. "But I do! Your coin is welcome—I am a whore, for all that, and claim myself no better—but it is *you* I care for!"

He swore raggedly and released her so abruptly she fell back against the wall. He unpinned the brooch and dropped it into her lap. "You will not see me again."

"My lord!" A hand beseeched. "Why? What have I done?"

"You said you cared." His eyes were black in poor light. "And that I will not have."

"Kellin!" She dared to use his name, but he turned away in a swirl of green wool and was gone. The door swung shut behind him.

The brooch that would buy her freedom was cold comfort in the night as she cried herself to sleep.

PART II

PART II

Chapter One

Kellin stepped out of the slope-roofed hovel into the slushy alley and stopped. He stared blankly at the darkened dwelling opposite and expelled a smoking breath. He inhaled deeply, almost convulsively, and the cold air filled his lungs with the anticipated burning. The alley stank of peat, filth, ordure. Even winter could not overcome the stench of depression and poverty.

He heard movement inside the hovel, through the cracks of ill-made walls: a woman crying.

Too harsh with her. Kellin gritted his teeth. Self-contempt boiled up to replace the thought. *What does she expect? I warned her. I told her not to care. There is nothing in me for anyone to care about, least of all a father . . . I will not risk losing another who claims to care for me.*

The sobs were soft but audible because he made himself hear them. He used them to flagellate; he deserved the punishment.

She was well-paid. That is what she cries for.

But he wondered if there were more, if the woman *did* care—

Kellin gritted his teeth, fighting off the part of his nature that argued for fairness, for a renunciation of the oath he had sworn ten years before. *She is a whore, nothing more. They all of them are whores. Where better to spill the seed for which I am so valued?*

Kellin swore, hissing invective between set teeth. His mood was foul. He detested the duality that ravaged his spirit. He had no use for softness, for compassion; he wanted nothing at all to do with the kind of relationship he saw binding his grandsire and his granddame. That kind of honor and respect simply begged for an ending, and therefore begged for pain.

And what was there for him in a relationship such as that shared by the Mujhar and his queen? Had they not made it clear, all of them, that it was not *Kellin* whom they cared about, but the seed he would provide?

Bitterness engulfed. *Let the whores have it. It will serve them better; expelling it serves ME.*

But the conscience he had believed eradicated was not entirely vanquished. Despite his wishes, he *did* regret his harshness with the woman; did regret he could not see her again, for she had been good to him. There had been a quiet dignity about her despite her life, and a simple acceptance that the gods had seen fit to give her this fate.

Self-contempt made it easy to transfer resentment to the woman. *She would make a good Cheysuli. Better than I do; I, after all, am at war with the gods.*

It was time to leave, lest he give in to the temptation to go back inside the hovel and offer comfort. He could not afford that. It was too easy to succumb, too easy to give in to the weakness that would lead in time to pain. Far better to keep pain at bay by permitting it no toehold in the ordering of his spirit.

Kellin glanced over and saw the familiar guardsmen waiting in the shadows between two ramshackle dwellings. Four shapes. Four watchdogs, set upon his scent by the Mujhar. Even now, even in adulthood, no matter where Kellin went or what he chose to do, they accompanied him. Discreetly, usually, for he was after all the Prince of Homana, but their loyalty was the Mujhar's.

As a boy, he had accepted it as perfectly natural and never thought to question the policy and protection. As a man, however, it chafed his spirit because such supervision, in his eyes, relegated his own abilities, his own opinions, to insignificance. Initially his protests were polite, but the Mujhar's intransigence soon triggered an angrier opposition. Yet the Mujhar remained obdurate. His heir could not—*would* not, by his order—be permitted to walk unaccompanied in Mujhara. Ever.

Kellin had tried losing his dogs, but they tracked him down. He tried tricking them, but they had proved too smart. He tried ordering them, but they were the Mujhar's men. And at last, terribly angry, he tried to fight them. To a man, despite his insults, they refused to honor him so.

He was accustomed to them now. He had trained them to stay out of his tavern brawls. It had taken time; they did not care to see their prince risk himself, but they had learned it was his only escape, and so they left him to it.

Kellin shivered, wrapping the heavy cloak more tightly around his shoulders. It was cold and very clear. The cloud cover had blown away, which meant the nights would be bitter cold until the next snowstorm came. Already he felt the chill in his bones; mouthing a curse, he moved on.

He did not know his destination. He had thought to spend the night with the woman, but that was over now. She had committed the unpardonable; the only punishment he knew was to deny her the comfort of his body, so that he, too, was denied the contentment he so desperately desired despite his vow.

He splashed through crusted puddles. It did not matter to him how it damaged his boots. He had many more at home. This sort of revenge offered little comfort, but it was something. Let the servants gossip as they would. It gave him some small pleasure to know he was entirely unpredictable in mood as well as actions.

Better to keep them off guard. Better to make them wonder.

As he wondered himself; it was a twisted form of punishment Kellin meted out to bind himself to his vow. If he relaxed his vigilance, he might be tempted to renounce his oath. He would not permit himself that, lest the gods win at last and turn him into a Cheysuli who thought only of his *tahlmorra*, instead of such things as a son badly in need of a father.

Behind him, the watchdogs also splashed. Kellin wondered what they thought of their honorable duty: to spend the night out of doors while their prince poured his royal seed into a whore's body. *They will get no Firstborn of her, or of any other whore.*

Ahead in wan moonlight, a placard dangled before a door. A tavern. *Good. I am of a mind to start a game not entirely like any other.*

Kellin shouldered open the cracked door and went in, knowing the dogs would follow along in a moment. He paused just inside, accustoming his eyes to greasy candlelight, and found himself in a dingy common room. The tables were empty save one, where five men gathered to toss dice and rune-sticks.

For a moment only, Kellin considered joining them. But instead he went to another table and hooked over a stool, motioning with a jerk of his head to the man in the stained cloth apron.

The watchdogs came in, marked where he was, and went to another table. He saw the tavern-keeper waver, for they wore tunics of the Mujharan Guard and doubtless meant more coin than a lone stranger.

Smiling faintly, Kellin drew his knife and stuck the point into wood, so that the heavy hilt stood upright. The rampant lion curled around the hilt, single ruby eye glinting in greasy light.

As expected, the tavern-keeper arrived almost at once. "My lord?"

"*Usca,*" Kellin ordered. "A jug of it."

The man nodded, but his gaze flicked to the guardsmen. "And for them?"

Kellin favored him with a humorless smile. "They drink what they like. Ask *them.*"

The man was clearly puzzled. "My lord, they wear the Mujhar's crest. And you have it here, on your knife. Doesn't that mean—"

Kellin overrode him curtly. "It means we have something in common, but it does not mean we sleep together." He yanked the broochless cloak from his shoulders and slapped it across the table. He waited. The man bowed and hastened away.

When the *usca* was brought, Kellin poured the crude cup full. He downed it all rapidly, waiting for the fire. It came, burning his belly and clear down into his toes. All at once there was life in his body, filling up flesh and blood, and the pain that accompanied it.

He had fought it so very long. Because of his oath, because of his need, he had shut himself off to emotions, severing his spirit from the Kellin he had been, because he could not bear the pain. He had seen the bewildered hurt in his grandmother's eyes and learned to ignore it, as he learned to withstand even the scorn in his grandfather's voice; eventually, in fact, he learned to cultivate that scorn, because it was a goad that drove him to maintain his vow even when, in moments of despair and self-hatred, he desired to unswear it.

One day intent became habit, despite the occasional defiance of a conscience battered for ten years into compliance. He was what he *was;* what he had made himself to be. No one could hurt him now.

Kellin drank *usca.* He wanted to fight very badly. When the fire filled head and belly, he rose and prepared to make his way to the table full of Homanans who laughed and wagered and joked.

A man stepped into his path, blocking his way. "Well met, my lord. Shall we share a cup of wine?"

Kellin's tongue was thick, but the words succinct enough. "I am drinking *usca.*"

"Ah, of course; forgive me." The stranger smiled faintly. A lifted hand and a slight gesture beckoned *usca* from the tavern-keeper.

Kellin stared hard at the stranger, struggling to make out the face. The room shifted and ran together so that the colors all seemed one. *Too much* usca *for conversation.*

When the new jug came, the stranger poured two cups full and offered one to Kellin. "Shall we sit, my lord?"

Kellin did not sit. He set his hand around the hilt of his knife, still standing upright in the table, and snapped it from the wood.

The stranger inclined his head. "I am unarmed, my lord, and offer no threat to you."

Kellin stared into the face. It was bland, beguiling; all mask and no substance. *Perhaps* he *will give me my fight.* He wanted the fight badly; needed it desperately, to assuage the guilt he felt despite his desire not to. *Physical pain is easier to bear than emotional pain.*

For years he had sought it, finding it in taverns among men who held back nothing. It was a release from self-captivity more wholly satisfying than any other he knew.

This man, perhaps? Or another. Kellin gestured and sat down, laying the knife atop the table as he took the brimming cup.

"A fortune-game?" the other man suggested.

It suited. Kellin nodded and the man took from beneath his cloak a wooden casket, all carved about its satiny sides with strange runic devices.

Kellin frowned. *Wait—*

But the man turned the casket over and spilled out sticks and cubes. The sticks were blank and black. The cubes turned lurid purple and began a dervish-dance.

"Aye," the man said softly, "you *do* remember me."

Kellin was abruptly sober. He marked the familiar blue eyes, the russet hair, the maddeningly serene expression. *How could I have forgotten?*

"Aye," Corwyth said. "Would you care to play out the game?"

Kellin looked for his watchdogs and saw them spilled slackly across their table. Their attitudes bespoke drunkenness to a man who knew no better; Kellin knew better.

He looked then at the other men who wagered near his own table, and saw they seemed not to know anyone else was in the room.

Breath ran shallowly. Kellin tensed on his stool and quietly took up the knife. "You have come for me."

Corwyth watched the bright cubes spin, seemingly undismayed

by the presence of a weapon. "Oh," he said lightly, "presently. I am in no hurry." He gestured briefly, and the knife fell out of Kellin's hand. "There is no need for that here."

Kellin swore and grabbed at it, only to find the metal searingly hot. "*Ku'reshtin—*" He dropped the knife at once, desiring to blow on burned fingers but holding himself in check. He would not give the Ihlini any measure of satisfaction.

Corwyth's eyes narrowed assessively. "No more the boy," he observed, "but a man well-grown, and dangerous. Someone who must be dealt with."

Kellin did not much care for the implication. "You tried before to 'deal' with me and failed."

"Aye. I misjudged you. A failing I shall not be moved to repeat."

The rune-sticks joined the cubes in an obscene coupling upon the table. Neither man watched. They looked at each other instead.

A vicious joy welled up in Kellin's soul. Here was the fight he had wanted. "I will not accompany you."

"One day," Corwyth said. "Be certain of it, Kellin." He gestured, and the cubes and rune-sticks fell into a pattern: one arrow pointed at Kellin, the other directly north. "You see? Even the game agrees."

As he had done so many years before, Kellin made a fist and banged it down upon the table. The arrows broke up and fell in disarray to the floor. Sticks and cubes scattered.

Corwyth showed good teeth. "This is a game," he said, "mere prelude to what will follow. If you think you have the power to prevent it, you are indeed a fool." Slender fingers were unmoving on scarred wood. "I do not threaten, Kellin; I come to warn instead. Lochiel is too powerful. You cannot hope to refuse him."

"I can. I do." Kellin displayed equally good teeth, but his grin was more feral. "He has tried before and failed, just as you did. I begin to think Lochiel is not so powerful as he would have us believe."

Corwyth's tone was mild. "He need only put out his hand, and you will be in it. He need only close that hand and crush the life from you."

Kellin laughed. "Then tell him to do it."

Corwyth's gaze was steady. "Before, you were a boy. They kept you close, and safe. But you are no longer a boy, and such chains as you have known will bind more than body, but the spirit as well.

Do you not fight those chains? Do you not come often into the Midden, fighting a battle within your soul as well as the war with the constraints of your station?"

Kellin's laughter died. Corwyth knew too much. He was overly conversant with what was in Kellin's mind. "I do what I desire to do. That has nothing to do with Lochiel."

"Ah, but it has *everything* to do with Lochiel. You have a choice, my lord: keep yourself to Homana-Mujhar and away from sorcery, yet know there will always be the threat of a traitorous Homanan." His smile was slight as he purposely evoked the memory of Rogan. "Or come out as you will, as you *desire* to, and know that each step you take is watched by Lochiel."

Kellin controlled the anger. Such a display was what Corwyth wanted to provoke; he would not satisfy him. "Then I challenge Lochiel to try me here and now."

Corwyth shook his head. "A game requires time, my lord, or the satisfaction is tainted . . . much like a man who spends himself too quickly between a woman's thighs. There are the rules to be learned first, before the game commences." The smile was banished. Corwyth leaned forward. "This night, you shall go free. This night you may go home to Homana-Mujhar—or to whatever whore you are keeping—and may sleep without fear for your soul. But you are to know this: you are not free. Your soul is not unclaimed. Lochiel waits in Valgaard. When he touches you, when he deigns to gather you up, be certain you shall know it."

The Ihlini sat back but his gaze did not waver from Kellin's. He smiled again, if faintly, and took something else from beneath his cloak. He set it flat on the table between them.

Sorcerer's Tooth.

The years fell away. Kellin was a frightened boy again lost in Homanan forests, with a tutor slain and a best friend dying, and the Lion on his trail.

"Keep it," Corwyth said, "as a token of my promise."

Kellin leapt to his feet, groping for the knife, but a sheet of purple flame drove him away from the table. When the smoke of it shredded away, the Ihlini was gone.

Chapter Two

Coughing, Kellin went at once to his watchdogs and found them dead. There were no wounds, no marks, no blood to prove what had befallen them, the four men were simply *dead*. They slumped across the table with blank eyes bulging and their flesh a pallid white.

He looked then for the Homanans, expecting some manner of comment, and discovered they no longer existed. The tavernkeeper had vanished as well. Kellin was quite alone in the common room save for the bodies Corwyth had left behind.

Kellin stood perfectly still. Silence was loud, so loud it filled his head and slid down to stuff his belly, until he wanted to choke on it, to spew it forth and deny everything; to somehow put back to rights the horror that had occurred.

The way I wanted Rogan to be alive again— Kellin shut his teeth. *Rogan was a traitor.*

His grip tightened on the knife. Its heat had dissipated. No longer tainted by Corwyth's wishes, it was merely a knife again, if a royal one. The lion hilt mocked him.

He looked around again. All was as before: four dead watchdogs sprawled across the table in a stinking common room of a Midden tavern Kellin was no longer certain truly existed.

Did Corwyth conjure the Homanans? Is this tavern no more than illusion? If so, he was trapped in it.

Kellin shivered, then swore at the response he interpreted as weakness. He went hastily back to his table, caught up his cloak and threw it around his shoulders. With the knife still clutched in one hand, hilt slick with sweat, he went out into the darkness where the air smelled like air, redolent of winter, but without the stink of Corwyth's sorcery.

The walk to Homana-Mujhar was the longest of Kellin's life.

His back was spectacularly naked of watchdogs; he had hated them before but had never wished them dead.

He avoided puddles now. His mouth was filled with the sour aftertaste of *usca*. Drunkenness had passed, as had hostility and the desire to fight. What he wanted most now was to reach Homana-Mujhar and deliver unpleasant news to Brennan, so the burden of the knowledge was no longer his alone.

There were few cobblestones in the Midden. Boots sank into muck, denying easy egress from winding, narrow alleys shut in by top-heavy dwellings. Between his shoulder blades Kellin felt a tingling; the hairs on the nape of his neck rose. He was *lir*less by choice, which left him vulnerable. A bonded warrior would know if an Ihlini was near. He had only his instincts to trust, and they told him it would be a simple thing for Corwyth to take him now, with a Tooth flung into his back.

But the Tooth was back in the tavern. Nothing could have induced him to touch it, let alone to keep it.

Kellin shivered despite the fur-lined cloak. His lips were excessively dry no matter how often he licked them. Corwyth had promised him his freedom tonight; that he might spend the time as he wished. Lochiel was patient.

Muck oozed up, capturing a boot. Kellin paused to free himself, then froze into stillness. A new noise had begun in place of his audible breathing and heartbeat.

The sound was one he knew: a raspy, throaty grunting; the chesty cough of a huge lion.

Gods— He turned convulsively, shoulders slamming against the wall. He heard the scrape of his cloak against brick. Moonlight sparked on the ruby as he lifted the knife.

For one insane moment Kellin saw his shadow on the wall across the narrow alley: the image of a small boy desperate to flee. And then the illusion was banished, replaced with the truth, and he saw himself clearly. No longer the boy. Nightmares were long behind him.

This is how Lochiel intends to take me. This is some trick—

Or perhaps not. After what had happened in the tavern, Kellin was not so certain.

Still, he would not prove such easy prey, to be terrorized by childhood nightmares.

He raised the knife higher. He saw the length of supple fingers, the sinewy back of his hand, the muscle sheathing wrist. He was a man now, and a very different kind of prey.

"Come, then," he said. "If that is you, Corwyth, be certain I am ready. Lochiel will find me no easier to defeat despite opportunity. I am, after all, Cheysuli."

The Lion paused. Noise ceased.

"Come," Kellin goaded. "Did you think to find me so frightened I soiled my leggings? Did you believe it would be *easy?*" He forced a laugh, relying on bravado that was genuine only in part. "Why not banish the Lion's aspect and face me as a man? Or do you fear me after all?"

Grunting and panting faded. The night was silent again.

Kellin laughed as tension fled, leaving him atremble despite his bravado. "So, you prefer to test a boy instead of a man. Well, now you know the truth of it. To take me now, you will have to try harder."

He waited. He thought perhaps Corwyth would resort to ordinary means to attack. But the night was silent, and empty; threat was dispersed.

Kellin drew in a deep breath. *Surely they told stories of my fears when I was a child. It would be a simple matter to shape a lion out of magic now merely to remind me of childhood fears.*

It was a simple explanation, and perhaps a valid one. But a nagging thought remained.

What of Tanni? She was truly gutted.

But men had been bought before: a cook, and Rogan. What if the beast who had slain Blais' *lir* was nothing but a man meant to *make* it look like a beast?

Kellin gripped the knife more tightly. *Corwyth is right. I am no safer now than I was as a child. But I will not order my life around fear; it would be a victory for Lochiel. I will be what I am. If the Ihlini is to take me, he will find it difficult.*

When Kellin reached Homana-Mujhar, he went at once to the watch commander and gave him the news. "Have them brought home," he said. "But also tell those sent to fetch them to touch nothing else. There was an Ihlini abroad tonight."

The captain, a hardened veteran, did not scoff. But Kellin saw the lowered lids, the shuttered thoughts, and knew very well his words were not wholly accepted. Men might be dead, but no Ihlini had come into Mujhara for years. More likely it was his fault, from trouble he had started.

It infuriated him. Kellin grabbed a handful of crimson tunic. "Do you doubt *me?*"

The captain did not hesitate. "Who speaks of doubt, my lord? I will of course do your bidding when the Mujhar confirms it."

"The Mujhar—" Kellin cut it off, gritting teeth against the anger he wanted to spew into the man's face. "Aye, tell the Mujhar; it will save me the trouble." He let go of the crumpled tunic and turned on his heel, striding across to a side entrance so as not to disturb the palace with his late return. *Let the captain tell his beloved Mujhar. I will spend my time on other things.*

He climbed the stairs two at a time, shedding cloak with a shrug of shoulders. He hooked it over an arm, heedless of the dragging hem. When he entered his chamber, he flung the cloak across a stool and hastily stripped out of soiled clothing. Naked, he paced to one of the unshuttered casements and scowled blackly into darkness.

He felt stifled. He felt young *and* old, exquisitely indifferent to life, and yet so filled with it he could not ignore its clamor. Something surged through his veins, charging his body with a vigor so intense he thought he was on fire. His hands trembled as if palsied; Kellin suppressed it with a curse.

A surfeit of energy. It set his bones ablaze. He was burning, *burning.*

"Too bright—" Kellin dug fingers into the sill until at last the burning faded. Emptiness replaced it; he was desolate now, with a spirit wholly diminished. Weakness replaced the hideous strength that had knotted all his muscles.

It is only reaction to what occurred earlier. No more than that.

But Kellin was not certain. Panting, he pressed his head into the wall, letting the stone pit flesh. Fingertips were sore, scraped raw by his grip upon the sill. Everything in him shook.

"Tired." It was much more than that. Kellin staggered to his bed and climbed between the curtains, blessing the servant who had left the warming pan.

But he could not stay there. A restlessness consumed his body and mind and made him accede to its wishes: that he forsake his bed for a physical release that had nothing to do with sex and everything to do with his spirit.

Breeches, no boots. Bare-chested, gripping the knife, Kellin left his chambers and went into the shadowed corridors. He felt as if *he* were a knife, honed sharp and clean and true, balanced in the hand as his own knife was balanced, but the hand which held *him* was none that he knew.

The gods? Kellin wanted to laugh. The old Cheysuli saying about a man's fate resting in the hands of the gods was imagery, no more, and yet he felt as if he fit. As if the hand merely waited.

This is madness. He went to the Great Hall. It had been a long time since he had entered it; it was his grandsire's place. Until Kellin could make it his, he was content to wait: a lean and hungry wolf intently watching its promised meal.

Guilt flickered; was suppressed. *I was bred for it. All the blood that flows in me cries out to rule Homana . . . I was not made of patient clay, and the firing is done.*

He halted before the dais, before the throne, and looked upon the Lion. An old beast, he thought, guarding its pride with aging eyes and older heart, its body tough and stringy, its mouth nearly empty of teeth.

Time runs out for the Lion. Time ran out for them all.

Kellin laughed softly. Slowly he mounted the steps to the throne and sat himself upon it, moving back into the shadows until his spine touched wood. He placed his arms on the armrests, curled his fingers over the paws and felt the extended claws.

"This is Homana," he said. "*This* is Homana—and one day it will be mine."

His fear of the throne was gone. As a child it had frightened him, but he was no longer a child.

Kellin stared out into the hall. "The lion must swallow the lands. The lion must swallow us all."

He roused at the scrape of a boot upon stone floor. "Not a comfortable bed," the Mujhar remarked.

Kellin jerked upright, blinking blearily, stiff and sore and intensely uncomfortable. He had spent what little remained of the night in the bosom of the Lion. The knife was still in his fist. He was warrior enough for that.

Brennan's expression was masked. "Was there any point to it?"

Kellin challenged him immediately. "I do nothing without a point."

His grandfather's mouth twisted scornfully. "What you do is your concern, as you have made it. I gave up years ago asking myself what could be in your mind, to explain your behavior." He gestured sharply. "Get up from there, Kellin. You do not suit it yet."

The insult was deliberate, and he felt it strike true. He wanted to shout back, but knew it would gain him nothing but additional scorn. Of late he and his grandfather had played a game with the stakes residing in dominance. Brennan was the old wolf, Kellin the new; one day the old would die.

Kellin tapped the blade against wooden claws. "Perhaps better suited than you believe."

"Get up from there," Brennan repeated, "or I shall pull you up myself."

Kellin considered it. At a few years beyond sixty the Mujhar was an aging man, but he was not infirm. His hair was completely silver with white frost around his face, but the fierce eyes were steady, the limbs did not tremble, and the arms with their weight of *lir*-gold did not shrivel and sag. *He is taller and heavier than I, and he might be able to do it.*

Kellin rose with practiced elegance. He made an elaborate bow to his grandfather and turned to walk away, but Brennan reached out and caught one arm.

"How much longer?" he rasped. "This comedy we play? Or is it a tragedy?"

Kellin knew the answer. "Tragedy, my lord. What else could these walls house?"

Brennan's mouth flattened into a thin, compressed line of displeasure. "What these walls will house, I cannot say. But what they have housed in the past I can and do say: greater men than you, though they were merely servants."

Killin wrenched his arm away. "You offer insult, my lord."

"I offer whatever I choose. By the gods, Kellin—will you never grow up?"

Kellin spread his hands in mock display. "Am I not a man?"

"No." Brennan's tone was cold. "You are but a boy grown larger in size than in sense."

"Insult yet again." Kellin was unoffended; it was all part of the game though the Mujhar did not view it as such.

"What is your excuse?" Brennan demanded. "That you lost people close to you? Well, do you think I have not? Do you think none of us has suffered as you do?"

Stung, Kellin glared. "What I suffer is my own concern!"

"*And* mine." Brennan faced him down squarely. "You lack a

jehan. You know why. You lost a tutor to sorcery, a friend to treachery, and a liege man to Cheysuli custom. You know how. And yet you choose to wallow in grief and make all of Mujhara suffer."

"Mujhara has nothing to do with this!"

"It does." Brennan's tone did not waver. "How many fights have you sought out—or caused, or joined—because of childish vindictiveness? How many men have you fought—and injured— because they were easy prey for your anger? How many bastards have you sired, duly packed off to Clankeep where you need not concern yourself with them?" More quietly, he said, "And how many guardsmen have died because of you?"

"*None* because of me!"

"Oh? Then what of the four men who died last night?"

"But that was not *my* fault."

"Whose was it, then? I thought you led them there on one of your Midden tours."

Anger boiled up. "Only because you put them on my trail like hounds upon a fox!" Kellin glared. "Call them off, grandsire. Then no more will die."

Brennan's expression was implacable. "Did you do it?"

"Did *I*—?" Kellin was aghast. "You believe I would *kill* them?"

"Aye," Brennan answered evenly. "I believe you might."

"How?" Kellin swallowed the painful lump in his throat. "I am your own grandson. And you accuse me of murder?"

"You have labored assiduously to make me believe you are capable of anything."

"But . . ." Kellin laughed once, expelling air rather than amusement. "I never thought you would *hate* me so."

"Do you think a man must hate another to believe him capable of things another would not do?" Brennan shook his head. "I do not hate you. I know you better than you think, and why you have twisted yourself into this travesty of the Kellin you once were. I cannot understand it, but I am cognizant of *why.*"

"Are you?" The anger was banished now, replaced with bitter helplessness. "You are not me."

"Thank the gods, no." Brennan lifted his shoulders briefly, as if shedding unwanted weight. "You are not as hard as you believe. I see it in you, Kellin. You still care what people think. It all matters to you, but you will not permit yourself to admit it. You fight with yourself; do you think I am blind? I need no *kivarna* to see that two men live in your soul."

"You cannot begin to know—"

"I *can*. I see what drives you, I see what shapes you. I only wish you would not give into it. It does *you* more harm than anyone else."

Kellin lashed out. "I do not care what anyone else thinks, only *you*—" He checked abruptly; he had divulged too much.

Brennan closed his eyes a moment. "Then why this charade? If you truly do care what I think—"

"I do. I know what I have done; it was done intentionally. I do not intend to alter it." Kellin's smile was humorless. "This way, I cannot be hurt."

Lines were graven deeply into Brennan's dark face. "You hurt yourself, this way."

"I can live with myself."

"Can you? Can you cohabit with both men? Or must you destroy one to allow the other more freedom?"

Kellin spat his answer between his teeth. "This is what I wanted. This is what *I* decided. This is what I am."

Brennan made a dismissive gesture. "Another time, then, for this; there is something more important. Tell me what occurred last night."

Kellin sighed and stared down at the knife still clenched in his hand. "It was Corwyth, the Ihlini who killed Rogan and Urchin. He came to the tavern and told me Lochiel still wants me, and will take me whenever he likes. Whenever he wishes, I was told, the Ihlini will put out his hand and I will fall into it."

Brennan nodded. "An old Ihlini trick. He terrorizes victims long before he confronts them."

"I have vanquished the lion," Kellin said, "but he will look for something else. Corwyth has convinced me Lochiel will be as patient as necessary."

"Kellin—"

"They were dead when I reached them." Kellin looked at the knife, recalling the bulging eyes and pallid faces. "There was nothing I could do."

"Then you must stay here," Brennan said. "Homana-Mujhar will shield you."

Kellin barked a laugh. "I would go mad inside a ten-day!"

"There may be no choice."

"*Mad,* grandsire! I am halfway there already." He flipped the knife in his hand, then again, until it spun so the hilt and blade became alternating blurs. In mid-flip he caught it. "I will not stay here."

Brennan's anger showed for the first time since his arrival. "Is this some manner of expiation for your guilt? A twisted version of *i'toshaa-ni?*"

"I feel no guilt," Kellin told him. "*That* is for my *jehan* to do . . . but I think it quite beyond him."

Brennan groaned in sheer frustration. "How many times have I told you? I have said again and again—"

Kellin cut him off. "You have said, and I have heard. But it means nothing. Not until he says it directly to me."

Brennan shook his head. "I will not send word to him again. That is finished."

Kellin nodded. "Because the last time he refused to extend hospitality to your messenger and packed him off home again. So, slighted, you surrender. I think my *jehan* must be mad as well, to speak so to the Mujhar of Homana."

"Aidan does not speak for himself, Kellin. He speaks for the gods."

"Facile words, grandsire. But listen first to yourself—and then recall that he is your *son.* I know very well who should have the ordering of the other."

Brennan lost his temper. Kellin listened in startled surprise; he had never thought to hear such language from his grandfather.

"Go, then." At last the royal fury was spent. "Go into the taverns and drink yourself into a stupor. Go to your light women and sire all the bastards you wish so you may leave them as your *jehan* left you, wondering what manner of man you are to desert a child." A pale indented ring circled Brennan's mouth. "Risk your life and the lives of honorable men so you may enter the game with Lochiel. I no longer care. You are Homana's heir for now, but if I must I can find another."

Kellin laughed at him. "Who can you find? From where? There are no more sons, grandsire; your *cheysula* gave you but one. And no more grandsons, either; Aidan's loins are empty. He is in all ways but half a man."

"Kellin—"

He raised his head. "There is no heir to be found other than the one you invested twenty years ago."

Brennan reached out and caught the flipping knife easily. "You are a fool," he said clearly. "Perhaps Homana would be better off without you."

Kellin looked at the hand that held his knife. He had not expected the weapon to be caught. Brennan was at least as quick as he; a forcible reminder that the Mujhar of Homana was more than merely a man, but a Cheysuli as well.

He met his grandfather's eyes. "May I have it back?"

"No."

He did not avoid the packleader's eyes. To do so was to submit. "I have need of a knife."

"You have another. Use it."

Kellin clenched his teeth. "That one belonged to Blais. I have sworn never to touch it."

"Then unswear it," the Mujhar said. "*Tu'halla dei,* Kellin. Such things as that come easily to a man who cares for nothing."

It was more than he had anticipated. It twisted within his belly. "It shall be as this, then?"

Brennan did not move. "As you have made it."

After a long moment, Kellin averted his stare. The young wolf, he acknowledged ruefully, could not yet pull down the old.

Chapter Three

In his chambers, Kellin sat on the edge of his bed, and stared at the small darkwood chest for a very long time. It rested inoffensively on a bench against the wall, where he had placed it many years before. He had looked at it often, stared at it, hated it, knowing what it contained, but once locked it had never been opened again.

He drew in a deep breath, wishing he need not consider doing what was so difficult, because he had made it so. He realized that in truth he need *not* consider it; it was more than possible for him to get another knife despite his grandfather's suggestion. He could buy one in Mujhara, or find one in the palace, or even go to Clankeep and have one of the warriors make him one; everyone knew Cheysuli long-knives were superior to all others, and only one Cheysuli-made was worth the coin. But the challenge had been put forth. The old wolf mocked the young. The young wolf found it intolerable.

His palms were damp. In disgust Kellin wiped them against his breech-clad thighs. *He tests you with this. Prove to him you are stronger than he thinks.*

Muttering an oath, Kellin slid off his bed and strode without hesitation directly across to the chest. The lid and the key atop it was layered with dust; he had ordered no one to touch the chest. Dust fell away as he picked up the key, smearing fingertips. He blew the iron clean, squinting against motes, hesitated a moment longer, then swore and unlocked the chest. Kellin flung back the lid so sharply it thumped against the wall.

His lips were dry. He wet them. A flutter of anticipation filled his belly. *I would do better to leave this here, as I vowed. I want no part of this. Blais is dead ten years, but it feels like ten hours.* Kellin's jaw clenched so hard his teeth ached. Then he thrust a hand inside and drew out the contents: a single Cheysuli long-knife.

The grief had not lessened with the passage of years, and the act of retrieving the knife intensified it tenfold. Kellin felt the tightening of his belly, the constriction of his throat, the anguish of his spirit. The wound, despite the decade, was still too fresh.

Kellin held the knife lightly, so that it lay crosswise across his palm. Candlelight glinted off steel because the hand beneath it trembled; he could not help himself. He recalled in precise detail the instant of realization, the comprehension that Blais was doomed because his *lir* was dead. In that moment he had come to understand the true cost of the magic that lived in a Cheysuli's blood. And knew how much he feared it.

The gods give warriors lir *not to bless them, but to curse them; to make them vulnerable, so they can never be men but minions instead, set to serve spiteful gods. They give warriors* lir *simply to take them away.*

Kellin stared hard at the knife, daring himself to break down. Beautifully balanced, the steel blade was etched with Cheysuli runes denoting Blais' name and Houses: Homana first, and Erinn. The grip itself was unadorned so as not to interfere with the hand, but the pommel made up for the plainness. An elaborate snarling wolf's head was set with emeralds for eyes.

Kellin's throat closed. To swallow was painful. "A waste," he said tightly. "The gods would have done better to take me in his place."

But they had not, despite his pleas, and he had cursed them for it often. Now he simply ignored them; there was no place in Kellin's life for gods so vindictive and capricious as to first steal his father, then permit his liege man to die.

Anger goaded his bruised spirit. Kellin slammed shut the chest and turned to his belt with its now-empty sheath. He slid the knife home with a decisive motion so that only the wolf's head showed, snarling a warning to the world. *Apropos,* Kellin thought. *Let them all be forewarned.*

He dressed rapidly, replacing soiled breeches with new; a plain wool shirt and velvet doublet, both brown; and Homanan-style boots. Over it all he fastened the belt, brushing the knife hilt with the palm of his hand to make certain of its presence. *Time I tested Corwyth's promise.*

The Mujhar had assigned new watchdogs. Kellin wondered briefly if they knew or were curious about what had become of the last four, but he did not trouble himself to ask. He merely told them curtly to keep their distance, making no effort to befriend them or endear himself to them; he did not want them as friends, and did not particularly care what they thought of him.

This time Kellin rode; so did they. They followed closely, but not so closely as to tread upon his mount's hooves. Testing them—and himself—he led them deep into the Midden to its very heart, where the weight of filth and poverty was palpable.

No one will know me here. And so they would not; Kellin wore nothing to give away his identity save his ruby signet ring, but if the stone were turned inward against his palm no one would see it. He preferred anonymity. Let those of the Midden believe he was a rich Mujharan lordling gone slumming for a lark; he knew better. He wanted a game, and a fight. As he had told the Mujhar, he did nothing without a point.

The tavern he selected lay at the dead end of a narrow, dark street little better than the manure trench behind the hall garderobe in Hornana-Mujhar. It was a slump-shouldered hovel with a haphazard slantwise roof; the low door, badly cracked, hung crooked in counterpoint to the roof. The building resembled nothing so much as a drunkard gone sloppy on too much liquor.

Kellin smiled tightly. *This will do.* He dropped off his horse and waited impatiently for his watchdogs to join him on the ground. "Three of you shall remain here," he said briefly. "One I will take with me, because I must in compromise; it seems I have no choice." He thrust the reins to one of the guardsmen. "Wait here, in the shadows. Do what you are honor-bound to do; I make no claim on your loyalty. You answer the Mujhar's bidding, but answer also a little of mine: leave me to myself this night." He gestured toward one of them. The man was young, tall, blocky-shouldered, with pale blond hair and blue eyes. "You will come in with me, but see you it is done without excess attention. And strip off that tunic."

The young guardsman was startled. "My lord?"

"Strip it off. I want no royal dogs at my heels tonight." Kellin appraised him closely. "What is your name?"

"Teague, my lord."

Kellin gestured. "Now."

Slowly Teague stripped out of his crimson tunic with its black rampant lion. He handed it reluctantly to another guardsman, then looked back at Kellin. "Anything else, my lord?"

"Rid yourself of your sword. Do not protest—you have a knife still." He allowed derision to shape the tone. "Surely more than enough weaponry for a member of the Mujharan Guard."

Cheeks burning, Teague slowly divested himself of the sword-belt and handed it over to the man who held his tunic.

Kellin assessed him again, chewing the inside of his cheek. Finally he sighed. "Even a horse with winter hair still shows its blood." He bent and scooped up a handful of mud, then smeared it purposefully across Teague's mail shirt to dull the polished links and to foul the pristine breeches. He ignored the young man's rigidity and pinched mouth. When he was done, Kellin washed his hands in slushy snow, then nodded at the discomfited guardsman. "They will not know you at once."

Distaste was not entirely suppressed though Teague made the effort. "They will not know me at *all*, my lord."

Kellin grinned. "Better. Now, my orders." He waited until his expectant silence gained Teague's complete attention. "Once we are through that door I am not to be called 'my lord,' nor do I desire your interference in anything I undertake."

Teague's jaw was tight. "We are charged with your life, my lord. Would you have me turn my back on a knife meant for yours?"

Kellin laughed. "Any knife meant for *my* back would have to be fast indeed. I doubt I will come to harm—though the gods know I would welcome the challenge." He gestured at the remaining three guardsmen. "Take the horses and move into the shadows."

"My lord?" Teague clearly had not forsaken the honorific. "It is not for me to reprove you—"

"No. It is not."

"—but I think you should know this is not the best of all places to spend your time drinking or dicing."

"Indeed," Kellin agreed gravely. "That is precisely the point. Now—you are to go in and find your own table. I require two things of you only: to sit apart from me, and to be silent."

Teague cast a scowl at his companions waiting in the shadows, then grudgingly nodded. "Aye."

Kellin jerked a thumb at the door, and the muck-smeared guardsman went in muttering under his breath. Kellin waited until enough time had passed to nullify the appearance of companionship, then went in himself.

The stench of the hovel tavern struck him first. Soiled rushes littered the packed earthen floor in crumbled bits and pieces Kellin was certain harbored all manner of vermin. Only a handful of greasy, sputtering tallow candles illuminated the room, exuding an acrid, rancid aroma and wan, ocherous light easily dominated by shadows. An hour in such a place would render his clothing irredeemable, but Kellin had every intention of remaining longer than that. He anticipated a full night.

Teague sat at a small flimsy table in the corner nearest the door. A crude clay jug stood at his elbow and an equally lumpy cup rested in his hands, but he paid attention to neither.

Their eyes met, slid away. Kellin was faintly surprised that Teague would enter so convincingly into subterfuge. There was no hint of recognition in the guardsman's face and nothing about his posture that divulged his true purpose. Mud clung to his mail shirt; a little had spattered across a cheekbone, altering the angle. His hair now also was mussed, as if he had scrubbed a hand through it hastily. Teague's expression was closed, almost sullen, which suited Kellin's orders and the surroundings.

Kellin was deliberate in his perusal of the room and its occupants, knowing the men measured him as carefully. He allowed them time to mark his clothing, bearing, and size, as well as the heavy knife at his belt. He wanted no one to undervalue him, so that when the fight came it would be on equal terms. He admired the elegant simplicity of organized viciousness.

The tavern was crowded, but mostly because its size was negligible. Most of the men spoke in quiet tones lacking aggression or challenge, as if each knew the other's worth and standing within the context of the tavern, and did not overstep. There would be rivals, Kellin knew, because it was the nature of men, but with the arrival of a stranger old rivalries would be replaced with unity. He and Teague, apart or as one, would be suspect, and therefore targets.

He grinned, and let them see it. He let them see everything as he strode to the lone empty table and sat down upon a stool, shouting to the wine-girl to bring him a jug of *usca.*

She came almost at once to judge the cut of his cloth and the color of his coin. Kellin dropped a silver piece onto the table and let it ring, flicking it in her direction with a single practiced finger. Only the gold of his ring showed; the ruby with its etched rampant lion rested against his palm.

"Usca," he repeated, "and beef."

She was a greasy, unkempt girl with soiled clothing and filthy nails. She offered him a lone grimy dimple and a smile with two teeth missing. "Mutton and pork, my lord."

"Mutton," he said easily, "and do not stint it." She wore a stained, threadbare apron over soiled gray skirts, and the sagging bodice gaped to display her breasts. She bent over to give him full benefit of her bounty. He saw more than she intended: flesh aplenty, aye, and wide, darkened nipples pinching erect under his perusal, but also a rash of insect bites. Dark brown hair swung down in its single braid. A louse ran across her scalp.

"My lord," the woman said, "we have more than just mutton and pork."

She was certain of her charms. In this place, he knew, no man would care about her filth, only the fit of his manhood between her diseased thighs. "Later," he said coolly. "Do not press me."

The brief flash of dismay was overtaken at once by enmity. She opened her mouth as if to respond, then shut it tight again. He saw her reassess his clothing, the coin, then forcibly alter hostility into a sullen acceptance. "Aye, my lord. Mutton and *usca*."

Kellin watched her walk away. Her hips swung invitation as if by habit; the rigidity of her shoulders divulged her injured feelings. He laughed softly to himself; he had frequent congress with Midden whores, but not with one such as she. He did not think much of acquiring lice as boon companions in exchange for a dip in her well-plumbed womanhood.

As he waited for *usca* and mutton, Kellin again assessed the room. His entrance, as expected, had caused comment, but that had died. Men gambled again, paying him no mind except for the occasional sidelong glance. Impatiently he pressed the tip of a fingernail into the edge of the silver piece and flipped the coin on the table. Again and again he did it, so that the coin rang softly, and the wan light from greasy candles glinted dully on the sheen of clean silver.

The woman returned with a boiled leather flask, no cup; and a platter of mutton. She thumped down the platter as he tested the smell of the flask. "Well?"

Kellin caught the tang of harsh liquor through the bitterness of boiled leather. He nodded, then flipped the coin in her direction. She caught it deftly, eyed his intent to discern if his mood toward her had changed; plainly it had not, but she bobbed a quick curtsy in deference to the silver. The overpayment was vast, but she accepted it readily enough with no offer of coppers in change. He had expected none.

"Do ye game?" she asked, jerking her head toward a neighboring table.

And so the dance commenced; Kellin felt the knot of anticipation tie itself into his belly. "I game."

"Do ye wager well?"

Kellin drew the Cheysuh long-knife and sliced into the meat. "As well as the next man."

Emerald wolf's-eyes glinted. She marked them, and stared. "Would ye dice with a stranger?"

Kellin bit into the chunk of meat. It was tough, stringy, foul; he ate it anyway, because it was part of the test. "If his coin is good enough, no man is a stranger."

Indecisive, she chewed crookedly at her lip. Then blurted her warning out. "You lords don't come here. The game is sometimes rough."

"Tame ones bore me." He cut more mutton. Emeralds winked.

Her own eyes shone with avarice. "Luce will throw with you. Will ye have him?"

Kellin downed a hearty swallow of *usca*, then tipped the flask again. Deliberately, he said, "I came here for neither the drink nor the meat. Do not waste my time on idle chatter."

She inhaled a hissing breath. Her spine was stiff as she swung away, but he noted it did not prevent her from walking to the closest table. She bent and murmured to one of the table's occupants, then went immediately into the kitchen behind a tattered curtain.

Kellin waited. He ate his way through most of the mutton, then shoved aside the platter with a grimace of distaste. The rest of the *usca* eventually burned away the mutton's aftertaste.

A second flask was slapped down upon the table even as Kellin set aside the first. The hand that held it was not the woman's. It was wide-palmed and seamed with scars. Thick dark hair sprouted from the back. "Purse," the man said. "I dice against rich men, not poor."

Kellin glanced up eventually. "Then we are well suited."

The man did not smile or otherwise indicate emotion. He merely untied a pouch from his belt, loosened the puckered mouth, and poured a stream of gemstones into his hand. With a disdainful gesture he scattered the treasure across scarred wood. His authority was palpable as he stood beside the table, making no motion to guard his wealth. No one in the tavern would dare test him by attempting to steal a gemstone.

Real, every one. Rubies, sapphires, emeralds, and a diamond or two for good measure. All were at least the size of a man's thumbnail; some were larger yet.

Kellin looked at Luce again. The man was huge. The imagery flashed into Kellin's mind: *A bull*. And so Luce seemed, with his thick neck, and a wide-planed, saturnine face hidden in bushy brown beard. His eyes were dark, nearly black. His crooked teeth were yellow, and he lacked his left thumb.

A *thief*. But caught only once, or the Mujhar's justice would have required more than a thumb.

On thick wrists Luce wore heavy leather bracers studded with grime-rimmed metal. His belt was identical, fastened with a massive buckle of heavy greenish bronze. His clothing was plain homespun wool, dark and unexceptional, but in a concession to personal vanity—and as a mark of his status—he wore a chunky bluish pearl in his right earlobe. In the Midden the adornment marked him a wealthy man.

A *good* thief, then. And undoubtedly dangerous.

Kellin smiled. He understood why the girl had gone to Luce rather than to another. She intended to teach the arrogant lordling a very painful lesson in payment for his rudeness.

He untied his belt-purse, loosened the mouth, then dumped the contents out onto the table. Gold spilled across stained wood, mingling with the glitter of Luce's stones. With it spilled also silver, a handful of coppers, and a single bloody ruby Kellin carried for good luck.

The pile of coins and lone ruby marked Kellin a rich man also, but it did not begin to match the worth of Luce's treasure. He knew that at once and thought rapidly ahead to alternatives. Only one suggested itself. Only one was worth the risk.

The bearded Homanan grunted and began to scoop the gemstones back into his pouch. "A poor man, then."

"No." Kellin's tone was deliberate, cutting through the faint clatter of stone against stone. "Look again." With an elegant gesture he pushed the long-knife into the pile.

He heard the sibilance of indrawn breaths. Luce's presence at Kellin's table had attracted an audience. The huge man was among friends in the Midden; Kellin had none. Even Teague, ostensibly there to guard him, slouched at the back of the crowd and appeared only marginally interested in Luce and the lordling who was not, after all, so rich a man as that—except he had now raised the stakes higher than anyone might expect.

The fingers on Luce's right hand twitched once. His eyes, dark and opaque, showed no expression. "I'll touch it."

"You know what it is," Kellin said. "But aye, you may touch it—for a moment."

The insult was deliberate. As expected, it caused a subtle shifting among the audience. Luce's mouth tightened fractionally in the hedgerow of his beard, then loosened. He picked up the knife and smoothed fingers over the massive pommel, closed on the grip itself, then eventually tested the clean steel as an expert does: he plucked a hair from his beard and pulled it gently across the edge. Satisfied, he twisted his mouth. Then it loosened, slackened, and the tip of his tongue showed as he turned the knife in poor light. Emerald eyes glinted.

Luce wet thick lips. "Real."

Kellin's hands were slack on the table top. Compared to Luce's bulky palms and spatulate fingers, Kellin's were almost girlish in their slender elegance. "I carry no false weapons."

Near-black eyes flicked an assessive glance at Kellin. "Cheysuli long-knife."

"Aye."

Flesh folded upon itself at the corners of Luce's eyes. "You'd risk this."

Kellin shrugged in elaborate negligence. "When I dice, there is no risk."

Thus the challenge was made. Luce's brows met, then parted. "This is worth more than I have."

"Of course it is." Kellin smiled faintly. "A Cheysuli knife cannot be bought, stolen, or copied . . . only earned." Idly he rolled his ruby back and forth on the splintered wood. "Be certain, Homanan—if you win that knife from me, you will have earned it. But if it concerns you now that you cannot match my wager, there is something else you may add."

Luce's eyes narrowed. "What?"

"If you lose," Kellin said, "your other thumb."

The tavern thrummed with low-toned growls of outrage and murmurs of surprise. In its tone Kellin heard the implicit threat, the promise of violence; he had challenged one of their own. But the audacity, once absorbed, was worth a grudging admiration. It was a wager to measure the courage of any man, and Luce had more pride than most to risk. They believed in him, Kellin knew, and that alone would move a reluctant man to accept a wager he would not otherwise consider.

Luce set the knife down very deliberately next to Kellin's hand. It was a subtle display of fairness that was, Kellin believed, uncommon to the Midden, and therefore all the more suspect, but was also a salute to Kellin's ploy. The handsome young lordling was no friend to them, but no longer precisely an enemy. He understood the tenor of their world.

Luce smiled. "A wager worth the making, but over too quickly. Let's save us the knife—and the thumb—for last."

Kellin suppressed a smile. "Agreed."

"One more," Luce cautioned, as Kellin moved to sweep the coins into his pouch, "if you lose the knife, an answer to a question."

Easy enough. "If I can give it."

Luce's gaze did not waver. "You'll tell me how you came by such a knife."

That was unexpected. Kellin was accustomed to those in better taverns recognizing him and therefore knowing he was Cheysuli. But Luce clearly knew nothing at all about him, least of all his race, which suited him perfectly. "It is important to you?"

Luce bent and spat. "I have no love of the shapechangers," he said flatly. "If you got a knife from one of them, it can be done again. I want to find the way. Then I would be on equal ground."

It was puzzling. "Equal ground? With the Cheysuli?"

Luce hitched massive shoulders. "They're sorcerers. Their weapons are bound with spells. If I had a knife, I'd share in the power. If I had two, I could rule it."

Kellin smiled. "Ambitious, for a thief."

Luce's eyes narrowed. "A thief, aye—for now. But these men'll tell you what my ambition earns them." One meaty hand swung out to encompass the room. "Without me they earn scraps. *With* me, they earn feasts." His stare was malignant. "The Midden is mine, lordling, and I'll be keeping it so. It'd be easier done with Cheysuli sorcery."

Kellin displayed his teeth in an undiluted grin then gestured with a sweep of one eloquent hand. "Sit you down, my lord of the Midden, and we shall see precisely what power there is to be won."

Chapter Four

By the time Kellin had won some of Luce's jewels and Luce a portion of Kellin's gold, even Teague had joined the crowd surrounding the table. No one paid him the slightest attention, including the prince he was commanded to protect.

Sweat stippled Kellin's upper lip. Except for the cracked door and holes broken in daub-and-wattle walls, the small room was mostly airless. Now that so many had moved in close to watch, ringing the table, he could not draw a single breath without inhaling also the stench of the tavern and the overriding stink of wool- and grime-swathed men who had not bathed since summer.

Kellin impatiently wiped the dampness from his face with the edge of his hand, knowing his nervousness came as much from belated acknowledgment of Luce's dicing skills as the closeness of the room. He had always been good himself, but Luce was better.

The luck has turned. Kellin tossed back a swallow of *usca* from his third flask, trying to diffuse the nagging sense of trepidation. *It favors Luce, not me—and we are nearly through my coin.*

Left were two silver pieces and a handful of coppers, pitiful remainders of Kellin's once-plump purse. Though he had briefly owned a few of Luce's jewels, the giant had easily won them back and more, including the lone ruby.

That is where my luck went. Kellin eyed the bloody glint in Luce's pile. *He has it now.*

Luce slapped one meaty hand down across the table, scattering the dice and the last few coins of the current wager. Dark eyes glittered. "Enough," he said. "Put up the rest of it, *all* of it—it's time for the final wager."

To buy time, Kellin assessed him. The big man had consumed cup after cup of *usca,* but nothing of it showed in eyes or manner. There was no indication Luce was any less sober than when the wine-girl first approached him, only a fixed desire to begin the final pattern of the dance.

Kellin inhaled slowly and deeply, trying to clear his head. An unexpected desperation made him nervous and irritable, doubling the effects of his overindulgence in *usca*. His belly was unsettled as well as his spirit. He could not bear the knowledge he might well lose Blais' knife. He had only risked the weapon because he had been certain of keeping it.

Luce smiled for the first time. Behind him, Kellin heard the murmuring of the Homanans. Their anticipation was clearer, as was their absolute faith in Luce's ability. Kellin found it particularly annoying.

He shoved all that remained of his wealth into the center of the table, mingling it with jewels, coins, and dice, then challenged Luce in silence.

The big man laughed. "All, is it?" He flicked onto the pile a glittering diamond. "Worth more than yours," he said offhandedly, "but I'll have it back anyway." Then, with abject contempt, he jabbed a hand toward Kellin. "Your throw. Boy."

The insult stung, as it was intended, but not so much after all. To Luce, he *was* a boy, for the man was much older—but something else was far more imperative than answering a gibe at his youth and inexperience.

If I could win this throw, I could yet string out the game awhile and avoid offering the knife. Teeth set tightly, Kellin scooped up the six ivory dice. Carved markings denoted their value. He threw, and counted the values before the dice stopped rolling.

Leijhana tu'sai— Relief crowded out the desperation in Kellin's belly. Sweat dried on his face. He maintained a neutral expression only with great effort, and only because he knew it would annoy Luce. "*Your* throw," he said negligently, relaxing on his stool. Inwardly jubilant, he waited. The crowd around the table stirred; only one value could beat the total on Kellin's dice, and it was not easily accomplished.

Luce grunted and grabbed the dice. His mouth moved silently as he whispered something and shook the cubes in his hand.

A body shifted behind Kellin, breaking his concentration. A voice said irritably: "Don't push!"

Kellin ignored it, watching Luce entreat the dice to fall his way, but within a moment the body pressed close again, brushing his shoulder. Kellin leaned forward in an attempt to escape the crowding. *If they take no care, they will upset the table—*

And they did so just as Luce threw. A body fell into Kellin, who was in turn shoved against the table. Coins, jewels, and dice spilled, showering the rush-littered floor.

Even as Kellin, swearing, rose to avoid overturned *usca,* he recognized the miscreant. The expression in Teague's eyes was one of calculation and satisfaction, not regret or anger, though he voiced a sharp protest against the man who had caused him to fall.

For only a moment Kellin's curiosity roused. Then he turned back to Luce, who cursed savagely and dropped to his knees, scrabbling for dice. Others were on the floor also, gathering coin and gemstones.

How many will make their way into purses and pockets? And then Kellin reflected that probably none would; Luce's hold over the men was too strong. A copper here and there might disappear, but nothing of significance.

Luce came up from the floor, broad face dark in anger. A malignancy glittered in near-black eyes. "The dice," he grated. "I have them all, but one."

Teague held it aloft. "I have it." His smile was odd as he tossed the cube in his left hand; the right lingered very near his knife.

Luce thrust out a hand. "Give it here."

"I think not." Teague had discarded his truculence and sloppy posture. He looked directly at Kellin. "The die is weighted improperly. You have been cheated."

"A *lie!*" Luce thundered.

Teague tossed the cube to Kellin. "What say you?"

Frowning, Kellin rolled the smooth ivory in his fingers. It felt normal enough. The ploy could well be Teague's way of rescuing him from a difficult situation.

He flashed a glance at the guardsman and saw nothing but a cool, poised patience. Nothing at all indicated Teague might be lying.

Kellin considered. A second test of the cube divulged a faint roughness at one rounded corner, but that could come from years of tavern use rather than purposeful weighting.

"A lie," Luce declared. "Give it here."

Kellin stared back. "You deny the charge."

"I do!"

"Then you will have no objection if we test it." Kellin kicked aside bits and pieces of soiled rushes. He grimaced in distaste as he knelt down on the packed earthen floor. It was a vulnerable position, with Luce towering over him, but he assumed it with as much nonchalance as he could muster. He dared not hesitate now, not before the ring of hostile faces.

"A lie," Luce repeated.

Kellin draped one forearm across a doubled knee. He gripped the die loosely in his right hand. "If it is a fair roll, you shall have the knife." He saw it in Teague's hand, emerald eyes glittering. "Otherwise, your remaining thumb is forfeit."

Luce breathed audibly. "Throw it, then."

Kellin opened his fingers and dropped the cube. It bounced, rattled, then stilled.

"You see?" Luce declared.

Kellin smiled. "Patience is not your virtue." He retrieved the die. "If the identical value shows four more times, I think there will be no question—"

Luce bellowed an order.

Kellin uncoiled from the floor and caught the knife easily as Teague slapped it into his hand. The blade rested against Luce's massive belly, forestalling any attack by others. "I offer you two things," Kellin said clearly. "First, your life; I have no desire to gut you here. It would only add to the stench." He showed the big man his teeth. "The other is the answer to your question. You see, I got this knife—" he pressed the tip more firmly against Luce's belly above the bronze buckle, "—in a sacred ritual. Few Homanans know about it; only one has witnessed it. His name was Carillon." Jubilation welled up in Kellin's spirit. He had risked himself, and won. "It is the custom to exchange knives when a Cheysuli liege man swears blood-oath to serve the Prince of Homana."

Luce's disbelief and fury began as a belly-deep growl and rose to a full-throated roar. *"Prince—"*

Kellin cut it off with a firmer pressure against the heavy belly. "Cheysuli as well, Homanan. *Tahlmorra lujhala mei wiccan, cheysu.*" He laughed, delighted to see the comprehension in Luce's face. "Now, perhaps we should discuss your thumb."

"Gut me, then!" Luce roared, and brought his knee up sharply.

The knife did not by much beat the knee to its target, but Kellin's thrust was almost immediately rendered ineffective. He *intended* to sheath the steel in Luce's belly, but the man's upthrust knee, driving home with speed and accuracy, deprived Kellin of everything except a burst of incredible pain, and the knowledge—even as he collapsed—that he had made a deadly mistake.

—*never hesitate*— But he had. Now he lay writhing on the filthy floor of a dirtier tavern, wondering if he would survive long enough to find out if he could bed a woman again.

He had cut Luce, perhaps deeply, but not deeply enough to kill; he heard the man shouting orders to his confederates. Hands closed on Kellin even as he groaned and tried to swallow the *usca* that threatened to exit his body. Bile burned in the back of his throat.

Teague. Somewhere. But they were two against too many.

For a fleeting moment Kellin wished he had not been so adamant about posting the remaining watchdogs outside, but there was no time for recriminations. He had lost his knife on the floor and had only his wits and skills with which to save his life.

Hands dragged him upright. Kellin wanted very badly to lie down again, but he dared not if he were to preserve his life. So he tapped the pain, used the pain as a goad, and channeled it into a weapon.

He tore loose of the hands holding him, jabbing with elbows and stomping with booted feet. One man he butted so firmly beneath the chin that teeth crunched. Something sharp sliced across his outflung hands, grated across knuckles; a second knife jabbed him in the back. But its tip fouled on the heavy winter doublet as he spun away.

Kellin lashed out with a boot and smashed a knee, then jammed an elbow into the man's face as he doubled over. Blood spurted as the nose broke, spraying Kellin as well as the Homanan.

Teague. Near, he knew; he could hear the guardsman swearing by the name of the Mujhar. Kellin hoped Teague was armed with more than oaths. *If I could find the door—*

A table was shoved into his path. Kellin braced, then swung up onto it, kicked out again, caught one man's jaw flush. The head snapped back on its neck. The man fell limply even as another replaced him.

Someone slashed at his leg. Kellin leapt high into the air and avoided the knife, but as he came down again the flimsy table collapsed. In a spray of shattered wood and curses, Kellin went down with it.

Something blunt dug into his spine as he rolled. *Wood, not blade—*

"Mine!" Luce roared. "He's mine to kill!"

"Teague!" Kellin shouted.

"My lord—" But the answering shout was cut off.

Kellin thrust himself upward. Arms closed around his chest, trapping his own arms in a deadly hug. His spine was pressed against the massive belt buckle; his head beneath Luce's chin. The Homanan's strength was immense.

A sharp, firm squeeze instantly expelled what little breath was left in Kellin's lungs. The human vice around his chest denied him another. Speckles crept into the corners of his eyes, then spread to threaten his vision.

Kellin writhed in Luce's grasp. He kicked but struck air, and the big man laughed. "Boy," Luce said, "your gods can't hear you now."

He had not petitioned the gods. Now he did, just in case, even as he snapped his head backward in a futile attempt to smash Luce's face. He struck nothing but muscled neck. Luce's grip tightened.

Frenziedly, Kellin fought. His breath was gone, and his strength, but desperation drove him. He would not give up. A Cheysuli warrior never gave up.

Luce, laughing, shook him. A rib protested. "Little prince," he baited, "where is your liege man now?"

Blais would not permit this— Kellin arched his body in a final attempt at escape, then went limp. Blood dripped from the corner of his mouth. He hung slackly in thick arms.

Luce squeezed him a final time, threw him down. "I'll have that knife, now."

Kellin's breath came back in a rush. He heard himself gasping and whooping as his lungs filled slowly, then understood what Luce intended to do. "No knife—*mine*—" And it was there, kicked beneath shattered wood; Kellin clawed for it, touched it, closed trembling fingers upon it even as Luce saw his intent. But before the big man could react, Kellin's hand closed over the hilt.

He came up from the floor in one awkward lunge, still gasping for breath, still doubled up from the pain of his bruised ribs. But to hesitate or protect himself guaranteed death; Kellin slashed out repeatedly, carving himself a clearing. He saw the glint of a swordblade—*no, two*—and realized the watchdogs were present at last. Teague had reached the door, or else they had heard the commotion.

Luce?

The man was there, armed as well. The knife he held was not so elaborate as Kellin's, but its blade was equally deadly. Near-black eyes were fastened on Kellin's face. "I'll have that long-knife yet."

Blood trickled into Kellin's right eye as he sucked at air. He scrubbed a forearm across his brow, shook back damp hair, then grinned at the big man. Without the breath to answer, Kellin beckoned Luce on with the waggle of one hand.

By now most of the fighting had been stopped, or stopped of its own accord. It had come down to Kellin and Luce. The silence in the tavern was heavy with expectation.

Luce still watched him, judging his condition. Kellin knew it well enough: he was half-sick on *usca* and the blow from Luce's knee, as well as bruised about the ribs. He was stippled by half a dozen nicks and slices, and a cut across his brow bled sluggishly, threatening his vision.

Kellin forced a ragged laugh. "Are you truly the king of the Midden? Do you think yourself fit to rule? Then *show* me, little man. Prove to a Cheysuli you are fit to hold his knife."

Luce came on, as expected. Kellin stood his ground, watching the man's posture and the subtle movements of his body; when Luce's momentum was fully engaged, his intent divulged, Kellin slipped aside and thrust out a boot. Luce stumbled, cursed, then fell against a table. His hands thrust out to brace himself.

With a single definitive blow of Blais' knife, Kellin chopped down and severed the thief's remaining thumb. "There," he said, "the debt now is paid."

Luce screamed. He clutched his bleeding hand against his chest. "Shapechanger sorcery!"

Kellin shook his head, still trying to regain his breath. "Just a knife in the hand of a man. But enough for you, it seems."

The conquest of Luce ended the fight entirely. Kellin saw bloodied faces and gaping mouths, torn clothing and gore-splattered hair. The crimson tunics of the watchdogs glowed like pristine beacons in the smoky shadows of the tavern.

He ached. His profaned manhood throbbed. He wanted no more than to lie down in the slushy snow and cool the heat of pain, to drive away the sickness, to regain in the bite of winter the self-control he had forfeited to a despised desperation.

Kellin wanted no one, thief or guardsman, to see how much he hurt. Without a word, without an order, he turned and walked through the crowd and pushed open the cracked door, taking himself from the tavern into the cold clarity of the alley. The stench was no better there, but the familiar glitter of stars was an infinite improvement over the opaque malignancy of Luce's enraged stare.

Kellin looked at the horses and very nearly flinched. He could not bear the idea of riding.

"My lord?" It was Teague, exiting the tavern. He was bloodied and bruised and very taut around the mouth. "We should get you to Homana-Mujhar."

The response was automatic. "If I choose to go."

Teague neither flinched nor colored. His tone was pitched to neutrality. "Are you done for the evening, my lord?"

Kellin gifted him with a scowl as the other guardsmen filed out of the tavern. "Is there something else you wished to do?"

Teague shrugged. "I thought perhaps you might desire to find another game." He paused. "My lord."

As he collected breath and wits, Kellin considered any number of retorts. Most of them were couched in anger or derision. But after what Teague had done, he thought the guardsman deserved better.

He blew out a frosted breath, then drew another into a sore chest. He wanted to lie down, or bend over, or lean against the wall, but he would do none of those things or risk divulging discomfort. Instead, he asked a question. "*Was* the die improperly weighted?"

Teague grinned. "As to that, I could not swear. But when Luce spread his hand down across the pile and challenged you to the final throw, I saw one die replaced with another. It seemed logical to assume it was weighted to favor Luce."

Kellin grunted agreement. "But it was not replaced before."

"No, my lord."

"You are certain?"

"My lord—" With effort, Teague suppressed a smile and did not look at his companions. "I am moved to say your luck was bad tonight."

"And, no doubt, my tavern selection." Kellin sighed and pressed a hand against sore ribs. "I am going home. You may come, or go, as you wish. It is nothing to me."

Teague considered it. "I think I will come, my lord." The faintest glint brightened his eyes. "I would like to hear what the Mujhar has to say when you arrive on his front step."

It was momentarily diverting. "To me, or to you?"

"To you, my lord. I have done my duty."

Kellin scowled. "It is not the Mujhar who concerns me."

"Who, then?"

It was an impertinence, but Kellin was too tired and sore to remind Teague of that. "The queen," he muttered. "She is Erinnish, remember? And possessed of a facile tongue." He sighed. "My ears will be burning tonight, as she can no longer redden my rump."

Teague surrendered his dignity to a shout of laughter. Then he recalled whom it was he served—the royal temper, Kellin knew, was notorious—and quietly gathered up the reins of his own mount and Kellin's. "I will walk with you, my lord."

The assumption stung. "And if I mean to ride?"

"Then I will ride also." Teague lowered his eyes and stared inoffensively at the ground. "But I daresay my journey will be more comfortable than yours."

Kelin's face burned. "I daresay."

The Prince of Homana walked all the way home as his faithful watchdogs followed.

Chapter Five

The Queen of Homana pressed a wine-soaked cloth against the wound in her grandson's scalp. "Sit still, Kellin! 'Tis a deep cut."

He could not help himself; he lapsed into an Erinnish lilt in echo of her own. "You'll be making it deeper, with this! D'ye mean to go into my brain?"

" 'Twould keep you from further idiocy, now, wouldn't it?" The pressure was firm as she worked to stanch the dribbling blood.

"That I doubt," Brennan said. "Kellin courts idiocy."

" 'Twould seem so," Aileen agreed equably. Then, when Kellin meant to protest, "Sit *still*."

Between them, they will slice me into little pieces. Kellin sat bolt upright in a stool in his chambers, bare to the waist. He was not in the slightest disposed to remain still as she pressed liquor into his scalp, because he could not. It stung fiercely. The right side of his chest was beginning to purple from Luce's affectionate hug, but Kellin was not certain Aileen's ministrations—or her words—would be gentler.

"You could bind his ribs," she suggested crisply to Brennan, "instead of standing there glowering like an old wolf."

"No," Kellin answered, knowing the Mujhar's hands would be far less gentle than hers. "You do it, granddame."

"Then stop twitching."

"It *hurts*."

Aileen sighed as she peeled back the cloth and inspected the oozing cut beneath. "For a Cheysuli warrior, my braw boyo, you're not so very good at hiding your pain."

"The *Erinnish* in me," he muttered pointedly. "Besides, how many Cheysuli warriors must suffer a woman to pour liquid fire into their skulls?"

Aileen pressed closed the cut. "How many *require* it?"

Kellin hissed. He slanted a sidelong glance at his grandfather. "I am not the first to rebel against the constraints of his rank."

The gibe did not disturb the Mujhar in the least. He stood quietly before his battered grandson with gold-weighted arms folded, observing his queen's ministrations. "Nor will you be the last," Brennan remarked. "But as that comment was aimed specifically at me, let me answer you in like fashion: dying before you inherit somewhat diminishes the opportunity to break free of my authority." He arched a brow. "Does it not?"

Kellin gritted his teeth. "I'm not looking to die, grandsire—"

"You give every indication of it."

"—merely looking for entertainment, something to fill my days, something to quench my taste—"

"—for rebellion." Brennan smiled a little. "Nothing you tell me now cannot be countered, Kellin. For that matter, you may as well save your breath, which is likely at this moment difficult to draw through bruised ribs—" the Mujhar cast him an ironic glance, "—because I know very well what you will say. I even know what *I* will say; it was said to me and to my *rujholli* several decades ago."

Kellin scowled. "I am not you, or Hart, or Corin—"

"—or even Keely," Aileen finished, "and I've heard this before, myself." Her green eyes were bright. "Now both of you be silent while I wrap up your ribs."

Kellin subsided into glum silence, punctuated only by an occasional hissed inhalation. He did not look again at his grandsire, but stared fixedly beyond him so he would not provoke a comment in the midst of intense discomfort.

He had told them little of the altercation in the tavern, saying merely that a game had gone bad and the fight was the result. No deaths, he pointed out; the Mujhar, oddly, asked about fire, to which Kellin answered in puzzlement that there was no fire, only a little blood. It had satisfied Brennan in some indefinable way; he had said little after that save for a few caustic comments.

Kellin sat very still as Aileen worked, shutting his teeth against the pain—he would *not* permit her to believe he was less able than anyone else to hold his tongue—and said nothing. But he was aware of an odd sensation that had little to do with pain.

"—still," she murmured, as a brief tremor claimed his body.

Kellin frowned as she snugged the linen around his ribs. *What is—?* And then again the tremor, and Aileen's muttered comment, and his own unintended reaction: every inch of flesh burned so intensely he sweated with it.

Brennan frowned. "Perhaps I should call a surgeon."

"No!" Kellin blurted.

"If there is that much pain—"

"—isn't *pain*," Kellin gritted. "Except—for that—" He sucked in a hissing breath as Aileen pulled linen taut against sore flesh. "Call no one. Grandsire."

He held himself still with effort. It *wasn't* pain, but something else entirely, something he could not ignore, that burned through flesh into bone with a will of its own, teasing at self-control. Fingers and toes tingled. It spread to groin and belly, then crept upward to his heart.

"Kellin?" Aileen's hands stilled. "*Kel*lin—"

He heard her only dimly, as if water filled his ears. His entire being was focused on a single sensation. It was very like the slow build toward the physical release of man into woman, he thought, but with a distinct difference he could not voice. He could not find the words. He knew only there was a vast and abiding *thing* demanding his attention, demanding his body and soul.

"Ihlini?" he murmured. "Lochiel?"

He need only put out his hand, Corwyth had said, and Kellin would be in it.

His ribs were strapped and tied. He could not breathe.

—could not *breathe*—

"Kellin!" Aileen's hands closed on his naked shoulders. "Can you hear me?"

He could. Clearly. The stuffy distance was gone. The burning subsided, as did the tremors. He felt it all go, leaching him of strength. He sat weak and trembling upon the stool, sweat running down his face. Damp hair stuck to his brow.

Gods— But he cut it off. He would not beg aid or explanation from those he could not honor.

Kellin clenched his teeth within an aching jaw. For a moment the room wavered around him, running together until all the colors were gone. Everything was a fleshy gray, lacking depth or substance.

"Kellin?" The Mujhar.

He could make no answer. He blinked, tried to focus, and vision eventually steadied. His hearing now was acute, so incredibly acute he heard the soughing of the folds of Aileen's skirts as she turned to Brennan. He could smell her, smell *himself:* the bitter tang of his own fear, the acrid bite of rebelling flesh.

"Brighter—" he blurted, and then the desolation swept in, and emptiness, and a despair so powerful he wanted to cry out. He was a shell, not a man; a hollow, empty shell. Shadow, not warrior, a man lacking in heart or substance, and therefore worthless among his clan.

In defiance of pain, Kellin lurched up from the stool. He shuddered. Tremors began again. He felt the protest of his ribs, but they did not matter. He took a step forward, then caught himself. For a moment he lingered, trapped upon the cusp, then somehow found the chamberpot so he could spew his excesses into pottery instead of onto the floor.

Even as Aileen murmured sympathy, Brennan cut her off. "He deserves it. The gods know Hart and Corin did, *and* Keely, when they followed such foolish whims."

"And what of *your* whims?" she retorted. "You did not drink overmuch, but you found Rhiannon instead."

Kellin stood over the chamberpot, one arm cradling his chest. It hurt to bend over, hurt to expell all the *usca,* hurt worse to draw a breath.

He straightened slowly, irritated by his grandparents' inconsequential conversation, but mostly humiliated by the dictates of his body. He felt no better for purging his belly. Sickness yet lurked within, waiting for the moment he least expected its return.

Brennan's tone was uncharacteristically curt, but also defensive as he answered his *cheysula.* "Rhiannon has nothing to do with *this.*"

"She was your downfall as much as gambling was Hart's and *I* was Corin's!" Aileen snapped. "Don't be forgetting it, Brennan. We all of us do things better left undone. Why should Kellin be different?"

He shivered once more, and then his body stilled. In quiescence was relief, carefully Kellin sought and found a cloth to wipe his mouth. It hurt too much to move; he leaned against the wall. Brickwork was cool against overheated flesh.

Distracted by his movement, Aileen turned from her husband. "Are you well?"

"How can he be well?" Brennan asked. "He has drunk himself insensible and now suffers for it, as well as for a fight that nearly stove in his chest." His mouth hooked down in derision. "But he is young, for all of that; he will begin again tomorrow."

"No," Kellin managed. "Not tomorrow." The room wavered again. He caught at brickwork to keep from falling.

"Kellin." The derision was banished from Brennan's tone. "Sit down."

The floor moved beneath Kellin's feet. Or was *he* moving?

"He's ill!" Aileen cried. "Brennan—*catch*—"

But the command came too late. Kellin was aware of a brief detached moment of disorientation, then found himself sprawled across the floor with his head in the Mujhar's arms.

He was cold, so *cold*—and a wail of utter despair rose from the depths of his spirit. "—empty—" he mouthed. "—*lost*—"

Brennan sat him upright and held him steady, examining his eyes. "Look at me."

Kellin looked. Then vision slid out of focus and the wail came back again. A sob tore loose in his chest. "Grandsire—"

"Be still. Look at me." Brennan cradled Kellin's head in his hands, holding it very still.

"Are you wanting a surgeon?" Aileen asked crisply.

"No."

"Earth magic, then."

"No."

"Then—"

"*Shansu,*" Brennan told her. "This is something else, *meijhana.* Something far beyond the discontent caused by too much *usca.*"

It was indeed. If not for the Mujhar's hands holding him in place, Kellin believed he might fall through the floor and beyond. "—too hard—" he whispered. "Too—"

"—empty," Brennan finished, "and cold, and alone, torn apart from the world and everything in it."

"—*lost*—"

"And angry and terribly frightened, and very small and worthless."

Kellin managed to nod. The anguish and desolation threatened to overwhelm him. "How can—how can you know?"

Brennan's severity softened. "Because I have felt it also. Every Cheysuli does when it is time to bond with his *lir.*"

"*Lir!*"

"Did you really believe you would never have one?" Brennan's smile was faint. "Did you believe you would not need one?"

"I renounced it!" Kellin cried. "When Blais left—I *swore*—"

"Some oaths are as nothing."

"I renounced a *lir*, and the gods." It was incomprehensible that now, after so long without one, he might require a *lir*, or that he should have to battle the interference of gods he did not honor.

"Clearly the gods did not renounce *you*," Brennan said dryly. "Now the time is come."

Kellin summoned all his strength; it was a pathetic amount. "I refuse."

The Mujhar smiled. "You are welcome to try."

Aileen was shocked. "You are overharsh!"

"No. There is nothing he can do. It is his time, Aileen. He will drive himself mad if he continues this foolishness. He must go. He is Cheysuli."

"And—Erinnish . . . and Homanan—and all the other lines—" Kellin shivered. " 'Tis all I count for, is it not? My seed. My blood. Not Kellin at *all!*" His spirit felt as cold and hard as the floor. Desperately, he said, "I renounce my *lir*."

"Renounce as you will," Brennan said, "but for now, get up on the stool."

Kellin gritted his teeth. "You are the Mujhar, blessed by the gods. I charge you to take it away."

"What—the pain? You earned it. The emptiness? I cannot. It can only be filled with a *lir*."

"Take it away!" Kellin shouted. "I cannot live like this!"

Brennan rose. His eyes, so intensely yellow, did not waver. "You have the right of *that*," he agreed. "You cannot live like this."

"Grandsire—"

"Get up, Kellin. There is nothing to be done."

He got up. He ached. He swore, even before Aileen. He was profoundly empty, bereft of all save futility and a terrifying *apartness*. "I renounced it," he said, "just as I renounced the gods. They have no power over me."

Brennan turned to Aileen. "I will have *usca* sent up. Best he dulls his pain with that which caused it; in the morning he will be better—" he slanted a glance at his grandson, "—or he will be worse."

She was clearly displeased. "Brennan."

The Mujhar of Homana extended a hand to his queen. "There is *nothing* to be done, Aileen. Whether or not he likes it, Kellin is Cheysuli. The price is always high, but no warrior refuses to pay it."

"I do," Kellin declared. "*I* refuse. I will not accept a *lir*."

Brennan nodded sagely. "Then perhaps you should spend the next few hours explaining that to the gods."

Chapter Six

"Leijhana tu'sai," Kellin murmured as his grandparents shut the door behind them. He was sick to death of Brennan's dire predictions and Aileen's contentiousness; could they not simply let him alone? *They try to shape me to fit their own idea of how a prince should be.*

Or perhaps they attempted to shape him into something other than his father who had renounced his rank and title as Kellin renounced his *lir*.

He drew in a hissing breath and let it out again, trying to banish pain as he banished the previous thought. Kellin had no desire to consider how his behavior might affect his grandparents, or that the cause of his own rebellion was incentive for the very expectations he detested. Such maunderings profited no one, save perhaps the occasional flicker of guilt searching for brighter light. He had no time for such thoughts; his ribs ached, and his manhood as yet reminded him of its abuse. Best he simply took to his bed; perhaps he would fall asleep, and by morning be much improved in health and spirit.

But restlessness forbade it even as he approached the bed. He was dispirited, disgruntled, highly unsettled. Even his bones itched. His body would not be still, but clamored at him for *something*—

"What?" Kellin gritted. "What is it I'm to do?"

He could not be *still*. Frustrated, Kellin began to pace, hoping to burn out the buzz in blood and bones. But he managed to stop only when he reached the polished plate hanging cockeyed on the wall.

He stared gloomily at his reflection: a tall man, fair of skin—*for a Cheysuli,* he thought, *though dark enough for a Homanan!*—with green eyes dilated dark and new bruises on his face.

Aileen's applications of wine had stiffened his hair. Kellin impatiently scrubbed a hand through it, taking care to avoid the crusting cut. The raven curls of youth were gone, banished by adulthood, but his hair still maintained a springy vigor. He scratched idly at his chest, disliking the tautness of the wrappings. The linen bandages stood out in stark relief against the nakedness of his torso.

Kellin stared at his reflection, then grinned as he recalled the cause of sore ribs. "And what of the thumbless thief?"

But the brief jolt of pleasure and vindication dissipated instantly. Luce was not important. Luce did not matter. Nothing at *all* mattered except the despair that welled up so keenly to squash his spirit flat.

Kellin turned from the plate abruptly. Better he not look; better he not *see*—

Emptiness overwhelmed, and the savage desire to tear down all the walls, brick by brick, so he could be free of them.

He burned with it. Cursing weakly, Kellin lurched to the narrow casement. Beyond lay Homana of the endless skies and meadows, the freedom of the air. He was confined by walls, oppressed by brickwork; every nerve in his body screamed its demand for freedom.

"Get out—" he blurted.

He needed desperately to get out, get free, get *loose*—

"Shadow," he murmured. "Half-man, hollow-man—" And then he squeezed shut his eyes as he dug fingers into stone. "I will not . . . will not be what they expect me to be—"

Cold stone bit into his brow, hurting his bruised face; he had pressed himself against the wall beside the window. Flame washed his flesh and set afire every nick, scratch, and cut. Rising bruises ached as blood throbbed in them, threatening to break through the fragile warding of his skin.

He paced because he could not help himself; he could not be still. A singing was in his blood, echoing clamorously. He paced and paced and paced, trying to suppress the singing, the overriding urge to squeeze himself through the narrow casement and fling himself into the air.

"—fall—" he muttered. "Fall, and break all my bones—"

Hands fisted repeatedly: a cat flexing its claws, testing the power in his body, the urge to slash into flesh.

He sweated. Panted. Swore at capricious gods. He wanted to

open the door, to tear it from its hinges, to shatter the wood completely and throw aside iron studs.

Kellin sat down on the stool and hugged bare arms against wrapped chest, ignoring the pain. He rocked and rocked and rocked: a child in need of succor; a spirit in need of release.

Tears ran down his face. "Too many—" he said. "Too *many* . . . I will not risk losing a *lir*—" Only to lose himself to an arcane Cheysuli ritual that robbed the world of another warrior despite his perfect health.

*Lir*less warriors went mad, he had been taught, as all Cheysuli were taught. Mad with the pain and the grief, the desperate emptiness.

"—mad *now*—" he panted. "Is this different?"

Perhaps not. Perhaps what he did now was invite the very madness he did not desire to risk in bonding with a *lir*.

Brickwork oppressed him. The walls and roof crushed his spirit.

"Out—" he blurted. But to go out was to surrender.

He rocked and rocked and rocked until he could rock no more; until he could not countenance sitting on the stool another moment and rose to pace again, to move from wall to wall, to stand briefly at the casement so as to test his will, to dare the desperate need that drove him to pace again, until he reached the door.

Unlocked. Merely latched. He need only *lift* the latch—

"No." A tremor wracked Kellin's body. He suppressed it. He turned away, jubilant in his victory, in the belief he had overcome it—and then felt his will crumble beneath the simplicity of sheer physical need.

It took but a moment: boots, doublet, russet wool cloak, long-knife. Emeralds winked in candlelight.

Kellin stared at the knife. Vision blurred: tears. Tears for the warrior who had once sworn by the blade, by his blood, by the *lir* whose death had killed him.

He thought of the words Blair had offered him a decade before.

It hurt. It *squeezed,* until no room was left for his heart; no room remained for his spirit.

"Y'ja'hai," Kellin breathed, then unlatched and jerked open the door.

*   *   *

He did not awaken the horse-boy sleeping in straw. He simply took a bridle, a horse—without benefit of blankets or saddle—and swung up bareback.

Pain thundered in Kellin's chest. He sat rigidly straight, daring himself to give in as sweat trickled down his temples. Scrapes stung from the taste of salt, but he ignored them. A smaller pain, intrusive but less pronounced, reminded him of his offended netherparts, but that pain, too, he relegated to nothing in the face of his compulsion.

Winter hair afforded him a better purchase bareback than the summer season, when mounts were slick-haired and the subsequent ride occasionally precarious. It was precarious now, but not because of horsehair; a rider was required to adapt to his mount's movements by adjustments in body both large and small, maintaining flexibility above all else, but the skill was stripped from Kellin. With ribs bruised and tightly strapped, he was forced to sit bolt upright without bending his spine, or risk significant pain.

He knew the way so well: a side-gate in the shadows, tucked away in the wall; he had used it before. He used it now, leaving behind the outer bailey, then Mujhara herself as he rode straight through the city to the meadowlands beyond. The narrow track was hard footing in the cold, glinting with frost rime in the pallor of the moon.

No more walls— Kellin gritted his teeth. *No more stone and brick, no more streets and buildings—*

Indeed, no more. He had traded city for country, replacing cobbles with dirt and turf, and captivity for freedom.

But the emptiness remained.

If I give myself over to the lir-*bond, I will be no different from any warrior whose promise to* cheysula *and children to care for them always is threatened by that very bond.*

It seemed an odd logic to Kellin. How could one promise supersede the other, yet still maintain its worth? How could any warrior swear himself so profoundly to *lir* and family knowing very well one of the oaths might be as nothing?

For that matter, how could *cheysula* or child believe anything the warrior promised when it was made very clear in the sight of gods and clan that a *lir* came first always?

Kellin shook his head. *A selfish oath demanded from selfish gods—*

The horse stumbled. Jarred, sore ribs protested; fresh sweat broke on Kellin's brow and ran down his face. Cold air against dampness made him shiver convulsively, which set up fresh complaint.

He cast a glance at the star-freighted sky. *Revenge for my slight? That I dare to question such overweening dedication to you?*

The horse did not stumble again. If the gods heard, they chose not to answer.

Kellin, for his part, laughed—until the despair and emptiness shattered into pieces the dark humor of his doubts, reminding him once again that he was, if nothing else, subject to such whims as the gods saw fit to send him.

Merely because I am Cheysuli— He gripped the horse with both knees, clutching at reins. He recalled all too well what his grandsire had said regarding madness. He recalled even more clearly the wild grief in Blais' eyes as the warrior acknowledged a far greater thing than that he must give up his life; Tanni's death and the severing of the *lir*-bond had been, in that moment, the only thing upon which Blais could focus himself, though it promised his death as well.

Irony blossomed. *Certainly he focused nothing upon me, who had from him a blood-oath of service.*

One sworn to the gods, at that.

Kellin and his mount exchanged meadowlands for the outermost fringes of the forest. His passage stirred the woods into renewed life, startling birds from branches and field warren from burrows. Here the moon shone more fitfully, fragmented by branches. Kellin heard the sound of his horse and his own breath expelled in pale smoke. He pulled the russet cloak more closely around his shoulders.

The horse stopped. It stood completely still, ears erect. Its nostrils expanded hugely, fluttered, then whuffed closed as he expelled a noisy snort of alarm.

"Shansu—" Even as Kellin gathered rein to forestall him, the horse quivered from head to toe.

From the shadows just ahead came the heavy, throaty coughing of a lion.

"Wait—" But even as Kellin clamped his legs, the horse lunged sideways and bolted.

Chapter Seven

In the first awkward lunge, Kellin felt the slide of horsehair against breeches and the odd, unbalanced weightlessness of a runaway. With it came a twofold panic: first, the chance of injury; the second because of the lion.

He had ridden runaways before. He had fallen off of or been thrown from runaways before. It was a straightforward hazard of horsemanship regardless how skilled the rider, regardless how docile the horse. A horseman learned to halt a runaway mount with various techniques when footing afforded it; here, footing was treacherous, and vision nonexistent. This particular runaway—at night, in the dark, with customary reflexes obliterated by pain and disorientation—was far more dangerous than most.

Kellin's balance was off. He could not sit properly. He was forced to ride mostly upright, perching precariously, breaking the fluid melding of horse and rider. Vibrations of the flight, instead of dissipating in his body, reverberated painfully as the horse broke through tangled undergrowth and leapt fallen logs.

Branches snagged hair, slapped face, cut into Kellin's mouth. A clawing vine hooked the bridge of his nose and tore flesh. He felt something dig at one eye and jerked his head aside, cursing helplessly. *One misstep—*

He tried to let reflexes assume control, rather than trusting to himself. But reflexes were banished. His spine was jarred as the horse essayed a depression in the ground, which in turn jarred his ribs. Kellin sucked in a noisy breath and tried to ease his seat, to let the response of muscles to his mount's motion dictate the posture of his body, but failed to do so.

The horse stumbled, then dodged and lurched sideways as it shied from an unseen terror. Kellin blurted discomfort, biting into his cheek; he thought of snubbing the horse's nose back to his left knee in the classic technique, but the trees were too close, the foliage too dense. He had no leeway, no leverage.

The horse hesitated, then leapt again, clearing an unseen impediment. It seemed then to realize it bore an unwanted rider. Kellin felt the body shifting beneath his buttocks, away from clamping legs; then it bunched and twisted, elevating buttocks, and flung its rider forward.

Awkwardly Kellin slid toward the horse's head, dangling briefly athwart one big shoulder. Hands caught frenziedly at mane as he tried to drag himself upright, clutching at reins, digging in with left heel, but the horse ducked out from under him.

Kellin was very calm as he hung momentarily in the air. He was aware of weighty darkness, encroaching vines and branches, the utter physical incomprehensibility that he was unconnected to his mount—and the unhappy acknowledgment that when he landed momentarily it would hurt very much.

He tucked up as best he could, cursing strapped ribs. One shoulder struck the ground first. He rolled through the motion, smashing hip against broken branches shrouded in tangled fern, then flopped down onto his back as the protest of his ribs robbed him of control. He landed flat and very hard, human prey for the hidden treacheries of unseen ground.

For a moment there was no pain. It terrified him. He recalled all too clearly the old Homanan soldier who had taken a tumble from his horse in the bailey of the castle. The fall had not been bad; but as fellow soldiers—and Kellin with them—gathered to trade jests, it became clear that though old Tammis lived, his neck was broken. He would not walk again.

The panic engendered by that image served as catalyst for the bruised strength in legs and arms. Kellin managed one huge jerking contortion against broken boughs and fern. It renewed all the pain, but he welcomed it. Pain was proof he could yet move.

I will *walk again.* But just now, he was not certain he wanted to. Now that he *could* move he did not, but lay slack and very still against a painful cradle. He forced himself not to gasp but to draw shallow breaths through the wreckage of his chest.

When he at last had wind again, Kellin gasped out a lengthy string of the vilest oaths he knew in Homanan, Old Tongue, and Erinnish. It used up the breath he had labored so carefully to recover, but he felt it worth it. Dead men did not swear.

The horse was gone. Kellin did not at that moment care; he could not bear the thought of trying to mount. He wished the animal good riddance, suppressing the flicker of dismayed apprehension—a long and painful walk all the way to Mujhara—then set about making certain he was whole. Everything *seemed* to be, but he supposed he could not tell for certain until he got up from the ground.

Sound startled him into stillness. But a stride or two away came the coughing grunt of beast, and the stink of its breath.

It filled Kellin's nostrils and set him to flight. It might be bear, mountain cat— He flailed, then stilled himself.

Lion?

It bore Corwyth's hallmark.

With effort Kellin pulled his elbows in to his sides and levered his torso upright, lifting a battered chest until he no longer lay squashed and helpless. "Begone," he said aloud, using the scorn of royalty. "You have no power over me."

The odor faded at once, replaced with the damp cold smells of winter. A man laughed softly from the shadows shielding the beast. "The lion may not," he said, "but be certain that *I* do."

Kellin's breath hissed between set teeth as Corwyth exited the shadows for the star-lighted hollow in which the prince lay. The Ihlini wore dark leathers and a gray wool cloak. Pinned by a heavy knot of silver at one shoulder, the cloak glowed purple in the livid shadows of its folds.

Knowledge diminished pain; made it no longer important. "Corwyth the Lion. But the guise is now ineffective; I have learned what you are."

Corwyth affected a negligent shrug. "I am whatever it serves me—and my master—to be. For you, it was a lion." The Ihlini walked quietly toward Kellin, crackling no branches, snagging no vegetation. His hands were gloved in black. "Indeed, we heard of the small prince's fear of lions. It permitted us certain liberties, even though we were powerless within the palace itself. Fear alone can prove effective, as it did in your case. You believed. That belief has shaped you, Kellin; it has made you what you are in heart and spirit, and placed you here within my grasp."

Kellin longed to repudiate it, but he could not speak. What Corwyth said was true. His own weakness had provided the Ihlini with a weapon.

The gloved hands spread, displaying tiny white flames that transformed themselves to pillars. They danced against Corwyth's palms. "Ian's death in particular was most advantageous. Your certainty that the Lion had killed him was unfounded—it was but a child's imagination gone awry, interpreting a passing comment into something of substance—but that substance, given life, nearly consumed you." The flames within his palms bathed Corwyth's smiling face with lurid illumination. His eyes were black pockets in a white-limned mask. "That, too, served, though it was none of ours. A fortuitous death, was Ian's. We could not have hoped for better."

Kellin stirred in protest, then suppressed a grunt of pain. He wanted very badly to rise and face the Ihlini as he would face a man, but pain ate at his bones. "Lochiel," he said.

Corwyth nodded. "The hand at last is outstretched. It beckons, Kellin. You are cordially invited to join your kinsman in the halls of Valgaard."

"Kinsman!"

Corwyth laughed. "You recoil as if wounded, my lord! But what else are you? Shall I recount your heritage?"

Kellin's silence was loud.

The Ihlini continued regardless. "Lochiel was Strahan's son. Strahan was Tynstar's son, who got him on Electra of Solinde. She was, at the time, married to Carillon and was therefore Queen of Homana; but her tastes lay with her true lord rather than the Mujhar who professed to be." White teeth shone briefly. "Strahan was her son. He was brother—*rujholli?*—to Aislinn, who bore Niall, who sired Brennan—and a multitude of others—who in turn sired Aidan. Your very own *jehan*." Corwyth nodded. "The line is direct, Kellin. You and Lochiel are indeed kinsmen, no matter what you might prefer."

Something slow and warm trickled into Kellin's eyes. He was bleeding—the cut Aileen had stanched? Or another, newer one?

Corwyth laughed. "Poor prince. So battered, so bruised . . . and so entirely helpless."

Kellin pressed himself up from the ground in a single painful lunge, jerking from its sheath the lethal Cheysuli long-knife. It fit his grasp so well, as if intended for him. *Blais could not have known—* He flipped it instantly in his hand and threw, arcing it cleanly across the darkness toward the Ihlini sorcerer. *My own brand of Tooth!*

But Corwyth put up a gloved hand now free of flames. The knife stopped in midair. Emerald eyes turned black.

"No!" Kellin's blurted denial was less of fear than of the
knowledge of profanation. *Not Blais' long-knife!*

Corwyth plucked the weapon from the air. He studied it a moment, then tucked it away into his belt. His eyes were bright. "I
have coveted one of these for a century. I thank you for your gift."
The young-looking Ihlini smiled. "Without you, I might never
have acquired one; Cheysuli warriors are, after all, well-protected
by their *lir*." Corwyth paused to consider. "But you lack a *lir* and
therefore lack the protection. *Leijhana tu'sai,* my lord."

Kellin wavered. His fragile strength, born of panic and fury,
was spent. Nothing was left to him, not even anger, nor fear. An
outthrust hand earned him nothing but empty air, certainly little
balance. Fingers closed, then the hand fell limply as Kellin bit into
his lip to forestall collapse. He would not, *would not,* show such
weakness to the Ihlini.

"Give in to it," Corwyth suggested gently. "I am not here to be
cruel, Kellin . . . you paint us so, I know, and it is a personal grief;
but there is no sense in maintaining such rigid and painful control
merely out of pride."

The darkness thickened. Sorcery? Or exhaustion compounded
by pain? "I am Cheysuli. I do not in any way, in words or deed or
posture, even by implication, suggest that I am inferior to an Ihlini."

Corwyth laughed. "Inferior, no. Never. We are *equal,* my lord,
in every sense of the word. Sired by the gods, we are now little
more than petty children quarreling over a toy." His hand closed
over the wolf-headed knife tucked into his belt. "Once, we might
have been brothers. *Rujheldi,* as *we* say—is it not close to *rujholli?*" Corwyth did not smile. "Uncomfortably close, I see, judging by your expression. But it is too late now for anything more
than enmity. The Cheysuli are too near fulfillment. The time is
now to stop the prophecy before it can be completed. Before *you,*
my Cheysuli *rujheldi,* can be permitted to sire a child upon an Ihlini woman."

Kellin wanted very much to spit. He did not because he thought
it was time he showed self-restraint. He, who had so little. With
careful disdain, he asked, "Do you believe I would so soil my manhood as to permit it entry into the womb of the netherworld?"

Corwyth laughed. It was a genuine sound kiting into darkness.
It stirred birds from a nearby tree and reawakened Kellin's apprehension. "A man is a fool to trust to taste and preference in a mat-

ter so important. I recite to you your own history, Kellin: Rhiannon, Lillith's daughter, sired by Ian himself—"

"Ian was tricked. He was bespelled. He was *lir*less, and therefore helpless."

"—and Brennan, your grandsire, who lay with Rhiannon and sired the halfling Ihlini woman at whose breast you suckled."

Kelfin's belly clenched. "My grandsire was seduced."

"But *you* are above such things?" Corwyth shook his head. "A single birth, Kellin . . . a single seed of yours sowed in fertile Ihlini soil, and the thing is done." His eyes were black and pitiless in the frosted darkness. "We are not all of us sworn to Asar-Suti. There are those Ihlini who would, to throw us down, try very hard to insure the child was conceived. The prophecy is not dependent upon *whose* blood mingles with yours, merely that it be Ihlini."

Kellin summoned the last of waning strength. In addition to battered chest, a hip and shoulder ached. Welts and scratches stung. Bravado was difficult. "So, will you kill me here?"

Corwyth smiled. "You are meant for Lochiel's disposition."

Kellin dredged up scorn. "If you mean to take me to Valgaard, you will do it against my will. That much you cannot take from me, *lir*less or no."

"That may be true," Corwyth conceded, "but there are other methods. And all of them equally efficient."

He gestured. From the shadows walked two cloaked men and a saddled horse. Kellin looked at them, looked at the mount, and knew what they meant to do.

"A long ride," Corwyth said, "and as painful as I can make it." He glanced to the horse, then looked back at Kellin. "How long do you think you can last?"

Chapter Eight

Kellin awoke with his mouth full of blood. He gagged, spat it out, felt more flow in sluggishly from the cut on the inside of his cheek. Pressure pounded in his head. It roused him fully, so that he could at last acknowledge the seriousness of his situation.

Corwyth's companions had flung him belly-down across the saddle, little more than a battered carcass shaped in the form of a man. Ankles were tied to the right stirrup, wrists to the left. The position was exceedingly uncomfortable; the binding around his ribs had loosened with abuse and provided no support.

He recalled his defiant challenge: Cheysuli to Ihlini. He recalled losing that challenge, though little of anything afterward; the pain had robbed him of consciousness. Now consciousness was back. He wished it were otherwise.

Kellin gagged and coughed again, suppressing the grunt of pain that exited his throat and was trapped with deliberate effort behind locked teeth. Regardless of the discomfort, despite the incipient rebellion of his discontented belly, he would not disgrace himself by losing that belly's contents in front of an Ihlini.

A thought intruded: *Had I listened to my grandsire—* But Kellin cut it off. Self-recrimination merely added to misery.

The horse moved on steadily with its Cheysuli burden. Every stride of the animal renewed Kellin's discomfort. He wanted very much to sit upright, to climb down from the horse, to lie down quietly and let his headache subside. But he could do none of those things.

A crackling of underbrush forewarned him of company as a horse fell in beside him. Kellin's limited head-down view provided nothing more of the world than stirrup leather and horsehair.

Then Corwyth spoke, divulging identity. "Awake at last, my lord? You have slept most of the night."

Slept? I have been in more comfortable beds. Kellin lifted his head. His skull felt heavy, too heavy; it took effort to hold it up. The light now was better; he could see the Ihlini plainly. Dawn waited impatiently just outside the doorflap.

Corwyth smiled. There was no derision in his tone, no contempt in his expression. "One would hardly recognize you. A bath would undoubtedly benefit. Would you care to visit a river?"

The thought of being dumped into an ice-cold river bunched the flesh of Kellin's bones. He suppressed a shiver with effort and made no answer.

The Ihlini's smile widened. "No, that would hardly do. You might sicken from it, and die . . . and then my lord would be very wroth with me." Blue eyes glinted. "I pity you, Kellin. I have seen Lochiel's anger before, and the consequences of it."

Kellin's mouth hurt. "Lochiel has tried to throw down my House before." It was mostly a croak; he firmed his voice so as not to sound so diminished. "Why do you believe he will succeed this time?"

"He has you," Corwyth said simply.

"*You* have me," Kellin corrected. "And I would not count a Cheysuli helpless while his heart still beats."

Russet brows arched. "Shall I stop it, then? To be certain of my safety? To convince you, perhaps, that you are indeed helpless despite your Cheysuli bravado?"

Kellin opened his mouth to retort but found no words would come. Corwyth's gloved hand was extended, fingers slack. They curled slowly inward.

There was no pain. Just a vague breathlessness that increased as the fingers closed, and a constriction in his chest that banished the ache of his ribs because this was much worse. Bruised ribs, even cracked ones, offered little danger when a man's heart was threatened.

Kellin stirred in protest, but his bonds held firm. The horse walked on, led by Corwyth's minions. The Ihlini's fingers closed.

He felt each of them: four fingers and a thumb, distinct and individual. Each was inside his chest. They touched him intimately, caressing the very muscle that kept him alive.

It was, he thought, rape, if of a very different nature.

Kellin desired very much to protest, to cry out, to shout, to swear, to scream imprecations. But his mouth would not function. Hands and feet were numb. He thought the pressure in his head might cause his eyes and ears to burst.

He could not *breathe.*

Corwyth's hand squeezed.

Kellin thrashed once, expelling breath and blood in a final futile effort to escape the hand in his chest.

"Your lips are blue," Corwyth said. "It is not a flattering color."

Nothing more was left. *Piece of meat—*

It was, Kellin felt, a supremely inelegant way to die.

Then the hand stilled his heart, and he *was* dead.

Kellin roused as Corwyth grabbed a handful of hair and jerked his head up. "Do you see?" the Ihlini asked. "Do you understand now?"

He understood only that he had been dead, or very close to it. He sucked in a choking breath, trying to fill flaccid lungs. The effort was awkward, spasmodic, so that he recognized only the muted breathy roaring of a frightened man trying desperately to breathe.

I am *frightened*— And equally desperate; he felt intensely helpless, and angry because of it. Lochiel's ambassador had humiliated him in the most elemental of ways: by stripping a Cheysuli of freedom, strength, and pride.

"Say it again," Corwyth suggested. "Say again Lochiel cannot throw down your House."

Kellin said nothing. He could not manage it.

The hand was cruel in his hair. Neck tendons protested. "You have seen nothing. *Nothing,* Kellin. I am proud, but practical; I admit my lesser place without hesitation or compunction. The power I command is paltry compared to his."

Paltry enough to kill him with little more than a gesture.

Corwyth released his hair. Kellin's neck was too weak to support his skull. It flopped down again, pressing face against winter horsehair. He breathed in its scent, grateful that he could.

"Think on it," Corwyth said. "Consider your circumstances, and recall that your life depends entirely upon the sufferance of Lochiel."

Kellin rather thought his life depended entirely on his ability to breathe, regardless of Lochiel's intentions. As he lay flopped across the saddle, he concentrated merely on in- and exhalations. Lochiel could wait.

*   *   *

When they cut him from the horse and dragged him down, Kellin wondered seriously if death might be less painful. He bit into his tongue to keep from disgracing himself further by verbal protestation, but the sudden sheen of perspiration gave his weakness away. Corwyth saw it, weighed it, then nodded to himself.

"Against the tree," the Ihlini ordered his companions.

The two hauled Kellin bodily to the indicated tree and left him at its foot to contemplate exposed roots as he fought to maintain consciousness. Sweat ran freely, dampening his hair. He lay mostly on one side. His wrists, though now cut free of the stirrup, were still tied together. He no longer was packed by horseback like so much fresh-killed meat, but the circumstances seemed no better.

Kellin blew grit from his lips. The taste in his mouth was foul, but he had been offered no water.

The sun was full up. They had been riding for hours without a single stop. In addition to the residual aches of the Midden battle and the discomfort of the ride, Kellin's bladder protested. It was a small but signal irritant that compounded his misery.

Kellin eased himself into a sitting position against the tree trunk. He sagged minutely, testing the fit of his ribs inside their loosened wrappings and bruised flesh, then let wood provide false strength; his own was negligible.

I am young, strong, and fit . . . this is a minor inconvenience. Meanwhile, he hurt.

Corwyth strode from his own mount to Kellin, who could not suppress a recoil as the Ihlini touched the binding around his wrists. "There, my lord: freedom." The wrappings fell away. Corwyth smiled. "Test us as you like."

Kellin wanted to spit into the arrogant face. Corwyth knew *he* knew there was no reason to test. No man, Cheysuli or not, would risk his heart a second time to Ihlini magic.

"Are you hungry? Thirsty?" Corwyth gestured, and one of his companions answered with a wrapped packet and leather flask delivered to Kellin at once. "Bread, and wine. Eat. Drink." Corwyth paused. "And if you refuse, be certain I shall make you."

Immediately Kellin conjured a vision of his own hands made by sorcery to stuff his mouth full of bread until he choked on it. His heart had been stopped once; better to eat and drink as bidden than risk further atrocity.

With hands made stiff and clumsy by the weight of too much blood, he unwrapped the parcel. It was a lumpy, tough-crusted loaf of Homanan journey-bread. He set it aside carefully, ignoring Corwyth's interest, and unstoppered the flask. Without hesitation—he would give nothing to the Ihlini, not even distrust—he put the flask to his cut lips and poured wine down his throat.

It stung the inside of his mouth. Kellin drank steadily, then restoppered the flask. "A poor vintage," he commented. "Powerful you may be, but you have no knowledge of wine."

Corwyth grinned. "Bait me, my lord, and you do so at your peril."

Kellin stared steadily back. "Unless you heal me, Lochiel may well wonder what you have done to render his valuable kinsman so bruised."

Corwyth rose. "Lochiel knows you better than that. Everyone in Homana—*and* Valgaard—has heard of the Midden exploits undertaken by the Prince of Homana."

Midden exploits. He detested the words. He detested even more Lochiel's knowledge of them. To forestall his own comment, he put bread into his mouth.

"Eat quickly," Corwyth said. "We ride again almost immediately."

Kellin glared at him. "Then why stop at all?"

"Why, to keep you and anyone else from claiming me inhumane!" With a glint in blue eyes, the young-seeming Ihlini turned away to his mount, then paused and turned back. "Would you like me to help you rise so you may relieve yourself?"

Kellin's face caught fire. Every foul word he knew crowded into his mouth, which prevented him from managing to expel even one.

"Come now," Corwyth said, "it is an entirely natural thing. And, as you are injured—"

"No," Kellin declared.

Blue eyes glinted again. "Hold onto the tree, my lord. It might help you to stand up."

Kellin desired nothing more than to ignore the suggestion entirely. But to do so was foolish in the face of his need. Pride stung, but so did his bladder.

"I will turn my back," Corwyth offered. "Your condition presupposes an inability to escape."

The comment naturally triggered an urge to prove Corwyth wrong, but Kellin knew better than to try. If the Ihlini could play with his heart, Kellin had no desire to risk a threat to anything else.

"Hurry," Corwth suggested. He turned away in an elaborate swirl of heavy cloak.

"Ku'reshtin," Kellin muttered.

Silence answered him.

Corwyth's companions escorted Kellin to his horse when it was time to ride on. Corwyth met him there. "You may ride upright, if you like. Surely it will prove more comfortable than being tied onto a saddle."

Kellin gritted teeth. "What will it cost me?"

"Nothing at all, I think—save perhaps respect for my magic." Corwyth caught Kellin's wrists before he could protest. The Ihlini gripped tightly, crossed one wrist over the other, and pressed until the bones ached in protest. "Flesh into flesh, Kellin. Nothing so common as rope, nor so heavy as iron, but equally binding." He took his hands away, and Kellin saw the flesh of his wrists had been seamlessly fused together.

Gods— Immediately he tried to wrench his wrists apart but could no more do that than rip an arm from his body. His wrists had grown together at the bidding of the Ihlini.

He could not help himself: he gaped. Like a child betrayed, he stared at his wrists in disbelief so utterly overwhelming he could think of nothing else.

My own flesh— It sent a shudder of repulsion through his body. *My heart, now this . . . what will Lochiel do?*

"A simple thing," Corwyth said easily. Then he signaled to his companions. "Help him to mount his horse. I doubt he will resist." Corwyth moved away, then hesitated as if in sudden thought, and swung back. "If he does, I shall seal his eyelids together."

They rode north, toward the Bluetooth River, where they would cross into the Northern Wastes and then climb over the Molon Pass down into Solinde, the birthplace of the Ihlini, and on to Valgaard itself. Kellin had heard tales of the Ihlini fortress and knew it housed the Gate of Asar-Suti. It was, Brennan had said, the Ihlini version of the Womb of the Earth deep in the foundations of Homana-Mujhar.

Kellin rode upright with precise, careful posture, trying to keep his torso very still. His legs conformed to the shape of saddle and horse, but his hands did not control the horse. The reins had been split so that each of Corwyth's companions—*minions?*—led the prisoner's mount. Corwyth rode ahead.

They kept to the forest tracks, avoiding main roads that would bring them into contact with those who might know the Prince of Homana. Kellin doubted anyone would recognize him. His face was welted and bruised, his lower lip split and swollen. He stank of dried sweat mixed with a film of grit and soil, and leaves littered his hair. Little about him now recommended his rank.

Snow crackled in deep shadows, breaking up beneath shod hooves. As afternoon altered to evening, the temperature dropped. Kellin shrugged more deeply into his cloak as his breath fogged the air.

When at last they halted, it was nearly full dark. Kellin was so sore and weary he thought he might topple off the horse if he so much as turned his head. *Let them see none of it.* Slowly he kicked free of stirrups, slung a leg across the saddle, and slid from his mount before the Ihlini could signal him down; a small rebellion, but successful.

He made no attempt to escape because to try was sheerest folly. Better to bide his time until his strength returned, then wait for the best moment. Just now all he could do was stand.

Kellin leaned against the horse a moment to steady himself, flesh cold beneath a film of newborn perspiration. He shivered. Disorientation broke up the edge of consciousness. Weariness, perhaps— *Or—?* He stilled. *Sorcery? Corwyth's attempt to tease me?*

One of the minions put his hand on Kellin's shoulder; he shrugged it off at once. The rebuke came easily in view of who received it. "No one is permitted to touch the Prince of Homana without his leave."

Corwyth, dropping off his own mount, laughed in high good humor. "Feeling better, are we?"

Kellin felt soiled by the minion's touch. An urge to bare his teeth in a feral snarl was suppressed with effort. He swung from the black-eyed man, displaying a taut line of shoulder.

Corwyth pointed. "There."

Kellin lingered a moment beside his horse. His head felt oddly packed and tight, so that the Ihlini's order seemed muted. A second shiver wracked his body, jostling aching bones. *Not just cold— more—*

"Sit him down," Corwyth said, but before the minion could

force the issue, Kellin sat down by himself. "Better." Corwyth tended his own mount as his companions tended Kellin's.

Kellin itched. It had nothing to do with bruises and scrapes, because the itching wasn't in his skin but in his blood. Flesh-bound hands flexed, curling fingers into palms, then snapping out straight again.

He could not eat, though they gave him bread, nor could he drink, because his throat refused to swallow. Once again he leaned against a tree, but this time he needed its support even more than before. He felt as if all his bones were soft, stripped of rigidity. His spirit was as flaccid.

He shifted against wood, grimaced in discomfort, then shifted again. He could not be still.

Just like in Homana-Mujhar. He fixed his eyes on Corwyth, who sat quietly by a small fire. "Was it you who drove me from the palace?"

"Drove you?"

"With sorcery. Was it you?"

Corwyth shrugged. "That required neither magic nor skill. I know your habits. You gamble, you drink, you whore. All it required was the proper time."

Kellin shifted again, hiding flesh-bound wrists beneath a fold of his cloak because to look on them was too unsettling. "You set the trap. I put myself into it."

The Ihlini smiled. "A happy accident. It did save time."

"Accident? Or my *tahlmorra?*"

That provoked a response. "You believe the gods might have planned this? This?" Corwyth's surprise was unfeigned. "Would the Cheysuli gods risk the final link in the prophecy so willingly?"

Kellin scowled. "Who can say what the gods would do? I despise them . . . they have done me little good."

Corwyth laughed and fed a stick to the flames. "Then perhaps this *is* their doing, if you and the gods are on such bad terms."

Kellin shivered again. "If Lochiel knows so much about me, surely he knows I have already sired children. Why kill me now? Before, certainly—to prevent the precious seed from being sown—but now it is too late. The seed is well sowed."

"Three children," Corwyth agreed. "But all bastards, and none with the proper blood. Halfling brats gotten on Homanan whores." He shrugged elegantly. "Lochiel only fears the Firstborn child."

Kellin stilled. Was it a weapon? "Lochiel is afraid?"

Corwyth's expression was solemn. "Only a fool would deny he fears this outcome. I fear it. Lochiel fears it. Even the Seker fears fulfillment." Flames illuminated his face. It was starkly white in harsh light, black in hollowed contours. "Have you never thought what fulfillment will bring?"

Kellin laughed. "A beginning for the Cheysuli. An ending for the Ihlini."

Flames consumed wood. A pine knot cracked, shedding sparks. Corwyth now was solemn. "In your ignorance, you are certain."

"Of course I am certain. It has been promised us for centuries."

"By the very gods you despise." Corwyth did not smile, nor couch his words in contempt. "If that is true, how then can you honor their prophecy?"

Kellin licked a numb lip. His body rang with tension, as if he were a harp string wound much too taut on its pegs. "I am Cheysuli."

"*That* is your answer?" Corwyth shook his head. "Perhaps you are more Cheysuli than you believe, even *lir*less as you are. Only fools such as your people dedicate themselves to the fulfillment of a mandate that will destroy everything they know."

Kellin's mouth twisted. "I have heard that old tale before. When the Ihlini cannot win through murder or sorcery, they turn to words. You mean to undermine our customs."

"Of *course* I do!" Corwyth snapped. "And if you had any wit to see it, you would understand why. Indeed, the prophecy will destroy Ihlini such as myself . . . but it will also destroy the Cheysuli." He extended an empty hand. "The prophecy of the Firstborn will close its fist around the heart of the Cheysuli, just as I did yours, and stop it." He shut his hand. "Just like this."

It was immediate. "No." Kellin twitched, then rolled his head against bark. "You play with words, Ihlini."

"This is not play. This is truth. You see me as I am: a man, not an Ihlini, but simply a man who fears the ending of his race in the ascendancy of another."

"Mine, " Kellin agreed.

"No." Corwyth placed another stick on the fire. His gloved hand shook. "The ascendancy is that of the Firstborn." In firelight his eyes were hidden by deep pockets of shadow. "Your child. Your son. When he accepts the Lion, the new order replaces the old."

"*Your* order."

Corwyth smiled faintly. "Tell me," he said, "is your prophecy complete? No—I do not speak of the words all of you mouth." His tone was ironic. " 'One day a man of all blood shall unite, in peace, four warring realms and two magical races.' What I speak of is the prophecy *itself* in its entirety. It was passed down century after century, was it not?"

"The *shar tahls* make certain of that."

"But do they know the whole of it? Do they have record of it?"

"Written down?" Kellin frowned. "Such things can be lost if not entrusted to *shar tahls* in an oral tradition."

Corwyth nodded. "Such things *were* lost, Kellin. I know very well what the *shar tahls* teach are mere fragments . . . pieces of yarn woven together into a single skein. Because that is all they know. In the schism that split the Firstborn into Cheysuli and Ihlini, very little was left of the dogma on which your future hangs." He shook his head. "You know nothing of what may come, yet you serve it blindly. *We* are not such fools."

Kellin said nothing.

The Ihlini pulled his dark cloak more closely around his shoulders. "This profits nothing. I will leave it to my lord to prove what I say is true." Corwyth glanced at his companions. "I will leave it to Lochiel, and to Asar-Suti."

Kellin shivered. *Lochiel will kill me. Not for myself. For the child. For the seed in my loins.*

In the scheme of the gods he detested, it seemed he counted for very little.

Chapter Nine

Kellin watched the three Ihlini prepare to sleep. Though his wrists remained sealed, he was certain something more would be done to insure he could not escape. Perhaps Corwyth *would* seal his eyelids, or stop his heart again.

But Corwyth did not even look at his captive. The sorcerer quietly went about his business, pacing out distances. Each time he halted, he sketched something in the air. The rune glowed briefly purple, then died away.

Wards, Kellin knew. To keep him in, and others out.

He watched them lie down in their cloaks. Three dark-shrouded men, sorcerers all, who served a powerful god no sane man could possibly honor.

Unless there is something to what Corwyth says. But Kellin shut off the thought. Corwyth's declarations of a separate Ihlini prophecy—or of the Cheysuli one entire—was nothing but arrant nonsense designed to shake Kellin's confidence.

But one telling question had been posed. *How do I justify serving the prophecy for gods I cannot honor?*

Kellin shivered. He did not attempt to sleep. He sat against the tree, wrists still bound by flesh, and tried to think himself warm, tried to ease his mind so it did not trouble itself with questionings of Cheysuli customs.

But why not? It was a Cheysuli custom that killed Blais, not an Ihlini.

Heresy.

Is it?

Kellin inhaled carefully, held his breath a moment as he expanded cramped lungs, then blew the air out again in a steady, hissing stream. He stared across the dying fire to the three cloaked shapes beyond. To Corwyth in particular. Kellin knew very well the Ihlini worked merely to undermine his own convictions, which would in turn undermine a spirit that might yet protest its captivity; he was not stupid enough to believe there was no motive in Corwyth's contentions. But his mind was overactive, his thoughts too restless; even when he tried to think of nothing at all, an overabundance of *somethings* filled his head.

It is a long journey to Valgaard. The trick is to lure them into a false sense that I will attempt nothing.

A mountain cat screamed. The nearness of the sound was intensely unnerving. Kellin sat bolt upright and immediately regretted it. He reached for his knife and realized belatedly he had none, nor the freedom of hands to use it.

The scream came again from closer yet, shearing through darkness and foliage. Corwyth and the others, too, were up, shaking cloaks back from shoulders and arms. Corwyth said something in a low voice to the others—Kellin heard Lochiel's name mentioned—then scribed a shape in the air. Runes flared briefly, then went down. Corwyth's men were free to hunt.

Kellin could not remain seated. He climbed awkwardly to his feet and waited beside the tree. The cat's voice lacked the deep-chested timbre of the lion's, but its determination and alien sound echoed the beast that had haunted so much of Kellin's life.

Corwyth spared him a glance, as if to forestall any attempt on Kellin's part to escape. But Kellin was no more inclined to risk meeting the cat than he was to prompt Corwyth to use more sorcery on him.

The Ihlini bent and put new kindling on the fire, then waved a negligent hand; flames came to life. "The noise is somewhat discomfiting," he commented, "but even a mountain cat is not immune to sorcery. I will have a fine pelt to present my master."

It seemed an odd goal to Kellin, in view of his own value and Lochiel's desire for his immediate company. "You would take the time to kill and skin a cat?"

"Lochiel has an affinity for mountain cats. He says they are the loveliest and most dangerous of all the predators. Fleet where a bear is slow; more devious than the wolf; more determined than a boar. And armed far more effectively than any man alive." Corywth smiled. "He keeps them in Valgaard, in cages beneath the ground."

A fourth scream sounded closer yet. Even Corwyth got to his feet.

A shudder wracked Kellin. "What is—" he grittened his teeth

against another assault. "—*ku'reshtin*—" he managed. "What threat do I offer?"

Corwyth cast him a glance. "What inanities do you mouth?"

A third shudder shook him. Kellin gasped. His bones were on fire. "What are you—"

Lir, said a voice, *the wards are down. I have done what I could to lead the others astray. Now it is up to you.*

He understood then. "No!" Kellin cried. "I want none of you!"

I am your only escape.

Corwyth laughed. "You may want none of me, but I have you nevertheless."

Kellin was not talking for the Ihlini's benefit. What consumed him now was the knowledge his *lir* was near. If he gave in, it would win. And he would be no freer than any other Cheysuli bound by oaths and service.

He wavered on his feet. *I renounced you. I want no part of you.*

Would you rather go to Valgaard and let Lochiel destroy you? The tone was crisp. *His methods are not subtle.*

His spirit screamed with need. The *lir* was close, so close—he had only to give in, to permit the channel to be opened that would form a permanent link.

He repudiated it. *I will not permit it.*

Then die. Allow the Ihlini to win. Remove from the line of succession the prince known as Kellin, and destroy the prophecy.

He gritted his teeth. *I will not pay your price.*

There is no other escape.

It infuriated him. Kellin brought his fleshbound hands into the moonlight. *A test, then,* he challenged.

The *lir* sighed. *You believe too easily what the Ihlini tells you to. His art is in illusion. Banish this one as you banished the lion.*

Kellin stared hard at his wrists. The skin altered, flowing away, and his wrists were free of themselves.

Corwyth marked the movement. He turned sharply, saw the truth, and jerked the knife from his belt.

"The wards are down," Kellin said, "and your minions bide elsewhere. Now it is you and I."

You will have to kill him, lir. *He will never let you go.*

"Go away," Kellin said. "I want nothing to do with you."

Corwyth laughed. "Is this your attempt at escape? To bait me with babbled nonsense?"

You must kill him.

He wanted to shout at the *lir.* *He is armed,* Kellin said acidly. *He is also Ihlini.*

And has recourse to no arts now that I am here.

We have not bonded. I will not permit it.

The tone was implacable. *Then die.*

"Come out!" Kellin shouted. "By the gods, I will fight you both!"

Corwyth's laughter grated. "Have you gone mad? Or do you use this to bait me?"

Distracted by a battle fought on two fronts, Kellin glared. "I need no *lir* for you. I will take you as a man."

"Do try," Corwyth invited. "Or shall I stop your heart again?"

He cannot, the *lir* declared. *While I am here, such power is blunted.*

Then why do I hear you? Near an Ihlini, the link is obscured.

You forget who you are. There is that within you that breaks certain rules.

"My blood?" Kellin jeered. "Aye, always the blood!"

Old Blood is powerful. You have it in abundance. The voice paused. *Have you not read the birthlines lately?*

"Do you want your blood spilled?" Corwyth asked. "I can do that for you . . . Lochiel will not punish me for that."

Kill him, the *lir* said. *You are weary and injured. He will defeat you even without sorcery.*

Kellin laughed. *With what? My teeth?*

Those are your weapons, among others. The tone was dryly amused. *But mostly there is your blood. If a man's form does not serve, take on another.*

Yours? But I do not even know what animal you are!

You have heard me. Now hear me again. The scream of a mountain cat filled the darkness but a handful of paces away.

Corwyth's face blanched. "I am Ihlini! " he cried. "You have no power here!"

Show him, it said. *Let him see what you are.*

Kellin was desperate. "How?"

Forget you are a man. Become a cat instead.

Kellin looked at Corwyth. The knife in the Ihlini's hand had belonged to Blais. Kellin wanted it back.

Corwyth laughed. "You and I, then."

Kellin was angry, so angry he could hardly hold himself still. His bones buzzed with newfound energy and flesh hardened itself

over tensing muscle and tendon. He shook with the urge to shred
the Ihlini into a pile of cracked bone and bloodied flesh.

A beginning, the *lir* said.

And then he understood—to accomplish what was required he
must shed all knowledge of human form, all human instincts.
Anger could help that. Anger could assist him.

I want Corwyth dead. I want the knife back.

*There is only one way to gain what you desire. I have given you
the key. Now you must open the door.*

To what future?

To the one you make.

"Come, then," Corwyth said. "I will shatter all your bones, then
knit them together again. Lochiel need never know."

Kellin smiled. He forgot about his ribs and all the other nagging
pains. He thought about *lir*-shape instead. He thought about mountain cats, and the instincts that served them.

"You cannot," Corwyth declared. "This is a trick."

Kellin laughed. "Do you forget who I am? You know so much
about me and the others of my House—surely you recall that we
claim the Old Blood." He paused. "With all of its special gifts."

Corwyth lunged. He was quick, very quick, and exceedingly
supple. Kellin dodged the outthrust knife with no little effort or
pain, then ducked a second thrust.

Concentrate, the *lir* commanded. *Fingers and toes are claws.
Flesh is thickly furred. The body is lean and fit. Jaws are heavy
and powerful, filled with tongue and teeth. All you desire is the
taste of his flesh in your mouth—his blood spilling from his throat
into yours—and the hot sweet scent of his death.*

The knife nearly caught his side. Kellin twisted, grimacing as
ribs protested.

Mountain cat, it said. *Far superior to any beast bred by god or
demon.*

Kellin rolled as Corwyth struck a third time. He panted audibly,
trying to divorce his mind from his body, to let his instincts dictate
motion.

Now.

Anger fed his strength. Kellin saw the glint of the knife in Corwyth's hand—*Blais' knife!*—and then, briefly, everything faded.
The world was turned inside out, and when it came right again it
was a very different place.

His mouth dropped open to curse the Ihlini, but what issued

forth was a rising, angry wail. He felt the coiling of haunches to gather himself; the whip of a sinuous tail; the tightness in his empty—*too empty!*—belly. Kellin bunched, and sprang.

The knife glinted again. Kellin reached out in midair with a hind leg and slashed the weapon from Corwyth's hand. He heard the Ihlini's cry, and then Kellin was on him.

Corwyth went down easily. Lost in the killing frenzy, Kellin did not think about what he did. He simply closed powerful jaws on the fragile throat of a man and tore it away.

There was no sense of jubilation, vindication, or relief. Merely satiation as the cat fed on the prey's body.

Chapter Ten

What am I—? Comprehension was immediate. Kellin hurled himself away from the body on the ground. No more the cat but a man, appalled by what had occurred. *Gods—I did THAT?*

Corwyth was messily dead. He lay sprawled on the ground with blood-soaked cloak bunched up around him, gaping throat bared to the moon.

I did.

He was shaking. All over. He was bloodied to the elbows. Blood soaked his doublet. Blood was in his mouth. *Everywhere, blood*—and the taste of Corwyth's flesh.

Kellin thrust himself from the ground to his knees, then bent and hugged sore ribs as his belly purged itself. He wanted very much to purge his mind as well, to forget what he had seen, to forget what he had done, but the memory was livid. It excoriated him.

He scrubbed again and again at his face, trying to rid it of blood, but his hands, too, were bloody. Frantically Kellin scooped up double handfuls of dirt and damp leaves and scoured hands, then face, pausing twice to spit.

Lir.

Kellin jumped. He spun on his knees, panting, bracing himself on one stiff arm, and searched avidly for the mountain cat who had driven him beyond self. There was no sound. No cat. He saw nothing but star-weighted darkness and the scalloped outline of dense foliage.

Gone. Breathing steadied. He scraped the back of a hand across his chin. Fingers shook.

Lir. The tone was gentle. *The death was required. Just as the deaths of the minions were required.*

"You killed them?"

They are dead.

He barked a hoarse laugh. "Then you have broken one of the

most binding rules of the *lir*-bond. You are not supposed to kill Ih-lini."

The tone was peculiar. *We are reflections of one another.*

"What does *that* mean?"

You do that which you are commanded not to do. And now I as well.

It astounded him. "Because of *me* you broke the rule?"

We are very alike.

He contemplated that. He knew himself to be a rebel; could a *lir* be so also? If so, they were indeed well matched.

He cut it off at once. "I want nothing to do with you."

It is done. The men are dead.

Kellin stiffened. He refused to look at Corwyth's body. "There was no warning—you said nothing of what I would feel!"

You felt as a cat feels.

"But I am a *man*."

More, it said. *Cheysuli.*

Kellin spat again, wishing he had the strength of will to scour his mouth as well as his flesh. A quick glance across the tiny camp-site offered relief: Ihlini supplies laid out in a neat pile.

"Water." He pressed himself from the ground and walked un-steadily to the supplies. He found a leather flask and unstoppered it, then methodically rinsed his mouth and spat until the taste of blood and flesh was gone. As carefully, he poured the contents of a second flask into one hand and then the other, scraping flesh free of sticky blood with cold, damp leaves.

"*I'toshaa-ni,*" he murmured, and then realized that the ritual merely emphasized the heritage that had led him to this.

Dripping, Kellin rose again. He made himself look. The view was no better: a sprawled, stilled body with only the pallor of ver-tebrae glistening in the ruin of a throat.

He shuddered. "I renounced you," he declared. "I made it very plain. Now more than ever it is imperative that I do not bond with a *lir*. If *that* is what it means—"

"That" was necessary. "That" was required.

"No." He would not now speak inside his head but say it as a man, so there existed no doubt as to who—and what—he was. "It was butchery, no more."

It was to save your life. The tone was terse, as if the *lir* sup-pressed a great emotion. *What the Ihlini do, they do to preserve their power. Lochiel would have killed you. Or gelded you.*

"Gelded—"

Do you think he would permit you to breed? You are his ending. The moment your son is born, the world begins anew.

Kellin wiped damp hands across his face, warping it out of shape as if self-inflicted violence would banish acknowledgment. "I want nothing to do with this."

It is too late.

"No. Not if I renounce you, as I have. Not if I refuse to bond with you."

Too late, the *lir* repeated. The tone now was muted.

Suspicion flared. He had been taught to honor all *lir*, but at this moment, conversing with this *lir*, he was afraid to assume it benefic ent. "Why?" Alarm replaced suspicion. "What have you done?"

It was necessary.

It filled him with apprehension. "What have you done?"

Lent you a piece of myself.

"You!"

Required, it insisted. *Without that part of me, you would never have accomplished the shapechange.*

A shudder wracked Kellin from head to foot. The flesh on his scalp itched as if all his hairs stood up. "Tell me," he said intently. "Tell me what I have become."

Silence answered him.

"Tell me!" Kellin shouted. "By the gods, you beast, *what have you done to me?*"

The tone was odd. *Why does a man swear by gods he cannot honor?*

The inanity amazed him. "If I could see you—"

Then see me. A shadow moved at the edge of the trees. *See me as I am. Know who Sima is.*

A soft rustle, then nothing more. In the reflection of dying flames, gold eyes gleamed.

Kellin nearly gaped. "You are little more than a *cub*!"

Young, Sima conceded. *But old enough for a* lir.

"But—" Kellin blurted a choked laugh, then cut it off. "I want nothing to do with you. With you, or with any of it. No *lir*, no bonding, no shapechange. I want a full life . . . not a travesty al ways threatened by an arcane ritual that needlessly wastes a war rior."

Sima blinked. *I would die if you died. The cost is equally shared.*

"I do not *want* to share it! I want not to risk it at all."

A tail twitched. She was black, black as Sleeta, the Mujhar's magnificent *lir*. But she was small, as yet immature, gangly as a half-grown kitten. Incongruity, Kellin thought, in view of her intransigence.

I am empty, Sima said. *I am but a shadow. Do you sentence me to that?*

"Can I? I thought you said it was too late."

Gold eyes winked out, then opened again. *If you wish to renounce me, you may. But then the Ihlini will be victorious, because both of us will die.*

She did not sound young. She sounded ineffably old. "Sima." Kellin wet his lips. "What have you done to me?"

The sleek black head lowered. Tufted ears flattened. The tail whipped a branch to shreds.

"Sima!"

Caused you to change before the balance was learned.

Kellin's mouth felt dry. "And that is a bad thing?"

If balance is lost and not regained, if it is not maintained, a warrior in lir-*shape risks his humanity.*

His voice sounded rusty. "He would be locked in beast-shape?"

If he lost his balance and spent too long in lir-*shape, he could lose knowledge of what he was. Self-knowledge is essential. Forgotten, the man becomes a monster caught between two selves.*

After a long moment, Kellin nodded. "*Leijhana tu'sai,*" he said grimly, "for giving me the chance to become a child's nightmare."

I gave you the chance to survive. Corwyth would not have killed you, but he would have brought you pain. And Lochiel would have done worse.

Kellin did not argue. He would not speak to her. He would give her no opportunity to drag him deeper into the mess she had made of his life.

Because he could not stay in the clearing with the mutilated body, Kellin took Corwyth's horse for his own. He turned the other mounts loose; he had no time for ponying.

Sima did not honor his moratorium on speech. *They would have killed me.*

He knew immediately what she referred to. For the first time, he contemplated what it was to a *lir* to experience guilt. He understood there was no choice in killing the minions; they would have skinned her and taken the pelt to Valgaard for presentation to Lochiel.

Even as they presented me. Grimly Kellin said, "I would wish that on no one, beast or no."

Leijhana tu'sai. Sima twitched her tail.

Kellin slanted her a hard glance as he snugged the girth tight. "You know the Old Tongue?"

Better than you do.

He grunted. "Privy to the gods, are you? More favored than most?"

Of course. All lir *are.* The cat paused. *You are an angry man.*

"After what you have made of me, do you expect gratitude?"

No. You are angry all the time.

He slipped fingers between girth and belly to check for a horse's favorite trick: intentional bloating to keep the girth loose. "How would you know *what* I am?"

I know.

"Obscurity does not commend you."

Sima thumped her tail. *A difficult bonding, I see.*

"No bonding at all." As the horse released its breath in response to an elbow jab, Kellin snugged the girth tighter. "Go back to wherever it is *lir* come from."

I cannot.

"I will not have you with me."

You cannot NOT have me.

"Oh?" Kellin cast her an arch glance. "Will you stop me with violence?"

Of course not. I am sworn to protect you, not injure you.

"That is something." He looped reins over the bay gelding's neck. "Go back to the gods, cat. I will have none of you."

You have no choice.

"Have I not?" Kellin gritted his teeth and put a boot toe into the left stirrup. Swearing inventively, he swung up into the saddle and settled himself slowly. "—I think I have every choice, cat."

None. Not if you wish to survive.

"There have been *lir*less Cheysuli before."

None who survived.

Kellin gathered in reins. "General Rowan," he said briefly. "Rowan was meticulous in teaching my history. Rowan was one of Carillon's most trusted men. He was a *lir*less Cheysuli."

He did not lose a lir. *He never had one. He was kept from the bonding by the Ellasians who did not know what he was.*

"I know what I am. I know what you are." He swung the horse southwesterly. "Go back to the gods who sent you. I will have none of them, or you."

Lir—

"No." Kellin spared a final glance at the body beside the fire. In time the beasts would eat it. He would not be one of them; he had done his part already. "*Tu'halla dei*," he said. "Or whatever the terminology from warrior to renounced *lir*."

The sleek back cat rose. *I am Sima. I am for you.*

Kellin kicked the horse into a walk. "Find another *lir*."

There IS none! she cried.

For the first time he heard the fear in her tone. Kellin jerked the horse to a halt. He turned in the saddle to stare angrily at the mountain cat. "I saw what became of Tanni. I know what became of Blais. I am meant to hold the Lion and sire a Firstborn son—do you think I dare risk it all for you? To know that if you die, the prophecy dies also?"

Without me, you die. Without you, I do. With both of us dead, there is no need for the prophecy.

Kellin laughed. "Surely the gods must see the folly in this! A *lir* is a warrior's weakness, not his strength. I begin to think the *lir*-bond is nothing more than divine jest."

I am for you, she said. *Without you, I am empty.*

It infuriated him. "Tell it to someone who cares!"

But as he rode from the campsite, the mountain cat followed.

Chapter Eleven

Kellin was exhausted by the time he reached Clankeep. He had briefly considered riding directly to Homana-Mujhar—no doubt Brennan and Aileen wondered what had become of him—but decided against it. Clankeep was the answer. His problem had nothing at all to do with the Homanan portion of his blood, but was wholly a Cheysuli concern.

I will tell them what has happened. I will explain what I was forced to become, and the result—surely they cannot countenance a warrior who in lir-*shape compromises every bit of his humanity.* He steadfastly ignored the shadow slinking behind him with gold eyes fixed on his back. *They will understand that this kind of bonding cannot be allowed to stand.*

Kellin sighed relief. He felt better already. Once his plight was explained, all would be understood. He had spent portions of his childhood in Clankeep and knew the pureblood Cheysuli could be a stiff-necked, arrogant lot—he had been accused of his share of arrogance by the castle boys in childhood—but they had to acknowledge the difficulty of his position. Kellin knew very well his request would be neither popular nor readily accepted, but once they fully understood what had occurred the Cheysuli would not refuse. He was one of their own, after all.

I will speak to Gavan. Gavan was clan-leader, a man Kellin respected. *He will see this is serious, not merely an inconvenience. He will know what must be done.*

Kellin felt gingerly at the bridge of his nose. It was whole, but badly scratched. His left eyelid was swollen so that a portion of his vision was obstructed. His clothing was crusted with dried blood. *I can smell myself.* It shamed him to show himself to Gavan and the others this way, but how better to explain his circumstances save with the gory proof before them?

He was not hungry though his belly was empty. The idea of

food repulsed him. He had eaten the throat of a man; though he was free now of the taste, his memory recalled it. Kellin wanted nothing at all to do with food.

He listened for and heard the faint rustling behind. Sima did not hide her presence, nor make attempt to quiet her movements. She padded on softly, following her *lir.*

Kellin's jaws tautened. *Gavan will see what has happened. He will know what must be done.*

Clankeep, to Kellin, was perfectly ordinary in its appearance. He had been taught differently, of course; the keep had been razed twenty years before on the night of his birth, when Lochiel himself had ridden down from Valgaard with sorcerers at his beck. The Ihlini had meant to destroy Clankeep and kill every living Cheysuli; that they had failed was in no way attributable to their inefficiency, but to the forced premature birth of Aidan's son. Cut from his mother's belly before the proper time, Kellin was at risk. Lochiel had immediately returned to Valgaard. In that retreat, a portion of Clankeep and her Cheysuli were left alive.

Kellin, gazing with gritty, tired eyes on the painted pavilions clustered throughout the forest like chicks around a hen, saw nothing of the past, only of the present. That the unmortared walls surrounding the pavilions were, beneath cloaks of lichen and ivy, still charred or split by heat did not remind him of that night, because he recalled nothing of it. He had no basis for comparison when he looked on the present Clankeep. To Kellin it was simply another aspect of his heritage, without the depressing weight of personal recollection.

Despite the hour he was welcomed immediately by the warriors manning the gate and was escorted directly to the clan-leader's pavilion. In the dark it stood out because of its color: a pale saffron bedecked with ruddy-hued foxes. Moonlight set it softly aglow.

Kellin dismounted as his escort ducked into Gavan's pavilion; a second warrior took Corwyth's horse and led it away. Kellin was alone save for the cat-shaped shadow nearby. He ignored her utterly.

In only a moment the first warrior returned and beckoned him inside, pulling aside the doorflap. Kellin drew in a deep breath and went in, acutely aware of his deshabille. He paused inside as his eyes adjusted to the muted glow of a fire cairn, then inclined his head to the older man who waited. Gavan offered the ritual welcome in the Old Tongue, then indicated a place to sit upon a thick black bear pelt. Honey brew and dried fruit also were offered. Kellin sat down with a murmured word of thanks and accepted cup and platter. Irresolute, he stared at both, then set aside the fruit and drank sparingly of the liquor. Like the Ihlini wine, it burned his cut mouth.

Gavan wore traditional leathers, though tousled graying hair indicated he had risen hastily from bed. In coal-cast shadows his dark Cheysuli face was hollowed and eerily feral, dominated by yellow eyes above oblique, prominent cheekbones. Some of Gavan's face was reflected in Kellin's, though his own was less angular and lacked the sharpness of additional years.

The clan-leader sat quietly on a bear pelt before Kellin, a ruddy dog-fox curled next to one knee. His eyes narrowed minutely as he observed Kellin's state. "Harsh usage."

Kellin nodded as he swallowed, then set aside the cup. "Ihlini," he said briefly. He was flattered by the instant response in Gavan's eyes: sharp, fixed attention, and a contained but palpable tension. Kellin wondered fleetingly if Gavan had been present during the Ihlini attack. Then he dismissed it, thinking of the man instead. *I will have more care from him than from my own* jehan.

"Lochiel?" the clan-leader asked.

Kellin shook his head. "A minion. Corwyth. Powerful in his own right . . . but not the master himself."

Gavan's mouth compressed slightly. "So the war begins anew."

Kellin swallowed heavily. "Lochiel wants me captured and taken to Valgaard. No more does he want me killed outright, but brought to him *alive*." Though his mouth was clean, he tasted Corwyth's blood again. It was difficult to speak. "In my dying—or whatever he decrees is to be my fate—I am to be Lochiel's entertainment."

Gavan set aside his cup. "You have not gone to the Mujhar."

"Not yet. I came here first." Kellin suppressed a shudder as the image of throatless Corwyth rose in his mind; this man would not understand such weakness. "There is a thing I must discuss. A *frightening* thing—" he did not like admitting such to Gavan, but it was the simple truth, "—and a thing which must be attended." It was more difficult than expected. Kellin flicked a glance at the mountain cat who lay so quietly beside him. He longed to dismiss her, but until all was explained he did not dare transgress custom. A *lir* was to be honored; arrant dismissal would immediately predispose Gavan to hostility. "I killed Corwyth, as I said—but not through a man's means."

Gavan smiled faintly as he looked at Sima. "It is my great personal joy that the bonding has at last occurred. It is well past time. Now you may be welcomed into the clan as a fully bonded warrior . . . it was of some concern that the tardiness of the *lir*-bonding might cause difficulty."

Kellin's mouth dried. "Difficulty?"

Gavan gestured negligent dismissal. "But it is of no moment, now. No one can deny your right to the Lion."

This was a new topic. "*Did* someone deny it?"

A muscle jumped briefly in Gavan's cheek. "There was some talk that perhaps the mixture of so many Houses in your blood had caused improper dilution."

"But the mixture is *needed*." Kellin fought to control his tone; he realized in a desperation fraying into panic that things would not be sorted out so easily after all. "The prophecy is very explicit about a man of *all* blood—"

"Of course." Neatly, Gavan cut him off. "A man of all blood, aye . . . but a man clearly Cheysuli." He smiled at Sima. "With so lovely a *lir*, you need fear no warrior's doubts."

Kellin found it difficult to breathe. To gain time he looked around the interior of the pavilion: at the dog-fox next to Gavan; at the glowing fire cairn; at the bronze-bound trunk with a handful of Cheysuli ornaments scattered across its closed lid; at the compact warbow—once called a hunting bow—leaning against the trunk; at the shadows of painted *lir* on the exterior of the pavilion fabric.

Lastly, at Sima. Gold eyes were unblinking.

Kellin picked up the cup of liquor and drained it. It burned briefly, then mellowed into a warmth that, in an empty belly, set his vision to blurring.

His lips felt stiff. "Carillon had no *lir*."

Gavan's black brows, as yet untouched by the silver threading his hair, moved more closely together. Clearly, he was baffled by the non sequitur. "Carillon was Homanan."

"But the clans accepted him."

"He was the next link. After Shaine: Carillon. After Carillon: Donal."

"Because Carillon sired only a daughter. A Solindish halfling."

"Aislinn. Who wed Donal and bore Niall." Gavan smiled then,

his faint consternation clearing. "Is this because Niall, too, was late receiving his *lir?* Did you fear, as they say he did, that you would never receive one?" He smiled, nodding his head in Sima's direction. "You need fear nothing. Your future is secure."

Kellin drew in a deep breath, ignoring the twinge in his chest. Gavan's words seemed to come from a great distance. "What if—" He broke off, then began again. "What if I had never received a *lir?*"

Gavan shrugged. "There is no profit in discussing what did not occur."

Kellin forced a smiled. "Curiosity. What if I had never received, nor bonded with a *lir?*" He was no good at disingenuity; the smile broke up into pieces and fell away. "I am well beyond the age a warrior receives a *lir.* Surely before now there must have been some discussion in case I never did."

The clan-leader made a dismissive gesture. "Aye, it was briefly discussed; there is no sense in hiding it from you. It is a serious matter. Because you are the only direct descendant with all of the proper bloodlines—"

"Save one."

Gavan inclined his head slightly. "—save one, aye . . . still, it remains that you *are* the only one with all of the necessary lineage required to produce the man we await."

"The Firstborn."

"Cynric." Gavan's eyes were bright. "So your *jehan* has prophesied."

Kellin did not desire to discuss his *jehan.* "Had I not received my *lir,* what would have happened? Would you have questioned my right to inherit?"

"Certainly clan-council would have met to discuss it formally at some point."

"Would *you* have questioned it?" Suddenly, it mattered. It mattered very much. "Would the Cheysuli have rejected my claim to the Lion?"

"The Mujhar is in no danger of giving up *his* claim any time soon." Gavan smiled. "He is a strong man, and in sound health."

"Aye." Kellin's nerves frayed further. It seemed no matter how careful he was, how meticulous his phrasing, he could not get the answer he wanted; yet at the same time he knew what the answer was, and dreaded it. "Gavan—" He felt sweat sting a scrape on one temple as the droplet ran down beneath a lock of hair. "Would the Cheysuli accept a *lir*less Mujhar?"

Gavan did not hesitate. "Now? No. There is no question of it. We are too close to fulfillment . . . a *lir*less Cheysuli would prove a true danger to the prophecy. We cannot afford to support a Mujhar who lacks the most fundamental of all Cheysuli gifts. It would provide the Ihlini an opportunity to destroy us forever."

"Of course." The words were ash. If he opened his mouth too widely, he would spew it like a dismantled fire cairn.

Gavan laughed. Yellow eyes were bright and amused, and wholly inoffensive. "If you are feeling unworthy in the aftermath of bonding, it is a natural thing. The gift—and the power that comes with it—is entirely humbling." He arched black brows. "Even for Mujhars—and men who will *be* Mujhar."

All of Kellin's anticipated arguments in favor of severing the partial bond with Sima evaporated. He would get no understanding from Gavan; likely, he would get nothing even remotely approaching sympathy. He would simply be stricken from the birthlines and summarily removed from the succession.

Leaving no one. "Blais," he said abruptly. "There was a time when some warriors wanted Blais to be named prince in my place."

"That was many years ago."

Kellin felt the dampness of perspiration stipple his upper lip. He wanted to brush it dry, but to do so would call attention to his desperation. "The *a'saii* still exist, do they not? Somewhere in Homana, separate from here . . . they still desire to make their own *tahlmorras* without benefit of the prophecy."

Gavan lifted his cup of honey brew. "There are always heretics."

Kellin watched him drink. *If Blais had survived*— He put it into words. "If Blais had survived, and I had gained no *lir*, would he have been named to the Lion?"

Gavan's eyes were steady. "In lieu of a proper heir, there would have been no other. But such a thing would have delayed completion for another generation, perhaps more. Blais lacked the Solindish and Atvian bloodlines. It would have taken time—more time than we have . . ." Gavan drank, then set aside his cup. "But what profit in this, Kellin? You are a warrior. You have a *lir*. It falls to you, now, without question. It all falls to you."

Coals crumbled in the firecairn. Illumination wavered, then stilled. It glowed in Gavan's eyes.

"Too heavy," Kellin murmured, swallowing tightly.

Gavan laughed aloud. A hand indicated Sima. "No burden is too heavy if there is a *lir* to help you bear it."

Chapter Twelve

Though offered a place in Clankeep, Kellin did not accept it. There was something else he wanted—*needed*—to do; something he should have done years before. He had avoided it with a steadfast intransigence, taking a quiet, vicious pleasure in the wrong done him because it fanned the flames of rebellion. A part of him knew very well that without what he perceived as true cause, his defiance might yet be warped into something other than a natural maturing of personality. He was expected to be different from others because of his heritage and rank; hot temper and hasty words were often overlooked because of who he was. That in itself sometimes forced him to more rebellion because he needed to provoke a response that would mitigate self-contempt.

He knew very well what the mountain cat said was right. He *was* too angry, and had been for years. But he knew its cause; it was hardly his fault. A motherless infant prince willingly deserted by a father had little recourse to other emotions.

Kellin stood outside the pavilion. Like Gavan's, it also bore a fox painted on its sides, though the base color was blue instead of saffron. The pavilion was difficult to see in the darkness; moonlight was obscured by clustered trees and overhanging branches. The Cheysuli had moved Clankeep after the Ihlini attack, for a part of the forest had burned. Only rain a day or two later had prevented more destruction.

Accost him now, just after awakening, so he has no time to marshal defenses or rhetoric. Kellin drew in a deep breath that expanded sore ribs, then called through the closed doorflap that he desired to see the *shar tahl*.

A moment only, and then a hand drew aside the flap so that the man stood unobstructed. He wore leather in place of robes, and *lir*-gold weighted his arms. He was alert; Kellin thought perhaps the man had not been asleep after all.

"Aye?" And then the warrior's expression altered. An ironic arch lifted black brows. "I should have expected this. You would not come all the times I invited you in the daylight . . . this suits your character."

It sparked an instant retort. "You know nothing about my character!"

The older man considered it. "That is true," he said at last. "What I know of you—now—has to do with the tales they tell." He widened the doorflap. "By your expression, this is not intended to be a sanguine visit. Well enough—I had gathered by your continued silence you did not accept my offers of aid as anything other than insult."

"Not insult," Kellin said. "Unnecessary."

"Ah." The man was in his late fifties, not so much younger than the Mujhar. Thick hair grayed heavily, but the flesh of his face was still taut, and his eyes were intent. "But now there is necessity."

Kellin did not look at Sima. He simply pointed to her. "I want to be rid of that."

"Rid?" The *shar tahl*'s irony evaporated. "Come in," he said curtly.

Kellin ducked in beside him. Hostility banished the dullness engendered by Gavan's honey brew; nerves made him twitchy. He stood aside in stiff silence as the *shar tahl* permitted the mountain cat to enter.

He waited edgily. There were many things he wanted to say, and he anticipated multiple pointed responses designed to dissuade him. The *shar tahl* would no more understand his desire than Gavan would have; the difference was, Kellin was better prepared to withstand anything the *shar tahl* might suggest by way of argument. He disliked the man. Dislike lent him the strength of will to defy a man whose service was to the gods, and to the preservation of tradition within the clans.

"Be seated," the *shar tahl* said briefly. Then, to Sima, "You are well come to my pavilion."

The cat lay down. Her tail thumped once. Then she stilled, huge eyes fixed on Kellin.

With a grimace of impatience, Kellin sat down. Neither food nor drink was offered; tacit insult, designed to tell him a thing or two. *Then we are well matched. I have things to say as well.*

"So." The older man's expression was closed, severe in its

aloofness. "You want to be rid of your *lir.* Since it is well known you had none, I can only assume this is a very recent bonding."

"Aye, very recent; last night." Pointedly, Kellin added, "When I was a captive of the Ihlini."

The *shar tahl's* expression did not alter; he seemed fixed upon a single topic. "Yet now you wish to sever that bond."

Kellin's hands closed into fists against crossed legs. "Does it mean nothing to you that the Prince of Homana was captured by the Ihlini, and less that he escaped?"

The *shar tahl's* mouth tightened minutely. "We will speak of that later. At this moment the Prince of Homana's desire to sever what the gods have made for him is of greater concern."

"Because it has to do with gods, and you are a *shar tahl.*" Kellin did not bother to hide the derision in his tone. "By all means let us discuss that which you believe of more import; after all, what is the welfare of Homana's future Mujhar compared to his desire to renounce a gift of the gods?"

"Yet if you renounce this bond, there is no more need to concern ourselves with the welfare of Homana's future Mujhar, as he would no longer *be* heir." The *shar tahl's* eyes burned brightly. "But you know that. I can see it in your face." He nodded slightly. "So you have been to Gavan already and what you have heard does not please you. Therefore I must assume this meeting is meant merely to air your grievance, though you know very well nothing can come of it. You cannot renounce the *lir*-bond, lest you be stripped of your rank. And you would never permit that; it would echo your *jehan's* actions."

Kellin's response was immediate. "I did not come to speak of my *jehan!*"

"But we will." The older man's tone allowed no room for protest. "We should have had this conversation years ago."

"We will not have it now. My *jehan* has nothing to do with this."

"Your *jehan* has much to do with this. His desertion of you has to do with everything in your life."

"Enough."

"I have hardly begun."

"Then I will end it!" Kellin glared at the man. "I am still the Prince of Homana. My rank is higher than yours."

"Is it?" Black brows arched. "I think not. Not in the eyes of the gods . . . ah, of course—you do not recognize their sovereignty."

The *shar tahl* lifted a quelling hand. "In fact, you detest them because you believe they stole your *jehan* from you."

Much as he longed to, Kellin knew better than to shout. To give in to such a display was to weaken his position. "He was meant to be the heir. Not I. Not *yet;* my time was meant for later. They *did* steal him."

"A warrior follows his *tahlmorra.*"

"Or obstructs the prophecy?" Kellin shook his head. "I think what they say of him is true: he is mad. No madman bases his actions on what is real. He does as he does because his mind is addled."

"Aidan's mind is no more addled than your own," the *shar tahl* retorted. "In fact, some would argue it is more sane than yours."

"Mine!"

The warrior smiled grimly. "Your reputation precedes you."

For only an instant Kellin was silent. Then he laughed aloud, letting the sound fill the pavilion. "Because I drink? Because I wager? Because I lie with whores?" The laughter died, but the grin was undiminished. "These actions appear to be a tradition within my family. Shall I name you the names? Brennan, Hart, Corin—"

"Enough." The irony was banished. "You came because you wish to renounce your *lir*. Allow me to do my office. Bide a moment, my lord." The *shar tahl* rose abruptly and moved to the doorflap. He ducked out, leaving Kellin alone with a silent black mountain cat. After a moment the priest returned and resumed his seat. His smile was humorless. "How may I serve my lord?"

Kellin's impatience faded. Hostility dissipated. If the man *could* aid him, he had best mend his manner. "The bonding was done hastily, to enable me to escape the Ihlini. Even she admits it." He did not glance at Sima. "She speaks of balance, and the danger in lacking it. I have none."

The *shar tahl* now was serious. "You assumed *lir*-shape in anger?"

"In anger, fear, panic . . ." Kellin sighed; the vestiges of pride and hostility faded utterly. Quietly, he explained what had happened—and how he had killed a man by tearing out his throat.

The dark flesh by the older man's eyes folded upon itself. His eyes seemed to age. "A harsh bonding. But more than that, an improper one. It is only half done."

"Half?" Kellin looked at the cat. "Do you mean I *could* renounce her?"

"No. Not safely. Your *lir*lessness is ended; half-bonded or no, you will never be what you were. The question now is, what will you permit yourself to *be?*"

Alarm bloomed. "What do you mean?"

"You are angry," the *shar tahl* said. "I perhaps understand it better than most—your *jehan* and I have shared many confidences." The severity of the face now was replaced with a human warmth that nearly unmanned Kellin. "Aidan and I have spent much time together. It was why I desired to speak with you before, to explain his reasoning."

"Let *him* explain it!"

The *shar tahl* sighed. "The proper time is not yet come."

Bitterness engulfed. "There never *will* be a 'proper time'!" Kellin cried. "That is the point!"

"No." The *shar tahl* lifted a hand, then let it drop. "That is not the point. There will come a time, I promise . . . when the gods intend that you should meet."

"When *he* intends, you mean . . . and he never will." Kellin gathered himself to rise. "This is bootless. It wastes my time."

"*Sit down.*" The tone was a whipcrack. "You have come to me with a serious concern that needs to be addressed. Set aside your hatred and hostility long enough, if you will, to permit me to explain that you are in grave danger."

"I have escaped the Ihlini."

"This has nothing to do with the Ihlini. This has to do with yourself. It is of the balance I speak." The *shar tahl* glanced at Sima. "Has she explained what could happen?"

"That I might be locked in beast-form if I lose my balance?" Kellin's mouth twisted. "Aye. *After* she urged me to take *lir*-shape."

"Then she must have believed it necessary." The *shar tahl* studied Sima with something very akin to sympathy, which seemed an odd thing to Kellin; the *lir* were considered far wiser than their warriors. "The *lir* are proscribed from attacking Ihlini. If she urged you to assume *lir*-shape before the proper time, fully cognizant of the risk, it was because she believed it necessary to preserve your life." The yellow eyes were intent. "The life has been preserved. Now we must insure that the mind within the body is preserved as well."

"Burr—" Kellin cut it off. It was time for truth, not protest. Defiance crumbled in the face of his admission. "I have resented you for years."

"I know." The *shar tahl* reached for a jug and cups, then poured two full. "Drink. What you must know will dry your mouth; wet it first, and then we shall begin."

"Can I learn it by dawn?"

"A thing so vital as this cannot be learned in a night. It requires years." Burr sipped his honey brew. "A young warrior is taught from the day of his birth how to strike the balance in all things. We are a proud race, we Cheysuli, and surpassingly arrogant—" Burr smiled, "—because we are, after all, the children of the gods . . . but we are not an angry race, nor one much given to war except when it is required. The Homanans have called us beasts and predators, but it is because of what we can do with our bodies, not our desire for blood. We are a peaceful race. That desire for peace—in mind as well as lifestyle—is taught from birth. By the time a young man reaches the age to receive a *lir*, his knowledge of self-control is well-rooted. His longing for a *lir* supercedes the recklessness of youth—no young Cheysuli would risk the wrath of the gods that might result in *lir*lessness."

"Is that true?" Kellin asked. "You are a *shar tahl*—would the gods deny a boy a *lir* because he does not suit their idea of a well-behaved Cheysuli?"

Burr laughed. "You are the most defiant and reckless of Cheysuli I have ever known. Yet there is the proof that the gods do as they will." A hand indicated Sima. "You have your place, Kellin. You have a *tahlmorra*. Now it is your task to acknowledge the path before you."

"And take it?"

"If it is what the gods intend."

"Gods," Kellin muttered. "They clutter up a life. They bind a man's spirit so he cannot do as he will."

"You, I believe, are a perfect example of the fallacy in that logic. You do—and have always done—precisely as you desire." Burr sipped liquor, then set the cup aside. "You must fully accept your *lir*. To remain half-bonded sentences both of you to a life to which no man—or *lir*—should ever be subjected."

"Madness," Kellin said. He worked a trapped twig from the weave of soiled breeches. "What if I told you I believed it was arrant nonsense, this belief that *lir*lessness results in madness? That I believe it is no more than a means for a man's misplaced faith in his gods to control him, or destroy him?"

Burr smiled. "You would not be the first to suggest that. In fact, if you were not the heir to the Lion and therefore assured of your place, I would say your defiance and determination resembles the *a'saii.*" He drank, watching Kellin over the rim of his cup. "It is not easy for a man to accept that one moment he is in the fullness of his prime, healthy and strong, while the next he is sentenced to the death-ritual despite his continued health and strength. It is the true test of what we are, Kellin; do you know of any other race which willingly embraces death when there appears to be no reason to die?"

"No. No other race is so ludicrously constrained by the gods." Kellin shook his head, tapping the twig against his knee. "It is a *waste,* Burr! Just as *kin-wrecking* is!"

"That, I agree with," Burr said. "Once, the custom had its place . . . there was a need, Kellin."

"To cast out a man because he was maimed?" Kellin shook his head. "The loss of a hand does not render a man incapable of serving his clan or his kin."

"Once, it might have. If a one-handed warrior failed, because of his infirmity, to protect a single life, he was a detriment. There was a time we dared not permit such a risk, lest our people die out entirely."

Kellin gestured. "Enough. I am speaking now of the death-ritual. I contend it is nothing more than a means of control, a method by which the gods—and *shar tahls,* perhaps?—" he grinned in arch contempt, "—can force others to do their will."

Burr was silent. His eyes were partially hidden behind lowered lashes. Kellin thought perhaps he might at last have provoked the older man into anger, but when Burr at last met his eyes there was nothing of anger in his expression. "What the gods have required of men is duty, honor, reverence—"

"And self-sacrifice!"

"—and sacrifice," Burr finished. "Aye. I deny none of it. But if we had not offered any of these things, Kellin, you would not be seated here before me contesting the need for such service."

"Words!" Kellin snapped. "You are as bad as the Ihlini. You weave magic with words, to ensorcell me to your will."

"I do nothing but state the truth." Burr's tone was very quiet, lacking all emotion. "If a single man in your birthline had turned his back on his *tahlmorra,* you would not be the warrior destined to inherit the Lion."

"You mean if my *jehan* had turned his back on his *tahlmorra.*" Kellin wanted to swear. "This is merely another attempt to persuade me that what my *jehan* did was necessary. You said yourself you are friends . . . I hear bias in his favor."

"It was necessary," Burr said. "Who can say what might have become of you if Aidan had not renounced his title? Paths can be altered, Kellin—and prophecies. If Aidan had remained here, he would be Prince of Homana. You would merely be third in line behind Brennan and Aidan. That extra time could well have delayed completion of the prophecy, and destroyed it utterly."

"You mean, it might have prevented me from lying with whatever woman I am supposed to lie with—*according to the gods*—in order to sire Cynric." Kellin tossed aside the twig. "A convenience, nothing more. No one *knows* this. Just as no one knows for certain a warrior goes mad if his *lir* is killed." He smiled victory. "You see? We have come full circle."

Burr's answering smile was grim. "But I can name you the proofs: Duncan, Cheysuli clanleader, kept alive by Ihlini sorcery though his *lir* was dead, and used as a weapon to strike at his son, Donal, who was meant to be Mujhar."

Kellin felt cold; he knew this history.

"Teirnan, Blais' *jehan*, who assumed the role of clan-leader to the heretical *a'saii*. A warrior who would have, given the chance, pulled Brennan from the Lion and mounted it himself." Burr's tone was steady. "Tiernan renounced his *lir*. In the end, completely mad, he threw himself into the Womb of the Earth before the eyes of your *jehan* and *jehana* in an attempt to prove himself worthy to hold the Lion. He did not come out."

Kellin knew that also.

Burr said softly, "First we will speak of your *jehan*. Then of the balance."

Kellin wanted it badly. "No," he said roughly. "What I learn of my *jehan* will be learned from him."

Burr looked beyond him to the slack doorflap. He said a single word—a name—and a warrior came in. In his arms he held a small girl asleep against his shoulder; by his side stood a tousle-haired boy of perhaps three years.

"There is another," the *shar tahl* said. "Another son; do you recall? Or have you forgotten entirely that these are your children?"

"Mine—" Kellin blurted.

"Three royal bastards." Burr's tone was unrelenting. "Packed off to Clankeep like so much unwanted baggage, and never once visited by the man who sired them."

Chapter Thirteen

Kellin refused to look at the children, or at the warrior with them. Instead he stared at Burr. "Bastards," he declared, biting off the word.

The *shar tahl*'s voice was calm. "That they are bastards does not preclude the need for parents."

Kellin's lips were stiff. "Homanan halflings."

"And what are you, my lord, but Homanan, Solindish, Atvian, Erinnish . . . ?" Burr let it trail off. "*I* am pure Cheysuli."

"*A'saii?*" Kellin challenged. "You believe I should be replaced?"

"If you refuse your *lir*, assuredly." Burr was relentless. "Look at your children, Kellin."

He did not want to. He was desperate not to. "Bastards have no place in the line of succession—"

"—and therefore do not matter?" Burr shook his head. "That is the Homanan in you, I fear . . . in the clans bastardy bears no stigma." He paused. "Did Ian know you felt so? He, too, was a bastard."

"Enough!" Kellin hissed. "You try to twist me inside out no matter what I say."

"I shall twist you any way I deem necessary, if the result achieved is as I believe it should be." Burr looked at the boy. "Young, but he promises well. Homanan eyes—they are hazel— but the hair is yours. And the chin—"

"Stop it."

"The girl is too young yet to show much of what she shall be—"

"*Stop* it!"

"—and of course the other boy is but a handful of months." Burr looked at Kellin, all pretenses to neutrality dropped. "Explain it away, if you please. Justify your actions with regard to these children, though you refuse to permit your *jehan* the same favor."

"*He traded me for the gods!*" It was a cry from the heart Kellin regretted at once. "Can you not see—"

"What I see are two children without a *jehan*," Burr said. "Another yet sleeps at the breast of a Cheysuli woman who lost her own baby. I submit to you, my lord: for what did you trade *them?*"

Words boiled up in Kellin's mouth, so many at first he could not find a single one that would, conjoined with another, make any sense at all. Furious, he thrust himself to his feet. At last the words broke free. "I get nothing from you. No truths, no support, no honorable service! Nothing more than drivel mouthed by a man who is truer to the *a'saii* than to his own Mujhar!"

Burr did not rise. "Until you can look on those children and acknowledge your place in their lives, speak no word against Aidan."

Kellin extended a shaking hand. He pointed at Sima. "I want no *lir.*"

"You have one."

"I want to be rid of her."

"And open the door to madness."

"I do not believe it."

Burr's eyes glinted. "Then test it, my lord. Challenge the gods. Renounce your *lir* and withstand the madness." He rose and took the small girl from the silent warrior's arms, settling her against his shoulder. Over her head, he said, "It will be a true test, I think. Certainly as true as the one Teirnan undertook at the Womb of the Earth."

Desperate, Kellin declared, "I have no room in my life for the impediment of halfling bastards!"

"That," Burr said, "is between you and the gods."

Kellin shut his teeth. "You are wrong. All of you. I will prove you wrong."

"*Tahlmorra lujhalla mei wiccan, cheysu,*" Burr said. Then, as Kellin turned to flee, "*Cheysuli i'halla shansu.*"

Kellin did not stay the rest of the night in Clankeep but took back his borrowed mount and rode on toward Mujhara. He had moved beyond the point of weariness into the realm of an exhaustion so complex as to render him almost preternaturally alert. Small sounds were magnified into a clamor that filled his head, so that there was no room for thought. It pleased him. Thought renewed anger, reestablished frustration, reminded him yet again

that no matter what he said—no matter who he *was*—no Cheysuli
warrior would accept him as one of them so long as he lacked a *lir.*

They would sooner have me go mad with *a* lir *than go mad because I renounce one.*

It made no sense to Kellin. But neither did the mountain cat
who shadowed his horse, loping in its wake.

He had tried to send her away. Sima refused to go. Since he had
made very clear his intentions to forswear her, the cat had said
nothing. The link was suspiciously empty.

As if she no longer exists. And yet here she was; he had only to
glance over a shoulder to see her behind him.

Would it not be simpler if he shut off that link forever? Certainly less hazardous. If Sima died while as yet unbonded, he could
escape the death ritual.

Though Burr says I will not.

Kellin shifted in the saddle, attempting to lessen the discomfort
of his chest. The *shar tahl* had challenged him to test the conviction that a *lir*less warrior went mad. And he had accepted. Part of
the reason was pride, part a natural defiance; uneasily Kellin wondered what might happen if he lost the challenge. If, after all, the
Cheysuli belief was based on truth.

What does it feel like to go mad? He slowed his mount as he approached the city; star- and moonlight, now tainted by Mujhara's
illumination, made it difficult to see the road. *What was Teirnan
thinking, as he leapt into the Womb?*

What had his father thought, and his mother, as the warrior
without a *lir* tested his right to the Lion, and was repudiated?

*I would never throw myself into the Womb of the Earth. It
was*— He brought himself up short. *Madness?*

Kellin swore the vilest oaths he could think of. An arm
scrubbed roughly across his face did nothing to rid his head of
such thoughts. It smeared grime and crusted blood—he had left
Clankeep without even so much as a damp cloth for cleaning his
face—and tousled stiffened hair. His clothing was rigid with dried
blood and scratched at bruised flesh. Inside the flesh, bones ached.

He did not enter Mujhara by way of the Eastern Gate because
they knew him there. Instead he angled the horse right and rode for
the Northern Gate. Of all the gates it was the least used; the Eastern led toward Clankeep, the Southern to Hondarth, the Western to
Solinde. The Northern opened onto the road that, followed to its

end, led to the Bluetooth River; beyond lay the Northern Wastes, and Valgaard.

Kellin shivered. *I would have gone there, had Corwyth persevered.*

Through the Northern Gate lay the poorer sections of Mujhara, including the Midden. Kellin intended to ride directly through, bound for Homana-Mujhar on its low rise in the center of the city. He wanted a bath very badly, and a bed—

His horse—Corwyth's horse—shied suddenly, even as Kellin heard the low-pitched growling. He gathered rein, swearing, as the dog boiled out of the darkness.

Kellin took a deeper seat, anticipating trouble, but the dog streaked by him. Then he knew.

The link that had been so empty blazed suddenly to life, engulfing him utterly. He heard the frantic barking, the growls; then Sima's wailing cry. The link, half-made though it was, reverberated with the mountain cat's frenzied counterattack.

"Wait!" It was a blurt of shock. Stunned by the explosion within the link, Kellin sat immobile. His body rang with pain and outrage; yet none of it was his own. "Hers." She had said they were linked, even if improperly. He felt whatever the cat felt.

Freed of the paralysis, Kellin jerked the horse around, feeling for the long-knife retrieved from Corwyth. He saw a huddle of black in the shadows, and the gleam of pale slick hide as the dog darted in toward Sima. It was joined by another, and then a third; in a moment the noise would bring every dog at a run.

They will kill— The rest was lost. A man-shaped shadow stepped out of a dark doorway and, with a doubled fist, smashed the horse's muzzle.

Kellin lost control instantly, and very nearly his nose. The horse's head shot skyward, narrowly missing Kellin's bowed head. The animal fell back a step or two, scrabbling in mucky footing, flinging his head in protest.

Before Kellin could attempt to regain control of the reins, hands grabbed his left leg. It was summarily jerked out of the stirrup and twisted violently, so that Kellin was forced to follow the angle or risk having his ankle broken. The position made him vulnerable; a second violent twist and a heave tipped Kellin off backward even as he grabbed for the saddle.

"Ku'reshtin—" He twisted in midair, broke free of the hands, then landed awkwardly on his feet—*leijhana tu'sai!*—and caught

his balance haphazardly against the startled horse's quivering rump.

Before he could draw a breath, the man was on him.

Inconsequentially, even as he fought, Kellin believed it ironic. He had no coin. All anyone would get from him was a Cheysuli long-knife; which, he supposed, was reward enough.

His own breathing was loud, but over his noise he heard the yowling of the mountain cat and the clamor of dogs. His concentration was split—for all he wanted no *lir*, he did not desire her to be killed or injured—which made it that much harder to withstand his assault.

Booted feet slipped in muck. The alley was narrow, twisted upon itself, hidden in deep shadow because dwellings blocked out much of the moon. Kellin did not hesitate but grabbed at once for Blais' knife; massive hands grasped his right arm immediately and wrenched his hand away from the hilt. The grip on his arm was odd, but firm enough; then it shifted. Fingers closed tautly on flesh, shutting off strength and blood. Kellin's hand was naught but a lifeless blob of bone, flesh, and muscle on the end of a useless arm.

"Ku'resh—"

The grip shifted. A knee was brought up as Kellin's captive forearm was slammed down. The bones of his wrist snapped easily against the man's thigh.

Pain was immediate. Kellin's outcry echoed the frenzy of the mountain cat as she fought off the dogs. But the attacker was undeterred. Even as Kellin panted a shocked protest colored by angry oaths, the stranger wound his fists into the bloodstiffened doublet. He lifted Kellin from the ground, then slammed him against the nearest wall.

Skull smacked stone. Lungs collapsed, expelling air. A purposeful elbow was dug deeply into Kellin's laboring chest, rummaging imperiously amidst the wreckage of fragile ribs. Bones gave way.

He inhaled raggedly and managed a breathless string of foul words in a mixture of Homanan, Old Tongue, and Erinnish, depending on the words to give him something on which he might focus. The pain was all-consuming, but not nearly so astounding as the violence of the attack itself.

Sima's screaming echoed in the canyon of cheek-by-jowl

dwellings. A dog yelped, then another; others belled a call to join the attack.

Lir— It was instinctive. He meant nothing by it. The appeal faded immediately, though not the knowledge of it.

Kellin sagged against the wall, pinned there by a massive body. A shoulder leaned into his chest. His broken wrist remained trapped.

The odd grip tightened, shifting on his forearm. "First the thumb," the attacker grunted.

There was no air, no air at all—but *pain*—

"First the thumb, then the fingers—"

Kellin sucked frantically at air.

"—and lastly, the *hand*—"

He knew the truth then. "Luce!" Kellin gasped. "Gods—"

"None here, little princeling. Only me." A grin split Luce's beard in the pallor of the night. "I'll hold the hand just so—" He did it one-handed, while the other snagged the long-knife from Kellin's belt.

One word, no more, "*Wait*—"

"What? D'ye think to buy me, princeling? No, not Luce—he's enough coin to last him, and ways of getting more." Luce's breath stank. He hooked an elbow up and slammed it into Kellin's jaw. The back of Kellin's skull smashed against stone wall; he felt a tooth break from the blow, and weakly spat out the pieces. Luce laughed. "A love-tap, nothing more . . . and speaking of that, perhaps I should make you mine to use as I will—a royal sheath for my sword—"

Kellin squirmed against the wall. His vision yet swam from the blow, and he tasted blood in his mouth. He did not know if it came from the empty root socket, or was expelled from pierced lungs.

Luce still pinned the broken wrist against the wall. In the other hand gleamed the knife. He set the point between Kellin's spread legs and tapped cloth-warded genitals. "The Midden's a harsh place full of desperate people—but *Luce* would protect you. Luce would make you his—"

"Sima!" Kellin, shouted, spraying blood and desperation. In the distance he heard growls and yelps, and the wailing cry of an infuriated cat. "*Sim*—"

But Luce shut it off with a dig of an elbow into broken ribs. "First the thumb," he said.

Kellin understood what a *lir* was for. He had repudiated his own. What, then, was left?

He hurt very badly. The injuries were serious. Even if Luce did nothing else, he would probably die regardless.

Sima had said before she had given him the key. Now it was his task to open the door again.

Kellin used the pain. He used the pain, the fury, the frustration, the fear. He *feasted* on it, and allowed it to fill his spirit until there was nothing left of the man but the elemental drives to kill, and to feed.

As the knife came down to sever the thumb from his hand, the hand was no longer there. In its place was the flexing paw of a mountain cat.

Chapter Fourteen

With a shocked cry, Luce let go. The knife glinted briefly, then tumbled into muck. Kellin dropped four-footed to splayed, leathery pads, then twisted sinuously in the body made for fluid movement, like water over stone; like runoff in the ancient cut of a waterfall over sheer cliffs.

He will learn what it means to harm a Cheysuli— But then the thought spilled away into a jumble of crazed images tumbled one against another, all stuck together like layers of leaves adhered one on top of another, until vision fell out of focus and no longer mattered at all. What mattered now was scent and the stink of a frightened man; the sound of the man's sobbing; the taste of promised revenge.

The cat who was Kellin reached out. Easily—*so* easily!—he slapped a negligent paw across the giant's thigh. Claws dug in sharply; blood spurted through rent cloth.

Luce screamed. Thumbless hands clutched at his bleeding thigh, trying to stanch it. Lazily, exultant in his strength, Kellin reached out again and slapped at the other meaty thigh so that it, too, bled. As Luce sobbed and whimpered, he curved a playful paw around one ankle and dug claws into bone. With a snarl that warped his mouth slantways, he jerked the man to the ground. The sound of the skull splitting was swallowed by his snarl.

The noise of the hounds was gone. Tail lashed anticipation, beating against cold air. Kellin moved to stand over his meal so no one else could steal it.

Lir!

Kellin did not listen.

Lir! Do not!

It was easier to frame the feelings, the images, not the words. His mouth was no longer human. His response was built of instinct, not the logic of a man. *You want it.*

No. No, lir. *Leave it.* A bleeding Sima was free of dogs, though some lay dead, others dying, while another ran off yelping. *Leave it.*

He challenged her. *YOU want it.*

No.

I hunger. Here is food. He paused. *Are you my mate?*

Come away.

He panted. He drooled. Hunger was paramount, but pain ate at his spirit. It was easiest to give in, to let instinct rule a comprehension that was, even more quickly now, flowing away from him. *I hunger. Here is food.*

You are man, not cat.

Man? I wear a cat's shape.

You are man. Cheysuli. Shapechanger. You have borrowed this shape. Give it back. Let the earth magic have it back. When you have learned the proper balance, you can borrow the shape again.

He let his tail lash. *Who am I, then?"*

Kellin. Not cat. Man.

He considered it. *I do not feel like a man. THIS is man, this food here beneath me.* Saliva dripped from his jowls. *You want it for yourself.*

Come away, she said. *You have wounds to be healed. So have I.*

The dogs hurt you?

I have hurts. So do you. Come away, lir. *We will have them healed.*

Nearby a door was opened. Someone looked out into the street. He heard a gabble of voices. He understood none of the words. Noise, no more; the noise of puny humans.

He lowered his jaws. Blood, sweat, urine, fear, and death commingled in a powerful perfume. He would taste it—

NO. The female was at his side. She leaned a shoulder into his. Her chin rubbed at his head. *If you would feed here, there will be no choice but to kill you.*

Who would kill me? Who would dare?

Men.

Inner knowledge gloated. *They could not accomplish it.*

She leaned harder, rubbing against his neck. *They could. They would. Come away,* lir. *You are badly hurt.*

Another door opened. A slash of candlelight slanted into the street. In its illumination he saw the dead hounds, the slack hulk of a man. Voices cried out, full of terror.

Away? he asked. *But—the food—*

Leave it, she said. *There is better elsewhere.*

The big cat hurt. His wounds were uncounted, and untended; he required tending. He went with her then because the urge to feed had left him. He felt disoriented and distant, unsure of himself. She led him away from the alley to another not far away and found a hidden corner.

Here, she said, nudging at a shoulder.

She was wounded, he saw. Blood spiked the fur on her spine. He turned to her, tending the bites, licking to wash the blood away. She had been hurt by the hounds, torn and tainted by the audacity of mere beasts who did not know what it was to be gods-blessed.

Leave it, she said. *Remember what you are.*

He paused. *I am—* He checked.

Gold eyes were intent. *What are you?*

I am—as you see me.

No.

I am—I am—

Remember! she snapped. *Recall your knowledge of self.*

He could not. He was what he was.

She leaned against him. He smelled her fear, her blood. She was alien to him, who did not know what she was to him. *Stay here. You are too badly wounded to walk. Wait here for me.*

It frightened him. *Where are you going?*

For help. Stay here.

She left him. He crouched against the wall, tail whipping a counterpoint to the pain in his foreleg, in his ribs, in his jaws. Licking intensified pain. He flattened his ears against his head and pulled back his lips from his teeth in a feral grimace of pain and fear.

She had left him alone, and now he was helpless.

Men came. And torches. The big cat shied back, huddling into a corner as he snarled and growled a warning. He slitted eyes against the flame and saw silhouettes, man-shapes holding sticks with fire blooming from them. He smelled them: they stank of anticipation, apprehension; the giddy tang of an excitement nearly sexual, as if they hoped to mate once the task was done. The odor was strong. It filled up his nostrils and entered his head, causing the reflex response that dropped open his jaws. Raspy in- and exhalations as he scented the men made him sound like a bellows.

Lir. It was the female. Sima. Lir, *do not fear. They have come to help, not harm.*

Fire.

They will come no closer, save one. She slunk out of the blinding light into his slime-coated corner. Blood crusted across her shoulders; she had run, and bled again. *Let the man come.*

He permitted it. He pressed himself against the wall and waited, one swollen paw dangling. Breathing hurt. He hissed and shook his head; a tooth in his jaw was broken.

The man came away from the fire. Kellin could not judge him by any but a cat's standards: his hair was silver like frost in winter sunlight, and his eyes glowed like coals. Metal glinted on naked arms, bared by a shed cloak despite the winter's bite.

"Kellin." The man knelt down on one knee, unmindful of the muck that would soil his leathers. "Kellin."

The cat opened his mouth and panted. Pain caused him to drool.

"Kellin, you must loose the cat-shape. There is no more need."

The cat rumbled a growl; he could not understand.

The man sighed and rose, turned back to the men with flames. He spoke quietly, and they melted away. Light followed them, so that though empty of men the corner still shone with a sickly, frenzied pallor.

The men were gone. In their places was a void, a blurred nothingness that filled the alley. And then a tawny mountain cat stalked out of the fading flame-dazzle with another at his side: a magnificent black female well into her prime. Her grace denounced the gangliness of the young female with Kellin who was, after all, little more than a cub.

Three mountain cats: two black, one tawny gold. In his mind formed the images that in humans would have been speech; to him, now, the images made promises that they would lend him required strength, and the healing he needed so badly.

In their eyes he saw a man. Human, like the others. His hair was not winter-frost, but black as a night sky. His eyes were green coals in place of ruddy or yellow. He did not glint with gold; he wore no gold at all. He was smooth and sleek and strong, with the blood running hot in his veins.

Pain blossomed anew. Broken bones protested.

Three cats pressed close. The tawny male mouthed his neck; Kellin flattened his ears and lowered his head. He hurt too much to display dominance postures to one who was clearly much older and wiser than he.

Come home, the cat said. *Come home with me now.*

Kellin panted heavily. In the muck, his pads were damp with sweat. Weakness overrode caution. He let them guide his mind until he saw what "home" meant: the true-body that was his. Fingers and toes in place of claws. Hair in place of fur, and smooth, taut flesh too easily bruised by harsh treatment.

Come home, the tawny cat said, and in its place was a man with eyes that understood his pain and the turmoil in his soul. "I have been there," he said. "My weakness is my fear of small dark places . . . I will be with you in this. I understand what it is to fear a part of yourself over which you have no control." Then, very softly, "Come home, Kellin. Let the anger go."

He let it go. Exhaustion engulfed, and a blurred disorientation. Spent, he slumped against the half- grown female. She licked at his face and scraped a layer of skin; human skin, not feline.

Kellin recoiled. He pressed himself into the stone wall.

"Kellin." Brennan still knelt. Behind him torches flared. "*Shansu,* Kellin—it is over."

"I—I—" Kellin stopped. He swallowed hard against the sour taste of bile. He could frame no proper words, as if he had lost them in his transformation. "I."

The Mujhar's expression was infinitely gentle. "I know. Come with me." Brennan paused. "Kellin, you are hurt. Come with me."

He panted shallowly. He cradled his wrist against a chest that hurt as much. His legs were coiled under him so he could rise instantly in a single upward thrust.

Brennan's hand was on his shoulder.

Kellin tensed. And then it mattered no longer. He closed his eyes and sagged against the stone. Tears ran unchecked through grime, perspiration, and blood old as well as new. He was not ashamed.

Brennan's hand touched his blood-stiffened hair softly, tenderly, as if to frame words he could not say. And then the hand was gone from Kellin's hair, closing instead on the arm that was whole. "Come up from there, my lord."

His grandsire had offered him no honor in manner or words for a very long time, nor the deep and abiding affection that now lived in his tone.

Kellin looked at him. "I am not . . . not . . ." He was still too close to the cat. He wanted to wail instead of speak. "Am. Not. Deserving . . ." He tried again in desperation, needing to say it; to recover the human words. "—not of such *care*—"

Tears shone in Brennan's eyes. "You are deserving of many things, not the least of which is care. *Shansu* my young one—we will find a balance for you. Somehow, we will find a proper balance."

Torchlight streamed closer. Kellin looked beyond his grandfather and saw the royal guard. One of the men was Teague.

Their faces had been schooled to show no emotion. But he had seen it. He had seen them, and the fear in their eyes as they had looked upon the cat who had been to all of them before nothing more than a man.

Kellin shuddered. "I was—I was . . ." The wail was very near. He shut his mouth upon it, so as to give them no more reason to look upon him with fear and apprehension.

They were the elite guard of a warrior who became a mountain cat at will. It was not new to them, who had seen it before. But Brennan was nothing if not a dignified man of immense self-control. Kellin was not and had never been a dignified man; self-control was nonexistent. In him, as a human, they saw an angry man desirous of shedding blood.

In him now, as a cat, they saw the beast instead.

They know what I have become. What I will always be to them. It spilled from Kellin's mouth, accompanied by blood. "Grandsire—*help me*—"

Brennan did not shirk it. "We will mend the body first. Then we shall mend the mind."

Chapter Fifteen

He was but half conscious, drifting on fading awareness that told him very little save his wounds were healed at last, his broken bones made whole—yet the spirit remained flaccid. He wanted badly to sleep. Earth magic drained a man, regardless of which side he walked.

His eyes were closed, sticky lashes resting against drawn cheeks. Earth magic reknit bones, but did not dissipate bruises or prevent scarring from a wound that would otherwise require stitching. It merely restored enough health and strength to vanquish immediate danger; a warrior remade by the earth magic was nonetheless well cognizant of what had occurred to require it.

Kellin's face bore testimony to the violence done him. The flesh across the bridge of his nose had been torn by a thorn; welts distorted his cheeks; his bottom lip was swollen. He had drunk and rinsed out his mouth, but the tang of blood remained from the cuts in his lip and the inside of his cheek.

A hand remained on Kellin's naked shoulder. Fingertips trembled against smooth, freshly sponged flesh; Aileen had seen to the washing. *"Shansu,"* Brennan murmured hoarsely, lifting the hand. He, too, was drained, for he had undertaken the healing alone. It would have been better had there been another Cheysuli to aid him, but Brennan had not dared waste the time to send for a warrior. He had done the healing himself, and now suffered for it.

Kellin was dimly aware of Aileen's murmuring. The Mujhar said something unintelligible, then the door thumped closed. Kellin believed himself alone until he heard the sibilance of skirt folds against one another, the faint slide of thin slipper sole on stone where the rug did not reach. He smelled the scent she favored. Her presence was a beacon as she sat down by his bed.

"She is lovely," Aileen said quietly. "This must be very much what Sleeta looked like, before she and Brennan bonded."

He lay slumped on one side with his back to her. A shoulder jutted skyward. Along his spine and the curve of his buttocks lay warmth, incredible warmth; the living bulk of a mountain cat.

Kellin sighed. He wanted to sleep, not speak, but he owed Aileen something. Into the limp hand curled against his chin, he murmured, "I would sooner do without her, lovely or no."

"D'ye blame her, then? For being what you are?"

It jerked him out of lassitude into startled wakefulness. He turned over hastily, thrusting elbows beneath his spine to lever his sheet-draped torso upright. "Do you think *I*—"

"You," Aileen said crisply; she was not and had never been a woman who deferred, nor did she now blunt her words because of his condition. "Are you forgetting, my braw boyo, that I've lived with a Cheysuli longer than you've *been* one?"

It took him aback. He had expected sympathy, gentleness, her quiet, abiding support. What Aileen offered now was something other than that. "It is because of Sima that I—did that."

"Did what? Killed a man? Two?" Aileen did not smile. "I'm born of the House of Eagles; d'ye think the knowledge of killing's new to me? My House has been to war more times than I can count . . . my birthlines are as bloody as yours." She sat very straight upon the stool, russet-hued skirts puddled about slippered feet. "You've killed an Ihlini sorcerer, and a Homanan who meant to kill—or maim—you; as good as dead to the Cheysuli; I know about *kin-wrecking*." Aileen's tone was steady, as were her eyes. "The first killing won't be questioned; he was an *Ihlini*."

His mouth flattened into a grim, contemptuous line. "But the other was Homanan."

"Thief or no," she said, "some will call you a beast."

Memory was merciless. "I *was*."

"So now you're blaming your lovely *lir*."

"She is not my *lir*. Not yet. We are not fully bonded."

"Ah." Aileen's green eyes narrowed. She looked more catlike for it, with a fixed and unsettling stare. "And you're for ending it, are you?"

She read him too easily. Kellin slumped back onto bolsters and bedclothes. She was due honor and courtesy, but he was very tired. Bones were healed, but the body was yet unaware of its improved condition, save the blazing pain was gone. Stiffness persisted; after all that had happened in the space of two days, his resiliency was weakened. Youth could not usurp reality though its teeth be blunted. "I have no choice. *She* made me become—"

"I'm doubting that." Aileen's tone was level, unforgiving; she offered no platitudes designed to ease his soul, but harsher truths instead. "By the gods, I'm doubting *that!* You're the blood of my blood, Kellin, and I'll not hear a word against you from others— but *I* will say what I choose. In this instance, I hide none of it behind kindness and love, but tell it to you plainly: you've only yourself to blame."

His protest was immediate, if incomplete. *"Me?"*

"No Cheysuli warrior alive is without anger, Kellin. He merely controls it better. You control nothing at all, nor make any attempt."

He had no time to think, merely the need to fill the toothed silence yawning between them; to fight back with words from a heart that was filled to bursting with despair and desperation: could *she* not understand? She was his own blood. "I did not *want* to kill them, granddame—at least, aye, perhaps the Ihlini— he threatened *me*, after all!—but not the Homanan, not like *that*—he was a thief, aye, and deserving of roughness, but to kill him like that?" He gestured impatiently, disliking his incoherency; it obscured the strength of intent. "Kill him, aye, because he meant to kill me, or maim me in such a way as to cut me off from my clan, but I never wanted to kill *him*—at least, not as a cat . . . as a man, *aye*—"

"Kellin." She cut him off sharply with voice and gesture; a quick motion of eloquent hand. It was a Cheysuli gesture. "If you would listen to what you just said—or *tried* to say!—you would understand why it is imperative that you fully accept your *lir.*"

All his muscles stood up inside flesh in mute repudiation. "My *lir*—or the beast who would *be* my *lir*—has nothing to do with this."

Aileen rose. She was in that moment less his granddame than the Queen of Homana. "You are a fool," she declared. "A spoiled, petulant boy trapped in a man's body, and dangerous because of it. A boy filled to bursting on anger and bitterness can do little harm; a man may do more. A man who is half a beast may do more yet."

"I am *not*—"

"You are what you are," she said flatly. "What are we to think? Aye, a man under attack will do as he must to survive—d'ye think

I will *excuse* a man who means to kill my grandson?—but a man such as you, gifted so terribly, can never *be* a man."

Gifted so terribly. He had not looked on it as such. "Grandsire also wears the shape of a cat."

Her mouth was compressed. She permitted herself no latitude in the weight of her displeasure. "No man in all of Homana, not even a Midden thief, need fear that the Mujhar of Homana would ever lose himself to the point he sheds his humanity and *feeds* as a beast."

It shook him. Her face was taut and pale; his own felt worse. He felt it would stretch until the bones of his skull broke through, shredding thinning flesh, thereby displaying the true architecture lying too near the surface.

Human? Or beast? Kellin swallowed heavily. "I want nothing to do with it. *You* are not Cheysuli—surely you can understand how I feel. Does it not frighten you that the man whose bed you share becomes a cat at will?"

"I know the man," she said evenly. "I'm not knowing you at all."

"But—I am *me!*"

"No. You are a bared blade hungry for blood, with no hand on its hilt to steady its course."

"Granddame—"

"He is old," Aileen said, and the cracks of desperation in her self-control began abruptly to show. "He is the Mujhar of Homana, in whose veins the Old Blood flows, and he serves the prophecy. There is no doubt in him; what he does, he does for the Lion, and for the gods who made the Cheysuli. What I think does not matter, though he honors me for it; he does what he must do." Her hands trembled slightly until she hid them in skirt folds. "How do you think it felt to be given a tiny infant and told the future of a realm depended on that infant, because the infant's father was meant for the gods, not men?"

Kellin did not answer. There were no words in his mouth.

"How do you think it felt for him to realize the entire fate of Homana and his own race depended *solely* on that infant; that there would be no others to shore up the claim. If that infant died, the prophecy died with him. Aidan can sire no more."

Beside him, Sima stirred.

"How do you think it has been for him to watch what you became? To see you waste yourself on whores, when there is a cousin in Solinde . . . to see you risk yourself in the Midden, when there are safer games nearby . . . to hear you rant about fatherlessness when *he* has been a father in every way but seed, and even *then* he is your grandsire! How do you think it feels?"

He wet dry lips. "Granddame—"

Aileen's face was white and terrible. "How do you think it feels to know that your grandson—the only heir to the Lion—lacks the balance that will maintain his humanity; that if he does not gain it, the beast in him will prevail?" Aileen leaned close. "He is my husband," she declared. "He is my *man*. If you threaten him with this, be certain you shall suffer."

It shocked him. *"Granddame!"*

She was not finished. "I wasted too many years not honoring him enough. That time is past. I will do what I must do to keep him from destroying himself because a spoiled, defiant grandson refuses to grow up."

"Granddame, you cannot know—"

"I know," she said. "I saw his face when he looked at you. I saw his fear."

The Erinnish possessed his tongue. "I'm not knowing what to *do!*"

Aileen stepped close to the bed. Her hand touched Sima's head. "Be what you are. Be a Cheysuli warrior. You're in need of the gods' care more than any man I know."

It filled his mouth before he could prevent it, lashing out to punish. The question was utterly unexpected, yet even as he asked it, Kellin knew he had desired to frame the words for many, many years. "Does it mean nothing to you at all that your son repudiates you?"

Color spilled out of her face.

Kellin was appalled. But the words were said; he could not unsay them. "I only mean—"

"You only mean that he deserted his mother as well as his son, yet she does nothing?" Aileen's eyes were a clear, unearthly green, and empty of tears. "She has not done nothing, Kellin—she has done everything within her power to convince him to come home. But Aidan says—*said*—no, when he answered my letters at first. He answers nothing now; he said I need only ask the gods." Her chin trembled minutely. "He has a powerful faith, my son—so powerful it blinds him to the needs of other people."

"If you went there—"

"He forbids it."

"You are his *jehana!*"

Her fingers folded themselves into her skirts. "I will not go as a supplicant to my own son. I have some measure of pride."

"But it must hurt you!"

Her eyes dimmed behind a glaze of tears. "As it hurts you. As it hurts Brennan. We are all of us scarred by the absence of Aidan."

Cold fury filled Kellin. "And you wonder why I want nothing to do with a *lir*, or with the gods! You have only to look at *him*, and what obsession has made of him. I will not be so bound."

"You will be Mujhar one day. That will bind you even as it does your grandsire."

Kellin shook his head. "That is different. What kind of a Mujhar risks himself by bonding with an animal who might be the death of him? Does he not therefore risk his realm as well—*and* the prophecy?"

Aileen's voice was steady. "What is worth having if you are naught but a beast, and your people desire to kill you?"

Chapter Sixteen

One hundred and two steps. Kellin counted them as he climbed down from the Great Hall into the undercroft of Homana-Mujhar, where the Womb of the Earth lay within *lir*-warded walls. As a boy he had gone once with Ian, and once with the Mujhar. He had never gone alone.

Not entirely alone. The cat is with me.

He did not want her there. But she was the reason he went down to the Womb at all.

One hundred and two steps. He stood in a small closet made of stone and depressed the keystone. A wall turned on edge, and the Womb lay before him.

Air was stale, but did not stink of an ending. The passageway walls were damp-slicked and shiny. He carried a torch; it smoked and streamed, shedding fragile light as he put it forward to illuminate the Womb.

Kellin tensed, though he knew what to expect; three visits were not enough to diminish the impact. *Lir* leapt out of walls and ceiling, tearing free of stone. They were incredibly lifelike, as if a sculptor had captured living animals and *encased* them in marble rather than carving them. They stared back at him from hard, challenging eyes: creamy ivory veined with gold.

The Womb gaped. Its rim was nonexistent in distorting light, so that he could not see the rune-worked edge. Only the deeper blackness that marked its mouth.

Kellin wet drying lips and moved past the *lir*-carved door slowly, holding the torch outthrust so he did not mistake the footing and tumble to his death.

But would I die? I am meant to be Mujhar . . . those to be Mujhar can survive the rebirth.

He did not have the courage to accept the challenge.

Kellin stepped inside. The Womb's maw expanded as the torch, held in an unsteady hand, illuminated the truth: a perfectly rounded hole that had accepted men before and refused to give them a second birth.

"Carillon," he murmured. "The last Prince of Homana to enter into the Womb and be born in the shape of a king."

He had learned the histories. He knew his birthline. Carillon of Homana, the last Homanan Mujhar.

"After him, Donal. Then Niall. Then—Brennan." Kellin's jaws tightened. *The next should have been my* jehan, *had he the courage to understand.*

But Aidan had renounced it. Aidan had been a coward.

Should I leap into the Womb to prove my worthiness? Can I atone for my jehan*'s weakness with my own strength?* He stared hard at the marble *lir*. "Is that what they want?"

No answer. The *lir* stared back in silence.

Kellin turned and set the torch into a bracket. Carefully he took three steps to the edge of the Womb, then squatted down beside it. Buttocks brushed booted heels. Sore thighs protested, as did newly knit ribs.

Silence.

Kellin's mouth went dry. In the presence of the Lion, he had felt many things. But the Womb was not the Lion. It spoke to him of a heritage far older than the Lion's, who was, in the unbiased nature of measurement, naught but a newmade thing. A cub to the Womb's adulthood. The walls were man-made, and the *lir* carved within stone, but before men had meddled to glorify what they perceived as the tangible proof of power, there had been the Womb.

"A gate," Kellin murmured. "How many have gone through it?"

Movement caught his attention. A black shadow paced into the vault, then rounded the Womb. It sat down across from him so that the Womb lay between, black and impenetrable. Gold eyes threw back smoky torchlight, opaque and eerily slanted.

Now, she said. *Your choice.*

He did not speak as a *lir*. "Is it?"

It has always been your choice.

"According to the prophecy, there can be no choice. If a warrior repudiates his *tahlmorra,* his service to the prophecy, he is denied the afterlife."

Her tail twitched once, then folded over arched toes. He had seen housecats sit so; incongruity. She was not and could never be tame. *A man may turn his back on life after death. It is his right to do so. It is the price of living.*

"To choose how he will live after he is dead?" Kellin grinned derisively. "I sense obscurity. I smell the kind of argument that must content my *jehan,* who trafficks with the gods. How else could a man be made to repudiate his son?"

He did not. He answered his tahlmorra. Her tail twitched again. *He created* your tahlmorra *in the following of his own.*

Kellin frowned. "I mislike oblique speech. Say what there is to say."

That it is a warrior's choice to be other than the gods might prefer him to be.

"And therefore alter the prophecy?"

Your jehan *might say that altering of the prophecy also follows its path.*

Kellin swore and sat down upon his rump, letting his heels slide forward. With blatant disregard for proprieties, he dangled both legs into the void. "You are saying that a man who turns his back on the prophecy also *follows* it by that very repudiation. But how? It makes no sense. If I made myself celibate and sired no more children, there would be no Firstborn. How would that serve a prophecy that exists solely to *make* another Firstborn?"

You have already sired children.

He thought about it. So he had. They, too, each of them, claimed the proper blood. *Save for the final House, the final link in the chain.* Kellin drew in a deep breath. "If I went to Solinde and found myself an Ihlini woman with whom I could bear to lie and got a child upon her, the task is finished. The prophecy complete."

Sima's tail twitched. She offered no answer.

"I could do it tomorrow, if I decided to. Leave. Go to Solinde. Find myself a woman, and end this travesty."

Sima displayed her teeth. *No one ever said it would be difficult.*

Kellin exploded. "Then if it is so *easy* to do—" But he let it trail off. "The blood. It comes to that. Ian lay with Lillith and sired Rhiannon. Rhiannon lay with my grandsire and bore—who? A daughter? The one who in turn lay with Lochiel and bore *him* the daughter with whom I shared a cradle?" Kellin hitched his shoulders. "And who, no doubt, would be the unlikeliest woman with whom I should be matched—and therefore is, in the perversity of the gods, the very woman they *intend* for me to lie with. To sire the proper son. Cynric, the Firstborn.'"

Sima held her silence.

The image was vivid before him. "Lochiel will geld me. He will show the woman to me—or, rather, me to her—and then he will *geld* me! So that I know, and she knows, how very close we came—and how superior the Ihlini are despite our Cheysuli gifts."

Sima bent her head and licked delicately at a paw.

"No answer?" Kellin asked. "No commentary? But I believed the *lir* were put here to *aid* their warriors, not obfuscate the truth."

The cat lowered her paw. She stared directly at him across the black expanse of the Womb. Feral gold eyes dominated the darkness. *I am not your* lir. *Have you not declared it? Have you not renounced me as your* jehan *renounced you?*

Had he? Had he?

A *lir*less warrior was destined to go mad. A *lir*less Cheysuli was not a warrior at all. A *lir*less Cheysuli could never be Mujhar. Could never hold the Lion. Could never sire the Firstborn because the Cheysuli would look to another.

A solution presented itself. An answer to the questions.

Kellin shuddered once. Sweat ran down his temples and stung the scratches on his face. Breathing was shallow, though the ribs now were healed. A flutter filled his belly, then spilled to genitals.

He swallowed painfully because his throat was dry and tight. He pressed both hands against cold stone on either side of his thighs. Fingertips left damp marks. Within the link, he said, *Let the gods decide.*

Kellin, prince of Homana, thrust himself into the Womb.

No top. No bottom. No sides.

No beginning, nor an ending.

Merely a *being.*

Kellin bit his lips bloody so he would not scream. It would diminish him to scream. Such noise would dishonor the gods.

Gods? What did he know of gods? They were, he had said, little more than constructs invented by men who desired to rule others, to keep lesser men contained so that *they* maintained the power.

Gods. His father worshiped them. *Jehan*, father, sire . . . there were so many words. None of them made sense. Nothing at all made sense to a man who leapt into the Womb.

The only sense in such folly was the *search* for sense, so he might understand what manner of man he was and what he was meant to be in the context of the gods.

Gods. Yet again.

If he renounced them, if he repudiated them, would they permit him to die?

If there *were* no gods, then surely he was dead.

Kellin fell. There was no bottom. He did not scream at all.

What were the Cheysuli but children of the gods? It was what the word meant.

Upon such unflagging faith was a race made strong, so others could not destroy it.

Men who had nothing in which to believe soon believed in Nothing. Nothing destroyed a man. Nothing destroyed a race.

Was Nothing, then, a demon?

Belief replaced Nothing. Belief destroyed the demon.

The Cheysuli were, if nothing else, a dedicated race. Once a thing made sense within the context of their culture, belief was overriding. Belief was their champion; it overwhelmed Nothing so the demon died of disuse, of DisBelief.

In the Womb, Kellin laughed. What had Sima said as Kellin looked upon flesh-bound wrists?

"You believe too easily in what the Ihlini tells you to. His art is illusion. Banish this one as you banished the Lion."

Illusion was another's successful attempt to make a man believe in something that did not truly exist. The key to banishing illusion was to *dis*believe.

Corwyth, and other Ihlini, had tried very hard to make the Cheysuli disbelieve in the prophecy.

The Ihlini disbelieved. Teirnan and the *a'saii* had—and did—disbelieve. And if *dis*belief could defeat illusion, and yet the prophecy survived, was it therefore a true thing, a thing with substance?

Or was it simply that the Cheysuli who believed in it believed *so strongly* that the weight of their faith, the contents of their spirits, destroyed the disbelief?

The champion of the gods, called Belief, destroyed the demon whose true-name was DisBelief.

Kellin cried out in the confines of the Womb: *"I do not understand!"*

History rose up. So many lessons learned. The hours and days and weeks and months Rogan had spent with him, laboring to instruct so that Kellin comprehended the heritage of the races he represented.

He could name all his races, all the Houses in his blood. They were each of them necessary.

So was it necessary for him to have a *lir;* to renounce the bond was to renounce his very self and the legacy of the blood.

A *lir*less Cheysuli had hurled himself into the Womb. He had placed his fate within the hands of the gods.

Kellin's shout echoed: *"Tahlmorra lujhalla mei wiccan, cheysu!"*

He had invited them to decide. If a man did *not* believe, would he risk himself so? If DisBelief ruled him, he would therefore commit suicide by issuing such a challenge, for a challenge with no recipient was no challenge at all but the substanceless defiance of an ignorant child.

Suicide was taboo.

Paradox, Kellin thought: Suicide was taboo, yet a *lir*less Cheysuli undertook the death-ritual. His sojourn in the forest was meant to find his death however it chose to take him; it was nothing else *but* suicide, though a man did not stab himself, or drink poison knowingly.

He died because of beasts. He died as prey to predator, as meat for the gods' creatures.

From flesh-colored clay in the hands of the gods, a man became meat.

The Wheel of Life turned so that the clay was fired in the kiln of the gods and set upon the earth to live as the clay willed. Believing or DisBelieving.

Kellin understood.

"Y'ja'hai!" he shouted.

Clay without the blood of a *lir* was nothing but colorless powder. Unmixed. Unmade. Never thrown upon the Wheel.

Kellin understood.

Kellin Believed.

The image of Sima's face flashed before blind eyes.

"I accept," he said. *"Yja'hai."* Then, desperately, "Will you accept me?"

The words rang in his head. *Ja'hai-na,* she said. *Y'ja'hai.*

The *lir*-link meshed, locked, sealed itself together. Nothing could break it now but the death of warrior or *lir*.

That knowledge no longer mattered to Kellin. He was whole.
He was Cheysuli.

The Womb of the Earth was fertile. The *Jehana* gave birth once
again after nearly one hundred years, to suckle the newborn man
upon the bosom of his *tahlmorra*.

The Prince of Homana who would one day become Mujhar.

He roused to torch-smudged darkness and the gaze of marble
lir. He lay sprawled on his back with arms and legs splayed
loosely, without purpose or arrangement, as if a large negligent
hand had spilled him from its palm onto the vault floor.

He thought perhaps one had.

"Lir?" He gasped it aloud, because before he had refused to
honor her in the link. "Sima?" And then, scraping himself up from
the floor, he wrenched his body sideways, to grasp frenziedly at
the cat who sat quietly by the hole into which he had pushed himself. *Lir?* This time in the link, so there was no room for doubt.
There would never be doubt again. He would not permit it; could
not *allow* himself—

Sima blinked huge eyes.

He scrabbled to her on awkward knees, needing to touch
her fur; requiring to touch the body that housed the blazing spirit.
Lir? Lir?

Sima yawned widely to display fearsome fangs. Then she
shook her head, worked wiry whiskers, and rose. She padded all of
two steps, pressed her head into his shoulder, then butted him
down. She was ungentle; she wanted him to acknowledge the
power in her body despite its immaturity. She was *lir*, after all; far
superior to *cat*.

He could say nothing but her name. He said it many times despite the fur in his mouth as she leaned down upon him; despite the
weight on his chest as she lay down across him; despite the warping of his mouth as her tongue reshaped his lips.

Lir—lir—lir. He could not say it enough.

Sima kneaded his shoulders. Smugly, she said, *Better now than
never.*

While the tears ran down his face.

Chapter Seventeen

Kellin clattered down the stairs to the first floor, intent on his destination. Behind him came Sima, glossy in mid-morning light; gold eyes gleamed. Daily her gangliness faded and was replaced by a burgeoning maturity, as if full bonding had at last loosed the vestiges of cubhood. She would one day, Kellin believed, rival Sleeta for size and beauty.

A month ago you would not have considered it, she told him.

A month ago I was lirless, and therefore lacked a soul. What man without a soul can acknowledge his lir*'s promise?*

Within the link, she laughed. *How we have changed in four weeks!*

He left behind the staircase and strode on toward the entryway. *Some would argue I have not changed at all; that I still frequent taverns—*

But not those in the Midden.

No, but taverns all the same—

And the women in them?

Kellin grinned; its suddenness startled a passing serving-woman, who dropped into an awkward, red-faced curtsy even as he went by. *Is there something you have neglected to tell me? Is there more to a link between warrior and female* lir *than I have been led to believe?*

That is vulgarity, lir.

Of course it is. You had best get used to it. No one has ever argued for my kindness and decency—have you not heard the stories?

Sima padded beside him, bumping a shoulder into his knee. *I need hear nothing,* lir. *What you are is in your mind.*

So I gave up privacy when I linked with you.

She yawned. *When a warrior bonds with a* lir, *he no longer desires privacy.*

It was true. He shared everything with Sima, save the intimacy his vulgarity implied. And while she did not climb into the bed he shared with a woman, she nonetheless was fully aware of what passed within it; she merely curled herself on the floor and slept—or pretended to. Kellin had gotten used to it, though he supposed there was gossip exchanged regarding a certain perverse affinity for a mountain cat as onlooker; and he was not certain he disapproved. Let them wonder about him. He would sooner be of interest than taken for granted, as he believed the Mujhar was.

"Kellin! Kellin?" It was Aileen, silver threads more evident in fading hair. "Have you a moment?"

He paused as she came down the corridor. "Now?" He displayed the warbow he carried, and the suede quiver full of white-fletched arrows. "I was bound for a hunt with my watchdogs." Kellin grinned. "They require activity. Of late I bore them, now I am reformed."

Aileen arched an ironic eyebrow. "You are not 'reformed,' my lad, merely *diverted*. And 'twill only take a moment; a letter has come from Hart. Brennan wants you in the solar."

"Bad news?"

Aileen touched a fingertip to her upper lip. "I'm thinking not," she said neutrally, "depending on point of view."

"On point of—" His suspicions blossomed as he saw the glint in green eyes. "Gods—'tis Dulcie, isn't it? Grandsire's put off Hart long enough, waiting for me to measure up . . . and now that he believes I've done it, he begins a discussion about marriage!"

"There was discussion of it a decade ago," she reminded him. " 'Tis nothing new, and should not surprise you. You are both well-grown."

He put up a silencing hand. "Enough. I will go. Will you send word to the watchdogs I will be delayed?"

" 'Tis sent," Aileen said. "Now, go to Brennan. Whatever complaint you have to make is better made to him."

"Aye. You argued *against* the marriage that decade ago." Kellin sighed. "But now you are for it, undoubtedly; catch the feckless warrior before he becomes less malleable."

"You are not now and never will be malleable," Aileen retorted, "merely occasionally less inclined to defy." She pointed. "Go."

Kellin went.

*　　*　　*

The solar was less bright now that the sun had moved westward, but displayed no shadows. The Mujhar sat in his usual chair
with his legs propped on a stool and a wine cup in his hand.
Against his thigh rested a creased, wax-weighted parchment held
down by a slack hand.

The door stood ajar. Kellin shouldered it open more fully and
crossed the threshold, tapping rattling arrows against one knee.
"So, I am to be wed. This year, or next? In Homana, or Solinde?"

Brennan smiled. He showed more age now; the healing of his
grandson had left its mark. "Have you no objection?"

"A mouthful, but you will hear none of them." Kellin tapped
arrows again as he halted before his grandsire. "What does
Hart say?"

"That there is no sense in putting off what must be done."

"How cognizant of tenderness is my great-uncle of Solinde."
Kellin sighed. "I suppose it must, then. To link Houses, and bloodlines . . . and no doubt beget the child who will fulfill the
prophecy." Irony spilled away. "Neither of us has a choice, grandsire. Neither Dulcie, nor me. Like you and granddame; like Niall
and Gisella; like Donal and Aislinn."

"Nor did Carillon and Solindish Electra, through whose blood
comes the proper match." Brennan's mouth twisted. "So many
years, so many marriages—all designed to bring us to this point."

"Not to *this* point, surely; to the birth, grandsire. Wedding Dulcie means nothing at all to the gods, only the son born of the
union." Kellin gestured with the warbow. "Have it carved in stone,
if you will, like the *lir* within the Womb: Kellin of Homana shall
wed Dulcie of Solinde, and so beget the Firstborn."

Brennan's fingers creased soiled parchment. "Left to your own
devices—"

Kellin took it up. "Left to my own devices, I would doubtless
waste my seed on a dozen different whores for the rest of the
month, then turn to a dozen more." He shrugged. "Does it matter?
I have known since I was ten it would come to this . . . Dulcie
knew it, too. It may as well have been settled as we soiled our royal
wrappings; there never was a chance we could look another way."

"No," Brennan conceded. "We are so very close, Kellin—"

"Then be done with it. Have her come here, or I will go there.
I do not care." He waved bunched arrows. "Write it now, if you
will. Let me be about my hunt. My watchdogs wait."

Brennan's mouth compressed though the faint displeasure engendered by flippancy was less pronounced than resignation. "Be about it, then. I will have this sent tomorrow."

Glumly, Kellin nodded. "My last hunt in freedom."

Brennan barked a laugh. "I doubt *Dulcie* will curtail your hunting, Kellin! She is very much Hart's daughter, in spirit as well as tastes."

"Why? Does she wager? Well, then, perhaps we will make a match of it after all." But levity faded in the face of his future now brought so near. Kellin shrugged. "It will do well enough. At least she is half Cheysuli; she will understand about Sima."

"Indeed," Brennan said gravely; a glint in his eye bespoke the irony of the statement because but four weeks before Sima was sheer impediment rather than half of Kellin's soul.

Kellin, who knew it; who saw the look in his grandsire's eye and colored under it, lifted his arrows. "I will help replenish the larder." Erinn slid into his words. " 'Twill take a day or two— don't be expecting me back before then." He grinned. "And aye, I'll be taking my watchdogs; they'll be hunting as well!"

Spring had arrived fitfully, turning snow to slush, slush to mud, then freezing it all together in a brief defiant spasm before resolving itself to its work. Kellin felt an affinity for the season as he rode out with Teague and the others; now more than ever he longed to remember winter, because *then* there had been no cause to concern himself with a wife.

"Cheysula," he muttered.

Teague, next to him on a red roan, lifted inquisitive brows. "What?"

Kellin repeated the word. "Old Tongue," he said, "for 'wife.' "

"Ah." Teague understood at once. "That time at last, is it?"

Kellin knew the incident in the Midden tavern had sealed their friendship, though Teague was careful to keep a distance between them so familiarity did not interfere with service. The others also had relaxed now that their lord was easier in himself; he knew very well the prevailing opinion was that Sima had worked wonders with the prince's temperament. For all he had initially disturbed them the night he was trapped in cat-form, they did not in any way indicate residual fear.

"That time," he agreed glumly. "I hoped it might wait a year or two more—or three, or four—"

"—or five?—"

"—but they'll not wait any longer. I'll be wed before summer, I'll wager."

Teague laughed. "Then you know nothing of women, my lord. She will be wanting an elaborate wedding with all the Houses of the world invited so they can bring her gifts."

Kellin considered it. "She did not appear to be much concerned for such things when I saw her last."

"How old was she?"

"Twelve?" He shrugged. "Or thirteen; I have lost track."

The young watchdog grinned. "Then she'll be *just* the age to demand such elaboration! You will not escape, my lord. But it offers you respite; it will take at least until *next* winter to prepare for such a feast!"

Kellin slanted a glance at Sima across one shoulder. "I do not know which is worse: wedding immediately with little ceremony—" he turned back to guide his mount, "—or putting it off a year so that so much can be made of it!"

One of the others joined in: a man named Ennis, who was Teague's boon companion. "Better now than tomorrow," he offered. "That way we can be done with our duty that much the sooner."

Kellin looked at him blankly.

Ennis grinned. "Do you think the Princess of Homana will desire our company?"

He had not considered that. Perhaps his marriage *would* offer him respite from the watchdogs, but Kellin was not convinced trading one for the other would prove so good a thing.

They left Mujhara and headed directly north, toward the woods that fringed the road. Because not so many people traveled the North Road, hunting was better. It did not take long for Kellin and his watchdogs to flush game. He hung back slightly, letting the Homanans do much of the work, and waited until they were so caught up in chasing down a hart that they forgot about him entirely.

Satisfied, he glanced down at Sima. *Now we can test it.*

She fixed him with an unwavering stare. *Best to know now what the last four weeks have wrought.*

Kellin dismounted and dropped reins over a limb thrust slantwise from a tree. He left the horse, quiver, and warbow and walked farther into the woods, conscious of the anticipatory flutter in his belly.

Be not so fearful, Sima suggested, following on his heels. *We have time.*

How much? he asked uneasily. *What should happen if, driven to anger in the midst of political turmoil, I forget my human trappings and become nothing more than a beast?*

Time, she repeated. *What turmoil is there to be? You are prince, not king. You matter little yet for the turmoil to involve you.*

A humbling reminder. Kellin sighed and beat his way through brush to a small clearing, then closed his hand on the wolf's-head pommel of Blais' knife. "Strength," he murmured, invoking his kinsman's memory. "You had your share of it, and of courage; lend a measure to me."

Sima pressed against one knee, then flowed away to take up position nearby. She sat with tail tucked over toes, ear-tufts flicking minutely. *You have learned much in four weeks.*

Kellin rubbed at too-taut shoulders, trying to ease the tension. *I have learned advice in four weeks. The doing yet remains, and that is what I fear.*

Be what you are, Sima said. *Kellin. That is all you* can *be, regardless of your shape.*

"More," he said. "I was more, *twice.*"

Sima blinked. *That was before.*

"Before you?" He grinned. "Aye, and therefore did not count; I was *lir*less, and unblessed." Humor spilled away. "Well enough. Let us see what I become when I trade my shape for another."

He squeezed the hilt once more, then let his hand fall away. With careful deliberation Kellin detached himself from the moment and let his awareness drift from the *here and now* to the *there,* with no sense of time, where the magic resided deep in the earth.

Power pulsed. At first it was coy, caressing his awareness so he knew it was there for the taking, then flowing away to tease him yet again with insubstantiality.

It was frustrating. *Sima—*

Yours to do, she told him.

He concentrated. Power flirted, seduced; he wanted it very badly. His body rang with tension that was almost sexual, an intense and abiding need. He let himself go into it until awareness of self became awareness of need, of what would satisfy him, and then Power uncovered itself like a woman shedding draperies and let him touch it.

—different—

It was. Before he had merely thought of the beast, neglecting to recall that he was a man with a man's distinct needs. The beast had overtaken all that was man, until he was helpless and unaware, beaten down from his humanity into animal instinct. This time he knew. His name was Kellin, not cat, and he was a *man*. A fully bonded Cheysuli warrior who had recourse to the magic that lived in the Womb of the Earth.

He touched it. It set his fingertips atingle.

Kellin, he whispered. *Man, not cat—but lend me the shape, and I will do it honor.*

Senses flared. Images broke up his mind. No longer human images of a human world, but the patterns of a cat.

Am I—?

Not yet, Sima said. *There is more yet to be done.*

More. He did not know more.

He fell. He was in the Womb again, empty of everything save a vague but burning awareness that he was a man who desired, but briefly, to give his human form to the earth so he might, for only a while, walk the world as a cat.

Not so much to ask.

Vision exploded. His eyes were open, but he saw nothing save a disorientation so great it threatened equilibrium. Kellin thrust out a staying hand intended to hold him upright, but it broke through the crust of the earth and sank deep into the river of Homana's Power.

Earth magic. There for the taking.

Kellin took it.

There, Sima said. *Not so difficult after all.*

Smells engulfed, replacing reliance on sight. In cat-form, Kellin exulted.

Let us run, Sima suggested. *Let us run as cats, so you know what it is to honor the gods.*

He did not think much of gods. But in this form, filled with the glory of *lir*-shape, Kellin could not protest.

If it was gods who were responsible, he would honor them.

Chapter Eighteen

Kellin ran through the sun-dappled forest with Sima at his shoulder, lovely, magnificent Sima—no other warrior's *lir* was half so beautiful!—and took joy in the pure, almost sensual freedom the cat-shape gave him. He explored it as he ran, marking the differences within his brain, yet the samenesses as well. His awareness of self was unchanged despite the body's alteration; he knew perfectly well he was a man in a *borrowed* form that would, when he chose, be exchanged once again for the proper body. There was no division in his soul other than that his awareness permitted; he did not wish himself one or the other. He simply was what he was: a Cheysuli warrior with magic in his blood, who could, when he desired to, become a mountain cat.

You see? Sima asked.

Kellin exulted. He believed he understood himself at last, and the needs that lived in his soul; he could control himself in this shape as easily as he could in human form. He need only remember, to keep alive the spark of self-knowledge that recalled he was Kellin, and human, so as not to tip the balance from *lir*-shape into beast form.

Not so difficult. His muscled body stretched, fluid in graceful motion, stronger by far than the human shape. *She has taught me much in the past weeks. I understand better. I understand what it is.*

Sima interrupted. *A stag, just ahead. Fit for Homana-Mujhar?*

He saw it; it was. A fine, huge stag with a magnificent rack of antlers.

Kellin slowed, then stilled even as Sima did. The stag stood unmoving, poised in a patch of sunlight. Flanks heaved from exertion; was he prey to someone's hunt?

Kellin did not care. The stag was *theirs,* now, and indeed fit for Homana-Mujhar. He was large and would no doubt prove difficult to take down, but there were two of them. Together they could manage it.

First leap to you, Kellin said.

Sima was pleased. She crouched even as he did, tail barely twitching at the tip. She tensed in a perfect stillness, tufted ears motionless.

Now— She was instantly in motion: a black, sleek blur that sprang effortlessly from the ground and hurled herself through the air.

Sima screamed. For an instant Kellin pinned tufted ears, wondering why she would startle the stag into flight and risk losing the prey, then saw the feathered shaft of an arrow protruding from her flank as she twisted in midair and fell.

She screamed again, and so did he. Her pain was his own, and the shock that consumed her body. She was down, twisting to bite frenziedly at the shaft.

Kellin heard a human voice shouting in fear and horror. A man burst through the bushes on foot. His face was drained; when he saw both cats, his horror was redoubled. "My lord! My lord, I did not mean it! It was the stag—the arrow was loosed before I saw her!"

The *lir*-link was alive with Sima's pain. Kellin shuddered with it, and the hair along his spine stood up straight. The shout of rage that issued from his throat was not that of a man, but of the beast instead.

The arrow in Sima's flesh dug deeply into his own. Pain, shock, and weakness merged into fury, and the comprehension of hideous truth: his *lir* was dying; so, then, was he.

Kellin screamed, and leapt.

The man thrust up a warding arm, but made no effort to draw the knife that might have saved his life. His mouth warped open in horror, but he did not move. It was as if he did not believe that his Cheysuli lord, though bound now by *lir*-shape, would ever truly harm him.

The man went down beneath the cat and gave up his life in an instant. He did not even cry out as the throat was torn from his body.

Other men burst from the trees on horseback and drew up in a ragged, abrupt halt that set horses' mouths to gaping, and men to swearing. Kellin dared them to attack. He stood over the prey and dared them to take it.

The keening scream welled in his chest and burst from his throat. Their faces twitched and blanched. None of them moved.

"Teague," one said, though the word made little sense. "Gods—he has killed *Teague!*"

Sima panted behind him. Kellin turned his dripping head and saw her sprawled on her right side, feathered shaft buried deep in her left flank. It bore the Mujhar's colors, and the richer crimson of her blood.

She panted. Her tongue lolled. The gold eyes dimmed.

Lir! Kellin cried.

She was beyond speech. He felt only her fear and pain and the bewildered questioning of what had happened.

Anger burned fiercely. Kellin swung back to the others and took a single step toward them. Horses snorted uneasily; one jibbed at the bit.

"My lord," a man said; his hands shook on the reins. A companion broke and ran, then a third, then a fourth. The one who had named the prey remained behind. "My lord," he said again, and his young face twisted in a mingling of shock and outrage. "Do you even know whom you have killed?"

Kellin tried to say it: *"The man who nearly killed Sima!"* But none of the words came out. Only a keening growl.

"He was your friend!" the Homanan shouted, tears filling his eyes. "Or now that you are a beast, do you only count *them* as friends?" In his anger, the young man drew his knife and threw it to the ground. "There! You may have it. I want none of it! I forswear my service; I renounce my rank. I want nothing to do with a prince who kills his friends, for assuredly he is not the man I want as my king!" He scrubbed hastily at his face. "The Mujhar is a man I honor, but I owe you nothing. I *give* you nothing; I am quit of royal service as of this moment!"

Kellin could not form the words. With effort he beat back the pain within the link, the knowledge of Sima's condition, and concentrated long enough to banish the shape that prevented communication. Human-form came quickly, too quickly; he stumbled to his knees, bracing himself upright with one hand thrust into deadfall. *"Wait—"* he blurted.

"Wait? Wait?" It was Ennis; Kellin's human eyes recognized him now. "For what? So you may change again, and tear out *my* throat?" Ennis's grief was profound. "He was my friend, my lord.

We grew up together, and now you have killed him. Do you expect me to *wait* while you fashion an explanation?"

"Sima—" Kellin panted. He hung there on hands and knees, then scrubbed haphazardly at his bloodied face. "My *lir*—in her pain, I could not stop." Sima's pain still ruled him, though now he was a man. Breathlessly he insisted, "He attacked her! What else was I to do? Permit him to kill her? Then he kills *me!*"

"He wanted the *stag,* my lord! None of us saw the cat." Ennis reined in his restive horse. His anguished face was twisted. "Will you permit me, my lord, to recover the body? I would prefer to give it a proper burial before you decide to eat it!"

Disorientation faded. The link remained strong, as did the pain contained within it, but Kellin was no longer a cat and he felt Sima's pain another way. He understood the difference between her senses and his own.

A man dead? By his doing? Still weak from the abruptness of his shapechange, Kellin turned awkwardly and saw the body sprawled in deadfall; the torn and bloodied throat. He recognized the man, acknowledged the handiwork. In that moment he fully comprehended what he had done. *"NO!"*

"Aye," Ennis retorted. "You have blood on your mouth, my lord; royalty or not, you cannot hide the truth from a man who has seen the Prince of Homana murder an innocent man."

Nearby, Sima panted. Blood matted her flank.

Brief concentration broke up in response to renewed pain. The link was filled with it, stuffing Kellin's head. He could think of nothing else but his *lir.* "Sima—"

"May I take the body?" Ennis persisted. "You may find another dinner."

Teague. It was Teague. He had killed Teague.

Lir? Sima's tone was weak. *Lir, you must heal me. Waste no time.*

"Will you permit me the leave to take my friend back?" Ennis asked.

Now, Sima said. Her tongue lolled from her mouth. Lir—

Teague was dead. Sima was dying. No doubt at that moment Ennis would prefer his prince died also, but Kellin could not give in merely to please him. He would not permit the travesty to go forth.

"Take him," he rasped, moving toward the cat, thinking only of the cat so he could avoid the truth. "Take him to my grandsire."

Ennis blurted a laugh that was profound in its anguish. "Be certain I shall! The Mujhar shall be told of this. He needs to know what manner of beast is his heir."

The tone flayed. *"Go!"* Kellin shouted. "It is a matter of balance—I have no control! If *you* would live, take Teague and go!" He knelt down at Sima's side. *What am I to do? How do I heal you?*

You are Cheysuli, she said. *Rely on that which makes you a warrior, and use it to heal me.*

The instructions he found obscure, but her condition alarmed him. It was all he could do not to fling back his head and howl his fear and pain. "Magic," he panted. "Gods—give me the magic."

He *was* Cheysuli. The power came at his call.

When it was done, Kellin came awake with a snap and realized in his trance he tread close to sleep, or to collapse. His bloodied hands were yet pressed against Sima's side, but the arrow was gone. He saw a few bits of feathers lying on the ground with the arrowhead itself, but the shaft was gone, as if burned to ash.

The breath came back into his lungs all unexpectedly, expanding what had collapsed, refilling what was empty. He coughed painfully. The world slid sideways; braced arms failed and spilled him to the ground, so that he landed flat upon his spine. The back of his skull thumped dully against leaf-strewn ground.

Sima stirred next to him. *The healing is complete. You have done well.*

He could not so much as open his eyes. *Had I not, we would both be bound for the afterlife. I was not in so much of a hurry.*

Nor I. She shifted closer yet, pressing the warmth of her body against his right side. *The magic drains a man. There is balance in that, also . . . we have time,* lir. *No need to move at once.*

He did not much feel like moving ever, let alone at once. Kellin sighed, welcoming the coolness of the deadfall beneath him. His itching face felt crusted. He longed to scratch it, but to do that required him to move a hand. It was too much to attempt.

Lir. Sima again, resting her chin upon his shoulder. *I am sorry for the man.*

"What m—" He broke off. Kellin thrust himself to hands and knees and hurled himself over, to look, to seek, to reassure himself that none of it was true.

Teague's body was gone, but bloodied leaves and hoofprints

confirmed the truth Kellin desired to avoid. Teague indeed had died, and Ennis had carried him home.

Kellin touched his crusted face with fingers that shook. *Teague's blood.*

"Gods," he choked aloud, "why do you *permit* this?"

Lir. Sima rose, butted at an arm. *Lir, it is done. It cannot be undone.*

"I killed—" He could not voice it, could not find the words. "I killed *Teague*—"

Reflex, she told him. *A cat, to protect himself, strikes first. You struck to protect me.*

"Teague," Kellin mouthed.

Even the comfort of the *lir*-link was not enough.

He had killed a man who was not an Ihlini, not a thief, not an enemy.

I have killed a friend.

Kellin sank down to the ground and pressed his face against it, unmindful of bloodied leaves.

I have killed a friend.

He recalled Teague's presence in the Midden tavern where Luce held sovereignty, and how the Homanan had aided him. How Teague had, of them all, not looked upon him as a beast the night he had nearly killed Luce because Teague had a better understanding of what lived in his lord's mind.

I swore to have no friends because I lost them all—because they all died . . . and now when I let one come close again after so much time, I kill him MYSELF—

He wound rigid hands into his hair and knotted them there, then permitted himself to shout as a man might shout to declare his grief and torment.

But the sound, to Kellin, was naught but a beast's wail.

Chapter Nineteen

It was demonstrably obvious, when Kellin reached Homana-Mujhar, that Ennis and the others had carried word before him. The horse-boy who took his mount did so with eyes averted and led the horse away quickly, not even waiting for his customary coin. Off-duty men gathered before the guardhouse in the bailey fell silent as Kellin walked by them, breaking off conversation to stare from the corners of their eyes. They measured him, he knew; they looked for the proof in his face, in his clothing, in the expression in his eyes.

What do they see?

He had washed the blood from face and hands, and scrubbed at his jerkin. He believed no bloodstains remained, but possibly none were required; he wore guilt in his posture despite his desire not to.

Sima padded beside him. They watched her, too, marking her apparent health. She did not limp or show any indication an arrow had but hours before driven her toward death. It was a natural healing, but to the Homanans, who had little knowledge of such things, it seemed to suggest that Kellin's reaction was one of whim, not of need; as if he had killed Teague because the idea had occurred, and because he could.

Kellin paused inside the palace to inquire as to the Mujhar's whereabouts, and was told to go at once to the Great Hall. Inwardly, Kellin's spirit quailed. *Not in privacy? Or is it that he will discuss it with me as Mujhar, not grandsire, nor even Cheysuli warrior?*

Sima bumped his leg. *I am with you.*

No. Kellin paused. *This is for me to face alone. Go up to my chambers and wait.*

She hesitated, then turned and padded away.

Kellin brushed haphazardly at the perspiration stippling his upper lip, then went on toward the Great Hall. Foreboding weighted his spirit until he twitched with it, desiring to scratch at stinging flesh.

Brennan was on the throne. The Lion's head reared above the Mujhar in a display of wooden glory. Aged eyes stared blindly; Kellin was grateful the Lion could not see what had become of a prince who would one day inherit it.

It was nearing sundown. Light slanting through stained glass formed lattices on the stone floor, so that Kellin walked through sharp-etched pools of pure color. In spring, the firepit was un-lighted. Kellin walked its length steadily, though more slowly than was his wont; he would not shirk the confrontation but did not desire to hasten it. What would come, would come; no need to accelerate it.

He reached the dais all too soon. And then he saw Aileen stand-ing at Brennan's right side with one hand on the Lion. *It is seri-ous*— Kellin clamped closed his teeth, feeling again the emptiness in his jaw where Luce had broken a tooth. Healing had sealed it closed, but the tooth was banished forever.

His grandsire looked old. The years had been kind to him for a long time, but now the kindness was banished. The healing four weeks before had left its mark, and the knowledge Ennis had brought. Dark skin no longer was as supple and taut, permitting brackets to form at nose and mouth, and webwork patches beside his eyes. The Mujhar's hands rested lightly over the curving, clawed armrests, but the knuckles were distended.

Kellin halted before the dais. Briefly he inclined his head to Aileen, then offered homage to the Mujhar. He waited in tense si-lence, wishing Sima stood beside him; knowing it as weakness. It was time he acknowledged it.

Brennan's eyes did not waver. His voice was steady. "When a king has but a single heir, and no hope of any others, he often over-looks such things as the hot blood of youth, and the trouble a boy can rouse. Gold soothes injured pride and mends broken taverns. It will even, occasionally, placate an angry *jehan* whose daughter has been taken with child. But it does not buy back a life. Even a king dares not overlook that."

Kellin wet dry lips. "I do not ask you to overlook it. Merely un-derstand it."

"I have been told by Ennis and the others that they heard Teague cry out; that he knew he had made a mistake."

"My lord, he did."

"And yet you used the power of *lir*-shape to kill him anyway."

It would have been better, Kellin decided, if the Mujhar had shouted at him, because then he could rely upon anger. But Brennan did not; he merely made quiet statements in a grave and habitual dignity that Kellin knew very well he could never emulate.

He inhaled a trembling breath. "My lord, I am moved to remind you of what you already know: that a warrior in *lir*-shape encounters all of the pain his *lir* does. It—affects—him."

"I *do* know it," Brennan agreed. "But a warrior in *lir*-shape is yet a man, and understands that a Homanan who acknowledges his mistake is not to be murdered."

Behind his back, Kellin balled his hands into fists. It would undermine his appeal if he shouted; and besides, he *was* guilty. "Sima was wounded. She was dying. All I could think about was that he had shot her, that she was badly hurt, and that if *she* died, I died also." The words were hard to force past a tight throat. "He was my friend, my lord. I never meant to kill him."

"You did. In that moment, you did indeed intend to kill him." Brennan's hands closed more tightly over the armrest. "Do you think I cannot see it? I am Cheysuli also."

Grief and anguish commingled to overwhelm. "Then why confront me like this?" Kellin cried. "By the gods, grandsire—"

But Brennan's sharp gesture cut Kellin's protest off. "Enough. There are other things to concern ourselves with than whether I understand what led to the attack."

"What other things?" Kellin demanded. "You yourself have said we cannot buy back Teague's life, but I will do whatever I must to atone for my mistake."

Brennan leaned forward. "Do you hear what you are saying? You speak of Teague's death as a mistake, an unfortunate circumstance you could not avoid."

"It was!"

"Yet when Teague makes a mistake, you respond by killing him." Brennan's face was taut. "Tell me where the difference lies. Why is one mistake excused—because you are a prince?—while one results in murder?"

"I—" Kellin swallowed heavily. "I could not help myself."

"In *lir*-shape."

"Aye." He understood now what Brennan meant him to see. "I felt her pain, her fear—"

"And your own."

"And my own." Kellin's face warped briefly. "I feared for her, grandsire—I had not had her very long, yet I could not imagine what it would be like to lose her. The grief, the anguish—" He looked at Brennan. "I thought I might go mad."

"Had she died, you would have." The Mujhar sank back into the Lion. "It is the price we pay. All your arguments against the death-ritual now mean nothing."

Kellin stared hard at the stone beneath his boots. "Aye."

"Through the link, her pain was yours . . . and you feared she would die. Knowing what it would cost."

"My life," Kellin murmured.

"So you took his, even though you might have turned to Sima at once and begun the healing that would have saved two lives: hers, and Teague's."

His mouth was stiff, awkward. "I could not help myself."

"No," Brennan agreed in abject weariness, "you never have been able to. And that is why you are here before us now: to decide what must be done."

He looked up sharply. "What must be done?" he echoed. "But—what *is* there to do? There are rituals for Teague, and his family to tend, and *i'toshaa-ni* for me—"

"Kellin." Brennan's voice was steady. He glanced briefly at Aileen, whose expression was so taut as to break, then firmed his mouth and looked back at his grandson. "Tell me why the *qu'mahlin* came about."

It was preposterous. Kellin nearly gaped. "Now?"

"Now."

"You desire a history lesson?"

"I desire you to do whatever I require of you."

"Aye." It was blurted before Kellin thought about it. Frowning his perplexity, he began the lesson. "A Homanan princess ran away with a Cheysuli. Lindir, Shaine's daughter—she went away with Hale, Shaine's liege man." In the face of Brennan's expectant patience, Kellin groped for more. "She was meant to wed Ellic of Solinde, to seal an alliance between Homana and Solinde, but she ran away instead with Hale." He paused. "That is what I was taught, grandsire. Is there more you want?"

"Those are the political concerns, Kellin. What the elopement did as regards Homana and Solinde was to destroy any opportunity for peace to flourish; the two realms remained at war. But *that*

would not cause the birth of the *qu'mahlin,* which was a strictly
Homanan-Cheysuli conflict."

"Shaine's pride was such that he declared them attainted, subject to punishment."

"That is part of it, Kellin. But think a moment . . . consider
something more." Brennan's fingers tightened against aged wood.
"It is one thing for a king to declare his daughter and his liege man
attainted; he has the right to ask for their lives if he chooses to. It
is quite another for that king to declare an *entire race* attainted, and
set all of Homana against it."

Kellin waited for more. Nothing more was said. "Aye," he
agreed at last. "But Shaine was a madman—"

"Even a madman cannot lead his people into civil war if they
do not believe what he has said. What did he say, Kellin?"

He knew it very well; Rogan had been at some pains to instruct
him, and the Cheysuli at Clankeep as well. "He said we were
demons and sorcerers and had to be destroyed."

"*Why* were we demons and sorcerers? What was his foremost
proof?"

"That we could assume the shape of animals at will—" Kellin
broke it off. He stared blindly at his grandsire. "That we could assume beast-shape and kill all the Homanans." He felt ill. "As—I
killed Teague."

"As you killed Teague." Brennan sighed deeply. "In the days of
Shaine, the Homanans believed themselves in danger. It was far
easier to kill all the Cheysuli than risk their sovereignty. And so
they tried. Shaine began it, and others carried it out. It took many
years, including Ihlini and Solindish domination, before the Cheysuli were admitted again to Homana without fear of extermination."

"Carillon," Kellin murmured. "He ended the *qu'mahlin.*"

"And made a Cheysuli Prince of Homana when he sired no
sons of his own." A silver forelock had frosted to white. "Before
the Lion came into the hands of Homanans, it was a Cheysuli
legacy. The kingdom of Homana was a *Cheysuli* realm. But we
gave it up rather than have the Homanans fear us, knowing that
someday it would fall again to us, and to the Firstborn who would
bind four realms and two magical races in a true peace." Brennan
drew in a breath. "How can the Homanans permit a man to rule
them who cannot control himself when he assumes *lir*-shape? He

is, to them, nightmare; a beast without self-control. And I am not so certain, just at this moment, the Homanans are wrong."

It shocked. *"Grandsire—"*

"I know what it is to share pain through the link. I know what it is to be driven half-mad by fear—you have heard stories, I know, of how I am in small places—but I do not *kill*."

"Grandsire—"

"What if it happens again?"

"Again!" Kellin stared. "You believe it might?"

"I must. These four weeks you have achieved much, but obviously self-control in *lir*-shape is not one of them. I cannot risk it, Kellin."

"Given time, guidance—"

"Aye. But I cannot risk it while you remain in Homana-Mujhar. It gives the Homanans too broad a target,"

Kellin's belly clenched. "Clankeep, then." Where he would have to explain to Gavan, and to Burr, and to men and women who would not understand how a Cheysuli warrior could permit such atrocity in the name of his *lir,* whom once he had meant to banish. "Balance," he murmured. "If I can learn the balance . . ."

"There is another balance, Kellin. One which has eluded you through all of your life, and which I have, in my ignorance, permitted to warp that life. I am as much to blame as you are, in this."

Aileen stirred. "No. Not you. I will not allow you to blame yourself."

Kellin looked at her. Aileen's green eyes blazed with conviction as she stared at her husband; he would get no support from her. He longed for Sima, but would not call her to him. "Banishment, then."

"The Council has approved."

Kellin winced.

"It is not a permanent thing. You will be permitted home when I am assured you have learned what you need to know."

"And when the rumors have died down." Kellin sighed. "I understand, grandsire. But—"

"I know." Brennan's eyes were filled with compassion. "It has happened before. My own *jehan* grew weary of the excesses of his sons, and banished two of them. Hart he sent to Solinde, Corin to Atvia. Neither wanted to go any more than you desire to go. As for me—" he smiled briefly at Aileen, "—I was made to wed before either of us was ready."

Aileen's face was rigid. "I do not regret it now."

"We both did then." Brennan turned back to his grandson. "For a six-month, a year—no longer than is necessary."

Kellin nodded. "When?"

"In the morning. I have made arrangements for the journey, and a boat will be waiting."

"Boat?" Kellin stared. "A boat? Why? What need have I of a boat?" Trepidation flared into panic. "Where are you sending me?"

"To the Crystal Isle. To your *jehan*."

Panic transmuted itself to outrage. *"No!"*

"It is arranged."

"*Un*arrange it! I will not go!"

"You wanted this for years."

"Not now. Not for *ten* years, grandsire! I have no intention of going to my *jehan*."

Brennan's gaze was level. "You will go. For all your anger and bitterness, and the multiplicity of your small rebellions, you are still a warrior of the clan. I am Mujhar. If I bid you to do so, you will go."

"What has *he* to do with this? This is something I must deal with on my own! I do not require the aid of a man who cannot keep his son but must give up everything to live on an *island*—"

"—where you will go." Brennan rose. "Aidan has everything to do with this. We could not have predicted it then, and I doubt it occurred to him—he was in thrall to the gods, and thought of nothing else but the *tahlmorra* meant for him—but it is something we must deal with now. You will go to the Crystal Isle and see your *jehan*."

"Why? *Why* do you think this will help me?"

"Because perhaps he can remove the boy's anger and replace it with a man's understanding that what the world—and gods—mete out is what he must deal with in a rational, realistic manner, without recourse to an anger that, in asserting itself, kills men." The muscles flexed in Brennan's jaw. "Because there is nowhere else I can send you and not be afraid."

Kellin stared. Shame banished outrage. "Of me? You are afraid of *me?*"

"I must be. I have seen what happens when the anger consumes the man." His eyes were bleak. "You must go to the source of your pain. To someone who can aid you."

"I want nothing to do with *him!*"

"He shaped you. By his very distance, by his own *tahlmorra,* he shaped you. I think it is time the *jehan,* and not the grandsire, tended the clay that his own loins sired." Brennan pushed a trembling hand across his brow. "I am too old to raise you now. It is Aidan's turn."

"Why," Kellin spat out between clenched teeth, "did you wait so long for this? I begged it all those years!"

"He did not wish it, and I believed you did not need it."

"Does he wish it now?"

"No."

"But now you believe I need it."

"Aye."

It congealed into bitterness. "Would I need it now if I had had it *then?*"

Brennan shut his eyes. "Gods—I cannot say . . . if so, I *am* to blame for what you have become—"

"No!" Aileen cried. "By all the gods of Erinn, Brennan, I've said it before—I'll not have you blaming yourself for this! What must I do to convince you? He is what he is. Let him take it to his father. Aidan is more fit to deal with aberration than either of us!"

"Why?" Kellin asked. "Because he is 'aberration,' and now I am also?"

Aileen looked at him. "You are my grandson," she said. "I love you for that—I will *always* love you for that—but I cannot comprehend a man who lacks the self-control to prevent him from killing other men." Her hands balled into fists. "I am Erinnish, not Cheysuli—I cannot understand the soul of a Cheysuli. That it is wild, I know, and untamed, and unlike that of any other, I know. But it is an honorable soul also, well-bound by the gods, and duty . . . yours is unbound. Yours is as unlike Brennan's—or Corin's—than any I have known. It is most like Aidan's in its waywardness, but with a blackness of spirit that makes you dangerous. Aidan was never that." Aileen glanced at Brennan briefly, then back to her grandson. "Go to your father. 'Tis what you need—and, I'm thinking, Aidan also."

Kellin's jaws hurt. "You said—'no longer than is necessary.' How am I to know?"

Brennan reached for and took into his own one of Aileen's hands. "Until Aidan sends you back."

He looked at Aileen in desperation. "Was it your idea?"

She offered oblique answer though her face was wasted. "In

Erinn," she said quietly, "a man accepts his punishment. And the will of his lord."

Kellin stood there a long time. Then, summoning what little pride remained, he bowed and took his leave.

Interval

He had, since coming to the Crystal Isle, seen to it that much of its wildness was tamed, at least so much that a man might walk freely along a track without fearing to lose an eye to an importunate branch. And yet not so much wildness was vanquished that a man, a Cheysuli, might feel his spirit threatened by *too* much change.

It was incongruity: to make the wildness useful without diluting its strength. And to offer change within a culture whose very strength was wildness.

He wore leathers, as always, snug against flesh that did not as yet begin to wither with age, and *lir*-gold on bare arms that did not surrender muscle. He was fit, if but a few years beyond his prime; a young man of twenty would call him old—perhaps, more kindly, old*er*—but to another man he represented all that was remarkable about a Cheysuli.

He paused at the border between woodlands and beach. Sunlight glinted off water, scouring white sands paler yet, so that he was forced to lift his hand against the blinding glare.

Blobs swam before his eyes, robbed of distinctness by the brilliance of the sun. They coalesced along the horizon, where the sea lapped in. He saw the blobs take shape, forming legs, tails, heads. He whistled. The blobs paused, then came flying, transmuting sun-dazzled formlessness into spray-dampened bodies recognizable as canine.

Tongues lolled. Tails whipped. They lashed their own bodies in a frenzy to reach him, to display a devotion so complete as to render words obsolete.

They were his now. The big male had died nearly twenty years before—of grief, he believed—but the others had survived despite the death of the woman who had caused them to be born. Most of those were dead, now, also—giant dogs died sooner—but they had bred as well, so that the island never lacked for companionship of a sort no Cheysuli had known before; they did not keep pets.

Nor were *these* pets; they were, by their existence, in the beating of great hearts, living memorials to Shona.

To him, they were sanity.

He paused as they joined him. The exuberance of their greeting endangered those parts most revered by a man; grinning, he turned a hip each time a tail threatened, then grabbed two or three until the dogs, all astonished, spun to whip tails free. Then it began again, until he told them with false sternness that the game was over; that they were to be still.

He sat down there in the sand, warding off inquisitive noses, until the dogs, too, settled with grunts and great rumbling sighs. Wise eyes watched him, waiting for the sign that he meant to rise and find a stick to toss for their pleasure; but he did not, and after a time they slept, or lay quietly: an ocean of storm-hued wolf, hounds sprawled upon the beach of an island, in its begetting, very alien to their souls. They were Erinnish, though none of these had been there.

They were all he had of her. The son she had borne in the midst of her dying, in the flames of a burning keep, was not and never had been his to tend. Another man might have grieved, then done what he could to raise up the living soul whose heart was partly hers, but he was denied that comfort. All he had of her, in the days and the darkness, were memories and dogs.

He honored the gods with his service. He did not question its needs, or the path he had taken; it was his *tahlmorra*. A great security resided in the knowledge that what he did served a greater purpose; that sacrifices made in the name of that greater purpose, no matter how difficult, would in the end bear out his seeming madness. Let them attach scorn to his name now, but one day, long after his bones had rotted, they would call him something else.

"But my spark is nothing compared to the flame of his." Aidan smiled. "My name is a spark, and Kellin's a bonfire—but *Cynric's* will blaze with all the terrible splendor of a wildfire as it devours the land around it."

He knew they would curse him. Men were often blind when it came to needed change. When they acknowledged what had happened—and what still would come—they would claim him an emmissary of a demon not to their liking, when all he did was serve the gods who had decided to mend what had broken.

"Revolution," he said; the dogs twitched ears. "If they knew what was to come, they would none of them agree; they would all become *a'saii*."

But he would not permit it. That was his purpose, to guide his people closer to a true understanding that out of devouring flames would rise a new world.

It would be difficult. But the gods would see to it he had a means to persevere. If it required a weapon, a weapon would be given.

Aidan was content. He knew his path very well. All he had to do was wait for the weapon, then set it on *its* path.

PART III

Chapter One

The chapel was built of standing stones set into a tight circle. Most of them still leaned a little, like teeth settling badly in a diseased jaw, but someone had taken the time—probably years—to see that many of the stones had been pushed back into proper alignment. The circle was whole again, with a carved lintel stone set over the darkened entrance, and a heel stone put up in front. Kellin went slowly to it, drawn by its singular splendor.

The side facing him was unnaturally flat, chipped and rubbed smooth. Across the dark gray face ran runic symbols he had seen but once before, in his Ceremony of Honors. He recognized most of them, but he was not perhaps as conversant in the Old Tongue as he should be. *I have lived too long among Homanans.*

Kellin was transfixed by the shapes carved into the stone. The runes were incised deeply; he thought the carvings no more than fifteen or twenty years old. The heel stone was older yet, but not so ancient as the circle itself. *An infant standing within the shade of his fathers.*

Standing, the heel stone reached Kellin's chest. As he knelt, the runes became clearer. He put a finger upon their shapes to trace them out. "One day . . . blood . . . magic."

"One day a man of all blood shall unite, in peace, four warring realms and two magical races," said the voice. "And if those few words you mouthed are all you know of the Old Tongue, it is well you come to me for instruction."

Kellin did not move. His fingers remained extended to touch the runes. Only the tips trembled. *Not what I expected a* jehan *to say to his son as he sees him for the first time.* It served to fuel his anger.

Aidan stood in the chapel doorway. The sunlight was full on his face, glinting off the gold freighting arms and ear. It struck Kellin as incongruity; oddly, he had expected a simple man, not a warrior. But Aidan was that, and more; best Kellin remember it.

He wanted very badly to say all manner of things, but he desired more to find just the right challenge. Let Aidan lead him, then; he would await the proper moment.

"Get up from there," Aidan said. "I am not the sort of man to require homage."

He does not know me. It shook him; he had expected Aidan to know. It altered his intent. "You gave that up," Kellin said forgoing patience. "Homage."

Aidan smiled. "That, as well as other unnecessary things." He hesitated. "Well, will you rise? Or have you come with broken legs to have them made whole again?"

Kellin wanted to laugh but suppressed the sound. He was not certain he could control it. "No," he said only.

"Good. I am not a god; I do not perform miracles."

Delicate contempt. "Surely you can heal. You are Cheysuli."

"Oh, aye—I have recourse to the earth magic. But you are too healthy to require it." Aidan gestured. "Rise."

Kellin rose. He found no words in his mouth, only an awkward, wary patience inhabiting his spirit.

Aidan's ruddy brows arched. "Taller than I believed . . . are you certain the clan desires to lose you?"

It was perplexing. "Why should you believe the clan might lose me?"

"Have you not come for the teaching?" It was Aidan's turn to frown. "The clans send to me those men—and women—who wish to learn what it is a *shar tahl* must do. I serve the gods by interpreting and teaching divine intentions . . ." He shrugged. "*I* make no differentiation between a man who is physically more suited to war than to study, but the clans often do. I am persuaded they would labor most assiduously to talk you out of coming here." The glint in his eyes was fleeting. "Surely the women would."

It was disarming, but Kellin would not permit it to vanquish his irritation. He used the reminder that his appearance was considered by most, especially women, as pleasing to look for himself in Aidan. He saw little. Aidan's hair was a rich, deep auburn, almost black in dim light, save for the vivid white wing over his left ear. His eyes were what a Cheysuli would describe as ordinary, though their uncompromising yellowness Homanans yet found unsettling.

His flesh was not so dark as a clan-bred warrior, but then neither was Kellin's.

There we match; in the color of our flesh. But not, I am moved to say, in the color of our hearts.

Aidan's tone was polite. "Have you come to learn?"

It nearly moved him to a wild, keening laughter; what he wanted to learn had nothing to do with gods. In subtle derision, he said, "If you can teach me."

Aidan smiled. "I will do what I can, certainly. It is up to the gods to make you a *shar tahl.*"

"Is that—?" Kellin blurted a sharp sound of disbelief. "Is that what you think I want?"

"What else? It is what I do here: prepare those who desire to serve the gods more closely than others do."

Kellin moved around the heel stone. He marked that the sun had been in Aidan's eyes; that what his father saw of him was little but silhouette, or the pale shadow of three dimensions.

He sees a warrior, somewhat taller than expected, but nonetheless kneeling in communion with the gods. Well, I will have to see to it he knows me for what I am, not what he presupposes. He moved to the front of the stone, permitting Aidan to see him clearly. *Now what do you say?*

Aidan's skin turned a peculiar grayish-white. His flesh was a chalk cliff in the sun, showing the damage done by rain and damp and age. Even the lips, carved of granite, were pale as alabaster.

"Echoes—" Aidan blurted, "—but Shona. The *kivarna*—" He was trembling visibly.

Kellin had not believed he much resembled his dead mother; they said she was fair, and her eyes brown. But obviously there was something; Aidan had seen it too quickly. *Or perhaps only feels it because of his* kivarna.

Contempt welled up. He wanted badly to hurt the man. "She did bear me," he said. "There should be something of her in me."

Aidan's face was peeled to the bone so the shape of his skull was visible. The eyes, so calm before, had acquired a brittle intensity that mocked his former self-possession. His mouth was unmoving, as if something had sealed it closed.

Is this what I wanted, all those years? Or do I want more yet?

Aidan drew in a breath, then released it slowly. He smiled a sad, weary smile. The chalk cliff of his face had lost another layer to the onslaught of exposure; in this case, to knowledge. "I knew you would hate me. But it was a risk I had to take."

Kellin wanted to shout. "Was it?" he managed tightly. "And was it worth it?" He paused, then framed the single word upon years of bitterness. *"Jehan."*

In Aidan's eyes was reflected as many years of conviction. "Come inside," he said. "What I have to say is best said there."

He did not want to—he felt to do as asked would weaken his position—but Kellin followed. The chapel was not large inside, nor did it boast substantial illumination; a tight latticework roof closed out the sun. Kellin allowed his eyes to adjust, then glanced briefly around the interior. A rune-carved alter stood in the center. Set against the tilted walls were stone benches. Torch brackets pegged into seams in the stonework were empty.

"Where is your *lir?*" Aidan asked.

"She led me here, then disappeared."

"Ah." Aidan nodded. "Teel disappeared this morning as well, so that all I had were the dogs; it was a conspiracy, then, that we should meet without benefit of *lir.*"

Kellin did not care overmuch about what the *lir* conspired to do. He was wholly fixed on the acknowledgment that the man who stood before him had planted the seed which had grown in Shona's belly, only to be torn free on a night filled with flames. *He loved her, they say. Could he not have loved her son as well?*

Aidan sat down on one of the benches. Kellin, pointedly, remained standing. Bitterly he said, "Surely with your *kivarna*—aye, I know about it—you must have known I was coming."

Color had returned to Aidan's face. It was no longer stretched so taut, no longer empty of a tranquillity that annoyed one who lacked it. "I do not question your right to bitterness and hatred, but this is not the place for it."

Kellin barked a harsh laugh. "Is that why you brought me in here? To tame my tongue and render me less than a man?" He wanted to jeer. "You forget, *jehan*—I have none of your reverence, nor your humility. If I choose to honor the gods, I do it in my own fashion. And, I might add, with less elaboration." He cast a scornful glance over the chapel. "I did not know a man would exchange the flesh of his own son for the confines of *stone.*"

Aidan waited him out. "I would not expect you to offer reverence or humility. You are not the man for it."

It was veiled insult, if Kellin chose to take it so. Another might acknowledge it as simple statement of fact. "Do you believe me too weak to be as you are? No, *jehan:* too strong. I am not a coward. I do not turn my face from its proper place to hide upon an island with a mouth full of prophecies."

"Indeed, you are not weak. Nor are you a coward." Aidan shrugged. "Nor am I, but I give you the freedom to believe as you will—just now, there is more. What you are is a confused, angry young man who only now confronts his heritage—and knows his ultimate fate lies in other hands." He overrode the beginnings of Kellin's protest. "You mentioned my *kivarna* first—shall we let the gift guide me in the examination of your soul?" He smiled without intending offense, reminding quietly that what he could do was what few others could. "You will do as I did when the time has come: acknowledge and fully accept what the gods have designed for you in the ordering of your life."

"If you know it, then tell me!" Kellin cried. "You claim communion with the gods. *Tell* me now and save me time wasted in discovering it for myself!"

"And deny you the chance to grow into the man the gods intend you to be?" Aidan smiled. "A warrior cannot circumvent a *tahl-morra* so easily . . . he is charged to become what he is meant to become in the husbandry of his soul. Were I to *tell* you what becomes of you, I might well alter what is meant to happen."

"Obscurity," Kellin charged. "That is what you teach here: how to speak in riddles so no man can understand."

"A man *learns*," Aidan countered, "and then he understands."

Kellin laughed. "Tell me," he challenged. "If indeed you can. Prophesy for me. For your only son."

Aidan did not move upon the bench. His hands lay in his lap. "Do you forget who I am?"

"Who *you* are? How could I? You are the man I have sought all my life—even when I denied it—and now that I have found you I am at last able to tell you precisely what I think of you and your foolish claims!"

"I am the mouthpiece of the gods."

Kellin laughed at him.

And then his laughter died, for Aidan began to speak. "The Lion shall lie with the witch. Out of darkness shall come light; out of death: life; out of the old: the new."

"Words," Kellin began, meaning to defame the man who said them, to leech them of their power, but his challenge died away.

"The Lion shall lie with the witch, and the witch-child born of it shall join with the Lion to swallow the House of Homana and all of her children."

"*Jehan!*"

Yellow eyes had turned black. Aidan stared fixedly at Kellin, one hand raised to indicate his son. "The Lion," he said, "shall devour the House of Homana."

"Stop—"

His voice rose. "Do you think to escape the Lion? Do you think to escape your fate?" Lips peeled back. "Small, foolish boy—you are *nothing* to the gods. It is the Lion's cub they desire, not the Lion himself . . . you are the means to an end. *The Lion shall lie down with the witch.*"

Kellin was instantly taken out of himself, swept back ten years. To the time of Summerfair, when he had put on his second-best tunic to go among the crowds and see what he would see, to taste *suhoqla* again and challenge a Steppes warrior. To enter the tent filled with a sickly, sweetish odor; to see again the old man who sat upon his cushion and told who he was, and what would be his fate.

"Lion—" Kellin whispered, staring at his father. "There is a lion—after all—"

Aidan smiled an odd, inhuman smile. "Kellin," he said plainly, "you *are* the Lion."

Chapter Two

"I am sorry." Aidan's tone was quiet, lacking its former power. "But I warned you. It is never a simple thing—and rarely pleasant—to learn your *tahlmorra.*"

Kellin clung to the heel stone for support. He did not precisely recall how he had reached it. He remembered, if dimly, stumbling out of the shadow-clad chapel into clean sunlight—and then he had fallen to his knees, keeping himself upright only by virtue of clinging to the heel stone as a child to its mother's neck.

He continued to clutch it. He twisted his head to ask over a shoulder. "Do you know what you said?"

Aidan, squinting against sunlight, sighed and nodded. "Most of it. I can never recall clearly what I say when I prophesy, but the intent remains in my mind." His eyes were steady, if darkened by the acknowledgment of what had occurred. "Despite what you led me to believe with regard to your ignorance of your *tahlmorra,* it is not the first time you have heard such words."

"I was ten." Kellin stood up and relinquished his grip on the stone, aware of a cold clamminess in his palms. "But I did not *know*—"

"No," Aidan agreed, "a child could not. Nor many men. You were not ready. Even now you are not."

Resentment congealed. "So you did it to prove something."

Mildly, Aidan said, "You did ask. In plain and impolite words."

Another time he would have fought back. Just now something else struck him as more important. "You said—" He looked warily at the chapel, as if it were responsible for putting the thoughts inside his head. "You said *I* am the Lion."

"You are."

"But *how*? I am a man. Not even in *lir*-shape am I a lion!"

Aidan nodded. "Where words will not serve, symbols often

do." He traced the runes inscribed in the heel stone. "These are symbols. And so is the Lion."

"The Lion is a throne."

"That, too, is a symbol." Aidan smiled. "You are a man in all the ways in which a man is measured; fear nothing there. But you are also the next link in the prophecy of the Firstborn. It may somewhat devalue my dedication to say this so baldly, but prophecies are sometimes little more than colorful pictures, like the *lir* we paint on pavilions."

It gave Kellin something, a tiny bit of strength with which to reassert his challenge. "Then there is no truth to it."

"Of course there is truth to it. Does the painted animal shape mean there is no living *lir?*" Aidan shook his head. "A prophecy does not lie. At times circumstances change, and the fate itself is changed; they gave us free will, the gods. The ultimate result may be altered, but what served as catalyst was never a falsehood. It is not graven in stone." He tapped fingertips against the heel stone. "This will remain here forever—for as long as the world has—to speak of the prophecy and all it entails. Eighteen words." His smile was not condescending, but unadorned serenity; he was certain of his place within the prophecy. "Eighteen simple words that have ruled our lives since before we were even conceived."

Kellin looked at the runes. " 'One day—' " But he broke off reflexive quoting. There was another matter he considered more important. "How can I be the Lion?"

"You *are*. No more than that. You are the Lion . . . just as I was the broken link."

Kellin wanted to deny it all, to accuse the *shar tahl* who was also his father that purposeful obscurity offered no one an answer. But what came out of his mouth was a simple truth: "I do not understand."

"That is one of my purposes here: to explain things more fully."

Bitterness reasserted itself. "To other men whose lives have been twisted by their *tahlmorras?*"

"Come with me."

It provoked. "Where? To that palace? I have seen it. You do not live there."

"To my pavilion." The smile, now lacking the unearthly quality of prophecy, was freely offered again with nothing more in its shaping than hospitality. "I am Cheysuli, Kellin. Never forget that."

* * *

Aidan's pavilion clustered with others in a smaller version of Clankeep. It was pale green with ravens adorning its sides; on the ridgepole sat the model.

Sima, sprawled on a rug before the doorflap, blinked sleepily in the sun. *You found me.*

Kellin scowled. *As you meant me to. That is why you left me.*

She was unrepentent. *Teel and I thought it best.*

I do not appreciate such secrecy in my own lir.

Nor does your jehan. She twitched her tail. *Even now he chastises Teel.*

He deserves it. So do you. He did not stoop to pat the cat but went on by her and into the pavilion as his father pulled back the flap.

Aidan seated himself on a brown bear pelt and gestured for Kellin to make himself comfortable. "We built the Keep here because I saw no sense in inhabiting a palace. We are Cheysuli. We are here to rebuild what we can of the old religion, while imbuing it with new." He smiled. "I am somewhat controversial with regard to my beliefs; some elders name me a fool."

Kellin said nothing. He had come for none of this.

"This is a place of history and magic," Aidan continued, "and we treat it as such. Palaces have no place here."

He disputed at once. "I thought the Cheysuli built it. There are runes in the pillars. Old Tongue runes, like those on the heel stone." It was proof; it was enough; it trapped his traitorous father.

"Runes can be carved later, as those on the heel stone were."

Kellin exhaled patience. He was wrung dry of it. "So, it is a Homanan palace after all. Should that matter? The Homanans are our people, too."

Aidan smiled. "If that was a test, then assuredly you have passed it."

In succinct Homanan, Kellin swore. "I did not come for this!"

"No." Aidan rested his hands on his knees. "Ask what you will, Kellin."

Kellin did not hesitate. The question had been formed nearly twenty years before. He had mouthed it every night, practicing in his bed, secure in his draperies as a child in its mother's womb. Now he could ask it in the open, in the light, of the man who knew the answer. "Why did you give me up?"

Aidan did not, hesitate. "It was an infinitely Cheysuli reason, and one you will undoubtedly contest, though you should know better; you, too, are Cheysuli."

Kellin inhaled angrily on a hissing breath. "*Tahlmorra.* That is your answer."

"The gods required me to renounce my title, rank, and inheritance. I was the *broken* link. The chain could only be mended—and therefore made much stronger—if I gave precedence to the next link. Its name was Kellin." Aidan's eyes did not waver. His tone did not break. His demeanor was relaxed. All of his self-possession was very much in opposition to the words he spoke. "It was the hardest thing I have ever done."

Through his teeth, Kellin said, "Yet you did it easily enough."

The first crack in Aidan's facade appeared. "Not without regret. Not without pain. When I set you into my *jehana*'s arms—" Aidan broke it off, as if afraid to give up too much of himself after all. His tone was husky. "You were Shona's child. You were all I had of her. But I was, in that moment, a child of the gods—"

"It is a simple thing to blame gods."

Aidan's lips parted. "It was done for Homana."

"Homana! Homana, no doubt, would have been better off with a contented prince instead of one who lacked a *jehan.* Do you know what my life has been?"

"Now, aye—the *kivarna* has told me."

"And what does it mean? Nothing? That I spent my childhood believing myself unworthy, and my adulthood cognizant that *I* mean nothing at all, save I can sire a son?" Kellin's fists trembled against his thighs. "Use your famous *kivarna* and see what you did by renouncing a son in favor of the gods."

"Kellin." The chalk cliff sloughed another layer; soon it would be bare, and the true man uncovered. "I never intended for you to suffer so. I knew it would be hard, but it had to be done . . . and you are not, above all things, a malleable man. You choose your own path—have *always* chosen your path—no matter the odds."

"I was a *child*—"

"So was I!" Aidan cried. "I had *dreams,* Kellin—nightmares. To me, the Lion was a vastly frightening thing." With effort, he let it go. He smiled sadly, no longer hiding his truths. "Do you know what it is like for a *jehan* to at last acknowledge that the thing which frightens him most is his own son?"

Kellin was nearly incoherent with outrage. "Is this your excuse for giving me up? That you are *afraid*—"

"It was necessary. There was a purpose in it for me—and one, I believe, for you."

Kellin jeered. "Facile words, *jehan*."

"True words, Kellin."

"Why would you be afraid of me? I am your *son*."

"You are the Lion. You are meant to lie down with the witch. You are meant to sire the Firstborn." Aidan's eyes did not waver. "It is one thing to serve the gods, Kellin, knowing what you work toward—it is entirely another to realize that what you do *matters* in the ordering of the world." His smile was without humor. "Men who honor no gods, who fail to serve the gods, cannot understand the enormity of the truth: that the seed of a single man's loins can alter forever the shape of a world."

Kellin was furious. "You will not blame *me* for this! You will not for one moment lay this at *my* doorflap! Do you think I am a fool? Do you think me so ignorant as to be led by facile words? By the gods, *jehan*—by *any fool's gods*—I will not be turned aside by your faith, by your admirable devotion, by the mouthings of a madman when I want to know the answer to a single, simple question!"

"And I have told you why!" Kellin had at last shattered Aidan's composure. It loosed the final layer of cliff and laid bare the underside of the man, not the *shar tahl;* the once-born Prince of Homana who had bequeathed it all to his infant son. "My *tahlmorra*. You should understand a little of that, now that you know what yours is."

"*Jehan*—"

"Would you have me hold you by the hand and lead you through it? Are you so blind—or so selfish—that you cannot permit yourself to see another man's pain?"

Kellin expelled a curse framed upon the Old Tongue. "What manner of pain could lead a man to renounce his son?"

"The pain in knowing that if he did not, an entire race might be destroyed."

"*Jehan*—"

"The throne was never meant for me. *Here* is where I was bound. The link—*my* link—was shattered in Valgaard; do you understand what I mean? I was broken, Kellin . . . *I* was . . . my link—a symbol—was destroyed. Yours was left whole. *Whole*, Kellin—to be joined with the rest of the chain when Brennan is dead, and a new king ascends. Do you see? I was in the way. I was *unnecessary.* The gods required a prophet, not another rump upon the throne . . . someone to proclaim the coming of the Firstborn. Someone to prepare the way."

"*Jehan—*"

"You are the Lion. You are meant to devour the House of Homana."

Kellin's face spasmed. "You say first I am the Lion, and then I am a link in a chain . . ." He shook his head in emphatic denial. "I understand none of it!"

Aidan's voice was hoarse. "We are all but links. Mine was shattered. Its destruction sundered the chain. Even now it lies in Valgaard, in Lochiel's keeping."

"A *real* chain?"

"A real chain."

"Broken."

"I broke it. I broke *me* to strengthen you."

Kellin bared his teeth. "What good does it do, then, if Lochiel holds it?"

"Someone must get it back."

"From *Lochiel?*"

"Someone must take the two halves and make them one again."

Kellin understood. He sprang to his feet. "By the gods—not *I!* I will not be used in a personal revenge that concerns only you."

Aidan's eyes were infinitely yellow. "Lochiel killed your *jehana.*"

Kellin recognized the battle and struck back at once, using all his weapons. "I never knew her. What does it matter?"

"*He cut you from her body as he burned down all of Clankeep.*"

It hurt desperately. He had blamed himself so long for his mother's death. "No—"

"He wanted the seed," Aidan said. "He wanted to raise you as his own, to turn you against your House . . . to defang the Lion utterly before it reached maturity."

Kellin fastened on a thing, a small, cruel thing, because he needed to, to salvage his anger, to shore up his bitterness. They were things he knew. "Where were *you,*" he asked viciously, "while Lochiel the Ihlini cut open my mother's belly?"

Aidan's eyes mirrored Kellin's desperation. "Where do you think I got this?" A trembling hand touched the white wing in his hair. "A sword. It broke open my skull and spilled out all the wits, all the words, all the things that make a man . . . and turned me into someone no one, not even I, can truly understand." His face was wasted. "Do you think, in all your hatred, when you lie awake at night cursing the man who left you, that any man, any father, would *ask* the gods to give him such a fate?"

Kellin was shaking. He could not stop himself. "I want—I want . . ." He wet dry lips. "I want to be free of the beast."

"Then kill it," Aidan said.

"How?"

"Go to Valgaard. Rejoin two halves of a whole."

"And that will make *me* whole?" Kellin's wild laugh tore his throat. "Expiation for *your* weakness does nothing to destroy my own!"

"Go to Valgaard."

Kellin bared his teeth. "You have not seen what I have become!"

"Nor has Lochiel." Aidan rose and opened the doorflap. "Perhaps the beast in you is a weapon for us all."

"I killed a friend!" Kellin cried. "Do you say it was necessary, that the gods required *this* to fashion a weapon?"

The chalk cliff shapechanged itself to granite. "The gods required me to give up my son. Now that son provides a way for us to destroy an Ihlini who would, given the chance, bring down all of us. He would smash the Lion to bits, then feed it chip by chip into the Gate of Asar-Suti." Aidan's tone was unflinching. His eyes condemned the weakness that would permit a man to refuse. "Make the sacrifice worth it. Make the death of your friend count for something—as Shona's death did."

Kellin's throat hurt. "This is not what I came for."

"It is," Aidan said. "Have I not said I am the mouthpiece of the gods?"

Kellin gestured helplessness. "All I ever wanted—all I *ever* wanted—was some word, some indication you cared, that you knew I *existed* . . . but you gave me nothing. Nothing at all."

Silence lay heavy between them. Then the faintest of sounds, so subtle that in another time, in another moment, no one would have marked it. It was the soft sibilance of a man's hand crumpling fabric.

Tears stood in Aidan's eyes as he clung to the doorflap. "What I gave you—what I gave you was what I believed you had to have." His mouth worked briefly. "Do you think I did not know what it would cost you?"

"But you never *came*."

Aidan's laugh was a travesty. "Had I come, I would have taken you back. Had I sent word, I would have told you to come. For the sake of your son, Kellin, I had to give up my own."

"For *my* son!"

"Cynric," Aidan whispered, and the blackness in his eyes ate away the yellow. "The sword and the bow and the knife—"

"No!" Kellin shouted. "What of me? What of me? *I* am your son, not he! What about me?"

Aidan's eyes were empty of all save prophecy. "You are the Lion, and you shall lie down with the witch."

"*Jehan*—" he said brokenly. "Is this what they have done, your beloved gods? Made you over into this?"

"The Lion shall devour the lands."

For the first time in his life, Kellin put his hands on his father.

For the second time in Aidan's life, he put arms around his son. "Do not be ashamed," he said. "There is no shame in tears."

Muffled, Kellin said, "I am—a warrior."

"So am I," Aidan agreed. "But the gods gave us tears nonetheless."

Chapter Three

They stood upon the dock, facing toward the city of Hondarth sprawled indistinct on the distant shore: the former Prince of Homana, who might have been Mujhar, and the present prince, his son, who one day *would* be.

The sea-salt breeze blew into their faces, ruffling hair, tickling eyelashes, softly caressing mouths. Behind him, silent wolfhounds gathered at the border between wooden dock and paler sand, waiting for their master. Perched in a nearby tree sat the raven called Teel, while the lovely mountain cat, blue-black in the light of the sun, waited mutely beside her warrior.

Kellin slanted a pensive, sidelong glance at his father. They did not, he had decided, much resemble one another. The son of Shona and Aidan appeared to be a mixture of everyone in his ancestry—which was, he felt, a stew of hybrid spices—save that the cat at his side and the gold on his flesh marked him as something more distinct than merely human.

He does not look so old as I thought yesterday. Kellin stripped a wayward lock of hair from an eye, blinking away the sting. *Yet if one looks at the eyes, he seems older than anyone else.* "So—you expect me to go." He snapped his fingers. "Just like that."

Aidan's smile was faint, with a hint of irony in it. "It would be folly indeed to expect *quite* so much acquiescence . . . surely you still have questions."

"A multitude. This one, to begin: how can you say I am the Lion who is meant to lie down with the witch? What witch? Who is it? How can it be done?" Kellin gestured incomprehension. "Even now my grandsire discusses a marriage between me and Dulcie—and I sincerely doubt *Dulcie* is this witch."

Aidan's smile was unabated, as was the irony. "Marriages, no matter how well planned, do not always occur."

It provoked Kellin to retort sharply. "As one nearly did not occur between Aileen of Erinn and the Prince of Homana?"

Aidan laughed, unoffended. "Old history. They are well content, now; and that marriage *did* occur."

"What of mine?"

"Oh, I believe you will indeed be married." Aidan nodded. "One day."

It seemed important to know. "To this witch?"

Aidan's tone was deliberate, akin to Rogan's when the tutor labored to instruct an easily distracted student. "What *precisely* have I said, when I prophesy?"

"That the Lion will lie with the witch." Kellin sighed. "I have heard it more than once."

"Lying down with a 'witch' does not necessarily mean you will marry her."

"Ah." Black brows sprang upward. "Then you advocate infidelity."

Aidan showed his teeth in a challenging grin that Kellin saw, in surprise, was very like his own. "I advocate merely that you do what must be done. *How* it is done is up to you."

"To sleep with an Ihlini . . ." Kellin hitched his shoulders because the flesh between them prickled; the idea was unattractive. "That is what she is, this witch, is she not? An Ihlini?"

"It has been done before."

"Oh, aye—grandsire did. Ian did. I know the stories."

"Do you?" Aidan's brows slanted upward in subtle query. The wing of white hair, against deep russet, was blinding in the sunlight. "Do you also know that *I* slept with one?"

"You!" It was entirely unexpected from a man who was *shar tahl*. "They say you bedded no one after my *jehana* died."

"I did not. I cannot. Surely they told you the cost of *kivarna*, when the partner dies. It is much like a *lir*less warrior, save the body does not die. Only the portion of it that might, given opportunity, given the wherewithal, sire another child."

"But—I am the only one."

"And will ever be." Aidan looked at him. "In Atvia, before I married Shona, I bedded an Ihlini woman. And the second time, I knew it."

"*Willingly?*"

"With Lillith?" Aidan sighed. "To excuse myself, to justify my action, I might prefer to say that even that first time she ensorcelled me . . . but it would be a lie. What I did, I did because I desired it; because I could not, in my maleness, deny myself the gratification found in a woman's body, despite whom she might be."

"Lillith . . ." Kellin tasted the name and found it oddly seductive. "It was she who lay with Ian and bore him a child."

"Rhiannon, who later lay with my *jehan* and bore *him* a child. Melusine is her name."

"You know it?"

"She is the woman who sleeps with Lochiel. She bore *him* a child . . . while she herself, Melusine, was born of Cheysuli blood as well as Ihlini—yet chooses to serve Asar-Suti."

It seemed surpassing odd. "How do you know all this?"

"Lochiel sees to it I know. Lochiel and I—" Aidan's taut, angled smile was strangely shaped, "have long been adversaries on more battlefields than the obvious ones. He sends me messages."

"Lochiel?" Kellin found it incomprehensible. "Why?"

"To make certain I know." Wind ruffled the white wing against Aidan's temple. "Her name is Melusine, and she bore him a daughter. It was that daughter with whom you shared a cradle."

Kellin grunted. "I know something of that."

"Do you?" Aidan's gaze was steady. "Shall I tell you the whole of it, then, so you may have another thing for which to hate me?"

"What? More?" It might have stung once; it might have been a weapon Kellin took pride in wielding, but no longer. Much remained between them, but some of the pain was assuaged. "Then tell me, and I will decide if I should rekindle my hatred."

Aidan looked directly at him. "I *bargained* for you. It was little more, to him, than a simple trade. I was to *choose*—" He rubbed briefly at his forehead as if it ached, then glanced away toward distant Hondarth. "There were two babies, as you know: you, and Lochiel's daughter. I had no way of telling which was which. You were both of you swaddled, and asleep; it is somewhat difficult to tell one infant from another, in such circumstances."

"Aye. How did you?"

"I did not."

"But—you chose *me*."

"I left Valgaard with a child in my arms. I did not know which one it was." Aidan sighed. "Not until I unwrapped you and saw you were male. Then I knew, and *only* then, that my choice had been correct."

"But—if you had chosen the *girl . . .*" Kellin let it go. The repercussions he saw were too complex to consider.

"If I had, you would have been reared as Lochiel's son."

And the girl as a princess within the bosom of Homana-Mujhar, where she might have worked against us. The flesh rose on Kellin's bones. He rubbed at his arms viciously, disliking the weakness that made his fear so plain. "So." It seemed enough.

"So." Aidan nodded. "You know the whole of it."

Kellin stared fixedly across the lapping water. He could not look at his father. He had spent too long hating from a distance to give way easily, to admit to circumstances that might persuade a man to act in such a way as to ignore his son. "You risked a great deal."

"It was my only choice. It was Homana's only chance."

Kellin frowned fiercely. "You said—the Lion will devour the House. Is that not the same fate Lochiel aspires to give us?"

"There is a difference between swallowing the lands, and *destroying* them. Words, Kellin—symbols. Intent is divulged with words. Think of the prophecy."

"Eighteen words, again?"

" '—*shall unite, in peace*—' " Aidan said. "Well?"

Kellin sighed, nodding. "Then to unite the lands, I must swallow them. Swallowing, one might argue, is a form of uniting."

Aidan smiled. "Vivid imagery. It helps a man to remember." He looked at the waiting boat. "We all make choices. You shall make yours."

Kellin saw his father form the eloquent Cheysuli gesture he had detested so long. He matched it easily with his own hand. *"Tahlmorra."*

Aidan's answering smile was serene. "You have run from it long enough."

"So, now you send me *to* it. To Lochiel and Valgaard—and to the witch?"

"That," Aidan said, "is for the gods to know."

Kellin sighed disgust. "I have not had much congress with gods. They are, I am convinced, capricious, petty beings."

"They may indeed be so, as well as other things perhaps not so reprehensible." Aidan was unoffended. "The example for all manner of behavior lies before you; we all of us are their children."

"Even the Ihlini?"

"Stubborn, resentful children, too spoiled in their power. It is time they recalled who gave it to them."

Kellin chewed his lip. "*Why* am I to bring you this chain? What are you to do with it?"

"Tame the Lion."

"*Tame* me!" He paused. "Tame *me?*"

"Who shall, in his turn, swallow the Houses—*unite* them, Kellin!—and bring peace to warring realms."

He clamped his teeth together. "All because of a chain. Which you broke. And left, like a fool, in *Valgaard!*"

"Aye," Aidan admitted. "But then I have never suggested I am anything else."

"'Mouthpiece of the gods,'" Kellin muttered. "You claim yourself *that.*"

"And so I am. But the gods made all men, and there *are* foolish ones." He smiled. "Bring me back the chain, and the beast shall be tamed."

"A quest," Kellin gritted.

"The gods do appear to enjoy them. It passes the time."

Kellin shook his head. There was much he wanted to say, but too little time in which to say it. He had been given his release; time he took it, and went.

"*Shansu,*" Aidan said. "*Cheysuli i'halla shansu.*"

Kellin's tone was ironic. "If there is any such thing in Valgaard." He paused. "You said you would not go to Homana-Mujhar because you feared you would bring me back."

"Aye."

"I am here now. That risk is gone." He hesitated. "Will you go home now?"

The wind teased auburn hair. "This is my home."

"Then—to visit. To be hosted by the Mujhar and his queen." It was hard to force the words past the lump in his throat. "She wants nothing more, *jehan.* Nor does he. Can you give them that now?"

Aidan's soft laugh was hoarse. "You believe me so much a monster as that . . ." He sighed. "There is still much to be done here."

"But—"

"But one day I will return to Homana-Mujhar."

Kellin smiled faintly. "Is that prophecy?"

"No. That is a *jehan* who is also a son, and who would like to see his parents."

Kellin sighed. There yet remained one more thing.

He looked away to the distant shore, then turned back and stared hard at Aidan as Sima leapt into the boat. "Fathers desert their children." He used Homanan purposely; he did not in this moment intend to discuss his own sire, but those of other children.

The wind stripped auburn hair back from Aidan's face. It bared, beneath the skin, the architecture of bone that was ineffably Cheysuli, if housed in paler flesh. "Aye."

"Other fathers . . . Homanan, Ellasian, Solindish—they must do it all over the world—" *I did it myself. I banished three to Clankeep.* "—Is there ever a reason?"

"Many reasons."

It was not the proper answer. Kellin reshaped the question. "Is there ever *justification?*"

"Only that which resides in a man's soul," Aidan answered. "To the child, bereft of a father, bereft of the *kivarna* that might explain the feelings that caused the father to leave, there is nothing save an emptiness and a longing that lasts forever."

"Even if—" Kellin hesitated. "Even after the father is dead?"

"Then it is worse. A deserted child dreams of things being put to rights, of all the missing pieces being found and rejoined. A deserted child whose dreams die with the father's death knows only a quiet desperation, a permanent incompleteness; that the dream, even born in hatred, pain, and bitterness, can now never come true."

Kellin swallowed with difficulty. Unevenly he said, "A hard truth, *jehan.*"

"And the only one there is."

Chapter Four

Kellin bought a horse in Hondarth, rode it across the city, then traded it for another at a second livery. The second mount, a plain brown gelding disinclined to shake his entire body with violent dedication every four steps, proved considerably more comfortable. The ride commenced likewise.

It crossed his mind once, as he and Sima neared the turning to Mujhara, that he could go home. What would the Mujhar do, send him away again? But the order had been for him to remain with his father until Aidan saw fit to send him home; Kellin could, he thought, argue that it was done.

Except he knew better. It most decidedly was *not* done, it being the ludicrous quest to fetch out of Valgaard two halves of a chain his father had broken, then foolishly left behind.

He might have kept it for himself and saved me the trouble.

Sima flanked his horse. *Aye. Then we would be where we were three weeks ago: banished to the island.* She paused. *Where there are dogs.*

Kellin laughed aloud. "Fastidious, are we? Disinclined to consort with *dogs?*" He grinned at his horse's ears; he knew the cat sensed his amusement within the link. "They are good dogs, Sima, regardless of your tastes. They do not bark like terriers, snatching at ankles if you move . . . nor do they bell like hounds on the morning you most desire to sleep."

No, she admitted. *But I am quieter even than those Erinnish beasts.*

"Usually," he said. "Your purring, beside my ear, is enough to shatter my skull."

You told me once it helps you to go to sleep.

"If I *cannot* sleep, aye; there is something soothing about it. But when you sprawl down next to me and take up with rumbling when I am already asleep . . ." He let her fill in the rest. *You are not a housecat,* lir. *You are considerably larger in many aspects, most markedly in your noise—and in the kneading of your claws.*

Sima forbore to answer.

It grew cold as they drew closer to the Bluetooth River. Kellin was grateful he had thought to buy a heavier cloak in Hondarth; he wished now it was fur-lined. But it was nearly summer, and people in the lowlands did not think of such things when the sun shone so brightly.

He shivered. *If I were home in Homana-Mujhar, or within a woman's arms—* Kellin sighed. *That is my favorite warmth.*

I thought I was.

He grinned. *There are certain kinds of warmth not even a lir may provide.*

Then I must assume you would prefer a roadhouse woman and her bed to the cold ground tonight.

He straightened in the saddle. *Is there one?*

One? Or both?

Either. A woman without the roadhouse would prove warm enough, as would a roadhouse without a woman. But a woman in a roadhouse would be the best of all.

Then you may rest well tonight. There is one around the curve of the road.

So there was. Content, Kellin rode up to the stable and dropped off his horse with a sigh of relief. There was no boy to do the work for him, so he led the horse inside the daub-and-wattle building, stripped his mount of tack, then rubbed him down and put him into an empty stall with hay and a measure of grain. He left saddle and bridle beneath drying blankets, then went out into the twilight to look for Sima.

She waited beneath a tree, melding into dusk. Kellin dropped to one knee and butted his brow against hers. *Tomorrow we go on.*

She butted back. *Do we?*

You saw the cairn at the turning. It is but three leagues to the ferry. We will cross first thing . . . by sundown tomorrow, we will be in Solinde.

Sima twisted her head and slid it along his jaw, so that a tooth scraped briefly. *And by sundown the day after that, Valgaard?*

His belly tightened. *I would sooner avoid it—but aye, so we will.*

Sima butted his cheek, tickling his left eye with the tuft of an ear. He buried his face in the silk of her fur, then climbed back to his feet. *Keep yourself to the trees.*

Keep yourself to one wine.

Kellin grinned. *But not to one woman? So much faith in me, lir!*

No, Sima answered. *There is only one woman.*

Kellin did not care. One would be sufficient.

The common room was small but well-lighted, and the rushes were clean. *Prosperous place . . .* Kellin glanced around. As well it should be, so close to the ferry crossing and the North Road out of Ellas, frequently traveled by merchants. He made arrangements for a room, moved to a table nearer the kegs than the front door, and looked for the girl.

It did not take long to find her, nor for her to find him. Even as he hooked out the stool from beneath the small table, she was at his side. Deft hands unpinned his cloak, then stripped it from his shoulders.

The girl froze. Black eyes were avid as she saw the gold on his arms; a glance quickly flicked at his left ear assured her that her assessment was correct.

She smiled, black eyes shining bronze in the light as *lir*-gold glinted. She was young and pretty in a wild, black-eyed way, bold in manners and glances. Content with the weight of his wealth, she eyed the fit of his leggings.

She was quite striking, though in time her looks would coarsen. For now, she would do. *Better than most.* Kellin smiled back. It was an agreement they reached easily without speaking a word; when he tossed the silver coin down on the table to pay for his food and drink, she caught it before it bounced. *Indeed, she will do— much better than expected.*

"Pleasure, my lord?"

He grinned briefly. It was a two-part question, as she well knew when she asked it. "For now, *usca.* If you have it."

"We hae it." White teeth flashed as the coin disappeared into a pocket in her voluminous woolen skirt. She wore a faded crimson blouse and a yellow tabard-smock over it, but both were slashed low to show off small, high breasts. She had pinned her thick black hair at the back of her neck in a bundled mass, but locks had come loose and straggled down her back. Finer strands curled against the pallor of her slender neck.

Kellin found the disarray, and the neck, infinitely appealing. "And what else?" he asked.

She showed her teeth again. "Lamb."

"Lamb will do." He let her see his assessment of her; she would mark it flattery, in the glint of green eyes. "What do they call you?"

"*They* call me whate'er they like," she said frankly. "So may you. But my name be Kirsty."

"Kirsty." He liked it. "Mine is Kellin."

She measured him avidly. "You're a shapechanger, are ye no', wi' all that gold . . . ?" She nodded before he had a chance to answer. "I ne'er seen a shapechanger w'out the yellow eyes."

He found her northern speech as appealing as her slender neck with its weight of hair. He gave her the benefit of a slow, inviting smile he had found years before to be most effective. "Do I frighten you?"

Arched black brows shot up. "You?" Kirsty laughed. "I've been all my life a wine-girl . . . 'tisn't much a man *hae* to frighten me!" She paused consideringly. "Do ye *mean* to, then?"

Her hand rested against the table. He put out his own and gently touched the flesh that lacked the smooth silken feel of the court women he had known before turning to the Midden; he found her hand familiar in its toughened competence, and therefore all the more attractive. "No," he said softly. "I would never mean to hurt *you*."

Kirsty promised much with eyes that bespoke experience without prevarication. "I'll bring your lamb, then, and the *usca* . . . but I'm working, now. I canna gie ye my company till later."

He turned his hand against hers so she could see the bloody glow of the ring on his forefinger. It was unlikely a north country girl would recognize the crest, but she would know its value well enough.

Black brows rose again. "You'd nae gie me *that* for a night, nor a *week* of nights!"

"Not this, perhaps—" he could not; it signified his rank, "—but certainly this." He touched the torque at his neck.

Her eyed widened. " 'Tis too *much!* For a wine-girl? Hae ye no more coin?"

"I 'hae' coin." He mimicked her accent. "But you hae a pretty neck."

She assessed the torque again. "A man's, no' a woman's . . . t'would lie low—here—" She touched her collar bone, then drew her fingers more slowly to the cleft of her high breasts and smiled to see his eyes.

He understood the game. "Do you not want it, then?"

For her, the game was ended. Dreams filled her eyes as the breath rushed out of her mouth. "Wi' *that* I could go to Mujhara! Am I a fool? Nae, I'd take it. But what d'ye want for it?"

"Your company. Now."

"Bu' . . ." She glanced around. "Tam'd turn me out, did I no' tend the others."

"I will pay Tam, too."

A smooth brow knitted. "Hae it been so long, then, that ye're *that* hungry?"

"Hungry," he answered, "for all the things that satisfy a man." He clasped her fingers briefly, then released her hand. "Food and drink first. Come when you can."

Her eyes were on the torque. "Promises made are no' kept, sometimes. D'ye think I'm a fool, then?"

For answer Kellin rose and stripped the torque from his neck. He hooked it around her own, then settled its weight low, on delicate collar bones. Its patina glowed richly against the pallor of her skin.

Her fingertips touched it. "Oh . . ."

Kellin grinned. "But you will earn it, my lass, with *me*."

Kirsty laughed aloud, then bent close to him. "Nae, I think not—'tis a *gift!* I'd hae done you for naught at all."

"For naught!"

"Aye!" Her laugh was throaty. "I've no' seen a man like you in all o' my days!"

Chagrined, he clapped a hand to her rump and found it firm and round. "Lamb and *usca*, then, before I die of hunger."

"Won't be hunger *you* die of!" She swung and was gone before he could retort.

Kellin ate lamb, drank *usca*, and laid a few wagers on the fall of the dice in a friendly game at another table. He was marked as Cheysuli, but no one appeared to resent it. Eyes followed the glint of gold when he moved in the lamplight, but the greed was friendly and lacking in covetous intent.

Kirsty appeared at last and ran deft fingers down his arm. Then she touched the buckle of his belt and tugged. "I'm done," she said. "Are you?"

"That depends," he gathered up his modest winnings, "on which game you refer to. With this one, aye; most certainly I am done. The other is not yet begun—" he grinned, "—and like to last all night."

She laughed softly. "Then coom prove it to me."

He rose and hooked a finger through the torque. He lifted it; then, using it, he pulled her closer, very close, so his breath warmed her face. "What more proof of my intent is necessary?"

Her hand was skilled as she slid it between his legs. "There's proof—and there's *proof.*"

Kellin laughed quietly. "*Shansu, meijhana*—or would you prefer an audience?"

"Those words," she said, brows lifting. "What are those *words?*"

He said it into her ear. "I will explain them elsewhere."

Kirsty laughed and hooked an arm around his waist as his settled across her shoulders. "This way, my beastie—"

"No." He halted her instantly, humor dissipating. "Do not refer to me so."

" 'Twas just . . ." Her defense died. She nodded.

Kellin pulled her close, sorry he had broken the mood. "You know better where my room is."

Kirsty took him there.

He awakened hours later, aware of *usca* sourness in his mouth and a certain stiffness in his shoulders. Kirsty had proven her mettle, and had certainly drained him of his.

The room was dark. It took Kellin a moment to adjust his eyes. The stub of a candle had long since melted down, so that the only illumination was from the seam of moonlight between ill-fitted shutters. It lent just enough light to see the pallor of Kirsty's shoulder, jutting roofward. Raven hair and blankets obscured the rest of her.

I like black hair—and such white, white skin. She was curled against him like a cat, rump set against his left hip. *Would she purr, like Sima?*

But his mind drifted in search of an answer to an unknown question. He wondered what had wakened him. Usually he slept the night through, unless he dreamed of the Lion; but it had been weeks since the last nightmare, and he believed Kirsty had effectively banished the beast for the night. He lay in perfect silence, listening to her breathing.

Lir, Sima said, *has the girl stolen your senses along with other things? I have called for you three times.*

Ah. Kellin sighed and rubbed at his eyes. *What is it?*

If you wish to ride to Valgaard, you had better leave your bed.

Why? Do you want to leave now? It was ludicrous. *I said we would go in the morning.*

Your horse is leaving. Sima sounded smug.

My horse— He understood at once.

Kellin sat up, swearing, and tossed the covers aside. Kirsty mumbled a protest and dragged the blankets back. His clothing lay in a tangled heap on the floor, and no doubt the leather was cold. Kellin swore again and reached for leggings.

Kirsty turned as he buckled his belt. "Where d'ye go?"

"To rescue my horse." He meant to take his cloak, but Kirsty had pulled it up around her shoulders.

She stared at him. "How d'ye know it *wants* rescuing?"

"My *lir* told me." He bent to pull on his boots.

"Yer *beast?*"

"Not a beast. She is a mountain cat." He grinned briefly, tossing her the bone. "Her fur is as black and lovely as your hair."

Kirsty hunched up beneath blankets and cloak unsure of the compliment. "Will ye coom back?"

Kellin pulled open the door. "Would a man be so foolish as to desert *you* in the midst of a cold night?"

Kirsty laughed. "Then I'll gie ye sommat to remember me by." She flung back cloak and coverlet, displaying cold-tautened breasts, and it was only with great effort that Kellin departed the room.

Upon exiting the roadhouse, Kellin was sorry he had left the cloak behind. The night was clear and cold, belying the season. Bare arms protested with pimpled flesh; he rubbed them vigorously, sliding fingertips across cooling *lir*-gold, and strode on toward the stable intending to settle the business at once, then hasten back to bed.

The building was a black, square-angled blob in the moonlight, blocky and slump-roofed. He approached quietly, accustomed to making no sound in the litheness of his movements, and touched the knife hilt briefly.

Sima's tone was clear. *They are taking the saddle, too.*

Kellin swore beneath his breath. Just as he reached the stable two men appeared, and a horse. *His* horse. The gelding was bridled and saddled, as if they intended to ride immediately.

He recognized them from the common room. *Greedier than I thought*— Kellin moved out of shadow into moonlight. "I doubt you could pay my price. You lost in the game tonight."

They froze. One man clung to the horse, while his companion stiffened beside him. Then the first put up his chin. "Go back to Kirsty," he said, "and we'll let ye be. 'Twill be a gey cold night, the other."

The dialect was thick. Kellin deciphered it, then added his own comment. " 'Twill be a gey cold night, withal—for *one* of us. . . ." He slipped into the lilt he had learned from his grandmother. Erinnish was similar. "But I'll be keeping yon horse for myself as well as the bonny lass."

Both men showed their knives. Kellin showed his. The display resulted in a muttered conversation between the two Homanans, as Kellin waited.

Eventually his patience waned. "We each of us has a knife. In that, we are well-matched. But are you forgetting I am Cheysuli? If a knife will not do to persuade you who is better, *lir*-shape will."

It sufficed. The man holding the reins released the gelding at once as the other stepped away. The horse wandered back toward the warm stable.

Kellin sighed. "Go on your way. *That* way." He gestured. "You'll be bedding down elsewhere, my boyos."

The men goggled at him. "We have a room!"

"Not any more."

"Ye canna *do* this!"

" 'Tis done." He grinned at them. "You tried to steal my horse, but that's done for the night. Now I've stolen your bed." He gestured. "On your way.

They muttered something to one another, then turned toward the road.

Kellin raised his voice. "*Cheysuli i'halla shansu!*"

They did not, either of them, offer an answer he understood.

"No, I thought not." Kellin went after the horse, caught and gathered dragging reins, then led the gelding into the stable. "Disturbed your sleep, did they?" He reached for the knotted girth. "Then we are a proper pair—though I dare say I miss the woman more than—" He turned. The noise was slight, but his hearing better than most.

It was too late. Weight descended upon him. Kellin went down with only a blurted protest.

Chapter Five

It was the cold that finally woke him. The earthen floor was packed hard as stone and was twice as cold. The scattered straw offered no protection. Kellin's flesh, as he roused, rose up on his bones all at once and he shivered violently in a sustained convulsive shudder that jarred loose the fog from his head.

"Gods—" His teeth clicked together and stayed there, clamped against the chattering he would not acknowledge.

Awake again?

He started to hitch himself up on one elbow, thought better of it almost at once, and stayed where he was. He rolled his head to one side and felt at the back of his skull, marking the lump. Something crusted in his fingers: dried blood, he guessed; at least it wasn't still flowing.

"*Lir?* Where are—uh." He scowled as he found her seated very close to his side. Aggrievedly, he said, "You might have at least lay down *next* to me! Some warmth is better than none!"

The last time we spoke of warmth, you claimed a woman's better than mine.

"That was in *bed.* Am I in bed now? No! I am lying sprawled on an icy stable floor with not even a *saddle* blanket for my—" He broke it off in astonishment. "—nor any *clothing,* either! My leathers—"

Sima slitted gold eyes against a stream of invective. When he at last ran out of oaths he stopped, caught his breath, and shut his eyes against the pain in his battered head.

He felt *empty,* somehow—and then Kellin clutched a naked earlobe. "My *lir*-gold!" He sat upright, unmindful of his headache. "Gods—they took my *gold!*"

Sima twitched her tail. *Gold is gold. Blessed or no, its value to a man remains the same.*

"But—it took me so long to get it—"

You were in no hurry, she reminded him primly. *You denied it—* and *me—for a very long time.*

Kellin gingerly rubbed the back of his tender skull, then felt the stiffness of abused neck tendons and attempted to massage the pain away. "Gloating does not become you."

Everything becomes a lir.

"And Blais' knife, too." Acknowledgment of a further atrocity sent a shudder through his body. "Oh, gods—oh, *gods* . . . my ring. My signet ring. Gods, *lir*—that ring signifies my rank and title!" He clutched the naked finger. "It has adorned the hand of every Prince of Homana since, since—" He gave it up. "*Lir*—" And then a burst of ironic laughter crowded out his panic. "Fitting, is it not? For ten years I rebel against the constraints of my I rank—and now thieves steal its symbol from me. Surely the gods had a hand in this."

Or a foolish warrior.

Levity vanished. "You are not in the least surprised."

I warned you. She licked a paw.

"Does it mean nothing to you that what they have done is heretical? To rob a Cheysuli warrior of his *lir*-gold, and the Prince of Homana of his signet—"

—is brave, if nothing else; I admire them for their gall. Sima blinked, then slitted eyes. *You can fetch it back.*

"In a saddle blanket? They have taken everything else!"

Surely the girl can bring you clothing.

"The girl likely was part of this." Realization stabbed him. "What coin I have left is in my room—" he reconsidered it, "—or *was.*"

Then you will have to tend it yourself.

Kellin swore again. Then, with excessive care, he got off the cold ground at last, found the nearest saddle blanket, and wrapped it around his loins. He was just tucking in the end when the stable door creaked open.

Kirsty stood silhouetted in moonlight, swathed in his cloak. He saw the tabard and woolen skirt, and leather shoes. Unbound hair, tangled from the evening's sport, hung below her hips.

Sima blinked again. *A conclusion perhaps best not jumped to.*

"Thieves," Kellin declared in answer to Kirsty's expression. "Did you know nothing of it?"

She put up her chin. "If I knew aught, I'd be other than here, ye muddle-headed whelp! D'ye think me so foolish as to *coom* to ye if I knew?"

"A clever woman would, merely to mislead me." He was curt in his headache and humiliation. "Have you clothing I can put on?"

Kirsty tossed back her untamed mane. "Ye'd took gey foolish in *my* clothing, ye ken."

Kellin sighed. "Aye, so I would. Have you *men's* I might put on?"

"Tam'll hae some. T'will cost, and nae doot'll be no' to your liking, but better than ye wear now." Her grin was abruptly sly. "Not that *I'm* minding, ye ken."

"I ken," he said dryly. "And I will pay Tam. Though the gods know that torque alone would buy me a trunkful."

She clutched at it. " ' 'Tis mine! Ye said so!"

" 'Tis yours. I said so. Keep it, Kirsty—run and fetch the clothing." Silently he said, *If I can trust you to come back.*

Kirsty swung on her heels and hastened away while Kellin sat down on a haphazard pile of grain sacks and tried to ignore the cold and the thumping in his head.

She was back after all in but a handful of moments, and had the right of it; the clothing was not at all to his liking. But he put on the grimy smock and woolen baggy trews without complaint, then stuffed straw into the toes of Tam's oversized, decaying boots so they at least remained on his feet. The soles were worn through, the poor heels all run down, but even tattered leather was better than bare feet.

His earlobe hurt. The thieves had paid scant attention to the wire and how it hooked; they had wrenched it out of the hole with little regard to his flesh. But the lobe, if sore, was whole; he recalled very clearly that his grandsire lacked all of his.

Kirsty touched his arms. "No' the same wi' nae gold."

Anger got the best of him. "Is that what you wanted all along?"

She drew back, warding the torque against his eyes. "Nae! And I only meant ye dinna look the same wi'oot it, not that I *wanted* it! Now ye look like a Homanan, and a poor one at that!"

He laughed with little amusement. "So I do; one might mistake me altogether as a common lowborn roadhouse-keeper." He regretted the words at once; what had she done to deserve them? "I am sorry—I am poor company. My thanks for the clothing. Now—which way did they go?"

"They?"

"The thieves. You know them, do you not?"

Kirsty said nothing.

"I saw them earlier, in the common room. They knew you, Kirsty, and you knew them." He paused. "I do not intend to kill them, merely fetch back my things. What they took is—sacred." He left it at that.

Kirsty chewed on a lock of hair. "North," she said finally, "across the river."

It was very near dawn. Already the sky behind her began to lighten. "Into Solinde."

She shrugged. "They're Solindish. They coom onc't a four-week."

"To steal."

"To work."

"One and the same, perhaps?" Kellin sighed. "Which way across the river?"

"Westward." She jerked her head. "They might ha' hurt ye worse."

"I said I will not kill them." He glanced at the stalls. "I have need of a horse."

Sima questioned that. *What of lir-shape?*

Within the link, he refused. *Too dangerous. No balance, yet—and now no time to learn it.* Kellin shivered. *For now, I will ride a horse.*

Kirsty stared. "*Now* ye want a horse? Ye hae no such coin in your purse, ye ken. I looked—*here* 'tis—*I* dinna want it!" She slapped it into his hand. "I only meant, how will ye buy the horse?"

"On promises," he said.

"Promises o' what? You've naught left; you've said so."

He turned from her and moved to the nearest stall. "This one will do. Where is the bridle?—ah." He took it down from its peg, slipped the posts that fenced in the horse, and slipped inside.

"You'll no' turn *thief,*" she said. "That be Tam's horse."

"Not yours."

"Nae. I own nothing but what I wear—and this." She clutched the torque. Her black eyes were very bright, but it was not from good humor; Kellin thought perhaps tears. "Unless you mean to take it back."

"No, I will do no such thing. Here, have back the coin—it will pay for the clothing. But I also need a horse. If you would have Tam repaid for *that,* there is a thing you can do." He bridled the piebald horse, then led it from the stall. He would not take saddle also; he took too much already. "If you would pay back Tam—and put coin in your pockets, as well—you need only go to Mujhara, and then to Homana-Mujhar."

"Homana-Mujhar!" She gaped. "To the palace?"

"They'll give you coin for the torque." He swung up bareback onto the piebald back and winced; the spine was well delineated. "That way it will stay with like pieces instead of winding up with a money-lender . . . tell them I used it to pay a debt."

"Tell *who?*" She tossed back her head. "The Mujhar himself?"

He grinned. "They do know me there."

She was instantly suspicious. "I'm to tell them Kellin sent me to trade this for coin? Och, aye—they'll toss me oot i' the street!"

"Not immediately. After a meal, perhaps." He glanced at Sima. *Coming?*

She stood up from the shadows and shook her coat free of straw, then slid out of darkness into the dawn of a new day. Kirsty let out a startled shriek and leapt back three paces.

"My *lir,*" he said briefly. "Do you see what I mean about her fur and your hair? Both such a lovely, glossy black."

The girl clutched at the shining torque. "In the eyes," she mumbled, staring at him. "E'en wi'*oot* the gold!"

"I thank you," Kellin said. "It is a compliment."

As he rode away from the stable, Kirsty called a final farewell. "Homana-Mujhar, indeed! I'll be keeping this for *myself!*"

Kellin sighed as he settled himself carefully athwart the treacherous spine. "Worth a trunkful of clothing and an entire *herd* of horses."

But less than your missing lir-*gold, your ring—and your kinsman's knife.*

Kellin offered no answer. Sima, as always, was right.

By the time they reached the ferry, Kellin's discomfort in his nether regions matched the thumping in his head. He was altogether miserable, wishing for his horse back, and all his gold back, and the knife, and most particularly the saddle that would have made things, even on *this* horse, much easier to bear.

He thought his head might burst. A closer inspection with fingers had not divulged anything he did not already know—the swelling was soft and tender, the cut dried. He wondered what they had struck him with—the roadhouse, perhaps?

He began a complaint to Sima. *They might have been—*

Halfway through the comment he cut off the communication through the link. It made his head hurt worse. He waved a gesture at the cat that dismissed conversation; she flicked tufted ears and held her silence accordingly, but he thought she looked amused.

The ferry was docked this side of the river. Relieved, Kellin halted the piebald and slid off carefully, so as not to jar his head. A man was slumped against a cluster of posts roped together, the stub of a pipe clenched in his teeth. His eyes were closed, but he was not asleep.

Kellin led the horse up. "Did you give passage to two men early this morning? Just before dawn?"

One eye opened. Graying brown hair straggled around his face beneath a threadbare cap. " 'Twould be hard for a body to *walk* across, would ye no' say?"

Kellin suppressed a retort. "Then you did."

"Dinna see bodies in the river, do ye?—though they be carried awa' by now." The other eye opened. "She's angry in the spring."

Kellin looked beyond the man he took to be the ferry-master to the river beyond. It *was* spring, and the river did seem angry; the thaw had thickened the Bluetooth so that it ran nearly out of its banks, with a high, fast current that would suck a man down all too easily.

"They robbed me," Kellin said. "I am angry, also."

The ferry-master squinted. "Doesna look like ye had so much to steal."

"Now, no. Before, I did. This is the best I could do." He paused. "Did you give two Solindishmen passage across the river?"

"If I said aye, would ye be after passage, too?"

"The woman said it was where they were bound."

"Kirsty?" The man brightened. He was, Kellin judged, nearly as old as the Mujhar. "Did she send ye, then?"

"She sent me."

He raked Kellin with a glance from brown eyes set deeply in shadowed sockets. "Then ye must ha' pleased her. She's no' needing to be sending a robbed man after those who coom to see her onc't a four-week."

Kellin hung onto his patience with effort. The thudding in his head made it increasingly difficult. "We pleased each other well enough. Did the men cross here?"

"Dinna walk, did they?" He heaved himself from the planking and jabbed the pipe in Sima's direction. "She tame, yon cat?"

Kellin opened his mouth to vigorously deny that a *lir* could be tamed; he shut it once he recalled what Kirsty had said: that he could, in Tam's clothing, pass as a Homanan. This close to Solinde, this close to Valgaard, it might be better to keep his mouth shut with regard to *lir*. "Aye," he said. "Tame enough."

"Then you'd best go no farther north," the ferrymaster warned. "There's a man o'er the Pass who pays gold and jewels for cats like her."

He was indignant. "*Who* does?"

The ferry-master made a sign against evil. "A man," he said only. "He'd hae *her* faster than the river would eat a man." His truculence now was vanished. "Aye, they crossed. Will ye?"

"I will. At once."

The man unwound the coil of rope tying up the ferry. "Hae ye coin for it?"

"I have—" No. He did not. "—this horse."

"*That* horse! That one? What would I be doing wi' Tam's old nag?"

"Mine was stolen," Kellin said tightly through his teeth. "I bought this one to track the thieves, so I might get back my *own* mount—which is, I might add, considerably better than 'Tam's old nag.' "

"Aye, it would be, ye ken? Not many *worse* than Tam's old nag." He jerked his head toward the ferry. "Coom aboard, then, you and yon cat . . . if Kirsty sent ye after them, there's a reason for't. I'll no' take the nag." He grinned briefly. "Kirsty'll make it right."

Knowing how she spent her nights, Kellin judged she would. Nonetheless, he was grateful.

Almost as soon as he was aboard, Kellin was sorry. The Bluetooth fought the ferry every inch of the way, spuming over the sides of the flat, thick platform until the boards ran white with foam. The old piebald spread his legs and dropped his head even as Kellin grabbed hold of a rope; Sima dug claws into aged wood and lashed her tail angrily in counterpoint to the heaves the ferrymaster put to the ropes.

By the time they reached the other side, Kellin's tattered clothing was soaked. Sima bared her teeth and shook droplets free of her coat. As soon as the ferry thumped the bank she sprang for land; Kellin led the piebald off and thanks the gods for putting firm land beneath his feet.

"Aye," the ferry-master said, "she's a gey wicked bitch in the spring. Summer's better." He jerked his head westward. "That way, they went. They won't be expecting ye, so they willna be in a hurry. Ye'll hae them by sundoon."

Kellin nodded thanks. "Is this because of Kirsty?"

"Och, she's a right'un, that lass . . . but ye've a pinched look in the eyes that says they hit ye a mite too hard." He grinned around the pipe. "And ye speak too well for a man born to wear Tam's clothes." He jerked his head again. "Gi'on wi' ye, then. Ye'll be back by tomorrow, and ye can pay for your ride."

Kellin smiled. "*Cheysuli i'halla—*" He broke it off instantly, cursing the headache that mangled his wits so.

The ferry-master's eyebrows shot up beneath the lock of greasy hair. "Ah. Well, then. Not tame after all, is she?" He coughed. "Yon cat."

"No." Kellin swung up onto the piebald and wished immediately his pride had permitted him to find a log and mount, like a woman. "There are times I wish she were."

The brown eyes were sharp. "Then 'tisn't the horse you're wanting, or the coin . . . more like cat-shaped gold, is't?"

"More like," Kellin said. He kicked the horse into motion.

"Aye, well . . . I've no' known them to be so foolish before." He briefly showed a gap-toothed grin that gave way to the pipestem. "Be wary of Solinde. Up here so close to Valgaard—well . . ." He let it go. "They'd be wanting more than yon cat."

This time he did not hesitate. "*Leijhana tu'sai. Cheysuli i'halla shansu.*"

Chapter Six

The westward road was not so well-traveled as the one cutting down from the Bluetooth into the center of Homana. It was narrow and twisty, winding its way through silted huddles of downed trees and acres of water-smoothed boulders carried this way and that by a temperamental river gone over its banks to suck back again, leaving detritus in its wake. Tam's old nag was not a particularly coordinated horse, and Kellin spent much of his time trying to keep his head very still upon his neck as the horse stumbled its way along.

"By sundown," Kellin muttered in reference to the ferrymaster's prediction as the piebald tripped again. "By then, I may well be lacking a head entirely. It will have fallen off and rolled to a halt amidst that pile of boulders, *there,* and when the crows have picked it clean no one will know the difference between it and that rock, *there.*"

Sima chanced the *lir*-link. *I will go on ahead. Let me find them—I will come back and fetch you.*

It pulsed within his skull. Kellin hissed in pain and shut his eyes against it, then waved her on. "Go. I am little threat to them if I find them in this state. They will laugh, and be on about their business with no fear of me."

The cat whipped her tail, then left at a springy lope.

The horse stumbled on. After a while Kellin balanced himself, shut his eyes, and gave himself over to a state very akin to sleep, in hopes that when he awoke the pain would be dispersed.

He roused to a quiet voice pitched over a rush of water. "I had expected to eat alone, but your horse has other ideas." A pause. "I am glad of the company; will you share my meal?"

Kellin opened his eyes. He slumped atop the piebald, which had in turn wandered off the road to a cluster of tumbled boulders very near the river's edge. He smelled smoke and fish. It made his belly rumble.

The stranger laughed. "I will take that as acceptance."

"Where am I?" Kellin glanced around. The road was not so far; he could see it winding westward.

"Here," the man said, amused. "At my campsite, such as it is; but I have had good fortune in my fishing, and there is enough for us both." His hazel eyes were friendly. The piebald snorted against the hand that held his bridle; the stranger grinned and pushed the muzzle away. "You have been hard used; I have wine for the ache."

He was a young, fine-featured man, perhaps Kellin's age or a year or two older. His hair was dark, nearly black, and fell smoothly to his shoulders. His clothing was spun of good wool of uniform yarn. Kellin marked him a well-to-do man: linen tunic dyed blue, with black embroidery at the collar; black-dyed breeches; good boots, and a brilliant crimson cloak thrown on loosely over shoulders.

Kellin considered refusing. There were the thieves to think about. But his head did ache, his belly did rumble—and Sima was on their trail. He need only wait for her, and by the time she returned, his condition would be improved.

"My thanks," he said. Then recalled what he looked like. "But I have nothing—"

The stranger waved a hand. "Your company is enough. I am not so far from my destination; I can be generous." He smiled again. "You might do better to walk, then to go another step atop *this* horse."

"Aye." Kellin smiled crookedly and slid off, gritting his teeth against the pounding in his head. It was worse, not better; but the road was hard and the horse clumsy. He was lucky his head remained on his neck.

"My name is Devin," the stranger said as Kellin pulled the reins over the piebald's neck. "The wine I have is Solindish white; will it do?"

Kellin followed. "Any wine will do. I am not fit to judge its taste." A glance from Devin told Kellin he had perhaps misphrased his answer; he had meant because of his head, but Devin's quick assessment indicated the stranger believed he meant his station. *He thinks me a poor man; well, for the moment, I am.* He led the piebald to the water-wracked, uprooted tree at the riverbank and tied him to a branch next to Devin's mount, a fine glossy bay very like Kellin's stolen horse.

A fire was built between a tumble of clustered boulders and the water's edge, hosting two speckled fish speared and hung belly-up along two stripped branches resting in crotched braces. The lap of the river was but paces away, so the sound was loud. Devin squatted near the fire, digging through packs. "Here." He tossed the wineskin. "I have another; drink as you will. I will tend the fish."

Kellin caught the skin as he turned from the piebald and swallowed, glad of the liquor's bite. If he drank enough, it would dull the pounding in his head, but that would be poor manners. He owed Devin sober companionship, not the rudeness of a man undone by misfortune.

Devin made conversation as he inspected the sizzling fish. "I misjudged the distance," he said, "or I would have stayed the night in the last roadhouse I passed. The ground is a hard bed when one is used to better." He lifted one of the speared fish. "Here. Trout. I daresay it will complement the wine."

Kellin accepted the proffered fish-laden stick with thanks and sat down against the closest boulder. He thought Devin was indeed accustomed to better; a sapphire gleamed on one hand, while a band of twisted gold glinted on the other.

Devin took the other fish for himself and sat back against his packs, blowing to cool the meat. "Have you a wife?" he asked.

Kellin shook his head. His mouth was full of fish.

"Ah. Well, neither do I—for but a four-week more!" He grinned. "I am bound for my wedding. Wish me good fortune, my friend, and that the girl is comely . . . I have no wish to share my bed with a plain woman!"

Kellin swallowed. "You have never seen her?"

"No. A dynastic thing, this marriage. To bind the bloodlines closer." Devin chewed thoughtfully. "A man like you weds for love, or lust—or because the woman has conceived, and her father insists!—but a man like me, well . . ." He sighed. "No choice for either of us. The match was suggested by her father, and mine accepted eagerly; one cannot help but to rise in service to a powerful lord."

Kellin's smile was crooked. "No."

"I envy you. You need not wed at all, if that is your desire— well, I should not complain; my lot is better than yours." Devin's attitude was friendly enough, but all too obviously he believed Kellin lowborn. "What is your trade?"

Kellin wanted to laugh. If he told Devin the truth— He grinned, thinking of the thieves. "What other trade is there but to aspire to higher in life—and the coin to make it possible?"

Devin's eyes narrowed consideringly as he washed down trout with wine. "You are a passing fair mimic."

"A mimic?"

"Aye. Put on finer clothing, wash the grime from your face, you could pass for a highborn man." He stoppered the wineskin. "You might make a mummer."

Kellin laughed, thinking of his grandparents. "There are those who have accused me of that very thing. I did but play-act the role, they said—then admonished me to learn my part better." He jerked his head westward. "When you came down the road, did you pass two men with a bay very like your own?"

Devin shrugged. "I passed many people. I do not recall the horse." His eyes brightened over the fish. "Why?"

"The horse they have is mine. It was stolen from me . . ." He ran a hand through tousled hair. "You see, I am not precisely the man I appear to be." Kellin plucked at Tam's grimy tunic. "They took more than my horse."

"And left you with that piebald horse and another's clothing?" Devin shouted a laugh. "Aye, it makes sense—you have not the manner of a low-born man, either."

Kellin thought of the Midden and his visits. "Some might argue with that."

"Well, at least they left you your life. Did they knock you on the head?" He grinned as Kellin grimaced an answer. "I thought so. The dullness in your eyes . . . aye, well, drink more wine." He finished his fish. "If I were not expected, I would help you catch the thieves. I have certain gifts that would improve the sport."

"Gifts?"

Devin grinned. "Arts." He reached for the wineskin, then turned as movement on the road caught his eyes. Almost at once he froze. "Be still!" He put out a hand. "Do not move—gods, but what a beauty . . . and a fitting gift for the girl's father. He covets them. I shall have to see if I can take her."

Kellin turned, asking, "Covets what—?" And broke off immediately. Suspicion blossomed.

He dropped the fish, set down the wineskin quietly, and wished he had his knife. He stared hard at the friendly stranger.

"She is *lovely!*" Devin breathed.

Kellin did not answer. He reached out very carefully and closed his hand around the hilt of Devin's knife.

Devin twisted at once, slapping down at Kellin's grasping hand. "What are you—*wait*—" He rolled and scrambled up, poised for attack. The light in his eyes was gone, replaced by a cold, piercing stillness. Quietly, he said "Only a fool steals from an Ihlini."

The cold knot solidified in Kellin's belly. He knelt on one knee with the other booted foot planted, grasping a stolen knife. "And only a fool thinks he can capture a *lir*."

Realization kindled in Devin's eyes, then damped to coals. He shook his head. "You have no power before me."

"Nor you before me."

Devin raised his hands. "I have these."

"And I have your knife."

Devin's eyes narrowed. His young face was stretched taut across prominent cheekbones. His lips were bloodless. He studied Kellin carefully, then murmured something beneath his breath. "They say—" He shut his mouth, then began again. "They say we are very alike. Ihlini and Cheysuli. That we are bloodkin." He remained half crouched, prepared to receive an onrush. "Do you believe it?"

"Does it matter?"

"It does. If there is truth to it. If we are to kill one another."

"Are we?"

Devin shrugged. "To serve Asar-Suti, I will kill whomever I must—" In one smooth motion he ripped his cloak from his shoulders and swirled it at Kellin, snapping weighted corners.

The blaze of crimson came at his face, aimed for his eyes. Kellin ducked the cloak easily enough, but it served merely as distraction; Devin scooped up and hurled a river rock that nearly struck Kellin's head.

Ku'resh— As Kellin dodged it, the Ihlini hurled himself forward.

They went down together hard, smashing into rocks spewed up by the Bluetooth River. Devin's fingers dug into Kellin's throat. He squirmed beneath the Ihlini, thrashing legs to gain leverage, and managed to thrust a knee upward that imperiled Devin's balance. The Ihlini tensed, shifted, and Kellin bucked him off. The knife was lost somehow, but he scrambled to his feet even as Devin came up clawing.

It was an obscene dance, an intercourse of grasping hands reaching to crush a throat. Kellin was aware of Sima's nearness by the sound of her growls and snarls, but the link was completely empty. In its place was an odd disorientation, a buzzing interference that told him all too clearly what he should have known before; what he *would* have known before had his wits not been so muddled.

They were too near the river. Sand shifted. Rocks rolled. Kellin's feet slid inside oversized, straw-stuffed boots. *No foothold*— He slipped even as Devin changed grasp, and Kellin stumbled. He brought the heel of his right hand up against the underside of Devin's jaw, meaning to snap the neck, but the Ihlini twisted his head sharply aside.

This, then— Kellin hooked a foot and caught Devin's ankle. He dropped the Ihlini, then turned and lunged for the knife but a pace away.

Devin's feet scissored out. Kellin, caught, fell hard, trying to twist, but Devin's hands were on him. *—knife*—

The Ihlini had it. Kellin saw the brief glint, saw the tip meet Tam's grimy fabric, then plunge through.

Gods—Sima— He squirmed, sucking in his belly.

Devin gasped a triumphant laugh. Steel dug through flesh and slid between ribs. The Ihlini's mouth was a rictus of victory and exertion. "*Who* wins this one?"

Kellin jerked himself off the blade, willing himself not to think of the pain, the damage, the risk. He saw the blood smearing steel, saw the crimson droplets staining damp sand, but refused to acknowledge it.

He twisted his torso and brought up a booted foot. One thrashing thrust jarred against Devin's thigh, then glanced off. It was enough. Kellin levered himself up, grasping hair and tunic, and threw Devin over. He let his weight fall and pinned the Ihlini, then grabbed handfuls of dark hair and began to smash the skull against the sand.

The wound was bad. If he did not kill Devin soon, he would soon bleed to death. What a sweet irony if they killed one another.

Devin bucked. An upthrust knee missed Kellin's groin but not his belly. Pain blossomed anew, and bleeding. His tunic was sodden with it.

"—wait—" Devin gritted. "—only need to *wait*—" But he did not. He bucked again, broke Kellin's grasp, and scrambled away from him. "Now—"

Kellin staggered upright, sealing the wound closed with his left arm pressed hard against his ribs. He fell back two steps, stumbled over a rock, tried to steady his footing. Strength was fading fast.

Devin laughed. His face was scratched and reddened in patches; it would bruise badly if he lived long enough. "Cheysuli blood—" he gasped, "—is red as Ihlini—red as my *own* . . . are we kinsmen, then?" He smeared an arm across his face. "I have only to wait—you will do me the favor of dying even if I never touch you again."

"My *lir*—will touch—*you*—" It was all Kellin could manage as he labored to keep his breath.

"Your *lir?* I think not. The *lir* are proscribed against harming Ihlini. Have you ever wondered why?" Devin's breath was returning.

Kellin backed up. He heard the rush of the river, the promise of its song. What he needed was time to recover himself, but time he did not have. Devin had time.

He could not hold the blood in. It crept through his fingers, then dripped to the sand. A rock was red with it, turning slowly black. Behind Kellin the river roared louder.

"Enough," Devin said, bending to grab the knife. "I am expected in Valgaard. This foolish dance delays me."

Kellin bent and scooped up a round stone. He let fly, then scooped another and threw again. Devin ducked, but did not let go of the knife. He knew better; why loose the only weapon and chance the enemy's retrieval?

The Ihlini advanced. "One more throw, and your heart will burst. Do you think I cannot tell?"

Kellin retreated, clutching bloodied wool against his chest. The world around him blurred. *Not like this—not what I could ask for in the manner of my death—*

Sima screamed. Devin lunged.

Kellin twisted from the knife as the blade was thrust toward him. He caught the outstretched arm in both hands and wrenched, snapping it over, trying with grim determination to break the limb entirely.

Devin shouted. The knife fell free, then the Ihlini stumbled forward and threw his weight against Kellin.

A curious warmth flowed throughout his chest. Kellin saw the

Ihlini's mouth moving, but heard no words. He sagged, thrust out a braced foot to hold himself up, and clung to Devin.

The bank behind them broke. Both flailing bodies tumbled into the river.

Kellin loosed his grasp on Devin as the waters closed over his head. He thrust himself upward, thrashing; ill-fitting boots filled with water and dragged him down again.

Sima—

He clawed, sealing his mouth shut, trying to make his way upward where he could breathe again. The boots were pulled off his feet.

Sima—

The river rolled. He broke the surface briefly and sucked air. Then the beast caught him again, threw him over, hurled him downward. He tumbled helplessly, clawing at current, holding his breath in lungs that refused to serve him.

He was briefly embraced within the treacherous arms of a buried tree, deep in the water. Then the tunic tore loose and he was free of it, of snag and tunic; he thrashed again but could no longer tell which was surface and which was bottom.

He breathed water. He was hurled against a rocky protuberance, then scraped off again and tumbled, limbs flailing uselessly. His right leg caught, wedged into a cleft between the rocks. Kellin twisted in the current, was tumbled helplessly, and felt the dull snap.

No pain. His leg was numb. *Both* legs were numb. His entire body was nothing but a blob of useless flesh, too vulnerable, too fragile, to withstand the beast in full spate.

The river dragged him free, then threw him heedlessly against another promontory. He surfaced briefly, coughed a garbled plea for air, for aid, then the river reclaimed him.

This time she was cruel. She hurled him into her depths and kept him there, like a cork caught in a millrace, and when she threw him out again, into the lesser current, she did not notice if the broken body breathed or not.

Interval

The master of Valgaard was found deep in the undercroft of the fortress, feeding his cats. They did not cluster at his feet as housecats do, courting morsels, demanding affection, because they were not pets, but mountain cats, tawny, russet, and black, who prowled the confines of their cages baring great teeth, snarling as he dangled promised offal before them, and red, bloodied meat.

He was a handsome man, and knew it; it pleased him to know it, though breeding almost assured it. And young, less than thirty, clearly in his prime—though that was won from the Seker and was not a natural thing. He kept his dark, springy hair closely cropped against a well-shaped head balanced on an elegant neck, and adorned supple fingers with a clutch of rings. They glinted bloody and bronze in the torchlight.

A man arrived. He stood in the archway and did not step into the chamber. His voice was pitched very quietly, so as not to disturb the cats; more importantly, so as not to disturb the master. "My lord."

Lochiel did not look away from his cats; he enjoyed their ferocity. "Have you news of Devin?"

The man folded his hands before him, eyes fixed on the floor so as not to offer offense. "We are not certain, my lord. We believe so."

Lochiel turned. His eyes were a clear ale-brown set beneath winged brows that on another man might suggest femininity; on him, they did not. No one alive would suggest he was less than a man. The structure of his face was of peculiar clarity, as if the gods had labored long to make him perfect. "Why are you uncertain?"

"We found a horse, and packs containing certain articles belonging to Devin—included among them was the ring your daughter sent him—but Devin was not with the horse. There were signs of violence, my lord—bloodied sand, and a fallen knife . . . but no body. At least, not there." The servant did not look up from the floor. "We found a man downriver not far from the horse, thrown up in the bank like driftwood."

"Dead?"

"He was not when we found him. He might be now. He is sore hurt."

Lochiel threw meat to the cats, one by one, and smiled to see unsheathed claws trying to fish meat bestowed from one cage into another. "Where is my daughter?"

"With him, my lord. She was hawking out of the defile, in the canyon—she saw us bring him up."

Lochiel sighed. "Not the most impressive way to meet your bridegroom." He glanced at bloodied hands and wished them clean; they were. "It will be an annoyance if Devin dies. I researched his pedigree most carefully."

"Aye, my lord."

Lochiel observed the cats. His day was now disturbed. "They will have to wait. I will have them eat no meat save it comes from my hands."

"Aye, my lord. My lord?"

Lochiel arched an inquisitive brow.

"We saw a cat, my lord. As we came over the Pass. A sleek, black female, young but promising well. She hid herself almost at once."

"Had she a mate?"

"None we saw. We were thinking of the man, and came straight on to the fortress."

"Very well. I will send you out tomorrow to learn the truth of her." He glanced at the black male who eyed him hungrily. "Perhaps if you are good, I shall give you a mate." He frowned pensively. "It would be a pity if my daughter lost hers. I need children of them." He touched one of his rings. *If Cynric is born—* His mouth compressed, robbing the line of its purity.

If Cynric were born after all, there was only one sure way, one certain course to defeat him; but such insurance was costly and required a sacrifice. Yet *he* had failed in all his attempts. Asar-Suti did not countenance failure.

The Ihlini studied his rings, considering, knowing the answer already. If Kellin lived to sire the child, that sure way, that exacting, definitive course would have to be taken.

Lochiel sighed. *If we are to block the Firstborn, I shall have to make a child for the Seker to inhabit.*

PART IV

Chapter One

"You should not be here," my mother declared.

I heard the rustle of her skirts as they dragged across the threshold. She wears them long and full, using up bolts of costly cloth that might better be distributed among several women instead of only one. But that was my mother; she lived solely for her position as Lochiel's wife, as if it might mislead a stranger into forgetting what she herself detested: that the taint of Cheysuli blood also ran in her veins.

"Undoubtedly," I agreed. "But I am here now; proprieties no longer matter." I glanced at her then, and saw the skirts were the deep, rich red of the thickest Homanan wine. She glittered with jet. *All black and red, and white.* . . . Even to carmined lips against the pallor of her flesh. She bleaches it deathly white, to hide the Cheysuli taint.

"Who is he?" She moved closer.

"A man," I answered evenly, with off-handed negligence. Then, to prick her: "He may well be Devin."

She cast me a sharp, well-honed glance designed to discover the truth; I hid it behind the mask. I had learned it of my father, who said *he* had learned it to turn the witch from the door.

It was his jest to say so. We are all of us witches.

"Devin or no, you had best take yourself elsewhere," she said. "There are servants who can tend him, and I am better suited to intimacy than you."

Aye, so she would be; she encouraged it constantly.

I shrugged. "I have already seen him. I met them in the canyon when they brought him up; they wrapped him in a blanket, but that was taken off when they put him in the bed." I paused. "I know what a man looks like."

Carmined lips compressed into a thin, retentive seam. She looked at the man lying so still in the bed. He was well-covered now, but I had seen the naked flesh. It was blue from the water, and slick with bleeding scrapes reopened by the ride. They had brought him to Valgaard trussed like a new-killed stag. The marks still dented wrists and ankles.

"Will he live?" she asked.

I shrugged. "If my father desires him to."

Her glance was sharp. "If he *is* Devin, be certain your father will indeed desire it."

I shrugged again. Everyone in Valgaard knew I was meant to wed Devin of High Crags no matter what *I* wanted; men, particularly fathers, are not often disposed to ask women what they prefer.

My father was less disposed to ask anything at all of anyone; Lochiel need never do so. What was not given, he took. *Or* made.

Well, so did I. Given the chance.

I looked at the man in the bed. *Devin? Are you Devin?*

My mother made a noise. She bent, studied his scraped and swollen face, then shook her head slightly. "He is damaged."

"Somewhat," I agreed dryly. "Whoever he is, he survived the Bluetooth. Worth respect, for that . . . would you expect a man who goes in handsome to come out better for it?"

He was, at present, decidedly *un*handsome; the river robs a body of the blood that lends flesh color, the heart that maintains life, and the spirit to drive the heart. He was a slab of flesh made into the form of a man, with two arms, a head, and two legs, though one of the legs was broken. I had seen the end of the bone pressing hard against bruised flesh below the knee, turning it white and shiny, but it had not broken through.

"His ear is torn," she said, "and his lip badly split."

"Aye," I agreed. There was much more than that. The entire left side of his face was mottled black with bruising, and bled colorless fluid from abrasions. "Turn back the covers, lady mother. There is worse yet to see."

She did; I expected it. But she looked first at something that was not, so far as we knew, injured by the river. He was a man, and whole.

I shut my teeth very tightly. There is in my mother a quality of *need,* as if she requires a man to note her beauty, to remark upon it, and to profess his ardent interest. She is indeed beautiful, but no man in Valgaard is foolish enough to give her more than covert glances. She is Lochiel's wife.

It had never been so bad as the past two years. I knew its cause now, though realization was slow, and comprehension more sluggish yet. No daughter desires to see her mother made jealous by her daughter's ascension to adulthood. But she was. It had been a hard truth, but I understood it at last.

Lochiel's wife was jealous of Lochiel's daughter.

You bore me, I said inwardly. *How can you envy the child you yourself bore?*

But her power was negligible. She was Lochiel's wife, while I was his *daughter.* Her value therefore was finished; she had borne him a single girl-child and could bear him no more. Now the value passed to the daughter who would, if married wisely, insure the downfall of the Cheysuli.

It was what she lived for. Despite that she was the bastard daughter of the Cheysuli warrior who sat upon the Lion in the Great Hall of Homana-Mujhar.

"What is this?" She touched his chest. "A knife wound, and deep."

I could not see his body because of the way she held the blankets, but I did not need to look. I knew what was there. The Bluetooth is cruel. "He should have bled to death, but the river sealed it. When he warms, it will bleed anew. We shall have to be ready."

She studied him avidly, marking the shape of his battered nose, the muddying of his jawline by swollen bruises, the mutilated left ear. Even his mouth, as if she measured its shape against the way she might desire it to fit her own.

I drew in a sharp breath. It sickened me to see her behave so.

She looked on him, and smiled. Then she looked at me. Something dark moved in her eyes. "*You* may have him."

It stopped the breath in my chest. That she could *suggest* such a thing was monstrous. She would give me my bridegroom because he was so badly hurt as to make him unattractive, and therefore unworthy of her interest.

Revulsion filled me. I looked at the man in the bed, so battered, bruised, and broken. *I hope you are handsome. And I hope she chokes on it!*

"Now," she said, "I will order the women in. We will do what we can do . . . I must make certain my daughter does not lose the man before the bedding." She said a single word, very quietly— she is, after all, Ihlini—and women came into the chamber.

They stripped him of bedclothes and began to clean his body, swabbing gouges and scrapes, cleaning the knife wound. He made no sound or movement until they touched his leg, and then he roused.

The indrawn hiss was hardly audible in the fuss around his bed, but I heard it. The tendons in his neck stood up, hard and rigid, beneath pale flesh.

My mother put her hand on his brow, pushing away stiffened hair. It was black as my own, and thick, but lacking luster. Sand crusted the pillow.

"Fever," she said crisply. "*Malenna* root, then."

I looked at her sharply. "It will leave him too weak!"

"You see how he fights the pain. I need him weak, and compliant, so the root may do its work."

So you can assert your control. But I did not say it.

With no word spoken, the women melted against the walls, faces downturned. I knew, without looking, my father had come.

" 'Sore hurt,' I was told." He walked through the door. "The leg must be set."

"You could heal it," I blurted, then wished I had said nothing; one does not suggest to my father what he can or cannot do.

My father smiled. "We do not yet know who he is. He could well be Homanan—why waste the Seker's gift on a man who is unworthy?" He gestured. "I will set it by conventional means."

That meant splints and linen. They were brought, and my father motioned for the women to hold him down. He clasped the bruised ankle, then pulled the bone straight.

I watched the man who might be Devin, and therefore meant for me. Eyes rolled beneath pale, vein-threaded lids. His head thrashed until one of the woman caught it between her hands and stopped its movement. The tendons stood up again, warping his neck; the battered mouth opened. It split the lip again so that it bled, running down his chin to drip against his neck. It spilled into the creases and stained the pillow.

Brilliant crimson against the pallor of fragile flesh. Devin's flesh?

I felt a frisson of nervous anticipation. If he *were* Devin, he was to be, with me, a means to destroy the prophecy. I could not help but hope he was indeed Devin so that our plans could continue; we were close, too close, my father said, to losing the battle. Kellin, Prince of Homana, need only sire a son and the thing was done.

But I smiled as I thought of it. Indeed, he need only sire a son

upon a particular woman—but Kellin had proved all too selfish
with respect to his conduct. For years my father had laughed to
hear of the prince's exploits, saying that so long as Kellin behaved
in such a wayward manner he actually *aided* us, but I knew it could
not last. He would have to die, so that we could be certain.

It seemed a simple task. Kill Kellin of Homana—and produce
an Ihlini child blessed by the Seker so we need never concern ourselves with the prophecy ever again.

The blood ran freely from the split lip. My mother made a
sound of disgust. I wanted very badly to take up a clean cloth and
blot away the blood, to press it against his lip so he would not lose
more, but I dared not be so intimate before my father.

"There." My father placed the splints on either side of his leg,
then bound it tightly with linen.

The mouth went slack again. His struggle had done more then
reopen his lip; now blood flowed sluggishly from his swollen
nose.

My mother smiled to see it. "A most unfortunate accident."

My father's gaze was on her, steady and unflinching. I could
not discern his thoughts. "He will recover," he said, "provided
Asar-Suti desires him to." He looked now at me. "I will certainly
request it. We need this man."

I stiffened. "Is it Devin?"

"They have searched his baggage more closely. A pouch contained the ring you sent last year, a cache of ward-stones, and the
eagle claw charm against *lir* intrusion. And—this." He held it up
in the light. It was a gold ring set with a deep blood-red stone,
nearly black; in its heart light stirred as if roused from sleep. My
father smiled. "It knows me."

"A lifestone!" my mother said, then looked more closely at the
man in the bed.

I shut my teeth together. *It makes a difference, does it? You look
again to see if he might present a different face.*

"Devin would have one, of course; he is sworn to the Seker."
My father's pale brown eyes looked at me over the glinting lifestone. "Unless this man is a thief who stole from Devin, then fell
into the water, I think it unlikely he is anyone else."

My mother frowned. "It is set in a ring. Why would he not
wear it?"

His gaze dwelled on her face. "Solinde is not entirely ours, anymore. Even in High Crags, men honor the shapechanger who holds

court in Lestra. An Ihlini sworn to the god cannot move so freely now without taking precautions. He was wise to put it away."

My mother's carmined lips compressed. "That will be changed. *We* shall rule again, as in the days of Tynstar and Bellam."

Lochiel laughed. "Did you know them personally?"

Color flared in her cheeks; she, as I, heard the irony. "I know as much of our history as anyone, Lochiel. Despite my Cheysuli blood!"

"Ali, but my blood is *theirs.*" He smiled. "Tynstar was my grandsire."

It silenced her at once. Even among the Ihlini, who understood his power, Lochiel was different. It was easy to forget how old he was, and how long-lived his ancestors.

I smiled to myself. *Tynstar, Strahan, Lochiel—and now Ginevra. I am their legacy.* It was more than she claimed, and Melusine knew it.

"Shall we see if he is Devin?" My father held the ring in such a way that the light sparked from it. "If he is an opportunist who decides, upon awakening, he would benefit from our care, we can take steps now to present him with the lie."

I looked at the ring. Light moved within it sluggishly. Indeed, it did know my father; the blood of the god ran in his veins, as it did in the veins of all those sworn to Asar-Suti. I as yet claimed none of it outside of my natural inheritance; I was to drink the cup at my wedding, to seal my service forever to the Seker.

"Will it kill him?" my mother asked.

Lochiel smiled at her. "If he is not Devin, assuredly." He held the ring. "My gift to you, Melusine—adjudicate this man."

"Wait!" I blurted, and regretted it at once as my father turned to me.

Carmined lips stretched back to display my mother's white teeth. "No," she said venomously. "He gives you everything—this he gives to *me!*" She snatched the ring, bent over the unconscious man, grasped his left hand and pushed the ring onto his forefinger. "Burn," Melusine said. "If you are not Devin, let the *godfire* devour you!"

"You *want* it to!" I cried. "By the god himself, I think—" But my accusation died as *godfire* flared up from the ring, a clean and livid purple. I fell back a step even as my mother did, who laughed.

"You see?" she said. "Not Devin at all!"

But the burst of flame died. The hand was unblemished. Light glowed brilliantly deep in the lifestone's heart.

"Ah," Lochiel said. "A premature assumption."

"Then—it is he?" I looked at the ring upon the hand. "This is Devin."

"It appears so. A lifestone is linked to an Ihlini as a *lir* is linked to a Cheysuli." For a brief moment he frowned, looking at Devin. "It is but another parallel . . ." But he let it go. "We will have confirmation when he awakens."

I drew in a breath and asked it carefully. "Then why not heal him instead of relying on normal means?"

Lochiel smiled. "Because even Devin must learn that he is solely dependent on me for such paltry things as his life." He extended his hand. My mother took it. "Nurse him well, Ginevra. There is no better way to judge a man than from the depths of pain. It is difficult to lie when your world is afire."

He led my mother from the room. They would go to bed, I knew. It made my face burn; I did not understand what need it was they answered, save there was one, only that they seemed to be, in all ways such private things are measured, particularly well suited.

One of the women blotted away the blood on Devin's face. Another came forward with a cup. *Malenna* root, I knew, mixed in with water. I wanted to protest it, but did not; it was true he needed the fever purged. If it weakened him too much, I would prevail upon my father to make certain he survived.

My father wanted a child. An heir to Valgaard, and the legacy of the Ihlini. If I did not marry Devin, we would have to find someone else whose blood was proper. Why waste the time? The man was right here.

I sat down on a stool and stared at him. *Live,* I told him. *There is much for you to learn.*

And as much for me.

I had seen my parents' marriage. I was not so certain I desired the same for myself.

I sighed. *The Seker grant me the knowledge I need to make my way in this. I want to serve my father—but I want to serve me also!*

Chapter Two

The fever broke before dawn. The *malenna* root did its work, purging his body of impurities so that the sweat ran upon his flesh. The worst was done, I thought; now could come the healing. It would take much time because of the severity of his injuries, but I believed he would survive.

The women my mother had left to tend him slid sidelong glances at me as they cleaned him. They dared say nothing to me, though I knew they felt it improper for me to remain in attendance. But he was my bridegroom; how could they believe I would *not* be interested in whether he lived or died?

I sat upon a stool close to his side. He fascinated me. I wanted to study him covertly so he need never know. A man awake is too aware of his pride and the manner of his appearance; I wanted to know *him* without such impediments.

His breathing sounded heavy in his chest. The wad of bandage pressed over the knife wound came away soiled with blood and fluid, but seemed clean enough. It did not stink of infection. It was a simple wound, if deep; with care he would recover.

He stirred and moaned, twisting his head against the pillow. The oozing of the scrapes on his face had stopped and his skin had begun to dry, puckering the flesh into a crusted film. The hollows beneath his eyes were darkened by bruising. Eyelids flickered. His lashes were as long as mine, and as thick.

Incongruous thought; I banished it. Then summoned it back again as I studied the fit of his swollen nose into the space between his eyes, beneath arched black eyebrows. He was badly bruised, aye, but I thought my mother was blind. She could not see beyond the wreckage wrought by the river to the good bones beneath.

I think when you are healed, you might surprise us all. I drew in a breath. "Devin?"

Lids flickered again, then opened. His eyes were a clear brilliant green, but glazed with weakness. *Malenna* root, I knew; it would rob him of his wits for longer than I preferred. I wanted them back.

I scraped my stool closer, so he could see me. His lips were badly swollen and crusted with dried blood. He moved them, winced, then took more care as he shaped the words. They—*it*—was malformed, but clear enough. "Who—?"

I smiled. "Ginevra."

I waited. I expected him to respond at once that he was Devin, or to make some indication he knew who I was. Instead, he touched his mangled bottom lip with an exploratory tongue tip, felt its state, and withdrew the tongue. Lids closed a moment, then lifted again.

"Your name?" I persisted, desiring verbal confirmation in addition to the lifestone.

A faint frown puckered his forehead. With the hair swept back I could see it was unmarred; the river had spared him her savagery there, at least. "My leg . . ." A hand moved atop the furred coverlet, as if it would pull the blanket aside.

"No." I stopped the hand with my own. "Your leg is broken, but it has been set." The hand stilled. I removed mine. "Do you recall what happened?"

The forehead puckered again. "What place is this?"

"Valgaard."

There was no change of expression in his eyes. What I saw there was a puzzled blankness.

It had to be the *malenna*. "Valgaard," I repeated.

He moved his mouth carefully. His words were imprecise. "What is—Valgaard?"

It astounded me. I turned sharply to one of the women. "How much *malenna* was he given?"

She paled. "No more than usual, Lady."

"Too much," I declared. "No more—do you hear?"

"Aye, Lady." She stared hard at the floor.

He moved slightly, and I looked back at once. "Why am I here?" he asked.

"This is where you are supposed to be. But you were hurt. There was a fight—you fell into the river." Or was pushed; how better to hide a body?

"The river?"

Indeed, too much root. "The Bluetooth." I studied him more

closely, marking the dullness of his eyes. More black than green in reflection of the root. "Do you truly recall none of it? Not even the man who stabbed you?"

"I remember—being *cold*—" He paused. "—heavy." The eyes closed, then opened. Their clarity was improved, but not their knowledge. "No more . . ." He stirred. "—head hurts."

"The Bluetooth," I repeated, beginning to understand. If he had struck his head, which was entirely likely in the river, he would likely he confused for a day or two. Combined with the root, it was fortunate he was conscious at all. "It will come back on its own," I promised. "You will know where you are, and that you are safe . . ." I paused. "Devin."

"Is that—I am Devin?"

I grinned. "Tell me when *you* are certain."

He looked at me more closely. "Who are you?"

Your bride, I answered, but could not say it aloud. "Ginevra."

He repeated it after me, rolling the soft, sibilant first syllable between his teeth an extra moment. His accent was odd, more Homanan than Solindish, but Devin is a High Crags man, from high up on the border between the two lands. I had heard the speech before. "How long—?"

"You were brought yesterday. My father sent out a search party since you were so late." I smiled wryly. "You are valuable. It was of some concern."

"Why?" The struggle was in his eyes. "I remember none of it—"

"Hush." I leaned forward. "Do not tax yourself . . . it will come."

"I should remember." Dampness glistened on his forehead. He made more sense as consciousness solidified. "Who am I, that my tardiness is worth a search party?"

"Devin of High Crags." I hope it might light the snuffed candle of his mind.

He tried. "No . . ."

No help for it. It was best simply to say it. "We are meant to be wed."

The candle within lighted, blazing in his eyes, but the knowledge was not increased. "Wed! When?" His mouth taxed him badly. "I remember *nothing*—"

I sighed. "Know this, then, so you need not remain in ignorance. I am Ginevra of the Ihlini, daughter of Lochiel—and we are meant to wed so we can bring down the Cheysuli." I stopped short, seeing the expression in his eyes. "The Cheysuli," I repeated. "Do you recall nothing of them?"

"—a *word*—"

"A bad word." I sighed. "Let it go, Devin. It will come back, and all will be remembered."

"Who am I?"

"Devin of High Crags." I smiled. "Like me, you are Ihlini." It was a bond stronger than any, and he would know it once his mind was restored.

He sighed. "Ihlini, Cheysuli . . . nothing but words to me. I could be either and never know it."

I laughed. "You would know," I told him. "Be certain you would know, when you went before the god."

His eyes snapped open. "The god?"

"Asar-Suti." He knew all of it, but I would tell him regardless. "My father will take you before the Seker. The god requires your oath. You are to wed Lochiel's daughter, and Lochiel is the Seker's most beloved servant. It is necessary." I smiled. "There is no need for you to worry. You are Ihlini. The Seker will know it, just as your lifestone does."

He followed the line of my gaze and saw the ring upon his hand. He lifted the hand into the air to study the stone, saw how his fingers trembled and lowered it again. "I—have no memory of this ring."

That was of concern. He was indeed badly damaged in his mind if he forgot what a lifestone was. But I dared not tell him that. "It will come to you."

His eyes were slitted. "You—will have to teach me. I have forgotten it all."

"But surely not *this*." I drew a rune in the air. It was only a small one; it lacked the intricacy of my mother's handiwork, but was impressive enough if you have never seen it—or if one has forgotten what *godfire* looks like. It glowed livid purple.

He stared at it, transfixed. His fingers trembled upon the fur. "Can I—do that?"

"Once, you must have. It is the first one we ever learn." I left the rune glowing so he would have a model. "Try it."

He lifted his hand and I saw how badly it shook. Awkwardly he attempted to sketch the rune, but his fingers refused to follow the pattern. It was if they had never learned it.

The hand dropped to the bed. He was exhausted. "If I knew it once, I have forgotten."

I dismissed my own rune. It was somewhat discomfiting to discover an Ihlini who could not even form the simplest rune, but not surprising. He would recall it. For the moment his mind was empty of power, of the knowledge of his magic, like a young child. "It will come again." I paused. "If it does not, be certain I will teach you."

The lips moved faintly, as if to form a smile. But his eyelids dropped closed. The root was reasserting its control.

I rose quietly. He looked very young and vulnerable. Against his hand the lifestone was black.

Black, not red.

"It will come back," I said.

At the door, as I lifted the latch, I heard a sound. I turned back and saw the faint glint of green eyes. "Ginevra," he said, as if to try out the fit of my name within his mouth.

I smiled. "Aye."

The lids closed again. "Beautiful," he whispered.

Nonplussed, I did not answer. I did not know if he meant my name, or the woman who bore it.

Then I thought of my mother. I could not help but smile. *You gave him to me,* I thought. *Now let you see what comes of it.*

I went at once to my father. With him was my mother, who sat upon a window seat in my father's tower chamber and gazed down upon the smoky bestiary before the gates. I thought she was very like the fortress, strong, proud, and fierce. I wished I could like her, but that had died. I knew her heart now, and the knowledge bruised my own.

"He remembers nothing," I told them. "Not even his name."

My father stood before a burning tripod brazier. It turned his eyes bronze. He waited.

"I told him. I told him mine as well, and that we are to wed. I told him where he is. But he recalls none of it . . . not even that he is Ihlini."

That brought my mother's head around. Bells tinkled in her hair. "He forgets *that?*"

I refused to flinch beneath the contempt. "He has been badly injured. It will come back."

"Did you test him?" my father asked.

I flattened my palms against my skirts and held my hands very still. "What magic he knew is forgotten. Even *bel'sha'a*. He is a child, my lord father—an infant empty of power." I took a careful breath, knowing what I said was incredibly important. "If you sought a tool, you could not find a better one. He has nothing on which to rely save what we give him. There are no preconceptions. How better to teach the man how to serve the master than by replacing the old memories with the new?"

Only the faintest glint in his eyes betrayed his interest. I knew I had caught him. Now there was no need for subtlety.

My father smiled. I saw him glance at my mother, who watched him with narrowed eyes. Hers, too, are pale brown, though not like his; hers are almost golden except when the light hits them fully, and then the Cheysuli shows.

"He shall be mine," Lochiel said.

I put up my chin. It was time I declared myself lest she do it first. "But you will share him with me."

My father laughed. "I shall do better than that. He shall be your charge until I believe the time is right . . . you may have the training of him. In all things."

I could not help the burst of pride in my chest. Never had he bestowed upon me such a gift. It was a mark of his acknowledgment of my blood. He was giving me the opportunity to serve my heritage.

Still, I hesitated. "Are you sure I am worthy?"

He laughed. "You need not fear that you might tarnish the vessel. I will be here for you . . . I will see what you do. He is meant for the god, Ginevra, as you are. Do you think I would give him immortality only to have you watch him sicken and die the way others do?"

"Lochiel!" my mother cried. "You promise too much."

"Do I?" His tone was cool. "Do you wish it for you in place of your daughter?"

Color stained her face. "You have never suggested it. Even when I asked—"

He made a subtle gesture with his hand. I had seen it before; I had tried to mimic it desperately because it always silenced my mother. "Melusine," he said, "you live here on my sufferance."

Her red lips trembled, then firmed. "I am your wife."

"That does not make you worthy of the Seker's favor."

Her eyes blazed almost yellow. "You promise it to *her!*"

He stood next to me. His hand was on my shoulder. The fingers crept into my hair, which hung loose to my hips, and I felt the warmth of his flesh through the velvet of my gown. "Ginevra is the flesh of my flesh, the blood of my blood, the bone of my bone," he said quietly. "Her mind is mine as well. You are, none of these things . . . I used you to get the child, and now I have her."

"Lochiel!"

His other hand rose. I could see it from the corner of my eye. I looked at my mother because I could look nowhere else. "Melusine," he said, "I have cared for you. You bore me a child. You suckled Kellin of Homana when I bid you do it. You have served me well. But you surely must see that you and your daughter are destined for different ends."

"I bore her!" It was her only chance now.

"In blood and pain; I know it. But so do the mares, and the cows, and the ewes . . . and they are not elevated by the honor of the Seker." He paused. "Surely you must see."

Her face was very pale. "You mean me to die, then."

"Not before due time."

"Before *her* time!"

Lochiel sighed. "You are a shrew."

It was incongruous. He was the most powerful sorcerer in the entire world, yet all he did was call my mother a name.

It infuriated her; I saw then what he did. "A shrew! In the name of Asar-Suti, are you mad? A shrew?"

My father laughed. There was something between them I could not understand. "Melusine, do you believe you have displeased me? You are all I could wish for. You suit me."

Her eyes glinted yellow. "Then why do you threaten me?"

"To relieve my boredom." He smoothed my hair, then released it. "She is lovely, our Ginevra . . . and this binding of the blood-lines will insure our survival. But Devin must go before the god. The blessing is required."

My mother was less angry now, but still unsettled. She hated to be used; before, I had not seen it. I was old enough now to begin to understand. "And if the blessing is denied?" She cast me a glance. "What happens to Devin then?"

"He dies," Lochiel said.

My mother looked at me and laughed.

I could not echo her. I knew she hoped he would.

Chapter Three

"A fool," I told him.

He ignored me. He sat up anyway and swung his legs over the edge of the bed. I watched not the splinted leg itself, which was at issue, but the face of the man who struggled to redeem himself in the eyes of the woman he was meant to wed.

It meant something to him. It meant a great deal to him. It pleased me to know why; that of all things in the world to come unexpectedly, we would make a match between a man and a woman who loved one another.

His color was much improved. A lock of black hair, now clean and glossy, fell forward over his forehead. The swelling of his face was gone, so that the clean lines of nose and brow formed a perfect melding, complementing the oblique angles of his cheekbones and the clarity of his eyes framed in sooty lashes that rivaled my own.

"A fool," I murmured, applying it to myself though he believed it meant for him. Never had I thought I could love a man the way I loved Devin, and we not even wed yet. We were, as yet, nothing but *intendeds;* but they all knew, everyone, despite our circumspection. It was easier for them to know than for us to admit it. As yet, we said nothing of it.

The ends of the splint tapped down; Devin winced. It would not stop him, I knew; I had learned that much of him in the past few weeks. A stubborn, intransigent man.

And entirely beautiful, in the way a man can be who is clearly a man. *Male,* I thought. *Expressly, completely male, like the cats in the undercroft.*

I wanted to laugh. My mother had lost. It pleased me intensely that he was as I expected, as I had dreamed between sleep and wakefulness, when my body would not be quiet. I understood, now, what lay between my parents.

"Devin—" I shook my head. "It is not necessary. I *know* you are not a weakling . . . let it heal."

His mouth was compressed in a grim, flat line. He intended to try again. I sighed and set my teeth; he would only damage himself.

I made a slight gesture from my chair, so that the bindings undid themselves and the splints fell away. Unbound, the leg was ill-suited to standing.

Devin looked at the fallen linen and the wooden sticks. "*You* did that."

I arched my brows. "I did warn you."

"No—you called me a fool."

"That was my warning."

He scowled. Beneath black brows, his eyes glittered like glass. "I cannot stand without aid."

"No."

He sighed. "The lesson is duly learned. Will you bind it up again?"

He would not admit it, but the leg hurt. Forgoing magic, because I longed so much to touch him, I knelt on the ground and bound it up by hand again. The flesh was flaccid and soft. The bones inside knit, but the muscles were wasting.

He watched me as I tied the knots. His voice was hoarse, as if he held back something he longed to say. "If we Ihlini are truly as powerful as you say, why leave healing to splints and linen bindings? Why not ensorcell my leg?"

I sat down in my chair again. We spent much time together in the small chamber, as I taught him what he knew already but did not recall. "My father desired you to know limitations."

"Ah." His mouth hooked down.

"And there is another reason. Healing is a Cheysuli gift."

"It would seem a benevolent gift. Perhaps if I had a Cheysuli here . . ." He grinned. "I see a storm in your eyes."

"You should. Besides, a Cheysuli here in Valgaard would have no power. It is because of the Gate—the Seker is too strong. The only magic here is that which he makes himself."

Devin's expression was serious. "And when will I see him?"

"When my father wishes you to." I sketched *ori'neth.* "Try it, Devin."

"I *have* tried."

"Again."

He put his hand into the air. His other was naked of lifestone; he had taken it off because, in losing weight, the ring would not seat itself properly. "Your father has not come to me again. How is he to know when I am ready?"

"Make the rune. He will know."

"Because you will tell him?"

"No one tells Lochiel anything; no one *has* to. My father knows things." I sighed. "Devin—"

He tried. Fingers warped, twisted, mimicking the patterns. Only the barest outline appeared, and then he let his hand drop. "There. You see?"

"You mastered *bel'sha'a*," I reminded him. "*Ori'neth* comes next."

Devin was glum. "I have no aptitude."

I laughed at him outright. "Aptitude! You are Ihlini." I smiled at his disgruntlement. "It was better. This time I could see the air parting. When you can separate the air and put the *godfire* in the seam between air and air, you will have learned the trick." I paused. "You learned *bel'sha'a*."

"In six weeks," he said. "I will be an old man before I learn the third level, and useless as a husband." He scowled at me. "What use are such tricks, Ginevra? They could not stop a man."

"*These* could not, it is true . . . but these are the first runes, Devin. This is a baby's game, to keep the child occupied." I laughed as the scowl deepened. "But you *are* a baby! I could make *bel'sha'a* when I was three years old. A six-month later I mastered *ori'neth*. I have no doubt it was the same for you—you have only forgotten. The river stole your wits."

"I may never get them back."

He was depressed. I pulled my chair closer, hesitated a moment, then leaned forward and caught his hand. It was an intimacy I would not have dared two weeks before, but something I needed now. I wanted to lessen the pain of his weakness.

And increase your own?

I went on regardless, ignoring my conscience. "An Ihlini does not gain his powers until he reaches adolescence, and even then it takes years to focus all the skills. I am not so well-versed myself." I was, but no need to tell him that; I was Lochiel's daughter, and the blood showed itself. "I am a child leading an infant, but who better to recall the days when a simple trick proved difficult? See this?" I made a gesture and felt the tingling coldness in my fingertips. The *godfire* came as I bid it, luridly purple. It hung in a glowing sheet between Devin and me, but our hands remained linked. "This is—"

He jerked his hand from mine and lifted it as if to shred the *godfire*. I tore it aside before he burned himself; he did not yet know how to ward himself. A sheen of perspiration coated his face. "Ginevra—"

"What is it?" I left my chair and knelt by the bedside. "Devin—what is it?"

"That—*that*—" His eyes were frightened. "I remember. Dimly. Fire—flame . . ." He closed his eyes. His body went slack against the pillows. "Why can I remember no more?"

"It will come," I told him, as I had so many times.

He shifted against the bedclothes. "How can you be certain? How can you *know?* And if I am not able to master such things . . ." The chiseled lips compressed themselves flat, robbing them of shape. "An Ihlini with no arts is hardly fit to be wed to Lochiel's daughter."

I took his hand into my own and pressed it against my mouth. "He will be fit," I said. "I will see to it."

Devin's eyes were black. His breathing was shallow and quick. "Can you do such a thing?"

Against his flesh, I said, "I can do many things."

The hand turned in my own. He caught my fingers, carried my hand to his mouth, and let me feel the hardness of his teeth in the tenderness of his lips. "Show me," he breathed.

I shuddered once. "Not—yet."

"When?"

It was a difficult truth, but he was due it rather than lies. "When my father is convinced you are fit to serve the god."

Devin's breath was warm against my hand as he laughed softly. "Fathers need not always rule their daughters in such matters as this."

"Mine does." I pulled free of his grasp. "If you forget that, even once, it could be your death."

"Ginevra—"

"He is *Lochiel*," I said; I knew it was enough.

The tension in his body fled. His mouth moved faintly into an ironic smile. And then it, too, died, and I saw in its place a harrowing despair. "I have nothing," he said. "I *am* nothing—save what you make me."

It shook me. "You are Devin."

"I am no one," he said, "save what you tell me. I am defined by you." His eyes burned livid as *godfire,* save they were green in place of purple. "You are my sanity."

I petitioned the Seker to lend him the strength to find his own sanity, lest mine prove too weak. And then I left the room. I wanted too badly to give him what he asked.

When the splint at last came off and Devin was able to stand, I learned he was taller than I had expected. He had lost flesh in his illness, but movement and better meals would restore him.

Within the week the crutch was tossed away and he walked freely on his own. With renewed mobility came vigor and curiosity to see where I lived. He walked easily enough, but I saw the trace of tension in his mouth and around his eyes. I wanted him to see all of Valgaard so he would know it as I did; it was to be his home. It was important that he understand the kind of power contained in the fortress, so he would not forget himself—once he had relearned the arts—and wield it improperly.

He progressed at last from *ori'neth* to *li'ri'a.* The rune pattern was roughly worked, but achieved, glowing fitfully in the air. He was most pleased that it smoked and sputtered, shedding bits of *godfire;* I reminded him that control was more important than appearance.

"You require new clothing," I told him as we walked the cobbled courtyard.

"I have clothing. And you have already said appearance is unimportant."

"Not unimportant; *less* important—and that is in wielding magic, not wearing clothing." I cast a sidelong glance. "I want you to have better. These do not fit well enough."

"And if I gain back the weight you say I have lost, the new clothing will not." He touched my cheek. "Let it be, Ginevra. I am content with what I have."

"Then at least wear the ring." I took it from the pouch hanging from my girdle. "Here. I sent it to you last year. The least you can do is wear it in my presence."

He took the emerald from me, studying it. I saw the flattening of his mouth. "Even this I do not recall. Any more than the other ring."

"No matter. Put it on."

He did so. The gold band turned on his finger. I saw the look in his eye.

"Bind it with wool," I said. "When you are well, it will fit."

He was frustrated and angry. "Will I ever be well?"

"Dev—"

He stopped dead in his tracks, capturing my shoulders in hands well recovered from his illness. "*Will* my memory return? Or am I sentenced to spend the rest of my life but half a man, able only to form the rune a child of two could make?"

It hurt me to see him so affected. If I could provide help—

I could. It was up to me to risk it.

I sighed. "I think it is time . . . come with me."

"Where?"

"To my father."

The black in his eyes expanded. "You would shame me before Lochiel?"

"There is no shame in this. My father understands."

He shut up the ring in his hand as it turned on his finger. "Can Lochiel restore me? Or is that healing also, and therefore anathema?"

"Come, " I said firmly, putting my hand on his arm. "Ask him instead of me."

The room was empty as we entered. It was a small private chamber tucked up into one of the towers, draped with rune-worked cloth to soften the walls, filled with a jumble of chairs and tables, and candleracks sculpted to new forms by hardened streamers of creamy wax. My father preferred the chamber when he desired to have private discussions; he saw no need for opulence among his family.

Devin was nonetheless impressed. It takes people that way, to witness power incarnate. It lived in the room. It was woven into the very cloth that warded the stone walls.

None of the candles was lighted in my father's absence. I blew a gentle breath that set them all ablaze, laughed at Devin's expression, then threw myself down in a chair and hooked a leg over the arm. An undecorous position, perhaps, but modesty was protected by voluminous skirts; I had, of late, put off hunting trews to wear silks and velvets. Even my hair was tamed; I contained it with a simple silver circlet, so that it did not spring forth from my scalp quite so exuberantly. I knew Devin liked it loose; he watched me most avidly from his sickbed when I combed it out after a wash-ing. It took two days to dry; if I wanted it uncrimped, I had to leave it loose.

Devin heaved a sigh and examined the room. His spine was very rigid. *Nervous—and for what? He will be Lochiel's son.* "Be at ease," I suggested.

"*You* be at ease." Then he grinned at me. "I daresay you would feel as I do were you to face the Cheysuli Mujhar."

"Never." I smiled serenely. "But that is not the case—and you are Ihlini, not Cheysuli. What have you to fear?" I slanted an arch glance at him. "Besides, you say you have no memories. How are you to be nervous when you know nothing of the man?"

Devin jeered, though not unkindly. "You have a ready tongue. You put it to his name often enough . . . 'Lochiel' this—'Lochiel' that. What else am I to feel but unworthy of him?"

"Oh, you *are* unworthy—" I grinned, "—but he will lift that from you. When you face Asar-Suti, Lochiel will no longer seem half so bad as now."

"Ah. I am comforted." He folded his arms. "Are we to wait all day on the chance he might come? Or will you send someone for him?" He paused. "Is he even *in* the fortress?"

"He is here." I tilted my head. "Very much *here*."

And he was, all of a sudden, arriving as he does to impress whoever waits. I wanted to chide him for excess display, but one does not chide Lochiel.

Violet smoke roiled in the center of the chamber. Devin stepped back hastily, mouthing an oath he had learned from me, and stared transfixed as the smoke transformed itself into the shape of a man.

"Close your mouth," I hissed.

Devin acquiesced. My father smiled. "That," he said quietly, "is something *you* should be able to do."

The sun had returned color to Devin's flesh. Now he burned darker. "Perhaps I could, once."

Lochiel, in his youth, did not appear much older than Devin. "Has nothing come back?"

"No memories." He glanced at me. "Ginevra has told me what she could of myself, but the words mean nothing. I must believe whatever she tells me; it is the only truth I know."

My father's gaze was unrelenting. "What are you able to do?"

Devin laughed, though it lacked humor. He put out his hand. He drew *li'ri'a.* It was a child's trick, but he could do no better. I did not wonder at the bitterness of his laughter. "That," he said, and banished it.

My father's voice was gentle. "Do you find it amusing?"

"In no way. I find it pitiful, and myself."

"Ah." Lochiel smiled. "But I know who you are. I know what potential you hold. I would not have chosen you otherwise to sire sons upon my daughter." Briefly he looked at me, and I saw a light in his eyes. "That you have forgotten your power means nothing to me. It will be restored. But first you must acknowledge it, instead of relying on the belief that you have forgotten all."

"But I *have*—"

My father reached out and caught Devin's right wrist. By the look in Devin's eyes I knew the grasp was firm. "Call for it now," Lochiel commanded. "Summon it to you. Let the power fill you completely, and you will see what you must know."

Devin was tense. "I *have* tried—"

"Try again." Lochiel's tone was hard. "Do you forget I am with you?"

I saw the alteration in Devin's eyes. He did indeed reach for it, but clumsily. I held my breath, knowing what my father intended to do.

Devin cried out. Wonder filled his face so that his eyes glowed with it, and then the light was extinguished. He cried out again, this time as if in pain, and fell to his knees even as my father released his wrist. His breathing was loud. "You would have—have me be—*that*—?"

Lochiel looked down upon him. "*That* is what you are. It is what I desire of you: power augmented by service to the god, and a perfect obedience. Not powerlessness, Devin. Never that; more." My father put a hand upon Devin's head. "Together, with that power, we can tear down the House of Homana and destroy the prophecy. Do you think I want a fool? Do you think I desire a child? I need a *man,* Devin, who can augment my own strength. A man to lie with my daughter and sire children for the Seker."

Devin still knelt. His face was drained by the knowledge of what he had felt, of the power in my father. "How can I serve with such blankness within me?"

Lochiel smiled. "You are empty. It will pass. We will see to it you are filled. The god himself will do it." He looked at me and smiled, then stretched out his hand. "Take my daughter. Get a son upon her. The wedding shall follow when I am certain she has conceived." He put our hands together, flesh against flesh.

I could look at no one save Devin. My father's voice became a part of the chamber, like a chair or a hanging; one did not acknowledge such things when Devin was in the room.

His eyes burned brilliant green. His spirit could not contain the avidity of his desire.

No more than I could mine.

"There is no need to wait," Lochiel said. "Much is lost, in waiting. The Wheel of Life is turning; if we do not stop it soon, our own lives will end."

Chapter Four

We had blown out the candles and now lay abed, delighting in discovery. Devin's breath warmed my neck. "What did he mean?" His mouth shaped the words against my flesh. "Why do our lives end if the Wheel of Life keeps turning?"

"A Cheysuli thing . . ." I turned my head to kiss his chin; to savor the taste of his flesh. "Must we speak of this now?"

His laughter was soft, as were his fingertips as they cherished my flesh. "Aye. You said you would teach me everything—well, perhaps not *this*."

Indeed not this. It made me blush, to know myself so wanton. "I am not the one to speak—" I caught my breath short and bit into my lip as his hand grew more insistent, "—but—it seems to me— *gods, Devin!*—that with all the wits you have lost, you did not forget *this*." I used his emphasis.

Devin laughed again: a rumble deep in his chest. His hand moved to my breasts, tracing their contours. His flesh was darker than mine—I am Ihlini fair, and his eyes were green in place of my ice-gray—but our bones were similar. We Ihlini breed true.

His voice was vibrant. "A man forgets little in the way a body works in congress with a woman."

"So it would seem." Our hips were sealed together. I turned toward him again, glorying in the feel of his flesh against my own. "The Wheel of Life is a Cheysuli thing. They speak in images, often: the Wheel, the Loom, and so on. They are, if nothing else, a colorful race." I traced the flesh of his chest, glad I could no longer count his ribs. The muscle was firm again. I avoided the scar left over from the healed knife wound. "This prophecy of theirs bids to end our people by making a new race. The Firstborn. If we keep them from that, if we destroy the prophecy, their Wheel will stop turning, and the world as we know it will continue as it is."

"As it is?"

"Well—as it should be. It will take time to turn them away from their gods. They are ignorant people, all of them."

"The Cheysuli?"

It was difficult to concentrate as I explored his body. "And others. The Homanans. The Ellasians. The island savages." I touched his lips with my fingers. "Even the Solindish must suffer—it is a Cheysuli warrior who holds the throne in Lestra."

"Heresy," he whispered; his tone was amused.

"So it is."

"And if we make a child, we can stop this Wheel?"

"My father is convinced."

He turned then and put his hand on my belly, spreading his fingers. The warmth of his palm was welcome. "Have we made it, then?"

I laughed. "Would it please you so much to be quit of your duty after a single night?"

"Duty? Duty is something you do with no real desire for it." The hand tightened as he bent down to taste my mouth. "*This* is no duty."

Breathlessly, I asked, "And if I have not conceived?"

"Then we will continue with this 'duty.' " His tongue traced my eyelids. "Do you think I wish to *stop?*"

It was abrupt, the chill in my soul. I could not answer.

He sensed my mood immediately and ceased the slow seduction. "What is it?"

I was reluctant to say it but felt I owed him truth. "There is a—strangeness—in you."

The words were too facile. "When a man knows nothing of his past, strangeness is natural."

"Aye. But—" I broke it off, sighing; this was not a topic I wished to pursue. Now.

He did. "But?"

"I wish—I wish you were whole. I wish you knew yourself. I wish you were all of a piece, so I need not wonder what bits and pieces may yet be missing."

Devin laughed. "I am whole where it counts."

"I am serious."

In that moment, so was he. Seduction and irony fled. He turned onto his back. Our hair mingled, black on black against the pallor of pillows. Strands of mine were wound around his forearm. "Aye, I wish I recalled my past—every day, I wish it, and in the darkness of the nights . . . but it is gone. There is *nothing,* save a yawning emptiness."

It hurt to hear him so vulnerable. "I want it to be vanquished."

There was no light, save from the stars beyond the casement. I could see little of his face and nothing of his expression. "I cannot spend my life wondering what I might be if it never is recalled . . . the present is what matters. What I am is what you are making me. Ginevra—" But then he laughed softly, banishing solemnity, as if he could not bear to think about his plight. He twisted his head to look at me. "What woman would not desire such a man? You can meld me this way and that, until you have what you want."

My vehemence stunned us both. *"I have what I want."*

He caught his breath a moment; released it slowly. He turned onto a hip, moving to face me, to wind his fingers in my hair. He pulled my face to his even as he leaned to me. "Then we shall have to give your father the grandson *he* desires for the Seker, and then we shall make our own."

He was right. What counted was the *now,* not the yesterday. If the child were not conceived soon, the Wheel might turn far enough so that we were destroyed in place of the Cheysuli.

But I could not tell him what I most feared. That the emptiness in him, the bleakness in his eyes that he would not acknowledge, might rob us of our future.

My father gave us five days and nights together, and then he summoned Devin. It piqued me that he would give us so little time—did he think we could conjure a child with a rune?—but I did not complain. Devin was nervous enough without my poor temper, and I dared make no response to my father.

I told Devin to go, that it was necessary he spend much time with my father, to better prepare him for the role he would assume once he had received the god's blessing. I saw the look in his eye, the tension in his body, and wished I knew a way to banish the concern.

But it, too, was necessary; a man facing Lochiel must understand what he did, lest he forget his proper place in the ordering of the world.

And so I sent him off with a kiss upon his fingers and one upon his mouth, knowing very well my father would test him in ways no one, not even Lochiel's daughter, could predict. If he were to assume an aspect of power within the hierarchy of the Ihlini, he had to learn the way.

It was late afternoon when I sent Devin to my father; only the Seker and Lochiel knew when I might see him again. I set myself the task of embroidering a runic design into the tunic I made for him—green on black—and tried not to think bleak, empty thoughts about what might happen if my father decided, all on his own, that Devin's missing memory might render him weak in the ways of Ihlini power.

My mother came into our chambers. She wore deep, rich red. Matching color painted her lips. "So."

I gritted my teeth and did not look up, concentrating fiercely on the design beneath my hands. She would say what she had come to say; I would not permit provocation.

The sound of her skirts was loud as she came closer. "So, in all ways my daughter is a woman."

Do not be provoked— I nodded absently, taking immense care with a particularly elaborate rune.

She waited. She expected a response. When I made none, the air between us crackled. So close to the Gate, such anger is personified.

I completed one rune, then began another.

My mother's hand swooped down and snatched the tunic from me. "And did the earth move for you? Did the stars fall from the sky?"

Sparks snapped from my fingers. With effort, I snuffed them out. A single drop of blood welled on a fingertip, where the needle had wounded me as she snatched the tunic away. I looked up and saw her smile; it satisfied her to know she had won the battle of wills.

Or had she?

I shook back my hair and rose from my stool, folding hands primly in violet skirts. "Indeed," I said, "it did move. And will again, I trust, when he returns to me." I smiled inoffensively. "It should please you to know your daughter is well serviced. I have no complaints of his manhood, or the frequency of our coupling."

Breath hissed as she inhaled. The color in her cheeks vied for preeminence over the paint on her mouth. "I will have no such language from you!"

I laughed at her. "You began it!"

"Ginevra—"

"By the Seker himself," I said, "can you not let me have this? You would take everything else from me, even my father's attention . . . what wrong have I done you? I am neither enemy nor rival—I am your *daughter!*"

Her face was white. "He gives you everything. *I* have to beg his attention."

"Surely not. I know otherwise. I *see* otherwise." I kept my hands in skirt folds, so as not to divulge the tension in them. "You are only angry that you misjudged Devin. You looked upon his injuries and dismissed him at once, pleased your daughter would wed an unhandsome man. And now that he is healed and you see he is beautiful, you are angry with yourself. Now that we have bedded and you see I am content, you desire very much to destroy what we have." I lifted my head. "I will not permit it."

Melusine laughed. "He will break," she said. "When he meets the god, or before . . . perhaps now, with Lochiel. His head is empty of knowledge, his spirit empty of power. He is no better than a Cheysuli hauled here before the Gate, *lir*-less and powerless. Pleasing in bed or no, he is wholly expendable."

I gritted my teeth. "The lifestone knew him. If he had no power, it would have consumed him."

Crimson lips mocked a true smile. "There is another test."

"My father tends to such things."

"*You* should tend to this one; you share a bed with a stranger. What if Lochiel were to discover he is not Devin at all?"

It was a refrain. "The lifestone knew him."

"Test him," she said. "Break it."

"It would kill him!"

"A chip," she said scornfully. "The tiniest chip would divulge the truth."

The air crackled between us. This time it was my doing. "I pity you," I told her. "That you must stoop to this merely because he is a man who prefers the daughter to the mother."

"*What?*"

"I know your ways better than you think. I have seen you at meals, and other times. Do you think I am blind? You court his favor assiduously . . . but he gives it all to me."

Red lips writhed. "I challenge you," she said. "Break a chip from the stone. Otherwise you will always wonder if you sleep with Devin of High Crags, or a man of another heritage."

Sparks flew as I pointed at the door. "Go!"

Melusine smiled. She built an elaborate rune in the air between us; before I could build my own to ward away the spell, she breathed upon the rune. It was blown to the bed, where it sank into the coverlet and disappeared. "There," she said. "Let us see what pleasure it brings you when next he *services* you."

"There are other beds," I told her. "And if you ensorcell those, there is always the floor."

Melusine threw down the tunic. In her hands, all the stitching had come undone. My labor was for naught.

I waited until she was gone. Then I went to the chest and drew out the pouch in which he had put his lifestone. I loosened the thong-snugged mouth and poured the ring into my hand.

In my palm the stone was black. No life moved within it. But I had seen it burn twice; first, at my father's touch; then on Devin's hand.

A lifestone crushed ended an Ihlini's life. To kill a Cheysuli, you kill his *lir;* to kill us, you destroy the lifestone.

If he were not what he seemed and I struck a chip from the stone, nothing at all would happen and we would know the truth. But if he were Devin and I broke a piece of the stone, it would injure him.

I shut up the ring in my hand. Gold bit into my flesh. The stone was cool, lifeless. *There must be trust between us. If I doubt, I undermine the foundations we have built.*

At my mother's behest.

I bent and picked up the ruined tunic. With great care I picked out the tattered embroidery, gathered silk thread, then began with deliberation to wind it around the ring. I would have him wear the stone where my mother could see it.

When that was done, I would begin the painstaking spell to undo the binding she had put upon the bed. Kept close in my arms, where the emptiness did not matter, it was his only haven.

Five days later, after a night-long meeting with my father, Devin came to me high of heart just as dawn broke. He woke me with a kiss. The bleakness was replaced with good humor and an unbounded enthusiasm. He showed no effects from staying up all night. "He says the power is building. He can feel it, he says."

I sat upright. "Are you sure?"

He laughed joyously. "*I* cannot—I feel precisely the same today as I did when I awoke here—but he assures me it is true. And so I begin to think I may be of some use after all."

"*Some* use," I agreed. "But no one suggests how much." I laughed at his feigned heart-blow. "And what are you planning? I see the look in your eye."

His hand rose in the gesture I knew so well. Two rings glinted upon it: my emerald, and the lifestone. There was no hesitation in his manner. His fingers were steady, assured, and the rune was more elaborate than any I had seen from him before.

"*Kir'a'el!*" I cried. "Devin—"

It shimmered in the air. Then it snuffed out the candles and became the only illumination in the room, dominating the dawn. It set his eyes aflame.

"Only a trick," he said negligently, but he could not hide his satisfaction.

"Three months ago you could not bestir the air to save your soul." I raised my own hand and built a matching rune. It was the distaff side of *kir'a'el*. Mine met his; they melted together like wax, then twined themselves into one. The conjoined rune glowed with the purest form of *godfire*. I stared hard at Devin, filled with blazing pride. *This* was what we were born for. "Together we can make anything!"

"A child?"

"Not yet." We touched our hands together, let the new rune bathe our flesh, then bespoke the word that banished it. "We shall have to try again."

His eyes were still alight with the acknowledgment of power. "Come out with me now. I have horses waiting."

"*You* are sure of yourself."

"Then I will go by myself."

"Hah." I arched brows haughtily. "You could not even get beyond the Field of Beasts, let alone find the defile."

"I found it before."

"Tied to the back of a horse like so much dead meat? *Aye,* you found it." I caught his hand and kissed it. "Let us go, then. I could not bear to have you lost."

But even as I dressed, having banished him from the chamber—otherwise I would never progress beyond the disrobing stage—I was aware of a tiny flicker of trepidation. For so long he had been helpless, bereft of Ihlini power, yet now he promised power in full measure. I did not begrudge it—we are what we are—but I was concerned.

Would he become so consumed by the power and Lochiel's ambitions that he would neglect me? Once the child was born, would there be a need for me? Or would I become as my mother: valueless in their eyes because my duty was done?

Naked, I shivered. Before me I conjured his eyes, so avid in tenderness. I felt his arms, his mouth; knew the answer in a body perfectly attuned to his.

Lochiel had sired me. Melusine had borne me. But it was Devin of High Crags who had brought me to life. Without him, my flame dimmed.

I will not be defined by the man with whom I sleep.

Yet he was defined by me. I was his only water in a wasteland of emptiness.

Devin took me out of Valgaard into the rocky canyons. It was all new to him, who had seen none of it, and I gloried in the telling of our history. He was fascinated, asking many questions, until the cat squalled. The noise of it echoed eerily.

He reined his horse in at once. His face was stark white, bleached of color and substance. Even his lips cried out for my mother's paint.

"Only a cat," I said. "Snow cat, I would wager. They sometimes come into the canyons. Though usually in winter." I frowned. "It is early for it, but—"

The cat screamed again. Devin stared blindly.

I searched for any subject to break his mood. "My father will call for a hunt. Perhaps you would care to go. You could have the pelt for your own . . . or perhaps I could make a coverlet for the cradle—"

He turned to me then and fixed me with a gaze of such brittle intensity I thought he might shatter. His voice was a travesty. "The cat is calling for something."

I shrugged. "Its mate, perhaps. Devin—"

A shudder took him. The tendons stood up in his neck like rope knotted much too tightly. His mouth moved rigidly as if to form words, but no voice issued.

"Devin—"

"Do you hear it?" His eyes were wholly empty. "A lonely, unhappy beast."

"Devin, *wait*—" But he rode on, ignoring me. "Snow cats can be dangerous. If it is sick, or injured . . ." He heard none of it. I turned my own mount and followed, irritated. "Wait for me."

He halted his horse roughly. As I saw the cause, I reined mine in as well. "By the god," I whispered.

Not a snow cat after all, but a black mountain cat. She crouched upon a ledge not far above our heads, keening a wail that echoed throughout the canyon. Great golden eyes glared.

I caught my breath. "Beware—"

But the cat did not spring. She merely held her crouch, staring down at him. Then, as I rode forward, she looked directly at me and screamed.

I reined in abruptly, apologizing inwardly to my mount. But the spell was broken. The cat turned and ran, leaping up through a wide crack. She was gone almost at once.

I released a breath. "Thanks to Asar-Suti . . ." I rode up to Devin. "I thought she would have you."

He stared after the cat.

"Devin."

His eyes were empty.

"Devin!"

At last, he looked at me. "Lonely," he said. Then, "Let us go home."

I was glad to turn my horse and ride back toward the defile, side by side with Devin. I did not like the pallor of his face, or the bafflement in his eyes.

As if he were incomplete, and now knew it more than ever.

Chapter Five

He cried out in his sleep and woke me, so that I sat upright with a hand clutched to my breast to still the lurching of my heart. He was still asleep, but he thrashed; I saw him grasp at his naked hip as if he meant to draw a knife.

"Devin." I put a hand upon his shoulder and felt the rigidity of muscle. "Devin—no." He came awake at once and lunged upward, one hand grasping my throat as if he would kill me. *"Devin!"*

His eyes were wild in the shadows of the chamber. Then sense came back to him, and horror. He knew what he had done. "Gods—"

"I am well," I said at once, seeing the look in his face. "Only somewhat surprised by your ferocity." He seemed no better for all my irony. I dismissed it. "I promise. I am well."

One hand raked hair from his face. Moonlight was gentle, but I could see the scars on his back from where the river had embraced him. His eyes were still full of realization: he had nearly strangled me.

I touched his shoulder and felt it tense. "What did you dream?"

"The cat."

At first I did not understand. Then the memory came. "The mountain cat we saw two weeks ago?"

"No. Another." His eyes were black in the darkness. "It was a lion."

"A lion!" Lions were mythical beasts. "Why would you dream of a lion?"

"It stalks me . . ." He let his breath out on a long sigh, and the tension went with it. "Only a dream."

"Then I will chase it away." I caught the fallen forelock in my fingers and stripped it back from his face. "I know what to do."

"No." His hand was on my wrist, pushing it away. "Not—now."

He turned back the covers and slid out of the curtained bed. "I need to go out."

I was astonished. "In the middle of the night?"

"I need to walk. Just along the battlements. I need to be alone." He slipped into a linen shirt that glowed in the dimness. "I beg you, understand there is a demon in me. Let me exorcise it, and I will come back to you."

I reached again for irony, so I would not sound too petty, too clinging, too much in need of him. "By morning? Or is this a *difficult* demon?"

"Difficult." His smile was strained. "But my memory of you will vanquish it."

"Go, then." I yanked the covers back over my breasts. "But do not be surprised if I am fast asleep. It troubles me not at all to have an empty bed."

He knew it for what it was, but the smile did not reach his eyes. He finished dressing, pulled on a fur-lined cloak, and went out of the chamber.

I stared into darkness. Resolution set me afire. "I can banish a lion. I am *Lochiel's* daughter."

He came up hours later. I was not asleep. He knew it instantly and apologized for keeping me awake by his absence.

I held the blankets up so he could climb beneath them. "Do you think I care?" His face was worn and bleak as he stripped out of his clothing; we had but an hour before dawn. "Have you destroyed the demon?"

He climbed in beside me, shivering, and drew me very close. At first he was gentle; then he held me so tightly I thought I might shatter. He shuddered once, twice. "Ginevra—" It was muted against my hair, but a cry nonetheless. "*Gods—*"

I had known it was coming. He had been wound too tightly. Now the wire snapped.

I held him tightly, wrapping arms around his shoulders and legs around *his* legs, until he was cocooned in flesh and hair. "Be still," I whispered. "I am here for you. I will always be here for you."

"I think—I think I am going mad."

"No. No, Devin. There is no madness in you."

"I wake in the night, in the darkness—"

"I know."

"—and there is nothing *there,* nothing at all, save emptiness and anguish . . . and then I recall there is you, always you—Ginevra, *here,* for me. And I know that you are my salvation, my only chance for survival—and I am *afraid*—"

"What do you fear?"

"That—you will go. That I will prove myself unworthy. That I will be turned out of Valgaard. That you will repudiate me because I am not what Lochiel needs me to be."

I stroked hair from his face. "You said he is pleased by your progress. And I have seen it also. There is nothing to fear, Devin. What can come between us?" Then, when he did not answer, "Where did you go?"

He said nothing at first. Then he shifted onto his back, cradling me in one naked arm. My head rested in the hollow of his shoulder. "I went below," he said finally. "To the undercroft."

For the merest moment I believed he meant the Gate. "The cats," I blurted.

"Aye." He was very still. The storm had passed, but the aftermath was as painful to see. His expression was wasted. "They are wild things, Ginevra. They were not made to be caged." His breath gusted softly. "Nor was I."

A hollow fear began to beat in my breast. "They are cats."

"I looked in their eyes," he said. "I saw the truth in them. They know what they have lost. They long for it back."

More desperately, I repeated, "They are *cats*."

"So am I, in my own way. I am very like them. I am caged by ignorance."

I knew it suddenly. "You want to set them free."

His hand settled in my hair, winding it through his fingers. "If we did, he would only replace them with others. Perhaps even the black one we saw in the canyon. I think—I think I could not bear to see more imprisoned then he already has. No. Let them alone. They have known their cages too long."

I drew him closer yet, warming his body as I wished I could warm his spirit. *How long?* I wondered. *How long will you know your cage?*

How long would I know mine, in the prison of his arms?

As long as I permitted it. As long as I desired it.

Forever is frightening.

*   *   *

The door opened very quietly as I sat before the polished plate
and combed my hair. In the reflection I saw Devin's face, peeking
around the door, and the expression he wore.

I stopped combing instantly and turned on the stool. "What?"

The set of his brows was comical in dismay. "I wanted to surprise you." But he did not seem so disheartened that the smile left
his face.

"What?" I repeated.

He gestured me down as I made to rise. "No. Wait." His expression was serious now, and very intent. His outstretched hand
was held palm up. He watched it closely; I watched *him*. I saw the
concentration, the effort he used, and then the startled wonder he
suppressed instantly so as to hide his childlike pleasure in a task at
last accomplished.

In his palm danced a tiny column of pure white flame. Slowly
it twisted, knotting itself, then reshaped itself into the aspect of a
bird, brilliant as a diamond.

I held my breath. The bird made of flame became a bird in
truth.

Devin extended the hand. "For you."

I put out my own hand, took the bird onto a finger, and suppressed the urge to cry. It was a tiny white nightingale, perfect in
all respects, and very, very real. It cocked its head, observed me
from glittering eyes, then began a jubilant song.

Devin's eyes shone. "Lochiel says it is because of Valgaard.
That though I have no recollections of power, the power simply *is*.
We are so close to the Gate . . . he says there is power for the taking; that we breathe it every day. A man—or a woman—need only
know how to use it. Even a Cheysuli, given enough time, if he
claims the Old Blood."

The bird's tiny feet clung to my fingers. I could not look at
Devin for fear I would see the change as I gave him the truth not
all men would tolerate. "You do know, do you not . . . that I am
also Cheysuli?"

He laughed. "Since your mother is a halfling, one would assume so."

I set the nightingale on the edge of my mirror. "The House of
Homana and my own House are so thickly intertwined, it is a wonder we keep our identities straight." I looked at him now. "You do
not mind?"

He came to me and threaded fingers into my hair. "Cheysuli—

Ihlini . . . what difference does it make? What matters is that we have one another."

"It is tainted blood. The Cheysuli desire to destroy us."

"So we will destroy them first." He laughed. "It is a matter of upbringing, not blood. Prejudice and hatred is created, not born. You serve the Ihlini because you know nothing else . . . but had you been raised in Homana you would serve the Cheysuli instead."

"I never could!"

"If you knew no better, of course you would."

"But I *do*—"

"So you do. And so you serve the Seker."

It could not go unasked. "What about you?"

Devin smiled. "I will do what must be done. If the god grants us immortality, it would be a sorry thing to repudiate his grace—and therefore watch forever as our race dies out at the behest of the Cheysuli."

I guided his hands and pressed them against my belly. "We will not die out. Not while the child within me lives."

Wonder engulfed his face. His fingers were gentle as he pressed them against the folds of my skirts. "Here?"

I laughed. "Thereabouts. It is too small for you to feel. But in six months you shall have your son."

He cradled my face in his hands. "Thank you," he said. "You have made it possible for me to be a man."

I found it odd. "But you *are* a man!"

"An incomplete one. Do you understand? Now we can be wed. Now, at last, I can go before the god and let him weigh my value."

Against my ear I heard the beating of his heart. Behind us, the bird stopped singing. When I looked around, the nightingale was gone.

Illusions are transitory. At least Devin was not.

I had seen the Gate many times, and the cavern that housed it, but never through Devin's eyes. It made it new again.

I took his hand as we stepped out of the passageway into the cavern. He did first what everyone does: tipped his head back to stare up at the arches, the glasswork ceiling alive with reflected flame. The symmetry was incomparable. So many layers of ceilings, so many soaring arches, and massive twisted columns spiraling from the floor. We were required to pass through them; at the end of the colonnade lay the Gate itself.

Devin was puzzled. "Where does the light come from? I see no torches."

I smiled. "It comes from the Gate. See how it is reflected time and time again, multiplied one hundredfold in the columns and the arches?" I watched his avid eyes. "The Gate itself is in the ground, but it is open, and its light is uninhibited. It is *godfire,* Devin—it is the light of truth, so that the Seker can illuminate the dark corners of your soul."

The light was in his eyes. I could see no pupil in them, only a vast empty blackness filled now with livid *godfire.* "He will see my weakness."

"All men are weak. He will draw it from you and replace it with strength."

"Is that why you have no fear?"

"I have fear." I touched his hand. "His glory is terrible. When one looks upon his aspect, one knows he—or she—is insignificance incarnate." I closed my fingers on the still flesh of his hand. "The Seker awaits."

"Ginevra!" He drew me back as I turned toward the columns. "Ginevra—wait." His face was graven with lines of tension. "I need you."

I carried his hand to my mouth. I felt his minute trembling; he feared as all men do, who must face Asar-Suti. Against his palm, I said, "I am here for you. Before the god, I swear it: I will always be here for you. We are bound already by the child in my body. Once we share the nuptial cup, we will be bound forever."

His voice was raw. "I am—unworthy."

"Of the god?" I smiled. "Or of me?"

Devin laughed; it was what I had hoped for. "Of both," he said.

I arched haughty brows. "Then neither the god nor I have grounds for discontentment. Things are as they should be." I glanced toward the Gate, then looked back into his face. "Come," I said gently. "There is no sense in delaying the truth."

"Truth," he echoed, "is what I fear."

I held his hand tightly in mine. "Why?"

"I am what you have made me. Ginevra's Devin, whatever— *who*ever—that is. I know nothing at all of my past . . . what if Devin of High Crags is a man who aspires to waste his coin in tavern wagers and his seed in roadhouse whores?"

My laughter echoed throughout the cavern. "Then the greater truth will be that Devin of High Crags is now a changed man." I shook back hair. "And they may spin the tale that it was the god's doing—or lay credit where it is due."

He was suspicious now. "Where?"

I set his hand against my heart. "Here," I said, "deep in my soul. What other truth is there?"

Devin looked beyond me. "Then let us get it done. Have them bring the nuptial cup. I am very thirsty."

My father waited for us at the Gate of the netherworld, clothed in black that the *godfire* dyed purple. In his hand was a rune-scribed silver goblet; at his feet lay the god himself.

"Where is he?" Devin breathed.

"There." I dipped my head. "Beneath the ground—that pool is the Gate."

I heard vague surprise in the timbre of his tone. "That hole in the ground?"

"His greatness is such that he requires no sepulcher," I said it more tartly than I intended; I expected Devin to be more circumspect in his worship of the Seker. Everyone else was.

Devin stared at the Gate. Light lapped at the edges, and smoke rose up. It wound around my father and clung to the folds of his robe. His gaze was fixed solely on Devin.

"Come," Lochiel said.

Devin's grasp tightened. "What is that?" he whispered.

He meant the pedestal just behind my father. "A chain," I whispered back. "A keepsake from a Cheysuli who thought he could defeat my father."

"It is in two pieces."

"The Cheysuli broke it. He surrendered to my father and broke the chain in half." I squeezed his hand. "Enough. There is a task we must do. Or do you mean to put off the ceremony that will make us one in the eyes of the god?" Devin's smile was fleeting. He stared at the cup.

"Empty," Lochiel said from the other side of the Gate. He held out the goblet. "Fill it, Devin, if you would have my daughter."

The tension spilled out of Devin. He turned to face me, brought my hand to his lips, and kissed my fingers. Then he released my hand and turned to Lochiel. He extended his arm across the maw of the Gate.

So vulnerable, I thought. *The god has only to rise and swallow him whole.*

Jennifer Roberson

But the Seker did not do it. Devin accepted the cup from my father's hand, then knelt at the edge of the Gate. Without hesitation,
with no sign of fear, he dipped the silver goblet into the pulsing
godfire.

Illumination engulfed him. Devin laughed, then dipped the cup
lower. When it was filled, he rose and inclined his head in tribute
to Lochiel, then turned to me. The cup's smoking contents flared,
burning more brightly, so that the light stripped bare all shadows
from Devin's face, washing the darkness from him. His eyes
burned brilliant green.

I placed my hands over his and guided the cup to my mouth. I
drank liquid light and let it fill me. Cold fire burned as my blood
responded to it.

Gods, but it was sweet. Such a sweet, cold fire . . . I laughed
and shook back my hair, then guided the cup to Devin.

He drank. I saw the widening of his eyes in shock; I feared, for
a horrible moment, he might sprew it from his mouth. But he swallowed. He shivered once. When I saw the emerald of his eyes replaced with livid black, I knew it was done.

My father's voice was an intrusion. It took effort to listen. "You
have shared the blood of the god at the god's own Gate. His blood
is yours. There can be no parting you now."

Devin turned. "Is there more?"

"There is always more." Lochiel extended his hands, and Devin
placed the goblet in them. My father smiled, then dropped the goblet into the light and smoke. "But you have begun already. Kneel
down, Ginevra—here, beside the Gate."

I knew better than to question.

"Remain there. It must be you first, so the child, too, is
blessed."

I dared not look at Devin. I knelt there beside the Gate, thinking of my child, and waited for the god.

He came all at once, without warning. I knew only that I was
blinded as the light sprang forth, and then it engulfed me. I felt
hands touching me, reaching through my clothing to pluck at my
flesh, until I feared it might be stripped from my bones. I shuddered once, then stilled. The god's hand was upon me.

I knew only what my father had told me: that the hand of the
god, the light of the Seker, would reveal the inner soul. Hidden
truths would be uncovered. Small vanities displayed. The insignif-

icant desires of a human would be mocked for what they were, so they could be replaced with perfect service to the god.

My perfect service was to bear the god a child. A son for the Seker, Who Lives and Dwells in Light—

I laughed aloud. "A son!" I cried. "A son to bring down the House of the Cheysuli!"

And the god was gone. I felt him go as abruptly as he had come. I wavered there on the edge, enshrouded in swirling smoke, and then Devin raised me up to keep me from tumbling in. "Ginevra?"

It was vital that I know. I turned my head to look at my father. "Is it done? Is it *done?*"

Lochiel smiled. "The god is well pleased."

I drew back then from Devin. "Kneel," I said.

The blackness lived in his eyes, which once had been clear green, but I saw something more. The emptiness remained though he had drunk of the cup.

"Kneel," I repeated. To mitigate the tone, I touched his face. For him, and only for him, I offered the key. "Release the cat," I whispered, so my father would not hear. "Let him go free from the cage of your fear."

Devin knelt. He crossed his arms against his breast and bent low in homage beside the Gate. The god spewed forth.

I held my breath. *It will only take a moment—*

Devin screamed. He screamed and screamed in a language I did not know, shaping words I could not decipher. His head fell back as he flung out both arms. He hung there on his knees, transfixed by the god. Blackened eyes were wide and blind.

I could not help myself: I shouted a denial. I saw the transformation, the alteration of bone and flesh. From man into cat: the hands became paws, the fingernails claws, the teeth elongated into fangs, and the sound that issued from his throat changed itself in mid-note from the shouting of a man to the scream of an angry cat.

Black as night, he was. Like the one we had seen in the canyon. But the eyes were purest green.

I was rooted to the stone. *Cheysuli—Cheysuli—Cheysuli.*

"Punish him!" Lochiel shouted. "Punish the transgressor!"

God, he was *Cheysuli!*

The god made him a man again, so he would know. I looked very hard for the mark of a Cheysuli, the sign of a demon, but all I saw was Devin.

In one step I reached him. I struck with all my strength, smashing my hand across his face. "How could you do this?" I shouted. "How could you do this to us?"

To us, I said. Not *to me.*

It infuriated me.

"How?" I cried. And then, viciously, "Is this part of your *tahlmorra?* To seduce an Ihlini so she conceives of your child?"

There was no response in his eyes. The god held him immobile, crucified on air; was he deaf as well as blind?

"Step back," my father said. "The god will deal with him."

Trembling, I stepped back. I saw the flicker in green eyes. Then a shudder wracked the Cheysuli.

"Tahlmorra," he gasped, in the tongue I did not know. *"Tahlmorra lujhalla—"*

My father overrode him. "Have you ever wondered," he mused, "what it would be like to be trapped in *lir*-shape forever?"

"—lujhalla me wiccan—cheysu—" And then, "Not Devin—"

The god sprang forth again. In a man's place writhed a cat with eyes the color of emeralds.

All I could think of was the incongruity: *Not yellow at all.*

Lochiel looked at me. "We will turn it loose," he said, "and then we will call a hunt."

Chapter Six

Was it like this, I wondered, *that they first brought you here?*

The cat remained senseless, deep in enforced sleep; they had thrown him unresisting on his side across a horse, then tied him to the packframe.

"Ginevra," my father said.

The cat's tongue lolled from a slack-lipped mouth. The eyes were half-lidded, dulled by the touch of the god.

We shared a bed, you and I. We shared our hearts. We shared our souls. And now we share this: a hunt to the death.

"Ginevra."

Lochiel again; I did not tarry longer. I turned my horse away from the cat and rode to the head of the party, letting no one see weakness. I was Lochiel's daughter.

I led them out of Valgaard, across the Field of Beasts, through the narrow defile into the canyon beyond. Then my father stopped us and used his own knife to cut the beast free. The heavy black body fell flopping to the ground. It brought no response; dull green eyes remained slitted and senseless, and the red tongue fell out into the dirt.

"Ginevra." A third time.

I looked at them all; at five of my father's minions; at my mother who watched me with undiminished avidity. Lastly I looked at him, who served Asar-Suti with an unflagging, perfect service.

"Leave it," I said evenly. "The hunt may commence tomorrow."

My mother raised her voice for the first time since we had left the fortress. "I wonder," she said, "that you take no steps to insure he does not flee. Would it not be wiser to kill him now?"

Lochiel looked at the cat. "Where is he to go? He is bound to Ginevra, bound by the god. And bound also, perhaps, by the child in her body."

I could not look at him. I was ashamed, so *ashamed* that I had defiled myself. That I had permitted myself to love him.

"No," he shook his head, "our prey will not flee. He will wait here for us, until we choose to come."

"Sweet revenge," I declared. "When you have trapped him, will you put him with the others in the undercroft?"

"There? No. When I decide to take him, it will be for his pelt. I have a whim to rest my feet in winter on the hide of a dead Cheysuli."

My mother's carmined mouth gloated.

In Valgaard, I threw back the lids to all the trunks and pulled the clothing from them, then piled it on the bed. I took the caskets containing the gifts I had bestowed and dumped the contents on top of the clothing. Lastly I dug out the nightshift I had worn the first night we shared a bed and tossed it into the pile. Then I summoned *godfire.*

"A waste," my mother said, "of a comfortable bed."

I did not turn. I did not care. Let her stand there if she would; I wanted nothing more than to watch all of it burn.

All of it. *All* of it. Every bit of it.

"Will you burn yourself too?"

I swung. The flames were in her eyes. It turned them Cheysuli yellow. "You wanted him," I said viciously. "From the beginning, you wanted him. How does it feel to know he was *Cheysuli?*"

My mother smiled. "So am I. So are you. And aye, I would have bedded him. He was in every way a *man.*"

I drew back my lips from my teeth. "Shapechanger!"

The light in her eyes was livid. She looked beyond me to the bed as the *godfire* consumed it. "Which one pleased you most?" she asked. "The warrior—or the cat?"

I wanted to scream at her. I wanted to burn her, too. I wanted to tear the mirror from the wall and hurl it into the fire.

Even as I thought it, the mirror shattered.

Melusine shook her head. "A dangerous thing, when Lochiel's daughter is angry. The very walls are at risk."

"Why have you come?" I cried. "Are you hoping I will cry?"

She wore her hair pinned up. Light glittered off all the gemstones. "Once I wanted your father to care as much for me as Devin does for you. He does not. Once I wanted your father to care as much for me as he does for you. He does not, and never will.

And so I am soundly defeated in all patterns of the dances which are danced between men and women—even between fathers and daughters." Her face was very still, but her eyes were livid. "I bore a single living child. I nearly spent myself in the birth, and tore myself so badly I could never bear again."

Behind me the bed burned. So did all of his clothing, the jewels I had given him, the nightshift he had removed with avid tenderness. "You are punishing me."

In her eyes *godfire* dimmed; the bed was nearly consumed. "The child you carry is the child of prophecy."

I touched a hand to my belly.

" 'The Lion shall lie down with the witch,' " my mother quoted. "It is what their madman says, the *shar tahl* who was a prince."

"Aidan," I murmured; I was consumed by realization, by the knowledge of what I was: a vessel for the child that could destroy my race. "I shared a cradle with his son. My father told me."

"As an infant you shared his cradle. As a woman, you shared his bed."

It jerked me out of numbness. "That was *Kellin?* Him? But— he said nothing of it! He made no indication! He was—" I broke it off, then finished it by rote, "—Devin. We all thought he was Devin." I looked at her. "You are punishing me. That is why you have come."

Her eyes were yellow again. "You nearly killed me," she said. "But *you* were what he wanted, once I could not bear again. You were his only hope. I counted as nothing. And then *he* came—and once there was a child, Lochiel gave you both what should have been mine!"

The *godfire* died to ash. I grieved for the woman, that she could be so bitter. I grieved for myself, that I had lost my mother when I most needed her.

And I grieved for the child who was not, after all, the salvation of my race, but the herald of its destruction.

"I will be dead," she said, "but you will live to see it."

When I was certain she was gone, I closed the door and locked it with meticulous care. I put a rune upon the lock so not even my mother could open the door. Only my father might, but he would not come.

Godfire was gone. The bed, the jewelry, the nightshift—all had been consumed. All that remained were charred bits and pieces and a drift of violet ash.

Grief roused itself. Anguish awoke. The terrible anger was stilled.

I knelt. I plunged my hands into the ash and closed them on frosted remnants. They did not burn my flesh. The pain was all inside, where no one could see it.

But I would know.

I would always know.

It burns, such pain. It devours the heart and soul.

When the summons came, I did not shirk it. I did not delay. Clad in the tattered remnants of my pride, I went to the tower chamber and presented myself to him. My deference was plain; there was no latitude, in this, for anything save shame.

He sat upon a tall stool set before a grimoire on a tripod stand. He wore russet hunting leathers, as if he planned already how the chase would commence. With his hair freshly cropped close against his head, I saw the shape of the skull. A beautiful man, my father; but the beauty now was tarnished by the memory of another, who had so indelibly replaced Lochiel as the model, in my mind, of pure masculine beauty.

I hated myself for it, but I could not banish it. I looked at my father, saw my father's face, and superimposed the features of another man.

It was easy to do. I saw in that instant that they were very like.

My lips parted. Color drained. "—true," I blurted. "All of it *true*—"

Winged brows arched. "What is true?"

"I did not see it before—but now . . ." I shivered. "We are, both of us, linked by more than enmity."

Only a few candles shed illumination. Most were unlighted. "Aye," my father said; in smoky light, his eyes were bronze. "For years we denied it; for decades, so did they. We came to accept it sooner than the Cheysuli. Most of them still deny it." His smile was slight. "We are everything they cannot countenance, we who serve the Seker. I think it less taxing to us to admit the truth. After all, we merely desire to destroy them in order to maintain what we have fought so hard to win. Autonomy from gods."

I shivered. "But—the Seker."

"I said, '*gods*.' " He emphasized the plural. "They worship a pantheon of gods, while we comprehend true power lies only with one." He held his silence then, weighing me by expression. "It provides many answers." He rose from the stool and lifted something from the gutter in the pages of the grimoire. Candlelight glinted. A gold ring, set with jet. "It lives again," he said. "It knows my touch."

"But—it knew *his,* too! And he is Cheysuli!"

"Kellin is many things. Kellin of Homana is very nearly a Firstborn himself. He has the Old Blood in abundance, twice and thrice again . . . the earth magic lives in him." The ring sparked deep red. "Our lifestones answer power. This close to the Gate, it does not distinguish. It acknowledged his gifts, no more. But it would not kill him; his blood is very like ours."

"Old Blood," I said. "Ours is older yet."

"No." His tone was thoughtful as he contemplated the ring. "Exactly the same, Ginevra. In all ways, the same. If I were to cut into my left hand and spill my blood, then cut into Kellin's hand and spill *his* blood, we would see they were the same. But until we mixed the blood, until we clasped hands, nothing could come of it save we each would bleed to death if the cuts proved too deep."

The cut inside my heart was very deep indeed. "Then Devin of High Crags is dead."

"It would seem so." He shut his hand upon the ring and squeezed. When he opened it again, the ring was naught but shattered crystal. He blew it from his palm. "Now, certainly." His eyes were steady. "Come here, Ginevra."

I shuddered once. Suppressed it.

"Ginevra," he chided. "Do you fear me? Do you believe I would harm you?"

My lips were stiff. "There is no need," I said. "I have shamed you. I have dishonored you. You need do nothing save withhold your regard, and I am diminished."

"Diminished." He smiled. "Lochiel's daughter should never be *diminished.*"

"I am. I *am.*" I fell to my knees. "The god will know my shame each time I go before him. And I will *know* he knows!"

My father came to me. I bowed my head before him. He put hands upon my head and cradled it tenderly. "You are everything I could desire in a daughter. You have not failed me. You have not dishonored me. There is no shame in what you have done; you did it at my behest. If you castigate yourself, you also castigate me."

I turned my face to look up at him. "I would *never*—"

"I know." Lochiel smiled. His eyes, in dim light, were black instead of brown. "In anything we do, there is no shame. Do you understand? I will have it no other way. In anything we do, there is no shame."

I nodded, grateful he would do so much to discard my degradation.

"Good." His hands shifted. He lifted me up. Our faces were very close. He studied mine avidly, and then he smiled. "There is your mother in you, also. You are her daughter as well."

"Aye." Though I hated to admit it.

"There is much in Melusine I find most entertaining, especially her passion. Are you the same?"

My face burned against his hands.

"Was the Cheysuli content?"

I began to tremble.

"Did you play kitten to his cat?"

"God—" I blurted.

Lochiel smiled. "After the hunt tomorrow, I will come to your bed."

"My *bed?*"

"To destroy the Cheysuli's seed, we will replace it with my own."

In my chamber, alone, where there was no bed, I wondered if he would conjure another fitting for his state.

Could I burn that one, too?

He would simply conjure again.

Did he think I would submit?

Or would he also conjure submission?

I looked at the door. I looked at the latch. No ward I made would prevent Lochiel from entering my chamber. No defense I summoned could prevent him from entering *me*.

After the hunt.

After the cat is dead.

What would my mother say?

I caught back the laugh before it became a sob. I pressed my hands against my mouth to suppress another lest I shame myself.

There were drugs, I knew. There were all manner of ways.

I did not want the child. I desired the child to die.

There were other ways than this.

"There is your mother in you also."

He wanted it this way to gratify himself.

After he killed the cat.

I unlatched the door and went out of the chamber that no longer contained a bed. I thanked the god I had burned it. What the Cheysuli and I had shared, despite centuries of enmity, was cleaner by far than the union my father proposed.

I went down to the undercroft, to see the caged cats. They greeted me with snarls, with lashings of supple tails, with the fixed stare of the predator as they paced out the dimensions of their lives.

What had he said of them? *"They know what they have lost. They long for it back."*

He had lost humanity in the shaping of his self. Did he know he had lost it? Did he long for it back?

Did he know, in the great gulf of darkness, why he could not leave?

Do you remember my name?

Did he understand what had happened?

Did you remember the truths we discovered in our bed?

Did he recall the god at all, and how he had come to be locked forever in cat-shape?

Do you remember the oath I swore, when you said you needed me?

I remembered it all.

"Cheysuli," I said aloud. The word was alien, shaped of a foreign tongue. Its sibilant hissed.

He had said something as the god revealed the truth. Something about fate. I knew the word for that. The Cheysuli called it *tahlmorra.*

"Fate," I said aloud, "is another word for surrender." It was an Ihlini belief; we make our own fates dependent on our needs.

One of the cats snarled. It thrust a tawny, wide-toed paw through the iron bars and reached toward me, slapping air with half-sheathed claws.

What else had he said? *"Prejudice and hatred is created, not born. You serve the Ihlini because you know nothing else."*

"I *am* Ihlini," I said. "What else would you have me do?"

The cat waved its paw and snarled.

"Do you hate me?" I asked. "Because I am Ihlini?"

His words were in my head. *"Cheysuli—Ihlini . . . what difference does it make? What matters is that we have one another."*

I had sworn him an oath.

I looked at the cat. "Oaths are made to be broken."

He was the father of my child.

The father of the Firstborn.

Anguish welled up. "Let me be free of this!"

It echoed in the undercroft, disturbing all the cats.

They know what they have lost. They long for it back.

" 'Let them alone,' you said. 'They have known their cages too long.' "

He was not caged. He would not *be* caged. My father would kill him, then strip the pelt from his body and use it for a rug.

Would he have us couple on it when he saw I had no bed?

The jaws clenched together. "For that, then," I said. "I honor my oath that much—and then we are quit of each other."

I knew what I had lost. I longed for it back. But knew I could never have it.

In the hour before dawn I went out of Valgaard, crossed the smoky Field of Beasts, and passed through the defile into the canyon beyond. There I found the cat I had known as man, whose name was Kellin.

I was bundled in a heavy cloak. "You know what you are," I said. "*I* know what you are. According to my father, what you are is what you shall be—until he desires to add a new rug to his floor to keep his feet warm in winter."

The eyes were huge and green. Sense had returned to them. They glared balefully.

"I owe you an oath," I said. "I gave it freely, not knowing what you are, and could in all good conscience claim its meaning forfeit . . . but there are things between us that are not so easily governed." I looked at the female beside him. "Did you tell her there is a child? That the child of the prophecy, so beloved by the Cheysuli, lives here in my body?" I pressed my hand against cloak-swathed belly. "If I suffer this child to live, I bring down my people. I destroy an entire race. That I will not do. But neither will I permit my father to kill you. I have no desire to gaze each winter upon the stones they will put in the sockets that once were your eyes."

The black tail lashed. Green eyes did not blink.

"Then come," I said roughly, angry that I cared. "I will set you free of this shape so you may resume your own. We have fought for centuries, the Ihlini and Cheysuli—I think it will do no harm if we fight a while longer."

If it came, it came. But I would not, as my mother threatened, live to see it. The god would, in making the bargain, require something to seal it. All I had of value was what he had given me.

Worth giving up, I thought, *so I need not spend the centuries watching the descendants of our races waste lives trying to kill one another in the name of a prophecy.*

Worth giving up so I need not replace my mother in my father's bed for the balance of forever.

Interval

The woman knelt at the Gate, and fire bloomed in her hands. She held them out steadily, reached across the pool, and shaped living *godfire* into a reflection of itself. In her hands the god writhed as he writhed within the Gate.

She parted her hands and drew them apart. Flame surged in her palms, licking from her fingers as each gout of *godfire* stretched toward the other. Then she brought her hands together and joined the halves again. She built of flame a goblet, then fed it on itself. Bloody runes formed on the rim. In the bowl sparks snapped; smoke rose from the contents.

She raised it to her mouth and drank the flame away. The goblet was banished. *Godfire* glowed in her eyes.

She looked at the cat who crouched nearby, beside the rim of the Gate. Tufted ears were flattened. Fire blazed in green eyes as the tail beat basalt.

The woman's mouth opened and smoke issued forth. Her voice was alive with light. Each word was a spark that broke from her lips and formed into a rune. The words she spoke bound themselves into sentences, until the runes formed a necklet that dangled in midair.

"He did not know," she said. "He believed himself Ihlini. He came to you consenting, eager for your touch, eager to serve the Seker. He meant to bind himself to you. What you revealed in his soul was not what he expected."

Viscid liquid boiled. Smoke billowed up. The runes that had been words burned brightly in the darkness.

"I do not question the punishment; he is Cheysuli, and transgressor. But he meant only to serve. His heart was empty of hostility. He meant no sacrilege."

A second necklet was conjoined with the first into a glowing girdle. It moved from the air to bind itself around her hips; to seal her wrists together. Smoke issued from her nostrils. Her eyes wept blood.

"To the god of the netherworld, Who Made and Dwells in Light; who illuminates our souls, I offer this bargain: my immortal life in exchange for his true guise."

The blood she wept was black. It ran down her cheeks to fall into the Gate, where the *godfire* hissed in welcome to itself.

She prostrated herself. Her hair tumbled free of pins and fell down into the Gate, where the *godfire* crept up the strands. It lingered at her hairline, then spilled in a glistening net to sheathe her face in a glowing filigree.

Her breath was made of flames. "Let him go," she begged. "Let him be a man. I will give you my life. I will give you the child."

Godfire gouted forth. It broke in a wave over the cat, bound it in white fire, then dragged it inexorably toward the Gate.

"No!" she cried. "I promised you the child!"

Claws locked into stone. And then the claws were human fingers with bloodied, broken nails digging into smoking rock. "Ginevra!" he shouted, with the voice and mouth of a man. *"Ginevra!"*

She broke free of her bonds and thrust herself to her knees, hands locked around wrists that were fleshed in human flesh. She dragged him forth from the Gate, breaking bonds. He climbed out, dripping gouts of *godfire,* and was reborn as a man.

Her grasp on his wrists broke as she fell to her knees. "Done," she gasped.

The man's breathing was labored. He bared human teeth in a snarl that was wholly bestial, as if he had forgotten how to make his mouth form words.

"Go," she said raggedly. "The bargain is made. If you linger now, you invite his renewed interest."

The man laughed harshly. He knelt upon the floor in an aspect of obeisance, but the burning in his eyes was born of different loyalties. " *'The Lion shall lie down with the witch.'* "

She stared at him. "What?"

"My *jehan* had the right of it. And now we are wed—Lochiel's daughter and the Prince of Homana." The laughter broke again from a throat made raw from fire. "How the *shar tahls* will untangle our birthlines I dare not predict; it may take more decades than either of us has."

Her face spasmed. "Go."

"Not without you."

Her breath halted, then resumed. Color ebbed in a face of fragile, faceted planes, delicate as the arches that shattered overhead. "That is finished. That is over."

Green eyes burned in the clean, sculpted features that were, in their fierceness, in their avidity, far more feral than human. He was predator to her prey.

"Go," she said again, as the Gate behind her blazed. "There is nothing between us now."

He closed his hand around her wrist. "What is between us now is of an entirely different making than what we shared in bed."

The woman's laughter echoed in basalt, and crystal arches. "Enmity?"

He pulled her from the floor. "His name is Cynric."

PART V

Chapter One

Kellin knew it at once. *She does not understand—she has no comprehension of what we did here, in drinking from the cup.*

Ginevra tore free of his grasp. Between them she built a wall of conjoined, blazing runes.

His own shredded it. "I drank of the cup," he told her. "What I know is not forgotten."

Ice-gray eyes were black in comprehension. "What have I done?" she whispered. "What have I wrought?"

Oddly, he wanted to laugh. "I think—peace." His mind moved ahead to means. Kellin turned. "Only one thing remains—"

She saw what he meant to do. "No! Not that—"

He did not heed her but went straight to the glassy basalt pedestal, all twisted upon itself, and snatched up the heavy links. He would take the chain to his father and prove himself worthy of being Aidan's son.

He turned back to Ginevra. Her face was bathed in light, but the shadowed hollows beneath her cheeks underscored the exquisite architecture of her face. *Gods, but she is magnificent. They wrought well when they made her.* Hoarsely, he said, "Now we go."

"No! Not me!"

She was pride incarnate, and beautiful, blazing with determination. Light from the Gate glowed in her hair. All of it was silver now save for the pure white frame around her face. She did not know. She had not comprehended what the god had stolen from her in addition to what was offered.

Knowing what she is alters nothing. NOTHING. I want her as much now as I did before. And—I need her as badly.

Yet looking at her, knowing what he knew of the woman who was Ihlini, but also whom he loved, Kellin was keenly aware of a strange division in his soul. He, too, had been raised to believe in certain assurances, in certain absolutes, such as a conviction that only one race could—and should—survive. Assumptions were made predicated on traditional beliefs; he, wondered now if perhaps disservices were done in the name of service.

To the Ihlini, service to the Seker is as binding—and as honorable—as ours to Cheysuli gods. In that moment he understood. He comprehended at last how his father could, in the name of prophecy, give up a son.

Should *he* not be able to sacrifice something as well to serve a greater purpose?

He looked at the woman. A small part of him wanted to say she was Ihlini, and enemy, and therefore worthy of hatred; but the greater part of him recalled the other woman. Had he not said it himself? *"Prejucide and hatred is created, not born."* He had loved her as an Ihlini, knowing no different; now that he did know, why should all things change? Ginevra was simply *Ginevra.*

Kellin laughed painfully, cognizant of a truth that no child could comprehend. *He gave up his son's childhood, but will have him in adulthood. I give up old prejudice so I may have a woman, and therefore serve the greatest purpose of all.*

Ginevra scrambled up as he rounded the Gate. "I gave you your freedom! Now go!"

His hand closed upon her wrist. The other clutched the chain. As she struggled to break free he caught handfuls of her hair, all tangled with bloodied fingers and links of rune-wrought gold. He held her imprisoned skull very still between his palms. "I want—" He could not say it. It filled all of his being, he overflowed with it, but he could not say it.

Her face twisted. "You want the child!"

Lips drew back. He did not mean to snarl, to bare his teeth before her, but much of him recalled what it was to be a cat in place of a man.

She was Lochiel's daughter.

Kellin laughed. He saw the spasm in her face, the anguish in her eyes, and knew he had to explain. If he could but find the words. "Ginevra—" He shut his teeth together. *Why not let her believe it is because of the child? It would be easier.*

But he no longer desired to predicate decisions on what was easiest. "I have— I have lost too much . . ." He would say it; he *would.* "In the past—too many people." His breath stirred her hair, stark white around her face, silver in his hands. *Say the words. Say them so she knows—say them so YOU know.* "If—if it is heresy—" He drew in a hissing breath. "If it is heresy to love Lochiel's daughter, then burn me now."

Her eyes were blackened sockets. Ginevra said nothing.

His breath rushed out of his mouth. "I thought it was a lie. *This* Lion, I swore, would never lie down with the witch." His eyes were avid as he cradled her face. "But he has, and found it good—"

"How can you say that?" she cried. "Knowing what we are—"

"Knowing what we are is *why* I can say it." Kellin clung to her more fiercely, wanting very badly to find the proper words, but not knowing how. He was afraid, suddenly. Afraid he could not win. "Ginevra—"

A gout of *godfire* burst from the Gate. It showered them with sparks. An eerie wailing whistle accompanied smoke.

Ginevra flinched, then her eyes opened wide. "He knows—the god *knows*—"

The ground beneath their feet shook. High overhead, one of the arches shattered. Glass rained down.

"No more time—" Kellin dragged her with him as he headed toward the colonnade that led from the Gate to the passageway beyond. More glass shattered. The chime of its landing was swallowed by the keening from the Gate. *Godfire* lapped at the edges, then spilled onto the floor.

She staggered next to him, fighting to regain balance. "I told you to go *at once,* so he would not renew his interest! You lingered too long!"

He had, but it was for her. "Then we had best make haste."

The voice echoed in the cavern, carrying easily above the keening of the Gate. "Ginevra shall go nowhere. She is my daughter— and within the Seker's keeping."

They spun in place. Lochiel stood on the far side of the Gate. In his outstretched palms danced crimson runes. His cloak smoked of *godfire,* purling around his body. The ale-brown eyes, in lurid light, were molten bronze in their sockets. The clean architecture of bone, so clear and pure in line, was visible behind the human mask that hid perverted purpose.

"She made a mistake," he said, "but it is easily rectified." The runes in his hand flared higher, brighter, though the brilliance did not distract him. They twisted into knots, then broke apart and reformed. "First, there is the child. We cannot permit it to live. Ginevra knows that. You have only to look at her face."

Kellin did not. He knew what he would see there. She was profoundly Ihlini; he did not know if she loved him enough to bear the child whose presence in the world would alter hers forever.

Scalloped arches broke from the ceiling in sheets and fell behind them, shattering against basalt. A splinter cut Kellin's cheek. The floor trembled again. The Gate ran white with fire, bubbling over its edges. Kellin had mastered the art of working *godfire* in order to make runes, but he knew better than to believe he might turn back the flood. Lochiel was *Lochiel;* his arts were more powerful, and his intentions deadly.

Kellin moved back two paces and took Ginevra with him.

Lochiel's eyes were fixed on his daughter. "She knows what must be done."

Color stood high in her face. "I serve the Seker."

"Aye," he said, "You do. In all ways necessary—and in certain sacrifices."

"Wait—" Kellin blurted.

Ginevra cried out, then fell to her knees. Her body shuddered once. Her face was alive with pain as her mouth formed a rictus, then loosened its hideous tension into slack astonishment. "—kill me . . ." she gasped. "—to kill it, you kill *me*—"

"Sufficient punishment." Lochiel's runes blazed more brilliantly. "You made a mistake."

Kellin dragged her up and turned her from the Gate, pushing her onward. "Go on—*go* . . . get out of the cavern!"

Ginevra screamed. "—inside me—" she gasped. "—so *black*—" She thrust out her hands and clawed at the air. *Godfire* sparked from fingertips. Her hair, in the light, glowed silver. "My own—father—"

Lochiel said calmly, "I can make other children."

Kellin built his own rune and hurled it across the Gate, bleeding *godfire* as it flew. Lochiel's blazed up, then shattered Kellin's rune into a shower of impotent fragments. "Tricks," the Ihlini said, and looked again at his daughter. "I would kill a thousand Ginevras to destroy the Firstborn."

"You—will not . . . you will *not*—" She reached out to Kellin, clawing. "Take—" She bit deeply into her lip as his fingers closed on hers. "I—will not—permit—"

"What choice have you?" Lochiel asked. "This is your sacrifice. Accept it willingly, so you do not shame me."

"*Shame* you! You?" Ginevra writhed against the pain, laughing breathlessly. She clutched Kellin's hand. "I need make no choice . . . you have made it *for* me—"

Godfire rose up in the Gate, then fell back, splashing, to pool again on the floor.

She clutched his hand more tightly. *"Kellin."* Her grin was ghastly as she bared it to her father. "You are Lochiel the Ihlini, servant of the Seker—but we—*we*—are more . . . in my body lies the Firstborn. Do you think he will allow you to kill him?"

Lochiel laughed. "It is unborn, Ginevra! And will stay that way."

"No—" She bit again into her lip. Blood ran red, unsullied; she had given up immortality. "He drank . . . and I drank. The child has tasted also. What we are together is more than even you can withstand." She bared her bloodied teeth in the travesty of a smile. "The god, like your cats, is hungry. I think it is time he was fed."

Kellin felt her fingers bite into his own, setting fingernails. He saw then what she meant to do.

"—help—" she gasped. "I cannot do it without you—"

No. Nor could he without her, or the child in her body.

"Earth magic," Kellin murmured. "This is a Gate, like the Womb of the Earth. Here it is perverted, but there is still a stronger power—"

"Now!" Ginevra cried, and the walls around them trembled. Archways tumbled down, shattering to fragments against the floor.

Godfire blazed up. At its heart it burned white. In its reflection, as its servant, Lochiel's face was without feature. He was, in that moment, the avatar of the god. *"GINEVRA."*

"He is hungry!" Ginevra cried. "He cries out for food!"

"In the name of the Seker, in the name of Asar-Suti—"

"Aye!" she cried. "In his name always, in all ways. You are his creature; let the god have you!"

Lochiel's eyes were livid. "I will raze this fortress before I permit you to take that child from here!"

Ginevra laughed. "You wanted to kill it! Now you change your mind?"

"As I must," he said. "The Seker's aspect is of *godfire*. I think he would like to be human once again, that he may walk the land freely as he sunders it.Æ

She clung more tightly to Kellin's hand. "If you would give him a body, give him your own!"

"GINEVRA!"

"Your own!" she cried. And then, *"Now,* Kellin!"

With their power they burned out his eyes, leaving blackened, melted sockets, and exploded the runes in his hands. His clothing caught fire. The flesh of his face peeled away so the bone exposed itself. A rictus replaced his lips, displaying perfect teeth. Lochiel staggered forward, waving impotent stubs on the ends of blazing arms, then tumbled into the Gate.

The *godfire* within dimmed as if measuring its addition. And then it burst upward in a geyser of naked flame, licking at the jagged remains of shattered crystal arches. The Gate bled *godfire* in Lochiel's immolation.

A shudder wracked Ginevra. She fell to her knees. Silver hair streamed around her, tangling on the floor with steaming *godfire* and melting glass. In the rumbling of the Gate, her sobs went unheard.

"Come." Kellin urged her up. "If Asar-Suti desires a second helping . . ."

She caught great handfuls of god-bleached hair in rigid, trembling hands. Tears shone on her face. "What manner of man sires a child such as *I,* who murders her own father?"

A ripple moved through the floor. It fractured the massive columns that spiraled to the roof. Black glass rained down. With it came more arches, the fretwork of the ceiling, and then the roof itself.

"Ginevra!" Kellin dragged her to her feet one handed as he tucked the two pieces of chain into his belt.

Cracks appeared in the rim of the Gate. Fissures ran toward them. As the roof fell down, part of it splashed into the Gate, so that *godfire* gouted forth. In its depths, something screamed.

The floor beneath them rolled. From high over their heads, from the bulwark of the fortress, came a keening howl of fury.

"They know," Ginevra said. "The bonds are all broken. Lochiel is dead and so *they* die—and Valgaard is falling." She caught his hand tightly. "I have to find my mother."

As they burst from out of the passageway into the corridor, Melusine was waiting. In her hands was a sword made of livid *godfire.* "What have you done?" she cried. "What have you wrought?"

Ginevra laughed crazily to hear her own words repeated. "Lochiel is dead."

"The walls fall," Melusine said; in her eyes shone the light of madness, yellow as a Cheysuli's. "Valgaard is sundered . . ." She looked at Kellin. "Kinsman," she said, then raised the sword high.

"No!" Ginevra struck before he could, transfixing her mother's breast with a single blazing rune. The sword was snuffed out. "No," Ginevra repeated. Her eyes were anguished. "Go away," she said. "Get out of Valgaard now."

Melusine laughed. "Without Lochiel? You must be mad!"

"Mother—" But the floor between them fissured. A jagged hole appeared. Kellin staggered, righted himself, then caught Ginevra and yanked her back as Melusine, screaming, tumbled in. *"Mother!"*

He did not remonstrate, nor try to explain there was no hope as *godfire* gushed forth and drove them back. Ginevra knew. *"Shansu,"* he whispered, though she would not understand.

She pressed a hand across her face so he would not see her tears.

Kellin did not permit them to stop until they were through the defile on their Valgaard horses and safe within the canyon, where the floor did not split, the walls did not fall down, and the roof above their heads did not collapse upon them. There Sima waited.

He expected the link to be sundered by Ginevra's presence, but Sima's pattern was clear. *You did well,* his *lir* said, *to release my kin.*

He thought of the undercroft, where he had, with his power, torn the doors off their hinges and permitted the cats to escape. *They deserved a better* tahlmorra *than to die with Lochiel.*

Sima's eyes gleamed golden. Tufted ears slicked. *Do you understand?*

No. I was taught we could not link when an Ihlini was near.

There is some of the god in you. Not only in your magic, but in your tolerance. You are both children of the gods; the time for schism is ending. She glanced at Ginevra. *Tend her first. There will be time for us later.*

He climbed off his horse, hooked its reins over a branch, then went to Ginevra's. "Come down," he said, and reached out a hand.

Ginevra looked down at him from atop her mount. Ash marred

her cheek. Silver hair was a tangled tapestry on either side of her face. In her eyes was an anguish of such immensity he feared it might break her.

He could not help herself. "*Meijhana—*"

At the sound of the enemy tongue, spoken so close to sundered Valgaard, Ginevra flinched. Then, with careful deliberation, she unhooked a foot from a stirrup and got off on the other side. It put the horse between them.

She could not have taken a blade and stabbed any deeper. He was eviscerated.

Gods, he prayed, *let this woman never hate me. I could not bear it.*

Ginevra took the horse away to the far side of the canyon. She sat down there upon a broken stump clad in the stormwrack of her soul and stared blindly into shadows with ice-gray eyes glazed black.

With effort, Kellin turned back to his horse. He unbuckled girths, pulled off saddle and blankets, scrubbed down the damp back with a handful of leaves. When he was done, he went to her horse and did the same service. Ginevra said nothing.

Smoke crept into the canyon. It was laden now with odors: burned flesh, the stink of the netherworld, the smell of a world come undone.

"It is gone," Ginevra said.

Kellin turned from her horse.

"Gone." She sketched a rune in the air; he recognized *bal'sha'a* by the movement of her fingers. But nothing came of it. Her fingers moved deftly, yet nothing flared into brilliance in answer to her shaping. "The Gate is closed," she said. The hand, bereft of power, slapped down slackly and lay curled in her lap. "And so now there is no *godfire.*" Her eyes were oddly empty. "Everyone I knew is dead. Every*thing* I knew is gone."

His voice shook. "Ginevra—"

Her face was a wasteland. "Lochiel was right. We are truly destroyed."

"No." He drew a slow breath, treading carefully; he desired in no way to be misconstrued, or what they had built between them—that now was in jeopardy—would collapse into ruins. "No, not destroyed." He would not lie to her; would *never* lie to her. "This *aspect* of it, perhaps, but your race survives. Asar-Suti is defeated, but there are Ihlini in the world."

"Good Ihlini?" She smiled, but without amusement; it was a ghastly mockery of the smiles he had won before. "Those who repudiate the Seker will surely survive and be looked upon with favor, but what of—us? Those like my father, and Strahan before him, and Tynstar before *him*." The line of her jaw was blade-sharp as she set her teeth. "What of Ihlini like me?"

"You said it yourself: the Gate is closed."

She did not flinch. "Aye."

"I would like to think that as we end this war, such Ihlini as they were will turn from the dark arts to fashion a new world."

" 'Such Ihlini,' " she echoed. "Like me?"

He said it, deliberately: "You are not your father."

"No." Moonlight glinted in hair. "No, so I am not. Or surely I would have killed you there at the Gate." Her mouth warped briefly. "Perhaps I should have."

"Aye," he agreed. "Or left the cat loose so the hunt could commence."

It shook her. It shook her so badly he knew she as much as comprehended the precipice.

He gave her the truth. "I do not believe Cynric's task is to have the Ihlini killed."

Her tone was harsh. "As we killed my mother and my father?"

My poor meijhana. He went to her, and squatted down before her. "No matter how hard you strike at me, it will not bring them back."

Ginevra laughed harshly. "How can I strike at you? You only did as I asked, there in the cavern. What does it matter to me *how* it was done, or that we used an unborn child for his power?"

He caught her hand. "Do not punish yourself for choosing to live. You did—we did—what had to be done."

"All of it? *All* of it?" Her hand shook in his. "My father. My mother. My—home." Tears glazed her eyes as she put a hand against her belly. "So falls the Ihlini race. As according to prophecy—but before he is even born!" Her voice was raw. "Are you pleased by it?"

He put his hand on her hand and let it rest against her belly. "He is Ihlini, also."

She wrenched her hand away and pressed both against her mouth. Fingers trembled minutely. Through them, she said, "How can you love me? I am everything you hate."

"When I was Cheysuli—" He smiled to see her start. "When I

was Cheysuli, and knew it, I hated Ihlini. There was no choice. They meant to destroy my House. They had killed people I loved. They would kill *me,* if I gave them the chance to do so." He pulled her hands away and held them in his. "When I was Cheysuli but no longer knew it, I was free to understand that life is much more complex. That the gods, when they act, when they wish to humble a man, wield a weapon of irony."

"*Your* gods!"

"Mine. Yours also." He lifted a strand of her hair. In the sunset, the silver was gilt. "You knew what would happen."

Ginevra stiffened.

"You knew very well. It was what you implied when you came to me here, to fetch me to the Gate so you could win me back my human form." He looked into her eyes. "You grieve for more than their deaths. You grieve because of guilt. That Lochiel's daughter, bred to serve her people, preserved in the name of love the life of the only man who could destroy her race."

"You shame me," she said.

It shook him. "In what way?"

"The truth. The truth shames me. I have betrayed my race." She put trembling fingers against his mouth. "And I would do it again."

He wanted in that moment, recognizing her truth as an absolute, to give her a truth in return. To admit to her—and to himself as well—what demon had lived in his soul all his adult life.

Before, he had not known. And if someone had told him, if someone had dared, he would have taken solace in ridicule. *I have used weapons in my life, but none so sharp as the blade of honesty. It is time, I think, to use it on myself and lance the canker I have cherished.*

Kellin took her hand away, caught up the other one, then tucked both against his chest so she could feel his heartbeat. "I have been afraid of many things in my life, but none so much as the intimacy of loving a woman. I lay with many, aye, to assuage a physical need in vain attempts to dull the emotional pain, but nothing sufficed. I was always empty, always in despair, despite what I believed. Despite what I yearned for." His fingers warmed hers. He pressed her palms against his heart. "In fear of losing others, I distorted my soul on purpose. I cherished bitterness. I drove people away, even those whom I loved, because I wanted no one to care for me so *I* would not be required to care for them . . . to care was to lose them, and I could not bear it. Not after so many deaths." He carried her hands to his mouth and kissed them. "The river gave me the chance to become another man, perhaps the one I was meant to be all along. What you see before you now is not Kellin of Homana, but Kellin *the man,* of whom Ginevra had the shaping." He set his mouth against her palm. "I am your construct. If you would destroy me now, you need only withdraw your love."

She looked away from him. She gazed over his shoulder. Beyond the defile, beyond the Beasts, Valgaard yet burned. The air was laden with smoke.

He would not release her hands. "What we have shared could transfigure a world. Even this one."

The scent of smoke was thick. Ginevra's mouth warped briefly. "I have no roof," she said. "It has all fallen down."

Kellin cradled her face in his hands, threading fingers into the shining wealth of her hair. Softly he said, "Homana-Mujhar's still stands."

She flinched visibly; he saw she regretted it at once. "I am Lochiel's daughter."

He pressed his lips against her brow. He kissed it twice, thrice, then moved the great distance between forehead and mouth. *Cynric or no, prophecy or no, how could I even consider giving up this woman?*

He never had. Not once.

The truth seared his soul even as his lips shaped words on hers with careful tenderness. "I need you," he whispered, "as I have needed no one. *You* are my balance."

He knew it was not enough. But it was all he had to give her.

When her hand touched his shoulder, Kellin opened his eyes. It was full night. He had not slept. Neither had she.

He waited. He held his silence, his position. The tension in her fingers, as she touched his shoulder, was a reflection of his own.

The canyon stank of smoke. Valgaard burned. The full moon above them was dyed violet and black.

Her hand withdrew. When she touched him again, her fingers were cool on his face. They touched his mouth and clung.

Kellin sat up. He sat upon his heels even as she sat upon hers; their knees touched, and hands.

Ginevra stared into his face. Her own was shadowed in the

shroud of her hair. He saw the angle of a cheekbone, the curve of her brow. Her eyes were pockets of darkness. "If I am your balance, you are my lifestone."

In silence, Kellin waited.

She took one of his hands and carried it to her breast. She cupped his fingers around it. *"Make me feel again."*

Chapter Two

Ginevra stopped Kellin at the top of the steps leading into Homana-Mujhar. Rigid hands bit into his forearm as he turned immediately. *"Meijhana*—what is it?"

Her face was a sculpted mask with burning ice for eyes. "How will you say it?" she asked. "How will you tell them who I am?"

Kellin smiled, moving down a single step so he did not tower so much; she was shorter than he, and delicate, but her stature belied the dominance of her spirit. "Easily. I will say to all of them: 'This lady is Ginevra. This lady is my *cheysula*. All of you should be pleased the beast is tamed at last.'"

Color bloomed in her cheeks. Fingernails dug through fabric into flesh that was lighter than the norm for a Cheysuli, but darker than hers. "And will they want *me* tamed? The wicked Ihlini?" She had left tears in Solinde; what she gave him now was pride fierce as a Cheysuli's. "At least *you* came to my home without excess display!"

It took effort for him to keep his hands and mouth from her here and now, out of doors, before the palace entrance and all the bailey, and the soldiers from the guardhouse. "I was unconscious," he reminded her. "I have not the slightest idea if there was display, or no. For all I know, you might have hung me from my ankles and dried me over a fire."

Ginevra let go of his arm. "It never would have worked. Your brain was much too soggy!"

"Meijhana." He captured her hand and tucked it into his arm, warming it with his own hand, "I know you too well; you are not the one to hide from a truth, harsh or no. You will tell them yourself."

"Aye," she said, "I will. Just give me the chance!"

Kellin laughed. "Then come into my house."

"Gods—" she blurted, *"—wait—"*

He turned around promptly and sat down upon the steps, hooking arms around upraised knees as Sima sat down beside him. The cat's purr rumbled against his thigh. When Ginevra did not move, he eventually glanced up. "Well?"

Sunlight glinted on silver; he had loved her mass of black hair, but found this as much to his liking. *She could be hairless, and I would love her.* And then he grinned; who would have predicted Kellin of Homana would lose his heart at all, and to an Ihlini?

"What are you doing?" she asked.

"Waiting. You wanted me to." He paused, elated by her presence and the knowledge of what life with her would be; never dull, never quiet. The Prince and Princess of Homana did not harbor timid souls. "Should I have food sent out? If we are to be here so long . . ."

Ginevra's sharp inhalation hissed. New color stained her cheeks. She turned on her heel and marched directly into the palace.

He leaned his weight into Sima, who threatened to collapse his leg. *Contradictory.*

Then you are well-suited.

How could we not be? Was it not prophesied?

Sima's eyes slitted. *Not specifically. The prophecy merely said the Lion would lie down with the witch. Even the gods could not predict that you would be so much alike.*

He smiled. *By now she may well be in the Great Hall confronting the Mujhar himself.*

Or in your chamber confronting the knowledge of other women.

Kellin sat bolt upright, then got up at once.

Sima relented. *She is in the solar speaking with the Queen. Leave the women to one another—your place is with the Mujhar.*

And you?

Sima's tufted ears flicked. She stared past him into the sunlight, transfixed on a thought he could not decipher. The ears flattened once, then lifted again.

Kellin prodded. *Lir?*

She looked at him. Her stare was level. He felt in that instant she looked beyond the exterior to the soul within, and wondered how she found it. *It is for you to do,* she told him.

Kellin smiled. "He will understand. Once I have explained it. All of them will." He laughed aloud for joy. "Most assuredly

my *jehan*, who undoubtedly knew very well what was to become of me!"

The cat's glance was oblique as she shouldered by his knee into
the palace. *The Great Hall,* she said, *where the Lion lives.*

He went there at once, pushing open the hammered doors, and
saw, as expected, the Mujhar sitting quietly in the belly of the
Lion, contemplating his hall.

Kellin paused just inside the doors. It had been half a year since
he had been sent away by a man clearly desperate to salvage his
only heir. *Well, the heir is salvaged. Homana is preserved.* Kellin's
smile was slow, shaped by anticipation. There was much he longed
to say, much he meant to share, but especially Ginevra. *I will make
him understand. And how could he not? Lochiel is dead. The
Wheel of Life still turns.*

Kellin drew in a breath, lifted his head, then walked with steady
strides the length of the firepit to pause before the dais. There he
lowered his eyes out of respect for the man, and gave him Cheysuli greeting.

The Mujhar did not answer.

Anticipation waned. Kellin's belly tightened. *Does he know already? Has word come before us: "The Prince of Homana has
taken to wife an Ihlini witch!"*

The Mujhar offered nothing. When Kellin could no longer
stand it, he raised his head at last. "Grandsire—"

He checked. He stood there a long while. He denied it once, and
twice. The truth offended him. He longed to discard it and conjure
another.

But truth was truth. Magic could not change it.

His spirit withered within.

Kellin climbed the three steps and sank to his knees. His trembling hand, naked of signet, reached out to touch the dark Cheysuli
flesh that was still faintly warm.

He looked for Sleeta, but the mountain cat was gone.

Kellin thought of Sima. *She knew. When she sat upon the
steps*— But he let it go. He looked into the face of the Cheysuli
warrior who had ruled Homana for more than forty years. The
body slumped only slightly, tilted slantwise across the back of the
throne, as if he merely rested. One gold-freighted arm lay slack,
hand upturned against a leather-clad thigh; the other was draped
loosely along the armrest, so the dark Cheysuli fingers followed

the curve of the claws. On his forefinger the seal ring of Homana glinted dully.

Though the flesh had stilled, the bones as yet defied the truth. Brennan was, even dead, still very much a king.

Kellin's mouth moved stiffly as he managed a smile. He said it as he had told her on the steps before the palace. "The lady is Ginevra. The lady is my *cheysula*. You should be pleased the beast is tamed at last."

In the Lion, silence reigned. The Mujhar had abdicated.

"So much—" his grandson whispered, kneeling before the king. "So much I meant to say."

Mostly *leijhana tu'sai*, for being *jehan* as well as grandsire.

The Mujhar of Homana left the Great Hall and went directly to Aileen, where Ginevra was. He was aware of an odd dispassion, as if someone had wrung him empty of grief, and pain; with effort he put into words the requirements of state.

Then he put into words that which most required telling: that he had loved and honored her *cheysul* far more deeply than he had shown, as he loved and honored her.

In her face he saw his father's: chalk eroding in storm; crumbling beneath the sun. It ate below the layers and bared the granite of her grief, hard and sharp and impenetrable, and ageless as the gods.

Pale lips moved at last. "If this were Erinn, we would take him to the sacred tor and give him to the *cileann*."

But this was not Erinn. They would take him to his tomb and lay him to rest with other Mujhars.

Kellin kissed his granddame. He sent for a servant. He sent for a *shar tahl* and Clankeep's clanleader.

He sent for his *lir* to bide her time with Ginevra, whose eyes bespoke her empathy, and returned to the Great Hall.

People came. They took away the body. They gave him a ring. They called him "my lord Mujhar." They left him as he desired: alone in the hall as the day shapechanged to dusk.

Kellin felt sick to his stomach. He sat upon the dais and wished the day were different, that he could stop the Wheel of Life from turning and then start it up again, only this time moving backward, *backward, BACKWARD,* so the time was turned upside down and his grandsire could live again.

He stared into the blazing firepit. *I do not want to be Mujhar.*
He had wanted it all of his life.

I want him back. Grandsire. Let him be Mujhar.

They had trained him from birth to be king in his grandsire's
place.

A king must die to let another rule in his place.

Kellin shut his eyes. He heard in the silence all the arguments
they had shared, all the rude words he had shouted because his
grandsire wanted too much, demanded too much of him; chained
his grandson up so he would never know any freedom.

The words were gall in his mouth. "Too much left unsaid."

Behind him crouched the Lion. Its presence was demanding.
Kellin heaved himself up and turned to confront it. Gilded eyes
glared back.

He moved because he had to; he could no longer sit still. He
climbed the dais. Touched the throne. Moved around to the back of
it and turned to face the wall. He stared hard at the tapestry while
the lions within its folds blurred into shapeless blobs.

He remembered very clearly the day Ian had died. One small
hand, not much darker than a Homanan's, and one old hand,
bronzed flesh aging into brittle, yellowed flesh.

"Gods," he said aloud, "you should have made a better man
than me."

"The gods wrought very well. In time, you will know it. I already do."

Kellin turned. *"Jehan."* He was mostly unsurprised; it seemed
to fit perfectly. "You know."

"I know."

"Have you seen the Queen?"

Aidan's eyes were steady. "I did not see your *cheysula.*" He let
it register. "But aye, I saw my *jehana.*"

The words were hard to say. "Did you know—before?"

Aidan's face was graven with new lines at eyes and mouth. "I
am privileged to know things before others do. It is part of my service."

" 'Privileged' to know your father has died?"

"Privileged to know certain things so I may prepare the way for
greater purposes."

Kellin smiled a little. "A true *shar tahl,* couching his words in
obscurity."

Aidan smiled back. "I believe it is required."

Kellin nodded. His father walked very steadily toward the dais on which he stood. "How does one know if one is worthy of what he inherits?"

"One never does." Aidan stopped before the dais. "*I* know, Kellin. For now, it is enough."

Kellin swallowed heavily. "Did you come for him?"

"I came for you. I came to bind the Lion."

"Bind . . ." Kellin sighed. He felt very old. "I feared it, once." He stroked away a lock of hair. "The Lion lay down with the witch."

Aidan nodded. "I know."

Kellin wanted to smile, but his face felt old, and empty. "You prophesied for me, that day. You said I would marry."

A glint, purest yellow. "Most princes do."

"But you knew it would be Ginevra."

The glint died. Aidan's eyes were calm. "It seemed a tidy way of achieving what we all of us have worked for."

"The Lion lay down with the witch. And so the prophecy—"

"—continues." Aidan's expression was solemn. "Despite what you may hope, it is not yet complete. There are things we still must do."

"Ah." Kellin put his hands to his belt, then undid the buckle with fingers that felt thick and slow. He slid the links free. "Here. This is yours."

Aidan took the broken chain as Kellin redid his belt. "Sit down, my lord. It is time I chained the Lion."

He was too weary to question the task. He sat down. The Lion's mouth gaped. Kellin touched the wood and felt an echo of ancient power. *Mine?* he wondered. *Or left over from my grandsire?*

Aidan stood before the dais, before the firepit. His eyes burned feral yellow in the umber light of the dying day. In his hands were links. "Shaine," he said, "who began the *qu'mahlin*. His nephew Carillon, who took back Homana and ended the *qu'mahlin*. Then came Donal, son of Alix and Duncan—and after him, Niall, followed by Brennan." Gold chimed on gold. "The next link is broken. Its name was Aidan. I shattered it myself to bargain for my son. To know without a doubt that what I sacrificed would make Homana stronger." He held up the shorter length. "Two more links. One of them is Kellin. The other is named Cynric."

Kellin waited.

Aidan smiled. He turned to the firepit and dropped the two halves into flame.

Kellin started up from the throne, then checked.

Aidan said clearly, "The chain shall bind the Lion."

Their eyes locked. *He does not ask, he TELLS.* And then Kellin laughed. He stood up from the Lion and walked down the dais steps. He knelt beside the firepit with his back to the Lion, and knew what he must do.

Aidan waited.

What is fire, but fire? I have withstood godfire; *I have made* godfire. *This comes from my* jehan—*surely its flame is cleaner.* Kellin drew in a breath. He put his hand through flames, then farther into coals.

It burned, but did not consume. Fingers found metal. He sought the shape of the link and could not find it. What he found was something else.

"Free it," Aidan said.

Kellin brought it out of the flame, unsurprised to discover his hand was whole. He opened it. In the palm lay an earring. The head of a mountain cat stared back at him.

"More," Aidan said.

Kellin set the earring onto the rim of the firepit. He reached into the flame again, dug down into coals, and took from the pit two *lir*-bands.

Aidan was patient. "And again."

"Again?" But he set the armbands also on the rim and plunged both hands into the blazing coals.

Aidan smiled. "A king must have a crown."

Kellin drew it forth. A rune-wrought circlet of *lir* gleamed against his palms. Its workmanship was such that no man, looking upon it, could withstand the desire to set it on his brow.

The voice was light and calm, pitched to reach the dais. "So this is Cheysuli magic." Ginevra's winged brows rose as she walked the length of the hall. "Does all your gold come from fire?"

"No," Aidan answered. "Our gold is merely gold, though blessed by the gods in the Ceremony of Honors. *This* gold, however, is to replace that he lost in misadventure."

"Misadventure." Her gaze dwelled on Kellin. She had tamed the silvered hair by braiding it into quiescence with blood-red cord. "The sort of misadventure that rendered him without mem-

ory of name, of rank—of race." She looked now at Aidan. "You are
the one my father most feared."

In dying light, Aidan's hair glowed russet. "He never told
me so."

"He did fear you. He never told *me* so—my father was not a
man to admit to such things as fear—but I think he must have. He
spoke of you repeatedly, telling me how it was, in your madness,
that you came to him in Valgaard to bargain for your son. I think
he did not know what else you might do, and it frightened him."

Kellin clutched the circlet. The gold was warm in his hands.
What passed between his father and Ginevra was undivulged even
in gesture; he could not decipher it.

Aidan's face was relaxed. "I might have chosen you."

"Aye. And brought me here." She cast a glance at Kellin. "My
lord prevails upon me to insist that had I been, I would never once
have realized I was anything but Cheysuli."

"But you are," Aidan answered. "You are many things,
Ginevra . . . among them Cheysuli. Among them Ihlini."

Her chin firmed. "And the mother of the Firstborn."

Aidan looked at her belly. She did not show much yet, but her
cupped hands divulged the truth. He smiled into her eyes. "You
may choose what you will be. The gods give us free will—even to
Ihlini."

"Choose?" She glanced sidelong at Kellin, then returned her
gaze to Aidan. "In what way do I choose? And what?"

"How you shall be remembered." Aidan rose. "You may be
Kellin's *cheysula*. You may be Queen of Homana. You may be
merely a mother—or the mother of the Firstborn."

"I was and always will be Lochiel's daughter."

Aidan inclined his head.

"And it will mark me," she declared. "*That* is how they will
know me!"

"Aye," Aidan agreed, "because it is required." His eyes were
very feral in the waning light. Flames turned them molten. "As it
concerns you, my prophesying is done."

It startled her. "What?"

"You were the witch. But that is done. When Kellin lies down
again, it will be with his *cheysula*. If you mean to be anything
more, you yourself will make the choice."

Color stood in her face. "You mean if I choose to remind them

I am heir to Lochiel's power." She smiled. "I could. I could do it easily."

"That would depend," Aidan said calmly, "on how you chose to do it."

She stared fixedly at him, then looked at Kellin. She was, in that moment, pride and glory incarnate.

Leijhana tu'sai, he thought, *for giving me the wits—or robbing me of them!—so I might see beyond the wall of our people's enmity to the woman beyond.*

The fire kindled her eyes and melted Ihlini ice. The quality of her tone was pitched now to acknowledgment, and a warmth that left him breathless. "Then I would choose to be the woman who crowned a king. So they would know I want no war. So they would know I am Ginevra, and not merely Lochiel's daughter."

"Then do it," Aidan said.

Ginevra lifted her head. She advanced steadily. Beside the firepit she paused, stared up into the blind, gilded eyes of the Lion Throne of Homana, and smiled a tiny smile. *"Tahlmorra,"* she said dryly. "Is that not what you call this?"

Aidan's voice was quiet. "All men—and all women—have a *tahlmorra*. You were bred of Cheysuli gods as surely as of Ihlini . . . they were—and remain—the same. In their view we are all of us 'Cheysuli.' The word means 'children of the gods.' " His smile was gentle, lacking in threat, lacking in arrogance. "We have a saying, of twins: 'Two blossoms from the same vine.' Though our vine was split and the two halves borne away to separate gardens, the rootstock remains the same. It is time we replanted."

She hesitated. "Asar-Suti? The Seker?"

"We are but aspects of our creators. When there is evil among men, look first at those gods from whom they inherited it."

Kellin's belly clenched. "Then he is not dead."

"The Gate was closed in the destruction of Valgaard. It takes time to build another. While Asar-Suti labors, centuries may pass."

Ginevra's smile was crooked. "Then I had best crown the king before the Gate is rebuilt. " She held it out, above his head. Flames glinted off gold. Clearly she said, "In the name of all the gods, even the Seker who is but one among them, I declare you Mujhar of Homana."

Kellin bowed his head. The circlet was cool as she slid it onto his head with trembling fingers. It warmed against his brow.

"Done," Ginevra said.

Aidan smiled. "And so the Lion is chained by the witch with whom he lay."

Kellin picked up the earring. "But this is *lir*-gold! How could *this* chain me?"

"Memories," Aidan answered. "History and heritage, and an ancestry that reaches across centuries. When the Lion roars he must recall what went before, so he will rule the world wisely. Responsibility binds a man; it binds a king more. Do not discount its weight."

"No," Kellin said. "Not ever again, *jehan*."

One of the hammered doors scraped open. A man came in. Kellin got to his feet.

"Already," Aidan murmured.

Kellin stared at his kinsman. Hart's hair was white. His gaunt face was lined with grief. He looked briefly at Aidan and Ginevra, then fastened an unflinching gaze on his twin-born brother's grandson. "I came for Brennan," he said, "but it seems the gods have seen fit to deprive me of my *rujho*."

Mute, Kellin nodded.

Hart looked at Aidan. "It would have been yours, once. Is that why you are come home at last?"

Something moved in Aidan's eyes. "I am come home for many reasons, *su'fali*. I am come to honor my *jehan*, whom the gods have taken; to offer strength to my *jehana;* to pay homage to my son, the Mujhar; to witness the coming of the Firstborn." The yellow eyes were fierce. "But also to grieve. Will you permit me that?"

Abashed, Hart nodded. He looked from Aidan to Aidan's son. "Brennan is gone, and so I come to you, his heir." Anguish blossomed a moment, was damped down with effort. "I had a son once. Owain. Lochiel murdered him. Now I have no son. I have come to give you Solinde."

Kellin was astounded. "You have daughters!"

Hart's voice was steady. "Blythe has borne only girls, and will bear no more. Cluna bore three stillborn children and will not conceive again. Jennet died in childbed. Dulcie was wed to the High Prince of Ellas two months ago." Hart's tension lessened. "She grew tired of waiting for you."

Kellin smiled faintly.

"And so the sons she bears, if she bears sons—we run to girls, I fear—will be reared Ellasian."

Kellin stood very still. The back of his neck prickled. He looked sharply at his father and saw the light in Aidan's eyes. *He said he knows things. He is "privileged" to know. He knew this would come.* Realization was a knife plunged deep into his vitals. *And he knows the others will come.*

He would stop it. He knew the way. He looked back at his grandsire's brother. "You will not die so soon. This is unnecessary."

Hart said only, "Brennan died today."

After a stricken moment Kellin turned away and stared hard at the tapestry of lions. He could not bear Hart's eyes. He could not bear to see his own grief in his great-uncle's face.

Chapter Three

When at last Ginevra slept, wearied from long labor, Kellin sat beside her with their son in his arms, thinking thoughts of wonder, of pride, of relief; of the prophecy of the Firstborn.

Lochiel's daughter stirred, then slid again into sleep. He put one hand into the glorious hair and stroked it gently from her face. The long eyes were lidded, lost to him in sleep, but he knew what lived behind them: the blazing ice of Ihlini *godfire*, legacy of Lochiel's power.

Women had swaddled his son in countless linen wrappings. The child, he thought, was ugly, far uglier than foal or puppy, but he supposed time would alter the red-faced, wrinkled infant into a human child, and eventually into a man.

Kellin drew in a breath. *What manner of power will you claim? Will you be human at all?*

Sima, at his feet, sent a lazy suggestion through the link that he let the child grow up and discover for himself what his *tahlmorra* was. That a father could, if he watered the clay too much, turn it into sludge so that no one at all could use it.

Kellin smiled. *Is that what I was? Sludge?*

Sima blinked. *Clay with too much grit. You cut the flesh of an unsuspecting potter.*

Ah. He laughed softly. And then he thought of other children who had no father to water them at all. *I will have them come here.*

Sima yawned. *Be wary of asking too much. You gave them to those women; if you mean to take them back, you will do more harm than good.*

They are my children.

Bastards.

He heard the echo of his own arrogance, and knew what Sima intended. He acceded to a greater wisdom than his own; she was, after all, *lir.* "Then I will give them leave to come whenever they like, so they will know their heritage."

And?

He smiled. *And I will go to them, so I will share* their *lives.*

Better. She lashed her tail once. *What will you do with the others?*

What others? He stiffened. *Are there more?*

I mean the ones to come later.

Later! Sima, by all the gods, do you think me a selfish, rutting fool? What man in the world would turn to another woman with this one in his bed?

Sima purred more loudly and shut her golden eyes. She offered no comment. Her work was done.

Kellin laughed softly and looked down upon his son. *Where would a warrior be without a* lir *such as Sima? Or Sleeta? Or Teel? Or Ian's Tasha? Or Blais' Tanni?* He touched his son's brow. *What* lir *will you have—if you have a* lir *at all?*

"Kellin."

He glanced up. Hart stood in the doorway. He knew without being told what his kinsman had come to say. "They are here," Kellin said. "Corin. And Keely."

Hart's face spasmed. "Did Aidan forewarn you? Or have you your own measure of his power of prophecy?"

It hurt, but he knew the pain was shared. It goaded all of them. "I have no power at all, save what any of us do. I know only what we all do—that the Lion shall swallow the lands." He beckoned one of the women, gave her Cynric, and rose. "You came to give me Solinde. I think we will find they have come to do the same with their own realms."

In Hart's eyes was a measure of quiet respect. "Brennan wrote me of his fears, of his frustrations. He knew very well what you *could* be, if you permitted yourself to achieve it. I see now he was not wrong." He nodded slightly. "A fitting legacy for my *rujho.* He wrought well, did Brennan. And Homana shall prosper for it."

Kellin paused in the doorway; it was Corin he saw first. The Lord of Atvia stood with his back to the deep-silled casement. A ruddy fox sat beside one leg: Kiri. Midday sunlight glinted off *lir*-gold. The once-tawny hair had faded, intermixed with silver, and the beard Corin yet wore showed traces of white, but no sign of age softened the tension in his body or the pride in his stance. For all he had none of the color, he was Cheysuli to the bone.

Kellin was aware of them all within an instant of entering the chamber: Aileen's solar, with Aileen in it, seated on a chair; near Corin stood a dark-haired woman with eloquent brown eyes he knew was Glyn, Corin's *cheysula;* a second woman in a chair with hair a pristine white and eyes like ice—*Ginevra's eyes*—was Ilsa, Hart's Solindish queen; and Keely, Corin's twin, seated nearby with Sean of Erinn at her back. The Erinnish lord was huge, dominating the chamber. Even in quietude his presence was of the kind another man, even a king, could not ignore.

And lastly Aidan, his father, who stood quietly behind his mother with a raven close at hand, watching the tableau as if he knew very well what was to come.

No doubt he does know. Kellin looked back at Corin even as Hart moved by him into the chamber to join Ilsa. He wondered what had passed among his kinfolk as they awaited his arrival. They had spoken of Brennan certainly; a quiet grief lingered in Keely's eyes. Her face was tautly drawn over high, pronounced cheekbones. The stubborn jaw was set. But Kellin saw a softness there that she might not acknowledge; she was, they all said, a very proud woman.

He smiled faintly to see her in skirts. He had heard the stories of her tempestuous youth. *She belongs in jerkin and leggings, with a sword in her hands.* Shona, they said, had been very like Keely. In the face of his granddame, he looked for his mother. In the face of his grandsire, he looked for himself.

But Sean was all Erinnish, bred in the Aerie's mews; Kellin was Cheysuli. *As well as other things, which bring me to this point.*

Sean's rumble broke the silence. "Lad," he said, "we've come for other things, but we owe our respects to the Mujhar of Homana."

"Leijhana tu'sai," Kellin said, and saw the startled speculation in Keely's eyes; had she heard that Brennan's heir repudiated his race? Well, it was time they understood. "In the name of my other grandsire, I welcome you to his home."

"Yours," Keely said softly.

Corin's smile was grim. "I came to speak with Brennan on a matter of some importance. I find instead I must speak to his heir. It may be—difficult."

Kellin nodded. "You none of you know me." He looked at

Keely; at Sean. "Not even you, who raised a proud daughter well worthy of my *jehan*. And I, am I fortunate, will be worthy of them." He stepped aside and beckoned Sima in. The cat slid through with a rub against his leg, then padded to a deep-silled casement aglow with midday sun. She leapt up, curled herself, and settled on the sill. "You may have heard nonsense of a young, foolish prince desiring nothing of a *lir* for fear he would lose her, or himself if she were killed. But that man was ignorant. He did not know what manner of gift the gods offered." He looked at Sima and saw they did the same. "In time, he came to see that a warrior without a *lir* is not a man at all . . . and wholly unfit to inherit the Lion Throne."

Tension fled Corin's shoulders. His smile widened. "News travels slowly."

"Much more slowly than rumor."

Ruefully, Corin laughed. "I know your birthline as well as my own, as I am in much of it . . . I have no quarrel with it. But you are young to be Mujhar."

"I am the age you were when you sailed away to your island."

Corin looked at Keely. "A long time ago, *rujholla*."

Keely's hair also had begun to silver, altering the gold of younger years. "Much too long, I fear, for either of us to recall the feelings of youth, and why we did what we did," She smiled at her brother, then looked to Kellin. "We are informed there is a new Prince of Homana."

Kellin saw no reason to rely on courtesy, or the traditions of a culture that now would be altered. "More than that," he said easily. "Cynric is the Firstborn."

Tension reinfected the chamber. He wondered if they believed he would not acknowledge such a thing; that he would deny sleeping with an Ihlini despite what it had produced.

Kellin understood; it would be so for years, until old prejudices died. "Her name is Ginevra. Among the Houses in her blood is our own: she is, as am I, a grandchild of Brennan."

The silence was heavy. Keely broke it. "We do not question that. The gods made it clear that one day it would happen, though I admit none of us believed you might *marry* an Ihlini." She slanted a troubled glance at Aidan, who had served as Cynric's prophet. "But it is difficult for me to reconcile her as anything other than *Lochiel's* child. He killed my daughter—"

"—and nearly his own." Kellin saw it register; marked startled attention. "When he learned the child she carried was Cynric, he tried to murder her. Ginevra refused to submit to the sacrifice he and his god required. With my help—and the help of her unborn child—she killed her father. She destroyed him in the Gate of his own god." He looked at each of them, one at a time, until he knew he had them. "We have fought the Ihlini forever. It was Ginevra's choice that this war be ended."

Keely's gaze did not waver. Her smile was bittersweet. "If it is possible for you to care so much for her, then perhaps I should take instruction in the art of forgiveness. I would like to forgive; she is, by marriage, my granddaughter. But such things do not come easy to a childless woman."

"Childless!" Kellin looked at Sean and saw anguished affirmation. "But—you also had a *son*—"

The upstanding veins of Keely's hand knotted. "Sean and Riordan went to Atvia to visit Corin and Glyn. This time, I did not go." A spasm of grief wracked her face. "This *once,* I did not go—"

"Keely." Sean put a big hand upon her shoulder. " 'Twas a storm in the Dragon's Tail. I was injured . . . in saving me, my son risked himself." His eyes glazed abruptly though the voice remained steady. "In Erinn, men rule. There is no one else left of my line."

Kellin drew in a breath. "Will Erinn have me?"

Aileen laughed softly. Grief had deeply marked her, but she was still profoundly Erinnish in coloring and speech. "With your eyes, my lad? They'll be needing no *kivarna* . . . there's no mistaking your blood! They'll be having themselves an Erinnish lord even if he is Mujhar of Homana."

"As for me," Corin said, "I have always known I would go elsewhere for my heir." His hand enfolded Glyn's. "A barren queen is worthless, some men might declare—but I know better. I would trade her for nothing, and no one." He exchanged a smile with the woman who could not speak, and looked back at Kellin. "It seemed natural to me that Brennan be my heir should I predecease him, despite the arguments of our youth. He was withal a supremely compassionate and *competent* man, a man who understood responsibility; he was far better fit to rule than I." For a moment his voice faltered. "That now is moot, but there is another man to whom I might entrust my realm."

Kellin did not immediately answer. He was intensely aware that all of them looked at him expectantly, awaiting his response. He knew what it would be, but he wondered if *they* did; if they understood at all what was about to happen in the ordering of their world.

It has nothing to do with me. But they do not see it; they see only me, and think of immediacies instead of the future. They have not yet reconciled what it is I have done by siring a son with Ginevra. I am Kellin to them, no more—except perhaps to my jehan, who understands very well.

He smiled at Aidan and saw the answer in yellow eyes; indeed, his father knew. The *shar tahl* knew many things. He was, after all, the mouthpiece of the gods.

One day they will know. They will come to understand. It has nothing to do with me.

Kellin glanced at Sima. Then he looked back at the others and gave them their answer. "*I* will have none of your realms." Their startlement was palpable in the minute stirring of their bodies, the intensity in their eyes. "Should you predecease me, you may be certain I shall respect and cherish your lands, doing what I must to keep the people content—but I will name none of them mine. I will serve only as regent until such a time as my son comes of age." He looked at his father; Aidan's smile was content. "The Lion may swallow the lands, but it is the Firstborn who shall rule them in the name of ancient gods."

Epilogue

The Lion's claws curled down beneath Kellin's hands. His fingers followed the line, tracing gilt-etched wood. He sought the Lion's strength to carry him through the ceremony that would, in its celebration, herald a new age.

His arms were heavy with *lir*-gold; his brow ablaze with more. The weight at his left ear, after its emptiness, was infinitely reassuring. He was, at last, Cheysuli in all things; a *lir*-blessed warrior who also knew his balance.

Kellin drew in a deep breath, held it a long moment, then released it slowly. He was aware of approval emanating from beside his right leg, snugged between Mujhar and Queen to offer them both support: Sima sat in silence with tail tucked over paws. Great golden eyes were fixed on those gathering to witness the investiture of a new Prince of Homana.

So many people. His kinfolk, of course, grouped near the firepit: Aileen first, wearing the *lir*-torque Brennan had given her decades before. Their son, Aidan, with a raven upon his shoulder and his mother's hand in his. Hart with Rael, and Ilsa; Corin and Kiri with mute Glyn; Keely flanked by Sean. And *lir*, so many *lir*, in rafters and windows and corners.

Others also: the Homanan Council, complete in all regards, and the castle staff; Gavan, clan-leader of Clankeep, with Burr and other *shar tahls;* plus the multitudes of warriors, and women with large-eyed children, from all the keeps of Homana. Ihlini also, from Solinde, who did not honor Asar-Suti. No one was turned away. Those who could not fit into the Great Hall gathered in corridors, in other chambers, in the baileys; even, he had been told, in the castle kitchens.

The firepit blazed. The sun beyond stained glass slanted into the crowded hall, glinting off *lir*-gold and other ornamentation, tinting into a likeness the fair Homanan faces and dark Cheysuli ones.

Kellin noted it. He noted everything, but nothing stood out so much as the woman at his side.

She stood quietly at his right, holding linen-swathed Cynric. She wore a velvet robe of deep bloodied wine that was, in its folds, in its richness, very nearly black. At her ears she wore rubies and jet; her slender neck was weighted with the gold of his *lir*-torque. Unbound silver hair fell in sheets to her knees. The white around her face framed an exquisite, alien beauty even more remarkable for her pride, for the blazing of her spirit, for the determination housed in icy Ihlini eyes.

This was *her* son. If it be her task alone, they would none of them forget it.

Kellin smiled. *They will remember her from this day. No matter what else may happen, they will never forget Ginevra.*

He looked out again at the multitude, then rose from the throne. He extended his right hand. Ginevra put into it her left, as her right arm cradled Cynric. Two steps only, and they stood at the edge of the marble dais steps.

Aidan moved out from the throng. His voice was pitched quietly, but no one in the hall could not hear what he said. "He is the sword." A shower of sparks rose up from the firepit. "He is the sword and the bow and the knife. He is darkness and light. He is good and evil. He is the child and the elder; the girl and the boy; the wolf and the lamb."

No one spoke. No child protested, no *lir* ruffled wing.

Aidan's eyes were black. *"I am no one; I am everyone. I am the child of the prophecy; child of darkness, and light; of like breeding with like until the blood is one again."*

Stained glass shattered. Empty casements displayed a sudden darkness: the moon slid across the sun and did not depart. Inside, the hall was black; outside, the world was.

People cried out in fear; Homanans, Kellin knew. Cheysuli feared no gods.

Aidan's voice whispered: *"The sword—and the bow—and the knife."*

Flames roared up in the firepit. The iron lid that covered the stairway to the Womb was flung back on its hinges, crashing into piled wood. In the flurry of ash and flame came a greater, more complex motion: the rushing torrent of dozens of *lir* issuing from the hole. In the flames they were creamy marble, with blind creamy eyes, but as they burst forth into the light, into the darkness of eclipse, marble shapechanged itself into the clothing of living *lir.*

Ginevra's hand gripped Kellin's. He felt her trembling; sensed the wonder in her heart, and his own, that their son could be the inheritor of so much power.

"I am Cynric," Aidan said, *"and I am Firstborn of those who have returned."*

Lir upon *lir,* freed of imprisonment, joined brother and sister *lir* in hammer-beamed rafters, in rune-rimmed sills, at the edge of the firepit. Others gathered the dais.

Firepit flames died. The hall was left in darkness.

"Cynric," Aidan said, *"who will bring light to the darkness so all men may see."*

The darkness was complete. Silence was loud.

Then Kellin understood. He looked at Ginevra, marking the sheen of silver hair in the dimness of the hall. "Unwrap him."

Her mouth parted as comprehension filled her eyes. Ginevra deftly freed the week-old infant from embroidered linen wrappings. With an avid tenderness she handed him to Kellin, who raised him up, naked, to the multitudes.

Tiny arms waved. In the darkness fire bloomed. A pale, luminous gold born of infant-etched runes, that encompassed the darkness and defeated it. Its heart was livid white.

Upturned faces were illuminated. Kellin heard murmurings, saw groping hands reach out to one another. Homanans and Cheysuli were bound together by awe.

He looked at his kinfolk standing near the dais: Aileen, crying; Hart and Ilsa; Corin and Glyn; Keely and Sean, all clasping hands. Their expressions were rapt.

Aidan raised his hands to encompass everyone. "From among them shall come a *lir* worthy of the Firstborn. Worthy of the child who had united, in peace, four warring realms and two magical races." His voice soared above them. "Cynric, child of prophecy; the Firstborn come again!"

There was a shifting among the crowd as warriors looked at *lir,* and an abrupt apprehension that was palpable. Kellin himself felt it.

He looked sharply at Sima. *What is this? Will we lose the* lir *after all?*

Sima's eyes were fixed on him in an unwavering intentness. Pupils were nonexistent. *You have wrought well. Decade after decade, until years became centuries, the Cheysuli have labored well. It is time now for two races to become one; for the power to be fixed as it was once before. From you and Lochiel's daughter will come others, and they in their turn shall sire their own, until the Firstborn as a race is viable again.*

He felt a clutch of trepidation. *What of us? What becomes of the Cheysuli and the Ihlini? Do we die out? Are we replaced?* He cast a harried glance at the gathered *lir*. Desperately he asked, *Have I destroyed my own race to elevate yours?*

The tip of her tail twitched.

Kellin began to tremble. *Sima—am I to lose you after all? To my son?* He could not bear it. He could not bear the idea. *Gods— do not do this! Would you have me be a monster to my people?*

Behold, Sima said.

"Behold!" Aidan cried.

Kellin heard it. At first he was not certain. Then he heard Ginevra's gasp and swung awkwardly, clasping the infant against his shoulder. He could not help himself; he stepped off the dais even as Sima preceded him; even as Ginevra fled.

But he knew. He *knew*. And his doubts spilled away.

He looked at Sima. She was fully grown and magnificent. *You knew all along.*

Golden eyes blinked. *I know many things. I am, after all,* lir.

"Look," Ginevra whispered. "Look what we have done!"

Kellin looked again. Words filled his mind, his mouth; too many words. He could not say them all; could not *think* them all.

In the end, he said the only ones he could manage. *"Leijhana tu'sai—"* he whispered, "for a *lir* such as this."

With meticulous precision, the throne unbent itself. Wood split and peeled away; gilt cracked and was sloughed as dust. The shoulders broke through first, heaving free of imprisonment, and then the head, twisting, as it freed itself from an ancient, rigid wood. The gaping jaws closed. The crouching beast dropped to all fours and shook its heavy mane, spraying chips of wood and gilt.

In the hall, people cried out: Homanan, Cheyuli, Ihlini. Some fell to their knees. Others mouthed petitions to various gods.

Wood cracked and popped. From the tattered prison emerged a male lion full-fleshed and in his prime. Golden eyes gleamed, stripped now of age-soiled gilt to display the soul inside. A flame burned there, kindling into a bonfire as he gazed upon the hall.

The lion shook himself. Wood chips flew into the hall; those that landed in the firepit popped once and hissed into smoke.

The grime of antiquity, the sheen of a thousand hands, was sloughed off with a single shrug of massive, mane-clad shoulders. Littering the dais was the wooden pelt newly shed; what stood before them now was the Lion of Homana as he once was, before a power wholly perverted had shapechanged him to wood.

The massive jaws opened, displaying fearsome teeth. His roar filled the hall. Fragments of glass still clinging to their casements shattered into colored spray.

The roar died. The lion scented, tasting the air, then took note of the tiny infant. Golden eyes sharpened. He padded forth to stand at the edge of the steps, gazing down upon the child who was unafraid of his roar. The rumble deep in his chest was one of abiding contentment, of a *lir* newly bonded.

Ja'hai-na, Kellin thought. *Imprisoned or no, this moment alone, here within the hall, has always been his* tahlmorra.

He looked down at the infant he cradled in his arms. The eyes were not open. The fists were impotent. But Kellin knew his son would never be measured by such things; he was Cynric, and Firstborn; he would measure himself against a personal criteria more demanding than any other.

The lion roared again. The moon moved off the sun. Sunlight filled the Great Hall, where a week-old, naked infant shaped tiny glowing runes.

Ginevra cried in silence. Kellin clasped and kissed her hand, raising it in tribute; he would have everyone know he honored his queen. *"Shansu,"* he whispered. "The war is ended."

As the Lion lay down behind them, Kellin turned to the gathering and raised his son once more. "His name is Cynric. In the name of Cheysuli gods, who conceived and bore us all, I ask you to accept him as my heir, the Prince of Homana—and the Firstborn come again!"

He was met at first by silence. Then a murmuring, a rustling of clothing, a clattering of jewelry; and at last the acclamation, wholly unrestrained, echoed in the rafters. The tongues conjoining were two: Homanan and Cheysuli. But the answer was encompassed in single word said twice.

"Ja'hai-na!"

"Accepted!"

Aidan came first, followed by Aileen. And Hart, Corin, Keely. Sean, Glyn, and Ilsa. Each of them approached the infant Prince of Homana to offer the kiss of kinfolk; only they could.

And then the others came: one by one by one—Cheysuli, Ihlini, Homanan—to pay homage to the heir, to the son, to the Firstborn, while on the dais behind the child, where Deirdre's tapestry hung, the Lion of Homana guarded his newborn *lir*.

Author's Note

The *Chronicles of the Cheysuli* was not originally intended as a series, but a single book only, titled *The Shapechangers*. It was my first foray into *written* fantasy, although I'd been reading it for many years; I'd written other (unpublished) novels, but no fantasy, because I was afraid. I loved the genre too much, and feared I couldn't do it justice.

But my favorite authors—Marion Zimmer Bradley, C.J. Cherryh, Katherine Kurtz, Patricia McKillip, Anne McCaffrey, etc.—simply didn't write fast enough to suit my reading addiction; I decided the only way to survive was to manufacture a "fix" by writing my own novel.

And so I concocted a plot about a race of shapechangers and their animal familiars, and a girl born of a mundane culture being absorbed into a magical one.

But plots always require thickening . . . I added royalty, a prophecy, created the Ihlini. And then one day, immediately following a cultural anthropology class in which we'd spent fifty minutes drawing triangles and circles as a generational exercise, I decided to apply my newfound knowledge to my stand-alone fantasy novel.

A trilogy was born.

More triangles and circles got added to the chart. The trilogy became a seven-book series. And when I realized seven didn't *quite* cover everything, I added another and brought it to eight, whereupon I promised myself to end it. *Finis.*

Twelve years later, it was ended. The prophecy was complete.

As I write this, it's been seventeen years to the month since the first volume, *Shapechangers*, was published. No author likes to turn her back on a world and its people after spending so much time creating them; Homana's root, after all, is *home.* But she does it, because to linger longer is to risk creative stagnation.

The *Chronicles of the Cheysuli* have covered approximately a century in the history of Homana and her races, blessed and un-blessed alike. It may be that someday there will be more stories to tell, but in the meantime I'm discovering new worlds, new characters, new races I want to write about, such as the denizens of my upcoming fantasy series, *Karavans*. I hope readers will join me on that journey as well.

—J.R.
Flagstaff, Arizona
February 2001

Visit Jennifer Roberson's Web site at:
www.cheysuli.com

APPENDIX
CHEYSULI/OLD TONGUE
GLOSSARY
(with pronunciation guide)

a'saii (uh-SIGH)—Cheysuli zealots dedicated to pure line of descent.

bu'lasa (boo-LAH-suh)—grandson

bu'sala (boo-SAH-luh)—foster-son

cheysu (chay-SOO)—man/woman; neuter; used within phrases.

cheysul (chay-SOOL)—husband

cheysula (chay-SOO-luh)—wife

cheysuli (chay-SOO-lee)—(*literal translation*): children of the gods.

Cheysuli i'halla shansu (chay-SOO-lee i-HALLA shan-SOO)—(*lit.*): May there be Cheysuli peace upon you.

godfire (god-fire)—common manifestation of Ihlini power; cold, lurid flame; purple tones.

harana (huh-RAH-na)—niece

harani (huh-RAH-nee)—nephew

homana (ho-MAH-na)—(*literal translation*): of all blood.

i'halla (ih-HALL-uh)—upon you: used within phrases.

i'toshaa-ni (ih-tosha-NEE)—Cheysuli cleansing ceremony; atonement ritual.

ja'hai ([French *j*] zshuh-HIGH)—accept

ja'hai-na (zshuh-HIGH-nuh)—accepted

jehan (zsheh-HAHN)—father

jehana (zsheh-HAH-na)—mother

ku'reshtin (koo-RESH-tin)—epithet; name-calling

leijhana tu'sai (lay-HAHN-uh too-SIGH)—(*lit.*): thank you very much.

lir (leer)—magical animal(s) linked to individual Cheysuli; title used indiscriminately between *lir* and warriors.

meijha (MEE-hah)—Cheysuli: light woman; (*lit.*): mistress.

meijhana (mee-HAH-na)—slang: pretty one

Mujhar (moo-HAR)—king

qu'mahlin (koo-MAH-lin)—purge; extermination

Resh'ta-ni (resh-tah-NEE)—(*lit.*): As you would have it.

rujho (ROO-ho)—slang: brother (diminutive)

rujholla (roo-HALL-uh)—sister (formal)

rujholli (roo-HALL-ee)—brother (formal)

ru'maii (roo-MY-ee)—(*lit.*): in the name of

Ru'shalla-tu (roo-SHAWL-uh TOO)—(*lit.*) May it be so.

Seker (Sek-AIR)—formal title: god of the netherworld.

shansu (shan-SOO)—peace

shar tahl (shar TAHL)—priest-historian; keeper of the prophecy.

shu'maii (shoo-MY-ee)—sponsor

su'fala (soo-FALL-uh)—aunt

su'fali (soo-FALL-ee)—uncle

sul'harai (sool-hah-RYE)—moment of greatest satisfaction in union of man and woman; describes shapechange.

tahlmorra (tall-MORE-uh)—fate; destiny; kismet.

Tahlmorra lujhala mei wiccan, cheysu (tall-MORE-uh loo-HALLA may WICK-un, chay-SOO)—(*lit.*): The fate of a man rests always within the hands of the gods.

tetsu (tet-SOO)—poisonous root given to allay great pain; addictive, eventually fatal.

tu'halla dei (too-HALLA-day-EE)—(*lit.*): Lord to liege man.

usca (OOIS-kuh)—powerful liquor from the Steppes.

y'ja'hai (EE-zshuh-HIGH)—(*lit.*): I accept.

The House of Homana

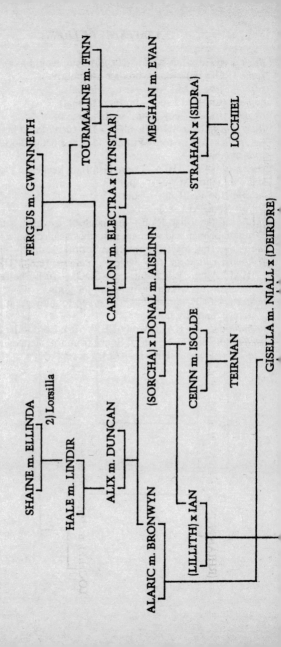

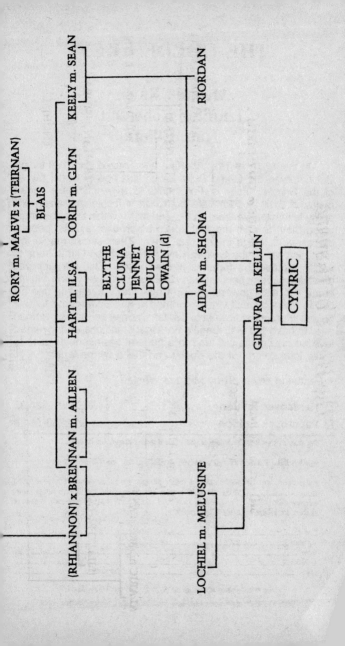

THE GOLDEN KEY
by
Melanie Rawn
Jennifer Roberson
Kate Elliott

In the duchy of Tira Virte fine art is prized above all things. But not even the Grand Duke knows just how powerful the art of the Grijalva family is. For thanks to a genetic fluke certain males of their bloodline are born with a frightening talent—the ability to manipulate time, space, and reality within their paintings, using them to cast magical spells which alter events, people, places, and things in the real world. Their secret magic formula, known as the Golden Key, permits those Gifted sons to vastly improve the fortunes of their family. Still, the Grijalvas are fairly circumspect in their dealings until two young talents come into their powers: Sario, a boy who will learn to use his Gift to make himself virtually immortal; and Saavedra, a female cousin who, unbeknownst to her family, may be the first woman ever to have the Gift. Sario's personal ambitions and thwarted love for his cousin will lead to a generations-spanning plot to seize total control of the duchy and those who rule it.

• Featuring cover art by Michael Whelan